A Whisper in the Dark

A Whisper in the Dark

Twelve Thrilling Tales
by Louisa May Alcott

Edited by Stefan Dziemianowicz

Introduction by Susie Mee

BARNES
&NOBLE
BOOKS
NEW YORK

Contents

Foreword

The secret is out: Louisa May Alcott led a double literary life! During the same years in which she carved a niche for herself in American letters with publication of her short stories in the prestigious *Atlantic Monthly* and her children's classic *Little Women*, she also wrote nearly three dozen thrillers steeped in violent emotion and cliff-hanging suspense. This may shock readers who know her solely as the celebrant of domestic virtues incarnated in the characters of *Little Women*, but it should come as no surprise to anyone who ever wondered how much autobiography she poured into her chronicle of the March family. Like the Marches, the Alcotts were in a constant state of financial need, and like the industrious Jo, whom she modeled on herself, Louisa undertook to supplement her family's income through the sale of "sensation stories."

It's not difficult to understand why Louisa May Alcott devoted so much energy to writing sensational stories in which virtue undergoes trial by ordeal and women are wronged and revenged: the stories paid well, and the demand for them was constant. More important, she had an obvious talent for this type of writing. An omnivorous reader in her youth, she was no doubt familiar with the Gothic romances that had entertained readers for a century through their personifications of good and evil, brooding atmospheric settings, and chilling supernaturalism. In her hands, the basic materials of these stories—the diabolical villain, the imperiled innocent, the conflict of the heart—became tools for shaping character studies as vibrant as those in her non-thrillers. Hints of her interest in this type of writing appear in her fiction as early as 1854 and recur throughout her work thereafter.

Nevertheless, Louisa felt ambivalent toward her thrillers and refused to allow them to appear under her own name, even when publishers interested in exploiting her reputation offered her more money to do so. Several appeared bylined "L. M. Alcott" or attributed cryptically to "A Well-Known Author," but the majority were published anonymously or under the pseudonym A. M. Barnard. Their steady output continued until 1870, by which time the runaway success of *Little Women* ensured that she would never have to write another such story unless she chose to—which she did in 1877, when a publisher encouraged her to follow through on an idea that had been simmering in her imagination for more than a decade: her Gothic opus, *A Modern Mephistopheles*. Louisa planned to own up to her authorship of this novel and her earlier thriller, "A Whisper in the Dark," when the two were reprinted in a single volume in 1889, but she died shortly before the book's publication.

Louisa May Alcott's reticence to acknowledge her thrillers in her lifetime is understandable from her standpoint as a professional, but unfortunate as far as her literary legacy is concerned. Although she dismissed these efforts as mere commercial necessities—a verdict she also rendered for her children's books, indicating that she may *not* have been the best judge of how posterity would see her—any embarrassment she felt toward them is wholly unjustified. The literary quality that distinguished these stories from others of their kind is still evident today.

The earliest of this volume's selections, "Marion Earle; or, Only an Actress!" was first published in 1858, and the latest, *A Modern Mephistopheles*, nearly two decades later. This period coincides with her most fruitful years as a writer, and all of the work she produced during that time reflects her growth and maturation into the writer who is today a recognized figure in America's literary pantheon. It is hard to believe that someone as committed to her art as Louisa May Alcott was would devote the care and attention she clearly lavished on her thrillers if she thought of them only as anomalous creations undeserving of preservation. If, as Alcott scholar Madeleine Stern has written, the unmarried Louisa took "her pen as her bridegroom," then we must consider *all* of her stories her progeny and her thrillers her prodigal children. It is time to welcome them back into the family after their long exile.

—*Stefan Dziemianowicz*
New York City, 1996

Introduction

Louisa May Alcott
The "Spinning Spider"

Louisa May Alcott is known to most readers as the woman who penned one of the most warm-hearted and eloquent tributes ever paid to the American family. What middle-class American girl has reached the throes of puberty without having immersed herself, at least once, in the tribulations and victories of Meg, Jo, Beth, and Amy in *Little Women*? It's a novel that both extols and subverts the value of domesticity; that triumphantly portrays the courage of nineteenth-century women at the same time that it notes the barriers inhibiting them; that reveals the conflicts between love and career, home and the workplace, individual freedom and familial commitment—conflicts that still exist today. In fact, it has been said that "few other books in American literary history . . . have had so enormous an impact on the imagination of [women]." The atmosphere within the March household, with loving Marmee in charge during the father's absence, is benign enough to keep at bay all the demons—except death—that lurk outside, which perhaps accounts for the book's continuing ability to inspire and soothe.

Yet sooner or later demons must be reckoned with if we (meaning men *and* women) are to experience moral growth—at least this seems to be the theme of the majority of Alcott's stories in the present volume. Alcott wrote these works both before and after *Little Women* as she persisted in widening her imaginative landscape and testing her literary wings. There are echoes here of Poe, Hawthorne, and the English gothic writers, but the voice itself, no matter what the guise, is unremittingly Alcott's: graceful, emotionally heightened, teetering on the brink of sentimentality but never quite allowing herself to plunge into it.

A Modern Mephistopheles is the longest and perhaps the most ambitious tale.

Essentially it's a rewriting of Goethe's *Faust*—there is even a Walpurgis Night—but with fascinating differences. In Alcott's version, the heroine, Gladys, possesses a purity that's endangered by the machinations of a jaded aristocrat, Jasper Helwyze.

> Helwyze liked to see her [Gladys] among the flowers; for there was something peculiarly innocent and fresh about her then, as if the woman forgot her griefs, and was a girl again. It struck him anew, as she stood there in the sunshine, leaning down to tend the soft leaves and cherish the delicate buds with a caressing hand.
>
> "Like seeks like: you are a sort of cyclamen yourself . . . the likeness is quite striking. . . . This is especially like you," continued Helwyze, touching one of the freshest. "Out of these strong sombre leaves rises a wraith-like blossom, with white, softly folded petals, a rosy color on its modest face, and a most sweet perfume for those whose sense is fine enough to perceive it. Most of all, perhaps, it resembles you in this—it hides its heart, and, if one tries to look too closely, there is danger of snapping the slender stem."

Here, as in her other stories, Alcott employs flower imagery to symbolize the beauty and fragility of the human soul, and insect imagery as a similitude for the delicate though enduring quality of women's work—indeed, Alcott often referred to herself as "spinning tales like a spider."

There's a secret at the heart of *A Modern Mephistopheles* that I suspect will be difficult for today's readers to guess (at least it was for me). In any case, the tale can be read a number of ways, including allegorically. To me, Jasper Helwyze represents the kind of malevolent cynicism that ultimately destroys innocence, even that of children.

In another long story, "V. V.; or Plots and Counterplots," Alcott examines the evil nature of women—particularly women who use their beauty and intelligence to serve their own selfish ends. Alcott's descriptive powers help prepare the way for the melodramatic elements of the story, thereby making them more palatable, and sometimes even arresting:

> Everything about her was peculiar and piquant. Her dress was of that vivid, silvery green, which is so ruinous to any but the purest complexion, so ravishing when worn by one whose fresh bloom defies all hues. The skirt swept long behind her, and the Pompadour waist, with its flowing sleeves, displayed a neck and arms of dazzling fairness, half concealed by a film of costly lace. No jewels but an antique opal ring, attached by a slender chain to a singular bracelet, or wide band of enchased gold. A single deep-hued flower

glowed on her bosom, and in that wonderful hair of hers, a chaplet of delicate ferns seemed to gather back the cloud of curls, and encircle coil upon coil of glossy hair, that looked as if it burdened her small head.

This is, of course, a more florid writing style than any that prevails today, although it's certainly consistent with Alcott's exotic settings and characters. As scholars have noted, there was a theatrical side to her nature—she flirted with the idea of becoming an actress—that seemed to require an occasional respite from the mundane. Perhaps this is the reason so many of her characters wear masks, and why she was so profoundly aware of the tensions between the exterior self and interior self, tensions that figure prominently in her gothic prose. Perhaps it's also the reason so many of her tales have a rich European or English setting. Considering the fact that she was brought up in a household of strong democratic beliefs and practices, these same aristocratic leanings must have posed some uncertainties. After all, her father, Bronson Alcott, was a close friend of Emerson (Emerson referred to him as "a tedious archangel"), who in the 1830s had called for an indigenous American literature, and also of Thoreau, who in *Walden* had the will and vision to make Emerson's call a reality.

Yet what did "indigenous literature" mean to a female writer of this period except in strictly domestic terms, and what did a woman's skills have to do with taming a wilderness or describing a backwoods culture that was predominantly male? Even Hawthorne recognized the problem. "No author, without a trial," he earlier observed, "can conceive of the difficulty of writing a romance about a country where there is no shadow, no antiquity, no mystery, no picturesque and gloomy wrong, nor anything but a commonplace prosperity, in broad and simple daylight." For Alcott, the artistic dilemma must have been doubly perplexing. Where were the customs, artifices, airs, and psychological nuances that would occupy Edith Wharton decades later? Her chief recourse—unless she wished to go on writing endless extensions of *Little Women*—was to seek creative impetus elsewhere, and this is what she did. (This impetus, by the way, had its commercial aspect: like today's celebrity worship, the burgeoning middle class wished to read about their "betters.")

Her demons, too, were almost always highborn, or at the very least, cosmopolitan—it was as if she sent her New World morality abroad to combat Old World pathologies. If so, morality invariably won, though not without considerable sacrifice—a struggle that, incidentally, figured in the trajectory of Alcott's own career. She never married, and although she enjoyed a certain amount of success, she also suffered numerous rejections, and some of her stories remained unpublished during her lifetime.

So what does this literary "spinning spider" have to teach us today? What can we learn from her stories? Though her tenacity of purpose and willingness to experiment both are traits to admire, she is, above all, a superb storyteller. She was one of the first "popular" female writers to recast traditional classics, such as *Faust* and *Pilgrim's Progress*, in order to examine women's roles; in this sense, it's little wonder that feminists have claimed her as their own. But Alcott, by virtue of her broad empathy, rises above such facile classification. Her compassion extended to men, too, and she never stopped studying the emotional makeup of both sexes. Though she looked back to Europe for many customs and artifacts, she still had both feet firmly planted on American soil. And if she was aware that home is woman's special province, she also knew that one has to explore what lies beyond the threshold. As a result, she spread her cobweb wide and caught many strange and wondrous creatures in it, some of whom are contained within these pages.

—*Susie Mee*
1996

Slowly the charcoal caught and kindled, while a light smoke filled the room. Slowly the youth staggered up, and, gathering the torn sheets, thrust them into his bosom, muttering bitterly, "Of all my hopes and dreams, my weary work and patient waiting, nothing is left but this. Poor little book, we'll go together, and leave no trace behind."

Throwing himself into a chair, he laid his head down upon the table, where no food had been for days, and, closing his eyes, waited in stern silence for death to come and take him.

Nothing broke the stillness but the soft crackle of the fire, which began to flicker with blue tongues of flame, and cast a lurid glow upon the motionless figure with its hidden face. Deeper grew the wintry gloom without, ruddier shone the fateful gleam within, and heavy breaths began to heave the breast so tired of life.

Suddenly a step sounded on the stair, a hand knocked at the door, and when no answer came, a voice cried, "Open!" in a commanding tone, which won instant obedience, and dispelled the deathful trance fast benumbing every sense.

"The devil!" ejaculated the same imperious voice, as the door swung open, letting a cloud of noxious vapor rush out to greet the new-comer—a man standing tall and dark against the outer gloom.

"Who is it? Oh! come in!" gasped the youth, falling back faint and dizzy, as the fresh air smote him in the face.

"I cannot, till you make it safe for me to enter. I beg pardon if I interrupt your suicide; I came to help you live, but if you prefer the other thing, say so, and I will take myself away again," said the stranger, pausing on the threshold, as his quick eye took in the meaning of the scene before him.

"For God's sake, stay!" and, rushing to the window, the youth broke it with a blow, caught up the furnace, and set it out upon the snowy roof, where it hissed and glowed like an evil thing, while he dragged forth his one chair, and waited, trembling, for his unknown guest to enter.

"For my own sake, rather: I want excitement; and this looks as if I might find it here," muttered the man, with a short laugh, as he watched the boy, calmly curious, till a gust of fresh air swept through the room, making him shiver with its sharp breath.

"Jasper Helwyze, at your service," he added aloud, stepping in, and accepting courteously the only hospitality his poor young host could offer.

The dim light and shrouding cloak showed nothing but a pale, keen face,

A Modern Mephistopheles

Editor's Note: In 1866, Alcott wrote *A Modern Mephistopheles, or the Long Fatal Love Chase*, a short gothic novel featuring a satanic villain. Her publishers rejected the story as "too long & too sensational," and it remained unpublished until 1995, when it appeared as *A Long Fatal Love Chase*. Eleven years later, clearly still intrigued by the idea of the devil incarnate, Alcott produced an entirely new short novel titled *A Modern Mephistopheles* for a fiction series that specialized in anonymous works by well-known writers. The longest of the gothic thrillers published in her lifetime, the tale is modeled noticeably on Goethe's *Faust*.

I

Without, a midwinter twilight, where wandering snowflakes eddied in the bitter wind between a leaden sky and frost-bound earth.

Within, a garret; gloomy, bare, and cold as the bleak night coming down.

A haggard youth knelt before a little furnace, kindling a fire, with an expression of quiet desperation on his face, which made the simple operation strange and solemn.

A pile of manuscript lay beside him, and in the hollow eyes that watched the white leaves burn was a tragic shadow, terrible to see—for he was offering the first-born of heart and brain as sacrifice to a hard fate.

with dark penetrating eyes, and a thin hand, holding a paper on which the youth recognized the familiar words, "Felix Canaris."

"My name! You came to help me? What good angel sent you, sir?" he exclaimed, with a thrill of hope—for in the voice, the eye, the hand that held the card with such tenacious touch, he saw and felt the influence of a stronger nature, and involuntarily believed in and clung to it.

"Your bad angel, you might say, since it was the man who damned your book and refused the aid you asked of him," returned the stranger, in a suave tone, which contrasted curiously with the vigor of his language. "A mere chance led me there to-day, and my eye fell upon a letter lying open before him. The peculiar hand attracted me, and Forsythe, being in the midst of your farewell denunciation, read it out, and told your story."

"And you were laughing at my misery while I was making ready to end it?" said the youth, with a scornful quiver of the sensitive lips that uttered the reproach.

"We all laugh at such passionate folly when we have outlived it. You will, a year hence; so bear no malice, but tell me briefly if you can forget poetry, and be content with prose for a time. In plain words, can you work instead of dream?"

"I can."

"Good! then come to me for a month. I have been long from home, and my library is neglected; I have much for you to do, and believe you are the person I want, if Forsythe tells the truth. He says your father was a Greek, your mother English, both dead, and you an accomplished, ambitious young man who thinks himself a genius, and will not forgive the world for doubting what he has failed to prove. Am I right?"

"Quite right. Add also that I am friendless, penniless, and hopeless at nineteen."

A brief, pathetic story, more eloquently told by the starvation written on the pinched face, the squalor of the scanty garments, and the despair in the desperate eye, than by the words uttered with almost defiant bluntness.

The stranger read the little tragedy at a glance, and found the chief actor to his taste; for despite his hard case he possessed beauty, youth, and the high aspirations that die hard—three gifts often peculiarly attractive to those who have lost them all.

"Wait a month, and you may find that you have earned friends, money, and the right to hope again. At nineteen, one should have courage to face the world, and master it."

"Show me how, and I *will* have courage. A word of sympathy has already made it possible to live!" and, seizing the hand that offered help, Canaris kissed it with the impulsive grace and ardor of his father's race.

"When can you come to me?" briefly demanded Helwyze, gathering his cloak about him as he rose, warned by the waning light.

"At once, to-night, if you will! I possess nothing in the world but the poor clothes that were to have been my shroud, and the relics of the book with which I kindled my last fire," answered the youth, with eager eyes, and an involuntary shiver as the bitter wind blew in from the broken window.

"Come, then, else a mightier master than I may claim you before dawn, for it will be an awful night. Put out your funeral pyre, Canaris, wrap your shroud well about you, gather up your relics, and follow me. I can at least give you a warmer welcome than I have received," added Helwyze, with that sardonic laugh of his, as he left the room.

Before he had groped his slow way down the long stairs the youth joined him, and side by side they went out into the night.

A month later the same pair sat together in a room that was a dream of luxury. A noble library, secluded, warm, and still; the reposeful atmosphere that students love pervaded it; rare books lined its lofty walls: poets and philosophers looked down upon their work with immortal satisfaction on their marble countenances; and the two living occupants well became their sumptuous surroundings.

Helwyze leaned in a great chair beside a table strewn with books which curiously betrayed the bent of a strong mind made morbid by physical suffering. Doré's "Dante" spread its awful pages before him; the old Greek tragedies were scattered about, and Goethe's "Faust" was in his hand. An unimpressive figure at first sight, this frail-looking man, whose age it would be hard to tell; for pain plays strange pranks, and sometimes preserves to manhood a youthful delicacy in return for the vigor it destroys. But at a second glance the eye was arrested and interest aroused, for an indefinable expression of power pervaded the whole face, beardless, thin-lipped, sharply cut, and colorless as ivory. A stray lock or two of dark hair streaked the high brow, and below shone the controlling feature of this singular countenance, a pair of eyes, intensely black, and so large they seemed to burden the thin face. Violet shadows encircled them, telling of sleepless nights, days of languor, and long years of suffering, borne with stern patience. But in the eyes themselves all the vitality of the man's indomitable spirit seemed concentrated, intense and brilliant as a flame, which nothing could quench. By turns melancholy, meditative, piercing, or contemptuous, they varied in expression with startling rapidity, unless mastered by an art stronger than nature; attracting or repelling with a magnetism few wills could resist.

Propping his great forehead on his hand, he read, motionless as a statue, till a restless movement made him glance up at his companion, and fall to studying him with a silent scrutiny which in another would have softened to admiration, for Canaris was scarcely less beautiful than the Narcissus in the niche behind him.

An utter contrast to his patron, for youth lent its vigor to the well-knit frame, every limb of which was so perfectly proportioned that strength and grace were most harmoniously blended. Health glowed in the rich coloring of the classically moulded face, and lurked in the luxuriant locks which clustered in glossy rings from the low brow to the white throat. Happiness shone in the large dreamy eyes and smiled on the voluptuous lips; while an indescribable expression of fire and force pervaded the whole, redeeming its beauty from effeminacy.

A gracious miracle had been wrought in that month, for the haggard youth was changed into a wonderfully attractive young man, whose natural ease and elegance fitted him to adorn that charming place, as well as to enjoy the luxury his pleasure-loving senses craved.

The pen had fallen from his hand, and lying back in his chair with eyes fixed on vacancy, he seemed dreaming dreams born of the unexpected prosperity which grew more precious with each hour of its possession.

"Youth surely *is* the beauty of the devil, and that boy might have come straight from the witches' kitchen and the magic draught," thought Helwyze, as he closed his book, adding to himself with a daring expression, "Of all the visions haunting his ambitious brain not one is so wild and wayward as the fancy which haunts mine. Why not play fate, and finish what I have begun?"

A pause fell, more momentous than either dreamed; then it was abruptly broken.

"Felix, the time is up."

"It is, sir. Am I to go or stay?" and Canaris rose, looking half-bewildered as his brilliant castles in the air dissolved like mist before a sudden gust.

"Stay, if you will; but it is a quiet life for such as you, and I am a dull companion. Could you bear it for a year?"

"For twenty! Sir, you have been most kind and generous, and this month has seemed like heaven, after the bitter want you took me from. Let me show gratitude by faithful service, if I can," exclaimed the young man, coming to stand before his master, as he chose to call his benefactor, for favors were no burden yet.

"No thanks, I do it for my own pleasure. It is not every one who can have antique beauty in flesh and blood as well as marble; I have a fancy to keep my handsome secretary as the one ornament my library lacked before."

Canaris reddened like a girl, and gave a disdainful shrug; but vanity was tickled, nevertheless, and he betrayed it by the sidelong glance he stole towards the polished doors of glass reflecting his figure like a mirror.

"Nay, never frown and blush, man; 'beauty is its own excuse for being,' and you may thank the gods for yours, since but for that I should send you away to fight your dragons single-handed," said Helwyze, with a covert smile, adding, as he leaned forward to read the face which could wear no mask for him, "Come, you shall give me a year of your liberty, and I will help you to prove Forsythe a liar."

"You will bring out my book?" cried Canaris, clasping his hands as a flash of joy irradiated every lineament.

"Why not? and satisfy the hunger that torments you, though you try to hide it. I cannot promise success, but I *can* promise a fair trial; and if you stand the test, fame and fortune will come together. Love and happiness you can seek for at your own good pleasure."

"You have divined my longing. I do hunger and thirst for fame; I dream of it by night, I sigh for it by day; every thought and aspiration centres in that desire; and if I did not still cling to that hope, even the perfect home you offer me would seem a prison. I *must* have it; the success men covet and admire, suffer and strive for, and die content if they win it only for a little time. Give me this and I am yours, body and soul; I have nothing else to offer."

Canaris spoke with passionate energy, and flung out his hand as if he cast himself at the other's feet, a thing of little worth compared to the tempting prize for which he lusted.

Helwyze took the hand in a light, cold clasp, that tightened slowly as he answered with the look of one before whose will all obstacles go down—

"Done! Now show me the book, and let us see if we cannot win this time."

II

Nothing stirred about the vine-clad villa, except the curtains swaying in the balmy wind, that blew up from a garden where midsummer warmth brooded over drowsy flowers and whispering trees. The lake below gleamed like a mirror garlanded about with water-lilies, opening their white bosoms to the sun. The balcony above burned with deep-hearted roses pouring out their passionate perfume, as if in rivalry of the purple heliotrope, which overflowed great urns on either side of the stone steps.

Nothing broke the silence but the breezy rustle, the murmurous lapse of waters upon a quiet shore, and now and then the brief carol of a bird waking from its noontide sleep. A hammock swung at one end of the balcony, but it was empty; open doors showed the wide hall tenanted only by statues gleaming, cool and coy, in shadowy nooks; and the spirit of repose seemed to haunt the lovely spot.

For an hour the sweet spell lasted; then it was broken by the faint, far-off warble of a woman's voice, which seemed to wake the sleeping palace into life; for, as if drawn by the music, a young man came through the garden, looking as Ferdinand might, when Ariel led him to Miranda.

Too beautiful for a man he was, and seemed to protest against it by a disdainful negligence of all the arts which could enhance the gracious gift. A picturesque carelessness marked his costume, the luxuriant curls that covered his head were in riotous confusion; and as he came into the light he stretched his limbs with the graceful abandon of a young wood-god rousing from his drowse in some green covert.

Swinging a knot of lilies in his hand, he sauntered up the long path, listening with a smile, for as the voice drew nearer he recognized both song and singer.

"Little Gladys must not see me, or she will end her music too soon," he whispered to himself; and, stepping behind the great vase, he peered between the plumy sprays to watch the coming of the voice that made his verses doubly melodious to their creator's ear.

Through the shadowy hall there came a slender creature in a quaint white gown, who looked as if she might have stepped down from the marble Hebe's pedestal; for there was something wonderfully virginal and fresh about the maidenly figure with its deep, soft eyes, pale hair, and features clearly cut as a fine cameo. Emerging from the gloom into a flood of sunshine, which

touched her head with a glint of gold, and brought out in strong relief the
crimson cover of the book, held half-closed against her breast, she came
down the steps, still singing softly to herself.

A butterfly was sunning its changeful wings on the carved balustrade, and
she paused to watch it, quite unconscious of the picture she made, or the
hidden observer who enjoyed it with the delight of one whose senses were
keenly alive to all that ministers to pleasure. A childish act enough, but it
contrasted curiously with the words she sung—fervid words, that seemed to
drop lingeringly from her lips as if in a new language; lovely, yet half learned.

"Pretty thing! I wish I could sketch her as she stands, and use her as an
illustration to that song. No nightingale ever had a sweeter voice for a love-
lay than this charming girl," thought the flattered listener, as, obeying a
sudden impulse, he flung up the lilies, stepped out from his ambush, and
half-said, half-sung, as he looked up with a glance of mirthful meaning—

> "Like a high-born maiden
> In a palace tower,
> Soothing her love-laden
> Soul in secret hour,
> With music sweet as love which overflows her bower."

The flowers dropped at her feet, and, leaning forward with the supple
grace of girlhood, she looked down to meet the dangerous dark eyes, while
her own seemed to wake and deepen with a sudden light as beautiful as the
color which dawned in her innocent face. Not the quick red of shame, nor
the glow of vanity, but a slow, soft flush like the shadow of a rosy cloud on
snow. No otherwise disconcerted, she smiled back at him, and answered with
unexpected aptness, in lines that were a truer compliment than his had
been—

> "Like a poet hidden
> In the light of thought,
> Singing hymns unbidden,
> Till the world is wrought
> To sympathy with hopes and fears it heeded not."

It was this charm of swift and subtle sympathy which made the girl seem
sometimes like the embodied spirit of all that was most high and pure in his
own wayward but aspiring nature. And this the spell that drew him to her

now, glad to sun himself like the butterfly in the light of eyes so clear and candid, that he could read therein the emotions of a maiden heart just opening to its first, half-conscious love.

Springing up the steps, he said with the caressing air as native to him as his grace of manner, "Sit here and weave a pretty garland for your hair, while I thank you for making my poor verses beautiful. Where did you find the air that fits those words so well?"

"It came itself; as the song did, I think," she answered simply, as she obeyed him, and began to braid the long brown stems, shaping a chaplet fit for Undine.

"Ah! you will never guess how that came!" he said, sitting at her feet to watch the small fingers at their pretty work. But though his eyes rested there, they grew absent; and he seemed to fall into a reverie not wholly pleasant, for he knit his brows as if the newly won laurel wreath sat uneasily upon a head which seemed made to wear it.

Gladys watched him in reverential silence till he became conscious of her presence again, and gave her leave to speak, with a smile which had in it something of the condescension of an idol towards its devoutest worshipper.

"Were you making poetry, then?" she asked, with the frank curiosity of a child.

"No, I was wondering where I should be now if I had never made any;" and he looked at the summer paradise around him with an involuntary shiver, as if a chill wind had blown upon him.

"Think rather what you will write next. It is so lovely I want more, although I do not understand all this," touching the book upon her knee with a regretful sigh.

"Neither do I; much of it is poor stuff, Gladys. Do not puzzle your sweet wits over it."

"That is because you are so modest. People say true genius is always humble."

"Then, I am not a true genius; for I am as proud as Lucifer."

"You may well be proud of such work as this;" and she carefully brushed a fallen petal from the silken cover.

"But I am *not* proud of that. At times I almost hate it!" exclaimed the capricious poet, impetuously, then checked himself, and added more composedly, "I mean to do so much better, that this first attempt shall be forgotten."

"I think you will never do better; for this came from your heart, without a thought of what the world would say. Hereafter all you write may be more perfect in form but less true in spirit, because you will have the fear of the world, and loss of fame before your eyes."

"How can you know that?" he asked, wondering that this young girl, so lately met, should read him so well, and touch a secret doubt that kept him idle after the first essay, which had been a most flattering success.

"Nay, I do not know, I only feel as if it must be so. I always sing best when alone, and the thought of doing it for praise or money spoils the music to my ear."

"I feel as if it would be possible to do *any thing* here, and forget that there is a world outside."

"Then it is not dull to you? I am glad, for I thought it would be, because so many people want you, and you might choose many gayer places in which to spend your summer holiday."

"I have no choice in this; yet I was willing enough to come. The first time is always pleasant, and I am tired of the gayer places," he said, with a *blasé* air that ill concealed how sweet the taste of praise had been to one who hungered for it.

"Yet it must seem very beautiful to be so sought, admired, and loved," the girl said wistfully, for few of fortune's favors had fallen into her lap as yet.

"It is, and I was intoxicated with the wine of success for a time. But after all, I find a bitter drop in it, for there is always a higher step to take, a brighter prize to win, and one is never satisfied."

He paused an instant with the craving yet despondent look poets and painters wear as they labor for perfection in "a divine despair;" then added, in a tone of kindly satisfaction which rung true on the sensitive ear that listened—

"But all that nonsense pleases Helwyze, and he has so few delights, I would not rob him of one even so small as this, for I owe every thing to him, you know."

"I do not know. May I?"

"You may; for I want you to like my friend, and now I think you only fear him."

"Mr. Canaris, I do not dislike your friend. He has been most kind to me; I am grieved if I seem ungrateful," murmured Gladys, with a vague trouble in her artless face, for she had no power to explain the instinctive recoil which had unconsciously betrayed itself.

"Hear what he did for me, and then it may be easier to show as well as to feel gratitude; since but for him you would have had none of these foolish rhymes to sing."

With a look askance, a quick gesture, and a curious laugh, Canaris tossed the book into the urn below, and the heliotrope gave a fragrant sigh as it closed above the treasure given to its keeping. Gladys uttered a little cry, but her companion took no heed, for clasping his hands about his knee he looked off into the bloomy wilderness below as if he saw a younger self there, and spoke of him with a pitiful sort of interest.

"Three years ago an ambitious boy came to seek his fortune in the great city yonder. He possessed nothing but sundry accomplishments, and a handful of verses which he tried to sell. Failing in this hope after various trials, he grew desperate, and thought to end his life like poor Chatterton. No, not like Chatterton—for this boy was not an impostor."

"Had he no friend anywhere?" asked Gladys—her work neglected while she listened with intensest interest to the tale so tragically begun.

"He thought not, but chance sent him one at the last hour, and when he called on death, Helwyze came. It always seemed to me as if, unwittingly, I conjured from the fire kindled to destroy myself a genie who had power to change me from the miserable wretch I was, into the happy man I am. For more than a year I have been with him—first as secretary, then *protégé*, now friend, almost son; for he asks nothing of me except such services as I love to render, and gives me every aid towards winning my way. Is not that magnificent generosity? Can I help regarding him with superstitious gratitude? Am I not rightly named Felix?"

"Yes, oh yes! Tell me more, please. I have led such a lonely life, that human beings are like wonder-books to me, and I am never tired of reading them." Gladys looked with a rapt expression into the face upturned to hers, little dreaming how dangerous such lore might be to her.

"Then you should read Helwyze; he is a romance that will both charm and make your heart ache, if you dare to try him."

"I dare, if I may, because I would so gladly lose my fear of him in the gentler feeling that grows in me as I listen."

Canaris was irresistibly led on to confidences he had no right to make, it was so pleasant to feel that he had the power to move the girl by his words, as the wind sways a leaf upon its delicate stem. A half-fledged purpose lurked in a dark corner of his mind, and even while denying its existence to himself, he yielded to its influence, careless of consequences.

"Then I will go on and let compassion finish what I have begun. Till thirty, Helwyze led a wonderfully free, rich life, I infer from hints dropped in unguarded moments—for confidential moods are rare. Every good gift was his, and nothing to alloy his happiness, unless it was the restless nature which kept him wandering like an Arab long after most men have found some ambition to absorb, or some tie to restrain, them. From what I have gathered, I know that a great passion was beginning to tame his unquiet spirit, when a great misfortune came to afflict it, and in an hour changed a life of entire freedom to one of the bitterest bondage such a man can know."

"Oh, what?" cried Gladys, as he artfully paused just there to see her bend nearer, and her lips part with the tremor of suspense.

"A terrible fall; and for ten years he has never known a day's rest from pain of some sort, and never will, till death releases him ten years hence, perhaps, if his indomitable will keeps him alive so long."

"Alas, alas! is there no cure?" sighed Gladys, as the violet eyes grew dim for very pity of so hard a fate.

"None."

A brief silence followed while the shadow of a great white cloud drifted across the sky, blotting out the sunshine for a moment.

All the flowers strayed down upon the steps and lay there forgotten, as the hands that held them were clasped together on the girl's breast, as if the mere knowledge of a lot like this lay heavy at her heart.

Satisfied with his effect, the story-teller was tempted to add another stroke, and went on with the fluency of one who saw all things dramatically, and could not help coloring them in his own vivid fancy.

"That seems very terrible to you, but in truth the physical affliction was not so great as the loss that tried his soul; for he loved ardently, and had just won his suit, when the misfortune came which tied him to a bed of torment for some years. A fall from heaven to hell could hardly have seemed worse than to be precipitated from the heights of such a happiness to the depths of such a double woe; for she, the beautiful, beloved woman proved disloyal, and left him lying there, like Prometheus, with the vulture of remembered bliss to rend his heart."

"Could he not forget her?" and Gladys trembled with indignation at the perfidy which seemed impossible to a nature born for self-sacrifice.

"He never will forget or forgive, although the man she married well avenged him while he lived, and bequeathed her a memory which all his gold could not gild. *Her* fate is the harder now; for the old love has revived, and Helwyze is dearer than in his days of unmarred strength. He knows it, but will not accept the tardy atonement; for contempt has killed *his* love, and with him there is no resurrection of the dead. A very patient and remorseful love is hers: for she has been humiliated in spirit, as he can never be, by the bodily ills above which he has risen so heroically that his courage has subdued the haughtiest woman I ever met."

"You know her, then?" and Gladys bent to look into his face, with her own shadowed by an intuition of the truth.

"Yes."

"I am afraid to listen any more. It is terrible to know that such bitterness and grief lie hidden in the hearts about me. Why did you tell me this?" she demanded, shrinking from him, as if some prophetic fear had stepped between them.

"Why did I? Because I wished to make you pity my friend, and help me put a little brightness into his hard life. You can do it if you will, for you soothe and please him, and few possess the power to give him any comfort. He makes no complaint, asks no pity, and insists on ignoring the pain which preys upon him, till it grows too great to be concealed; then shuts himself up alone, to endure it like a Spartan. Forgive me if in my eagerness I have said too much, and forget whatever troubled you."

Canaris spoke with genuine regret, and hoped to banish the cloud from a face which had been as placid as the lake below, till he disturbed it by reflections that affrighted her.

"It is easy to forgive, but not to forget, words which cannot be unsaid. I was so happy here; and now it is all spoilt. She was a new-made friend, and very kind to me when I was desolate. I shall seem a thankless beggar if I go away before I have paid my debt as best I can. How shall I tell her that I must?"

"Of whom do you speak? I gave no name. I thought you would not guess. Why must you go, Gladys?" asked the young man, surprised to see how quickly she felt the chill of doubt, and tried to escape obligation, when neither love nor respect brightened it.

"I need give no name, because you know. It is as well, perhaps, that I have guessed it. I ought not to have been so content, since I am here through charity. I must take up my life and try to shape it for myself; but the world seems very large now I am all alone."

She spoke half to herself, and looked beyond the safe, secluded garden, to the gray mountains whose rough paths her feet had trod before they were led here to rest.

Quick to be swayed by the varying impulses which ruled him with capricious force, Canaris was now full of pity for the trouble he had wrought, and when she rose, like a bird startled from its nest, he rose also, and, taking the hand put out as if involuntarily asking help, he said with regretful gentleness—

"Do not be afraid, we will befriend you. Helwyze shall counsel and I will comfort, if we can. I should not have told that dismal story; I will atone for it by a new song, and you shall grow happy in singing it."

She hesitated, withdrew her hand, and looked askance at him, as if one doubt bred others. An approaching footstep made her start, and stand a moment with head erect, eye fixed, and ear intent, like a listening deer, then whispering, "It is she; hide me till I learn to look as if I did not know!"— Gladys sprung down the steps, and vanished like a wraith, leaving no token of her presence but the lilies in the dust, for the young man followed fleetly.

III

~

A woman came into the balcony with a swift step, and paused there, as if disappointed to find it deserted. A woman in the midsummer of her life, brilliant, strong, and stately; clad in something dusky and diaphanous, unrelieved by any color, except the pale gold of the laburnum clusters, that drooped from deep bosom and darkest hair. Pride sat on the forehead, with its straight black brows, passion slept in the Southern eyes, lustrous or languid by turns, and will curved the closely folded lips of vivid red.

But over all this beauty, energy, and grace an indescribable blight seemed to have fallen, deeper than the loss of youth's first freshness, darker than the trace of any common sorrow. Something felt, rather than seen, which gave her the air of a dethroned queen; conquered, but protesting fiercely, even while forced to submit to some inexorable decree, whose bitterest pang was the knowledge that the wrong was self-inflicted.

As she stood there, looking down the green vista, two figures crossed it. A smile curved the sad mouth, and she said aloud, "Faust and Margaret, playing the old, old game."

"And Mephistopheles and Martha looking on," added a melodious voice, behind her, as Helwyze swept back the half-transparent curtain from the long window where he sat.

"The part you give me is not a flattering one," she answered, veiling mingled pique and pleasure with well-feigned indifference.

"Nor mine; yet I think they suit us both, in a measure. Do you know, Olivia, that the accidental reading of my favorite tragedy, at a certain moment, gave me a hint which has afforded amusement for a year."

"You mean your fancy for playing Mentor to that boy. A dangerous task for you, Jasper."

"The danger is the charm. I crave excitement, occupation; and what but something of this sort is left me? Much saving grace in charity, we are told; and who needs it more than I? Surely I have been kinder to Felix than the Providence which left him to die of destitution and despair?"

"Perhaps not. The love of power is strong in men like you, and grows by what it feeds on. If I am not mistaken, this whim of a moment has already hardened into a purpose which will mould his life in spite of him. It is an occupation that suits your taste, for you enjoy his beauty and his promise; you like to praise and pamper him till vanity and love of pleasure wax strong, then you check him with an equal satisfaction, and find excitement in curbing his high spirit, his wayward will. By what tie you hold him I cannot tell; but I know it must be something stronger than gratitude, for, though he chafes against the bond, he *dares* not break it."

"Ah, that is my secret! What would you not give if I would teach you the art of taming men as I once taught you to train a restive horse?"—and Helwyze looked out at her with eyes full of malicious merriment.

"You have taught me the art of taming a woman; is not that enough?" murmured Olivia, in a tone that would have touched any man's heart with pity, if with no tenderer emotion.

But Helwyze seemed not to hear the reproach, and went on, as if the other topic suited his mood best.

"I call Canaris my Greek slave, sometimes, and he never knows whether to feel flattered or insulted. His father was a Greek adventurer, you know (ended tragically, I suspect), and but for the English mother's legacy of a trifle of moral sense, Felix would be as satisfactory a young heathen as if brought straight from ancient Athens. It was this peculiar mixture of un-scrupulous daring and fitful virtue which attracted me, as much as his unusual beauty and undoubted talent. Money can buy almost any thing, you know; so I bought my handsome Alcibiades, and an excellent bargain I find him."

"But when you tire of him, what then? You cannot sell him again, nor throw him away, like a book you weary of. Neither can you leave him neglected in the lumber-room, with distasteful statues or bad pictures. Affection, if you have it, will not outlast your admiration, and I have much curiosity to know what will become of your 'handsome Alcibiades' then."

"Then, my cousin, I will give him to you, for I have fancied of late that you rather coveted him. You could not manage him now—the savage in him is not quite civilized yet—but wait a little, and I will make a charming plaything for you. I know you will treat him kindly, since it is truly said, 'Those who have served, best know how to rule.' "

The sneer stung her deeply, for there was no humiliation this proud woman had not suffered at the hands of a brutal and unfaithful husband. Pity was as bitter a draught to her as to the man who thus cruelly reminded her of the long bondage which had left an ineffaceable blight upon her life. The wound bled inwardly, but she retaliated, as only such a woman could.

"Love is the one master who can rule and bind without danger or disgrace. I shall remember that, and when you give me Felix he will find me a gentler mistress than I was ten years ago—to you."

The last words dropped from her lips as softly as if full of tender reminiscence, but they pricked pride, since they could not touch a relentless heart. Helwyze betrayed it by the sombre fire of his eye, the tone in which he answered.

"And I will ask of you the only gift I care to accept—your new *protégée*, Gladys. Tell me where you found her; the child interests me much."

"I know it;" and, stifling a pang of jealous pain, Olivia obeyed with the docility of one in whom will was conquered by a stronger power.

"A freak took me to the hills in March. My winter had been a vain chase after happiness, and I wanted solitude. I found it where chance led me—in this girl's home. A poor, bleak place enough; but it suited me, for there were only the father and daughter, and they left me to myself. The man died suddenly, and no one mourned, for he was a selfish tyrant. The girl was left quite alone, and nearly penniless, but so happy in her freedom that she had no fears. I liked the courage of the creature; I knew how she felt; I saw great capacity for something fine in her. I said, 'Come with me for a little, and time will show you the next step.' She came; time has shown her, and the next step will take her from my house to yours, unless I much mistake your purpose."

Leaning in the low, lounging chair, Helwyze had listened motionless, except that the fingers of one thin hand moved fitfully, as if he played upon some instrument inaudible to all ears but his own. A frequent gesture of his, and most significant, to any one who knew that his favorite pastime was touching human heart-strings with marvellous success in producing discords by his uncanny skill.

As Olivia paused, he asked in a voice as suave as cold—

"My purpose? Have I any?"

"You say she interests you, and you watch her in a way that proves it. Have you not already resolved to win her for your amusement, by some bribe as cunning as that you gave Canaris for his liberty?"

"I have. You are a shrewd woman, Olivia."

"Yet she is not beautiful;" and her eye vainly searched the inscrutable countenance, that showed so passionless and pale against the purple cushion where it leaned.

"Pardon me, the loveliest woman I have seen for years. A beautiful, fresh soul is most attractive when one is weary of more material charms. This girl seems made of spirit, fire, and dew; a mixture rare as it is exquisite, and the spell is all the greater because of its fine and elusive quality. I promise myself much satisfaction in observing how this young creature meets the trials and temptations life and love will bring her; and to do this she must be near at hand."

"Happy Gladys!"

Olivia smiled a scornful smile, but folded her arms to curb the rebellious swelling of her heart at the thought of another woman nearer than herself. She turned away as she spoke; but Helwyze saw the quiver of her lips, and read the meaning of the piercing glance she shot into the garden, as if to find and annihilate that unconscious rival.

Content for the moment with the touch of daily torture which was the atonement exacted for past disloyalty, he lifted the poor soul from despair to delight by the utterance of three words, accompanied by a laugh as mirthless as musical—

"Happy Felix, rather."

"Is *he* to marry her?" and Olivia fronted him, glowing with a sudden joy which made her lovely as well as brilliant.

"Who else?"

"Yourself."

"I!" and the word was full of a bitterness which thrilled every nerve the woman had, for an irrepressible regret wrung it from lips sternly shut on all complaint, except to her.

"Why not?" she cried, daring to answer with impetuous warmth and candor. "What woman would not be glad to serve you for the sake of the luxury with which you would surround her, if not for the love you might win and give, if you chose?"

"Bah! what have I to do with love? Thank Heaven my passions are all dead, else life would be a hell, not the purgatory it is," he said, glancing at his wasted limbs, with an expression which would have been pathetic, had it not been defiant; for that long discipline of pain had failed to conquer the spirit of the man, and it seemed to sit aloof, viewing with a curious mixture of compassion and contempt the slow ruin of the body which imprisoned it.

With an impulse womanly as winning, Olivia plucked a wine-dark rose from the trellis nearest her, and, bending towards him, laid it in his hand, with a look and gesture of one glad to give all she possessed, if that were possible.

"Your love of beauty still survives, and is a solace to you. Let me minister to it when I can; and be assured I offer my little friend as freely as I do my choicest rose."

"Thanks; the flower for me, the friend for Felix. Young as he is, he knows how to woo, and she will listen to his love-tale as willingly as she did to the highly colored romance he was telling her just now. You would soon find her a burden, Olivia, and so should I, unless she came in this way. We need do nothing but leave the young pair to summer and seclusion; they will make the match better and more quickly than we could. Then a month for the honeymoon business, and all can be comfortably settled before October frosts set in."

"You often say, where women are is discord; yet you are planning to bring one into your house in the most dangerous way. Have you no fears, Jasper?"

"Not of Gladys; she is so young, I can mould her as I please, and that suits me. She will become my house well, this tender, transparent little creature, with her tranquil eyes, and the sincere voice which makes truth sweeter than falsehood. You must come and see her there; but never try to alter her, or the charm will be destroyed."

"You may be satisfied: but how will it be with Felix? Hitherto your sway has been undivided, now you must share it; for with all her gentleness she is strong, and will rule him."

"And I, Gladys. Felix suits me excellently, and it will only add another charm to the relation if I control him through the medium of another. My young lion is discovering his power rapidly, and I must give him a Una before he breaks loose and chooses for himself. If matters must be complicated, I choose to do it, and it will occupy my winter pleasantly to watch the success of this new combination."

While he talked, Helwyze had been absently stripping leaf after leaf from the great rose, till nothing but the golden heart remained trembling on the thorny stem.

Olivia had watched the velvet petals fall one by one, feeling a sad sympathy with the ill-used gift; yet, as the last leaf fluttered to the ground, she involuntarily lifted up her hand to break another, glad if even in the destruction of so frail a thing he could find a moment's pleasure.

"No, let them hang; their rich color pleases best among the green; their cloying perfume is too heavy for the house. A snowdrop, leaning from its dainty sheath undaunted by March winds, is more to my taste now," he said, dropping the relics of the rose, with the slow smile which often lent such significance to a careless word.

"I cannot give you that: spring flowers are all gone long ago," began Olivia, regretfully.

"Nay, you give me one in Gladys; no spring flower could be more delicate than she, gathered by your own hand from the bleak nook where you found her. It is the faint, vernal fragrance of natures, coyly hidden from common eye and touch, which satisfies and soothes senses refined by suffering."

"Yet you will destroy it, like the rose, in finding out the secret of its life. I wondered why this pale, cold innocence was so attractive to a man like you. There was a time when you would have laughed at such a fancy, and craved something with more warmth and brilliancy."

"I am wiser now, and live here, not here," he answered, touching first his forehead then his breast, with melancholy meaning. "While my brain is spared me I can survive the ossification of all the heart I ever had, since, at best, it is an unruly member. Almost as inconvenient as a conscience; that, thank fortune, I never had. Yes; to study the mysterious mechanism of human nature is a most absorbing pastime, when books weary, and other sources of enjoyment are forbidden. Try it, and see what an exciting game it becomes, when men and women are the pawns you learn to move at will. Goethe's boyish puppet-show was but a symbol of the skill and power which made the man the magician he became."

"An impious pastime, a dearly purchased fame, built on the broken hearts of women!" exclaimed Olivia, walking to and fro with the noiseless step and restless grace of a leopardess pacing its cage.

Helwyze neither seemed to see nor hear her, for his gloomy eyes stared at a little bird tilting on a spray that swung in the freshening wind, and his thoughts followed their own path.

" 'Pale, cold innocence.' It *is* curious that it should charm me. A good sign, perhaps; for poets tell us that fallen angels sigh for the heaven they have lost, and try to rise again on the wings of spirits stronger and purer than themselves. Would they not find virtue insipid after a fiery draught of sin? Did not Paradise seem a little dull to Dante, in spite of Beatrice? I wish I knew."

"Is it for this that you want the girl's help?" asked Olivia, pausing in her march to look at him. "I shall wait with interest to see if she lifts you up to sainthood, or you drag her down to your level, where intellect is God, conscience ignored, and love despised. Unhappy Gladys! I should have said, because I cannot keep her from you, if I would; and in your hands she will be as helpless as the dumb creatures surgeons torture, that they may watch a living nerve, count the throbbing of an artery, or see how long the poor things will live bereft of some vital part. Let the child alone, Jasper, or you will repent of it."

"Upon my word, Olivia, you are in an ominously prophetic mood. I hear a carriage; and, as I am invisible to all eyes but your gifted ones, pardon me if I unceremoniously leave the priestess on her tripod."

And the curtain dropped between them as suddenly as it had been lifted, depriving the woman of the one troubled joy of her life—companionship with him.

IV

"Felix, are you asleep?"

"No, sir, only resting."

"Have you been at work?"

"Decidedly; I rowed across the lake and back."

"Alone?"

"Gladys went with me, singing like a mermaid all the way."

"Ah!"

Both men were lounging in the twilight; but there was a striking difference in their way of doing it. Canaris lay motionless on a couch, his head pillowed on his arms, enjoying the luxury of repose, with the *dolce far niente* only possible to those in whose veins runs Southern blood. Helwyze leaned in a great chair, which looked a miracle of comfort; but its occupant stirred restlessly, as if he found no ease among its swelling cushions; and there was an alert expression in his face, betraying that the brain was at work on some thought or purpose which both absorbed and excited.

A pause followed the brief dialogue, during which Canaris seemed to relapse into his delicious drowse, while Helwyze sat looking at him with the critical regard one bestows on a fine work of art. Yet something in the spectacle of rest he could not share seemed to annoy him; for, suddenly turning up the shaded lamp upon his table, he dispelled the soft gloom, and broke the silence.

"I have a request to make. May I trouble you to listen?"

There was a tone of command in the courteously worded speech, which made Canaris sit erect, with a respectful—

"At your service, sir."

"I wish you to marry," continued Helwyze, with such startling abruptness that the young man gazed at him in mute amazement for a moment. Then, veiling his surprise by a laugh, he asked lightly—

"Isn't it rather soon for that, sir? I am hardly of age."

"Geniuses are privileged; and I am not aware of any obstacle, if *I* am satisfied," answered Helwyze, with an imperious gesture, which seemed to put aside all objections.

"Do you seriously mean it, sir?"

"I do."

"But why such haste?"

"Because it is my pleasure."

"I will not give up my liberty so soon," cried the young man, with a mutinous flash of the eye.

"I thought you had already given it up. If you choose to annul the agreement, do it, and go. You know the forfeit."

"I forgot this possibility. Did I agree to obey in all things?"

"It was so set down in the bond. Entire obedience in return for the success you coveted. Have I failed in my part of the bargain?"

"No, sir; no."

"Then do yours, or let us cancel the bond, and part."

"How can we? What can I do without you? Is there no way but this?"

"None."

Canaris looked dismayed—and well he might, for it seemed impossible to put away the cup he had thirsted for, when its first intoxicating draught was at his lips.

Helwyze had spoken with peculiar emphasis, and his words were full of ominous suggestion to the listener's ear; for he alone knew how much rebellion would cost him, since luxury and fame were still dearer than liberty or honor. He sprung up, and paced the room, feeling like some wild creature caught in a snare.

Helwyze, regardless of his chafing, went on calmly, as if to a willing hearer, eying him vigilantly the while, though now his own manner was as persuasive as it had been imperative before.

"I ask no more than many parents do, and will give you my reasons for the demand, though that was not among the stipulations."

"A starving man does not stop to weigh words, or haggle about promises. I was desperate, and you offered me salvation; can you wonder that I clutched the only hand held out to me?" demanded Canaris, with a world of conflicting emotions in his expressive face, as he paused before his master.

"I am not speaking of the first agreement, that was brief as simple. The second bargain was a more complicated matter. You were not desperate then; you freely entered into it, reaped the benefits of it, and now wish to escape the consequences of your own act. Is that fair?"

"How could I dream that you would exact such obedience as this? I am too young; it is a step that may change my whole life; I must have time," murmured Canaris, while a sudden change passed over his whole face; his eye fell before the glance bent on him, as the other spoke.

"It need not change your life, except to make it freer, perhaps happier. Hitherto you have had all the pleasure, now I desire my share. You often speak of gratitude; prove it by granting my request, and, in adding a new solace to my existence, you will find you have likewise added a new charm to your own."

"It is so sudden—I do desire to show my gratitude—I have tried to do my part faithfully so far," began Canaris, as if a look, a word, had tamed his high spirit, and enforced docility sorely against his will.

"So far, I grant that, and I thank you for the service which I desire to lessen by the step you decline to take. I have spoilt you for use, but not for ornament. I still like to see you flourish; I enjoy your success; I cannot free you; but I *can* give you a mate, who will take your place and amuse me at home, while you sing and soar abroad. Is that sufficiently poetical for a poet's comprehension?" and Helwyze smiled, that satiric smile of his, still watching the young man's agitated countenance.

"But why need *I* marry? Why cannot"—there Canaris hesitated, for he lacked the courage to make the very natural suggestion Olivia had done.

Helwyze divined the question on his lips, and answered it with stern brevity.

"That is impossible;" then added, with the sudden softening of tone which made his voice irresistibly seductive, "I have given one reason for my whim: there are others, which affect you more nearly and pleasantly, perhaps. Little more than a year ago, your first book came out, making you famous for a time. You have enjoyed your laurels for a twelvemonth, and begin to sigh for more. The world has petted you, as it does any novelty, and expects to be paid for its petting, else it will soon forget you."

"No fear of that!" exclaimed the other, with the artless arrogance of youth.

"If I thought you would survive the experiment, I would leave you to discover what a fickle mistress you serve. But frost would soon blight your budding talent, so we will keep on the world's sunny side, and tempt the Muse, not terrify her."

Nothing could be smoother than the voice in which these words were said; but a keen ear would have detected an accent of delicate irony in it, and a quick eye have seen that Canaris winced, as if a sore spot had been touched.

"I should think marriage would do that last, most effectually," he answered, with a scornful shrug, and an air of great distaste.

"Not always: some geniuses are the better for such bondage. I fancy you are one of them, and wish to try the experiment. If it fails, you can play Byron, to your heart's content."

"A costly experiment for some one." Canaris paused in his impatient march, to look down with a glance of pity at the dead lily still knotted in his button-hole.

Helwyze laughed at the touch of sentiment—a low, quiet laugh; but it made the young man flush, and hastily fling away the faded flower, whose pure loveliness had been a joy to him an hour ago. With a half docile, half defiant look, he asked coldly—

"What next, sir?"

"Only this: you have done well. Now, you must do better, and let the second book be free from the chief fault which critics found—that, though the poet wrote of love, it was evident he had never felt it."

"Who shall say that?" with sudden warmth.

"I, for one. You know nothing of love, though you may flatter yourself you do. So far, it has been pretty play enough, but I will not have you waste yourself, or your time. You need inspiration, this will give it to you. At your age, it is easy to love the first sweet woman brought near you, and almost impossible for any such to resist your wooing. An early marriage will not only give heart and brain a fillip, but add the new touch of romance needed to keep up the world's interest in the rising star, whose mysterious advent piques curiosity as strongly as his work excites wonder and delight."

Composure and content had been gradually creeping back into the listener's mien, as a skilful hand touched the various chords that vibrated most tunefully in a young, imaginative, ardent nature. Vivid fancy painted the "sweet woman" in a breath, quick wit saw at once the worldly wisdom of the advice, and ambition found no obstacle impassable.

"You are right, sir, I submit; but I claim the privilege of choosing my inspirer," he said, warily.

"You have already chosen, if I am not much mistaken. A short wooing, but a sure one; for little Gladys has no coquetry, and will not keep you waiting for her answer."

"Gladys is a child," began Canaris, still hesitating to avow the truth. "The fitter mate for you."

"But, sir, you are mistaken: I do not love her."

"Then, why teach her to love you?"

"I have not: I was only kind. Surely I cannot be expected to marry every young girl who blushes when I look at her," he said, with sullen petulance, for women had spoilt the handsome youth, and he was as ungrateful as such idols usually are.

"Then, who?—ah! I perceive; I had forgotten that a boy's first *tendresse* is too often for a woman twice his age. May I trouble you?" and Helwyze held up the empty glass with which he had been toying while he talked.

Among the strew of books upon the table at his elbow stood an antique silver flagon, coolly frosted over by the iced wine it held. This Canaris obediently lifted; and, as he stooped to fill the rosy bowl of the Venetian goblet, Helwyze leaned forward, till the two faces were so close that eye looked into eye, as he said, in one swift sentence, "It was to win Olivia for *yourself*, then, that you wooed Gladys for *me*, three hours ago?"

The flagon was not heavy, but it shook in the young man's grasp, and the wine overflowed the delicate glass, dyeing red the hand that held it. One face glowed with shame and anger; the other remained unmoved, except a baffling smile upon the lips, that added, in mild reproach—

"My Ganymede has lost his skill; it is time I filled his place with a neat-handed Hebe. Make haste, and bring her to me soon."

Mutely Canaris removed all traces of the treacherous mishap, inwardly cursing his imprudent confidences, wondering what malignant chance brought within ear-shot one who rarely left his own apartments at the other end of the villa; and conscious of an almost superstitious fear of this man, who read so surely, and dragged to light so ruthlessly, hidden hopes and half-formed designs.

Vouchsafing no enlightenment, Helwyze sipped the cool draught with an air of satisfaction, continuing the conversation in a tone of exasperating calmness.

"Among other amusing fables with which you beguiled poor Gladys, I think you promised counsel and comfort. Keep your word, and marry her. It is the least you can do, after destroying her faith in the one friend she possessed. A pleasant, but a dangerous pastime, and not in the best taste; let me advise you to beware of it in future."

There was a covert menace in the tone, a warning in the significant grip of the pale fingers round the glass, as if about to snap its slender stem. Canaris was white now with impotent wrath, and a thrill went through his vigorous young frame, as if the wild creature was about to break loose, and defy its captor.

But the powerful eye was on him, with a spark of fire in its depths, and controlled till words, both sweet and bitter, soothed and won him.

"I know that any breath of tenderness would pass by Olivia as idly as the wind. You doubt this, and a word will prove it. I am not a tyrant, though I seem such; therefore you are free to try your fate before you gratify my whim and make Gladys happy."

"You think the answer will be 'No'?" and Canaris forgot every thing but the hope which tempted, even while reason told him it was vain.

"It always has been; it always will be, if I know her."

"Will be till *you* ask."

"Rest easy; I am done with love."

"But if she answers 'Yes'?"

"Then bid good-bye to peace—and me."

The answer startled the young lover, and made him shrink from what he ardently desired; for the new passion was but an enthralment of the senses, and he knew it by the fine instinct which permits such men to see and condemn their lower nature, even while yielding to its sway.

But pride silenced doubt, and native courage made it impossible to shun the trial or accept the warning. His eye lit, his head rose, and he spoke out manfully, though unconsciously he wore the look of one who goes to lead a forlorn hope—

"I shall try my fate to-night, and, if I fail, you may do what you like with me."

"Not a coward, thank Heaven!" mused Helwyze, as he looked after the retreating figure with the contemptuous admiration one gives to any fool-hardy enterprise bravely undertaken. "He must have his lesson, and will be the tamer for it, unless Olivia takes me at my word, and humors the boy, for vengeance' sake. That would be a most dramatic complication, and endanger my winter's comfort seriously. Come, suspense is a new emotion; I will enjoy it, and meantime make sure of Gladys, or I may be left in the lurch. A reckless boy and a disappointed woman are capable of any folly."

V

Helwyze folded the black velvet *paletot* about him, stroked the damp hair off his forehead, and, with hands loosely clasped behind his back, went walking slowly through the quiet house, to find the bright drawing-room and breezy balcony already deserted.

No sound of voice or step gave him the clew he sought; and, pausing in the hall, he stood a moment, his finger on his lip, wondering whither Gladys had betaken herself.

"Not with them, assuredly. Dreaming in the moonshine somewhere. I must look again."

Retracing his noiseless steps, he glanced here and there with eyes which nothing could escape, for trifles were significant to his quick wit; and he found answers to unspoken queries in the relics the vanished trio left behind them. Olivia's fan, flung down upon a couch, made him smile, as if he saw her toss it there when yielding half-impatiently to the entreaties of Canaris. An ottoman, pushed hastily aside, told where the young lover sat, till he beguiled her out to listen to the pleading which would wax eloquent and bold under cover of the summer night. The instrument stood open, a favorite song upon the rack, but the glimmering keys were mute; and the wind alone was singing fitfully. A little hat lay in the window, as if ready to be caught up in glad haste when the summons came; but the dew had dimmed the freshness of its azure ribbons, and there was a forlorn look about the girlish thing, which told the story of a timid hope, a silent disappointment.

"Where the deuce is the child?" and Helwyze cast an ireful look about the empty room; for motion wearied him, and any thwarting of his will was dangerous. Suddenly his eye brightened, and he nodded, as if well pleased; for below the dark drapery that hung before an arch, a fold of softest white betrayed the wearer.

"Now I have her!" he whispered, as if to some familiar; and, parting the curtains, looked down upon the little figure sitting there alone, bathed in moonlight as purely placid as the face turned on him when he spoke.

"Might one come in? The house seems quite deserted, and I want some charitable soul to say a friendly word to me."

"Oh, yes! What can I do, sir?" With the look of a suddenly awakened child, Gladys rose up, and involuntarily put out her hand as if to heap yet more commodiously the pillows of the couch which filled the alcove; then paused, remembering what Canaris had told her of the invalid's rejection of all sympathy, and stood regarding him with a shy, yet wistful glance, which plainly showed the impulse of her tender heart.

Conscious that the surest way to win this simple creature was by submitting to be comforted—for in her, womanly compassion was stronger than womanly ambition, vanity, or interest—Helwyze shed a reassuring smile upon her, as he threw himself down, exclaiming, with a sigh of satisfaction, doubly effective from one who so seldom owned the weariness that oppressed him—

"Yes: you shall make me comfortable, if you kindly will; the heat exhausts me, and I cannot sleep. Ah, this is pleasant! You have the gift of piling pillows for weary heads, Gladys. Now, let the moonlight make a picture of you, as it did before I spoilt it; then I shall envy no man."

Pleased, yet abashed, the girl sank back into her place on the wide window-ledge, and bent her face over the blooming-linden spray that lay upon her lap, unconsciously making of herself a prettier picture than before.

"Musing here alone? Not sorrowfully, I hope?"

"I never feel alone, sir, and seldom sorrowful."

" 'They never are alone that are accompanied with noble thoughts;' yet it would not be unnatural if you felt both sad and solitary, so young, so isolated, in this big, bad world of ours."

"A beautiful and happy world to me, sir. Even loneliness is pleasant, because with it comes—liberty."

The last word fell from her lips involuntarily; and, with a wonderfully expressive gesture, she lifted her arms as if some heavy fetter had newly dropped away.

Ardent emphasis and forceful action both surprised and interested Helwyze, confirming his suspicion that this girlish bosom hid a spirit as strong as pure, capable of deep suffering, exquisite happiness, heroic effort. His eye shone, and he gave a satisfied nod; for his first careless words had struck fire from the girl, making his task easier and more attractive.

"And how will you use this freedom? A precious, yet a perilous, gift for such as you."

"Can any thing so infinitely sweet and sacred be dangerous? He who planted the longing for it here, and gave it me when most needed, will surely teach me how to use it. I have no fear."

The bent head was erect now; the earnest face turned full on Helwyze with such serene faith shining in it, that the sneer died off his lips, and something like genuine compassion touched him, at the sight of such brave innocence tranquilly confronting the unknown future.

"May nothing molest, or make afraid. While here, you are quite safe—you *do*, then, think of going?" he added, as a quick change arrested him.

"I do, sir, and soon. I only wait to see how, and where."

It was difficult to believe that so resolute a tone could come into a voice so gentle, or that lips whose shape was a smile could curl with such soft scorn. But both were there; for the memory of that other woman's story embittered even gratitude, since in the girl's simple creed disloyalty to love was next to disloyalty to God.

Helwyze watched her closely, while his fingers fell to tapping idly on the sofa scroll; and the spark brightened under the lids that contracted with the intent expression of concentrated sight.

"Perhaps I can show you how and when. May I?" he asked, assuming a paternal air, which inwardly amused him much.

Gladys looked, hesitated, and a shade of perplexity dimmed the clear brightness of her glance, as if vaguely conscious of distrust, and troubled by its seeming causelessness.

Helwyze saw it, and quickly added the magical word which lulled suspicion, roused interest, and irresistibly allured her fancy.

"Pardon me; I should not have ventured to speak, if Felix had not hinted that you began to weary of dependence, as all free spirits must; your own words confirm the hint; and I desired to share my cousin's pleasure in befriending, if I might, one who can so richly repay all obligation. Believe me, Gladys, your voice is a treasure, which, having discovered, we want to share between us."

If the moonlight had been daybreak, the girl's cheek could not have shown a rosier glow, as she half-averted it to hide the joy she felt at knowing Canaris had taken thought for her so soon. Her heart fluttered with tender hopes and fears, like a nestful of eager birds; and, forgetting doubt in delight, she yielded to the lure held out to her.

"You are most kind: I shall be truly grateful if you will advise me, sir. Mrs. Surry has done so much, I can ask no more, but rather hasten to relieve her of all further care of me."

"She will be loth to lose you; but the friend of whom I am about to speak needs you much, and can give you what you love better even than kindness— independence."

"Yes: that is what I long for! I will do any thing for daily bread, if I may earn it honestly, and eat it in freedom," leaning nearer, with clasped hands and eager look.

"Could you be happy to spend some hours of each day in reading, singing to, and amusing a poor soul, who sorely needs such pleasant comforting?"

"I could. It would be very sweet to do it; and I know how, excellently well, for I have had good training. My father was an invalid, and I his only nurse for years."

"Fortunate for me in all ways," thought Helwyze, finding another reason for his purpose; while Gladys, bee-like, getting sweetness out of bitter-herbs, said to herself, "Those weary years had their use, and are not wasted, as I feared."

"I think these duties will not be difficult nor distasteful," continued

Helwyze, marking the effect of each attraction, as he mentioned it with modest brevity. "It is a quiet place; plenty of rare books to read, fine pictures to study, and music to enjoy; a little clever society, to keep wits bright and enliven solitude; hours of leisure, and entire liberty to use them as you will. Would this satisfy you, Gladys, till something better can be found?"

"Better!" echoed the girl, with the expression of one who, having asked for a crust, is bidden to a feast. "Ah, sir, it sounds too pleasant for belief. I long for all these lovely things, but never hoped to have them. Can I earn so much happiness? Am I a fit companion for this poor lady, who must need the gentlest nursing, if she suffers in the midst of so much to enjoy?"

"You will suit exactly; have no fear of that, my good child. Just be your own happy, helpful self, and you can make sunshine anywhere. We will talk more of this when you have turned it over in that wise young head of yours. Olivia may have some more attractive plan to offer."

But Gladys shook "the wise young head" with a decided air, as piquant as the sudden resolution in her artless voice.

"I shall choose for myself; your plan pleases me better than any Mrs. Surry is likely to propose. She says I must not work, but rest and enjoy myself. I will work; I love it; ease steals away my strength, and pleasure seems to dazzle me. I must be strong, for I have only myself to lean upon; I must see clearly, for my only guide is my own conscience. I *will* think of your most kind offer, and be ready to accept it whenever you like to try me, sir."

"Thanks; I like to try you now, then; sit here and croon some drowsy song, to show how well you can lull wakeful senses into that blessed oblivion called sleep."

As he spoke, Helwyze drew a low seat beside the couch, and beckoned her to come and take it; for she had risen as if to go, and he had no mind to be left alone yet.

"I am so pleased you asked me to do this, for it is my special gift. Papa was very stubborn, but he always had to yield, and often called me his 'sleep-compeller.' Let me drop the curtain first, light is so exciting, and draws the insects. I shall keep them off with this pretty fan, and you will find the faint perfume soothing."

Full of the sweetest good-will, Gladys leaned across the couch to darken the recess before the lullaby began. But Helwyze, feeling in a mood for investigation and experiment, arrested the outstretched hand, and, holding it in his, turned the full brilliance of his fine eyes on hers, asking with most seductive candor—

"Gladys, if *I* were the friend of whom we spoke, would you come to me? You compel truth as well as sleep, and I cannot deceive you, while you so willingly serve me."

A moment she stood looking down into the singular countenance before her with a curious intentness in her own. A slight quickening of the breath was all the sign she gave of a consciousness of the penetrative glance fixed upon her, the close grasp of his hand; otherwise unembarrassed as a child, she regarded him with an expression maidenly modest, but quite composed. Helwyze keenly enjoyed these glimpses of the new character with which he chose to meddle, yet was both piqued and amused by her present composure, when the mere name of Felix filled her with the delicious shamefacedness of a first love.

It was a little curious that during the instant the two surveyed each other, that, while the girl's color faded, a light red tinged the man's pale cheek, her eye grew clear and cold as his softened, and the small hand seemed to hold the larger by the mere contact of its passive fingers.

Slow to arrive, the answer was both comprehensive and significant, but very brief, for three words held it.

"Could I come?"

Helwyze laughed with real enjoyment.

"You certainly have the gift of surprises, if no other, and it makes you charming, Gladys. I fancied you as unsophisticated as if you were eight, instead of eighteen, and here I find you as discreet as any woman of the world—more so than many. Where did you learn it, child?"

"From myself; I have no other teacher."

"Ah! 'instinct is a fine thing, my masters.' *You* could not have a better guide. Rest easy, little friend, the proprieties shall be preserved, and you *can* come, if you decide to do me the honor. My old housekeeper is a most decorous and maternal creature, and into her keeping you will pass. Felix pleased me well, but his time is too valuable now; and, selfish as I am, I hesitate to keep for my own comfort the man who can charm so many. Will you come, and take his place?"

Helwyze could not deny himself the pleasure of calling back the tell-tale color, for the blushes of a chaste woman are as beautiful as the blooming of a flower. Quickly the red tide rose, even to the brow, the eyes fell, the hand thrilled, and the steady voice faltered traitorously, "I could not fill it, sir."

Still detaining her, that he might catch the sweet aroma of an opening heart, Helwyze added, as the last temptation to this young Eve, whom he was beguiling out of the safe garden of her tranquil girlhood into the unknown world of pain and passion, waiting for womankind beyond—

"Not for my own sake alone do I want you, but for his. Life is full of perils for him, and he needs a home. I cannot make one for him, except in this way, for my house is my prison, and he wearies of it naturally. But I *can* give it a new charm, add a never-failing attraction, and make it homelike by a woman's presence. Will you help me in this?"

"I am not wise enough; Mrs. Surry is often with you: surely she could make it homelike far better than I," stammered Gladys, chilled by a sudden fear, as she remembered Canaris' face as he departed with Olivia an hour ago.

"Pardon; that is precisely what she cannot do. Such women weary while they dazzle, the gentler sort win while they soothe. We shall see less of her in future; it is not well for Felix. Take pity on *me*, at least, and answer 'Yes.' "

"I do, sir."

"How shall I thank you?" and Helwyze kissed the hand as he released it, leaving a little thorn of jealousy behind to hoodwink prudence, stimulate desire, and fret the inward peace that was her best possession.

Glad to take refuge in music, the girl assumed her seat, and began to sing dreamily to the slow waving of the green spray. Helwyze feigned to be courting slumber, but from the ambush of downcast lids he stole sidelong glances at the countenance so near his own, that he could mark the gradual subsiding of emotion, the slow return of the repose which made its greatest charm for him. And so well did he feign, that presently, as if glad to see her task successfully ended, Gladys stole away to the seclusion of her own happy thoughts.

Busied with his new plans and purposes, Helwyze waited till his patience was rewarded by seeing the face of Canaris appear at the window, glance in, and vanish as silently as it came. But one look was enough, and in that flash of time the other read how the rash wooing had sped, or thought he did, till Olivia came sweeping through the room, flung wide the curtains, and looked in with eyes as brilliant as if they had borrowed light of the fire-flies dancing there without.

"A fan, a cigarette, a scarlet flower behind the ear, and the Spanish donna would be quite perfect," he said, surveying with lazy admiration the richly colored face, which looked out from the black lace, wrapped mantilla-wise over the dark hair and whitely gleaming arms.

"Is the snowdrop gone? Then I will come in, and hear how the new handmaid suits. I saw her at her pleasing task."

"So well that I should like to keep her at it long and often. Where is Felix?"

His words, his look, angered Olivia, and she answered with smiling ambiguity—

"Out of his misery, at last."

"Cruel as ever. I told him it would be so."

"On the contrary, I have been kind, as I promised to be."

"Then his face belied him."

"Would it please you, if I had ventured to forestall your promised gift, and accepted all Felix has to offer me, himself. I have my whims, like you, and follow them as recklessly."

Helwyze knit his brows, but answered negligently, "Folly never pleases me. It will be amusing to see which tires first. I shall miss him; but his place is already filled, and Gladys has the charm of novelty."

"You have spoken, then?"

"Forewarned, forearmed; I have her promise, and Felix can go when he likes."

Olivia paled, dropped her mask, and exclaimed in undisguised alarm—

"There is no need: I have no thought of such folly! My kindness to Felix was the sparing him an avowal, which was simply absurd. A word, a laugh, did it, for ridicule cures more quickly and surely than compassion."

"I thought so. Why try to fence with me, Madame? you always get the worst of it," and Helwyze made the green twig whistle through the air with a sharp turn of the wrist, as he rose to go; for these two, bound together by a mutual wrong, seldom met without bitter words, the dregs of a love which might have blest them both.

He found Felix waiting for him, in a somewhat haughty mood; Olivia having judged wisely that ridicule, though a harsh, was a speedy cure for the youthful delusion, which had been fostered by the isolation in which they lived, and the ardent imagination of a poet.

"You were right, sir. What are your commands?" he asked, controlling disappointment, pique, and unwillingness with a spirit that won respect and forbearance even from Helwyze, who answered with a cordial warmth, as rare as charming—

"I have none: the completion of my wish I leave to you. Consult your own time and pleasure, and, when it is happily accomplished, be assured I shall not forget that you have shown me the obedience of a son."

Quick as a child to be touched, and won by kindness, Canaris flushed with grateful feeling and put out his hand impulsively, as he had done when selling his liberty, for now he was selling his love.

"Forgive my waywardness. I *will* be guided by you, for I owe you my life, and all the happiness I have known in it. Gladys shall be a daughter to you; but give me time—I must teach myself to forget."

His voice broke as he stumbled over the last words, for pride was sore, and submission hard. But Helwyze soothed the one and softened the other by one of the sympathetic touches which occasionally broke from him, proving that the man's heart was not yet quite dead. Laying his hand upon the young man's shoulder, he said in a tone which stirred the hearer deeply—

"I feared this pain was in store for you, but could not save you from it. Accept the gentle comforter I bring you, for I have known the same pain, and *I* had no Gladys."

VI

So the days went by, fast and fair in outward seeming, while an undercurrent of unquiet emotion rolled below. Helwyze made no sign of impatience, but silently forwarded his wish, by devoting himself to Olivia; thereby making a green oasis in the desert of her life, and leaving the young pair to themselves.

At first, Canaris shunned every one as much as possible; but sympathy, not solitude, was the balm he wanted, and who could give it him so freely as Gladys? Her mute surprise and doubt and grief at this capricious coldness, after such winning warmth, showed him that the guileless heart was already his, and added a soothing sense of power to the reluctance and regret which by turns tormented him.

Irresistibly drawn by the best instincts of a faulty but aspiring nature to that which was lovely, true, and pure, he soon returned to Gladys, finding in her sweet society a refreshment and repose Olivia's could never give him. Love he did not feel, but affection, the more helpful for its calmness; confidence, which was given again fourfold; and reverence, daily deepening as time showed him the gentle strength and crystal clarity of the spirit he was linking to his own by ties which death itself could not sever. But the very virtues which won, also made him hesitate, though rash enough when yielding to an attraction far less noble. A sense of unworthiness restrained him, even when reluctance had passed from resignation to something like desire, and he paused, as one might, who longed to break a delicate plant, yet delayed, lest it should wither too quickly in his hand.

Helwyze and Olivia watched this brief wooing with peculiar interest. She, being happy herself, was full of good hope for Gladys, and let her step, unwarned, into the magic circle drawn around her. He sat as if at a play, enjoying the pretty pastoral enacted before him, content to let "summer and seclusion" bring the young pair together as naturally and easily as spring-time mates the birds. Suspense gave zest to the new combination, surprise added to its flavor, and a dash of danger made it unusually attractive to him.

Canaris came to him one day, with a resolute expression on his face, which rendered it noble, as well as beautiful.

"Sir, I will not do this thing; I dare not."

"Dare not! Is cowardice to be added to disobedience and falsehood?" and Helwyze looked up from his book with a contemptuous frown.

"I will not be sneered out of my purpose; for I never did a braver, better act than when I say to you, 'I dare not lie to Gladys.' "

"What need of lying? Surely you love her now, or you are a more accomplished actor than I thought you."

"I have tried—tried too faithfully for her peace, I fear; but, though I reverence her as an angel, I do *not* love her as a woman. How can I look into her innocent, confiding face, and tell her—she who is all truth—that I love as she does?"

"Yet that is the commonest, most easily forgiven falsehood a man can utter. Is it so hard for *you* to deceive?"

Quick and deep rose the hot scarlet to Canaris's face, and his eyes fell, as if borne down by the emphasis of that one word. But the sincerity of his desire brought courage even out of shame; and, lifting his head with a humility more impressive than pride or anger, he said, steadily—

"If this truth redeems that falsehood, I shall, at least, have recovered my own self-respect. I never knew that I had lost it, till Gladys showed me how poor I was in the virtue which makes her what she is."

"What conscientious qualm is this? Where would this truth-telling bring you? How would your self-respect bear the knowledge that you had broken the girl's heart? for, angel as you call her, she has one, and you have stolen it."

"At your bidding."

"Long before I thought of it. Did you imagine you could play with her, to pique Olivia, without harm to Gladys? Is yours a face to smile on a woman, day after day, and not teach her to love? In what way but this *can* you atone for such selfish thoughtlessness? Come, if we are to talk of honor and honesty, do it fairly, and not shift the responsibility of your acts upon my shoulders."

"Have I done that? I never meant to trouble her. Is there no way out of it but this? Oh, sir, I am not fit to marry her! What am I, to take a fellow-creature's happiness into my hands? What have I to offer her but the truth in return for her love, if I must take it to secure her peace?"

"If you offer the truth, you certainly *will* have nothing else, and not even receive love in return, perhaps; for her respect may go with all the rest. If I know her, the loss of that would wound her heart more deeply than the disappointment your silence will bring her now. Think of this, and be wise as well as generous in the atonement you should make."

"Bound, whichever way I look; for when I meant to be kindest I am cruel."

Canaris stood perplexed, abashed, remorseful; for Helwyze had the art to turn even his virtues into weapons against him, making his new-born regard for Gladys a reason for being falsely true, dishonorably tender. The honest impulse suddenly looked weak and selfish, compassion seemed nobler than sincerity, and present peace better than future happiness.

Helwyze saw that he was wavering, and turned the scale by calling to his aid one of the strongest passions that rule men—the spirit of rivalry—knowing well its power over one so young, so vain and sensitive.

"Felix, there must be an end of this; I am tired of it. Since you are more enamoured of truth than Gladys, choose, and abide by it. I shall miss my congenial comrade, but I will not keep him if he feels my friendship slavery. I release you from all promises: go your way, in peace; I can do without you."

A daring offer, and Helwyze risked much in making it; but he knew the man before him, and that in seeming to set free, he only added another link to the invisible chain by which he held him. Canaris looked relieved, amazed, and touched, as he exclaimed, incredulously—

"Do you mean it, sir?"

"I do; but in return for your liberty I claim the right to use mine as I will."

"Use it? I do not understand."

"To comfort Gladys."

"How?"

"You do not love her, and leave her doubly forlorn, since you have given her a glimpse of love. I must befriend her, as you will not; and when she comes to me, as she has promised, if she is happy, I shall keep her."

"As *fille adoptive.*"

Canaris affirmed, not asked, this; and, in the changed tone, the suspicious glance, Helwyze saw that he had aimed well. With a smile that was a sneer, he answered coldly—

"Hardly that: the paternal element is sadly lacking in me; and, if it were not, I fear a man of forty could not adopt a girl of eighteen without compromising her, especially one so lonely and so lovely as poor little Gladys."

"You will marry her? Yet when I hinted it, you said, 'Impossible!' "

"I did; but then I did not know how helpful she could be, how glad to love, how easy to be won by kindness. *Ennui* drives one to do the rashest things; and when you are gone, I shall find it difficult to fill your place. 'Tis a pity to tie the pretty creature to such a clod. But, if I can help and keep her in no other way, I may do it, remembering that her captivity would be a short one; it should be my care that it was a very light one while it lasted."

"But she loves *me!*" exclaimed Canaris, with jealous inconsistency.

"I fear so; yet you reject her for a scruple. Hearts are easily caught in the rebound; and who will hold hers more gently than I? Olivia will tell you I *can* be gentle when it suits me."

The name stung Canaris, where pride was sorest; and the thought, that this man could take from him both the woman whom he loved and the girl who loved him, roused an ignoble desire to silence the noble one. He showed it instantly, for his eye shot a quick glance at the mirror; a smile that was almost insolent passed over his face; and his air was full of the proud consciousness of youth, health, comeliness, and talent.

"Thanks for my freedom; I shall know how to use it. Since I may tell Gladys the truth, I do not dread her love so much; and will atone generously, if I can. I think she will accept poverty with me rather than luxury with you. At least she shall have her choice."

"Well said. You will succeed, since you possess all the gifts which win women except wealth and"—

"Stop! you shall *not* say it," cried Canaris, hotly. "Are you possessed of a devil, that you torment me so?" He clenched his hands, and walked fast through the room, as if to escape from some fierce impulse.

A certain, almost brutal, frankness characterized the intercourse of these men at times; for the tie between them was a peculiar one, and fretted both, though both clung to it with strange tenacity. With equal candor and entire composure Helwyze answered the excited question.

"We are all possessed, more or less; happy the man who is master. My demon is a bad one; for your intellectual devil is hard to manage, since he demands the best of us, and is not satisfied or cheated as easily as some that are stronger, yet less cunning. Yours is ambition—an insatiable fellow, who gives you no rest. I had a fancy to help you rule him; but he proves less interesting than I thought to find him, and is getting to be a bore. See what you can do, alone; only, when he gets the upper hand again, excuse me from interfering: once is enough."

Canaris made no reply, but dashed out of the room, as if he could bear no more, leaving Helwyze to throw down his book, muttering impatiently—

"Here is a froward favorite, and excitement with a vengeance! He will not speak yet; for with all his fire he is wary, and while he fumes I must work. But how? but how?"

VII

A storm raged all that night; but dawn came up so dewy and serene, that the world looked like a child waking after anger, with happy smiles upon its lips, penitential tears in its blue eyes.

Canaris was early astir, after a night as stormy within as without, during which he had gone through so many alternations of feeling, that, weary and still undecided, he was now in the mood to drift whithersoever the first eddy impelled him. Straight to Gladys, it seemed; and, being superstitious, he accepted the accident as a good omen, following his own desire, and calling it fate.

Wandering in the loneliest, wildest spot of all the domain, he came upon her as suddenly as if a wish had brought her to the nook haunted for both by pleasant memories. Dew-drenched her feet, hatless her head; but the feet stood firmly on the cliff which shelved down to the shore below, and the upturned head shone bright against the deep blue of the sky. Morning peace dwelt in her eyes, morning freshness glowed on her cheek, and her whole attitude was one of unconscious aspiration, as she stood there with folded hands and parted lips, drinking in the storm-cooled breeze that blew vigorous and sweet across the lake.

"What are you doing here so early, little dryad?" and Canaris paused, with an almost irresistible desire to put out his arms and hold her, lest she fly away, so airy was her perch, so eager her look into the boundless distance before her.

"Only being happy!" and she looked down into his face with such tender and timid joy in her own, he hardly had need to ask—

"Why, Gladys?"

"Because of this," showing a string of pearls that hung from her hand, half-hidden among the trailing bits of greenery gathered in her walk.

"Who gave you that?" demanded Canaris, eying it with undisguised surprise; for the pearls were great, globy things, milk-white, and so perfect that any one but Gladys would have seen how costly was the gift.

"Need you ask?" she said, blushing brightly.

"Why not? Do you suspect me?"

"You cannot deceive me by speaking roughly and looking stern. Who but you would put these in my basket without a word, and let me find them there when I laid my work away last night? I was so pleased, so proud, I could not help keeping them, though far too beautiful for me."

Then Canaris knew who had done it; and his hand tightened over the necklace, while his eye went towards the lake, as if he longed to throw it far into the water. He checked himself, and, turning it about with a disdainful air, said, coldly—

"If *I* had given you this, it should have been quite perfect. The cross is not large nor fine enough to match the chain. Do you see?"

"Ah, but the little cross is more precious than all the rest! That is the one jewel my mother left me, and I put it there to make my rosary complete;" and Gladys surveyed it with a pretty mixture of devout affection and girlish pleasure.

"I'll give you a better one than this—a string of tiny carved saints in scented wood, blessed by holy hands, and fit to say prayers like yours upon. You will take it, though my gift is not half so costly as his?" he said, eagerly.

"Whose?"

"Helwyze gave you that."

"But why?" and Gladys opened wide her clear, large eyes in genuine astonishment.

"He is a generous master; your singing pleases him, and he pays you so," replied Canaris, bitterly.

"He is not my master!"

"He will be."

"Never! I shall not go, if I am to be burdened with benefits. I will earn my just due, but not be overpaid. Tell him so."

Gladys caught back the chain, unclasped the cross, and threw the pearls upon the grass, where they lay, gleaming, like great drops of frozen dew, among the green. Canaris liked that; thought proudly, "*I* have no need to bribe;" and hastened to make his own the thing another seemed to covet. Drawing nearer, he looked up, asking, in a tone that gave the question its true meaning—

"May *I* be your master, Gladys?"

"Not even you."

"Your slave, then?"

"Never that."

"Your lover?"

"Yes."

"But I can give you nothing except myself."

"Love is enough;" and finding his arms about her, his face, warm and wistful, close to hers, Gladys bent to give and take the first kiss, which was all they had to bestow upon each other.

Singularly unimpassioned was the embrace in which they stood for a brief instant. Canaris held her with a clasp more jealous than fond; Gladys clung to him, yet trembled, as if some fear subdued her joy; and both vaguely felt the incompleteness of a moment which should be perfect.

"You do love me, then?" she whispered, wondering at his silence.

"Should I ask you to be my wife if I did not?" and the stern look melted into an expression of what seemed, to her, reproach.

"No; ah, no! I fancied that I might have deceived myself. I am so young, you are so kind. I never had a—friend before;" and Gladys smiled shyly, as the word which meant "lover" dropped from her lips.

"I am not kind: I am selfish, cruel, perhaps, to let you love me so. You will never reproach me for it, Gladys? I mean to save you from ills you know nothing of; to cherish and protect you—if I can."

Verily in earnest now; for the touch of those innocent lips reminded him of all his promise meant, recalled his own unfitness to guide or guard another, when so wayward and unwise himself. Gladys could not understand the true cause of his beseeching look, his urgency of tone; but saw in them only the generous desire to keep safe the creature dearest to him, and loved him the more for it.

"I never can think you selfish, never will reproach you but will love and trust and honor you all my life," she answered, with a simplicity as solemn as sincere; and, holding out the hand that held her dead mother's cross, Canaris pledged his troth upon it with the mistaken chivalry which makes many a man promise to defend a woman against all men but himself.

"Now you can be happy again," he said, feeling that he had done his best to keep her so.

She thought he meant look out upon the lake, dreaming of him as when he found her; and, turning, stretched forth her arms as if to embrace the whole world, and tell the smiling heaven her glad secret.

"Doubly happy; then I only hoped, now I *know!*"

Something in the exultant gesture, the fervent tone, the radiant face, thrilled Canaris with a sudden admiration; a feeling of proud possession; a conviction that he had gained, not lost; and he said within himself—

"I am glad I did it. I will cherish her; she will inspire me; and good *shall* come out of seeming evil."

His spirits rose with a new sense of well-being and well-doing. He gathered up the rejected treasure, and gave it back to Gladys, saying lightly—

"You may keep it as a wedding-gift; then he need give no other. He meant it so, perhaps, and it will please him. Will you, love?"

"If you ask it. But why must brides wear pearls? They mean tears," she added, thoughtfully, as she received them back.

"Perhaps because then the sorrows of their lives begin. Yours shall not: I will see to that," he promised, with the blind confidence of the self-sacrificing mood he was in.

Gladys sat down upon the rock to explore a pocket, so small and empty that Canaris could not help smiling, as he, too, leaned and looked with a lover's freedom.

"Only my old chain. I must put back the cross, else I shall lose it," laughed Gladys, as she brought out a little cord of what seemed woven yellow silk.

"Is it your hair?" he asked, his eye caught by its peculiar sunshiny hue.

"Yes; I could not buy a better one, so I made this. My hair is all the gold I have."

"Give it to me, and you wear mine. See, I have an amulet as well as you."

Fumbling in his breast, Canaris undid a slender chain, whence hung a locket, curiously chased, and tarnished with long wear. This he unslung, and, opening, showed Gladys the faded picture of a beautiful, sad woman.

"That is my Madonna."

"Your mother?"

"Yes."

"Mine now." The girl touched it with her lips, then softly closed and laid it on her lap.

Silently Canaris stood watching her, as she re-slung both poor but precious relics, while the costlier one slipped down, as if ashamed to lie beside them. He caught and swung it on his finger, thinking of something he had lately read to Helwyze.

"Kharsu, the Persian, sent a necklace to Schirin, the princess, whom he loved. She was a Christian, and hung a cross upon his string of pearls, as you did," he said aloud.

"But I am not a princess, and Mr. Helwyze does not love me; so the pretty story is all spoiled."

"This thing recalled it. *I* have given you a necklace, and you are hanging a cross upon it. Wear the one, and use the other, for my sake. Will you, Gladys?"

"Did Schirin convert Kharsu?" asked the girl, catching his thought more from his face than his words; for it wore a look of mingled longing and regret, which she had never seen before.

"That I do not know; but you must convert me: I am a sad heathen, Helwyze says."

"Has *he* tried?"

"No."

"Then I will!"

"You see I've had no one to teach me any thing but worldly wisdom, and I sometimes feel as I should be better for a little of the heavenly sort. So when you wear the rosary I shall give you—'Fair saint, in your orisons be all my sins remembered;' " and Canaris put his hand upon her head, smiling, as if half-ashamed of his request.

"I am no Catholic, but I *will* pray for you, and you shall not be lost. The mother in heaven and the wife on earth will keep you safe," whispered Gladys, in her fervent voice, feeling and answering with a woman's quickness the half-expressed desire of a nature conscious of its weakness, yet unskilled in asking help for its greatest need.

Silently the two young lovers put on their amulets, and, hand in hand, went back along the winding path, till they reached the great eglantine that threw its green arches across the outlet from the wood. All beyond was radiantly bright and blooming; and as Canaris, passing first to hold back the thorny boughs, stood an instant, bathed in the splendor of the early sunshine, Gladys exclaimed, her face full of the tender idolatry of a loving woman—

"O Felix, you are so good, so great, so beautiful, if it were not wicked, I should worship you!"

"God forbid! Do not love me too much, Gladys: I do not deserve it."

"How can I help it, when I feel very like the girl who lost her heart to the Apollo?" she answered, feeling that she never could love *too much.*

"And broke her heart, you remember, because her god was only a stone."

"Mine is not, and he will answer when I call."

"If he does not, he will be harder and colder than the marble!"

When Canaris, some hours later, told Helwyze, he looked well pleased, thinking, "Jealousy is a helpful ally. I do not regret calling in its aid, though it has cost Olivia her pearls." Aloud he said, with a gracious air, which did not entirely conceal some secret anxiety—

"Then you have made a clean breast of it, and she forgives all peccadilloes?"

"I have not told her; and I will not, till I have atoned for the meanest of them. May I ask you to be silent also for her sake?"

"You are wise." Then, as if glad to throw off all doubt and care, he asked, in a pleasantly suggestive tone—

"The wedding will soon follow the wooing, I imagine, for you make short work of matters, when you do begin?"

"You told me to execute your wish in my own way. I will do so, without troubling Mrs. Surry, or asking you to give us your blessing, since playing the father to orphans is distasteful to you."

Very calm and cool was Canaris now; but a sense of wrong burned at his heart, marring the satisfaction he felt in having done what he believed to be a just and generous act.

"It is; but I will assume the character long enough to suggest, nay, *insist,* that however hasty and informal this marriage may be, you will take care that it *is* one."

"Do you mean that for a hint or a warning, sir? I have lied and stolen by your advice; shall I also betray?" asked Canaris, white with indignation, and something like fear; for he began to feel that whatever this man commanded he must do, spite of himself.

"Strong language, Felix. But I forgive it, since I am sincere in wishing well to Gladys. Marry when and how you please, only do not annoy me with another spasm of virtue. It is a waste of time, you see, for the thing is done."

"Not yet; but soon will be, for you are fast curing me of a too tender conscience."

"Faster than you think, my Faust; since to marry without love betrays as surely as to love without marriage," said Helwyze to himself, expressing in words the thought that had restrained the younger, better man.

A week later, Canaris came in with Gladys on his arm, looking very like a bride in a little bonnet tied with white, and a great nosegay of all the sweet, pale flowers blooming in the garden that first Sunday of September.

"Good-bye, sir; we are going."

"Where, may I ask? To church?"

"We have been;" and Canaris touched the ungloved hand that lay upon his arm, showing the first ring it had ever worn.

"Ah! then I can only say, Heaven bless you, Gladys; a happy honeymoon, Felix, and welcome home when—you are tired of each other."

VIII

~

"Home at last, thank Heaven!" exclaimed Canaris, as the door opened, letting forth a stream of light and warmth into the chilly gloom of the October night. Gladys made no answer but an upward look, which seemed to utter the tender welcome he had forgotten to give; and, nestling her hand in his, let him lead her through the bright hall, up the wide stairway to her own domain.

"As we return a little before our time, we must not expect a jubilee. Look about you, love, and rest. I will send Mrs. Bland presently, and tell Helwyze we are home."

He hurried away, showing no sign of the *ennui* which had fitfully betrayed itself during the last week. Gladys watched him wistfully, then turned to see what home was like, with eyes that brightened beautifully as they took in the varied charms of the luxurious apartments prepared for her. The newly kindled light filled the room with a dusky splendor; for deepest crimson glowed everywhere, making her feel as if she stood in the heart of a great rose whose silken petals curtained her round with a color, warmth, and fragrance which would render sleep a "rapture of repose." Woman-like, she enjoyed every dainty device and sumptuous detail; yet the smile of pleasure was followed by a faint sigh, as if the new magnificence oppressed her, or something much desired had been forgotten.

Stepping carefully, like one who had no right there, she passed on to a charming drawing-room, evidently intended for but two occupants, and all the pleasanter to her for that suggestion. Pausing on the threshold of another door, she peeped in, expecting to find one of those scented, satin boudoirs, which are fitter for the coquetries of a Parisian belle, than for a young wife to hope and dream and pray in.

But there was no splendor here; and, with a cry of glad surprise, its new owner took possession, wondering what gentle magic had guessed and gathered here the simple treasures she best loved. White everywhere, except the pale green of the softly tinted walls, and the mossy carpet strewn with mimic snowdrops. A sheaf of lilies in a silver vase stood on the low chimney-piece above the hearth, where a hospitable fire lay ready to kindle at a touch; and this was the only sign of luxury the room displayed. Quaint furniture, with no ornament except its own grace or usefulness, gave the place a homelike air; and chintz hangings, fresh and delicate as green leaves scattered upon snow could make them, seemed to shut out the world, securing the sweet privacy a happy woman loves.

Gladys felt this instantly, and, lifting her hand to draw the pretty draperies yet closer, discovered a new surprise, which touched her to the heart. Instead of looking out into the darkness of the autumn night, she found a little woodland nook imprisoned between the glass-door and the deep window beyond. A veritable bit of the forest, with slender ferns nodding in their sleep, hardy vines climbing up a lichened stump to show their scarlet berries, pine-needles pricking through the moss, rough arbutus leaves hiding coyly till spring should freshen their russet edges, acorns looking as if just dropped by some busy squirrel, and all manner of humble weeds, growing here as happily as when they carpeted the wood for any careless foot to tread upon.

These dear familiar things were as grateful to Gladys as the sight of friendly faces; and, throwing wide the doors, she knelt down to breathe with childish eagerness the damp, fresh odors that came out to meet her.

"How sweet of him to make such a lovely nest for me, and then slip away before I could thank him," thought the tender-hearted creature, with tears in the eyes that dwelt delightedly upon the tremulous maiden-hair bending to her touch, and the sturdy grasses waking up in this new summer.

A sound of opening doors dispelled her reverie; and with girlish trepidation she hastened to smooth the waves of her bright hair, assume the one pretty dress she would accept from Olivia, and clasp the bridal pearls about her neck; then hastened down before the somewhat dreaded Mrs. Bland appeared.

It pleased her to go wandering alone through the great house, warmed and lighted everywhere; for Helwyze made this his world, and gathered about him every luxury which taste, caprice, or necessity demanded. A marvellously beautiful and varied home it seemed to simple Gladys, as she passed from picture-gallery to music-room, eyed with artless wonder the subdued magnificence of the *salon*, or paused enchanted in a conservatory whose crystal walls enclosed a fairyland of bloom and verdure.

Here and there she came upon some characteristic whim or arrangement, which made her smile with amusement, or sigh with pity, remembering the recluse who tried to cheer his solitude by these devices. One recess held a single picture glowing with the warm splendor of the East. A divan, a Persian rug, an amber-mouthed *nargileh*, and a Turkish-coffee service, all gold and scarlet, completed the illusion. In another shadowy nook tinkled a little fountain guarded by one white-limbed nymph, who seemed to watch with placid interest the curious sea-creatures peopling the basin below. The third showed a study-chair, a shaded lamp, and certain favorite books, left open, as if to be taken up again when the mood returned. In one of these places Gladys lingered with fresh compassion stirring at her heart, though it looked the least inviting of them all. Behind the curtains of a window looking out upon the broad street on which the mansion faced stood a single chair, and nothing more.

"He shall not be so lonely now, if I can interest or amuse him," thought Gladys, as she looked at the worn spot in the carpet, the crumpled cushion on the window-ledge; mute witnesses that Helwyze felt drawn towards his kin, and found some solace in watching the activity he could no longer share.

Knowing that she should find him in the library, where most of his time was spent, she soon wended her way thither. The door stood hospitably open; and, as she approached, she saw the two men standing together; marked, as never before, the sharp contrast between them, and felt a glow of wifely pride in the young husband whom she was learning to love with all the ardor of a pure and tender soul.

Canaris was talking eagerly, as he turned the leaves of a thin manuscript which lay between them. Helwyze listened, with his eyes fixed on the speaker so intently that it startled the new-comer, when, without a sound to warn him of her approach, he turned suddenly upon her with the smile which dazzled without warming those on whom it was shed.

"I have been chiding this capricious fellow for the haste which spoils the welcome I hoped to give you. But I pardon him, since he brings the sunshine with him," he said, going to meet her, with genuine pleasure in his face.

"I could not have a kinder welcome, sir. I was glad to come; Felix feared you might be needing him."

"So duty brought him back a week too soon? A poet's honeymoon should be a long one; I regret to be the cause of its abridgement."

Something in the satirical glimmer of his eye made Gladys glance at her husband, who spoke out frankly—

"There were other reasons. Gladys hates a crowd, and so do I. Bad weather made it impossible to be romantic, so we thought it best to come home and be comfortable."

"I trust you will be; but I have little to offer, since the attractions of half a dozen cities could not satisfy you."

"Indeed, we should be most ungrateful if we were not happy here," cried Gladys, eagerly. "Only let me be useful as well as happy, else I shall not deserve this lovely home you give us."

"She is anxious to begin her ministrations; and I can recommend her, for she is quick to learn one's ways, patient with one's whims, fruitful in charming devices for amusement, and the best of comrades," said Canaris, drawing her to him with a look more grateful than fond.

"From that speech, and other signs, I infer that Felix is about to leave me to your tender mercies, and fall to work upon his new book; since it seems he could not resist making poetry when he should have been making love. Are you not jealous of the rival who steals him from you, even before the honeymoon has set?" asked Helwyze, touching the little manuscript before him.

"Not if she makes him great, and I can make him happy," answered Gladys, with an air of perfect content and trust.

"I warn you that the Muse is a jealous mistress, and will often rob you of him. Are you ready to give him up, and resign yourself to more prosaic companionship?"

"Why need I give him up? He says I do not disturb him when he writes.

He allowed me to sit beside him while he made these lovely songs, and watch them grow. He even let me help with a word sometimes, and I copied the verses fairly, that he might see how beautiful they were. Did I not, Felix?"

Gladys spoke with such innocent pride, and looked up in her husband's face so gratefully, that he could not but thank her with a caress, as he said, laughing—

"Ah, that was only play. I've had my holiday, and now I must work at a task in which no one can help me. Come and see the den where I shut myself up when the divine frenzy seizes me. Mr. Helwyze is jailer, and only lets me out when I have done my stint."

Full of some pleasurable excitement, Canaris led his wife across the room, threw open a door, and bade her look in. Like a curious child, she peeped, but saw only a small, bare *cabinet de travail*.

"No room, you see, even for a little thing like you. None dare enter here without my keeper's leave. Remember that, else you may fare like Bluebeard's Fatima." Canaris spoke gayly, and turned a key in the door with a warning click, as he glanced over his shoulder at Helwyze. Gladys did not see the look, but something in his words seemed to disturb her.

"I do not like this place, it is close and dark. I think I shall not want to come, even if you *are* here;" and, waiting for no reply, she stepped out from the chill of the unused room, as if glad to escape.

"Mysterious intuition! she felt that we had a skeleton in here, though it is such a little one," whispered Canaris, with an uneasy laugh.

"Such a sensitive plant will fare ill between us, I am afraid," answered Helwyze, as he followed her, leaving the other to open drawers and settle papers, like one eager to begin his work.

Gladys was standing in the full glare of the fire, as if its cheerful magic could exorcise all dark fancies. Helwyze eyed the white figure for an instant, feeling that his lonely hearth-stone had acquired a new charm; then joined her, saying quietly—

"This is the place where Felix and I have lived together for nearly two years. Do you like it?"

"More than I can tell. It does not seem strange to me, for he has often described it; and when I thought of coming here, I was more curious to see this room than any other."

"It will be all the pleasanter henceforth if Felix can spare you to me sometimes. Come and see the corner I have prepared, hoping to tempt you here when he shuts us out. It used to be his; so you will like it, I think."

Helwyze paced slowly down the long room, Gladys beside him, saying, as she looked about her hungrily—

"So many books! and doubtless you have read them all?"

"Not quite; but you may, if you will. See, here is your place; come often, and be sure you never will disturb me."

But one book lay on the little table, and its white cover, silver lettered, shone against the dark cloth so invitingly that Gladys took it up, glowing with pleasure as she read her own name upon the volume she knew and loved so well.

"For me? you knew that nothing else would be so beautiful and precious. Sir, why are you so generous?"

"It amuses me to do these little things, and you must humor me, as Felix does. You shall pay for them in your own coin, so there need be no sense of obligation. Rest satisfied I shall get the best of the bargain." Before she could reply a servant appeared, announced dinner, and vanished as noiselessly as he came.

"This has been a bachelor establishment so long that we are grown careless. If you will pardon all deficiencies of costume, we will not delay installing Madame Canaris in the place she does us the honor to fill."

"But I am not the mistress, sir. Please change nothing; my place at home was very humble; I am afraid I cannot fill the new one as I ought," stammered Gladys, somewhat dismayed at the prospect which the new name and duty suggested.

"You will have no care, except of us. Mrs. Bland keeps the machinery running smoothly, and we lead a very quiet life. My territory ends at that door; all beyond is yours. I chiefly haunt this wing, but sometimes roam about below stairs a little, a very harmless ghost, so do not be alarmed if you should meet me."

Helwyze spoke lightly, and tapped at the door of the den as he passed.

"Come out, slave of the pen, and be fed."

Canaris came, wearing a preoccupied air, and sauntered after them, as Helwyze led the new mistress to her place, shy and rosy, but resolved to do honor to her husband at all costs.

Her first act, however, gave them both a slight shock of surprise; for the instant they were seated, Gladys laid her hands together, bent her head, and whispered Grace, as if obeying a natural impulse to ask Heaven's blessing on the first bread she broke in her new home. The effect of the devoutly simple act was characteristically shown by the three observers. The servant paused, with an uplifted cover in his hand, respectfully astonished; Canaris looked intensely annoyed; and Helwyze leaned back with the suggestion of a shrug, as he glanced critically from the dimpled hands to the nugget of gold that shone against the bended neck. The instant she looked up, the man whisked off the silver cover with an air of relief; Canaris fell upon his bread like a hungry boy, and Helwyze tranquilly began to talk.

"Was the surprise Felix prepared for you a satisfactory one? Olivia and I took pleasure in obeying his directions."

"It was lovely! I have not thanked him yet, but I shall. You, also, sir, in some better way than words. What made you think of it?" she asked, looking at Canaris with a mute request for pardon of her involuntary offence.

Glad to rush into speech, Canaris gave at some length the history of his fancy to reproduce, as nearly as he could, the little room at home, which she had described to him with regretful minuteness; for she had sold every thing to pay the debts which were the sole legacy her father left her. While they talked, Helwyze, who ate little, was observing both. Gladys looked more girlish than ever, in spite of the mingled dignity and anxiety her quiet but timid air betrayed. Canaris seemed in high spirits, talking rapidly, laughing often, and glancing about him as if glad to be again where nothing inharmonious disturbed his taste and comfort. Not till dessert was on the table, however, did he own, in words, the feeling of voluptuous satisfaction which was enhanced by the memory that he had been rash enough to risk the loss of all.

"It is not so very terrible, you see, Gladys. You eat and drink like a bird; but I know you enjoy this as much as I do, after those detestable hotels," he said, detecting an expression of relief in his young wife's face, as the noiseless servant quitted the room for the last time.

"Indeed I do. It is so pleasant to have all one's senses gratified at once, and the common duties of life made beautiful and easy," answered Gladys, surveying with feminine appreciation the well-appointed table which had that air of accustomed elegance so grateful to fastidious tastes.

"Ah, ha! this little ascetic of mine will become a Sybarite yet, and agree with me that enjoyment *is* a duty," exclaimed Canaris, looking very like a young Bacchus, as he held up his wine to watch its rich color, and inhale its bouquet with zest.

"The more delicate the senses, the more delicate the delight. I suspect Madame finds her grapes and water as delicious as you do your olives and old wine," said Helwyze, finding a still more refined satisfaction than either in the pretty contrast between the purple grapes and the white fingers that pulled them apart, the softly curling lips that were the rosier for their temperate draughts, and the unspoiled simplicity of the girl sitting there in pearls and shimmering silk.

"When one has known poverty, and the sad shifts which make it seem mean, as well as hard, perhaps one does unduly value these things. I hope I shall not; but I do find them very tempting," she said, thoughtfully eying the new scene in which she found herself.

Helwyze seemed to be absently listening to the musical chime of silver against glass; but he made a note of that hope, wondering if hardship had given her more of its austere virtue than it had her husband.

"How shall you resist temptation?" he asked, curiously.

"I shall work. This is dangerously pleasant; so let me begin at once, and sing, while you take your coffee in the drawing-room. I know the way; come when you will, I shall be ready;" and Gladys rose with the energetic expression which often broke through her native gentleness. Canaris held the door for her, and was about to resume his seat, when Helwyze checked him—

"We will follow at once. Was I not right in my prediction?" he asked, as they left the room together.

"That we should soon tire of each other? You were wrong in that."

"I meant the ease with which you would soon learn to love."

"I have not learned—yet."

"Then this vivacity is a cloak for the pangs of remorse, is it?" and Helwyze laughed incredulously.

"No: it is the satisfaction I already feel in the atonement I mean to make. I have a grand idea. I, too, shall work, and give Gladys reason to be proud of me, if nothing more."

Something of her own energy was in his mien, and it became him. But Helwyze quenched the noble ardor by saying, coldly—

"I see: it is the old passion under a new name. May your virtuous aspirations be blest!"

IX

H elwyze was right, and Canaris found that his sudden marriage did
stimulate public interest wonderfully. There had always been something
mysterious about this brilliant young man and his relations with his patron;
who was as silent as the Sphinx regarding his past, and tantalizingly enigmatical about his plans and purposes for the future. The wildest speculations
were indulged in: many believed them to be father and son; others searched
vainly for the true motive of this charitable caprice; and every one waited
with curiosity to see the end of it. All of which much amused Helwyze, who
cared nothing for the world's opinion, and found his sense of humor tickled
by the ludicrous idea of himself in the new *rôle* of benefactor.

The romance seemed quite complete when it was known that the young
poet had brought home a wife whose talent, youth, and isolation seemed to
render her peculiarly fitted for his mate.

Though love was lacking, vanity was strong in Canaris, and this was
gratified by the commendation bestowed on the new ornament he wore; for
as such simple Gladys was considered, and shone with reflected lustre, her
finer gifts and graces quite eclipsed by his more conspicuous and self-
asserting ones.

With unquestioning docility she gave herself into his hands, following
where he led her, obeying his lightest wish, and loving him with a devotion
which kept alive regretful tenderness when it should have cherished a loyal
love. He gladly took her into all the gayety which for a time surrounded
them, and she enjoyed it with a girl's fresh delight. He showed her wise and
witty people whom she admired or loved; and she looked and listened with
an enthusiast's wonder. He gave her all he had to give, novelty and pleasure;
though the one had lost its gloss for him, and too much of the other he was
forced to accept from Helwyze's hands. But through all the experiences that
now rapidly befell her, Gladys was still herself; innocently happy, stanchly
true, characteristically independent, a mountain stream, keeping its waters
pure and bright, though mingled with the swift and turbid river which was
hurrying it toward the sea.

Curiosity being satisfied, society soon found some fresher novelty to
absorb it. Women still admired Canaris, but marriage lessened his attractions
for them; men still thought him full of promise, but were fast forgetting the
first successful effort which had won their applause; and the young lion

found that he must roar loud and often, if he would not be neglected. Shutting himself into his cell, he worked with hopeful energy for several months, often coming out weary, but excited, with the joyful labor of creation. At such times there was no prose anywhere; for heaven and earth were glorified by the light of that inner world, where imagination reigns, and all things are divine. Then he would be in the gayest spirits, and carry Gladys off to some hour of pleasant relaxation at theatre, opera, or ball, where flattery refreshed or emulation inspired him; and next day would return to his task with redoubled vigor.

At other times his fickle mistress deserted him; thought would not soar, language would not sing, poetry fled, and life was unutterably "flat, stale, and unprofitable." Then it was Gladys, who took possession of him; lured him out for a brisk walk, or a long drive into a wholesomer world than that into which he took her; sung weary brain to sleep with the sweetest lullabies of brother bards; or made him merry by the display of a pretty wit, which none but he knew she could exert. With wifely patience and womanly tact she managed her wayward but beloved lord, till despondency yielded to her skill, and the buoyant spirit of hope took him by the hand, and led him to his work again.

In the intervals between these fits of intellectual intoxication and succeeding depression, Gladys devoted herself to Helwyze with a faithfulness which surprised him and satisfied her; for, as she said, her "bread tasted bitter if she did not earn it." He had expected to be amused, perhaps interested, but not so charmed, by this girl, who possessed only a single talent, a modest share of beauty, and a mind as untrained as a beautiful but neglected garden. This last was the real attraction; for, finding her hungry for knowledge, he did not hesitate to test her taste and try her mental mettle, by allowing her free range of a large and varied library. Though not a scholar, in the learned sense of the word, he had the eager, sceptical nature which interrogates all things, yet believes only in itself. This had kept him roaming solitarily up and down the earth for years, observing men and manners; now it drove him to books; and, as suffering and seclusion wrought upon body and brain, his choice of mute companions changed from the higher, healthier class to those who, like himself, leaned towards the darker, sadder side of human nature. Lawless here, as elsewhere, he let his mind wander at will, as once he had let his heart, learning too late that both are sacred gifts, and cannot safely be tampered with.

All was so fresh and wonderful to Gladys, that her society grew very attractive to him; and pleasant as it was to have her wait upon him with quiet zeal, or watch her busied in her own corner, studying, or sewing with the little basket beside her which gave such a homelike air, it was still pleasanter to have her sit and read to him, while he watched this face, so intelligent, yet so soft; studied this mind, at once sensitive and sagacious, this nature, both serious and ardent. It gave a curious charm to his old favorites when she read them; and many hours he listened contentedly to the voice whose youth made Montaigne's worldly wisdom seem the shrewder; whose music gave a certain sweetness to Voltaire's bitter wit or Carlyle's rough wisdom; whose pitying wonder added pathos to the melancholy brilliancy of Heine and De Quincy. Equally fascinating to him, and far more dangerous to her, were George Sand's passionate romances, Goethe's dramatic novels, Hugo and Sue's lurid word-pictures of suffering and sin; the haunted world of Shakespeare and Dante, the poetry of Byron, Browning, and Poe.

Rich food and strong wine for a girl of eighteen; and Gladys soon felt the effects of such a diet, though it was hard to resist when duty seconded inclination, and ignorance hid the peril. She often paused to question with eager lips, to wipe wet eyes, to protest with indignant warmth, or to shiver with the pleasurable pain of a child who longs, yet dreads, to hear an exciting story to the end. Helwyze answered willingly, if not always wisely; enjoyed the rapid unfolding of the woman, and would not deny himself any indulgence of this new whim, though conscious that the snowdrop, transplanted suddenly from the free fresh spring-time, could not live in this close air without suffering.

This was the double life Gladys now began to lead. Heart and mind were divided between the two, who soon absorbed every feeling, every thought. To the younger man she was a teacher, to the elder a pupil; in the one world she ruled, in the other served; unconsciously Canaris stirred emotion to its depths, consciously Helwyze stimulated intellect to its heights; while the soul of the woman, receiving no food from either, seemed to sit apart in the wilderness of its new experience, tempted by evil as well as sustained by good spirits, who guard their own.

One evening this divided mastery was especially felt by Helwyze, who watched the young man's influence over his wife with a mixture of interest and something like jealousy, as it was evidently fast becoming stronger than his own. Sitting in his usual place, he saw Gladys flit about the room, brushing up the hearth, brightening the lamps, and putting by the finished books, as if the day's duties were all done, the evening's rest and pleasure honestly earned, eagerly waited for. He well knew that this pleasure consisted in carrying Canaris away to her own domain; or, if that were impossible, she would sit silently looking at him while he read or talked in his fitful fashion on any subject his master chose to introduce.

The desire to make her forget the husband whose neglect would have sorely grieved her if his genius had not been his excuse in her eyes for many faults, possessed Helwyze that night; and he amused himself by the effort, becoming more intent with each failure.

As the accustomed hour drew near, Gladys took her place on the foot-stool before the chair set ready for Felix, and fell a-musing, with her eyes on the newly replenished fire. Above, the unignited fuel lay black and rough, with here and there a deep rift opening to the red core beneath; while to and fro danced many colored flames, as if bent on some eager quest. Many flashed up the chimney, and were gone; others died solitarily in dark corners, where no heat fed them; and some vanished down the chasms, to the fiery world below. One golden spire, tremulous and translucent, burned with a brilliance which attracted the eye; and, when a wandering violet flame joined it, Gladys followed their motions with interest, seeing in them images of Felix and herself, for childish fancy and womanly insight met and mingled in all she thought and felt.

Forgetting that she was not alone, she leaned forward, to watch what became of them, as the wedded flames flickered here and there, now violet, now yellow. But the brighter always seemed the stronger, and the sad-colored one to grow more and more golden, as if yielding to its sunshiny mate.

"I hope they will fly up together, out into the wide, starry sky, which is their eternity, perhaps," she thought, smiling at her own eagerness.

But no; the golden flame flew up, and left the other to take on many shapes and colors, as it wandered here and there, till, just as it glowed with a splendid crimson, Gladys was forced to hide her dazzled eyes and look no more. Turning her flushed face away, she found Helwyze watching her as intently as she had watched the fire, and, reminded of his presence, she glanced toward the empty chair with an impatient sigh for Felix.

"You are tired," he said, answering the sigh. "Mrs. Bland told me what a notable housewife you are, and how you helped her set the upper regions to rights to-day. I fear you did too much."

"Oh, no, I enjoyed it heartily. I asked for something to do, and she allowed me to examine and refold the treasures you keep in the great carved wardrobe, lest moths or damp or dust had hurt the rich stuffs, curious coins, and lovely ornaments stored there. I never saw so many pretty things before," she answered, betraying, by her sudden animation, the love of "pretty things," which is one of the strongest of feminine foibles.

He smiled, well pleased.

"Olivia calls that quaint press from Brittany my bazaar, for there I have collected the spoils of my early wanderings; and when I want a *cadeau* for a fair friend, I find it without trouble. I saw in what exquisite order you left my shelves, and, as you were not with me to choose, I brought away several trifles, more curious than costly, hoping to find a thank-offering among them."

As he spoke, he opened one of the deep drawers in the writing-table, as if to produce some gift. But Gladys said, hastily—

"You are very kind, sir; but these fine things are altogether too grand for me. The pleasure of looking at and touching them is reward enough; unless you will tell me about them: it must be interesting to know what places they came from."

Feeling in the mood for it, Helwyze described to her an Eastern bazaar, so graphically that she soon forgot Felix, and sat looking up as if she actually saw and enjoyed the splendors he spoke of. Lustrous silks sultanas were to wear; misty muslins, into whose embroidery some dark-skinned woman's life was wrought; cashmeres, many-hued as rainbows; odorous woods and spices, that filled the air with fragrance never blown from Western hills; amber, like drops of frozen sunshine; fruits, which brought visions of vineyards, olive groves, and lovely palms dropping their honeyed clusters by desert wells; skins mooned and barred with black upon the tawny velvet, that had lain in jungles, or glided with deathful stealthiness along the track of human feet; ivory tusks that had felled Asiatic trees, gored fierce enemies, or meekly lifted princes to their seats.

These, and many more, he painted rapidly; and, as he ended, shook out of its folds a gauzy fabric, starred with silver, which he threw over her head, pointing to the mirror set in the door of the *armoire* behind her.

"See if that is not too pretty to refuse. Felix would surely be inspired if you appeared before him shimmering like Suleika, when Hatem says to her—

" 'Here, take this, with the pure and silver streaking,
        And wind it, Darling, round and round for me;

What is your Highness? Style scarce worth the speaking,
When thou dost look, I am as great as He.' "

Gladys did look, and saw how beautiful it made her; but, though she did
not understand the words he quoted, the names suggested a sultan and his
slave, and she did not like either the idea or the expression with which
Helwyze regarded her. Throwing off the gauzy veil, she refolded and put it
by, saying, in that decided little way of hers, which was prettier than petulance—

"My Hatem does not need that sort of inspiration, and had rather see his
Suleika in a plain gown of his choosing, than dressed in all the splendors of
the East by any other hand."

"Come, then, we must find some better *souvenir* of your visit, for I never let
any one go away empty-handed;" with that he dipped again into the drawer,
and held up a pretty bracelet, explaining, as he offered it with unruffled
composure, though she eyed it askance, attracted, yet reluctant, a charming
picture of doubt and desire—

"Here are the Nine Muses, cut in many-tinted lava. See how well the
workman suited the color to the attribute of each Muse. Urania is blue;
Erato, this soft pink; Terpsichore, violet; Euterpe and Thalia, black and
white; and the others, these fine shades of yellow, dun, and drab. That
pleases you, I know; so let me put it on."

It did please her; and she stretched out her hand to accept it, gratified, yet
conscious all the while of the antagonistic spirit which often seized her when
with Helwyze. He put on the bracelet with a satisfied air; but the clasp was
imperfect, and, at the first turn of the round wrist, the Nine Muses fell to the
ground.

"It is too heavy. I am not made to wear handcuffs of any sort, you see:
they will not stay on, so it is of no use to try;" and Gladys picked up the
trinket with an odd sense of relief; though poor Erato was cracked, and
Thalia, like Fielding's fair Amelia, had a broken nose. She rose to lay it on
the table, and, as she turned away, her eye went to the clock, as if reproaching
herself for that brief forgetfulness of her husband. Half amused, half annoyed, and bent on having his own way, even in so small a thing as this,
Helwyze drew up a chair, and, setting a Japanese tray upon the table, said,
invitingly—

"Come and see if these are more to your taste, since fine raiment and
foolish ornaments fail to tempt you."

"Oh, how curious and beautiful!" cried Gladys, looking down upon a collection of Hindoo gods and goddesses, in ebony or ivory: some hideous, some lovely, all carved with wonderful delicacy, and each with its appropriate symbol—Vishnu, and his serpent; Brahma, in the sacred lotus; Siva, with seven faces; Kreeshna, the destroyer, with many mouths; Varoon, god of the ocean; and Kama, the Indian Cupid, bearing his bow of sugar-cane strung with bees, to typify love's sting as well as sweetness. This last Gladys examined longest, and kept in her hand as if it charmed her; for the minute face of the youth was beautiful, the slender figure full of grace, and the ivory spotless.

"You choose him for your idol? and well you may, for he looks like Felix. Mine, if I have one, is Siva, goddess of Fate, ugly, but powerful."

"I will have no idol—not even Felix, though I sometimes fear I may make one of him before I know it;" and Gladys put back the little figure with a guilty look, as she confessed the great temptation that beset her.

"You are wise: idols are apt to have feet of clay, and tumble down in spite of our blind adoration. Better be a Buddhist, and have no god but our own awakened thought; 'the highest wisdom,' as it is called," said Helwyze, who had lately been busy with the Sâkya Muni, and regarded all religions with calm impartiality.

"These are false gods, and we are done with them, since we know the true one," began Gladys, understanding him; for she had read aloud the life of Gautama Buddha, and enjoyed it as a legend; while he found its mystic symbolism attractive, and nothing repellent in its idolatry.

"But do we? How can you prove it?"

"It needs no proving; the knowledge of it was born in me, grows with my growth, and is the life of my life," cried Gladys, out of the fulness of that natural religion which requires no revelation except such as experience brings to strengthen and purify it.

"All are not so easily satisfied as you," he said, in the sceptical tone which always tried both her patience and her courage; for, woman-like, she could feel the truth of things, but could not reason about them. He saw her face kindle, and added, rapidly, having a mind to try how firmly planted the faith of the pretty Puritan was: "Most of us agree that Allah exists in some form or other, but we fall out about who is the true Prophet. You choose Jesus of Nazareth for yours; I rather incline to this Indian Saint. They are not unlike: this Prince left all to devote his life to the redemption of mankind, suffered persecutions and temptations, had his disciples, and sent out the first apostles of whom we hear; was a teacher, with his parables, miracles, and belief in transmigration or immortality. His doctrine is almost the same as the other; and the six virtues which secure Nirvâna, or Heaven, are charity, purity, patience, courage, contemplation, and wisdom. Come, why not take him for a model?"

Gladys listened with a mixture of perplexity and pain in her face, and her hand went involuntarily to the little cross which she always wore; but, though her eye was troubled, her voice was steady, as she answered, earnestly—

"Because I have a nobler one. My Prince left a greater throne than yours to serve mankind; suffered and resisted more terrible persecution and temptation; sent out wiser apostles, taught clearer truth, and preached an immortality for all. Yours died peacefully in the arms of his friends, mine on a cross; and, though he came later, he has saved more souls than Buddha. Sir, I know little about those older religions; I am not wise enough even to argue about my own: I can only believe in it, love it, and hold fast to it, since it is all I need."

"How can you tell till you try others? This, now, is a fine one, if we are not too bigoted to look into it fairly. Wise men, who have done so, say that no faith—not even the Christian—has exercised so powerful an influence on the diminution of crime as the old, simple doctrine of Sâkya Muni; and this is the only great historic religion that has not taken the sword to put down its enemies. Can you say as much for yours?"

"No; but it is worth fighting for, and I *would* fight, as the Maid of Orleans did for France, for this is my country. Can you say of *your* faith that it sustained you in sorrow, made you happy in loneliness, saved you from temptation, taught, guided, blessed you day by day with unfailing patience, wisdom, and love? I think you cannot; then why try to take mine away till you can give me a better?"

Seldom was Gladys so moved as now, for she felt as if he was about to meddle with her holy of holies; and, without stopping to reason, she resisted the attempt, sure that he would harm, not help, her, since neither his words nor example had done Felix any good.

Helwyze admired her all the more for her resistance, and thought her unusually lovely, as she stood there flushed and fervent with her plea for the faith that was so dear to her.

"Why, indeed! You would make an excellent martyr, and enjoy it. Pity that you have no chance of it, and so of being canonized as a saint afterward. That is decidedly your line. Then, you won't have any of my gods? not even this one?" he asked, holding up the handsome Kama, with a smile.

"No, not even that. I will have only one God, and you may keep your idols for those who believe in them. My faith may not be the oldest, but it *is* the best, if one may judge of the two religions by the happiness and peace they give," answered Gladys, taking refuge in a very womanly, yet most convincing, argument, she thought, as she pointed to the mirror, which reflected both figures in its clear depths.

Helwyze looked, and though without an atom of vanity, the sight could not but be trying, the contrast was so great between her glad, young face, and his, so melancholy and prematurely old.

"Satma, Tama—Truth and Darkness," he muttered to himself; adding aloud, with a vengeful sort of satisfaction in shocking her pious nature—

"But *I* have no religion; so that defiant little speech is quite thrown away, my friend."

It did shock her; for, though she had suspected the fact, there was something dreadful in hearing him confess it, in a tone which proved his sincerity.

"Mr. Helwyze, do you really mean that you believe in nothing invisible and divine? no life beyond this? no God, no Christ to bless and save?" she asked, hardly knowing how to put the question, as she drew back dismayed, but still incredulous.

"Yes."

He was both surprised, and rather annoyed, to find that it cost him an effort to give even that short answer, with those innocent eyes looking so anxiously up at him, full of a sad wonder, then dim with sudden dew, as she said eagerly, forgetting every thing but a great compassion—

"O sir, it is impossible! You think so now; but when you love and trust some human creature more than yourself, then you will find that you do believe in Him who gives such happiness, and be glad to own it."

"Perhaps. Meantime *you* will not make me happy by letting me give you any thing; why is it, Gladys?"

The black brows were knit, and he looked impatient with himself or her. She saw it, and exclaimed with the sweetest penitence—

"Give me your pardon for speaking so frankly. I mean no disrespect; but I cannot help it when you say such things, though I know that gratitude should keep me silent."

"I like it. Do not take yourself to task for that, or trouble about me. There are many roads, and sooner or later we shall all reach heaven, I suppose—if there is one," he added, with a shrug, which spoiled the smile that went before.

X

Gladys stood silent for a moment, with her eyes fixed on the little figures, longing for wisdom to convince this man, whom she regarded with mingled pity, admiration, and distrust, that he could not walk by his own light alone. He guessed the impulse that kept her there, longed to have her stay, and felt a sudden desire to reinstate himself in her good opinion. That wish, or the hope to keep her by some new and still more powerful allurement, seemed to actuate him as he hastily thrust the gods and goddesses out of sight, and opened another drawer, with a quick glance over his shoulder towards that inner room.

At that instant the clock struck, and Gladys started, saying, in a tone of fond despair—

"Where *is* Felix? Will he never come?"

"I heard him raging about some time ago, but perfect silence followed, so I suspect he caught the tormenting word, idea, or fancy, and is busy pinning it," answered Helwyze, shutting the drawer as suddenly as he opened it, with a frown which Gladys did not see; for she had turned away, forgetting him and his salvation in the one absorbing interest of her life.

"How long it takes to write a poem! Three whole months, for he began in September; and it was not to be a long one, he said."

"He means this to be a masterpiece, so labors like a galley-slave, and can find no rest till it is done. Good practice, but to little purpose, I am afraid. Poetry, even the best, is not profitable now-a-days, I am told," added Helwyze, speaking with a sort of satisfaction which he could not conceal.

"Who cares for the profit? It is the fame Felix wants, and works for," answered Gladys, defending the absent with wifely warmth.

"True, but he would not reject the fortune if it came. He is not one of the ethereal sort, who can live on glory and a crust; his gingerbread must not only be gilded, but solid and well spiced beside. You adore your poet, respect also the worldly wisdom of your spouse, madame."

When Helwyze sneered, Gladys was silent; so now she mused again, leaning on the high back of the chair which she longed to see occupied. He mused also, with his eyes upon the fire, fingers idly tapping, and a furtive smile round his mouth, as if some purpose was taking shape in that busy brain of his. Suddenly he spoke, in a tone of kindly interest, well knowing where her thoughts were, and anxious to end her weary waiting.

"Perhaps the poor fellow has fallen asleep, tired out with striving after immortality. Go and wake him, if you will, for it is time he rested."

"May I? He does not like to be disturbed; but I fear he is ill: he has eaten scarcely any thing for days, and looks so pale it troubles me. I will peep first; and if he is busy, creep away without a word."

Stepping toward the one forbidden, yet most fascinating spot in all the house, she softly opened the door and looked in. Canaris was there, apparently asleep, as Helwyze thought; for his head lay on his folded arms as if both were weary. Glancing over her shoulder with a nod and a smile, Gladys went in, anxious to wake and comfort him; for the little room looked solitary, dark, and cold, with dead ashes on the hearth, the student lamp burning dimly, and the food she had brought him hours ago still standing, untasted, among the blotted sheets strewn all about. At her first touch he looked up, and she was frightened by the expression of his face, it was so desperately miserable.

"Dear, what is it?" she asked, quickly, with her arms about him, as if defying the unknown trouble to reach him there.

"Disappointment—nothing else;" and he leaned his head against her, grateful for sympathy, since she could give no other help.

"You mean your book, which does not satisfy you even yet?" she said, interpreting the significance of the weary, yet restless, look he wore.

"It never will! I have toiled and tried, with all my heart and soul and mind, if ever a man did; but I cannot do it, Gladys. It torments me, and I cannot escape from it; because, though it is all here in my brain, it *will not* be expressed in words."

"Do not try any more; rest now, and by and by, perhaps, it will be easier. You have worked too hard, and are worn out; forget the book, and come and let me take care of you. It breaks my heart to see you so."

"I was doing it for your sake—all for you; and I thought this time it would be very good, since my purpose was a just and generous one. But it is not, and I hate it!"

With a passionate gesture, Canaris hurled a pile of manuscript into the further corner of the room, and pushed his wife from him, as if she too were an affliction and a disappointment. It grieved her bitterly; but she would not be repulsed; and, holding fast in both her own the hand that was about to grasp another sheaf of papers, she cried, with a tone of tender authority, which both controlled and touched him—

"No, no, you shall not, Felix! Put me away, but do not spoil the book; it has cost us both too much."

"Not you; forgive me, it is myself with whom I am vexed;" and Canaris penitently kissed the hands that held his, remembering that she could not know the true cause of his effort and regret.

"I *shall* be jealous, if I find that I have given you up so long in vain. I must have something to repay me for the loss of your society all this weary time. I have worked to fill your place: give me my reward."

"Have you missed me, then? I thought you happy enough with Helwyze and the books."

"Missed you! happy enough! O Felix! you do not know me, if you think I *can* be happy without you. He is kind, but only a friend; and all the books in the wide world are not as much to me as the one you treat so cruelly." She clasped tightly the hands she held, and looked into his face with eyes full of unutterable love. Such tender flattery could not but soothe, such tearful reproach fail to soften, a far prouder, harder man than Canaris.

"What reward will you have?" he asked, making an effort to be cheerful for her sake.

"Eat, drink, and rest; then read me every word you have written. I am no critic; but I would try to be impartial: love makes even the ignorant wise, and I shall see the beauty which I know is in it."

"I put you there, or tried; so truth and beauty should be in it. Some time you shall hear it, but not now. I could not read it to-night, perhaps never; it is such a poor, pale shadow of the thing I meant it to be."

"Let me read it," said a voice behind them; and Helwyze stood upon the threshold, wearing his most benignant aspect.

"You?" ejaculated Canaris; while Gladys shrunk a little, as if the proposition did not please her.

"Why not? Young poets never read their own verses well; yet what could be more soothing to the most timorous or vain than to hear them read by an admiring and sympathetic friend? Come, let me have my reward, as well as Gladys;" and Helwyze laid his hand upon the unscattered pile of manuscript.

"A penance, rather. It is so blurred, so rough, you could not read it; then the fatigue"—began Canaris, pleased, yet reluctant still.

"I can read any thing, make rough places smooth, and not tire, for I have a great interest in this story. He has shown me some of it, and it *is* good."

Helwyze spoke to Gladys, and his last words conquered her reluctance, whetted her curiosity; he looked at Canaris, and his glance inspired hope, his offer tempted, for his voice could make music of any thing, his praise would be both valuable and cheering.

"Let him, Felix, since he is so kind, I so impatient that I do not want to wait;" and Gladys went to gather up the leaves, which had flown wildly about the room.

"Leave those, I will sort them while you begin. The first part is all here. I am sick of it, and so will you be, before you are through. Go, love, or I may revoke permission, and make the bonfire yet."

Canaris laughed as he waved her away; and Gladys, seeing that the cloud had lifted, willingly obeyed, lingering only to give a touch to the dainty luncheon, which was none the worse for being cold.

"Dear, eat and drink, then *my* feast will be the sweeter."

"I will; I'll eat and drink stupendously when you are gone; I wish you *bon appetit,*" he said, filling the glass, and smiling as he drank.

Contented now, Gladys hurried away, to find Helwyze already seated by the study-table, with the manuscript laid open before him. He looked up, wearing an expression of such pleasurable excitement, that it augured well for what was coming, and she slipped into the chair beside the one set ready for Canaris on the opposite side of the hearth, still hoping he would come and take it. Helwyze began, and soon she forgot every thing—carried away by the smoothly flowing current of the story which he read so well. A metrical romance, such as many a lover might have imagined in the first inspiration of the great passion, but few could have painted with such skill. A very human story, but all the truer and sweeter for that fact. The men and women in it were full of vitality and color; their faces spoke, hearts beat, words glowed; and they seemed to live before the listener's eye, as if endowed with eloquent flesh and blood.

Gladys forgot their creator utterly, but Helwyze did not; and even while reading on with steadily increasing effect, glanced now and then towards that inner room, where, after a moment of unnecessary bustle, perfect silence reigned. Presently a shadow flickered on the ceiling, a shadow bent as if listening eagerly, though not a sound betrayed its approach as it seemed to glide and vanish behind the tall screen which stood before the door. Gladys saw nothing, her face being intent upon the reader, her thoughts absorbed in following the heart-history of the woman in whom she could not help finding a likeness to herself.

Helwyze saw the shadow, however, and laughed inwardly, as if to see the singer irresistibly drawn by his own music. But no visible smile betrayed this knowledge; and the tale went on with deepening power and pathos, till at its most passionate point he paused.

"Go on; oh, pray go on!" cried Gladys, breathlessly.

"Are you not tired of it?" asked Helwyze, with a keen look.

"No, no! You are? Then let me read."

"Not I; but there is no more here. Ask Felix if we *may* go on."

"I must! I will! Where is he?" and Gladys hurried round the screen, to find Canaris flung down anyway upon a seat, looking almost as excited as herself.

"Ah," she cried, delightedly, "you could not keep away! You know that it is good, and you are glad and proud, although you will not own it."

"Am I? Are you?" he asked, reading the answer in her face, before she could whisper, with the look of mingled awe and adoration which she always wore when speaking of him as a poet—

"Never can I tell you what I feel. It almost frightens me to find how well you know me and yourself, and other hearts like ours. What gives you this wonderful power, and shows you how to use it?"

"Don't praise it too much, or I shall wish I had destroyed, instead of resorting, the second part for you to hear." Canaris spoke almost roughly, and rose, as if about to go and do it now. But Gladys caught his hand, saying gayly, as she drew him out into the fire-light with persuasive energy—

"That you shall never do; but come and enjoy it with us. You need not be so modest, for you know you like it. Now I am perfectly happy."

She looked so, as she saw her husband sink into the tall-backed chair, and took her place beside him, laughing at the almost comic mixture of sternness, resignation, and impatience betrayed by his set lips, silent acquiescence, and excited eyes.

"Now we are ready;" and Gladys folded her hands with the rapturous contentment of a child at its first fairy spectacle.

"All but the story. I will fetch it;" and Helwyze stepped quickly behind the screen before either could stir.

Gladys half rose, but Canaris drew her down again, whispering, in an almost resentful tone—

"Let him, if he will; you wait on him too much. I put the papers in order; he will read them easily enough."

"Nay, do not be angry, dear; he does it to please me, and surely no one could read it better. I know you would feel too much to do it well," she answered, her hand in his, with its most soothing touch.

There was no time for more. Helwyze returned, and, after a hasty resettling of the manuscript, read on, without pausing, to the story's end, as if unconscious of fatigue, and bent on doing justice to the power of the *protégé* whose success was his benefactor's best reward. At first, Gladys glanced at her husband from time to time; but presently the living man beside her grew less real than that other, who, despite a new name and country, strange surroundings, and far different circumstances, was so unmistakably the same, that she could not help feeling and following his fate to its close, with an interest almost as intense as if, in very truth, she saw Canaris going to his end. Her interest in the woman lessened, and was lost in her eagerness to have the hero worthy of the love she gave, the honor others felt for him; and, when the romance brought him to defeat and death, she was so wrought upon by this illusion, that she fell into a passion of sudden tears, weeping as she had never wept before.

Felix sat motionless, his hand over his eyes, lips closely folded, lest they should betray too much emotion; the irresistible conviction that it *was* good, strengthening every instant, till he felt only the fascination and excitement of an hour, which foretold others even more delicious. When the tale ended, the melodious voice grew silent, and nothing was heard but the eloquent sobbing of a woman. Words seemed unnecessary, and none were uttered for several minutes, then Helwyze asked briefly—

"Shall we burn it?"

As briefly Canaris answered "No;" and Gladys, quickly recovering the self-control so seldom lost, looked up with "a face, clear shining after rain," as she said in the emphatic tone of deepest feeling—

"It would be like burning a live thing. But, Felix, you must not kill that man: I cannot have him die so. Let him live to conquer all his enemies, the worst in himself; then, if you must end tragically, let the woman go; she would not care, if he were safe."

"But she is the heroine of the piece; and, if it does not end with her lamenting over the fallen hero, the dramatic point is lost," said Helwyze; for

Canaris had sprung up, and was walking restlessly about the room, as if the spirits he had evoked were too strong to be laid even by himself.

"I know nothing about that; but I feel the moral point would be lost, if it is not changed. Surely, powerful as pity is, a lofty admiration is better; and this poem would be nobler, in every way, if that man ends by living well, than by dying ignominiously in spite of his courage. I cannot explain it, but I am sure it is so; and I will not let Felix spoil his best piece of work by such a mistake."

"Then you like it? You would be happy if I changed and let it go before the world, for your sake more than for my own?"

Canaris paused beside her, pale with some emotion stronger than gratified vanity or ambitious hope. Gladys thought it was love; and, carried out of herself by the tender pride that overflowed her heart and would not be controlled, she let an action, more eloquent than any words, express the happiness she was the first to feel, the homage she would be the first to pay. Kneeling before him, she clasped her hands together, and looked up at him with cheeks still wet, lips still tremulous, eyes still full of wonder, admiration, fervent gratitude, and love.

In one usually so self-restrained as Gladys such joyful abandonment was doubly captivating and impressive. Canaris felt it so; and, lifting her up, pressed her to a heart whose loud throbbing thanked her, even while he gently turned her face away, as if he could not bear to see and receive such worship from so pure a source. The unexpected humility in his voice touched her strangely, and made her feel more deeply than ever how genuine was the genius which should yet make him great, as well as beloved.

"I will do what you wish, for you see more clearly than I. You *shall* be happy, and I *will* be proud of doing it, even if no one else sees any good in my work."

"They will! they must! It may not be the grandest thing you will ever do, but it is so human, it cannot fail to touch and charm; and to me that is as great an act as to astonish or dazzle by splendid learning or wonderful wit. Make it noble as well as beautiful, then people will love as well as praise you."

"I will try, Gladys. I see now what I should have written, and—if I can— it shall be done."

"I promised you inspiration, you remember: have I not kept my word?" asked Helwyze, forgotten, and content to be forgotten, until now.

Canaris looked up quickly; but there was no gratitude in his face, as he answered, with his hand on the head he pressed against his shoulder, and a certain subdued passion in his voice—

"You have: not the highest inspiration; but, if *she* is happy, it will atone for much."

XI

~

A nd Gladys *was* happy for a little while. Canaris labored doggedly till all was finished as she wished. Helwyze lent the aid which commands celerity; and early in the new year the book came out, to win for itself and its author the admiration and regard she had prophesied. But while the outside world, with which she had little to do except through her husband, rejoiced over him and his work, she, in her own small world, where he was all in all, was finding cause to wonder and grieve at the change which took place in him.

"I have done my task, now let me play," he said; and play he did, quite as energetically as he had worked, though to far less purpose. Praise seemed to intoxicate him, for he appeared to forget every thing else, and bask in its sunshine, as if he never could have enough of it. His satisfaction would have been called egregious vanity, had it not been so gracefully expressed, and the work done so excellent that all agreed the young man had a right to be proud of it, and enjoy his reward as he pleased. He went out much, being again caressed and fêted to his heart's content, leaving Gladys to amuse Helwyze; for a very little of this sort of gayety satisfied her, and there was something painful to her in the almost feverish eagerness with which her husband sought and enjoyed excitement of all kinds. Glad and proud though she was, it troubled her to see him as utterly engrossed as if existence had no higher aim than the most refined and varied pleasure; and she began to feel that, though the task was done, she had not got him back again from that other mistress, who seemed to have bewitched him with her dazzling charms.

"He will soon have enough of it, and return to us none the worse. Remember how young he is; how natural that he should love pleasure over-much, when he gets it, since he has had so little hitherto," said Helwyze, answering the silent trouble in the face of Gladys; for she never spoke of her daily increasing anxiety.

"But it does not seem to make him happy; and for that reason I sometimes think it cannot be the best kind of pleasure for him," answered Gladys, remembering how flushed and weary he had been when he came in last night, so late that it was nearly dawn.

"He is one who will taste all kinds, and not be contented till he has had his fill. Roaming about Europe with that bad, brilliant father of his gave him glimpses of many things which he was too poor to enjoy then, but not too young to remember and desire now, when it is possible to gratify the wish. Let him go, he will come back to you when he is tired. It is the only way to manage him, I find."

But Gladys did not think so; and, finding that Helwyze would not speak, she resolved that she would venture to do it, for many things disturbed her, which wifely loyalty forbade her to repeat; as well as a feeling that Helwyze would not see cause for anxiety in her simple fears, since he encouraged Felix in this reckless gayety.

Some hours later, she found Canaris newly risen, sitting at his *escritoire* in their own room, with a strew of gold and notes before him, which he affected to be counting busily; though when she entered she had seen him in a despondent attitude, doing nothing.

"How pale you look. Why will you stay so late and get these weary headaches?" she asked, stroking the thick locks off his forehead with a caressing touch.

" 'Too late I stayed, forgive the crime;
Unheeded flew the hours;
For lightly falls the foot of time,
That only treads on flowers.' "

sang Canaris, looking up at her with an assumption of mirth, sadder than the melancholy which it could not wholly hide.

"You make light of it, Felix; but I am sure you will fall ill, if you do not get more sleep and quieter dreams," she said, still smoothing the glossy dark rings of which she was so proud.

"*Cara mia*, what do you know about my dreams?" he asked, with a hint of surprise in the manner, which was still careless.

"You toss about, and talk so wildly sometimes, that it troubles me to hear you."

"I will stop it at once. What do I talk about? Something amusing, I hope," he asked, quickly.

"That I cannot tell, for you speak in French or Italian; but you sigh terribly, and often seem angry or excited about something."

"That is odd. I do not remember my dreams, but it is little wonder my poor wits are distraught, after all they have been through lately. Did I talk last night, and spoil your sleep, love?" asked Canaris, idly piling up a little heap of coins, though listening intently for her reply.

"Yes: you seemed very busy, and said more than once, 'Le jeu est fait, rien ne va plus.' 'Rouge gagne et couleur'—or, 'Rouge perd et couleur gagne.' I know what those words mean, because I have read them in a novel; and they trouble me from your lips, Felix."

"I must have been dreaming of a week I once spent in Homberg, with my father. We don't do that sort of thing here."

"Not under the same name, perhaps. Dear, do you ever play?" asked Gladys, leaning her cheek against the head which had sunk a little, as he leaned forward to smooth out the crumpled notes before him.

"Why not? One must amuse one's self."

"Not so. Please promise that you will try some safer way? This is not— honest." She hesitated over the last word, for his tone had been short and sharp, but uttered it bravely, and stole an arm about his neck, mutely asking pardon for the speech which cost her so much.

"What is? Life is all a lottery, and one must keep trying one's luck while the wheel goes round; for prizes are few and blanks many, you know."

"Ah, do not speak in that reckless way. Forgive me for asking questions; but you are all I have, and I must take care of you, since no one else has the right."

"Or the will. Ask what you please. I will tell you any thing, my visible conscience;" and Canaris took her in the circle of his arm, subdued by the courageous tenderness that made her what he called her.

"Is that all yours?" she whispered, pointing a small forefinger rather sternly at the money before him, and sweetening the question with a kiss.

"No, it is yours, every penny of it. Put it in the little drawer, and make merry with it, else I shall be sorry I won it for you."

"That I cannot do. Please do not ask me. There is always enough in the little drawer for me, and I like better to use the money you have earned."

"Say, rather, the salary which *you* earn and *I* spend. It is all wrong, Gladys; but I cannot help it!" and Canaris pushed away his winnings, as if he despised them and himself.

"It is my fault that you did this, because I begged you not to let Mr. Helwyze give me so much. I can take any thing from you, for I love you, but not from him; so you try to make me think you have enough to gratify my every wish. Is not that true?"

"Yes: I hate to have you accept any thing from him, and find it harder to do so myself, than before you came. Yet I cannot help liking play; for it is an inherited taste, and he knows it."

"And does not warn you?"

"Not he: I inherit my father's luck as well as skill, and Helwyze enjoys hearing of my success in this, as in other things. We used to play together, till he tired of it. There is nothing equal to it when one is tormented with *ennui!*"

"Felix, I fear that, though a kind friend, he is not a wise one. Why does he encourage your vices, and take no interest in strengthening your virtues? Forgive me, but we all have both, and I want you to be as good as you are gifted," she said, with such an earnest, tender face, he could not feel offended.

"He does not care for that. The contest between the good and evil in me interests him most, for he knows how to lay his hand on the weak or wicked spots in a man's heart; and playing with other people's passions is his favorite amusement. Have you not discovered this?"

Canaris spoke gloomily, and Gladys shivered as she held him closer, and answered in a whisper—

"Yes, I feel as if under a microscope when with him; yet he is very kind to me, and very patient with my ignorance. Felix, is he trying to discover the evil in me, when he gives me strange things to read, and sits watching me while I do it?"

"*Gott bewahre!*—but of this I am sure, he will find no evil in you, my white-souled little wife, unless he puts it there. Gladys, refuse to read what pains and puzzles you. I will not let him vex your peace. Can he not be content with me, since I am his, body and soul?"

Canaris put her hastily away, to walk the room with a new sense of wrong hot within him at the thought of the dangers into which he had brought her against his will. But Gladys, caring only for him, ventured to add, with her kindling eyes upon his troubled face—

"I will not let him vex *your* peace! Refuse to do the things which you feel are wrong, lest what are only pleasures now may become terrible temptations by and by. I love and trust you as he never can; I will not believe your vices stronger than your virtues; and I will defend you, if he tries to harm the husband God has given me."

"Bless you for that! it is so long since I have had any one to care for me, that I forget my duty to you. I am tired of all this froth and folly; I will stay at home hereafter; that will be safest, if not happiest."

He began impetuously, but his voice fell, and was almost inaudible at the last word, as he turned away to hide the expression of regret which he could not disguise. But Gladys heard and saw, and the vague fear which sometimes haunted her stirred again, and took form in the bitter thought, "Home is not happy: am I the cause?"

She put it from her instantly, as if doubt were dishonor, and spoke out in the cordial tone which always cheered and soothed him—

"It shall be both, if I can make it so. Let me try, and perhaps I can do for you what Mr. Helwyze says I have done for him—caused him to forget his troubles, and be glad he is alive."

Canaris swung round with a peculiar expression on his face.

"He says that, does he? Then he is satisfied with his bargain! I thought as much, though he never condescended to confess it to me."

"What bargain, Felix?"

"The pair of us. We were costly, but he got us, as he gets every thing he sets his heart upon. He was growing tired of me; but when I would have gone, he kept me, by making it possible for me to win you for myself—and him. Six months between us have shown you this, I know, and it is in vain to hide from you how much I long to break away and be free again—if I ever can."

He looked ready to break away at once, and Gladys sympathized with him, seeing now the cause of his unrest.

"I know the feeling, for I too am tired of this life; not because it is so quiet, but so divided. I want to live for you alone, no matter how poor and humble my place may be. Now I am so little with you, I sometimes feel as if I should grow less and less to you, till I am nothing but a burden and a stumbling-block. Can we not go and be happy somewhere else? must we stay here all our lives?" she asked, confessing the desire which had been strengthening rapidly of late.

"While he lives I must stay, if he wants me. I cannot be ungrateful. Remember all he has done for me. It will not be long to wait, perhaps."

Canaris spoke hurriedly, as if regretting his involuntary outburst, and anxious to atone for it by the submission which always seemed at war with some stronger, if not nobler, sentiment. Gladys sat silent, lost in thought; while her husband swept the ill-gotten money into a drawer, and locked it up, as if relieved to have it out of sight. Soon the cloud lifted, however; and going to him, as he stood at the window, looking out with the air of a caged eagle, she said, with her hand upon his arm—

"You are right: we *will* be grateful and patient; but while we wait we must work, because in that one always finds strength and comfort. What can we do to earn the wherewithal to found our own little home upon when this is gone? I have nothing valuable; have you?"

"Nothing but this;" and he touched the bright head beside him, recalling the moment when she said her hair was all the gold she had.

Gladys remembered it as well, and the promise then made to help him, both as wife and woman. The time seemed to have come; and, taking counsel of her own integrity, she had dared to speak in the "sincere voice that made truth sweeter than falsehood." Now she tried, in her simple way, to show how the self-respect he seemed in danger of losing might be preserved by a task whose purpose would be both salvation and reward.

"Then let the wit inside this head of mine show you how to turn an honest penny," she began, unfolding her plan with an enthusiasm which redeemed its most prosaic features. "Mr. Helwyze says that even the best poetry is not profitable, except in fame. That you already have; and pride and pleasure in the new book is enough, without spoiling it by being vexed about the money it may bring. But you can use your pen in other ways, before it is time to write another poem. One of these ways is the translation of that curious Spanish book you were speaking of the other day. That will bring something, as it is rare and old; and you, that have half a dozen languages at your tongue's end, can easily find plenty of such work, now that you do not absolutely need it."

"That sounds a little bitter, Gladys. Don't let my resentful temper spoil your sweet one."

"I am learning fast; among other things, that to him who hath, more shall be given; so you, being a successful man, may hope for plenty of help from all *now*, though you were left to starve, when a kind word would have saved you so much suffering," Gladys answered, not bitterly, but with a woman's pitiful memory of the wrongs done those dearest her.

"God knows it would!" ejaculated Canaris, with unusual fervor.

"Mr. Helwyze remembers that, I think; and this is perhaps the reason why he is so generous now. Too much so for your good, I fear; and so I speak, because, young as I am, I cannot help trying to watch over you, as a wife should."

"I like it, Gladys. I am old, in many things, for my years, but a boy still in love, and you must teach me how to be worthy of all you give so generously and sweetly."

"Do I give the most?"

"All women do, they say. But go on, and tell the rest of this fine plan of yours. While I use my polyglot accomplishments, what becomes of you?" he asked, hastily returning to the safer subject; for the wistful look in her eyes smote him to the heart.

"I work also. You are still Mr. Helwyze's *homme d'affaires,* as he calls you; I am still his reader. But when he does not need me, I shall take up my old craft again, and embroider, as I used at home. You do not know how skilful I am with the needle, and never dreamed that the initials on the handkerchiefs you admired so much were all my work. Oh, I am a thrifty wife, though such a little one!" and Gladys broke into her clear child's laugh, which seemed to cheer them both, as a lark's song makes music even in a cloud.

Canaris laughed with her; for these glimpses of practical gifts and shrewd common sense in Gladys were very like the discovery of a rock under its veil of moss, or garland of airy columbines.

"But what will *he* say to all this?" asked the young man, with a downward gesture of the finger, and in his eye a glimmer of malicious satisfaction at the thought of having at least one secret in which Helwyze had no part.

"We need not tell him. It is nothing to him what we do up here. Let him find out, if he cares to know," answered Gladys, with a charmingly mutinous air, as she tripped away to her own little room.

"He *will* care, and he *will* find out. He has no right; but that will not stop him," returned Canaris, following to lean in the door-way, and watch her kneeling before a great basket, from which she pulled reels of gay silk, unfinished bits of work, and fragments of old lace.

"See!" she said, holding up one of the latter, "I can both make and mend; and one who is clever at this sort of thing can earn a pretty penny in a quiet way. Through my old employer I can get all the work I want; so please do not forbid it, Felix: I should be so much happier, if I might?"

"I will forbid nothing that makes you happy. But Helwyze will be exceeding wroth when he discovers it, unless the absurdity of beggars living in a palace strikes him as it does me."

"I am not afraid!"

"You never saw him in a rage: I have. Quite calm and cool, but rather awful, as he withers you with a look, or drives you half wild with a word that stings like a whip, and makes you hate him."

"Still I would not fear him, unless I *had* done wrong."

"He makes you feel so, whether you have or not; and you ask pardon for doing what you know is right. It is singular, but he certainly does make black seem white, sometimes," mused Canaris, knitting his brows with the old perplexity.

"I am afraid so;" and Gladys folded up a sigh in the parcel of rosy floss she laid away. Then she chased the frown from her husband's face by talking blithely of the home they would yet earn and enjoy together.

Conscious that things were more amiss with him than she suspected, Canaris was glad to try the new cure, and soon found it so helpful, that he was anxious to continue it. Very pleasant were the hours they spent together in their own rooms, when the duties they owed Helwyze were done; all the pleasanter for them, perhaps, because this domestic league of theirs shut him out from their real life as inevitably as it drew them nearer to one another.

The task now in hand was one that Canaris could do easily and well; and Gladys's example kept him at it when the charm of novelty was gone. While he wrote she sat near, so quietly busy, that he often forgot her presence; but when he looked up, the glance of approval, the encouraging word, the tender smile, were always ready, and wonderfully inspiring; for this sweet comrade grew dearer day by day. While he rested, she still worked; and he loved to watch the flowery wonders grow beneath her needle, swift as skilful. Now a golden wheat-ear, a scarlet poppy, a blue violet; or the white embroidery, that made his eyes ache with following the tiny stitches, which seemed to sow seed-pearls along a hem, weave graceful ciphers, or make lace-work like a cobweb.

Something in it pleased his artistic sense of the beautiful, and soothed him, as did the conversation that naturally went on between them. Oftenest he talked, telling her more of his varied life than any other human being knew; and in these confidences she found the clew to many things which had pained or puzzled her before; because, spite of her love, Gladys was clear-sighted, even against her will. Then she would answer with the story of her monotonous days, her lonely labors, dreams, and hopes; and they would comfort one another by making pictures of a future too beautiful ever to be true.

Helwyze was quick to perceive the new change which came over Felix, the happy peace which had returned to Gladys. He "did care, and he did find out," what the young people were about. At first he smiled at the girl's delusion in believing that she could fix a nature so mercurial as that of Canaris, but did not wonder at his yielding, for a time at least, to such tender persuasion; and, calling them "a pair of innocents," Helwyze let them alone, till he discovered that his power was in danger.

Presently, he began to miss the sense of undivided control which was so agreeable to him. Canaris was as serviceable as ever, but no longer made him sole confidant, counsellor, and friend. Gladys was scrupulously faithful still, but her intense interest in his world of books was much lessened: for she was reading a more engrossing volume than any of these—the heart of the man she loved. Something was gone which he had bargained for, thought he had secured, and now felt wronged at losing—an indescribable charm, especially pervading his intercourse with Gladys; for this friendship, sweet as honey, pure as dew, had just begun to blossom, when a chilly breath seemed to check its progress, leaving only cheerful service, not the spontaneous devotion which had been so much to him.

He said nothing; but for all his imperturbability, it annoyed him, as the gnat annoyed the lion; and, though scarcely acknowledged even to himself, it lurked under various moods and motives, impelling him to words and acts which produced dangerous consequences.

"Pray forgive us, we are very late."

"Time goes so fast, we quite forgot!" exclaimed Felix and Gladys both together, as they hurried into the library, one bright March morning, looking so blithe and young, that Helwyze suddenly felt old and sad and bitter-hearted, as if they had stolen something from him.

"I have learned to wait," he said, with the cold brevity which was the only sign of displeasure Gladys ever saw in him.

In remorseful silence she hastened to find her place in the book they were reading; but Canaris, who seemed bubbling over with good spirits, took no notice of the chill, and asked, with unabated cheerfulness—

"Any commissions, sir, beside these letters? I feel as if I 'could put a girdle round the earth in forty minutes,' it is such a glorious, spring-like day."

"Nothing but the letters. Stay a moment, while I add another;" and, taking up the pen he had laid by, Helwyze wrote hastily—

To Olivia at the South:—

    The swallows will be returning soon; return with them, if you can. I am deadly dull: come and make a little mischief to amuse me. I miss you.

                                         JASPER.

Sealing and directing this, he handed it to Canaris, who had been whispering to Gladys more like a lover than a husband of half a year's standing. Something in the elder man's face made the younger glance involuntarily at the letter as he took it.

"Olivia? I promised to write her, but I"—

"Dared not?"

"No: I forgot it;" and Canaris went off, laughing at the *grande passion,* which now seemed very foolish and far away.

"This time, I think, you *will* remember, for I mean to fight fire with fire," thought Helwyze, with a grim smile, such as Louis XI. might have worn when sending some gallant young knight to carry his own death-warrant.

XII

~

Olivia came before the swallows; for the three words, "I miss you," would have brought her from the ends of the earth, had she exiled herself so far. She had waited for him to want and call her, as he often did when others wearied or failed him. Seldom had so long a time passed without some word from him; and endless doubts, fears, conjectures, had harassed her, as month after month went by, and no summons came. Now she hastened, ready for any thing he might ask of her, since her reward would be a glimpse of the only heaven she knew.

"Amuse Felix: he is falling in love with his wife, and it spoils both of them for my use. He says he has forgotten you. Come often, and teach him to remember, as penalty for his bad taste and manners," was the single order Helwyze gave; but Olivia needed no other; and, for the sake of coming often, would have smiled upon a far less agreeable man than Canaris.

Gladys tried to welcome the new guest cordially, as an unsuspicious dove might have welcomed a falcon to its peaceful cote; but her heart sunk when she found her happy quiet sorely disturbed, her husband's place deserted, and the old glamour slowly returning to separate them, in spite of all her gentle arts. For Canaris, feeling quite safe in the sincere affection which now bound him to his wife, was foolhardy in his desire to show Olivia how heart-whole he had become. This piqued her irresistibly, because Helwyze was looking on, and she would win *his* approval at any cost. So these three, from divers motives, joined together to teach poor Gladys how much a woman can suffer with silent fortitude and make no sign.

The weeks that followed seemed unusually gay and sunny ones; for April came in blandly, and Olivia made a pleasant stir throughout the house by her frequent visits, and the various excursions she proposed. Many of these Gladys escaped; for her pain was not the jealousy that would drive her to out-rival her rival, but the sorrowful shame and pity which made her long to hide herself, till Felix should come back and be forgiven. Helwyze naturally declined the long drives, the exhilarating rides in the bright spring weather, which were so attractive to the younger man, and sat at home watching Gladys, now more absorbingly interesting than ever. He could not but admire the patience, strength, and dignity of the creature; for she made no complaint, showed no suspicion, asked no advice, but went straight on, like one who followed with faltering feet, but unwavering eye, the single star in all the sky that would lead her right. A craving curiosity to know what she felt and thought possessed him, and he invited confidence by unwonted kindliness, as well as the unfailing courtesy he showed her.

But Gladys would not speak either to him or to her husband, who seemed wilfully blind to the slowly changing face, all the sadder for the smile it always wore when his eyes were on it. At first, Helwyze tried his gentlest arts; but, finding her as true as brave, was driven, by the morbid curiosity which he had indulged till it became a mania, to use means as subtle as sinful—like a burglar, who, failing to pick a lock, grows desperate and breaks it, careless of consequences.

Taking his daily walk through the house, he once came upon Gladys watering the *jardinière*, which was her especial care, and always kept full of her favorite plants. She was not singing as she worked, but seriously busy as a child, holding in both hands her little watering-pot to shower the thirsty ferns and flowers, who turned up their faces to be washed with the silent delight which was their thanks.

"See how the dear things enjoy it! I feel as if they knew and watched for me, and I never like to disappoint them of their bath," she said, looking over her shoulder, as he paused beside her. She was used to this now, and was never surprised or startled when below stairs by his noiseless approach.

"They are doing finely. Did Moss bring in some cyclamens? They are in full bloom now, and you are fond of them, I think?"

"Yes, here they are: both purple and white, so sweet and lovely! See how many buds this one has. I shall enjoy seeing them come out, they unfurl so prettily;" and, full of interest, Gladys parted the leaves to show several baby buds, whose rosy faces were just peeping from their green hoods.

Helwyze liked to see her among the flowers; for there was something peculiarly innocent and fresh about her then, as if the woman forgot her griefs, and was a girl again. It struck him anew, as she stood there in the sunshine, leaning down to tend the soft leaves and cherish the delicate buds with a caressing hand.

"Like seeks like: you are a sort of cyclamen yourself. I never observed it before, but the likeness is quite striking," he said, with the slow smile which usually prefaced some speech which bore a double meaning.

"Am I?" and Gladys eyed the flowers, pleased, yet a little shy, of compliment from him.

"This is especially like you," continued Helwyze, touching one of the freshest. "Out of these strong sombre leaves rises a wraith-like blossom, with white, softly folded petals, a rosy color on its modest face, and a most sweet perfume for those whose sense is fine enough to perceive it. Most of all, perhaps, it resembles you in this—it hides its heart, and, if one tries to look too closely, there is danger of snapping the slender stem."

"That is its nature, and it cannot help being shy. I kneel down and look up without touching it; then one sees that it has nothing to hide," protested Gladys, following out the flower fancy, half in earnest, half in jest, for she felt there was a question and a reproach in his words.

"Perhaps not; let us see, in my way." With a light touch Helwyze turned the reluctant cyclamen upward, and in its purple cup there clung a newly fallen drop, like a secret tear.

Mute and stricken, Gladys looked at the little symbol of herself, owning, with a throb of pain, that if in nothing else, they *were* alike in that.

Helwyze stood silent likewise, inhaling the faint fragrance while he softly ruffled the curled petals as if searching for another tear. Suddenly Gladys spoke out with the directness which always gave him a keen pleasure, asking, as she stretched her hand involuntarily to shield the more helpless flower—

"Sir, why do you wish to read my heart?"

"To comfort it."

"Do I need comfort, then?"

"Do you not?"

"If I have a sorrow, God only can console me, and He only need know it. To you it should be sacred. Forgive me if I seem ungrateful; but you cannot help me, if you would."

"Do you doubt my will?"

"I try to doubt no one; but I fear—I fear many things;" and, as if afraid of saying too much, Gladys broke off, to hurry away, wearing so strange a look that Helwyze was consumed with a desire to know its meaning.

He saw no more of her till twilight, for Canaris took her place just then, reading a foreign book, which she could not manage; but, when Felix went out, he sought one of his solitary haunts, hoping she would appear.

She did; for the day closed early with a gusty rain, and the sunset hour was gray and cold, leaving no after-glow to tint the western sky and bathe the great room in ruddy light. Pale and noiseless as a spirit, Gladys went to and fro, trying to quiet the unrest that made her nights sleepless, her days one long struggle to be patient, just, and kind. She tried to sing, but the song died in her throat; she tried to sew, but her eyes were dim, and the flower under her needle only reminded her that "pansies were for thoughts," and hers, alas! were too sad for thinking; she took up a book, but laid it down again, since Felix was not there to finish it with her. Her own rooms seemed so empty, she could not return thither when she had looked for him in vain; and, longing for some human voice to speak to her, it was a relief to come upon Helwyze sitting in his lonely corner—for she never now went to the library, unless duty called her.

"A dull evening, and dull company," he said, as she paused beside him, glad to have found something to take her out of herself, for a time at least.

"Such a long day! and such a dreary night as it will be!" she answered, leaning her forehead against the window-pane, to watch the drops fall, and listen to the melancholy wind.

"Shorten the one and cheer the other, as I do: sleep, dream, and forget."

"I cannot!" and there was a world of suffering in the words that broke from her against her will.

"Try my sleep-compeller as freely as I tried yours. See, these will give you one, if not all the three desired blessings—quiet slumber, delicious dreams, or utter oblivion for a time."

As he spoke, Helwyze had drawn out a little *bonbonnière* of tortoise-shell and silver, which he always carried, and shaken into his palm half a dozen white comfits, which he offered to Gladys, with a benign expression born of real sympathy and compassion. She hesitated; and he added, in a tone of mild reproach, which smote her generous heart with compunction—

"Since I may not even try to minister to your troubled mind, let me, at least, give a little rest to your weary body. Trust me, child, these cannot hurt you; and, strong as you are, you will break down if you do not sleep."

Without a word, she took them; and, as they melted on her tongue, first sweet, then bitter, she stood leaning against the rainy window-pane, listening to Helwyze, who began to talk as if he too had tasted the Indian drug, which "made the face of Coleridge shine, as he conversed like one inspired."

It seemed a very simple, friendly act; but this man had learned to know how subtly the mind works; to see how often an apparently impulsive action is born of an almost unconscious thought, an unacknowledged purpose, a deeply hidden motive, which to many seem rather the child than the father of the deed. Helwyze did not deceive himself, and owned that baffled desire prompted that unpremeditated offer, and was ready to avail itself of any self-betrayal which might follow its acceptance, for he had given Gladys hasheesh.

It could not harm; it might soothe and comfort her unrest. It surely would make her forget for a while, and in that temporary oblivion perhaps he might discover what he burned to know. The very uncertainty of its effect added to the daring of the deed; and, while he talked, he waited to see how it would affect her, well knowing that in such a temperament as hers all processes are rapid. For an hour he conversed so delightfully of Rome and its wonders, that Gladys was amazed to find Felix had come in, unheard for once.

All through dinner she brightened steadily, thinking the happy mood was brought by her prodigal's return, quite forgetting Helwyze and his bitter-sweet bonbons.

"I shall stay at home, and enjoy the society of my pretty wife. What have you done to make yourself so beautiful to-night? Is it the new gown?" asked Canaris, surveying her with laughing but most genuine surprise and satisfaction as they returned to the drawing-room again.

"It is not new: I made it long ago, to please you, but you never noticed it before," answered Gladys, glancing at the pale-hued dress, all broad, soft folds from waist to ankle, with its winter trimming of swan's down at the neck and wrists; simple, but most becoming to her flower-like face and girlish figure.

"What cruel blindness! But I see and admire it now, and honestly declare that not Olivia in all her splendor is arrayed so much to my taste as you, my Sancta Simplicitas."

"It is pleasant to hear you say so; but that alone does not make me happy: it must be having you at home all to myself again," she whispered, with shining eyes, cheeks that glowed with a deeper rose each hour, and an indescribably blest expression in a face which now was both brilliant and dreamy.

Helwyze heard what she said, and, fearing to lose sight of her, promptly challenged Canaris to chess, a favorite pastime with them both. For an hour they played, well matched and keenly interested, while Gladys sat by, already tasting the restful peace, the delicious dreams, promised her.

The clock was on the stroke of eight, the game was nearly over, when a quick ring arrested Helwyze in the act of making the final move. There was a stir in the hall, then, bringing with her a waft of fresh, damp air, Olivia appeared, brave in purple silk and Roman gold.

"I thought you were all asleep or dead; but now I see the cause of this awful silence," she cried. "Don't speak, don't stir; let me enjoy the fine tableau you make. Retsch's 'Game of Life,' quite perfect, and most effective."

It certainly was to an observer; for Canaris, flushed and eager, looked the young man to the life; Helwyze, calm but intent, with his finger on his lip, pondering that last fateful move, was an excellent Satan; and behind them stood Gladys, wonderfully resembling the wistful angel, with that new brightness on her face.

"Which wins?" asked Olivia, rustling toward them, conscious of having made an impressive entrance; for both men looked up to welcome her, though Gladys never lifted her eyes from the mimic battle Felix seemed about to lose.

"I do, as usual," answered Helwyze, turning to finish the game with the careless ease of a victor.

"Not this time;" and Gladys touched a piece which Canaris in the hurry of the moment was about to overlook. He saw its value at a glance, made the one move that could save him, and in an instant cried "Checkmate," with a laugh of triumph.

"Not fair, the angel interfered," said Olivia, shaking a warning finger at Gladys, who echoed her husband's laugh with one still more exultant, as she put her hand upon his shoulder, saying, in a low, intense voice never heard from her lips before—

"I have won him; he is mine, and cannot be taken from me any more."

"Dearest child, no one wants him, except to play with and admire," began Olivia, rather startled by the look and manner of the lately meek, mute Gladys.

Here Helwyze struck in, anxious to avert Olivia's attention; for her undesirable presence disconcerted him, since her woman's wit might discover what it was easy to conceal from Canaris.

"You have come to entertain us, like the amiable enchantress that you are?"

he asked, suggestively; for nothing charmed Olivia more than permission to amuse him, when others failed.

"I have a thought—a happy thought—if Gladys will help me. You have given me one living picture: I will give you others, and she shall sing the scenes we illustrate."

"Take Felix, and give us 'The God and the Bayadere,' " said Helwyze, glancing at the young pair behind them, he intent upon their conversation, she upon him. "No, I will have only Gladys. You will act and sing for us, I know?" and Olivia turned to her with a most engaging smile.

"I never acted in my life, but I will try. I think I should like it for I feel as if I could do any thing to-night;" and she came to them with a swift step, an eager air, as if longing to find some outlet for the strange energy which seemed to thrill every nerve and set her heart to beating audibly.

"You look so. Do you know all these songs?" asked Olivia, taking up the book which had suggested her happy thought.

"There are but four: I know them all. I will gladly sing them; for I set them to music, if they had none of their own already. I often do that to those Felix writes me."

"Come, then. I want the key of the great press, where you keep your spoils, Jasper."

"Mrs. Bland will give it you. Order what you will, if you are going to treat us to an Arabian Night's entertainment."

"Better than that. We are going to teach a small poet, by illustrating the work of a great one;" and, with a mischievous laugh, Olivia vanished, beckoning Gladys to follow.

The two men beguiled the time as best they might: Canaris playing softly to himself in the music-room; Helwyze listening intently to the sounds that came from behind the curtains, now dropped over a double door-way leading to the lower end of the hall. Olivia's imperious voice was heard, directing men and maids. More than once an excited laugh from Gladys jarred upon his ear; and, as minute after minute passed, his impatience to see her again increased.

XIII

~

Aften what would have seemed a wonderfully short time to a more careless
waiter, three blows were struck, in the French fashion, and Canaris had
barely time to reach his place, when the deep blue curtains slid noiselessly
apart, showing the visible portion of the hall, arranged to suggest a mediæval
room. An easy task, when a suit of rusty armor already stood there; and
Helwyze had brought spoils from all quarters of the globe, in the shape of
old furniture, tapestry, weapons, and trophies of many a wild hunt.

"What is it?" whispered Canaris eagerly.

"An Idyl of the King."

"I see: the first. How well they look it!"

They did; Olivia, as

> "An ancient dame in dim brocade;
> And near her, like a blossom, vermeil-white,
> That lightly breaks a faded flower-sheath,
> Stood the fair Enid, all in faded silk."

Gladys, clad in a quaint costume of tarnished gray and silver damask, singing, in "the sweet voice of a bird"—

> "Turn, Fortune, turn thy wheel, and lower the proud;
> Turn thy wild wheel through sunshine, storm, and cloud;
> Thy wheel and thee we neither love nor hate.
>
> "Turn, Fortune, turn thy wheel with smile and frown;
> With that wild wheel we go not up nor down;
> Our hoard is little, but our hearts are great.
>
> "Smile and we smile, the lords of many lands;
> Frown and we smile, the lords of our own hands;
> For man is man and master of his fate.
>
> "Turn, turn thy wheel above the staring crowd;
> Thy wheel and thou art shadows in the cloud;
> Thy wheel and thee we neither love nor hate."

There was something inexpressibly touching in the way Gladys gave
the words, which had such significance addressed to those who listened
so intently, that they nearly forgot to pay the tribute which all actors, the

greatest as the least, desire, when the curtain dropped, and the song was done.

"A capital idea of Olivia's, and beautifully carried out. This promises to be pleasant;" and Helwyze sat erect upon the divan, where Canaris came to lounge beside him.

"Which comes next? I don't remember. If it is Vivien, they will have to skip it, unless they call you in for Merlin," he said, talking gayly, because a little conscience-stricken by the look Gladys wore, as she sung, with her eyes upon him—

"Our hoard is little, but our hearts are great."

"They will not want a Merlin; for Gladys could not act Vivien, if she would," answered Helwyze, tapping restlessly as he waited.

"She said she could do 'any thing' to-night; and, upon my life, she looked as if she might even beguile you 'mighty master,' of your strongest spell."

"She will never try."

But both were mistaken; for, when they looked again, the dim light showed a dark and hooded shape, with glittering eyes and the semblance of a flowing, hoary beard, leaning half-hidden in a bower of tall shrubs from the conservatory. It was Olivia, as Merlin; and, being of noble proportions, she looked the part excellently. Upon the wizard's knee sat Vivien—

"A twist of gold was round her hair;
A robe of samite without price, that more exprest
Than hid her, clung about her lissome limbs,
In color like the satin-shining palm
On sallows in the windy gleams of March."

In any other mood, Gladys would never have consented to be loosely clad in a great mantle of some Indian fabric, which shimmered like woven light, with its alternate stripes of gold-covered silk and softest wool. Shoulders and arms showed rosy white under the veil of hair which swept to her knee, as she clung there, singing sweet and low, with eyes on Merlin's face, lips near his own, and head upon his breast—

"In Love, if Love be Love, if Love be ours,
Faith and unfaith can ne'er be equal powers;
Unfaith in aught is want of faith in all.

"It is the little rift within the lute
      That by and by will make the music mute,
      And ever widening, slowly silence all.

"The little rift within the lover's lute,
      Or little pitted speck in garner'd fruit,
      That, rotting inward, slowly moulders all.

"It is not worth the keeping: let it go:
      But shall it? Answer, darling, answer 'No;'
      And trust me not at all or all in all."

There Gladys seemed to forget her part, and, turning, stretched her arms towards her husband, as if in music she had found a tongue to plead her cause. The involuntary gesture recalled to her that other verse which Vivien added to her song; and something impelled her to sing it, standing erect, with face, figure, voice all trembling with the strong emotion that suddenly controlled her—

"My name, once mine, now thine, is closelier mine,
      For fame, could fame be mine, that fame were thine;
      And shame, could shame be thine, that shame were mine;
      So trust me not at all or all in all."

Down fell the curtain there, and the two men looked at one another in silence for an instant, dazzled, troubled, and surprised; for in this brilliant, impassioned creature they did not recognize the Gladys they believed they knew so well.

"What possessed her to sing that? She is so unlike herself, I do not know her," said Canaris, excited by the discoveries he was making.

"She is inspired to-night; so be prepared for any thing. These women will work wonders, they are acting to the men they love," answered Helwyze, warily, yet excited also; because, for him, a double drama was passing on that little stage, and he found it marvellously fascinating.

"I never knew how beautiful she was!" mused Canaris, half aloud, his eyes upon the blue draperies which hid her from his sight.

"You never saw her in such gear before. Splendor suits her present mood, as well as simplicity becomes her usual self-restraint. You have made her jealous, and your angel will prove herself a woman, after all."

"Is that the cause of this sudden change in her? Then I don't regret playing truant, for the woman suits me better than the angel," cried Canaris, conscious that the pale affection he had borne his wife so long was already glowing with new warmth and color, in spite of his seeming neglect.

"Wait till you see Olivia as Guinevere. I know she cannot resist that part, and I suspect she is willing to efface herself so far that she may take us by storm by and by."

Helwyze prophesied truly; and, when next the curtains parted, the stately Queen sat in the nunnery of Almesbury, with the little novice at her feet. Olivia *was* right splendid now, for her sumptuous beauty well became the costly stuffs in which she had draped herself with the graceful art of a woman whose physical loveliness was her best possession. A trifle *too* gorgeous, perhaps, for the repentant Guinevere; but a most grand and gracious spectacle, nevertheless, as she leaned in the tall carved chair, with jewelled arms lying languidly across her lap, and absent eyes still full of love and longing for lost Launcelot.

Gladys, in white wimple and close-folded gown of gray, sat on a stool beside the "one low light," humming softly, her rosary fallen at her feet—

> "the Queen looked up, and said,
> 'O maiden, if indeed you list to sing
> Sing, and unbind my heart, that I may weep.
> Whereat full willingly sang the little maid,
>
> Late, late, so late! and dark the night and chill!
> Late, late, so late! but we can enter still.
> Too late! too late! ye cannot enter now.
>
> No light had we: for that we do repent,
> And, learning this, the bridegroom will relent.
> Too late! too late! ye cannot enter now.
>
> No light, so late! and dark and chill the night!
> O let us in, that we may find the light!
> Too late! too late! ye cannot enter now.
>
> Have we not heard the bridegroom is so sweet?
> O let us in, tho' late, to kiss his feet!
> No, no, too late! ye cannot enter now."

Slowly the proud head had drooped, the stately figure sunk, till, as the last lament died away, nothing remained of splendid Guinevere but a hidden face, a cloud of black hair from which the crown had fallen, a heap of rich robes quivering with the stormy sobs of a guilty woman's smitten heart. The curtains closed on this tableau, which was made the more effective by the strong contrast between the despairing Queen and the little novice telling her beads in meek dismay.

"Good heavens, that sounded like the wail of a lost soul! My blood runs cold, and I feel as if I ought to say my prayers," muttered Canaris, with a shiver; for, with his susceptible temperament, music always exerted over him an almost painful power.

"If you knew any," sneered Helwyze, whose eyes now glittered with something stronger than excitement.

"I do: Gladys taught me, and I am not ashamed to own it."

"Much good may it do you." Then, in a quieter tone, he asked, "Is there any song in 'Elaine'? I forget; and that is the only one we have not had."

"There is 'The Song of Love and Death.' Gladys was learning it lately; and, if I remember rightly, it was heart-rending. I hope she will not sing it, for this sort of thing is rather too much for me;" and Canaris got up to wander aimlessly about, humming the gayest airs he knew, as if to drown the sorrowful "Too late! too late!" still wailing in his ear.

By this time Gladys was no longer quite herself: an inward excitement possessed her, a wild desire to sing her very heart out came over her, and a strange chill, which she thought a vague presentiment of coming ill, crept through her blood. Every thing seemed vast and awful; every sense grew painfully acute; and she walked as in a dream, so vivid, yet so mysterious, that she did not try to explain it even to herself. Her identity was doubled: one Gladys moved and spoke as she was told—a pale, dim figure, of no interest to any one; the other was alive in every fibre, thrilled with intense desire for something, and bent on finding it, though deserts, oceans, and boundless realms of air were passed to gain it.

Olivia wondered at her unsuspected power, and felt a little envious of her enchanting gift. But she was too absorbed in "setting the stage," dressing her prima donna, and planning how to end the spectacle with her favorite character of Cleopatra, to do more than observe that Gladys's eyes were luminous and large, her face growing more and more colorless, her manner less and less excited, yet unnaturally calm.

"This is the last, and you have the stage alone. Do your best for Felix; then you shall rest and be thanked," she whispered, somewhat anxiously, as she placed Elaine in her tower, leaning against the dark screen, which was unfolded, to suggest the casement she flung back when Launcelot passed below—

> "And glanced not up, nor waved his hand,
> Nor bade farewell, but sadly rode away."

The "lily-maid of Astolat" could not have looked more wan and weird than Gladys, as she stood in her trailing robes of dead white, with loosely gathered locks, hands clasped over the gay bit of tapestry which simulated the cover of the shield, eyes that seemed to see something invisible to those about her, and began her song, in a veiled voice, at once so sad and solemn, that Helwyze held his breath, and Canaris felt as if she called him from beyond the grave—

> "Sweet is true love, tho' given in vain, in vain;
> And sweet is death, who puts an end to pain;
> I know not which is sweeter, no, not I.
>
> Love, art thou sweet? then bitter death must be;
> Love, thou art bitter; sweet is death to me.
> O Love, if death be sweeter, let me die.
>
> Sweet love, that seems not made to fade away,
> Sweet death, that seems to make us loveless clay,
> I know not which is sweeter, no, not I.
>
> I fain would follow love, if that could be;
> I needs must follow death, who calls for me:
> Call and I follow, I follow! let me die!"

Carried beyond self-control by the unsuspected presence of the drug, which was doing its work with perilous rapidity, Gladys, remembering only that the last line should be sung with force, and that she sung for Felix, obeyed the wild impulse to let her voice rise and ring out with a shrill, despairing power and passion, which startled every listener, and echoed through the room, like Elaine's unearthly cry of hapless love and death.

Olivia dropped her asp, terrified; the maids stared, uncertain whether it was acting or insanity; and Helwyze sprung up aghast, fearing that he had dared too much. But Canaris, seeing only the wild, woful eyes fixed on his, the hands wrung as if in pain, forgot every thing but Gladys, and rushed between the curtains, exclaiming in real terror—

"Don't look so! don't sing so! my God, she is dying!"

Not dying, only slipping fast into the unconscious stage of the hasheesh dream, whose coming none can foretell but those accustomed to its use. Pale and quiet she lay in her husband's arms, with half-open eyes and fluttering breath, smiling up at him so strangely that he was bewildered as well as panic-stricken. Olivia forgot her Cleopatra to order air and water; the maids flew for salts and wine; Helwyze with difficulty hid his momentary dismay; while Canaris, almost beside himself, could only hang over the couch where lay "the lily-maid," looking as if already dead, and drifting down to Camelot.

"Gladys, do you know me?" he cried, as a little color came to her lips after the fiery draught Olivia energetically administered.

The eyes opened wider, the smile grew brighter, and she lifted her hand to bring him nearer, for he seemed immeasurably distant.

"Felix! Let me be still, quite still; I want to sleep. Good-night, good-night."

She thought she kissed him; then his face receded, vanished, and, as she floated buoyantly away upon the first of the many oceans to be crossed in her mysterious quest, a far-off voice seemed to say, solemnly, as if in a last farewell—

"Hush! let her sleep in peace."

It was Helwyze; and, having felt her pulse, he assured them all that she was only over-excited, must rest an hour or two, and would soon be quite herself again. So the brief panic ended quietly; and, having lowered the lights, spread Guinevere's velvet mantle over her, and reassured themselves that she was sleeping calmly, the women went to restore order to ante-room and hall, Canaris sat down to watch beside Gladys, and Helwyze betook himself to the library.

"Is she still sleeping?" he asked, with unconcealable anxiety, when Olivia joined him there.

"Like a baby. What a high-strung little thing it is. If she had strength to bear the training, she would make a cantatrice to be proud of, Jasper."

"Ah, but she never would! Fancy that modest creature on a stage for all the world to gape at. She was happiest in the nun's gown to-night, though simply ravishing as Vivien. The pretty, bare feet were most effective; but how did you persuade her to it?"

"I had no sandals as a compromise: I therefore insisted that the part *must* be so dressed or undressed, and she submitted. People usually do, when I command."

"She was on her mettle: I could see that; and well she might be, with you for a rival. I give you my word, Olivia, if I did not know you were nearly forty, I should swear it was a lie; for 'age cannot wither nor custom stale' my handsome Cleopatra. We ought to have had that, by the by: it used to be your best bit. I could not be your Antony, but Felix might: he adores costuming, and would do it capitally."

"Not old enough. Ah! what happy times those were;" and Olivia sighed sincerely, yet dramatically, for she knew she was looking wonderfully well, thrown down upon a couch, with her purple skirts sweeping about her, and two fine arms banded with gold clasped over her dark head.

Helwyze had flattered with a purpose. Canaris was in the way, Gladys might betray herself, and all was not safe yet; though in one respect the experiment had succeeded admirably, for he still tingled with the excitement of the evening. Now he wanted help, not sentiment, and, ignoring the sigh, said, carelessly—

"If all obey when you insist, just make Felix go home with you. The drive will do him good, for he is as nervous as a woman, and I shall have him fidgeting about all night, unless he forgets his fright."

"But Gladys?"

"She will be the better for a quiet nap, and ready, by the time he returns, to laugh at her heroics. He will only disturb her if he sits there, like a mourner at a death-bed."

"That sounds sensible and friendly, and you do it very well, Jasper; but I am impressed that something is amiss. What is it? Better tell me; I shall surely find it out, and will not work in the dark. I see mischief in your eyes, and you cannot deceive me."

Olivia spoke half in jest; but she had so often seen his face without a mask, that it was difficult to wear one in her presence. He frowned, hesitated, then fearing she would refuse the favor if he withheld the secret, he leaned towards her and answered in a whisper—

"I gave Gladys hasheesh, and do not care to have Felix know it."

"Jasper, how dared you?"

"She was restless, suffering for sleep. I know what that is, and out of pity gave her the merest taste. Upon my honor, no more than a child might safely take. She did not know what it was, and I thought she would only feel its soothing charm. She would, if it had not been for this masquerading. I did not count on that, and it was too much for her."

"Will she not suffer from the after-effects?"

"Not a whit, if she is let alone. An hour hence she will be deliciously drowsy, and to-morrow none the worse. I had no idea it would affect her so powerfully; but I do not regret it, for it showed what the woman is capable of."

"At your old tricks. You will never learn to let your fellow-creatures alone, till something terrible stops you. You were always prying into things, even as a boy, when I caught butterflies for you to look at."

"I never killed them: only brushed off a trifle of the gloss by my touch, and let them go again, none the worse, except for the loss of a few invisible feathers."

"Ah! but that delicate plumage is the glory of the insect; robbed of that, its beauty is marred. No one but their Maker can search hearts without harming them. I wonder how it will fare with yours when He looks for its perfection?"

Olivia spoke with a sudden seriousness, a yearning look, which jarred on nerves already somewhat unstrung, and Helwyze answered, in a mocking tone that silenced her effectually—

"I am desperately curious to know. If I can come and tell you, I will: such pious interest deserves that attention."

"Heaven forbid!" ejaculated Olivia, with a shiver.

"Then I will *not*. I have been such a poor ghost here, I suspect I shall be glad to rest eternally when I once fall asleep, if I can."

Weary was his voice, weary his attitude, as, leaning an elbow on either knee, he propped his chin upon his hands, and sat brooding for a moment with his eyes upon the ground, asking himself for the thousandth time the great question which only hope and faith can answer truly.

Olivia rose. "You are tired; so am I. Good-night, Jasper, and pleasant dreams. But remember, no more tampering with Gladys, or I must tell her husband."

"I have had my lesson. Take Felix with you, and I will send Mrs. Bland to sit with her till he comes back. Good-night, my cousin; thanks for a glimpse of the old times." Such words, uttered with a pressure of the hand, conquered Olivia's last scruple, and she went away to prefer her request in a form which made it impossible for Canaris to refuse. Gladys still slept quietly. The distance was not long, the fresh air grateful, Olivia her kindest self, and he obeyed, believing that the motherly old woman would take his place as soon as certain housewifely duties permitted.

Then Helwyze did an evil thing—a thing few men could or would have done. He deliberately violated the sanctity of a human soul, robbing it alike of its most secret and most precious thoughts. Hasheesh had lulled the senses which guarded the treasure; now the magnetism of a potent will forced the reluctant lips to give up the key.

Like a thief he stole to Gladys' side, took in his the dimpled hands whose very childishness should have pleaded for her, and fixed his eyes upon the face before him, untouched by its helpless innocence, its unnatural expression. The half-open eyes were heavy as dew-drunken violets, the sweet red mouth was set, the agitated bosom still rose and fell, like a troubled sea subsiding after storm.

So sitting, stern and silent as the fate he believed in, Helwyze concentrated every power upon the accomplishment of the purpose to which he bent his will. He called it psychological curiosity; for not even to himself did he dare confess the true meaning of the impulse which drove him to this act, and dearly did he pay for it.

Soon the passive palms thrilled in his own, the breath came faint and slow, color died, and life seemed to recede from the countenance, leaving a pale effigy of the woman; lately so full of vitality. "It works! it works!" muttered Helwyze, lifting his head at length to wipe the dampness from his brow, and send a piercing glance about the shadowy room. Then, kneeling down beside the couch, he put his lips to her ear, whispering in a tone of still command—

"Gladys, do you hear me?"

Like the echo of a voice, so low, expressionless, and distant was it, the answer came—

"I hear."

"Will you answer me?"

"I must."

"You have a sorrow—tell it."

"All is so false. I am unhappy without confidence," sighed the voice.

"Can you trust no one?"

"No one here, but Felix."

"Yet he deceives, he does not love you."

"He will."

"Is this the hope which sustains you?"

"Yes."

"And you forgive, you love him still?"

"Always."

"If the hope fails?"

"It will not: I shall have help."

"What help?"

No answer now, but the shadow of a smile seemed to float across the silent lips as if reflected from a joy too deep and tender for speech to tell.

"Speak! what is this happiness? The hope of freedom?"

"It will come."

"How?"

"When you die."

He caught his breath, and for an instant seemed daunted by the truth he had evoked; for it was terrible, so told, so heard.

"You hate me, then?" he whispered, almost fiercely, in the ear that never shrank from his hot lips.

"I doubt and dread you."

"Why, Gladys, why? To you I am not cruel."

"Too kind, alas, too kind!"

"And yet you fear me?"

"God help us. Yes."

"What is your fear?"

"No, no, I will *not* tell it!"

Some inward throe of shame or anguish turned the pale face paler, knotted the brow, and locked the lips, as if both soul and body revolted from the thought thus ruthlessly dragged to light. Instinct, the first, last, strongest impulse of human nature, struggled blindly to save the woman from betraying the dread which haunted her heart like a spectre, and burned her lips in the utterance of its name. But Helwyze was pitiless, his will indomitable; his eye held, his hand controlled, his voice commanded; and the answer came, so reluctantly, so inaudibly, that he seemed to divine, not hear it.

"What fear?"

"Your love."

"You see, you know it, then?"

"I do not see, I vaguely feel; I pray God I may never know."

With the involuntary recoil of a guilty joy, a shame as great, Helwyze dropped the nerveless hands, turned from the mutely accusing face, let the troubled spirit rest, and asked no more. But his punishment began as he stood there, finding the stolen truth a heavier burden than baffled doubt or desire had been; since forbidden knowledge was bitter to the taste, forbidden love possessed no sweetness, and the hidden hope, putting off its well-worn disguise, confronted him in all its ugliness.

An awesome silence filled the room, until he lifted up his eyes, and looked at Gladys with a look which would have wrung her heart could she have seen it. She did not see; for she lay there so still, so white, so dead, he seemed to have scared away the soul he had vexed with his impious questioning.

In remorseful haste, Helwyze busied himself about her, till she woke from that sleep within a sleep, moaned wearily, closed the unseeing eyes, and drifted away into more natural slumber, dream-haunted, but deep and quiet.

Then he stole away as he had come, and, sending the old woman to watch Gladys, shut himself into his own room, to keep a vigil which lasted until dawn; for all the poppies of the East could not have brought oblivion that night.

XIV

~

It seemed as if some angel had Gladys in especial charge, bringing light out of darkness, joy out of sorrow, good out of evil; for no harm came to her—only a great peace, which transfigured her face till it was as spiritually beautiful, as that of some young Madonna.

Waking late the next day she remembered little of the past night's events, and cared to remember little, having clearer and calmer thoughts to dwell upon, happier dreams to enjoy.

She suspected Helwyze of imprudent kindness, but uttered no reproach, quite unconscious of how much she had to forgive; thereby innocently adding to both the relief and the remorse he felt. The doubt and dread which had risen to the surface at his command, seemed to sink again into the depths; and hope and love, to still the troubled waters where her life-boat rode at anchor for a time.

Canaris, as if tired of playing truant, was ready now to be forgiven; more conscious than ever before that this young wife was a possession to be proud of, since, when she chose, she could eclipse even Olivia. The jealousy which could so inspire her flattered this man's vanity, and made her love more precious; for not yet had he learned all its depth, nor how to be worthy of it. The reverence he had always felt increased fourfold, but the affection began to burn with a stronger flame; and Canaris, for the first time, tasted the pure happiness of loving another better than himself. Glad to feel, yet ashamed to own, a sentiment whose sincerity made it very sweet, he kept it to himself, and showed no sign, except a new and most becoming humility of manner when with Gladys, as if silently asking pardon for many shortcomings. With

Helwyze he was cold and distant, evidently dreading to have him discover the change he had foretold, and feeling as if his knowledge of it would profane the first really sacred emotion the young man had known since his mother died.

Anxious for some screen behind which to hide the novel, yet most pleasurable, sensations which beset him, he found Olivia a useful friend, and still kept up some semblance of the admiration, out of which all dangerous ardor was fast fading. She saw this at once, and did not regret it: for she had a generous nature, which an all-absorbing and unhappy passion had not entirely spoiled.

Obedience to Helwyze was her delight; but, knowing him better than any other human being could, she was troubled by his increasing interest in Gladys, more especially since discovering that the girl possessed the originality, fire, and energy which were more attractive to him than her youth, gentleness, or grace. Jealousy was stronger than the desire to obey; and, calling it compassion, Olivia resolved to be magnanimous, and spare Gladys further pain, letting Canaris return to his allegiance, as he seemed inclined to do, unhindered by any act of hers.

"The poor child is so young, so utterly unable to cope with me, it is doubly cruel to torment her, just to gratify a whim of Jasper's. Better make my peace handsomely, and be her friend, than rob her of the only treasure she possesses, since I do not covet it," she thought, driving through the May-day sunshine, to carry Jasper the earliest sprays of white and rosy hawthorn from the villa garden, whither she had been to set all in order for the summer.

Helwyze was not yet visible; and, full of her new design, Olivia hastened up to find Gladys, meaning by some friendly word, some unmistakable but most delicate hint, to reassure her regarding the errant young husband, whom she had not yet learned to hold.

There was no answer to her hasty tap, and Olivia went in to seek yet further. Half-way across the larger apartment she paused abruptly, and stood looking straight before her, with a face which passed rapidly from its first expression of good-will to one of surprise, then softened, till tears stood in the brilliant eyes, and some sudden memory or thought made that usually proud countenance both sad and tender.

Gladys sat alone in her little room, her work lying on her knee, her arms folded, her head bent, singing to herself as she rocked to and fro, lost in some reverie that made her lips smile faintly, and her voice very low. She often sat so now, but Olivia had never seen her thus; and, seeing, divined at once the hope which lifted her above all sorrow, the help sent by Heaven, when most she needed it. For the song Gladys sang was a lullaby, the look she wore was that which comes to a woman's face when she rocks her first-born on her knee, and above her head was a new picture, an angel, with the Lily of Annunciation in its hand.

The one precious memory of Olivia's stormy life was the little daughter, who for a sweet, short year was all in all to her, and whose small grave was yearly covered with the first spring flowers. Fresh from this secret pilgrimage, the woman's nature was at its noblest now; and seeing that other woman, so young, so lonely, yet so blest, her heart yearned over her—

> "All her worser self slipped from her
> Like a robe"—

and, hurrying in, she said, impulsively—

"O child, I wish you had a mother!"

Gladys looked up, unstartled from the calm in which she dwelt. Olivia's face explained her words, and she answered them with the only reproach much pain had wrung from her—

"*You* might have been one to me."

"It is not too late! What shall I do to prove my sincerity?" cried Olivia, stricken with remorse.

"Help me to give my little child an honest father."

"I will! show me how."

Then these two women spent a memorable hour together; for the new tie of motherhood bridged across all differences of age and character, made confession easy, confidence sweet, friendship possible. Yet, after all, Gladys was the comforter, Olivia the one who poured out her heart, and found relief in telling the sorrows that had been, the temptations that still beset her, the good that yet remained to answer, when the right chord was touched. She longed to give as much as she received; but when she had owned, with a new sense of shame, that she was merely playing with Canaris for her own amusement (being true to Helwyze even in her falsehood), there seemed no more for her to do, since Gladys asked but one other question, and that she could not answer.

"If he does not love you, and, perhaps, it is as you say—only a poet's admiration for beauty—what *is* the trouble that keeps us apart? At first I was too blindly happy to perceive it; now tears have cleared my eyes, and I see that he hides something from me—something which he longs, yet dares not tell."

"I know: I saw it long ago; but Jasper alone can tell that secret. He holds Felix by it, and I fear the knowledge would be worse than the suspicion. Let it be: time sets all things right, and it is ill thwarting my poor cousin. I have a charming plan for you and Felix; and, when you have him to yourself, you may be able to win his confidence, as, I am sure, you have already won his heart."

Then Olivia told her plan, which was both generous and politic; since it made Gladys truly happy, proved her own sincerity, secured her own peace and that of the men whose lives seemed to become more and more inextricably tangled together.

"Now I shall go to Jasper, and conquer all his opposition; for I know I am right. Dear little creature, what is it about you that makes one feel both humble and strong when one is near you?" asked Olivia, looking down at Gladys with a hand on either shoulder, and genuine wonder in the eyes still soft with unwonted tears.

"God made me truthful, and I try to keep so; that is all," she answered, simply.

"That is enough. Kiss me, Gladys, and make me better. I am not good enough to be the mother that I might have been to you; but I *am* a friend; believe that, and trust me, if you can?"

"I do;" and Gladys sealed her confidence with both lips and hand.

"Jasper, I have invited those children to spend the summer at the villa, since you have decided for the sea. Gladys is mortally tired of this hot-house life, so is Felix: give them a long holiday, or they will run away together. Mrs. Bland and I will take care of you till they come back."

Olivia walked in upon Helwyze with this abrupt announcement, well knowing that persuasion would be useless, and vigorous measures surest to win the day. Artful as well as courageous in her assault, she answered in that one speech several objections against her plan, and suggested several strong reasons for it, sure that he would yield the first, and own the latter.

He did, with unexpected readiness; for a motive which she could not fathom prompted his seemingly careless acquiescence. He had no thought of relinquishing his hold on Canaris, since through him alone he held Gladys; but he often longed to escape from both for a time, that he might study and adjust the new power which had come into his life, unbidden, undesired.

Surprise and disappointment were almost instantaneously followed by a sense of relief when Olivia spoke; for he saw at once that this project was a wiser one than she knew.

Before her rapid sentences were ended, the thought had come and gone, the decision was made, and he could answer, in a tone of indifference which both pleased and perplexed her—

"Amiable woman, with what helpful aspirations are you blest. Seeing your failure with Felix, I have been wondering how I should get rid of him till he recovers from this comically tardy passion for his wife. They can have another and a longer honeymoon up at the villa, if they like: the other was far from romantic, I suspect. Well, why that sphinx-like expression, if you please?" he added, as Olivia stood regarding him from behind the fading hawthorn which she forgot to offer.

"I was wondering if I should ever understand you, Jasper."

"Doubtful, since I shall never understand myself."

"You ought, if any man; for you spend your life in studying yourself."

"And the more I study, the less I know. It is very like a child with a toy ark: I never know what animal may appear first. I put in my hand for a dove, and I get a serpent; I open the door for the sagacious elephant, and out rushes a tiger; I think I have found a favorite dog, and it is a wolf, looking ready to devour me. An unsatisfactory toy, better put it away and choose another."

Helwyze spoke in the half-jesting, half-serious way habitual to him; but though his mouth smiled, his eyes were gloomy, and Olivia hastened to turn his thoughts from a subject in which he took a morbid interest.

"Fanciful, but true. Now, follow your own excellent advice, and find wholesome amusement in helping me pack off the young people, and then ourselves. It is not too early for them to go at once. Canaris can come in and out as you want him for a month longer, then I will have all things ready for you in the old cottage by the sea. You used to be happy there: can you not be so again?"

"If you can give me back my twenty years. May-day is over for both of us; why try to make the dead hawthorn bloom again? Carry out your plan, and let the children be happy."

They *were* very happy; for the prospect of entire freedom was so delicious, that Gladys had some difficulty in concealing her delight, while Canaris openly rejoiced when told of Olivia's offer. All dinner-time he was talking of it; and afterward, under pretence of showing her a new plant, he took his wife into the conservatory, that he might continue planning how they should spend this unexpected holiday.

Helwyze saw them wandering arm in arm; Canaris talking rapidly, and Gladys listening, with happy laughter, to his whimsical suggestions and projects. Their content displeased the looker-on; but there was something so attractive in the flower-framed picture of beauty, youth, and joy, that he could not turn his eyes away, although the sight aroused strangely conflicting thoughts within him.

He wished them gone, yet dreaded to lose the charm of his confined life, feeling that absence would inevitably become estrangement. Canaris never would be entirely his again; for he was slowly climbing upward into a region where false ambition could not blind, mere pleasure satisfy, nor license take the place of liberty. He had not planned to ruin the youth, but simply to let "the world, the flesh, and the devil" contend against such virtues as they found, while he sat by and watched the struggle.

As Olivia predicted, however, power was a dangerous gift to such a man; and, having come to feel that Canaris belonged to him, body and soul, he was ill-pleased at losing him just when a new interest was added to their lives.

Yet losing him he assuredly was; and something like wonder mingled with his chagrin, for this girl, whom he had expected to mould to his will, exerted over him, as well as Canaris, a soft control which he could neither comprehend nor conquer. Its charm was its unconsciousness, its power was its truth; for it won gently and held firmly the regard it sought. She certainly did possess the gift of surprises; for, although brought there as a plaything, "little Gladys," without apparent effort, had subjugated haughty Olivia, wayward Felix, ruthless Helwyze; and none rebelled against her. She ruled them by the irresistible influence of a lovely womanhood, which made her daily life a sweeter poem than any they could write.

"Why did I not keep her for myself? If she can do so much for him, what might she not have done for me, had I been wise enough to wait," thought Helwyze, watching the bright-haired figure that stood looking up to the green roof whence Canaris was gathering passion-flowers.

As if some consciousness of his longing reached her, Gladys turned to look into the softly lighted room beyond, and, seeing its master sit there solitary in the midst of its splendor, she obeyed the compassionate impulse which was continually struggling against doubt and dislike.

"It must seem very selfish and ungrateful in us to be so glad. Come, Felix, and amuse him as well as me," she said, in a tone meant for his ear alone. But Helwyze heard both question and answer.

"I have been court-fool long enough. 'Tis a thankless office, and I am tired of it," replied Canaris, in the tone of a prisoner asked to go back when the door of his cell stands open.

"*I* must go, for there is Jean with coffee. Follow, like a good boy, when you have put your posy into a song, which I will set to music by and by, as your reward," said Gladys, turning reluctantly away.

"You make goodness so beautiful, that it is easy to obey. There is my posy set to music at once, for you are a song without words, *cariña;*" and Canaris threw the vine about her neck, with a look and a laugh which made it hard for her to go.

Jean not only brought coffee, but the card of a friend for Felix, who went away, promising to return. Gladys carefully prepared the black and fragrant draught which Helwyze loved, and presented it, with a sweet friendliness of mien which would have made hemlock palatable, he thought.

"Shall I sing to you till Felix comes to give you something better?" she asked, offering her best, as if anxious to atone for the sin of being happy at the cost of pain to another.

"Talk a little first. There will be time for both before he remembers us again," answered Helwyze, motioning her to a seat beside him, with the half-imperative, half-courteous, look and gesture habitual to him.

"He will not forget: Felix always keeps his promises to me," said Gladys, with an air of gentle pride, taking her place, not beside, but opposite, Helwyze, on the couch where Elaine had laid not long ago.

This involuntary act of hers gave a tone to the conversation which followed; for Helwyze, being inwardly perturbed, was seized with a desire to hover about dangerous topics: and, seeing her sit there, so near and yet so far, so willing to serve, yet so completely mistress of herself, longed to ruffle that composure, if only to make her share the disquiet of which she was the cause.

"Always?" he said, lifting his brows with an incredulous expression, as he replied to her assertion.

"I seldom ask any promise of him, but when I do, he always keeps it. You doubt that?"

"I do."

"When you know him as well as I, you will believe it."

"I flatter myself that I know him better; and, judging from the past, should call him both fickle and, in some things, false, even to you."

Up sprung the color to Gladys's cheek, and her eyes shone with sudden fire, but her voice was low and quiet, as she answered quickly—

"One is apt to look for what one wishes to find: *I* seek fidelity and truth, and I shall not be disappointed. Felix may wander, but he will come back to me: I have learned how to hold him *now.*"

"Then you are wiser than I. Pray impart the secret;" and, putting down his cup, Helwyze regarded her intently, for he saw that the spirit of the woman was roused to defend her wifely rights.

"Nay, I owe it to you; and, since it has prevailed against your enchantress, I should thank you for it."

The delicate emphasis on the words, "your enchantress," enlightened him to the fact that Gladys divined, in part at least, the cause of Olivia's return. He did not deny, but simply answered, with a curious contrast between the carelessness of the first half of his reply, with the vivid interest of the latter—

"Olivia has atoned for her sins handsomely. But what do you owe *me?* I have taught you nothing. I dare not try."

"I did not know my own power till you showed it to me; unintentionally, I believe, and unconsciously, I used it to such purpose that Felix felt pride in the wife whom he had thought a child before. I mean the night I sang and acted yonder, and did both well, thanks to you."

"I comprehend, and hope to be forgiven, since I gave you help or pleasure," he answered, with no sign of either confusion or regret, though the thought shot through his mind, "Can she remember what came after?"

"Questionable help, and painful pleasure, yet it was a memorable hour and a useful one; so I pardon you, since after the troubled delusion comes a happy reality."

There was a double meaning in her words, and a double reproach in the glance which went from the spot where she had played her part, to the garland still about her neck.

"Your yoke is a light one, and you wear it gracefully. Long may it be so."

Helwyze thought to slip away thus from the subject; for those accusing eyes were hard to meet. But Gladys seemed moved to speak with more than her usual candor, as if anxious to leave no doubts behind her; and, sitting in the self-same place, uttered words which moved him even more than those which she had whispered in her tormented sleep.

"No, my yoke is not light;" she said, in that grave, sweet voice of hers, looking down at the mystic purple blossom on her breast, with the symbols of a divine passion at its heart. "I put it on too ignorantly, too confidingly, and at times the duties, the responsibilities, which I assumed with it weigh heavily. I am just learning how beautiful they are, how sacred they should be, and trying to prove worthy of them. I know that Felix did not love as I loved, when he married me—from pity, I believe. No one told me this: I felt, I guessed it, and would have given him back his liberty, if, after patient trial, I had found that I could not make him happy."

"Can you?"

"Yes, thank God! not only happy, but good; and henceforth duty is delight, for I can teach him to love as I love, and he is glad to learn of me."

Months before, when the girl Gladys had betrayed her maiden tenderness, she had glowed like the dawn, and found no language but her blushes; now the woman sat there steadfast and passion-pale, owning her love with the eloquence of fervent speech; both pleading and commanding, in the name of wifehood and motherhood, for the right to claim the man she had won at such cost.

"And if you fail?"

"I shall not fail, unless you come between us. I have won Olivia's promise not to tempt Felix's errant fancy with her beauty. Can I not win yours to abstain from troubling his soul with still more harmful trials? It is to ask this that I speak now, and I believe I shall not speak in vain."

"Why?"

Helwyze bent and looked into her face as he uttered that one word below his breath. He dared do no more; for there was that about her, perilously frank and lovely though she was, which held in check his lawless spirit, and made it reverence, even while it rebelled against her power over him.

She neither shrank nor turned aside, but studied earnestly that unmoved countenance which hid a world of wild emotion so successfully, that even her eyes saw no token of it, except the deepening line between the brows.

"Because I am bold enough to think I know you better even than Olivia does; that you are not cold and cruel, and, having given me the right to live for Felix, you will not disturb our peace; that, if I look into your soul, as I looked into my husband's, I shall find there what I seek—justice as well as generosity."

"You shall!"

"I knew you would not disappoint me. For this promise I am more grateful than words can express, since it takes away all fear for Felix, and shows me that I was right in appealing to the heart which you try to kill. Ah! be your best self always, and so make life a blessing, not the curse you often call it," she added, giving him a smile like sunshine, a cordial glance which was more than he could bear.

"With you I am. Stay, and show me how to do it," he began, stretching both hands towards her with an almost desperate urgency in voice and gesture.

But Gladys neither saw nor heard; for at that moment Felix came through the hall singing one of the few perfect love songs in the world—

"Che faro senza Eurydice."

"See, he does keep his promise to me: I knew he would come back!" she cried delightedly, and hurried to meet him, leaving Helwyze nothing but the passion-flowers to fill his empty hands.

XV

~

B ack again, earlier than before. But not to stay long, thank Heaven! By another month we will be truly at home, my Gladys," whispered Canaris, as they went up the steps, in the mellow September sunshine.

"I hope so!" she answered, fervently, and paused an instant before entering the door; for, coming from the light and warmth without, it seemed as dark and chilly as the entrance to a tomb.

"You are tired, love? Come and rest before you see a soul."

With a new sort of tenderness, Canaris led her up to her own little bower, and lingered there to arrange the basket of fresh recruits she had brought for her winter garden: while Gladys lay contentedly on the couch where he placed her, looking about the room as if greeting old friends; but her eyes always came back to him, full of a reposeful happiness which proved that all was well with her.

"There! now the little fellows sit right comfortably in the moss, and will soon feel at home. I'll go find Mother Bland, and see what his Serene Highness is about," said the young man, rising from his work, warm and gay, but in no haste to go, as he had been before.

Gladys remembered that; and when, at last, he left her, she shut her eyes to re-live, in thought, the three blissful months she had spent in teaching him to love her with the love in which self bears no part. Before the happy reverie was half over, the old lady arrived; and, by the time the young one was ready, Canaris came to fetch her.

"My dearest, I am afraid we must give up our plan," he said, softly, as he led her away: "Helwyze is so changed, I come to tell you, lest it should shock you when you see him. I think it would be cruel to go at once. Can you wait a little longer?"

"If we ought. How is he changed?"

"Just worn away, as a rock is by the beating of the sea, till there seems little left of him except the big eyes and greater sharpness of both tongue and temper. Say nothing about it, and seem not to notice it; else he will freeze you with a look, as he did me when I exclaimed."

"Poor man! we will be very patient, very kind; for it must be awful to think of dying with no light beyond," sighed Gladys, touching the cross at her white throat.

"A Dante without a Beatrice: I am happier than he;" and Canaris laid his cheek against hers with the gesture of a boy, the look of a man who has found the solace which is also his salvation.

Helwyze received them quietly, a little coldly, even; and Gladys reproached herself with too long neglect of what she had assumed as a duty, when she saw how ill he looked, for *his* summer had not been a blissful one. He had spent it in wishing for her, and in persuading himself that the desire was permissible, since he asked nothing but what she had already given him—her presence and her friendship. It was her intellect he loved and wanted, not her heart; that she might give her husband wholly, since he understood and cared for affection only: her mind, with all its lovely possibilities, Helwyze coveted, and reasoned himself into the belief that he had a right to enjoy it, conscious all the while that his purpose was a delusion and a snare. Olivia had mourned over the moody taciturnity which made a lonely cranny of the cliffs his favorite resort, where he sat, day after day, watching, with an irresistible ever-changing sea—beautiful and bitter as the hidden tide of ling in his own breast, where lay the image of Gladys, as werful, as the moon which ruled the ebb and flow of that g a fatalist for want of a higher faith, he left all to chance, imply resolved to enjoy what was left him as long and as ssible; since Felix owed him much, and Gladys need never prayed *not* to know.

ble, as they sat almost a year ago, he watched the two young faces as he had done then, finding each, unlike his own, changed for the better. Gladys was a girl no longer; and the new womanliness which had come to her was of the highest type, for inward beauty lent its imperishable loveliness to features faulty in themselves, and character gave its indescribable charm to the simplest manners. Helwyze saw all this; and perceiving also how much heart had already quickened intellect, began to long for both, and to grudge his pupil to her new master.

Canaris seemed to have lost something of his boyish comeliness, and had taken on a manlier air of strength and stability, most becoming, and evidently a source of pardonable pride to him. At his age even three months could work a serious alteration in one so easily affected by all influences; and Helwyze felt a pang of envy as he saw the broad shoulders and vigorous limbs, the wholesome color in the cheeks, and best of all, the serene content of a happy heart.

"What have you been doing to yourself, Felix? Have you discovered the Elixir of Life up there? If so, impart the secret, and let me have a sip," he said, as Canaris pushed away his plate after satisfying a hearty appetite with the relish of a rustic.

"Gladys did," he answered, with a nod across the table, which said much. "She would not let me idle about while waiting for ideas: she just set me to work. I dug acres, it seemed to me, and amazed the gardener with my exploits. Liked it, too; for she was overseer, and would not let me off till I had done my task and earned my wages. A wonderfully pleasant life, and I am the better for it, in spite of my sunburn and blisters;" and Canaris stretched out a pair of sinewy brown hands with an air of satisfaction which made Gladys laugh so blithely it was evident that their summer had been full of the innocent jollity of youth, fine weather, and congenial pastime.

"Adam and Eve in Eden, with all the modern improvements. Not even a tree of knowledge or a serpent to disturb you!"

"Oh, yes, we had them both; but we only ate the good fruit, and the snake did not tempt me!" cried Gladys, anxious to defend her Paradise even from playful mockery.

"He did me. I longed to kill him, but my Eve owed him no grudge, and would not permit me to do it; so the old enemy sunned himself in peace, and went into winter quarters a reformed reptile, I am sure."

Canaris did not look up as he spoke, but Helwyze asked hastily—

"I hope you harvested a few fresh ideas for winter work? We ought to have something to show after so laborious a summer."

"I have: I am going to write a novel or a play. I cannot decide which; but rather lean toward the latter, and, being particularly happy, feel inclined to write a tragedy;" and something beside the daring of an ambitious author sparkled in the eyes Canaris fixed upon his patron. It looked too much like the expression of a bondman about to become a freeman to suit Helwyze; but he replied, as imperturbably as ever—

"Try the tragedy, by all means: the novel would be beyond you."

"Why, if you please?" demanded Canaris, loftily.

"Because you have neither patience nor experience enough to do it well. Goethe says: 'In the novel it is *sentiments* and *events* that are exhibited; in the drama it is *characters* and *deeds*. The novel goes slowly forward, the drama must hasten. In the novel, some degree of scope may be allowed to chance; but it must be led and guided by the sentiments of the personages. Fate, on the other hand, which, by means of outward, unconnected circumstances, carries forward men, without their own concurrence, to an unforeseen catastrophe, can only have place in the drama. Chance may produce pathetic situations, but not tragic ones.' "

Helwyze paused there abruptly; for the memory which served him so well outran his tongue, and recalled the closing sentence of the quotation—words which he had no mind to utter then and there—"Fate ought always to be terrible; and it is in the highest sense tragic, when it brings into a ruinous concatenation the guilty man and the guiltless with him."

"Then you think I *could* write a play?" asked Canaris, with affected carelessness.

"I think you could act one, better than imagine or write it."

"What, I?"

"Yes, you; because you are dramatic by nature, and it is easier for you to express yourself in gesture and tone, than by written or spoken language. You were born for an actor, are fitted for it in every way, and I advise you to try it. It would pay better than poetry; and that stream *may* run dry."

Gladys looked indignant at what she thought bad advice and distasteful pleasantry; but Canaris seemed struck and charmed with the new idea, protesting that he would first write, then act, his play, and prove himself a universal genius.

No more was said just then; but long afterward the conversation came back to him like an inspiration, and was the seed of a purpose which, through patient effort, bore fruit in a brilliant and successful career: for Canaris, like many another man, did not know his own strength or weakness yet, neither the true gift nor the power of evil which lay unsuspected within him.

So the old life began again, at least in outward seeming; but it was impossible for it to last long. The air was too full of the electricity of suppressed and conflicting emotions to be wholesome; former relations could not be resumed, because sincerity had gone out of them; and the quiet, which reigned for a time, was only the lull before the storm.

Gladys soon felt this, but tried to think it was owing to the contrast between the free, happy days she had enjoyed so much, and uttered no complaint; for Felix was busy with his play, sanguine as ever, inspired now by a nobler ambition than before, and happy in his work.

Helwyze had flattered himself that he could be content with the harmless shadow, since he could not possess the sweet substance of a love whose seeming purity was its most delusive danger. But he soon discovered "how bitter a thing it is to look into happiness through another man's eyes;" and, even while he made no effort to rob Canaris of his treasure, he hated him for possessing it, finding the hatred all the more poignant, because it was his own hand which had forced Felix to seize and secure it. He had thought to hold and hide this new secret; but it held him, and would not be hidden, for it was stronger than even his strong will, and ruled him with a power which at times filled him with a sort of terror. Having allowed it to grow, and taken it to his bosom, he could not cast it out again, and it became a torment, not the comfort he had hoped to find it. His daily affliction was to see how much the young pair were to each other, to read in their faces a hundred happy hopes and confidences in which he had no part, and to remember the confession wrung from the lips dearest to him, that his death would bring to them their much-desired freedom.

At times he was minded to say "Go," but the thought of the utter blank her absence would leave behind daunted him. Often an almost uncontrollable desire to tell her that which would mar her trust in her husband tempted him; for, having yielded to a greater temptation, all lesser ones seemed innocent beside it; and, worse than all, the old morbid longing for some excitement, painful even, if it could not be pleasurable, goaded him to the utterance of half truths, which irritated Canaris and perplexed Gladys, till she could no longer doubt the cause of this strange mood. It seemed as if her innocent hand gave the touch which set the avalanche slipping swiftly but silently to its destructive fall.

One day when Helwyze was pacing to and fro in the library, driven by the inward storm which no outward sign betrayed, except his excessive pallor and unusual restlessness, she looked up from her book, asking compassionately—

"Are you suffering, sir?"

"Torment."

"Can I do nothing?"

"Nothing!"

She went on reading, as if glad to be left in peace; for distrust, as well as pity, looked out from her frank eyes, and there was no longer any pleasure in the duties she performed for Canaris's sake.

But Helwyze, jealous even of the book which seemed to absorb her, soon paused again, to ask, in a calmer tone—

"What interests you?"

" 'The Scarlet Letter.' "

The hands loosely clasped behind him were locked more closely by an involuntary gesture, as if the words made him wince; otherwise unmoved, he asked again, with the curiosity he often showed about her opinions of all she read—

"What do you think of Hester?"

"I admire her courage; for she repented, and did not hide her sin with a lie."

"Then you must despise Dimmesdale?"

"I ought, perhaps; but I cannot help pitying his weakness, while I detest his deceit: he loved so much."

"So did Roger;" and Helwyze drew nearer, with the peculiar flicker in his eyes, as of a light kindled suddenly behind a carefully drawn curtain.

"At first; then his love turned to hate, and he committed the unpardonable sin," answered Gladys, much moved by that weird and wonderful picture of guilt and its atonement.

"The unpardonable sin!" echoed Helwyze, struck by her words and manner.

"Hawthorne somewhere describes it as 'the want of love and reverence for the human soul, which makes a man pry into its mysterious depths, not with a hope or purpose of making it better, but from a cold, philosophical curiosity. This would be the separation of the intellect from the heart: and this, perhaps, would be as unpardonable a sin as to doubt God, whom we cannot harm; for in doing this we must inevitably do great wrong both to ourselves and others.' "

As she spoke, fast and earnestly, Gladys felt herself upon the brink of a much-desired, but much-dreaded, explanation; for Canaris, while owning to her that there *was* a secret, would not tell it till Helwyze freed him from his promise. She thought that he delayed to ask this absolution till she was fitter to bear the truth, whatever it might be; and she had resolved to spare her husband the pain of an avowal, by demanding it herself of Helwyze. The moment seemed to have come, and both knew it; for he regarded her with the quick, piercing look which read her purpose before she could put it into words.

"You are right; yet Roger was the wronged one, and the others deserved to suffer."

"They did; but Hester's suffering ennobled her, because nobly borne; Dimmesdale's destroyed him, because he paltered weakly with his conscience. Roger let his wrong turn him from a man into a devil, and deserves the contempt and horror he rouses in us. The keeping of the secret makes the romance; the confession of it is the moral, showing how falsehood can ruin a life, and truth only save it at the last."

"Never have a secret, Gladys: they are hard masters, whom we hate, yet dare not rebel against."

His accent of sad sincerity seemed to clear the way for her, and she spoke out, briefly and bravely—

"Sir, *you* dare any thing! Tell me what it is which makes Felix obey you against his will. He owns it, but will not speak till you consent. Tell me, I beseech you!"

"Could you bear it?" he asked, admiring her courage, yet doubtful of the wisdom of purchasing a moment's satisfaction at such a cost; for, though he could cast down her idol, he dared not set up another in its place.

"Try me!" she cried: "nothing can lessen my love, and doubt afflicts me more than the hardest truth."

"I fear not: with you love and respect go hand in hand, and some sins you would find very hard to pardon."

Involuntarily Gladys shrunk a little, and her eye questioned his inscrutable face, as she answered slowly, thinking only of her husband—

"Something very mean and false *would* be hard to forgive; but not some youthful fault, some shame borne for others, or even a crime, if a very human emotion, a generous but mistaken motive, led to it."

"Then this secret is better left untold; for it would try you sorely to know that Felix *had* been guilty of the fault you find harder to forgive than a crime—deceit. Wait a little, till you are accustomed to the thought, then you shall have the facts; and pity, even while you must despise him."

While he spoke, Gladys sat like one nerving herself to receive a blow; but at the last words she suddenly put up her hand as if to arrest it, saying, hurriedly—

"No! do not tell me; I cannot bear it yet, nor from you. He shall tell me; it will be easier so, and less like treachery. O sir," she added, in a passionately pleading tone, "use mercifully whatever bitter knowledge you possess! Remember how young he is, how neglected as a boy, how tempted he may have been; and deal generously, honorably with him—and with me."

Her voice broke there. She spread her hands before her eyes, and fled out of the room, as if in his face she read a more disastrous confession than any Felix could ever make. Helwyze stood motionless, looking as he looked the night she spoke more frankly but less forcibly: and when she vanished, he stole away to his own room, as he stole then; only now his usually colorless cheek burned with a fiery flush, and his hand went involuntarily to his breast, as if, like Dimmesdale, he carried an invisible scarlet letter branded there.

XVI

~

Neither had heard the door of that inner room open quietly; neither had seen Canaris stand upon the threshold for an instant, then draw back, looking as if he had found another skeleton to hide in the cell where he was laboring at the third act of the tragedy which he was to live, not write.

He had heard the last words Gladys said, he had seen the last look Helwyze wore, and, like a flash of lightning, the truth struck and stunned him. At first he sat staring aghast at the thing he plainly saw, yet hardly comprehended. Then a sort of fury seized and shook him, as he sprang up with hands clenched, eyes ablaze, looking as if about to instantly avenge the deadliest injury one man could do another. But the half-savage self-control adversity had taught stood him in good stead now, curbing the first natural but reckless wrath which nerved every fibre of his strong young body with an almost irresistible impulse to kill Helwyze without a word.

The gust of blind passion subsided quickly into a calmer, but not less dangerous, mood; and, fearing to trust himself so near his enemy, Canaris rushed away, to walk fast and far, unconscious where he went, till the autumnal gloaming brought him back, master of himself, he thought.

While he wandered aimlessly about the city, he had been recalling the past with the vivid skill which at such intense moments seems to bring back half-forgotten words, apparently unnoticed actions, and unconscious impressions; as fire causes invisible letters to stand out upon a page where they are traced in sympathetic ink.

Not a doubt of Gladys disturbed the ever-deepening current of a love the more precious for its newness, the more powerful for its ennobling influence. But every instinct of his nature rose in revolt against Helwyze, all the more rebellious and resentful for the long subjection in which he had been held.

A master stronger than the ambition which had been the ruling passion of his life so far asserted its supremacy now, and made it possible for him to pay the price of liberty without further weak delay or unmanly regret.

This he resolved upon, and this he believed he could accomplish safely and soon. But if Helwyze, with far greater skill and self-control, had failed to guide or subdue the conflicting passions let loose among them, how could Canaris hope to do it, or retard by so much as one minute the irresistible consequences of their acts? "The providence of God cannot be hurried," and His retribution falls at the appointed time, saving, even when it seems to destroy.

Returning resolute but weary, Canaris was relieved to find that a still longer reprieve was granted him; for Olivia was there, and Gladys apparently absorbed in the tender toil women love, making ready for the Christmas gift she hoped to give him. Helwyze sent word that he was suffering one of his bad attacks, and bade them all good-night; so there was nothing to mar the last quiet evening these three were ever to pass together.

When Canaris had seen Olivia to the winter quarters she inhabited near by, he went up to his own room, where Gladys lay, looking like a child who had cried itself to sleep. The sight of the pathetic patience touched with slumber's peace, in the tear-stained face upon the pillow, wrung his heart, and, stooping, he softly kissed the hand upon the coverlet—the small hand that wore a wedding-ring, now grown too large for it.

"God bless my dearest!" he whispered, with a sob in his throat. "Out of this accursed house she shall go to-morrow, though I leave all but love and liberty behind me."

Sleepless, impatient, and harassed by thoughts that would not let him rest, he yielded to the uncanny attraction which the library now had for him, and went down again, deluding himself with the idea that he could utilize emotion and work for an hour or two.

The familiar room looked strange to him; and when the door of Helwyze's apartment opened quietly, he started, although it was only Stern, coming to nap before the comfortable fire. Something in Canaris's expectant air and attitude made the man answer the question his face seemed to ask.

"Quiet at last, sir. He has had no sleep for many nights, and is fairly worn out."

"You look so, too. Go and rest a little. I shall be here writing for several hours, and can see to him," said Canaris, kindly, as the poor old fellow respectfully tried to swallow a portentous gape behind his hand.

"Thank you, Mr. Felix: it would be a comfort just to lose myself. Master is not likely to want any thing; but, if he should call, just step and give him his drops, please. They are all ready. I fixed them myself: he is so careless when he is half-asleep, and, not being used to this new stuff, an overdose might kill him."

Giving these directions, Stern departed with alacrity, and left Canaris to his watch. He had often done as much before, but never with such a sense of satisfaction as now; and though he carefully abstained from giving himself a reason for the act, no sooner had the valet gone than he went to look in upon Helwyze, longing to call out commandingly, "Wake, and hear me!"

But the helplessness of the man disarmed him, the peaceful expression of the sharp, white features mutely reproached him, the recollection of what he would awaken to made Canaris ashamed to exult over a defeated enemy; and he turned away, with an almost compassionate glance at the straight, still figure, clearly defined against the dusky background of the darkened room.

"He looks as if he were dead."

Canaris did not speak aloud, but it seemed as if a voice echoed the words with a suggestive emphasis, that made him pause as he approached the study-table, conscious of a quick thrill of comprehension tingling through him like an answer. Why he covered both ears with a sudden gesture, he could not tell, nor why he hastily seated himself, caught up the first book at hand and began to read without knowing what he read. Only for an instant, however, then the words grew clear before him, and his eyes rested on this line—

$$\text{``}σύ\ θην\ ἃ\ χρήζεις,\ ναῦν'\ ἐπιγλωσσᾷ\ Διός.\text{''}*$$

He dropped the book, as if it had burnt him, and looked over his shoulder, almost expecting to see the dark thought lurking in his mind take shape before him. Empty, dim, and quiet was the lofty room; but a troubled spirit

---

* "Thy ominous tongue gives utterance to thy wish."
ÆSCHYLUS.

and distempered imagination peopled it with such vivid and tormenting phantoms of the past, the present, and the future, that he scarcely knew whether he was awake or dreaming, as he sat there alone, waiting for midnight, and the spectre of an uncommitted deed.

His wandering eye fell on a leaf of paper, lying half-shrivelled by the heat of the red fire. This recalled the hour when, in the act of burning that first manuscript, Helwyze had saved him, and all that followed shortly after.

Not a pleasant memory, it seemed; for his face darkened, and his glance turned to a purple-covered volume, left on the low chair where Gladys usually sat, and often read in that beloved book. A still more bitter recollection bowed his head at sight of it, till some newer, sharper thought seemed to pierce him with a sudden stab, and he laid his clenched hand on the pile of papers before him, as if taking an oath more binding than the one made there nearly three years ago.

He had been reading Shakespeare lately, for one may copy the great masters; and now, as he tried with feverish energy to work upon his play, the grim or gracious models he had been studying seemed to rise and live before him. But one and all were made subject to the strong passions which ruled him; jealousy, ambition, revenge, and love wore their appropriate guise, acted their appropriate parts, and made him one with them. Othello would only show himself as stabbing the perfidious Iago; Macbeth always grasped at the air-drawn dagger; Hamlet was continually completing his fateful task; and Romeo whispered, with the little vial at his lips—

> "Oh, true apothecary!
> Thy drugs are quick."

Canaris tried to chase away these troubled spirits; but they would not down, and, yielding to them, he let his mind wander as it would, till he had "supped full of horrors," feeling as if in the grasp of a nightmare which led him, conscious, but powerless, toward some catastrophe forefelt, rather than foreseen. How long this lasted he never knew; for nothing broke the silence growing momently more terrible as he listened to the stealthy tread of the temptation coming nearer and nearer, till it appeared in the likeness of himself, while a voice said, in the ordinary tone which so often makes dreams grotesque at their most painful climax—

"Master is so careless when half-asleep; and, not being used to this new stuff, an overdose might kill him."

As if these words were the summons for which he had been waiting, Canaris rose up suddenly and went into that other room, too entirely absorbed by the hurrying emotions which swept him away to see what looked like a new phantom coming in. It might have been the shade of young Juliet, gentle Desdemona, poor Ophelia, or, better still the *eidolen* of Margaret wandering, pale and pensive, through the baleful darkness of this *Walpurgis Nacht.*

He did not see it; he saw nothing but the glass upon the table where the dim light burned, the little vial with its colorless contents, and Helwyze stirring in his bed, as if about to wake and speak. Conscious only of the purpose which now wholly dominated him, Canaris, without either haste or hesitation, took the bottle, uncorked, and held it over the glass half-filled with water. But before a single drop could fall, a cold hand touched his own, and, with a start that crushed the vial in his grasp, he found himself eye to eye with Gladys.

Guilt was frozen upon his face, terror upon hers; but neither spoke, for a third voice muttered drowsily, "Stern, give me more; don't rouse me."

Canaris could not stir; Gladys whispered, with white lips, and her hand upon the cup—

"Dare I give it?"

He could only answer by a sign, and cowered into the shadow, while she put the draught to Helwyze's lips, fearing to let him waken now. He drank drowsily, yet seemed half-conscious of her presence; for he looked up with sleep-drunken eyes, and murmured, as if to the familiar figure of a dream—

"Mine asleep, his awake," then whispering brokenly about "Felix, Vivien, and daring any thing," he was gone again into the lethargy which alone could bring forgetfulness.

Gladys feared her husband would hear the almost inaudible words; but he had vanished, and when she glided out to join him, carefully closing the door behind her, a glance showed that her fear was true.

Relieved, yet not repentant, he stood there looking at a red stain on his hand with such a desperate expression that Gladys could only cling to him, saying, in a terror-stricken whisper—

"Felix, for God's sake, come away! What are you doing here?"

"Going mad, I think," he answered, under his breath; but added, lifting up his hand with an ominous gesture, "I would have done it if you had not stopped me. It would be better for us all if he were dead."

"Not so; thank Heaven I came in time to save you from the sin of murder!" she said, holding fast the hand as yet unstained by any blood but its own.

"I *have* committed murder in my heart. Why not profit by the sin, since it is there? I hate that man! I have cause, and you know it."

"No, no, not all! You shall tell me every thing; but not now, not here."

"The time has come, and this is the place to tell it. Sit there and listen. I must untie or cut the snarl to-night."

He pointed to the great chair; and, grateful for any thing that could change or stem the dangerous current of his thoughts, Gladys sank down, feeling as if, after this shock, she was prepared for any discovery or disaster. Canaris stood before her, white and stern, as if he were both judge and culprit; for a sombre wrath still burned in his eye, and his face worked with the mingled shame and contempt warring within him.

"I heard and saw this afternoon, when you two talked together yonder, and I knew then what made you so glad to go away, so loath to come back. *You* have had a secret as well as I."

"I was never sure until to-day. Do not speak of that: it is enough to know it, and forget it if we can. Tell your secret: it has burdened you so long, you will be glad to end it. *He* would have done so, but I would not let him."

"I thought it would be hard to tell you, yet now my fault looks so small and innocent beside his, I can confess without much shame or fear."

But it was not easy; for he had gone so far into a deeper, darker world that night, it was difficult to come to lesser sins and lighter thoughts. As he hesitated for a word, his eye fell upon the purple-covered book, and he saw a way to shorten his confession. Catching up a pen, he bent over the volume an instant, then handed it to Gladys, open at the title-page. She knew it—the dear romance, worn with much reading—and looked wonderingly at the black mark drawn through the name, "Felix Canaris," and the words, "Jasper Helwyze," written boldly below.

"What does it mean?" she asked, refusing to believe the discovery which the expression of his averted face confirmed.

"That I am a living lie. He wrote that book."

"He?"

"Every line."

"But not the other?" she said; clinging to a last hope, as every thing seemed falling about her.

"All, except half a dozen of the songs."

Down dropped the book between them—now a thing of little worth—and, trying to conceal from him the contempt which even love could not repress, Gladys hid her face, with one reproach, the bitterest she could have uttered—

"O my husband! did you give up honor, liberty, and peace for so poor a thing as that?"

It cut him to the soul: for now he saw how high a price he had paid for an empty name; how mean and poor his ambition looked; how truly he deserved to be despised for that of which he had striven to be proud. Gladys had so rejoiced over him as a poet, that it was the hardest task of all to put off his borrowed singing-robes, and show himself an ordinary man. He forgot that there was any other tribunal than this, as he stood waiting for his sentence, oppressed with the fear that out of her almost stern sense of honor she might condemn him to the loss of the respect and confidence which he had lately learned to value as much as happiness and love.

"You must despise me; but if you knew"—he humbly began, unable to bear the silence longer.

"Tell me, then. I will not judge until I know;" and Gladys, just, even in her sorrow, looked up with an expression which said plainer than words, "For better, for worse; this is the worse, but I love you still."

That made it possible for him to go on, fast and low, not stopping to choose phrases, but pouring out the little story of his temptation and fall, with a sense of intense relief that he was done with slavery for ever.

"Neither of us coolly planned this thing; it came about so simply and naturally, it seemed a mere accident.—And yet, who can tell what *he* might have planned, seeing how weak I was, how ready to be tempted.—It happened in that second month, when I promised to stay; he to help me with my book. It was *all* mine then; but when we came to look at it, there was not enough to fill even the most modest volume; for I had burnt many, and must recall them, or write more. I tried honestly, but the power was not in me, and I fell into despair again; for the desire to be known was the breath of my life."

"You will be, if not in this way, in some other; for power of some sort *is* in you. Believe it, and wait for it to show itself," said Gladys, anxious to add patience and courage to the new humility and sincerity, which could not fail to ennoble and strengthen him in time.

"Bless you for that!" he answered, gratefully, and hurried on. "It came about in this wise: one day my master—he was then, but is no longer, thank God!—sat reading over a mass of old papers, before destroying them. Here he came upon verses written in the diaries kept years ago, and threw them to me, 'to laugh over,' as he said. I did not laugh: I was filled with envy and admiration, and begged him to publish them. He scorned the idea, and bade me put them in the fire. I begged to keep them, and then—Gladys, I swear to you I cannot tell whether I read the project in his face, or whether my own evil genius put it into my head—then I said, audaciously, though hardly dreaming he would consent, 'You do not care for fame, and throw these away as worthless: I long for it, and see more power in these than in any I can hope to write for years, perhaps; let me add them to mine, and see what will come of it.' 'Put your own name to them, if you do, and take the consequences,' he answered, in that brusque way of his, which seems so careless, yet is so often premeditated. I assented, as I would have done to any thing that promised a quick trial of my talent; for in my secret soul I thought some of my songs better than his metaphysical verses, which impressed, rather than charmed me. The small imposture seemed to amuse him; I had few scruples then, and we did it, with much private jesting about Beaumont and Fletcher, literary frauds, and borrowed plumage. You know the rest. The book succeeded, but he saved it; and the critics left me small consolation, for my songs were ignored as youthful ditties, his poems won all the praise, and *I* was pronounced a second Shelley."

"But he? Did he claim no share of the glory? Was he content to let you have it all?" questioned Gladys, trying to understand a thing so foreign to her nature that it seemed incredible.

"Yes; I offered to come down from my high place, as soon as I realized how little right I had to it. But he forbade me, saying, what I was fool enough to believe, that my talent only needed time and culture, and the sunshine of success to ripen it; that notoriety would be a burden to him, since he had neither health to sustain nor spirits to enjoy it; that in me he would live his youth over again, and, in return for such help as he could give, I should be a son to him. That touched and won me; now I can see in it a trap to catch and hold me, that he might amuse himself with my folly, play the generous patron, and twist my life to suit his ends. He likes curious and costly toys; he had one then, and has not paid for it yet."

"This other book? Tell me of that, and speak low, or he may hear us," whispered Gladys, trembling lest fire and powder should meet.

With a motion of his foot Canaris sent the book that lay between them spinning across the hearth-rug out of sight, and answered, with a short, exultant laugh—

"Ah! there the fowler was taken in his own snare. I did not see it then, and found it hard to understand why he should exert himself to please you by helping me. I thought it was a mere freak of literary rivalry; and, when I taxed him with it, he owned that, though he cared nothing for the world's praise, it *was* pleasant to know that his powers were still unimpaired, and be able to laugh in his sleeve at the deluded critics. That was like him, and it deceived me till to-day. Now I know that he begrudged me your admiration, wanted your tears and smiles for himself, and did not hesitate to steal them. The night he so adroitly read *his* work for mine, he tempted me through you. I had resolved to deserve the love and honor you gave me; and again I tried, and again I failed, for my romance was a poor, pale thing to his. He had read it; and, taking the same plot, made it what you know, writing as only such a man could write, when a strong motive stimulated him to do his best."

"But why did you submit? Why stand silent and let him do so false a thing?" cried poor Gladys, wondering when the end of the tangle would come.

"At first his coolness staggered me; then I was curious to hear, then held even, against my will, by admiration of the thing—and you. I meant to speak out, I longed to do it; but it was very hard, while you were praising me so eloquently. The words were on my lips, when in his face I saw a look that sealed them. He meant that I should utter the self-accusation which would lower me for ever and raise him in your regard. I could not bear it. There was no time to think, only to feel, and I vowed to make you happy, at all costs. I hardly thought he would submit; but he did, and I believed that it was through surprise at being outwitted for the moment, or pity towards you. It was neither: he fancied I had discovered his secret, and he *dared* not defy me then."

"But when I was gone? You were so late that night: I heard your voices, sharp and angry, as I went away."

"Yes; that was *my* hour, and I enjoyed it. He had often twitted me with the hold he had on my name and fame, and I bore it; for, till I loved you, they were the dearest things I owned. That night I told him he *should not* speak; that you should enjoy your pride in me, even at his expense, and I refused to release him from his bond, as he had, more than once, refused to release me:

for we had sworn never to confess till both agreed to it. Good heavens! how low he must have thought I had fallen, if I could consent to buy your happiness at the cost of my honor! He did think it: that made him yield; that is the cause of the contempt he has not cared to hide from me since then; and that adds a double edge to my hatred now. I was to be knave as well as fool; and while I blinded myself with his reflected light, he would have filched my one jewel from me. Gladys, save me, keep me, or I shall do something desperate yet!"

Beside himself with humiliation, remorse, and wrath, Canaris flung himself down before her, as if only by clinging to that frail spar could he ride out the storm in which he was lost without compass or rudder.

Then Gladys showed him that such love as hers could not fail, but, like an altar-fire, glowed the stronger for every costly sacrifice thrown therein. Lifting up the discrowned head, she laid it on her bosom with a sweet motherliness which comforted more than her tender words.

"My poor Felix! you have suffered enough for this deceit; I forgive it, and keep my reproaches for the false friend who led you astray."

"It was so paltry, weak, and selfish. You *must* despise me," he said, wistfully, still thinking more of his own pain than hers.

"I do despise the sin, not the dear sinner who repents and is an honest man again."

"But a beggar."

"We have each other. Hush! stand up; some one is coming."

Canaris had barely time to spring to his feet, when Stern came in, and was about to pass on in silence, though much amazed to see Gladys there at that hour, when the expression of the young man's face made him forget decorum and stop short, exclaiming, anxiously—

"Mr. Felix, what's the matter? Is master worse?"

"Safe and asleep. Mrs. Canaris came to see what I was about."

"Then, sir, if I may make so bold, the sooner she gets to bed again the better. It is far too late for her to be down here; the poor young lady looks half-dead," Stern whispered, with the freedom of an old servant.

"You are right. Come, love;" and without another word Canaris led her away, leaving Stern to shake his gray head as he looked after them.

Gladys *was* utterly exhausted; and in the hall she faltered, saying, with a patient sigh, as she looked up the long stairway, "Dear, wait a little; it is so far—my strength is all gone."

Canaris caught her in his arms and carried her away, asking himself, with a remorseful pang that rent his heart—

"Is this the murder I have committed?"

XVII

S tern!"

"Yes, sir."

"What time is it?"

"Past two, sir."

"What news? I see bad tidings of some sort in that lugubrious face of yours; out with it!"

"The little boy arrived at dawn, sir," answered old Stern, with a paternal air.

"What little boy?"

"Canaris, Jr., sir," simpered the valet, venturing to be jocose.

"The deuce he did! Precipitate, like his father. Where is Felix?"

"With her, sir. In a state of mind, as well he may be, letting that delicate young thing sit up to keep him company over his poetry stuff," muttered Stern, busying himself with the shutters.

"Sit up! when? where? what are you maundering about, man?" and Helwyze himself sat up among the pillows, looking unusually wide-awake.

"Last night, sir, in the study. Mr. Felix made me go for a wink of sleep, and when I came back, about one, there sat Mrs. Canaris as white as her gown, and him looking as wild as a hawk. Something was amiss, I could see plain enough, but it wasn't my place to ask questions; so I just made bold to suggest that it was late for her to be up, and he took her away, looking dazed-like. That's all I know, sir, till I found the women in a great flustration this morning."

"And I slept through it all?"

"Yes, sir; so soundly, I was a bit anxious till you waked. I found the glass empty and the bottle smashed, and I was afraid you might have taken too much of that *choral* while half-asleep."

"No fear; nothing kills me. Now get me up;" and Helwyze made his toilet with a speed and energy which caused Stern to consider *"choral"* a wonderful discovery.

A pretence of breakfast; then Helwyze sat down to wait for further tidings—externally quite calm, internally tormented by a great anxiety, till Olivia came in, full of cheering news and sanguine expectations.

"Gladys is asleep, with baby on her arm, and Felix adoring in the background. Poor boy! he cannot bear much, and is quite bowed down with remorse for something he has done. Do you know what?"

As she spoke, Olivia stooped to pick up a book half-hidden by the fringe of a low chair. It lay face downward, and, in smoothing the crumpled leaves before closing it, she caught sight of a black and blotted name. So did Helwyze; a look of intelligence flashed over his face, and, taking the volume quickly, he answered, with his finger on the title-page—

"Yes, now I know, and so may you; for if one woman is in the secret, it will soon be out. Felix wrote that, and it is true."

"I thought so! One woman *has* known it for a long time; nevertheless, the secret was kept for your sake;" and Olivia's dark face sparkled with malicious merriment, as she saw the expression of mingled annoyance, pride, and pleasure in his.

"My compliments and thanks: you are the eighth wonder of the world. But what led you to suspect this little fraud of ours?"

"I did not, till the last book came; then I was struck here and there by certain peculiar phrases, certain tender epithets, which I think no one ever heard from your lips but me. These, in the hero's mouth, made me sure that you had helped Canaris, if not done the whole yourself, and his odd manner at times confirmed my suspicion."

"You have a good memory: I forgot that."

"I have had so few such words from you that it is easy to remember them," murmured Olivia, reproachfully.

It seemed to touch him; for just then he felt deserted, well knowing that he had lost both Felix and Gladys; but Olivia never would desert him, no matter what discovery was made, or who might fall away. He thanked her for her devotion, with the first ray of hope given for years, as he said, in the tone so seldom heard—

"You shall have more henceforth; for you are a stanch friend, and now I have no other."

"Dear Jasper, you shall never find me wanting. *I* will be true to the death!" she cried, blooming suddenly into her best and brightest beauty, with the delight of this rare moment. Then, fearing to express too much, she wisely turned again to Felix, asking curiously, "But why did you let this young daw deck himself out in your plumes? It enrages me, to think of his receiving the praise and honor due to you."

He told her briefly, adding, with more than his accustomed bitterness—

"What did *I* want with praise and honor? To be gaped and gossiped about would have driven me mad. It pleased that vain boy as much as fooling the public amused me. A whim, and, being a dishonest one, we shall both have to pay for it, I suppose."

"What will he do?"

"He has told Gladys, to begin with; and, if it had been possible, would have taken some decisive step to-day. He can do nothing sagely and quietly: there must be a dramatic *dénouement* to every chapter of his life. I think he has one now." Helwyze laughed, as he struck back the leaves of the book he still held, and looked at the dashing signature of his own name.

"*He* wrote that, then?" asked Olivia.

"Yes, here, at midnight, while I lay asleep and let him tell the tale as he liked to Gladys. No wonder it startled her, so tragically given. The sequel may be more tragic yet: I seem to feel it in the air."

"What shall *you* do?" asked Olivia, more anxiously than before; for Helwyze looked up with as sinister an expression as if he knew how desperate an enemy had stood over him last night, and when his own turn came, would be less merciful.

"Do? Nothing. They will go; I shall stay; tongues will wag, and I shall be tormented. I shall seem the gainer, he the loser; but it will not be so."

Involuntarily his eye went to the little chair where Gladys would sit no longer, and darkened as if some light had gone out which used to cheer and comfort him. Olivia saw it, and could not restrain the question that broke from her lips—

"You do love her, Jasper?"

"I shall miss her; but you shall take her place."

Calm and a little scornful was his face, his voice quite steady, and a smile was shed upon her with the last welcome words. But Olivia was not deceived: the calmness was unnatural, the voice *too* steady, the smile too sudden; and her heart sank as she thanked him, without another question. For a while they sat together playing well their parts, then she went away to Gladys, and he was left to several hours of solitary musing.

Had he been a better man, he would not have sinned; had he been a worse one, he could not have suffered; being what he was, he did both, and, having no one else to study now, looked deeply into himself, and was dismayed at what he saw. For the new love, purer, yet more hopeless than the old, shone like a star above an abyss, showing him whither he had wandered in the dark.

Sunset came, filling the room with its soft splendor; and he watched the red rays linger longest in Gladys's corner. Her little basket stood as she left it, her books lay orderly, her desk was shut, a dead flower drooped from the slender vase, and across the couch trailed a soft white shawl she had been wont to wear. Helwyze did not approach the spot, but stood afar off looking at these small familiar things with the melancholy fortitude of one inured to loss and pain. Regret rather than remorse possessed him as he thought, drearily—

"A year to-morrow since she came. How shall I exist without her? Where will her new home be?"

An answer was soon given to the last question; for, while his fancy still hovered about that nook, and the gentle presence which had vanished as the sunshine was fast vanishing, Canaris came in wearing such an expression of despair, that Helwyze recoiled, leaving half-uttered a playful inquiry about "the little son."

"I have no son."

"Dead?"

"Dead. I have murdered both."

"But Gladys?"

"Dying; she asks for you—come!" No need of that hoarse command; Helwyze was gone at the first word, swiftly through room and hall, up the stairs he had not mounted for months, straight to that chamber-door. There a hand clutched his shoulder, a breathless voice said, "Here I am first;" and Canaris passed in before him, motioning away a group of tearful women as he went.

Helwyze lingered, pale and panting, till they were gone; then he looked and listened, as if turned to stone, for in the heart of the hush lay Gladys, talking softly to the dead baby on her arm. Not mourning over it, but yearning with maternal haste to follow and cherish the creature of her love.

"Only a day old; so young to go away alone. Even in heaven you will want your mother, darling, and she will come. Sleep, my baby, I will be with you when you wake."

A stifled sound of anguish recalled the happy soul, already half-way home, and Gladys turned her quiet eyes to her husband bending over her.

"Dear, will he come?" she whispered.

"He is here."

He was; and, standing on either side of the bed, the two men seemed unconscious of each other, intent only upon her. Feebly she drew the white cover over the little cold thing in her bosom, as if too sacred for any eyes but hers to see, then lifted up her hand with a beseeching glance from one haggard face to the other. They understood; each gave the hand she asked, and, holding them together with the last effort of failing strength, she said, clear and low—

"Forgive each other for my sake."

Neither spoke, having no words, but by a mute gesture answered as she wished. Something brighter than a smile rested on her face, and, as if satisfied, she turned again to Canaris, seeming to forget all else in the tender farewell she gave him.

"Remember, love, remember we shall be waiting for you. The new home will not be home to us until you come."

As her detaining touch was lifted, the two hands fell apart, never to meet again. Canaris knelt down to lay his head beside hers on the pillow, to catch the last accents of the beloved voice, sweet even now. Helwyze, forgotten by them both, drew back into the shadow of the deep red curtains, still studying with an awful curiosity the great mystery of death, asking, even while his heart grew cold within him—

"Will the faith she trusted sustain her now?"

It did; for, leaning on the bosom of Infinite Love, like a confiding child in its father's arms, without a doubt or fear to mar her peace, a murmur or lament to make the parting harder, Gladys went to her own place.

XVIII

~

For in that sleep of death, what dreams may come. Is this one?" was the vague feeling, rather than thought, of which Helwyze was dimly conscious, as he lay in what seemed a grave, so cold, so dead he felt; so powerless and pent, in what he fancied was his coffin. He remembered the slow rising of a tide of helplessness which chilled his blood and benumbed his brain, till the last idea to be distinguished was, "I am dying: shall I meet Gladys?" then came oblivion, and now, what was this?

Something was alive still—something which strove to see, move, speak, yet could not, till the mist, which obscured every sense, should clear away. A murmur was in the air, growing clearer every instant, as it rose and fell, like the muffled sound of waves upon a distant shore. Presently he recognized human voices, and the words they uttered—words which had no meaning, till, like an electric shock, intelligence returned, bringing with it a great fear.

Olivia was mourning over him, and he felt her tears upon his face; but it was not this which stung him to sudden life—it was another voice, saying, low, but with a terrible distinctness—

"There is no hope. He may remain so for some years; but sooner or later the brain will share the paralysis of the body, and leave our poor friend in a state I grieve to think of."

"No!" burst from Helwyze, with an effort which seemed to dispel the trance which held his faculties. Stir he could not, but speak he did, and opened wide the eyes which had been closed for hours. With the unutterable relief of one roused from a nightmare, he recognized his own room, Olivia's tender face bent over him, and his physician holding a hand that had no feeling in it.

"Not dead yet;" he muttered, with a feeble sort of exultation, adding, with as feeble a despair and doubt, "but *she* is. Did I dream that?"

"Alas, no!" and Olivia wiped away her own tears from the forehead which began to work with the rush of returning memory and thought.

"What does this numbness mean? Why are you here?" he asked, as his eye went from one face to the other.

"Dear Jasper, it means that you are ill. Stern found you unconscious in your chair last night. You are much better now, but it alarmed us, for we thought you dead," replied Olivia, knowing that he would have the truth at any cost.

"I remember thinking it was death, and being glad of it. Why did you bring me back? I had no wish to come."

She forgave the ingratitude, and went on chafing the cold hand so tenderly, that Helwyze reproached no more, but, turning to the physician, demanded, with a trace of the old imperiousness coming back into his feeble voice—

"Is this to be the end of it?"

"I fear so, Mr. Helwyze. You will not suffer any more, let that comfort you."

"My body may not, but my mind will suffer horribly. Good heavens, man, do you call this death in life a comfortable end? How long have I got to lie here watching my wits go?"

"It is impossible to say."

"But certain, sooner or later?"

"There is a chance—your brain has been overworked: it must have rest," began the doctor, trying to soften the hard facts, since his patient would have them.

"Rest! kill me at once, then; annihilation would be far better than such rest as that. I will not lie here waiting for imbecility—put an end to this, or let me!" cried Helwyze, struggling to lift his powerless right hand; and, finding it impossible, he looked about him with an impotent desperation which wrung Olivia's heart, and alarmed the physician, although he had long foreseen this climax.

Both vainly tried to soothe and console; but after that one despairing appeal Helwyze turned his face to the wall, and lay so for hours. Asleep, they hoped, but in reality tasting the first bitterness of the punishment sent upon him as an expiation for the sin of misusing one of Heaven's best gifts. No words could describe the terror such a fate had for him, since intellect had been his god, and he already felt it tottering to its fall. On what should he lean, if that were taken? where see any ray of hope to make the present endurable? where find any resignation to lighten the gloom of such a future?

Restless mind and lawless will, now imprisoned in a helpless body, preyed on each other like wild creatures caged, finding it impossible to escape, and as impossible to submit. Death would not have daunted him, pain he had learned to endure; but this slow decay of his most precious possession he could not bear, and suffered a new martyrdom infinitely sharper than the old.

How time went he never knew; for, although merciful unconsciousness was denied him, his thoughts, like avenging Furies, drove him from one bitter memory to another, probing his soul as he had probed others, and tormenting him with an almost supernatural activity of brain before its long rest began. Ages seemed to pass, while he took no heed of what went on about him. People came and went, faces bent over him, hands ministered to him, and voices whispered in the room. He knew all this, without the desire to do so, longing only to forget and be forgotten, with an increasing irritation, which slowly brought him back from that inner world of wordless pain to the outer one, which must be faced, and in some fashion endured.

Olivia still sat near him, as if she had not stirred, though it was morning when last he spoke, and now night had come. The familiar room was dim and still, every thing already ordered for his comfort, and the brilliant cousin had transformed herself into a quiet nurse. The rustling silks were replaced by a soft, gray gown; the ornaments all gone; even the fine hair was half-hidden by the little kerchief of lace tied over it. Yet never had Olivia been more beautiful; for now the haughty queen had changed to a sad woman, wearing for her sole ornaments constancy and love. Worn and weary she looked, but a sort of sorrowful content was visible, a jealous tenderness, which plainly told that for her, at least, there was a drop of honey even in the new affliction, since it made him more her own than ever.

"Poor soul! she promised to be faithful to the death; and she will be—even such a death as this."

A sigh, that was almost a groan, broke from Helwyze as the thought came, and Olivia was instantly at his side.

"Are you suffering, Jasper? What can I do for you?" she said, with such a passionate desire to serve or cheer, that he could not but answer, gently—

"I am done with pain: teach me to be patient."

"Oh, if I could! we must learn that together," she said, feeling with him how sorely both would need the meek virtue to sustain the life before them.

"Where is Felix?" asked Helwyze, after lying for a while, with his eyes upon the fire, as if they would absorb its light and warmth into their melancholy depths.

"Mourning for Gladys," replied Olivia, fearing to touch the dangerous topic, yet anxious to know how the two men stood toward one another; for something in the manner of the younger, when the elder was mentioned, made her suspect some stronger, sadder tie between them than the one she had already guessed.

"Does he know of this?" and Helwyze struck himself a feeble blow with the one hand which he could use, now lying on his breast.

"Yes."

"What does he say of me?"

"Nothing."

"I must see him."

"You shall. I asked him if he had no word for you, and he answered, with a strange expression, 'When I have buried my dead I will come, for the last time.'"

"How does he look?" questioned Helwyze, curious to see, even through another's eyes, the effect of sorrow upon the man whom he had watched so long and closely.

"Sadly broken; but he is young and sanguine: he will soon forget, and be happy again; so do not let a thought of him disturb you, Jasper."

"It does not: we made our bargain, and held each other to it, till he chose to break it. Let him bear the consequences, as I do."

"Alas, they fall on him far less heavily than on you! He has all the world before him where to choose, while you have nothing left—but me."

He did not seem to hear her, and fell into a gloomy reverie, which she dared not break, but sat, patiently beguiling her lonely watch with sad thoughts of the twilight future they were to share together—a future which might have been so beautiful and happy, had true love earlier made them one.

Another day, another night, then there were sounds about the house which told Helwyze what was passing, without the need of any question. He asked none; but lay silent for the most part, as if careless or unconscious of what went on around him. He missed Olivia for an hour, and when she returned, traces of tears upon her cheeks told him that she had been to say farewell to Gladys. He had not spoken that name even to himself; for now an immeasurable space seemed to lie between him and its gentle owner. She had gone into a world whither he could not follow her. A veil, invisible, yet impenetrable, separated them for ever, he believed, and nothing remained to him but a memory that would not die—a memory so bitter-sweet, so made up of remorse and reverence, love and longing, that it seemed to waken his heart from its long sleep, and kindle in it a spark of the divine fire, whose flame purified while it consumed; for even in his darkness and desolation he was not forgotten.

Late that day Canaris came, looking like a man escaped from a great shipwreck, with nothing left him but his life. Unannounced he entered, and, with the brevity which in moments of strong feeling is more expressive than eloquence, he said—

"I am going."

"Where?" asked Helwyze, conscious that any semblance of friendship, any word of sympathy, was impossible between them.

"Out into the world again."

"What will you do?"

"Any *honest* work I can find."

"Let me"—

"No! I will take nothing from you. Poor as I came, I will go—except the few relics I possess of her."

A traitorous tremor in the voice which was stern with repressed emotion warned Canaris to pause there, while his eye turned to Olivia, as if reminded of some last debt to her. From his breast he drew a little paper, unfolded it, and took out what looked like a massive ring of gold; this he laid before her, saying, with a softened mien and accent—

"You were very kind—I have nothing else to offer—let me give you this, in memory of Gladys."

Only a tress of sunny hair; but Olivia received the gift as if it were a very precious one, thanking him, not only with wet eyes, but friendly words.

"Dear Felix, for her sake let *me* help you, if I can. Do not go away so lonely, purposeless, and poor. The world is hard; you will be disheartened, and turn desperate, with no one to love and hope and work for."

"I must help myself. I am poor; but not purposeless, nor alone. Disheartened I may be: never desperate again; for I *have* some one to love and hope and work for. She is waiting for me somewhere: I must make myself worthy to follow and find her. I have promised; and, God helping me, I will keep that promise."

Very humble, yet hopeful, was the voice; and full of a sad courage was the young man's altered face—for out of it the gladness and the bloom of youth had gone for ever, leaving the strength of a noble purpose to confront a life which hereafter should be honest, if not happy.

Helwyze had not the infinite patience to work in marble; the power to chisel even his own divided nature into harmony, like the sculptor, who, in the likeness of a suffering saint, hewed his own features out of granite. He could only work in clay, as caprice inspired or circumstance suggested; forgetting that life's stream of mixed and molten metals would flow over his faulty models, fixing unalterably both beauty and blemish. He had found the youth plastic as clay, had shaped him as he would; till, tiring of the task, he had been ready to destroy his work. But the hand of a greater Master had dropped into the furnace the gold of an enduring love, to brighten the bronze in which suffering and time were to cast the statue of the *man.* Helwyze saw this now, and a pang of something sharper than remorse wrung from him the reluctant words—

"Take, as my last gift, the fame which has cost you so much. I will never claim it: to me it is an added affliction, to you it may be a help. Keep it, I implore you, and give me the pardon *she* asked of you."

But Canaris turned on him with the air of one who cries, "Get thee behind me!" and answered with enough of the old vehemence to prove that grief had not yet subdued the passionate spirit which had been his undoing—

"It is no longer in your power to tempt me, or in mine to be tempted, by my bosom sin. Forsythe knows the truth, and the world already wonders. I will earn a better fame for myself: keep this, and enjoy it, if you can. Pardon I cannot promise yet; but I give you my pity, 'for her sake.'"

With that—the bitterest word he could have uttered—Canaris was gone, leaving Helwyze to writhe under the double burden imposed by one more just than generous. Olivia durst not speak; and, in the silence, both listened to the hasty footsteps that passed from room to room, till a door closed loudly, and they knew that Canaris had set forth upon that long pilgrimage which was in time to lead him up to Gladys.

Helwyze spoke first, exclaiming, with a dreary laugh—

"So much for playing Providence! You were right, and I *was* rash to try it. Goethe could make his Satan as he liked; but Fate was stronger than I, and so comes ignominious failure. Margaret dies, and Faust suffers, but Mephistopheles cannot go with him on his new wanderings. Still, it holds—it holds even to the last! My end comes too soon; yet it is true. In loving the angel I lose the soul I had nearly won; the roses turn to flakes of fire, and the poor devil is left lamenting."

Olivia thought him wandering, and listened in alarm; for his thoughts seemed blown to and fro, like leaves in a fitful gust, and she had no clew to them. Presently, he broke out again, still haunted by the real tragedy in which he had borne a part; still following Canaris, whose freedom was like the thought of water to parched Tantalus.

"He will do it! he will do it! When or how, who shall say? but, soon or late, she will save him, since he believes in such salvation. Would that I did!"

Perhaps the despairing wish was the seed of a future hope, which might blossom into belief. Olivia trusted so, and tried to murmur some comfortable, though vague, assurance of a love and pity greater even than hers. He did not hear her; for his eyes were fixed, with an expression of agonized yearning, upon the sky, serene and beautiful, but infinitely distant, inexorably dumb; and, when he spoke, his words had in them both his punishment and her own—

"Life before was Purgatory, now it is Hell; because I loved her, and *I* have no hope to follow and find her again."

Marion Earle;

or, Only an Actress!

Editor's Note: Alcott nurtured a lifelong passion for acting and even adapted some of her early stories for the stage. In her journal for 1858, she wrote, "Perhaps it is acting, not writing, I'm meant for. Nature must have a vent somehow." "Marion Earle; or Only an Actress!" appeared that same year, shortly after an unfulfilled opportunity to appear on stage. The story clearly shows her sympathy for what many considered a disreputable profession. The first of her thrillers, it weaves a moral of virtue rewarded into an account of sexual betrayal and abandonment.

B ut, Mrs. Leicester, all are not weak, frivolous and vain. I have known actresses as virtuous and cultivated as any lady whom you honor with your friendship. Faithful wives, good mothers, and true-hearted women, who are an honor to their profession, and would be an ornament of any class of society, were it not—pardon me—for prejudices like your own."

"Show me one such, Mr. Lennox, and I will conquer my prejudices—as far as I can. But it seems impossible that they can be all you describe, surrounded by such influences, and leading such a life," and the lady glanced at the stage where a ballet was performing previous to the play.

"Ah, you see only the roses scattered in their way, and fancy them butter-flies," replied the gentleman; "there are more thorns than flowers, and their life is often a long and patient struggle with stern necessity. What is mere amusement to you, is daily bread to them, and we little know, as they pass before us with smiling faces, what heavy hearts they may have. There is many a sadder tragedy played behind those scenes, than any we see here before. You ask me to point you out an actress such as I have described; Marion Earle, whom you will see to-night, is such an one."

"You are a great admirer of Miss Earle's, and therefore, being an interested party, I fear I cannot depend on your opinion; with you, gentlemen, beauty veils so many blemishes," said the lady, with a reproving smile.

"Madam, I am proud to say that I am Miss Earle's friend," replied the gentleman, gravely, "and my grey hairs should give some weight to my opinion. Marion's beauty veils only a good and tender heart, and if you will allow me to tell you a little of her history, I think you will look upon her with different eyes."

Mrs. Leicester bowed her acquiescence, and the eager old gentleman con-tinued—

"She was left an orphan, with a little sister dependent on her for support. They were friendless and poor, but (after vainly trying to support herself by the few occupations left to women) Marion had the courage to enter the profession for which her talents fitted her. She knew the dangers and the labor through which she must pass, but for the child's sake she ventured it, and the motive has kept her safe through all.

"By her own indomitable energy and patience, she has struggled up through poverty, injustice, and temptation, till she has become a beloved, admired and respected actress—aye, respected, Mrs. Leicester, for not a breath of slander ever touched her name.

"The little sister is being educated well, and Marion, by her own efforts, has secured a quiet home, where she and May can be together all their lives. Surely such an aim is noble, and such a woman must win respect though she is only an actress!"

"O, surely, you have made me quite impatient to behold the embodiment of all the virtues," answered Mrs. Leicester, smiling at her friend's enthusi-asm. But she soon forgot both Mr. Lennox and his story, in the interest of the scenes passing before her.

It was a comedy, and Marion, for the hour, put by her cares, and was the gay and brilliant creature that she seemed.

Her beauty charmed the eye, her clear voice satisfied the ear, and the fire and feeling she threw into her part touched the heart, and lent a womanly grace to every look and action.

Even Mrs. Leicester felt and owned her power, forgetting her pride and prejudice in the excitement of the hour, and heartily applauded what she had just condemned.

Towards the close of the last act, after a splendidly played scene, Marion went out with a jest upon her lips; a moment afterward a cry rang through the theatre so sharp and bitter, it filled the listeners with wonder and dismay.

There was a stir among the audience, and the performers paused involuntarily for what should come, but nothing followed save a confused murmur behind the scenes.

The play went on, but it now received the divided attention of those who were absorbed before.

Contradictory rumors of the sudden cry were whispered about, and its mournful echo still seemed lingering in many ears.

When, after a long pause, Marion appeared, a quick murmur arose, for in her face there might be read a tale of suffering that brought tears of pity into womanly eyes, and changed the comedy to a tragedy, for those who saw that countenance so lately beautiful and gay, now resolute and white, with a fixed look of agony and grief in its large eyes. It was a pitiful sight to see and a still more pitiful thing to hear the jests and joyous words that fell so mockingly from lips that quivered and grew white in the vain effort to recall their vanished smiles.

Apparently unconscious of the sympathizing faces looking into hers, or the consoling whispers of her fellow-players, Marion went on, mechanically performing every action of her part like one in a dream, except that now and then there flitted across her face an expression of intense and eager longing, and her eyes seemed to look in vain for some means of escape; but the stern patience of a martyr seemed to bear her up, and she played on, a shadow in the scene whose brightness she had lately been.

Her task at length was done, all but a little song, which always won for her the plaudits of her delighted hearers.

With the same painful faithfulness, she tried to sing it; her voice faltered and failed—her heart was too full, and she could only shake her head with a smile so sad and weary, that it called forth the pity of her audience in the only way she could express it, by the heartiest applause they ever had bestowed upon her.

It touched her deeply, and feeling only the generous sympathy that made them friends, she forgot time and place, and stretching her hands to them said imploringly:

"Kind friends, pardon me—I cannot sing—for my little May is dead!"

The only sound that broke the silence, was the rustle of flowers falling at her feet, as, leaving her broken words and her great grief to plead for her, she bowed her thanks, and the curtain shut her and her sorrow from the world.

"My dear Grace, what are you weeping so bitterly for?" asked Mrs. Leicester, as they prepared to go.

"I cannot help it, aunt, I pity that poor girl so much. Who will comfort her, for she is an orphan, and all alone now?" sobbed the warm-hearted girl, too young to feel ashamed of her generous emotion.

"Don't be foolish, my love," whispered her aunt, wrapping her cloak about her; "Miss Earle has plenty of comforters; such people never feel these things very deeply. You see she made quite a good thing out of it; her tragedy air was vastly effective; so never waste your pity, child—she is only an actress."

"There is a young person below, who insists on seeing you. Shall I send her up?"

"Certainly not; I am engaged," and Mrs. Leicester sank back among the cushions of her lounge, and resumed her novel.

The servant lingered, saying—

"I am afraid she won't go, ma'am; this is the third time she has been this week begging to see you. Couldn't she come up and be done with it?"

"No impertinence, John; she wants work, probably; tell her I have none, and let me hear no more of her."

John departed, but the door had hardly closed behind him, when it was suddenly re-opened, and the "young woman" entered, locked it behind her, possessed herself of the bell-rope, and then turning to the startled lady, said, desperately—

"Madam, you must hear me; do not be alarmed, there was no way left but this; you would not see me, therefore I have forced myself upon you; only listen, and you will pardon me."

The girl's face was wan and wasted with recent suffering, and wore a look of mingled supplication, fear and anguish, as of some timid creature hunted till it stood at bay.

"Who and what are you?" demanded Mrs. Leicester, recovering her self-possession.

"You ask me sternly, madam, and you shall have a stern answer," replied the girl steadily, while the hot blood burnt in her thin cheek.

"I am a motherless girl, whom your son, promising to cherish and protect, robbed of the one treasure she possessed, and then left to the pity of a world which is merciless to the weak. I have watched and waited for him one long year, have borne pity, scorn and pain, most patiently, trusting he would come as he promised. But he never has, and when I learned that he had been across the sea, I forgave him, and came here to his home to seek and ask him if he had forgotten me. Let me see him for one hour, one moment—he will set my heart at rest, and I will never trouble you again."

Mrs. Leicester fixed her cold eye on the face before her, saying, haughtily:

"If you desire money, say so, boldly; but do not come to me with this old story, which I neither believe nor desire to hear."

"Heaven help us, madam, it *is* an old story, but Christian charity is never old; I only ask that from you, and justice from your son. It is all he can do now; let him keep the word he plighted to me, and give his little child a name!"

"Girl! how dare you come to me with a demand like this? You are an impostor, and your tale is false, utterly false!" cried Mrs. Leicester, with an indignant frown; "my son is an honorable gentleman, and you—what are you, that you have the audacity to demand justice for your own sin and folly?"

The girl's eyes flashed, and she smiled bitterly, as she replied:

"I am used to looks and words like these, and for your son's sake, I have borne them for a year. You speak of my sin, judge of his. I was an orphan, ignorant and young, trusting all who were kind to me—and he was very fond and tender for a while—God forgive me—how I loved him! Worldly fears disturbed our peace; he left me, promising to come again. He never has, and his falsehood has changed me from a happy child, into a most miserable woman. O, madam, which is the blacker sin, to love blindly, or to betray a trusting heart? Which of us two, the lonely orphan, or the 'honorable gentleman' is the greater sinner?"

Mrs. Leicester rose, with an angry flush upon her face, saying:

"I will listen to this no longer; were my son here, he would clear himself from your accusations at once; in his absence I will hear nothing, believe nothing against him; I know him too well. Go, and never venture here again."

The girl turned away, but remembering that it was her last hope, she made one more appeal, crying, humbly:

"By the sacred name of mother, which we both bear, do not cast me off! A little sympathy, a little pity, will save me now! O, by the love you bear your son, have compassion upon mine, and do not send us out, *two* helpless children into the cruel world, for I am very young in all but sorrow, and there are so few to take me in. Be merciful, and help me in my bitter strait!"

The hard face softened at the poor young creature's prayer, but wordly pride swept like a cloud across the ray of womanly compassion, and offering a well-filled purse, Mrs. Leicester pointed silently to the door.

The girl struck the money from her hand, and swept past her with the mien of an insulted queen; pausing on the threshold, she turned, saying:

"Madam, I did not sell my love, and gold cannot buy my peace. I shall remember this, and as you have dealt by my son, so will I deal by yours." Then, with a warning gesture, she was gone.

"Miss Earle, there is a poor girl below, who wants to see you; I made bold to say she could, for you bid me always let the poor souls in."

"Poor and in trouble, doubtless. Yes, I will see her, Janet," and Marion left her flowers, murmuring softly—

> "We do pray for mercy; and that same prayer
> Doth teach us all to render
> Deeds of mercy."

"My child, what can I do for you?" she asked, turning towards the slight figure entering at her door.

The stranger looked eagerly into the face before her, as if fearing a repulse. But in that countenance, so beautiful and benign, she read no contempt; a tender pity shown in the lustrous eyes, and the music of the poet's words still lingered in the voice that called her "child."

The wild anxiety passed from her young face, and overcome by one kind word, the poor heart that had borne so much gave way at last, and with a burst of grateful tears, she cried to Marion—

"I am fatherless and motherless; oh, help me in my trouble and keep me from despair."

Lost in the tumult of her own emotion, the girl was but dimly conscious of the arm that gently enfolded her, or the hand that uncovered her aching head and laid it to rest upon a friendly bosom.

But the low voice soon recalled her, saying tenderly—

"Dear child, be comforted; tell me your grief, and believe me that whatever it may be, you are no longer friendless and alone."

"Ah, madam," sighed the girl, "forgive my tears, but yours are the first kind words I have heard this many a day; I thought there was no charity in all the world for me, and when it came so bounteously I could not bear it."

"It has been a cruel world to you, I fear. But tell me your trouble and take heart, for you are too young to despair," said Marion, looking down upon the face so youthful, but so darkened by remorse and care.

The girl shrank timidly away, and answered brokenly:

"You will despise and turn from me as all have done when I have told you more, but oh, remember I was very young and very lonely, and it seemed so sweet to be beloved."

But Marion only drew her nearer, only lifted up the drooping head, and with a tenderer compassion shining in her eyes, said earnestly:

"It is not for me to judge you or your error, but remembering my own weakness, to comfort and console as I in my sorrow would have been consoled, and leave all judgment to a wise and pitying God, who knows our strength and our temptations. Look bravely up and tell me all."

And gazing steadfastly into the friendly face, the poor girl told her story, and through it all the arm about her never fell away, and the pitiful eyes looked down unchanged.

"What is this man's name?" asked Marion, with an indignant flush upon her cheek.

"That I shall never tell," was the resolute reply. "No one shall look coldly on him, and he shall never reproach me for bringing contempt upon him. He had a kind heart once, and it may lead him back to me at last; till then, I will trust and wait."

"True woman through it all," sighed Marion. "But tell me how I best can serve you; what are your present needs, your future hopes?"

"I ask only honest work to keep me and the child from suffering; I will do anything, however humble, anything for bread. My greatest fear has been that, cut off from human love, I should grow wild and wicked and be driven to despair and death."

"Never fear that again," said Marion. "I will see that you have a quiet home and simple work, a home where you can love your boy and lead a blameless life. But always remember that there is One who hears his children when they cry to him, and when human pity fails, his great love takes them in."

"I will never doubt again, for in my extremest need he led me here. Ah, madam, if there were more hearts like yours, there would be fewer fates like mine. I heard of you from those you had succored, and hoping and fearing, I came here to be consoled as tenderly as if I were a sister. God in heaven bless you forever and forever."

But Marion seemed unconscious of the grateful kisses pressed upon her hand; the one word "sister" touched a cord in her warm heart and stirred a tender memory that drew her closer to the lonely girl.

She caressed the bright head resting on her shoulder, as she had caressed another which could never lie there any more, and with a sudden dimness in her beautiful proud eyes, looked down upon it, saying softly:

"I had a sister once, a little clinging child, who was the blessing of my life. We had no mother, and I loved her as a mother might. For ten happy years she was my comfort and my joy, and then when I had gained the home for which I had toiled and struggled, this little sister died. Since then for every child I feel a yearning tenderness, and love for her sake. In every young girl blooming into womanhood I see my darling as she would have been had she been spared, and a great sympathy possesses me for all their innocent delights, their maiden hopes and fears. In every wronged and sorrowing woman I behold some likeness of the child she might have been had fate not proved unkind, and I feel a strong compassion and a longing wish to comfort and protect them out of love for her.

"So looking into your wan face I see my May's confiding eyes, and knowing that her feet might have faltered among the snares of this false world as yours have done, I thank God she is safe, and remembering what might have been, I take you to the shelter of my love, as I would have had some kind heart pity and protect my child."

They sat silent for a moment when Marion ceased; then, with a blissful smile flitting across her face, she said:

"I am to be married soon, and then I shall have no cares but those of home. Come to me in a month and I will do yet more for you. If meanwhile you are unhappy or in trouble write to me. I will not forget you even in my own great happiness. But tell me child, what is your name?"

"My name," echoed the girl, "I have disgraced the honest one my father bore, *he* who should have given me one denied me his; I have no name but Agnes; call me that alone."

"You have no other," Marion said, "that none can deny, none take away, a sweet and blessed name which will sanctify your life and half its bitterness away, when baby lips shall call you 'mother.' Be true to that name, and though your child may never know an earthly father, remember he has an Heavenly one who never will forsake you, though all the world may cast you off."

Agnes turned to go, but Marion bade her wait, and writing a few lines, offered them with a generous supply of money, saying, as the girl drew back:

"Here is the name of the good woman with whom you will find a home, and here a little sum for future needs; I give it you in my lost darling's name and I know that you will take it for her sake."

"It was offered once before, but not as now," murmured Agnes; "I will take it and pray with all my grateful heart that you may be a happy wife and mother, with no shadow to disturb you all your tranquil life." Then looking timidly up she faltered—"May I kiss you, madam."

The stately woman bent and gathered the outcast to her bosom, remembering nothing but that blessed charity which binds human hearts together and makes the whole world kin.

Had Robert Leicester been a poor man's son he would have found in hard experience a teacher who would have made a strong and noble man of him, for he had generous impulses and a kindly nature. But born to wealth and early left fatherless, he grew up beneath the care of a proud, world-minded mother, whom he loved tenderly and whose will became his law.

Hoping to make an accomplished gentleman, she forgot that better thing—an honest man, and was content when he grew up handsome, gay and courtly, with no ambition but to enjoy life, and no knowledge of the duties wherein its true enjoyment might be found.

Easily led to good or ill, his was a character dangerous both to himself and others, for with winning manners and a generous heart, he loved and was beloved by all who knew him, even by those who saw the weakness and mourned the high powers misdirected, talents wasted, and the wrong early done a noble nature.

Meeting Marion abroad, whither she had gone after her little sister's death, they had journeyed much together; and Robert, by his sympathy and kindness, had lightened her sorrow, won her confidence, and soon woke a warmer interest in the heart which longed to bless and be blessed. From friends they glided into lovers, from lovers they were soon to pass into that closer union which makes the happiness or misery of two lives.

Marion saw her lover's faults, but felt she had the power to strengthen and direct, and was glad to feel she could do something for the friend who had made her solitary life so beautiful with hope and love.

And Robert looked up to Marion loving yet fearing, for he felt he was unworthy the generous confidence she bestowed upon him, and though bitterly lamenting it, had not the courage to become more worthy in his own eyes and in hers by sacrificing her love to the higher sense of duty that oppressed him.

Mrs. Leicester had no affection for Marion; of high birth herself, she felt that her son stooped to take her as his wife. But Marion had made a name for herself and better men than he had thought it no dishonor to offer her their hands.

Marion was an actress, and the proud woman looked upon her profession with contempt. But Marion had buried down all doubts long ago and there was nobody in the land purer than she, nor prouder of the blameless life she led, and Mrs. Leicester, while she hated, must respect her.

Marion had fortune, too, partly gained by her own honest labor, partly bequeathed her by an admiring friend. The extravagance of Mrs. Leicester and her son had nearly squandered the property the elder Leicester left, so worldly caution triumphed over womanly dislike, and for her own sake the selfish mother left her son to the best and truest passion of his life.

Mrs. Leicester's spacious drawing-rooms were filled with a throng of friends in honor of her son's wedding, for Marion would have no public spectacle and shrank even from the eyes that had so often watched her play the part she felt so real and solemn now.

A sudden stillness reigned through the brilliant rooms, broken only by the voice which asked:

"Robert Leicester, will thou take this woman to be thy wedded wife?"

Before the answering words could fall from the bridegroom's lips a start and stir among the guests arrested them, and with an involuntary motion he turned—to see Agnes standing at his side with her child in her arms.

There was a fire in her eye before which his own fell, and her low voice rang like thunder in his startled ear.

"*Will* you take that woman for your wife while I stand here with your child upon my breast? What are the promises you made, the oath you swore? Will you deny them with this innocent face to testify against you? Oh, Robert! Robert! I have hoped and waited all this weary year to find you here at last false to yourself and me."

The young man as she spoke had cast one look of despair and dismay about him, then covering up his face had staggered to a seat and sunk into it crushed by the weight of his remorse and shame.

Mrs. Leicester clutched Agnes by the arm and hissed a warning in her ear, endeavoring to lead her away; but the girl's spirit was roused, and shaking off her grasp, she drew her slight figure proudly up, and lifting the boy from her bosom cried exultingly:

"I told you I would remember the hour when you cast me off! Have I not kept my word? I told you as you dealt by my son so would I deal by yours; you left this child to shame and sorrow; he smiles in your face. Look at *your* son, on whose head lies the shame heaviest now? You would not believe me; ask him whose word you cannot doubt if what I say be not the living truth. Here before these witnesses I tell you this is his child and in the eye of God I am his wife. Ask him if he can deny it?"

White as her bridal veil, with a bewildered countenance and eyes dilated with a growing fear Marion had stood motionless, while Agnes poured out her excited words and pointed to the bowed figure that never spoke nor stirred.

"Robert, is this true?" and the words came imploringly from Marion's lips, as she bent towards him with clasped hands, as if pleading him for life.

The young man writhed as if some conflict tore his heart, but lifted up his face and answered steadily:

"Yes, Marion, all true."

She heard him with an incredulous gaze, but as he turned away with a bitter groan, a scarlet flush of scorn and indignation burnt in her cheek, then paled and left it whiter than before, and with one look at her lover she drew her veil across her face and prayed inwardly for help.

Agnes had caught a single sentence dropped carelessly from the lips of a lady for whom she had worked.

"Young Leicester's wedding tonight."

It was enough for her; she had borne much, but she would see him once more, make one appeal, and then submit. She had not learned the bride's name, nor did she recognize her in her bridal robes until she heard her voice; then looking on the woman whose happiness she hoped to blast, she saw her benefactress.

Fierce and bitter were the passions surging in the poor girl's heart, but at the sight of that kind face, so blanched and sorrow-stricken, gratitude rose up and silenced the storm that raged within. She forgot herself, her wrongs, and only heard again the voice that comforted, only saw the friend who succored her, and dropping her boy upon the cushion, where the happy bride would soon have knelt, she flung herself at Marion's feet, and clinging to her she cried passionately:

"Oh, pardon me—I never knew that it was you who had come between me and my love. Forget what I have said, and I will go away never to disturb your peace again. You can make him happier than I, a poor, fond child, whose love has always been a sorrow to him. I forgive him all if he is but true to you. Heaven bless and keep you, dearest lady. See, I am going, never, never more to be a shame or grief to any heart that has been kind to me."

Snatching up her child, she turned away, and Mrs. Leicester, eager to spare her son, stepped forward, saying with affected calmness:

"Friends, forget this painful scene, and let the ceremony proceed."

"It shall proceed, madam," answered the voice few thought to hear, and Marion, plunging aside her veil, passed down the room, took Agnes by the hand and led her back, saying as she took the child into her arms:

"Agnes, this is your place, not mine; for your sake and the boy's obey me. Robert Leicester, this is the woman whom you promised to cherish and protect; take her by the hand, and here publicly atone for the wrong you have done her, by giving her the sacred name of wife."

"He shall not—Robert, at your peril do you obey this mad request!" cried Mrs. Leicester, looking defiantly at Marion.

"Madam, he shall—I am the one to set him free or hold him to his bond. He owes me reparation for the double wrong he has done me and this poor girl, whose cause I make my own. Robert, I appeal to you, as you are a man, and would win back some part of the regard I once bestowed on you. I command you to keep the word you plighted one year ago, as you would have kept that you vowed to me."

There was a flash in Marion's eye, and a command in her tones that rang like a silver trumpet through the room and awed both haughty mother and wavering son to a complete submission.

Robert put aside his mother's hand, and with a resolute pale face silently took his place at Agnes' side. Marion spoke a few words to the aged minister, who bowed his white head, and with a trembling voice pronounced the marriage ceremony.

Agnes never turned her gaze from Marion's countenance, and Marion, motionless and white as a marble image, stood with the child upon her arm, looking straight before her with eyes that saw only utter darkness.

As they rose up from their knees, Robert turned to Marion, hoarsely: "Are you content?"

She only bowed her head, and without a word or look for his young wife he rushed from the room. Then Mrs. Leicester was herself again, and sweeping disdainfully past Agnes' drooping form, she turned to Marion, saying haughtily:

"Miss Earle, my house has been made a stage long enough, where you may play the queen. Oblige me by leaving it at once, and taking with you your friend, for much as I admire the skill with which you have entrapped my son into this shameful marriage, believe me neither he nor I will ever accept, or disgrace our home with the presence of the wife you have thrust upon him."

Marion's eyes lit, but she answered calmly with a glance of pity and contempt, that stung the proud woman more deeply than her words could have done.

"Madam, your son's wife will never ask the shelter of your roof unless he claims her, as I trust he one day will; then you may feel some remorse for this most cruel deed. I have played out my part, not as a queen I trust, but as a Christian woman, and I only ask of those who witness my last act, to remember that when the lady and the mother cast forth that poor girl with scorn, the actress—at whom she sneered—taught by her own human errors, pitied the outcast, and remembering a divine example, comforted and took her in."

And with the little child upon her breast, and the forsaken mother on her arm, Marion passed through the sympathizing throng, stately and calm, as if no bitter pain and desolation were lying heavily at her brave heart.

She did it well, for she was "only an actress."

Three years had passed since that unhappy bridal, and Robert Leicester had not claimed his wife. She still dwelt under Marion's roof, finding her only happiness in her boy and the love of that true friend.

Friends had warned and enemies had sneered, but Marion heeded neither, and kept the forsaken mother and child safe in the shelter of her honorable home, answering both friends and foes by a few simple words, which silenced them forever.

"Let him who is without sin cast the first stone."

And so they lived, two solitary women bound together by one sorrow and one love.

Mrs. Leicester, meeting with heavy losses, left the city soon after her son's strange marriage, and for three long years no tidings had been heard of them.

Agnes had written to her husband once, but receiving no reply felt that she was deserted, and patiently waited, hoping for happier times to come.

Marion sat in the pleasant garden of her country home. The air was full of summer music, and Agnes' little son played in the sunshine at her feet. The wind idly fluttered the leaves of her neglected book, for her eyes were fixed upon the little face which daily grew more like the one she remembered well.

Time had passed lightly over Marion's head, bringing a riper beauty and a deeper experience. The first, last love of her life, abandoned as a hope, crushed as a passion, living only as a quiet grief and a pure remembrance, still kept its watch as guardian of her heart.

No bitter memories soured the gracious sweetness of her nature, no discontent darkened her brave spirit; she poured strength and happiness within herself, and led a tranquil, cheerful life, with Agnes and her son.

Marion's reverie was broken by old Janet, who came hurrying down the path exclaiming:

"Oh, Miss, a poor gentleman has just fainted in the hall; he asked for you, and before I could answer he fell like one dead; I've sent Joe for the doctor, but do you come and see what can be done for him."

Bidding the child to stay among the flowers, Marion hastened in, to recognize in the unconscious stranger her lover, Robert Leicester.

"Thank heaven he has come at last, though it be only to die near us," she murmured to herself, holding fast the icy hand.

Then with quiet energy she gave all necessary directions for the sick man's comfort.

When Dr. Murrey arrived, he found his patient recovering from the death-like swoon, but already delirious with the fever burning in his veins, and Marion hovering over him, resolute and calm, though harassed by fears that filled her with the deepest anxiety.

"This is no place for you, my dear Miss Earle," said the doctor, turning from the sick man to the eager woman at his side. "This fever is contagious, and you must not expose yourself. I trust it is not too late. Send Mrs. Leicester and her boy away, and take all proper precautions yourself, and we will have nurse Clay to take charge of the poor gentleman."

"Nurse Clay is with her sick daughter, sir, and no other woman in the village would risk her life for an utter stranger. This gentleman is Mrs. Leicester's husband, and for her boy's sake she must not see him; but I have no fear, and I shall not leave him till the danger is past, or he needs human help no longer."

As she spoke, there was a light in Marion's eye and a glow upon her cheek which told more eloquently than words the earnestness of her resolve, and the joy her perilous compassion would afford her.

In vain the good doctor sought to intimidate and dissuade—she would not yield, and soon won an unwilling consent from him to be allowed to stay.

The child was sent to its mother with a message from Marion, forbidding her to return from the friendly neighbors where she chanced to be, till all danger was over.

Agnes, trusting all to Marion, obeyed her in this as in everything, and lived upon the tidings that came hourly from her husband's room, to allay her fears.

Marion set her house in order; released the timid servants from their posts, keeping only old Janet, and then in the darkened room sat down to her long watch beside the pillow of the suffering man, who never knew her, though he called upon her day and night, imploring her to pardon him, and give him back his wife and his own dear little child.

A long night and a day passed since the wild voice echoed through the lonely house, and Marion still sat beside the bed, bathing the burning head that found no ease upon its tender resting-place, or lifting a cooling draught to parched lips that could not thank her for her patient and untiring care.

The shaded lamp was lit, and its soft light fell on Marion's anxious face; tears such as she had seldom shed were falling fast, and broken words of love and sorrow mingled with her whispered prayers.

A slight sound startled her, and looking up she saw a grey-haired woman standing on the threshold. Wild-eyed and wan was the face that watched her from the gloom, travel-stained and poor were the garments that covered the tall figure bending towards her, and there was a world of stifled fear and anguish in the voice that cried to her:

"Where is my son?"

Marion, pointing silently to the head upon her bosom, beckoned the wanderer in, and yielded up her place to the poor mother, who looked fearfully into the eyes that had no recognition in them, and listened to the voice that could not welcome.

A sudden thought roused Marion, as she stood aside watching that sad meeting, and drawing near, she said:

"Dear madam, he was brought to me unconsciously, and has never known me since. Forgive me for seeking to banish you from your son, but it is not safe for you to stay—there is danger of contagion."

"Danger?" echoed Mrs. Leicester; "then why are you here?"

"Because I could not leave him to a stranger's care, his mother was not here, his wife must live for her boy, I have neither child nor mother to lament my loss; I loved him once, and therefore I am here."

With a sudden impulse, Mrs. Leicester stretched her hand to Marion, and kissed the beautiful, mild face that smiled so cheerfully amid the danger and the gloom. Then, as if ashamed of the unwonted emotion, she said, with a proud humility that showed how much the effort cost her—

"Miss Earle, I once turned you from my home. Can you pardon my discourtesy, and for my son's sake shelter me a short time in your own?"

"Yes, Madam, I can freely pardon all the past; for, as I once foretold, your son has come to claim his wife. By his sad wanderings I have learned the remorse and penitence that led him here, and for Agnes' sake I can forgive a far greater wrong than you have ever done me."

And Marion proved the truth of her words, for no daughter could more anxiously forestall a mother's needs than she. Abating nothing of her own quiet dignity, she paid a respectful deference to her guest's wishes, which soon won its way to the proud woman's heart, grown softer through the sharp discipline of poverty and pain.

The three years which passed so quietly in Marion's home had been years of suffering to mother and son. Too proud to ask help from friends, they went among strangers, to conceal their poverty. Unused to labor, life had been a sore struggle to them both, and had taught them stern lessons for which both were made humbler and wiser.

For his mother, Robert labored patiently at any work he could obtain. For her son, Mrs. Leicester put away her pride and plied her needle as diligently as the poor seamstress she had so often pitied.

They might have been happy in spite of their fallen fortunes, but for the bitter thoughts that haunted the son, who in his hour of trouble learned compassion for the grief of others.

The loss of Marion's love he could have borne, but Marion's esteem he longed to win again, and would have come to claim his wife had it not been deterred by his mother's entreaties.

She never gave him the letter Agnes generously sent, and suppressed the few her son insisted upon writing, thus convincing him that Agnes and Marion would not forgive, and had cast him off forever.

Mrs. Leicester, in her humbled state, could not bring herself to ask pardon or relief from those she had wronged, and so they struggled on till Robert, worn out with unaccustomed labor and the grief that preyed upon him, yielded to the uncontrollable desire that possessed him, and in his mother's absence wandered away to find Marion, caring only to be forgiven, and set free from the burden of remorse that oppressed him.

All this Marion had learned from his unconscious lips, and Mrs. Leicester's inadvertent words. She never spoke of it to her guest, nor made inquiries into her past life—the worn and aged face told the sad history, and the altered manner showed that misfortune had softened the high spirit that was once so pitiless and stern.

Day and night the two women kept their watch in the sick-room, learning to know each other better, and drawn closer by the one anxiety that possessed them both.

"If your son wakes conscious from his death-like sleep, he is safe—if not, be prepared, dear madam, for the worst. I shall not leave you, so take heart, for I predict a favorable change," and with a cheerful smile old Dr. Murrey stole into the ante-room to guard the sleeper's rest.

Twilight faded into evening, evening deadened into night, and still the marchers, like pale images of patience, sat beside the quiet bed.

Marion, with folded hands and eyes that never left the white face on the pillow, prayed for the wavering life as it had been her own. Mrs. Leicester, from the deep shadow of the parted curtains, watched her long and keenly, reading the unconscious countenance like an open book, and musing bitterly within herself of the wrong she had done her.

"I thought her ambitious, loving my boy only for the high place to which he could lift her, but now I know she loved him for himself, and for the right gave him up. I see lines in her tranquil face that only a great sorrow could have left, a sorrow she has conquered, but can never forget. I hated and despised her, and she has repaid me thus. God forgive me for the wrong I did her noble nature, and spare my son that we may both atone for the injustice we have done her."

And Mrs. Leicester kept her word.

Night waned slowly, and the grey dawn came stealing in. A single ruddy gleam shot across the sky and shone into the room. Marion pointed to the ray as a blessed omen, and as if awakened by the light, the sleeper's eyes unclosed and looked into her own.

"Marion here, then all is well," he murmured feebly, with a faint smile of recognition, and then sank again into a healthful slumber.

Marion covered up her face, remembering nothing but her great gratitude, until she felt Mrs. Leicester's arms about her, and the mother's tears upon her cheek. No words were uttered, but heart spake to heart, and the silence was eloquent with the forgiveness so generously bestowed, so humbly received.

Robert Leicester, a pale shadow of his former self, sat in the sunny garden waiting for the wife he once cast so cruelly from him. As she had longed and watched for him, he now longed and watched for her, forgetting even the quiet figure at her side, who looked wistfully upon him with eyes dimmed by long vigils for his sake.

A child's voice broke the summer stillness, and at the sound Marion arose, and with a solemn beauty shadowing her quiet face, laid her hands on Robert's bended head, saying earnestly—

"God bless you in your happiness, dear friend, and send you a fair future to atone for your sad past. Be a true husband to my sister Agnes, a wise father to your little child, and sometimes think of Marion."

"How can I forget you, the good angel of my life," cried Robert fervently. "Where are you going, Marion? You were with me by my bedside, in my darkest hour—why leave me in the brightest I have ever known?" he asked, as she turned away with the solemn light still shining in her wistful eyes.

She only answered:

"It is better so," and stole away.

But from a distant nook she watched him still, forgetting the dizzy pain that dimmed her sight, and the fierce flame that burnt and throbbed in every vein. Watched, till she saw his mother place Agnes in the shelter of her husband's love, till she saw the grey head bent tenderly above the little golden one, and the divided family united once again. Then, with a blessing on them all, she went silently away to lie down upon the bed from which she never rose again.

Her fortune was left to Agnes' son. Her summer home to Mrs. Leicester, with the hope that she might "love it for the giver's sake." Then having bestowed all she possessed to give, her life, her love, and earthly wealth, as she had lived, she died, "quiet; amid grass and flowers and charitable deeds," and this home was Marion's monument—a noble one, though she was but an ACTRESS.

~~~~~~~~~~~~~~~~~~~~~~~~~~~

La Jeune;

or, Actress and Woman

Editor's Note: "La Jeune; or, Actress and Woman" is one of a handful of stories in which Alcott uses actresses or actors to express a theme that recurs in all her thrillers: People are not what they seem. In this tale, her emphasis is on how easily people misconstrue evidence to see what they want in others. This is hardly a surprising concern for a writer who published blood-and-thunder stories anonymously and pseudonymously in the hope that they would not give readers of her literary writing the wrong impression. Today's reader can only wonder how much the tale reflects Alcott's own ambivalence toward her double personas as a writer.

J ust in time for the theatre. You'll come, Ulster?"

"Decidedly not."

"And why?"

"Because I prefer a cigar, a novel, and my bottle of cliquot."

"But every one goes," began Brooke, in a dissatisfied tone.

"True, and for that reason, I keep away."

"You used to be as fond of it as I am."

"At your age I grant it; now, I'm ten years older and wiser. I'm tired of that as of most other pleasures, so go your way, my boy, and leave me in peace."

"Come, Ulster, don't play Timon yet. You are lazy, not used up nor misanthropic, so be obliging, and come like a good fellow."

Fanning away the cloud of smoke from before me, I took a look at my friend, for something in his manner convinced me that he had some particular reason for desiring my company. Arthur Brooke was a handsome young Briton, of four-and-twenty; blue-eyed, tawny-haired, ruddy and robust, with a frank face, cordial smile, and a heart both brave and tender. I loved him like a younger brother, and watched over him during his holiday in gay, delightful, wicked Paris. So far, he had taken his draught of pleasure with the relish of youth, but like a gentleman. Of late, he had turned moody, shunned me once or twice, and when I alluded to the change, affected surprise, assuring me that nothing was amiss. As I looked at him, I was surer than ever that all was not right. He was pale, and anxious lines had come on his smooth forehead; there was an excited glitter in his eyes, though he had scarcely touched wine at dinner; his smile seemed forced, his voice had lost its hearty ring, and his manner was half petulant, half pleading, as he stood undecidedly crushing up his gloves while he spoke.

"Why do you want me to go? Is it on your account, lad?" I asked, in an altered tone.

"Yes."

"Give me a reason, and I will."

He hesitated, colored all over his fair face, then looked me straight in the eyes, and answered steadily.

"I want you to see Mademoiselle Nairne."

"The deuce you do! Why, Brooke, you've not got into a scrape with La Jeune, I hope!" I exclaimed, sitting up, annoyed.

"Far from it; but I love, and mean to marry her if I can," he answered, in a resolute tone.

"Don't say that for heaven's sake. My dear boy, think of your father, your family, your prospects, and don't ruin yourself by such folly," I cried, in real anxiety.

"If you loved as I do, you wouldn't call it folly," he said, excitedly.

"Of course not, but it would be cursed folly nevertheless, and if some friend saved me from it, I should thank him for it when the delusion was over. Love her if you will, but don't marry her, I beg of you."

"That is impossible; she is as good as she is lovely, and will listen to none but honorable vows. Laugh, if you will, it's so, and actress as she is, there's not a purer woman than she in all Paris."

"Bless your innocence, that's not saying much for her. Why, my dear lad, she knows your fortune to a soul and makes her calculations accordingly. She sees that you are a simple, tender-hearted fellow, easy to catch, and not hard to manage when caught. She will marry you for your money, spend it like water, and when tired of the respectabilities, will elope with the first rich lover that comes along. Don't shoot me, I speak for your good; I know the world, and warn you of this woman."

"Do you know her?"

"No, but I know her class; they are all alike, mercenary, treacherous, and shallow."

"You are mistaken this time, Ulster. I know I'm young, easily gulled perhaps, and in no way your equal in such matters, but I'll stake my life that Natalie is not what you say."

"My poor boy, you are far gone, indeed! What can I do to save you?"

"Come and see her," he said, eagerly. "You don't know her, never saw her beauty or talent, yet you judge her, and would have me abide by your unjust decree."

"I'll go; the fever is on you, and you must be helped through the crisis, or you'll wreck your whole life. It always goes hard with your sort."

My indolence was quite conquered by anxiety, and away we went, Brooke armed with a great bouquet, and I mentally cursing his folly in wasting time, money, and the love of his honest heart on a painted butterfly.

We took a box, and from the intense interest we showed in the piece, both of us might have been taken for ardent admirers of "La Jeune." I had never seen her, though all Paris had been running after her that season, as it was after any novelty from a learned pig to a hero. Having been bored by her praises, and annoyed by urgent entreaties to go, I perversely set my face against her, and affected even more indifference than I really felt. I was tired of such follies, fancied my day was over, and for a year or two had felt no interest in any actress less famous than Ristori or Rachel.

The play was one of those brilliant trifles possible only in Paris; for there, wit without vulgarity is appreciated, and art is so perfect, one forgets the absence of nature. The stage represented a charming boudoir, all mirrors, muslins, flowers and light. A coquettish soubrette was arranging the toilet as she delivered a few words that put the house in good humor, by whetting curiosity and raising a laugh, in the midst of which Madame la Marquise entered, not as most actresses take the stage, but as a pretty woman really would enter her room, going straight to the glass to see if the effect of her costume was quite destroyed by the vicissitudes of a bal-masque. She was beautiful—I could not deny that, but answered Brooke's eager inquiry with a shrug and the cruel words:

"Paint, dress, wine or opium."

He turned his back to me, and I devoted myself to the study of the woman he loved. She looked scarcely twenty, so fresh and brilliant was her face, so beautifully molded her figure, so youthful her charming voice, so elastic her graceful gestures. Petite and piquant, fair hair, dark eyes, a ravishing foot and hand, a dazzling neck and arm, made this rosy, dimpled little creature altogether captivating, even to one as *blasé* as myself. Gay, arch, and full of that indescribable coquetry which is as natural to a pretty woman as her beauty, La Jeune well deserved the sobriquet she had won.

Being a connoisseur in dress, I observed that hers was in perfect taste—a rare thing, for the costume of the Louis Quatorze era is usually overdone on the stage. But this woman had evidently copied some portrait, for everything was in keeping, coiffure, jewels, lace brocade; and from the tiny patch on her white chin to the diamond buckles in her scarlet-heeled shoes, she was a true French marquise. Even in gesture, gait and accent, she kept up the illusion, causing modern France to be forgotten for the hour, and making that comedy a picture of the past, and winning applause from critics whose praise was tame.

Through the sparkling dialogue, the inimitable by-play, romantic incident and courtly intrigues of the piece, she played admirably, embodying not only the beauty and coquetry, but the wit, *finesse* and brilliancy of the part. I was interested in spite of myself; I forgot my anxiety, and found myself applauding more than once. Brooke heard my hearty "Bravo!" and turned with an exultant smile.

"You are conquering your prejudices fast, *mon ami.* Is she not charming?"

"Very. I never questioned her skill as an actress, and readily accord my praise, for she plays capitally. But I'd rather not see her my friend's wife. Just fancy presenting her to your family."

He winced at that as his eye followed mine to the stage, which just then showed the marquise languishing in a great *fauteuil* before her mirror, surrounded by several fops, while her lover, disguised as a *coiffeur*, powdered her hair and dropped *billet doux* into her lap.

Fascinating, fair and frivolous as she was, how could he dream of transplanting her to a decorous English home, where her name alone would raise a storm, if coupled, even in jest, with his. He looked, sighed and sat silent till the curtain fell, then applauded till his gloves were in tatters, threw his bouquet at her feet as she reappeared, and turned to me, saying, with unabated eagerness:

"Now come and see her at home; the woman is more charming than the actress. I am asked to supper, and may bring a friend with me. Come, I beg of you."

To his surprise and satisfaction I consented at once, but did not tell him what had induced me to comply. It was a trifle, but it had weight with me, and hoping still to save my headstrong friend, I went away to sup with La Jeune.

The trifle was this: After one of her best scenes she left the stage, but did not go to her dressing-room, as she must re-enter in a moment.

From our box we could command the opposite wings; a chair was placed there for her, and sinking into it, she waved away two or three devoted gentlemen who eagerly approached. They retired, and as if forgetting that she could be overlooked, La Jeune leaned back with a change of countenance that absolutely startled me. And the fire, the gayety, the youth, seemed to die out, leaving a weary, woeful face, the sadder for the contrast between its tragic pathos and the blithe comedy going on before us.

Brooke did not see her; he had seized the moment to sprinkle his flowers, already drooping in the hot air.

I said nothing, but watched that brief aside more eagerly than her best point. It was but an instant. Her cue came, and she swept on to the stage with a ringing laugh, looking the embodiment of joy.

This glimpse of the woman off the stage roused my curiosity, and made me anxious to see more of her.

As we drove away I asked Brooke if he had spoken yet, for I wished to know how to conduct myself in the affair.

"Not in words; my eyes and actions must have told her; but I delayed to speak till you had seen her, for willful as I seem, I value your advice, Ulster."

"Have you spoken of me?"

"Yes; once or twice. Some one asked why you never came with me, and I said you had forsworn theatres."

"How did she take that blunt reply?"

"Rather oddly, I thought, for, looking at me, she said, softly: 'It would be better for you if you followed the example of your mentor.'"

"Art, my child, all art; warn a man against anything, and he'll move heaven and earth to get it. How will you explain this visit of your mentor, who has forsworn theatres?" I said, nettled at having that sage and venerable name applied to me.

"It will be both gallant and truthful to say you came to see her. She bade me bring any friend I liked, and will be flattered at your coming, if you don't put on your haughty airs."

"I'll be amiable on your account. Here we are. Upon my word mademoiselle lodges sumptuously."

As we drove into a courtyard, lights shone in long windows of La Jeune's *appartement*, and the sound of music met us as we passed up the stairs.

Two large, luxurious rooms, brilliantly, yet tastefully decorated and furnished, received us as we stepped in unannounced. Half a dozen persons were scattered about, chatting, laughing and listening to a song from a member of the opera troupe then delighting Paris. Supper was laid in the further room, and while waiting till it was served, every one exerted themselves to amuse their hostess in return for the delight she had given them.

Mademoiselle seemed to have just arrived, for she was still *en costume*, and appeared to have thrown herself into a seat as if wearied with her labors.

The rich hue of the garnet velvet chair relieved her figure admirably, as she leaned back, with a white cloak half concealing her brilliant dress. The powder had shaken from her hair, leaving its gold undimmed as it hung slightly disheveled about her shoulders. She had wiped the rouge from her face, leaving it paler, but none the less lovely, for in resuming her own character, that face had changed entirely. No longer gay, arch, or coquetish, it was thoughtful, keen, and cold. She smiled graciously, received compliments tranquilly, and conversed wittily; but her heart evidently was not there, and she was still playing a part.

I made these observations and received these impressions during the brief pause at the door; then Brooke presented me with much *empressement*, plainly showing that he wished each to produce a favorable effect upon the other.

As my name was spoken a slight smile touched her lips, but her dark eyes scanned my face so gravely, that in spite of myself I paid my compliments with an ill grace.

"It is evident that this is not monsieur's first visit to Paris."

From another person, and in another mood, I should have accepted this speech as a compliment to my accent and manner, but from her I chose to see in it an ironical jest at my unwonted *maladresse*, a feminine return for my long negligence. Anxious to do myself justice, I gave a genuine French shrug and replied, with a satirical smile which belied my flattering words:

"I was about to say no, but I remember to whom I speak, and say yes, for by the magic of mademoiselle, modern Paris vanishes, and for the first time I visit Paris in the time of the Grand Monarque. The illusion was perfect, and like a hundred others, I am at a loss how to show my gratitude."

"That is easily done; madame is hungry; oblige her with a *morceau* of that *pâté* and a glass of champagne."

Her mocking tone, the sparkle of her eye, and the wicked smile on her lips, annoyed me more than the unromantic request that made my speech absurd.

I obeyed with feigned devotion, telling Brooke to keep out of the way still longer, as I passed him on my way back. He had withdrawn a little, that I might see and judge for myself, and stood in an alcove near by, affecting to talk with a gentleman in the same sentimental plight as himself.

Mademoiselle ate and drank as if she was really hungry, inviting me to do the same with such hospitable grace that I drew up a little table and continued our *tête-à-tête*, while the others stood or sat about in groups in a pleasantly informal manner.

"My friend is much honored, I perceive. Mademoiselle shows both taste and judgment in her selection, for though young for his years, Brooke is a true gentleman," I said, observing that of all the many bouquets thrown at her feet his was the only one she kept.

"Do you know why I selected this?" she asked, with a quick glance after a slight pause.

"I can easily guess," I replied, with a significant smile.

She glanced over her shoulder, took up the great bouquet, and plunging her dimpled hand into the midst of the flowers, drew out a glittering bracelet, saying, as she offered it to me, with an air of pride that surprised me very much:

"I kept it that I might return this. It may annoy your friend less to take it from you, therefore restore it with my thanks, and tell him I can accept nothing but flowers."

"Nothing, mademoiselle?"

"Nothing, monsieur."

I put my question with emphasis, and as she answered she flashed a look at me that perplexed me, though I thought it a bit of clever acting.

Taking the bracelet, I said, in a tone of feigned regret:

"Must I afflict the poor boy by returning his gift with such a cruel message?"

"If you would be a true friend to him do what I ask, and take him away from Paris."

Her urgent tone struck me even more than this unexpected frankness, and I involuntarily exclaimed:

"Does mademoiselle know what she banishes thus?"

"I know that Sir Richard Brooke would disinherit his only son if that son made a *mésalliance;* I know that I regard Arthur too much to mar his future, and—I banish him."

She spoke rapidly, and laid her hand upon her heart as if to hide its agitation, but her eyes were fixed steadily on mine with an expression which affected me with a curious sense of guilt for my hard judgment of her.

There was a pause, and in that pause I chid myself for letting a pair of lovely eyes ensnare my reason, or an enchanting smile bribe my judgment.

"Mademoiselle understands the perversity of mankind well. It will be impossible to get Arthur away after a command like yours," I said, coldly.

She deliberately examined my face, and a change passed over her own. The earnestness vanished, the soft trouble was replaced by an almost bitter smile, and her voice had a touch of scorn in it as she said, sharply:

"Then Telemachus had better find a truer Mentor."

A gentleman approached; she welcomed him with a genial look, and I retired, feeling more ruffled than I would confess.

As soon as I joined Brooke in the alcove he demanded in English, and with lover-like eagerness:

"What is your opinion of her?"

"Hush; she will overhear you!"

"She speaks no English—she is absorbed—answer freely."

"Well, then, I think her a charming, artful, dangerous woman, and the sooner you leave her the better," I answered, abruptly.

"But, Ulster, don't joke. How artful? Why dangerous? I'll *not* leave her till I've tried my fate," he cried, half angry, half hurt.

I told him our conversation, gave him the jewel, and advised him to disappoint her hopes by departing without another word.

"You think she means to win me by affecting to sacrifice her own heart to my welfare?" he said as I paused.

"Exactly; she did it capitally, but I am not to be duped; and I tell you she will never let so rich a prize escape her unless she has a richer in sight, which I doubt."

"I'll not believe it! You wrong us both; you distrust all women, and insult her by such bare suspicions. You are deceived."

"I *never* am deceived; I read men and women like books, and no character is too mysterious for me to decipher. I tell you, I am right, and I'll prove it if you will keep silent for a few weeks longer."

"How?" demanded Brooke, hotly.

"I'll study this woman, and report my discoveries to you; thus, step by step, I'll convince you that she is all I say, and save you from the folly you are about to commit. Will you agree to this?"

"Yes; but you'll take no unfair advantage, you'll deal justly by us both, and if you fail————"

"I *never fail*—but if such an unheard of thing occurs, I'll own I'm conquered, and pay any penalty you decree."

"Then, I say, done. Prove that I'm a blind fool, and I'll submit to your advice, will forget Natalie and leave Paris."

Grateful for any delay, and already interested in the test, I pledged my word to act fair throughout, and turned to begin my work. Mademoiselle was surrounded by several gentlemen, and seemed to have recovered from her fatigue. Her eyes shone, a brilliant color burned on her cheek, she talked gayly, and mingled her silvery laughter in the peals of merriment her witty sallies produced. As we joined the group, some one was speaking of tragedy, and assuring La Jeune that she would excel in that as in comedy.

"*Mon Dieu*, no; one has tragedy enough off the stage; let us feign gayety in public, and laugh on even though our hearts ache," she answered, with a charming smile.

"Yet I can testify that mademoiselle would act tragedy well, if I may judge by the sample I have seen."

I spoke significantly, and her eye was instantly upon me, as she exclaimed with visible surprise:

"Seen! where?"

"To-night, as mademoiselle reposed a moment in the wing, between the fourth and fifth acts."

She knit her brows, thought an instant, then as if recalling the fact, clapped her hands, and broke into that ringing laugh of hers, as she cried:

"Monsieur has penetration! It is true, I was in a tragic mood, for the spur of one of my buckles wounded my foot cruelly, and I could not complain. Behold how I suffered," and she showed a spot of scarlet that had stained through silk stocking and satin shoe.

"Great heaven! and does mademoiselle still wear the cruel ornament? Permit me to relieve this charming foot," cried one of the Frenchmen, in a pathetic tone; and going down upon his knee, undid the buckle.

I was leaning on the back of her chair just then, and during the little stir said quietly:

"I congratulate mademoiselle, for if a pin-prick can call up such a woeful expression, her rendering of a mighty sorrow would be wonderfully truthful."

"I believe it would."

She looked up at me as she spoke, and in those beautiful eyes I fancied I read something like reproach. For what? Had I touched some secret wound, and was her explanation a skillful feint, as I thought it? Or did she feel with a woman's quick instinct that I was an enemy, and set herself to disarm me by her beauty? I inclined to the latter belief, and instantly saw that if I would execute my purpose, I must convince her that I was a friend, an admirer, a lover even. It was evident that simple Brooke had allowed her to perceive that I did not approve his suit; this hurt her pride, and she distrusted me. Deciding to warm gradually, I looked back at her, saying gently, as if replying to that reproachful glance alone:

"I sincerely hope mademoiselle may never be called upon to play a part in any tragedy off the stage, for smiles, not tears, should be the portion of La Jeune."

Her face softened beautifully, and the dark-curled lashes fell as if to hide the sudden dew that dimmed her eyes.

"You are kind, I thank you," she murmured, in a tone that touched me, skeptic as I was. "I received much flattery, and value it for what it is worth; but a friendly wish, simple and sincere, is very sweet to me, for even a path strewn with flowers has its thorns."

She spoke as if to herself more than to me, and fancying that sentiment might succeed better than sarcasm, I began one of those speeches that may mean much or little; but in the middle of it detected her in a yawn behind her little hand, and stopped abruptly. She laughed, and with the arch expression that made her face piquant she said with a shake of the head:

"Ah, monsieur, that's but a waste of eloquence. I detect false sympathy in an instant, and betray that I do. Pardon my rudeness, and turn me a charming compliment; that is more in your style."

"Mademoiselle is fatigued; we are unmerciful to leave her no time for rest. Brooke, we should go," I said, repentantly.

"I *am* tired," she answered, with the air of a sleepy child. "*Au revoir*, not adieu, for you will come again."

"If mademoiselle permits," and with that we bowed ourselves away.

For a month I studied La Jeune in ways as skillful as unobtrusive. I made four discoveries, reported them to Brooke, and flattered myself that I should be able to save him from this fascinating, yet dangerous woman.

My first discovery was this. Fearing to rouse suspicion by too suddenly feigning admiration and regard, I began with an occasional call, contenting myself meantime with cultivating the friendship of a gossipy old Frenchman, who lodged in the same house. From him I learned various hints of Natalie, for the old gentleman adored her, and was as garrulous as an old woman. He said there was one room in mademoiselle's suite that none of the servants of the house were allowed to enter.

Several times a week, early in the morning, when her mistress was invisible to every one else, Jocelynd, the maid, admitted a man, who came and went as if anxious to escape observation. He was young, handsome, an Italian, and evidently deeply interested in all concerning Mademoiselle Nairne.

"A lover, without doubt," the old man said. I agreed with him, and Brooke, on learning this, could be with difficulty restrained from demanding an explanation from La Jeune.

My second discovery was made unexpectedly. One night, when she did not play, I went to see her on pretense of finding Brooke, who, I knew, was not there.

Mademoiselle was out, but expected momently, so I went in to wait. I heard her arrive soon after and enter an adjoining room, followed by the maid, who cast a glance into the *salon* as she passed. I stood in the deep window idly looking into the street below, and Jocelynd did not see me, for I heard her say:

"There is no one here, mademoiselle. Pierre was mistaken, and Monsieur Ulster did not wait."

"Thank heaven! I am so fatigued I can see no one to-night. Count this for me. I have been playing for a high stake, but I have won, and Florimond shall profit by my success."

I heard the clink of money, and noiselessly stole away, saying to myself as I went to join Brooke: "She gambles—so much the better."

A week afterward I chanced to be in one of those dark little stores in the Rue Bonaparte, where cigars, cosmetics, perfumery, and drugs are sold. I was standing in the back part of the shop selecting a certain sort of toilet soap which I fancied, when a woman came in, and, beckoning the wife of the shopman aside, handed her a peculiar little flask, saying in a low tone:

"The same quantity as usual, madame, but stronger."

The woman nodded, disappeared, and returned; but having left the stopper on the counter, she passed me with the flask uncorked, and I plainly perceived the acrid scent of laudanum. I knew it well, having used it during a nervous illness, and left the shop convinced that La Jeune was an opium-eater, like many of her class, for the woman I had seen was Jocelynd.

The fourth discovery was that some secret anxiety or grief preyed upon mademoiselle, for during that month she altered visibly. Her spirits were variable, her cheek lost its bloom, her form its roundness, and her eyes burned with feverish brilliancy, as if some devouring care preyed upon her life.

I could mark these changes carefully, for I was a frequent and a welcome guest now. By imperceptible degrees I had won my way, and making Brooke my pretext, often led her to speak of him, fancying that topic the one most likely to interest her. Soon I let her see that she had wakened my admiration as an actress, for I was as constant at the theatre as Brooke. Then I, with feigned reluctance, betrayed my susceptibility to her charms as a woman, and by look, sigh, act and word, permitted her to believe that I was one of her most devout adorers.

Upon my life, I sometimes felt as if in truth I was, and half longed to drop my mask and tell her that, with all her faults and follies, I found her more dangerous to my peace than any woman I had ever known. More than once I was tempted to believe that had I been a richer man she would have smiled upon me in spite of Brooke and the unknown Florimond.

As time passed this fancy of mine increased, for I observed that with others she was as careless, gay and witty as ever, but with me, especially if we were alone, her manner was subdued, her glance restless, timid and troubled, her voice often agitated or constrained, her whole air that of a woman whose heart is full and pride alone keeps her from letting it overflow.

To Brooke she was uniformly kind, but cold, and often shunned him. At first I believed this only a ruse to lure him to the point, but soon my own penetration, vanity, if you will, led me to think that for a time at least she would hold mercenary motives in check and let the master-passion rule her in spite of interest.

This belief of mine added new excitement to my task, and my undisguisable absorption in it roused Brooke's jealousy, and nothing but a promise to hold his peace till the month was up restrained him from ruining everything, for he refused to accept my discoveries without further proof.

On the last day of the month I went to Natalie at noon, knowing that Arthur would speak that night. I had never been admitted so early before, but sending in an urgent request, it was granted.

I scarcely knew what I meant to say or do, for although my friend and I were freed by mutual consent from the pledge we had given one another, I was hardly ready to fetter myself with a lifelong tie, even to Natalie, whom I no longer disguised from myself that I loved.

I dared make no other offer, for in spite of the gossip and prejudice which always surrounds a young and beautiful actress, I felt that Natalie was innocent, from pride if not from principle, and would be to me a wife or nothing. I loved my freedom well, yet half resolved to lose it for her sake, for in spite of past experiences, I was conscious of a more ardent love at eight-and-thirty than any I had known in my youth.

Natalie came in, looking pale, yet very lovely, for her eyes possessed the soft lustre that follows tears, and on her face there was a look I had never seen before.

She wore a white cashmere *peignoir*, and was wrapt in a soft white mantle. Her hair hung in loose, glittering masses about her face, and her only ornament was a rosary of ebony and gold that hung from her neck.

The room was shaded by heavy curtains, which she did not draw aside, and as she seated herself in the deep velvet chair, her face was much in shadow. I regretted this, for never having seen her by day, except driving, I wished to see and study her when free from the illusion which dress and lamp-light can throw about the plainest woman.

Her hand trembled as I kissed it, her eyes avoided mine, and while I paid my compliments, she listened with drooping lids, a shy smile on her lips, and such a quickly beating heart that the rosary on her bosom stirred visibly. This agitation, coupled with her unusual welcome, banished my last doubt, and before I had decided to betray my passion, the words passed my lips.

As I paused, breathless with the impetuous petition I had made, she looked up with an unmistakable flash of triumph in her eye, an irrepressible accent of joy in her voice, as she answered, with a smile that thrilled my heart:

"Then you love me? You ask my hand? and give your happiness into my keeping?"

"I do."

"You forget what I am—forget that you know nothing of my past; that my heart is a sealed book to you, and that you have seen only the gay, frivolous side I show the world."

"I forget nothing, and glory in your talent as in the fame it wins you. I know you better than you think, for during a month I have studied you deeply, and I read you like an open book. I have discovered faults and follies, mysteries and entanglements, but I can forgive all, forget all, for the sake of this crowning discovery. You love me; I guess it; but I long to hear you confess it, and to know in words that I am blest."

She had questioned eagerly, with her keen eyes full on my face as I replied, but in the act of answering my last speech she rose suddenly as a swift change passed across her face, and in a tone of bitterest contempt, uttered these startling words:

"You say you know me well; you boast that you never are deceived; you believe that you have discovered the secret passions, vices and ambitions of my life; you affirm that I have had a lover, that I gamble, eat opium, and— love you. That last is the blindest blunder of the four, for of all men living, *you* are the one for whom I have the supremest contempt."

I had risen involuntarily when she did, but dropped into my seat as if flung back by the forceful utterance of that last word. I was so entirely taken by surprise that speech, self-possession, and courage deserted me for the moment, and I sat staring at her in dumb amazement. In a voice full of passionate pride, she rapidly continued, with her steady eyes holding me fast by their glittering spell:

"You were wise in your own conceit, and needed humbling. I heard your boast, your plot and pledge, made in this room a month ago, and resolved to teach you a lesson. You flatter yourself you know me thoroughly, yet you have not caught even a glimpse of my true nature, and Arthur's honest instinct has won the day against your worldly wisdom."

"Prove it!" I cried, angrily, for her words, her glance, roused me like insults.

"I will. First let us dispose of the discoveries so honorably made, and used to blast my reputation in a good man's eyes. My lover is an Italian physician;

who comes to serve a suffering friend whom I shelter; the laudanum is for the same unhappy invalid. The money I won was honestly *played for*—on the stage, and the secret love you fancied I cherished was not for you—but Arthur."

"Hang the boy; it is a plot between you," I cried, forgetting self-command in my rising wrath.

"Wrong again; he knew nothing of my purpose, never guessed my love till to-day."

"To-day! he has been here already!" I exclaimed, "and you have snared him in spite of my sacrifice. Good! I am right in one thing, the richer prize tempts the mercenary enchantress."

"Still deceived; I have refused him, and no earthly power can change my purpose," she answered, almost solemnly.

"Refused him! and why?" I gasped, feeling more bewildered every moment.

"Because I am married, and—dying."

As the last dread word dropped from her lips, I felt my heart stand still, and I could only mutter hoarsely:

"No! no! it is impossible!"

"It is true; look here and believe it."

With a sudden gesture she swept aside the curtain, gathered back her clustered hair, dropped the shrouding mantle, and turned her face full to the glare of noonday light.

I did believe, for in the wasted figure, no longer disguised with a woman's skill, the pallid face, haggard eyes, and hollow temples, I saw that mysterious something which foreshadows death. It shocked me horribly, and I covered up my eyes without a word, suffering the sharpest pang I had ever known. Through the silence, clear and calm as an accusing angel's, came her voice, saying, slowly:

"Judge not, lest ye be judged. Let me tell you the truth, that you may see how much you have wronged me. You think me a Frenchwoman, and you believe me to be under five-and-twenty. I am English, and thirty-seven to-morrow."

"English! thirty-seven!" I ejaculated in a tone of utter incredulity.

"I come of a race whom time touches lightly, and till the last five years of my life, sorrow, pain, and care have been strangers to me," she said, in pure English, and with a faint smile on her pale lips. "I am of good family, but misfortune overtook us, and at seventeen I was left an orphan, poor, and nearly friendless. Before trouble could touch me, Florimond married and took me away to a luxurious home in Normandy. He was much older than myself, but he has been fond as a father, as faithful, tender and devoted as a lover all these years. I married him from gratitude, not love, yet I have been happy and heart-free till I met Arthur."

Her voice faltered there, and she pressed her hands against her bosom, as if to stifle the heavy sigh that broke from her.

"You love him; you will break the tie that binds you, and marry him?" I said, bitterly, forgetting in my jealous pain that she had refused him.

"Never! See how little you know my true character," she answered, with a touch of indignation in the voice that now was full of a pathetic weariness. "For years my husband cherished me as the apple of his eye; then, through the treachery of others, came ruin, sickness, and a fate worse than death. My poor Florimond is an imbecile, helpless as a child. All faces are strange to him but mine, all voices empty sounds but mine, and all the world a blank except when I am with him. Can I rob him of this one delight—he who left no wish of mine ungratified, who devoted his life to me, and even in this sad eclipse clings to the one love that has escaped the wreck? No, I cannot forget the debt I owe him. I am grateful, and in spite of all temptations, I remain his faithful wife till death."

How beautiful she was as she said that! Never in her most brilliant hour, on stage or in *salon,* had she shone so fair or impressed me with her power as she did now. That was art, this nature. I admired the actress, I adored the woman, and feeling all the wrong I had done her, felt my eyes dim with the first tears they had known for years. She did not see my honest grief; her gaze went beyond me, as if some invisible presence comforted and strengthened her. With every moment that went by I seemed passing further and further from her, as if she dropped me out of her world henceforth, and knew me no more.

"Now you divine why I became an actress, hid my name, my grief, and for his sake smiled, sung, and feigned both youth and gayety, that I might keep him from want. I had lived so long in France that I was half a Frenchwoman; I had played often, and with success, in my own pretty theatre at Villeroy. I was unknown in Paris, for we seldom came hither, and when left alone with Florimond to care for, I decided to try my fortune on the stage. Beginning humbly, I have worked my way up till I dared to play in Paris. Knowing that youth, beauty and talent attract most when surrounded by luxury, gayety and freedom, I hid my cares, my needs, and made my *debut* as one unfettered, rich, and successful. The bait took; I am flattered, fêted, loaded with gifts, lavishly paid, and, for a time, the queen of my small realm. Few guess the heavy heart I bear, or dream that a mortal malady is eating my life away. But I am resigned; for if I live three months and am able to play on, I shall leave Florimond secure against want, and that is now my only desire."

"Is there no hope, no help for you?" I said, imploringly, finding it impossible to submit to the sad decree which she received so bravely.

"None. I have tried all that skill can do, and tried in vain. It is too late, and the end approaches fast. I do not suffer much, but daily feel less strength, less spirit, and less interest in the world about me. Do not look at me with such despair; it is not hard to die," she answered, softly.

"But for one so beautiful, so beloved, to die alone is terrible," I murmured, brokenly.

"Not alone, thank heaven; one Friend remains, tender and true, faithful to the end."

A blissful smile broke over her face as she stretched her arms towards the place her eye had often sought during that interview. If any further punishment was needed, I received it when I saw Arthur gather the frail creature close to his honest heart, reading his reward in the tender, trusting face that turned so gladly from me to him.

It was no place for me, and murmuring some feeble farewell, I crept away, heart-struck and humbled, feeling like one banished from Paradise; for despite the shadow of sorrow, pain and death, love made a heaven for those I left behind.

I quitted Paris the next day, and four months later Brooke returned to England, bringing me the ebony rosary I knew so well, a parting gift from La Jeune, with her pardon and adieu, for Arthur left her and her poor Florimond quiet under the sod at Père la Chaise.

~~~~~~~~~~~~~~~~~~~~~~~~~~

A Pair of Eyes;

or, Modern Magic

Editor's Note: Most of Alcott's heroines show strength by maintaining their virtue and dignity in a world intent on destroying these qualities. Agatha Eure, the heroine of "A Pair of Eyes; or, Modern Magic," represents the flip side of this character type: She is jealous, possessive, and manipulative. The story is interesting in that it portrays marriage between two strong-willed people as a domestic hell in which one partner must ultimately dominate the other. Alcott, who spent most of her life providing for her family, never married, and it's possible that, like Agatha's husband, Max, she felt marriage would entail forsaking her art for a spouse.

I was disappointed—the great actress had not given me what I wanted, and my picture must still remain unfinished for want of a pair of eyes. I knew what they should be, saw them clearly in my fancy, but though they haunted me by night and day I could not paint them, could not find a model who would represent the aspect I desired, could not describe it to any one, and though I looked into every face I met, and visited afflicted humanity in many shapes, I could find no eyes that visibly presented the vacant yet not unmeaning stare of Lady Macbeth in her haunted sleep. It fretted me almost beyond endurance to be delayed in my work so near its completion, for months of thought and labor had been bestowed upon it; the few who had seen it in its imperfect state had elated me with commendation, whose critical sincerity I knew the worth of; and the many not admitted were impatient for a sight of that which others praised, and to which the memory of former successes lent an interest beyond mere curiosity. All was done, and well done, except the eyes; the dimly lighted chamber, the listening attendants, the ghostly figure with wan face framed in hair, that streamed shadowy and long against white draperies, and whiter arms, whose gesture told that the parted lips were uttering that mournful cry—

> "Here's the smell of blood still:
> All the perfumes of Arabia will not
> Sweeten this little hand—"

The eyes alone baffled me, and for want of these my work waited, and my last success was yet unwon.

I was in a curious mood that night, weary yet restless, eager yet impotent to seize the object of my search, and full of haunting images that would not stay to be reproduced. My friend was absorbed in the play, which no longer possessed any charm for me, and leaning back in my seat I fell into a listless reverie, still harping on the one idea of my life; for impetuous and resolute in all things, I had given myself body and soul to the profession I had chosen and followed through many vicissitudes for fifteen years. Art was wife, child, friend, food and fire to me; the pursuit of fame as a reward for my long labor was the object for which I lived, the hope which gave me courage to press on over every obstacle, sacrifice and suffering, for the word "defeat" was not in my vocabulary. Sitting thus, alone, though in a crowd, I slowly became aware of a disturbing influence whose power invaded my momentary isolation, and soon took shape in the uncomfortable conviction that some one was looking at me. Every one has felt this, and at another time I should have cared little for it, but just then I was laboring under a sense of injury, for of all the myriad eyes about me, none would give me the expression I longed for; and unreasonable as it was, the thought that I was watched annoyed me like a silent insult. I sent a searching look through the boxes on either hand, swept the remoter groups with a powerful glass, and scanned the sea of heads below, but met no answering glance; all faces were turned stageward, all minds seemed intent upon the tragic scenes enacting there.

Failing to discover any visible cause for my fancy, I tried to amuse myself with the play, but having seen it many times and being in an ill-humor with the heroine of the hour, my thoughts soon wandered, and though still apparently an interested auditor, I heard nothing, saw nothing, for the instant my mind became abstracted the same uncanny sensation returned. A vague consciousness that some stronger nature was covertly exerting its power over my own; I smiled as this whim first suggested itself, but it rapidly grew upon me, and a curious feeling of impotent resistance took possession of me, for I was indignant, without knowing why, and longed to rebel against—I knew not what. Again I looked far and wide, met several inquiring glances from near neighbors, but none that answered my demand by shy betrayal of especial interest or malicious pleasure. Baffled, yet not satisfied, I turned to myself, thinking to find the cause of my disgust there, but did not succeed. I seldom drank wine, had not worked intently that day, and except the picture had no anxiety to harass me; yet without any physical or mental cause that I could discover, every nerve seemed jangled out of tune, my temples beat, my breath came short, and the air seemed feverishly close, though I had not perceived it until then. I did not understand this mood and with an impatient gesture took the playbill from my friend's knee, gathered it into my hand and fanned myself like a petulant woman, I suspect, for Louis turned and surveyed me with surprise as he asked:

"What is it, Max; you seem annoyed?"

"I am, but absurd as it is, I don't know why, except a foolish fancy that some one whom I do not see is looking at me and wishes me to look at him."

Louis laughed—"Of course there is, aren't you used to it yet? And are you so modest as not to know that many eyes take stolen glances at the rising artist, whose ghost and goblins make their hair stand on end so charmingly? I had the mortification to discover some time ago that, young and comely as I take the liberty of thinking myself, the upturned lorgnettes are not levelled at me, but at the stern-faced, black-bearded gentleman beside me, for he looks particularly moody and interesting to-night."

"Bah! I just wish I could inspire some of those starers with gratitude enough to set them walking in their sleep for my benefit and their own future glory. Your suggestion has proved a dead failure, the woman there cannot give me what I want, the picture will never get done, and the whole affair will go to the deuce for want of a pair of eyes."

I rose to go as I spoke, and there they were behind me!

What sort of expression my face assumed I cannot tell, for I forgot time and place, and might have committed some absurdity if Louis had not pulled me down with a look that made me aware that I was staring with an utter disregard of common courtesy.

"Who are those people? Do you know them?" I demanded in a vehement whisper.

"Yes, but put down that glass and sit still or I'll call an usher to put you out," he answered, scandalized at my energetic demonstrations.

"Good! then introduce me—now at once—Come on," and I rose again, to be again arrested.

"Are you possessed to-night? You have visited so many fever-wards and madhouses in your search that you've unsettled your own wits, Max. What whim has got into your brain now? And why do you want to know those people in such haste?"

"Your suggestion has not proved failure, a woman can give me what I want, the picture will be finished, and nothing will go to the deuce, for I've found the eyes—now be obliging and help me to secure them."

Louis stared at me as if he seriously began to think me a little mad, but restrained the explosive remark that rose to his lips and answered hastily, as several persons looked round as if our whispering annoyed them.

"I'll take you in there after the play if you must go, so for heaven's sake behave like a gentleman till then, and let me enjoy myself in peace."

I nodded composedly, he returned to his tragedy, and shading my eyes with my hand, I took a critical survey, feeling more and more assured that my long search was at last ended. Three persons occupied the box, a well-dressed elderly lady dozing behind her fan, a lad leaning over the front absorbed in the play, and a young lady looking straight before her with the aspect I had waited for with such impatience. This figure I scrutinized with the eye of an artist which took in every accessory of outline, ornament and hue.

Framed in darkest hair, rose a face delicately cut, but cold and colorless as that of any statue in the vestibule without. The lips were slightly parted with the long slow breaths that came and went, the forehead was femininely broad and low, the brows straight and black, and underneath them the mysterious eyes fixed on vacancy, full of that weird regard so hard to counterfeit, so impossible to describe; for though absent, it was not expressionless, and through its steadfast shine a troubled meaning wandered, as if soul and body could not be utterly divorced by any effort of the will. She seemed unconscious of the scene about her, for the fixture of her glance never changed, and nothing about her stirred but the jewel on her bosom, whose changeful glitter seemed to vary as it rose and fell. Emboldened by this apparent absorption, I prolonged my scrutiny and scanned this countenance as I had never done a woman's face before. During this examination I had forgotten myself in her, feeling only a strong desire to draw nearer and dive deeper into those two dark wells that seemed so tranquil yet so fathomless, and in the act of trying to fix shape, color and expression in my memory, I lost them all; for a storm of applause broke the attentive hush as the curtain fell, and like one startled from sleep a flash of intelligence lit up the eyes, then a white hand was passed across them, and long downcast lashes hid them from my sight.

Louis stood up, gave himself a comprehensive survey, and walked out, saying, with a nod,

"Now, Max, put on your gloves, shake the hair out of your eyes, assume your best 'deportment,' and come and take an observation which may immortalize your name."

Knocking over a chair in my haste, I followed close upon his heels, as he tapped at the next door; the lad opened it, bowed to my conductor, glanced at me and strolled away, while we passed in. The elderly lady was awake, now, and received us graciously; the younger was leaning on her hand, the plumy fan held between her and the glare of the great chandelier as she watched the moving throng below.

"Agatha, here is Mr. Yorke and a friend whom he wishes to present to you," said the old lady, with a shade of deference in her manner which betrayed the companion, not the friend.

Agatha turned, gave Louis her hand, with a slow smile dawning on her lip, and looked up at me as if the fact of my advent had no particular interest for her, and my appearance promised no great pleasure.

"Miss Eure, my friend Max Erdmann yearned to be made happy by a five minutes audience, and I ventured to bring him without sending an *avant courier* to prepare the way. Am I forgiven?" with which half daring, half apologetic introduction, Louis turned to the chaperone and began to rattle.

Miss Eure bowed, swept the waves of silk from the chair beside her, and I sat down with a bold request waiting at my lips till an auspicious moment came, having resolved not to exert myself for nothing. As we discussed the usual topics suggested by the time and place, I looked often into the face before me and soon found it difficult to look away again, for it was a constant surprise to me. The absent mood had passed and with it the frost seemed to have melted from mien and manner, leaving a living woman in the statue's place. I had thought her melancholy, but her lips were dressed in smiles, and frequent peals of low-toned laughter parted them like pleasant music; I had thought her pale, but in either cheek now bloomed a color deep and clear as any tint my palette could have given; I had thought her shy and proud at first, but with each moment her manner warmed, her speech grew franker and her whole figure seemed to glow and brighten as if a brilliant lamp were lit behind the pale shade she had worn before. But the eyes were the greatest surprise of all—I had fancied them dark, and found them the light, sensitive gray belonging to highly nervous temperaments. They were remarkable eyes; for though softly fringed with shadowy lashes they were not mild, but fiery and keen, with many lights and shadows in them as the pupils dilated, and the irids shone with a transparent lustre which varied with her varying words, and proved the existence of an ardent, imperious nature underneath the seeming snow.

They exercised a curious fascination over me and kept my own obedient to their will, although scarce conscious of it at the time and believing mine to be the controlling power. Wherein the charm lay I cannot tell; it was not the influence of a womanly presence alone, for fairer faces had smiled at me in vain; yet as I sat there I felt a pleasant quietude creep over me, I knew my voice had fallen to a lower key; my eye softened from its wonted cold indifference, my manner grown smooth and my demeanor changed to one almost as courtly as my friend's, who well deserved his soubriquet of "Louis the Debonnair."

"It is because my long fret is over," I thought, and having something to gain, exerted myself to please so successfully that, soon emboldened by her gracious mood and the flattering compliments bestowed upon my earlier works, I ventured to tell my present strait and the daring hope I had conceived that she would help me through it. How I made this blunt request I cannot tell, but remember that it slipped over my tongue as smoothly as if I had meditated upon it for a week. I glanced over my shoulder as I spoke, fearing Louis might mar all with apology or reproof; but he was absorbed in the comely duenna, who was blushing like a girl at the half playful, half serious devotion he paid all womankind; and reassured, I waited, wondering how Miss Eure would receive my request. Very quietly; for with no change but a peculiar dropping of the lids, as if her eyes sometimes played the traitor to her will, she answered, smilingly,

"It is I who receive the honor, sir, not you, for genius possesses the privileges of royalty, and may claim subjects everywhere, sure that its choice ennobles and its power extends beyond the narrow bounds of custom, time and place. When shall I serve you, Mr. Erdmann?"

At any other time I should have felt surprised both at her and at myself; but just then, in the ardor of the propitious moment, I thought only of my work, and with many thanks for her great kindness left the day to her, secretly hoping she would name an early one. She sat silent an instant, then seemed to come to some determination, for when she spoke a shadow of mingled pain and patience swept across her face as if her resolve had cost her some sacrifice of pride or feeling.

"It is but right to tell you that I may not always have it in my power to give you the expression you desire to catch, for the eyes you honor by wishing to perpetuate are not strong and often fail me for a time. I have been utterly blind once and may be again, yet have no present cause to fear it, and if you can come to me on such days as they will serve your purpose, I shall be most glad to do my best for you. Another reason makes me bold to ask this favor of you, I cannot always summon this absent mood, and should certainly fail in a strange place; but in my own home, with all familiar things about me, I can more easily fall into one of my deep reveries and forget time by the hour together. Will this arrangement cause much inconvenience or delay? A room shall be prepared for you—kept inviolate as long as you desire it—and every facility my house affords is at your service, for I feel much interest in the work which is to add another success to your life."

She spoke regretfully at first, but ended with a cordial glance as if she had forgotten herself in giving pleasure to another. I felt that it must have cost her an effort to confess that such a dire affliction had ever darkened her youth and might still return to sadden her prime; this pity mingled with my expressions of gratitude for the unexpected interest she bestowed upon my work, and in a few words the arrangement was made, the day and hour fixed, and a great load off my mind. What the afterpiece was I never knew; Miss Eure stayed to please her young companion, Louis stayed to please himself, and I remained because I had not energy enough to go away. For, leaning where I first sat down, I still looked and listened with a dreamy sort of satisfaction to Miss Eure's low voice, as with downcast eyes, still shaded by her fan, she spoke enthusiastically and well of art (the one interesting theme to me) in a manner which proved that she had read and studied more than her modesty allowed her to acknowledge.

We parted like old friends at her carriage door, and as I walked away with Louis in the cool night air I felt like one who had been asleep in a closed room, for I was both languid and drowsy, though a curious undercurrent of excitement still stirred my blood and tingled along my nerves. "A theatre is no place for me," I decided, and anxious to forget myself said aloud:

"Tell me all you know about that woman."

"What woman, Max?"

"Miss Agatha Eure, the owner of the eyes."

"Aha! smitten at last! That ever I should live to see our Benedict the victim of love at first sight!"

"Have done with your nonsense, and answer my question. I don't ask from mere curiosity, but that I may have some idea how to bear myself at these promised sittings; for it will never do to ask after her papa if she has none, to pay my respects to the old lady as her mother if she is only the duenna, or joke with the lad if he is the heir apparent."

"Do you mean to say that you asked her to sit to you?" cried Louis, falling back a step and staring at me with undisguised astonishment.

"Yes, why not?"

"Why, man, Agatha Eure is the haughtiest piece of humanity ever concocted; and I, with all my daring, never ventured to ask more than an occasional dance with her, and feel myself especially favored that she deigns to bow to me, and lets me pick up her gloves or carry her bouquet as a mark of supreme condescension. What witchcraft did you bring to bear upon her? and how did she grant your audacious request?"

"Agreed to it at once."

"Like an empress conferring knighthood, I fancy."

"Not at all. More like a pretty woman receiving a compliment to her beauty—though she is not pretty, by the way."

Louis indulged himself in the long, low whistle, which seems the only adequate expression for masculine surprise. I enjoyed his amazement, it was my turn to laugh now, and I did so, as I said:

"You are always railing at me for my avoidance of all womankind, but you see I have not lost the art of pleasing, for I won your haughty Agatha to my will in fifteen minutes, and am not only to paint her handsome eyes, but to do it at her own house, by her own request. I am beginning to find that, after years of effort, I have mounted a few more rounds of the social ladder than I was aware of, and may now confer as well as receive favors; for she seemed to think me the benefactor, and I rather enjoyed the novelty of the thing. Now tell your story of 'the haughtiest piece of humanity' ever known. I like her the better for that trait."

Louis nodded his head, and regarded the moon with an aspect of immense wisdom, as he replied:

"I understand it now; it all comes back to me, and my accusation holds good, only the love at first sight is on the other side. You shall have your story, but it may leave the picture in the lurch if it causes you to fly off, as you usually see fit to do when a woman's name is linked with your own. You never saw Miss Eure before; but what you say reminds me that she has seen you, for one day last autumn, as I was driving with her and old madame—a mark of uncommon favor, mind you—we saw you striding along, with your hat over your eyes, looking very much like a comet streaming down the street. It was crowded, and as you waited at the crossing you spoke to Jack Mellot, and while talking pulled off your hat and tumbled your hair about, in your usual fashion, when very earnest. We were blockaded by cars and coaches for a moment, so Miss Eure had a fine opportunity to feast her eyes upon you, 'though you are not pretty, by the way.' She asked your name, and when I told her she gushed out into a charming little stream of interest in your daubs, and her delight at seeing their creator; all of which was not agreeable to me, for I considered myself much the finer work of art of the two. Just then you caught up a shabby child with a big basket, took them across, under our horses' noses, with never a word for me, though I called to you, and, diving into the crowd, disappeared. 'I like that,' said Miss Eure; and as we drove on she asked questions, which I answered in a truly Christian manner, doing you no harm, old lad; for I told all you had fought through, with the courage of a stout-hearted man, all you had borne with the patience of a woman, and what a grand future lay open to you, if you chose to accept and use it, making quite a fascinating little romance of it, I assure you. There the matter dropped. I forgot it till this minute, but it accounts for the ease with which you gained your first suit, and is prophetic of like success in a second and more serious one. She is young, well-born, lovely to those who love her, and has a fortune and position which will lift you at once to the topmost round of the long ladder you've been climbing all these years. I wish you joy, Max."

"Thank you. I've no time for lovemaking, and want no fortune but that which I earn for myself. I am already married to a fairer wife than Miss Eure, so you may win and wear the lofty lady yourself."

Louis gave a comical groan,

"I've tried that, and failed; for she is too cold to be warmed by any flame of mine, though she is wonderfully attractive when she likes, and I hover about her even now like an infatuated moth, who beats his head against the glass and never reaches the light within. No; you must thankfully accept the good the gods bestow. Let Art be your Leah, but Agatha your Rachel. And so, good-night!"

"Stay and tell me one thing—is she an orphan?"

"Yes; the last of a fine old race, with few relatives and few friends, for death has deprived her of the first, and her own choice of the last. The lady you saw with her plays propriety in her establishment; the lad is Mrs. Snow's son, and fills the rôle of *cavaliere-servente;* for Miss Eure is a Diana toward men in general, and leads a quietly luxurious life among her books, pencils and music, reading and studying all manner of things few women of two-and-twenty care to know. But she has the wit to see that a woman's mission is to be charming, and when she has sufficient motive for the exertion she fulfils that mission most successfully, as I know to my sorrow. Now let me off, and be for ever grateful for the good turn I have done you to-night, both in urging you to go to the theatre and helping you to your wish when you got there."

We parted merrily, but his words lingered in my memory, and half unconsciously exerted a new influence over me, for they flattered the three ruling passions that make or mar the fortunes of us all—pride, ambition, and self-love. I wanted power, fame, and ease, and all seemed waiting for me, not in the dim future but the actual present, if my friend's belief was to be relied upon; and remembering all I had seen and heard that night, I felt that it was not utterly without foundation. I pleased myself for an idle hour in dreaming dreams of what might be; finding that amusement began to grow dangerously attractive, I demolished my castles in the air with the last whiff of my meerschaum, and fell asleep, echoing my own words:

"Art is my wife, I will have no other!"

Punctual to the moment I went to my appointment, and while waiting an answer to my ring took an exterior survey of Miss Eure's house. One of an imposing granite block, it stood in a West End square, with every sign of unostentatious opulence about it. I was very susceptible to all influences, either painful or pleasant, and as I stood there the bland atmosphere that surrounded me seemed most attractive; for my solitary life had been plain and poor, with little time for ease, and few ornaments to give it grace. Now I seemed to have won the right to enjoy both if I would; I no longer felt out of place there, and with this feeling came the wish to try the sunny side of life, and see if its genial gifts would prove more inspiring than the sterner masters I had been serving so long.

The door opened in the middle of my reverie, and I was led through an anteroom, lined with warm-hued pictures, to a large apartment, which had been converted into an impromptu studio by some one who understood all the requisites for such a place. The picture, my easel and other necessaries had preceded me, and I thought to have spent a good hour in arranging matters. All was done, however, with a skill that surprised me; the shaded windows, the carefully-arranged brushes, the proper colors already on the palette, the easel and picture placed as they should be, and a deep curtain hung behind a small dais, where I fancied my model was to sit. The room was empty as I entered, and with the brief message, "Miss Eure will be down directly," the man noiselessly departed.

I stood and looked about me with great satisfaction, thinking, "I cannot fail to work well surrounded by such agreeable sights and sounds." The house was very still, for the turmoil of the city was subdued to a murmur, like the far-off music of the sea; a soft gloom filled the room, divided by one strong ray that fell athwart my picture, gifting it with warmth and light. Through a half-open door I saw the green vista of a conservatory, full of fine blendings of color, and wafts of many odors blown to me by the west wind rustling through orange trees and slender palms; while the only sound that broke the silence was the voice of a flame-colored foreign bird, singing a plaintive little strain like a sorrowful lament. I liked this scene, and, standing in the doorway, was content to look, listen and enjoy, forgetful of time, till a slight stir made me turn and for a moment look straight before me with a startled aspect. It seemed as if my picture had left its frame; for, standing on the narrow dais, clearly defined against the dark background, stood the living likeness of the figure I had painted, the same white folds falling from neck to ankle, the same shadowy hair, and slender hands locked together, as if wrung in slow despair; and fixed full upon my own the weird, unseeing eyes, which made the face a pale mask, through which the haunted spirit spoke eloquently, with its sleepless anguish and remorse.

"Good morning, Miss Eure; how shall I thank you?" I began, but stopped abruptly, for without speaking she waved me towards the easel with a gesture which seemed to say, "Prove your gratitude by industry."

"Very good," thought I, "if she likes the theatrical style she shall have it. It is evident she has studied her part and will play it well, I will do the same, and as Louis recommends, take the good the gods send me while I may."

Without more ado I took my place and fell to work; but, though never more eager to get on, with each moment that I passed I found my interest in the picture grow less and less intent, and with every glance at my model found that it was more and more difficult to look away. Beautiful she was not, but the wild and woful figure seemed to attract me as no Hebe, Venus or sweet-faced Psyche had ever done. My hand moved slower and slower, the painted face grew dimmer and dimmer, my glances lingered longer and longer, and presently palette and brushes rested on my knee, as I leaned back in the deep chair and gave myself up to an uninterrupted stare. I knew that it was rude, knew that it was a trespass on Miss Eure's kindness as well as a breach of good manners, but I could not help it, for my eyes seemed beyond my control, and though I momentarily expected to see her color rise and hear some warning of the lapse of time, I never looked away, and soon forgot to imagine her feelings in the mysterious confusion of my own.

I was first conscious of a terrible fear that I ought to speak or move, which seemed impossible, for my eyelids began to be weighed down by a delicious drowsiness in spite of all my efforts to keep them open. Everything grew misty, and the beating of my heart sounded like the rapid, irregular roll of a muffled drum; then a strange weight seemed to oppress and cause me to sigh long and deeply. But soon the act of breathing appeared to grow unnecessary, for a sensation of wonderful airiness came over me, and I felt as if I could float away like a thistledown. Presently every sense seemed to fall asleep, and in the act of dropping both palette and brush I drifted away into a sea of blissful repose, where nothing disturbed me but a fragmentary dream that came and went like a lingering gleam of consciousness through the new experience which had befallen me.

I seemed to be still in the quiet room, still leaning in the deep chair with half-closed eyes, still watching the white figure before me, but that had changed. I saw a smile break over the lips, something like triumph flash into the eyes, sudden color flush the cheeks, and the rigid hands lifted to gather up and put the long hair back; then with noiseless steps it came nearer and nearer till it stood beside me. For a while it paused there mute and intent, I felt the eager gaze searching my face, but it caused no displeasure; for I seemed to be looking down at myself, as if soul and body had parted company and I was gifted with a double life. Suddenly the vision laid a light hand on my wrist and touched my temples, while a shade of anxiety seemed to flit across its face as it turned and vanished. A dreamy wonder regarding its return woke within me, then my sleep deepened into utter oblivion, for how long I cannot tell. A pungent odor seemed to recall me to the same half wakeful state. I dimly saw a woman's arm holding a glittering object before me, whence the fragrance came; an unseen hand stirred my hair with the grateful drip of water, and once there came a touch like the pressure of lips upon my forehead, soft and warm, but gone in an instant. These new sensations grew rapidly more and more defined; I clearly saw a bracelet on the arm and read the Arabic characters engraved upon the golden coins that formed it; I heard the rustle of garments, the hurried breathing of some near presence, and felt the cool sweep of a hand passing to and fro across my forehead. At this point my thoughts began to shape themselves into words, which came slowly and seemed strange to me as I searched for and connected them, then a heavy sigh rose and broke at my lips, and the sound of my own voice woke me, drowsily echoing the last words I had spoken:

"Good morning, Miss Eure; how shall I thank you?"

To my great surprise the well-remembered voice answered quietly:

"Good morning, Mr. Erdmann; will you have some lunch before you begin?"

How I opened my eyes and got upon my feet was never clear to me, but the first object I saw was Miss Eure coming towards me with a glass in her hand. My expression must have been dazed and imbecile in the extreme, for to add to my bewilderment the tragic robes had disappeared, the dishevelled hair was gathered in shining coils under a Venetian net of silk and gold, a white embroidered wrapper replaced the muslins Lady Macbeth had worn, and a countenance half playful, half anxious, now smiled where I had last seen so sorrowful an aspect. The fear of having committed some great absurdity and endangered my success brought me right with a little shock of returning thought. I collected myself, gave a look about the room, a dizzy bow to her, and put my hand to my head with a vague idea that something was wrong there. In doing this I discovered that my hair was wet, which slight fact caused me to exclaim abruptly:

"Miss Eure, what have I been doing? Have I had a fit? been asleep? or do you deal in magic and rock your guests off into oblivion without a moment's warning?"

Standing before me with uplifted eyes, she answered, smiling:

"No, none of these have happened to you; the air from the Indian plants in the conservatory was too powerful, I think; you were a little faint, but closing the door and opening a window has restored you, and a glass of wine will perfect the cure, I hope."

She was offering the glass as she spoke. I took it but forgot to thank her, for on the arm extended to me was the bracelet never seen so near by my waking eyes, yet as familiar as if my vision had come again. Something struck me disagreeably, and I spoke out with my usual bluntness.

"I never fainted in my life, and have an impression that people do not dream when they swoon. Now I did, and so vivid was it that I still remember the characters engraved on the trinket you wear, for that played a prominent part in my vision. Shall I describe them as proof of it, Miss Eure?"

Her arm dropped at her side and her eyes fell for a moment as I spoke; then she glanced up unchanged, saying as she seated herself and motioned me to do the same:

"No, rather tell the dream, and taste these grapes while you amuse me."

I sat down and obeyed her. She listened attentively, and when I ended explained the mystery in the simplest manner.

"You are right in the first part of your story. I did yield to a whim which seized me when I saw your picture, and came down *en costume*, hoping to help you by keeping up the illusion. You began, as canvas and brushes prove; I stood motionless till you turned pale and regarded me with a strange expression; at first I thought it might be inspiration, as your friend Yorke would say, but presently you dropped everything out of your hands and fell back in your chair. I took the liberty of treating you like a woman, for I bathed your temples and wielded my vinaigrette most energetically till you revived and began to talk of 'Rachel, art, castles in the air, and your wife Lady Macbeth;' then I slipped away and modernized myself, ordered some refreshments for you, and waited till you wished me 'Good-morning."

She was laughing so infectiously that I could not resist joining her and accepting her belief, for curious as the whole affair seemed to me I could account for it in no other way. She was winningly kind, and urged me not to resume my task, but I was secretly disgusted with myself for such a display of weakness, and finding her hesitation caused solely by fears for me, I persisted, and, seating her, painted as I had never done before. Every sense seemed unwontedly acute, and hand and eye obeyed me with a docility they seldom showed. Miss Eure sat where I placed her, silent and intent, but her face did not wear the tragic aspect it had worn before, though she tried to recall it. This no longer troubled me, for the memory of the vanished face was more clearly before me than her own, and with but few and hasty glances at my model, I reproduced it with a speed and skill that filled me with delight. The striking of a clock reminded me that I had far exceeded the specified time, and that even a woman's patience has limits; so concealing my regret at losing so auspicious a mood, I laid down my brush, leaving my work unfinished, yet glad to know I had the right to come again, and complete it in a place and presence which had proved so inspiring.

Miss Eure would not look at it till it was all done, saying in reply to my thanks for the pleasant studio she had given me—"I was not quite unselfish in that, and owe you an apology for venturing to meddle with your property; but it gave me real satisfaction to arrange these things, and restore this room to the aspect it wore three years ago. I, too, was an artist then, and dreamed aspiring dreams here, but was arrested on the threshold of my career by loss of sight; and hard as it seemed then to give up all my longings, I see now that it was better so, for a few years later it would have killed me. I have learned to desire for others what I can never hope for myself, and try to find pleasure in their success, unembittered by regrets for my own defeat. Let this explain my readiness to help you, my interest in your work and my best wishes for your present happiness and future fame."

The look of resignation, which accompanied her words, touched me more than a flood of complaints, and the thought of all she had lost woke such sympathy and pity in my frosty heart, that I involuntarily pressed the hand that could never wield a brush again. Then for the first time I saw those keen eyes soften and grow dim with unshed tears; this gave them the one charm they needed to be beautiful as well as penetrating, and as they met my own, so womanly sweet and grateful, I felt that one might love her while that mood remained. But it passed as rapidly as it came, and when we parted in the anteroom the cold, quiet lady bowed me out, and the tender-faced girl was gone.

I never told Louis all the incidents of that first sitting, but began my story where the real interest ended; and Miss Eure was equally silent, through forgetfulness or for some good reason of her own. I went several times again, yet though the conservatory door stood open I felt no ill effects from the Indian plants that still bloomed there, dreamed no more dreams, and Miss Eure no more enacted the somnambulist. I found an indefinable charm in that pleasant room, a curious interest in studying its mistress, who always met me with a smile, and parted with a look of unfeigned regret. Louis railed me upon my absorption, but it caused me no uneasiness, for it was not love that led me there, and Miss Eure knew it. I never had forgotten our conversation on that first night, and with every interview the truth of my friend's suspicion grew more and more apparent to me. Agatha Eure was a strong-willed, imperious woman, used to command all about her and see her last wish gratified; but now she was conscious of a presence she could not command, a wish she dare not utter, and, though her womanly pride sealed her lips, her eyes often traitorously betrayed the longing of her heart. She was sincere in her love for art, and behind that interest in that concealed, even from herself, her love for the artist; but the most indomitable passion given humanity cannot long be hidden. Agatha soon felt her weakness, and vainly struggled to subdue it. I soon knew my power, and owned its subtle charm, though I disdained to use it.

The picture was finished, exhibited and won me all, and more than I had dared to hope; for rumor served me a good turn, and whispers of Miss Eure's part in my success added zest to public curiosity and warmth to public praise. I enjoyed the little stir it caused, found admiration a sweet draught after a laborious year, and felt real gratitude to the woman who had helped me win it. If my work had proved a failure I should have forgotten her, and been an humbler, happier man; it did not, and she became a part of my success. Her name was often spoken in the same breath with mine, her image was kept before me by no exertion of my own, till the memories it brought with it grew familiar as old friends, and slowly ripened into a purpose which, being born of ambition and not love, bore bitter fruit, and wrought out its own retribution for a sin against myself and her.

The more I won the more I demanded, the higher I climbed the more eager I became; and, at last, seeing how much I could gain by a single step, resolved to take it, even though I knew it to be a false one. Other men married for the furtherance of their ambitions, why should not I? Years ago I had given up love of home for love of fame, and the woman who might have made me what I should be had meekly yielded all, wished me a happy future, and faded from my world, leaving me only a bitter memory, a veiled picture and a quiet grave my feet never visited but once. Miss Eure loved me, sympathised in my aims, understood my tastes; she could give all I asked to complete the purpose of my life, and lift me at once and for ever from the hard lot I had struggled with for thirty years. One word would work the miracle, why should I hesitate to utter it?

I did not long—for three months from the day I first entered that shadowy room I stood there intent on asking her to be my wife. As I waited I lived again the strange hour once passed there, and felt as if it had been the beginning of another dream whose awakening was yet to come. I asked myself if the hard healthful reality was not better than such feverish visions, however brilliant, and the voice that is never silent when we interrogate it with sincerity answered, "Yes." "No matter, I choose to dream, so let the phantom of a wife come to me here as the phantom of a lover came to me so long ago." As I uttered these defiant words aloud, like a visible reply, Agatha appeared upon the threshold of the door. I knew she had heard me—for again I saw the soft-eyed, tender girl, and opened my arms to her without a word. She came at once, and clinging to me with unwonted tears upon her cheek, unwonted fervor in her voice; touched my forehead, as she had done in that earlier dream, whispering like one still doubtful of her happiness—

"Oh, Max! be kind to me, for in all the world I have only you to love."

I promised, and broke that promise in less than a year.

We were married quietly, went away till the nine days gossip was over, spent our honeymoon as that absurd month is usually spent, and came back to town with the first autumnal frosts; Agatha regretting that I was no longer entirely her own, I secretly thanking heaven that I might drop the lover, and begin my work again, for I was as an imprisoned creature in that atmosphere of "love in idleness," though my bonds were only a pair of loving arms. Madame Snow and son departed, we settled ourselves in the fine house and then endowed with every worldly blessing, I looked about me, believing myself master of my fate, but found I was its slave.

If Agatha could have joined me in my work we might have been happy; if she could have solaced herself with other pleasures and left me to my own, we might have been content; if she had loved me less, we might have gone our separate ways, and yet been friends like many another pair; but I soon found that her affection was of that exacting nature which promises but little peace unless met by one as warm. I had nothing but regard to give her, for it was not in her power to stir a deeper passion in me; I told her this before our marriage, told her I was a cold, hard man, wrapt in a single purpose; but what woman believes such confessions while her heart still beats fast with the memory of her betrothal? She said everything was possible to love, and prophesied a speedy change; I knew it would not come, but having given my warning left the rest to time. I hoped to lead a quiet life and prove that adverse circumstances, not the want of power, had kept me from excelling in the profession I had chosen; but to my infinite discomfort Agatha turned jealous of my art, for finding the mistress dearer than the wife, she tried to wean me from it, and seemed to feel that having given me love, wealth and ease, I should ask no more, but play the obedient subject to a generous queen. I rebelled against this, told her that one-half my time should be hers, the other belonged to me, and I would so employ it that it should bring honor to the name I had given her. But, Agatha was not used to seeing her will thwarted or her pleasure sacrificed to another, and soon felt that though I scrupulously fulfilled my promise, the one task was irksome, the other all absorbing; that though she had her husband at her side his heart was in his studio, and the hours spent with her were often the most listless in his day. Then began that sorrowful experience old as Adam's reproaches to Eve; we both did wrong, and neither repented; both were self-willed, sharp-tongued and proud, and before six months of wedded life had passed we had known many of those scenes which so belittle character and lessen self-respect.

Agatha's love lived through all, and had I answered its appeals by patience, self-denial and genial friendship, if no warmer tie could exist, I might have spared her an early death, and myself from years of bitterest remorse; but I did not. Then her forbearance ended and my subtle punishment began.

"Away again to-night, Max? You have been shut up all day, and I hoped to have you to myself this evening. Hear how the storm rages without, see how cheery I have made all within for you, so put your hat away and stay, for this hour belongs to me, and I claim it."

Agatha took me prisoner as she spoke, and pointed to the cosy nest she had prepared for me. The room was bright and still; the lamp shone clear; the fire glowed; warm-hued curtains muffled the war of gust and sleet without; books, music, a wide-armed seat and a woman's wistful face invited me; but none of these things could satisfy me just then, and though I drew my wife nearer, smoothed her shining hair, and kissed the reproachful lips, I did not yield.

"You must let me go, Agatha, for the great German artist is here, and I had rather give a year of life than miss this meeting with him. I have devoted many evenings to you, and though this hour is yours I shall venture to take it, and offer you a morning call instead. Here are novels, new songs, an instrument, embroidery and a dog, who never can offend by moody silence or unpalatable conversation—what more can a contented woman ask, surely not an absent-minded husband?"

"Yes, just that and nothing more, for she loves him, and he can supply a want that none of these things can. See how pretty I have tried to make myself for you alone; stay, Max, and make me happy."

"Dear, I shall find my pretty wife to-morrow, but the great painter will be gone: let me go, Agatha, and make me happy."

She drew herself from my arm, saying with a flash of the eye—"Max, you are a tyrant!"

"Am I? then you made me so with too much devotion."

"Ah, if you loved me as I loved there would be no selfishness on your part, no reproaches on mine. What shall I do to make myself dearer, Max?"

"Give me more liberty."

"Then I should lose you entirely, and lead the life of a widow. Oh, Max, this is hard, this is bitter, to give all and receive nothing in return."

She spoke passionately, and the truth of her reproach stung me, for I answered with that coldness that always wounded her:

"Do you count an honest name, sincere regard and much gratitude as nothing? I have given you these, and ask only peace and freedom in return. I desire to do justice to you and to myself, but I am not like you, never can be, and you must not hope it. You say love is all-powerful, prove it upon me, I am willing to be the fondest of husbands if I can; teach me, win me in spite of myself, and make me what you will; but leave me a little time to live and labor for that which is dearer to me than your faulty lord and master can ever be to you."

"Shall I do this?" and her face kindled as she put the question.

"Yes, here is an amusement for you, use what arts you will, make your love irresistible, soften my hard nature, convert me into your shadow, subdue me till I come at your call like a pet dog, and when you make your presence more powerful than painting I will own that you have won your will and made your theory good."

I was smiling as I spoke, for the twelve labors of Hercules seemed less impossible than this, but Agatha watched me with her glittering eyes; and answered slowly—

"I will do it. Now go, and enjoy your liberty while you may, but remember when I have conquered that you dared me to it, and keep your part of the compact. Promise this." She offered me her hand with a strange expression— I took it, said good-night, and hurried away, still smiling at the curious challenge given and accepted.

Agatha told me to enjoy my liberty, and I tried to do so that very night, but failed most signally, for I had not been an hour in the brilliant company gathered to meet the celebrated guest before I found it impossible to banish the thought of my solitary wife. I had left her often, yet never felt disturbed by more than a passing twinge of that uncomfortable bosom friend called conscience; but now the interest of the hour seemed lessened by regret, for through varying conversation held with those about me, mingling with the fine music that I heard, looking at me from every woman's face, and thrusting itself into my mind at every turn, came a vague, disturbing self-reproach, which slowly deepened to a strong anxiety. My attention wandered, words seemed to desert me, fancy to be frostbound, and even in the presence of the great man I had so ardently desired to see I could neither enjoy his society nor play my own part well. More than once I found myself listening for Agatha's voice; more than once I looked behind me expecting to see her figure and more than once I resolved to go, with no desire to meet her.

"It is an acute fit of what women call nervousness; I will not yield to it," I thought, and plunged into the gayest group I saw, supped, talked, sang a song, and broke down; told a witty story, and spoiled it; laughed and tried to bear myself like the lightest-hearted guest in the rooms; but it would not do, for stronger and stronger grew the strange longing to go home, and soon it became uncontrollable. A foreboding fear that something had happened oppressed me, and suddenly leaving the festival at its height, I drove home as if life and death depended on the saving of a second. Like one pursuing or pursued I rode, eager only to be there; yet when I stood on my own threshold I asked myself wonderingly, "Why such haste?" and stole in ashamed at my early return. The storm beat without, but within all was serene and still, and with noiseless steps I went up to the room where I had left my wife, pausing a moment at the half open door to collect myself, lest she should see the disorder of both mind and mien. Looking in I saw her sitting with neither book nor work beside her, and after a momentary glance began to think my anxiety had not been causeless, for she sat erect and motionless as an inanimate figure of intense thought; her eyes were fixed, face colorless, with an expression of iron determination, as if every energy of mind and body were wrought up to the achievement of a single purpose. There was something in the rigid attitude and stern aspect of this familiar shape that filled me with dismay, and found vent in the abrupt exclamation,

"Agatha, what is it?"

She sprang up like a steel spring when the pressure is removed, saw me, and struck her hands together, with a wild gesture of surprise, alarm or pleasure, which I could not tell, for in the act she dropped into her seat white and breathless as if smitten with sudden death. Unspeakably shocked, I bestirred myself till she recovered, and though pale and spent, as if with some past exertion, soon seemed quite herself again.

"Agatha, what were you thinking of when I came in?" I asked, as she sat leaning against me with half closed eyes and a faint smile on her lips, as if the unwonted caresses I bestowed upon her were more soothing than any cordial I could give. Without stirring she replied,

"Of you, Max. I was longing for you, with heart and soul and will. You told me to win you in spite of yourself, and I was sending my love to find and bring you home. Did it reach you? did it lead you back and make you glad to come?"

A peculiar chill ran through me as I listened, though her voice was quieter, her manner gentler than usual as she spoke. She seemed to have such faith in her tender fancy, such assurance of its efficacy, and such a near approach to certain knowledge of its success, that I disliked the thought of continuing the topic, and answered cheerfully,

"My own conscience brought me home, dear; for, discovering that I had left my peace of mind behind me, I came back to find it. If your task is to cost a scene like this it will do more harm than good to both of us, so keep your love from such uncanny wanderings through time and space, and win me with less dangerous arts."

She smiled her strange smile, folded my hand in her own, and answered, with soft exultation in her voice,

"It will not happen so again, Max; but I am glad, most glad you came, for it proves I have some power over this wayward heart of yours, where I shall knock until it opens wide and takes me in."

The events of that night made a deep impression on me, for from that night my life was changed. Agatha left me entirely free, never asked my presence, never upbraided me for long absences or silence when together. She seemed to find happiness in her belief that she should yet subdue me, and though I smiled at this in my indifference, there was something half pleasant, half pathetic in the thought of this proud woman leaving all warmer affections for my negligent friendship, the sight of this young wife laboring to win her husband's heart. At first I tried to be all she asked, but soon relapsed into my former life, and finding no reproaches followed, believed I should enjoy it as never before—but I did not. As weeks passed I slowly became conscious that some new power had taken possession of me, swaying my whole nature to its will; a power alien yet sovereign. Fitfully it worked, coming upon me when least desired, enforcing its commands regardless of time, place or mood; mysterious yet irresistible in its strength, this mental tyrant led me at all hours, in all stages of anxiety, repugnance and rebellion, from all pleasures or employments, straight to Agatha. If I sat at my easel the sudden summons came, and wondering at myself I obeyed it, to find her busied in some cheerful occupation, with apparently no thought or wish for me. If I left home I often paused abruptly in my walk or drive, turned and hurried back, simply because I could not resist the impulse that controlled me. If she went away I seldom failed to follow, and found no peace till I was at her side again. I grew moody and restless, slept ill, dreamed wild dreams, and often woke and wandered aimlessly, as if sent upon an unknown errand. I could not fix my mind upon my work; a spell seemed to have benumbed imagination and robbed both brain and hand of power to conceive and skill to execute.

At first I fancied this was only the reaction of entire freedom after long captivity, but I soon found I was bound to a more exacting mistress than my wife had ever been. Then I suspected that it was only the perversity of human nature, and that having gained my wish it grew valueless, and I longed for that which I had lost: but it was not this, for distasteful as my present life had become, the other seemed still more so when I recalled it. For a time I believed that Agatha might be right, that I was really learning to love her, and this unquiet mood was the awakening of that passion which comes swift and strong when it comes to such as I. If I had never loved I might have clung to this belief, but the memory of that earlier affection, so genial, entire and sweet, proved that the present fancy was only a delusion; for searching deeply into myself to discover the truth of this, I found that Agatha was no dearer, and to my own dismay detected a covert dread lurking there, harmless and vague, but threatening to deepen into aversion or resentment for some unknown offence; and while I accused myself of an unjust and ungenerous weakness, I shrank from the thought of her, even while I sought her with the assiduity but not the ardor of a lover.

Long I pondered over this inexplicable state of mind, but found no solution of it; for I would not own, either to myself or Agatha, that the shadow of her prophecy had come to pass, though its substance was still wanting. She sometimes looked inquiringly into my face with those strange eyes of hers, sometimes chid me with a mocking smile when she found me sitting idly before my easel without a line or tint given though hours had passed; and often, when driven by that blind impulse I sought her anxiously among her friends, she would glance at those about her, saying, with a touch of triumph in her mien, "Am I not an enviable wife to have inspired such devotion in this grave husband?" Once, remembering her former words, I asked her playfully if she still "sent her love to find and bring me home?" but she only shook her head and answered, sadly,

"Oh, no; my love was burdensome to you, so I have rocked it to sleep, and laid it where it will not trouble you again."

At last I decided that some undetected physical infirmity caused my disquiet, for years of labor and privation might well have worn the delicate machinery of heart or brain, and this warning suggested the wisdom of consulting medical skill in time. This thought grew as month after month increased my mental malady and began to tell upon my hitherto unbroken health. I wondered if Agatha knew how listless, hollow-eyed and wan I had grown; but she never spoke of it, and an unconquerable reserve kept me from uttering a complaint to her.

One day I resolved to bear it no longer, and hurried away to an old friend in whose skill and discretion I had entire faith. He was out, and while I waited I took up a book that lay among the medical works upon his table. I read a page, then a chapter, turning leaf after leaf with a rapid hand, devouring paragraph after paragraph with an eager eye. An hour passed, still I read on. Dr. L——— did not come, but I did not think of that, and when I laid down the book I no longer needed him, for in that hour I had discovered a new world, had seen the diagnosis of my symptoms set forth in unmistakable terms, and found the key to the mystery in the one word—Magnetism. This was years ago, before spirits had begun their labors for good or ill, before ether and hashish had gifted humanity with eternities of bliss in a second, and while Mesmer's mystical discoveries were studied only by the scientific or philosophic few. I knew nothing of these things, for my whole life had led another way, and no child could be more ignorant of the workings or extent of this wonderful power. There was Indian blood in my veins and superstition lurked there still; consequently the knowledge that I was a victim of this occult magic came upon me like an awful revelation, and filled me with a storm of wrath, disgust and dread.

Like an enchanted spirit who has found the incantation that will free it from subjection, I rejoiced with a grim satisfaction even while I cursed myself for my long blindness, and with no thought for anything but instant accusation on my part, instant confession and atonement on hers, I went straight home, straight into Agatha's presence, and there, in words as brief as bitter, told her that her reign was over. All that was sternest, hottest and most unforgiving ruled me then, and like fire to fire roused a spirit equally strong and high. I might have subdued her by juster and more generous words, but remembering the humiliation of my secret slavery I forgot my own offence in hers, and set no curb on tongue or temper, letting the storm she had raised fall upon her with the suddenness of an unwonted, unexpected outburst.

As I spoke her face changed from its first dismay to a defiant calmness that made it hard as rock and cold as ice, while all expression seemed concentrated in her eye, which burned on me with an unwavering light. There was no excitement in her manner, no sign of fear, or shame, or grief in her mien, and when she answered me her voice was untremulous and clear as when I heard it first.

"Have you done? Then hear me: I knew you long before you dreamed that such a woman as Agatha Eure existed. I was solitary, and longed to be sincerely loved. I was rich, yet I could not buy what is unpurchasable; I was young, yet I could not make my youth sweet with affection; for nowhere did I see the friend whose nature was akin to mine until you passed before me, and I felt at once, 'There is the one I seek!' I never yet desired that I did not possess the coveted object, and believed I should not fail now. Years ago I learned the mysterious gift I was endowed with, and fostered it; for, un-blessed with beauty, I hoped its silent magic might draw others near enough to see, under this cold exterior, the woman's nature waiting there. The first night you saw me I yielded to an irresistible longing to attract your eye, and for a moment see the face I had learned to love looking into mine. You know how well I succeeded—you know your own lips asked the favor I was so glad to give, and your own will led you to me. That day I made another trial of my skill and succeeded beyond my hopes, but dared not repeat it, for your strong nature was not easily subdued, it was too perilous a game for me to play, and I resolved that no delusion should make you mine. I would have a free gift or none. You offered me your hand, and believing that it held a loving heart, I took it, to find that heart barred against me, and another woman's name engraved upon its door. Was this a glad discovery for a wife to make? Do you wonder she reproached you when she saw her hopes turn to ashes, and could no longer conceal from herself that she was only a stepping-stone to lift an ambitious man to a position which she could not share? You think me weak and wicked; look back upon the year nearly done and ask yourself if many young wives have such a record of neglect, despised love, unavailing sacrifices, long-suffering patience and deepening despair? I had been reading the tear-stained pages of this record when you bid me win you if I could; and with a bitter sense of the fitness of such a punishment, I resolved to do it, still cherishing a hope that some spark of affection might be found. I soon saw the vanity of such a hope, and this hard truth goaded me to redouble my efforts till I had entirely subjugated that arrogant spirit of yours, and made myself master where I would so gladly have been a loving subject. Do you think I have not suffered? have not wept bitter tears in secret, and been wrung by sharper anguish than you have ever known? If you had given any sign of affection, shown any wish to return to me, any shadow of regret for the wrong you had done me, I should have broken my wand like Prospero, and used no magic but the pardon of a faithful heart. You did not, and it has come to this. Before you condemn me, remember that you dared me to do it—that you bid me make my presence more powerful than Art—bid me convert you to my shadow, and subdue you till you came like a pet dog at my call. Have I not obeyed you? Have I not kept my part of the compact? Now keep yours."

There was something terrible in hearing words whose truth wounded while they fell, uttered in a voice whose concentrated passion made its tones distinct and deep, as if an accusing spirit read them from that book whose dread records never are effaced. My hot blood cooled, my harsh mood softened, and though it still burned, my resentment sank lower, for, remembering the little life to be, I wrestled with myself, and won humility enough to say, with regretful energy:

"Forgive me, Agatha, and let this sad past sleep. I have wronged you, but I believed I sinned no more than many another man who, finding love dead, hoped to feed his hunger with friendship and ambition. I never thought of such an act till I saw affection in your face; that tempted me, and I tried to repay all you gave me by the offer of the hand you mutely asked. It was a bargain often made in this strange world of ours, often repented as we repent now. Shall we abide by it, and by mutual forbearance recover mutual peace? or shall I leave you free, to make life sweeter with a better man, and find myself poor and honest as when we met?"

Something in my words stung her; and regarding me with the same baleful aspect, she lifted her slender hand, so wasted since I made it mine, that the single ornament it wore dropped into her palm, and holding it up, she said, as if prompted by the evil genius that lies hidden in every heart:

"I will do neither. I have outlived my love, but pride still remains; and I will not do as you have done, take cold friendship or selfish ambition to fill an empty heart; I will not be pitied as an injured woman, or pointed at as one who staked all on a man's faith and lost; I will have atonement for my long-suffering—you owe me this, and I claim it. Henceforth you are the slave of the ring, and when I command you must obey, for I possess a charm you cannot defy. It is too late to ask for pity, pardon, liberty or happier life; law and gospel joined us, and as yet law and gospel cannot put us asunder. You have brought this fate upon yourself, accept it, submit to it, for I have bought you with my wealth, I hold you with my mystic art, and body and soul, Max Erdmann, you are mine!"

I knew it was all over then, for a woman never flings such taunts in her husband's teeth till patience, hope and love are gone. A desperate purpose sprung up within me as I listened, yet I delayed a moment before I uttered it, with a last desire to spare us both.

"Agatha, do you mean that I am to lead the life I have been leading for three months—a life of spiritual slavery worse than any torment of the flesh?"

"I do."

"Are you implacable? and will you rob me of all self-control, all peace, all energy, all hope of gaining that for which I have paid so costly a price?"

"I will."

"Take back all you have given me, take my good name, my few friends, my hard-earned success; leave me stripped of every earthly blessing, but free me from this unnatural subjection, which is more terrible to me than death!"

"I will not!"

"Then your own harsh decree drives me from you, for I will break the bond that holds me, I will go out of this house and never cross its threshold while I live—never look into the face which has wrought me all this ill. There is no law, human or divine, that can give you a right to usurp the mastery of another will, and if it costs life and reason I will not submit to it."

"Go when and where you choose, put land and sea between us, break what ties you may, there is one you cannot dissolve, and when I summon you, in spite of all resistance, you must come."

"I swear I will not!"

I spoke out of a blind and bitter passion, but I kept my oath. How her eyes glittered as she lifted up that small pale hand of hers, pointed with an ominous gesture to the ring, and answered:

"Try it."

As she spoke like a sullen echo came the crash of the heavy picture that hung before us. It bore Lady Macbeth's name, but it was a painted image of my wife. I shuddered as I saw it fall, for to my superstitious fancy it seemed a fateful incident; but Agatha laughed a low metallic laugh that made me cold to hear and whispered like a sibyl:

"Accept the omen; that is a symbol of the Art you worship so idolatrously that a woman's heart was sacrificed for its sake. See where it lies in ruins at your feet, never to bring you honor, happiness or peace: for I speak the living truth when I tell you that your ambitious hopes will vanish, the cloud of dust now rising like a veil between us, and the memory of this year will haunt you day and night, till the remorse you painted shall be written upon heart, and face, and life. Now go!"

Her swift words and forceful gesture seemed to banish me for ever, and, like one walking in his sleep, I left her there, a stern, still figure, with its shattered image at its feet.

That instant I departed, but not far—for as yet I could not clearly see which way duty led me. I made no confidante, asked no sympathy or help, told no one of my purpose, but resolving to take no decisive step rashly, I went away to a country house of Agatha's, just beyond the city, as I had once done before when busied on a work that needed solitude and quiet, so that if gossip rose it might be harmless to us both. Then I sat down and thought. Submit I would not, desert her utterly I could not, but I dared defy her, and I did; for as if some viewless spirit whispered the suggestion in my ear, I determined to oppose my will to hers, to use her weapons if I could, and teach her to be merciful through suffering like my own. She had confessed my power to draw her to me, in spite of coldness, poverty and all lack of the attractive graces women love; that clue inspired me with hope. I got books and pored over them till their meaning grew clear to me; I sought out learned men and gathered help from their wisdom; I gave myself to the task with indomitable zeal, for I was struggling for the liberty that alone made life worth possessing. The world believed me painting mimic woes, but I was living through a fearfully real one: friends fancied me busied with the mechanism of material bodies, but I was prying into the mysteries of human souls; and many envied my luxurious leisure in that leafy nest, while I was leading the life of a doomed convict; for as I kept my sinful vow so Agatha kept hers.

She never wrote, or sent, or came, but day and night she called me—day and night I resisted, saved only by the desperate means I used—means that made my one servant think me mad. I bid him lock me in my chamber; I dashed out at all hours to walk fast and far away into the lonely forest; I drowned consciousness in wine; I drugged myself with opiates, and when the crisis had passed, woke spent but victorious. All arts I tried, and slowly found that in this conflict of opposing wills my own grew stronger with each success, the other lost power with each defeat. I never wished to harm my wife, never called her, never sent a baneful thought or desire along that mental telegraph which stretched and thrilled between us; I only longed to free myself, and in this struggle weeks passed, yet neither won a signal victory, for neither proud heart knew the beauty of self-conquest and the power of submission.

One night I went up to the lonely tower that crowned the house, to watch the equinoctial storm that made a Pandemonium of the elements without. Rain streamed as if a second deluge was at hand; whirlwinds tore down the valley; the river chafed and foamed with an angry dash, and the city lights shone dimly through the flying mist as I watched them from my lofty room. The tumult suited me, for my own mood was stormy, dark and bitter, and when the cheerful fire invited me to bask before it I sat there wrapped in reveries as gloomy as the night. Presently the well-known premonition came with its sudden thrill through blood and nerves and with a revengeful strength never felt before I gathered up my energies for the trial, as I waited some more urgent summons. None came, but in its place a sense of power flashed over me, a swift exultation dilated within me, time seemed to pause, the present rolled away, and nothing but an isolated memory remained, for fixing my thoughts on Agatha, I gave myself up to the dominant spirit that possessed me. I sat motionless, yet I willed to see her. Vivid as the flames that framed it, a picture started from the red embers, and clearly as if my bodily eye rested on it, I saw the well-known room, I saw my wife lying in a deep chair, wan and wasted as if with suffering of soul and body, I saw her grope with outstretched hands, and turn her head with eyes whose long lashes never lifted from the cheek where they lay so dark and still, and through the veil that seemed to wrap my senses I heard my own voice, strange and broken, whispering:

"God forgive me, she is blind!"

For a moment the vision wandered mistily before me, then grew steady, and I saw her steal like a wraith across the lighted room, so dark to her; saw her bend over a little white nest my own hands placed there, and lift some precious burden in her feeble arms; saw her grope painfully back again, and sitting by that other fire—not solitary like my own—lay her pale cheek to that baby cheek and seem to murmur some lullaby that mother-love had taught her. Over my heart strong and sudden gushed a warmth never known before, and again, strange and broken through the veil that wrapped my senses, came my own voice whispering:

"God be thanked, she is not utterly alone!"

As if my breath dissolved it, the picture faded; but I willed again and another rose—my studio, dim with dust, damp with long disuse, dark with evening gloom—for one flickering lamp made the white shapes ghostly, and the pictured faces smile or frown with fitful vividness. There was no semblance of my old self there, but in the heart of the desolation and the darkness Agatha stood alone, with outstretched arms and an imploring face, full of a love and longing so intense that with a welcoming gesture and a cry that echoed through the room, I answered that mute appeal:

"Come to me! come to me!"

A gust thundered at the window, and rain fell like stormy tears, but nothing else replied; as the bright brands dropped, the flame died out, and with it that sad picture of my deserted home. I longed to stir but could not, for I had called up a power I could not lay, the servant ruled the master now, and like one fastened by a spell I still sat leaning forward intent upon a single thought. Slowly from the gray embers smouldering on the hearth a third scene rose behind the smoke wreaths, changeful, dim and strange. Again my former home, again my wife, but this time standing on the threshold of the door I had sworn never to cross again. I saw the wafture of the cloak gathered about her, saw the rain beat on her shelterless head, and followed that slight figure through the deserted streets, over the long bridge where the lamps flickered in the wind, along the leafy road, up the wide steps and in at the door whose closing echo startled me to the consciousness that my pulses were beating with a mad rapidity, that a cold dew stood upon my forehead, that every sense was supernaturally alert, and that all were fixed upon one point with a breathless intensity that made that little span of time as fearful as the moment when one hangs poised in air above a chasm in the grasp of nightmare. Suddenly I sprang erect, for through the uproar of the elements without, the awesome hush within, I heard steps ascending, and stood waiting in a speechless agony to see what shape would enter there.

One by one the steady footfalls echoed on my ear, one by one they seemed to bring the climax of some blind conflict nearer, one by one they knelled a human life away, for as the door swung open Agatha fell down before me, storm-beaten, haggard, spent, but loving still, for with a faint attempt to fold her hands submissively, she whispered:

"You have conquered, I am here!" and with that act grew still for ever, as with a great shock I woke to see what I had done.

Ten years have passed since then. I sit on that same hearth a feeble, white-haired man, and beside me, the one companion I shall ever know, my little son—dumb, blind and imbecile. I lavish tender names upon him, but receive no sweet sound in reply; I gather him close to my desolate heart, but meet no answering caress; I look with yearning glance, but see only those haunting eyes, with no gleam of recognition to warm them, no ray of intellect to inspire them, no change to deepen their sightless beauty; and this fair body moulded with the Divine sculptor's gentlest grace is always here before me, an embodied grief that wrings my heart with its pathetic innocence, its dumb reproach. This is the visible punishment for my sin, but there is an unseen retribution heavier than human judgment could inflict, subtler than human malice could conceive, for with a power made more omnipotent by death Agatha still calls me. God knows I am willing now, that I long with all the passion of desire, the anguish of despair to go to her, and He knows that the one tie that holds me is this aimless little life, this duty that I dare not neglect, this long atonement that I make. Day and night I listen to the voice that whispers to me through the silence of these years; day and night I answer with a yearning cry from the depths of a contrite spirit; day and night I cherish the one sustaining hope that Death, the great consoler, will soon free both father and son from the inevitable doom a broken law has laid upon them; for then I know that somewhere in the long hereafter my remorseful soul will find her, and with its poor offering of penitence and love fall down before her, humbly saying:

"You have conquered, I am here!"

The Abbot's Ghost

or, Maurice Treherne's Temptation

A Christmas Story

Editor's Note: When she wrote at length, Alcott had room to fill out her thrillers with all the gothic flourishes they could accommodate. "The Abbot's Ghost: or, Maurice Treherne's Temptation" is one of her longer tales, and it is chock-full of the fundamentals that made gothic fiction so popular: a dark family secret, an ancient curse, a miraculous healing, a haunted abbey, and a ghostly tryst. Although her stories abound with seemingly uncanny occurrences, this is one of the few in which she does not demystify the supernatural events with a rational explanation by the story's end. The intrusion of the supernatural gives the tale a genuine sense of foreboding not found in her other thrillers.

Chapter I

~

Dramatis Personæ

How goes it, Frank? Down first, as usual."

"The early bird gets the worm, major."

"Deuced ungallant speech, considering that the lovely Octavia is the worm," and with a significant laugh the major assumed an Englishman's favorite attitude before the fire.

His companion shot a quick glance at him, and an expression of anxiety passed over his face as he replied, with a well-feigned air of indifference:

"You are altogether too sharp, major; I must be on my guard while you are in the house. Any new arrivals? I thought I heard a carriage drive up not long ago."

"It was General Snowdon and his charming wife; Maurice Treherne came while we were out, and I've not seen him yet, poor fellow!"

"Ay, you may well say that; his is a hard case, if what I heard is true. I'm not booked up in the matter, and I should be, lest I make some blunder here, so tell me how things stand, major; we've a good half hour before dinner, Sir Jasper is never punctual."

"Yes, you've a right to know, if you are going to try your fortune with Octavia."

The major marched through the three drawing-rooms, to see that no inquisitive servant was eavesdropping, and finding all deserted, he resumed his place, while young Annon lounged on a couch as he listened with intense interest to the major's story.

"You know it was supposed that old Sir Jasper, being a bachelor, would leave his fortune to his two nephews. But he was an oddity, and as the title *must* go to young Jasper by right, the old man said Maurice should have the money. He was poor, young Jasper rich, and it seemed but just, though *Madame Mère* was very angry when she learned how the will was made."

"But Maurice didn't get the fortune, how was that?"

"There was some mystery there which I shall discover in time. All went smoothly till that unlucky yachting trip, when the cousins were wrecked. Maurice saved Jasper's life, and almost lost his own in so doing. I fancy he wishes he had, rather than remain the poor cripple he is. Exposure, exertion and neglect afterward brought on paralysis of the lower limbs, and there he is, a fine, talented, spirited fellow tied to that cursed chair like a decrepit old man."

"How does he bear it?" asked Annon, as the major shook his gray head, with a traitorous huskiness in his last words.

"Like a philosopher or a hero. He is too proud to show his despair at such a sudden end to all his hopes, too generous to complain, for Jasper is desperately cut up about it, and too brave to be daunted by a misfortune which would drive many a man mad."

"Is it true that Sir Jasper, knowing all this, made a new will, and left every cent to his namesake?"

"Yes, and there lies the mystery. Not only did he leave it away from poor Maurice, but so tied it up that Jasper cannot transfer it, and at his death it goes to Octavia."

"The old man must have been demented. What in Heaven's name did he mean by leaving Maurice helpless and penniless after all his devotion to Jasper? Had he done anything to offend the old party?"

"No one knows; Maurice hasn't the least idea of the cause of this sudden whim, and the old man would give no reason for it. He died soon after, and the instant Jasper came to the title and estate, he brought his cousin home, and treats him like a brother. Jasper is a noble fellow, with all his faults, and this act of justice increases my respect for him," said the major, heartily.

"What will Maurice do, now that he can't enter the army as he intended?" asked Annon, who now sat erect, so full of interest was he.

"Marry Octavia, and come to his own, I hope."

"An excellent little arrangement, but Miss Treherne may object," said Annon, rising with sudden kindling of the eye.

"I think not, if no one interferes. Pity, with women, is akin to love, and she pities her cousin in the tenderest fashion. No sister could be more devoted, and as Maurice is a handsome, talented fellow, one can easily foresee the end, if, as I said before, no one interferes to disappoint the poor lad again."

"You espouse his cause, I see, and tell me this that I may stand aside. Thanks for the warning, major; but as Maurice Treherne is a man of unusual power in many ways, I think we are equally matched, in spite of his misfortune. Nay, if anything, he has the advantage of me, for Miss Treherne pities him, and that is a strong ally for my rival. I'll be as generous as I can, but I'll *not* stand aside and relinquish the woman I love without a trial first."

With an air of determination, Annon faced the major, whose keen eyes had read the truth which he had but newly confessed to himself. Major Royston smiled as he listened, and said, briefly, as steps approached:

"Do your best, Maurice will win."

"We shall see," returned Annon, between his teeth.

Here their host entered, and the subject of course was dropped. But the major's words rankled in the young man's mind, and would have been doubly bitter, had he known that their confidential conversation had been overheard. On either side of the great fire-place, was a door leading to a suite of rooms which had been old Sir Jasper's. These apartments had been given to Maurice Treherne, and he had just returned from London, whither he had been to consult a certain famous physician. Entering quietly, he had taken possession of his rooms, and having rested and dressed for dinner, rolled himself into the library, to which led the curtained door on the right. Sitting idly in his light, wheeled chair, ready to enter when his cousin appeared, he had heard the chat of Annon and the major. As he listened, over his usually impassive face passed varying expressions of anger, pain, bitterness and defiance, and when the young man uttered his almost fierce "We shall see," Treherne smiled a scornful smile, and clenched his pale hand with a gesture which proved that a year of suffering had not conquered the man's spirit, though it had crippled his strong body.

A singular face was Maurice Treherne's; well cut and somewhat haughty features; a fine brow under the dark locks that carelessly streaked it, and remarkably piercing eyes. Slight in figure, and wasted by pain, he still retained the grace as native to him as the stern fortitude which enabled him to hide the deep despair of an ambitious nature from every eye, and bear his affliction with a cheerful philosophy more pathetic than the most entire abandonment to grief. Carefully dressed, and with no hint at invalidism but the chair, he bore himself as easily and calmly as if the doom of life-long helplessness did not hang over him. A single motion of the hand sent him rolling noiselessly to the curtained door, but as he did so, a voice exclaimed behind him:

"Wait for me, cousin," and as he turned, a young girl approached, smiling a glad welcome as she took his hand, adding, in a tone of soft reproach, "Home again, and not let me know it, till I heard the good news by accident."

"Was it good news, Octavia?" and Maurice looked up at the frank face with a new expression in those penetrating eyes of his. His cousin's open glance never changed as she stroked the hair off his forehead with the caress one often gives a child, and answered, eagerly:

"The best to me; the house is dull when you are away, for Jasper always becomes absorbed in horses and hounds, and leaves mamma and me to mope by ourselves. But tell me, Maurice, what they said to you, since you would not write."

"A little hope, with time and patience. Help me to wait, dear; help me to wait."

His tone was infinitely sad, and as he spoke, he leaned his cheek against the kind hand he held, as if to find support and comfort there. The girl's face brightened beautifully, though her eyes filled, for to her alone did he betray his pain, and in her alone did he seek consolation.

"I will, I will with heart and hand! Thank Heaven for the hope, and trust me it shall be fulfilled. You look very tired, Maurice, why go in to dinner with all those people? Let me make you cosy here," she added, anxiously.

"Thanks, I'd rather go in, it does me good; and if I stay away, Jasper feels that he must stay with me. I dressed in haste, am I right, little nurse?"

She gave him a comprehensive glance, daintily settled his cravat, brushed back a truant lock, and, with a maternal air that was charming, said:

"My boy is always elegant, and I'm proud of him. Now we'll go in." But with her hand on the curtain she paused, saying quickly, as a voice reached her, "Who is that?"

"Frank Annon, didn't you know he was coming?" Maurice eyed her keenly.

"No, Jasper never told me. Why did he ask him?"

"To please you."

"Me! when he knows I detest the man. No matter, I've got on the color he hates, so he wont annoy me, and Mrs. Snowdon can amuse herself with him. The general has come, you know?"

Treherne smiled, well pleased, for no sign of maiden shame or pleasure did the girl's face betray, and as he watched her while she peeped, he thought, with satisfaction.

"Annon is right, I have the advantage, and I'll keep it at all costs."

"Here is mamma, we must go in," said Octavia, as a stately old lady made her appearance in the drawing-room.

The cousins entered together and Annon watched them covertly, while seemingly intent on paying his respects to "Madame Mère," as his hostess was called by her family.

"Handsomer than ever," he muttered, as his eye rested on the blooming girl, looking more like a rose than ever in the peach-colored silk which he had once condemned because a rival admired it. She turned to reply to the major, and Annon glanced at Treherne with an irrepressible frown, for sickness had not marred the charm of that peculiar face, so colorless and thin that it seemed cut in marble; but the keen eyes shone with a wonderful brilliancy, and the whole countenance was alive with a power of intellect and will which made the observer involuntarily exclaim:

"That man must suffer a daily martyrdom, so crippled and confined; if it last long he will go mad or die."

"General and Mrs. Snowdon," announced the servant, and a sudden pause ensued as every one looked up to greet the new-comers.

A feeble, white-haired old man entered, leaning on the arm of an indescribably beautiful woman. Not thirty yet, tall and nobly moulded, with straight black brows over magnificent eyes; rippling dark hair gathered up in a great knot, and ornamented with a single band of gold. A sweeping dress of wine-colored velvet, set off with a dazzling neck and arms decorated like her stately head with ornaments of Roman gold. At the first glance she seemed a cold, haughty creature, born to dazzle but not to win. A deeper scrutiny detected lines of suffering in that lovely face, and behind the veil of reserve, which pride forced her to wear, appeared the anguish of a strong-willed woman, burdened by a heavy cross. No one would dare express pity or offer sympathy, for her whole air repelled it, and in her gloomy eyes sat scorn of herself mingled with defiance of the scorn of others. A strange, almost tragical-looking woman, in spite of beauty, grace and the cold sweetness of her manner. A faint smile parted her lips as she greeted those about her, and as her husband seated himself beside Lady Treherne, she lifted her head with a long breath, and a singular expression of relief, as if a burden was removed, and for the time being she was free. Sir Jasper was at her side, and as she listened, her eye glanced from face to face.

"Who is with you now?" she asked, in a low, mellow voice that was full of music.

"My sister and my cousin are yonder; you may remember Tavie as a child, she is little more now. Maurice is an invalid, but the finest fellow breathing."

"I understand," and Mrs. Snowdon's eyes softened with a sudden glance of pity for one cousin, and admiration for the other, for she knew the facts.

"Major Royston, my father's friend, and Frank Annon, my own. Do you know him?" asked Sir Jasper.

"No."

"Then allow me to make him happy by presenting him, may I?"

"Not now, I'd rather see your cousin."

"Thanks, you are very kind. I'll bring him over."

"Stay, let me go to him," began the lady, with more feeling in face and voice than one would believe her capable of showing.

"Pardon, it will offend him; he will not be pitied, nor relinquish any of the duties or privileges of a gentleman which he can possibly perform. He is proud, we can understand the feeling, so let us humor the poor fellow."

Mrs. Snowdon bowed silently, and Sir Jasper called out in his hearty, blunt way, as if nothing was amiss with his cousin:

"Maurice, I've an honor for you, come and receive it."

Divining what it was, Treherne noiselessly crossed the room, and with no sign of self-consciousness or embarrassment, was presented to the handsome woman. Thinking his presence might be a restraint, Sir Jasper went away. The instant his back was turned, a change came over both; an almost grim expression replaced the suavity of Treherne's face, and Mrs. Snowdon's smile faded suddenly, while a deep flush rose to her brow, as her eyes questioned his beseechingly.

"How dared you come?" he asked, below his breath.

"The general insisted."

"And you could not change his purpose; poor woman!"

"You will not be pitied, neither will I," and her eyes flashed; then the fire was quenched in tears, and her voice lost all its pride in a pleading tone.

"Forgive me, I longed to see you since your illness, and so I 'dared' to come."

"You shall be gratified; look, quite helpless, crippled for life, perhaps."

The chair was turned from the groups about the fire, and as he spoke, with a bitter laugh Treherne threw back the skin which covered his knees, and showed her the useless limbs once so strong and fleet. She shrunk and paled, put out her hand to arrest him, and cried in an indignant whisper:

"No, no, not that! you know I never meant such cruel curiosity, such useless pain to both—"

"Be still, some one is coming," he returned, inaudibly; adding aloud, as he adjusted the skin and smoothed the rich fur as if speaking of it:

"Yes, it is a very fine one, Jasper gave it me; he spoils me, like a dear, generous-hearted fellow as he is. Ah, Octavia, what can I do for you?"

"Nothing, thank you. I want to recall myself to Mrs. Snowdon's memory, if she will let me."

"No need of that; I never forget happy faces and pretty pictures. Two years ago I saw you at your first ball, and longed to be a girl again."

As she spoke, Mrs. Snowdon pressed the hand shyly offered, and smiled at the spirited face before her, though the shadow in her own eyes deepened, as she met the bright glance of the girl.

"How kind you were that night! I remember you let me chatter away about my family, my cousin, and my foolish little affairs, with the sweetest patience, and made me very happy by your interest. I was homesick, and aunt could never bear to hear of those things. It was before your marriage, and all the kinder, for you were the queen of the night, yet had a word for poor little me."

Mrs. Snowdon was pale to the lips, and Maurice impatiently tapped the arm of his chair, while the girl innocently chatted on:

"I am sorry the general is such an invalid; yet I dare say you find great happiness in taking care of him. It is so pleasant to be of use to those we love." And as she spoke, Octavia leaned over her cousin to hand him the glove he had dropped. The affectionate smile that accompanied the act made the color deepen again in Mrs. Snowdon's cheek, and lit a spark in her softened eyes. Her lips curled, and her voice was sweetly sarcastic, as she answered:

"Yes, it is charming to devote one's life to these dear invalids, and find one's reward in their gratitude. Youth, beauty, health and happiness are small sacrifices if one wins a little comfort for the poor sufferers."

The girl felt the sarcasm under the soft words, and drew back with a troubled face.

Maurice smiled, and glanced from one to the other, saying, significantly:

"Well for me that my little nurse loves her labor, and finds no sacrifice in it. I am fortunate in my choice."

"I trust it may prove so—" Mrs. Snowdon got no further, for at that moment dinner was announced, and Sir Jasper took her away. Annon approached with him, and offered his arm to Miss Treherne, but with an air of surprise and a little gesture of refusal, she said, coldly:

"My cousin always takes me in to dinner. Be good enough to escort the major." And with her hand on the arm of the chair, she walked away, with a mischievous glitter in her eyes.

Annon frowned, and fell back, saying, sharply:

"Come, major, what are you doing there?"

"Making discoveries."

Chapter II
~
By-Play

A right splendid old dowager was Lady Treherne, in her black velvet and point lace, as she sat, erect and stately, on a couch by the drawing-room fire, a couch which no one dare occupy in her absence, or share uninvited. The gentlemen were still over their wine, and the three ladies were alone. My lady never dozed in public, Mrs. Snowdon never gossiped, and Octavia never troubled herself to entertain any guests but those of her own age, so long pauses fell, and conversation languished, till Mrs. Snowdon roamed away into the library. As she disappeared, Lady Treherne beckoned to her daughter, who was idly making chords at the grand piano. Seating herself on the ottoman at her mother's feet, the girl took the still-handsome hand in her own, and amused herself with examining the old-fashioned jewels that covered it, a pretext for occupying her telltale eyes, as she suspected what was coming.

"My dear, I'm not pleased with you, and I tell you so at once, that you may amend your fault," began Madame Mère, in a tender tone, for though a haughty, imperious woman, she idolized her children.

"What have I done, mamma?" asked the girl.

"Say rather, what have you left undone. You have been very rude to Mr. Annon; it must not occur again; not only because he is a guest, but because he is your—brother's friend."

My lady hesitated over the word "lover," and changed it, for to her Octavia still seemed a child, and though anxious for the alliance, she forbore to speak openly, lest the girl should turn willful, as she inherited her mother's high spirit.

"I'm sorry, mamma, but how can I help it, when he teases me so that I detest him?" said Octavia, petulantly.

"How tease, my love?"

"Why, he follows me about like a dog, puts on a sentimental look when I appear; blushes, and beams, and bows at everything I say, if I am polite; frowns and sighs if I'm not, and glowers tragically at every man I speak to, even poor Maurice. O mamma, what foolish creatures men are!" And the girl laughed blithely, as she looked up for the first time into her mother's face.

Her mother smiled, as she stroked the bright head at her knee, but asked, quickly:

"Why say 'even poor Maurice,' as if it were impossible for any one to be jealous of him?"

"But isn't it, mamma? I thought strong, well men regarded him as one set apart, and done with, since his sad misfortune."

"Not entirely; while women pity and pet the poor fellow, his comrades will be jealous, absurd as it is."

"No one pets him but me, and I have a right to do it, for he is my cousin," said the girl, feeling a touch of jealousy herself.

"Rose and Blanche Talbot outdo you, my dear, and there is no cousinship to excuse them."

"Then let Frank Annon be jealous of them, and leave me in peace. They promised to come to-day; I'm afraid something has happened to prevent them;" and Octavia gladly seized upon the new subject. But my lady was not to be eluded.

"They said they could not come till after dinner, they will soon arrive. Before they do so, I must say a few words, Tavia, and I beg you to give heed to them. I desire you to be courteous and amiable to Mr. Annon, and before strangers to be less attentive and affectionate to Maurice. You mean it kindly, but it looks ill, and causes disagreeable remarks."

"Who blames me for being devoted to my cousin? Can I ever do enough to repay him for his devotion? Mamma, you forget he saved your son's life."

Indignant tears filled the girl's eyes, and she spoke passionately, forgetting that Mrs. Snowdon was within ear-shot of her raised voice. With a frown my lady laid her hand on her daughter's lips, saying, coldly:

"I do not forget, and I religiously discharge my every obligation by every care and comfort it is in my power to bestow. You are young, romantic, and tender-hearted. You think you must give your time and health, must sacrifice your future happiness to this duty. You are wrong, and unless you learn wisdom in season, you will find that you have done harm, not good."

"God forbid! How can I do that? tell me, and I will be wise in time."

Turning the earnest face up to her own, Lady Treherne whispered, anxiously:

"Has Maurice ever looked or hinted anything of love during this year he has been with us, and you his constant companion?"

"Never, mamma; he is too honorable and too unhappy to speak or think of that. I am his little nurse, sister and friend, no more, nor ever shall be. Do not suspect us, or put such fears into my mind, else all our comfort will be spoiled."

Flushed and eager was the girl, but her clear eyes betrayed no tender confusion as she spoke, and all her thought seemed to be to clear her cousin from the charge of loving her too well. Lady Treherne looked relieved, paused a moment, then said, seriously but gently:

"This is well, but, child, I charge you tell me at once, if ever he forgets himself, for this thing cannot be. Once I hoped it might; now it is impossible; remember that he continue a friend and cousin, nothing more. I warn you in time, but if you neglect the warning, Maurice must go. No more of this; recollect my wish regarding Mr. Annon, and let your cousin amuse himself without you in public."

"Mamma, do you wish me to like Frank Annon?"

The abrupt question rather disturbed my lady, but knowing her daughter's frank, impetuous nature, she felt somewhat relieved by this candor, and answered, decidedly:

"I do; he is your equal in all respects; he loves you, Jasper desires it, I approve, and you, being heart-whole, can have no just objection to the alliance."

"Has he spoken to you?"

"No, to your brother."

"You wish this much, mamma?"

"Very much, my child."

"I will try to please you, then." And stifling a sigh, the girl kissed her mother with unwonted meekness in tone and manner.

"Now I am well pleased. Be happy, my love; no one will urge or distress you; let matters take their course, and if this hope of ours can be fulfilled, I shall be relieved of the chief care of my life."

A sound of girlish voices here broke on their ears, and springing up, Octavia hurried to meet her friends, exclaiming, joyfully:

"They have come! they have come!"

Two smiling, blooming girls met her at the door, and being at an enthusiastic age, they "gushed" in girlish fashion for several minutes, making a pretty group as they stood in each other's arms, all talking at once, with frequent kisses and little bursts of laughter, as vents for their emotion. Madame Mère welcomed them, and then went to join Mrs. Snowdon, leaving the trio to gossip unrestrained.

"My dearest creature, I thought we never should get here, for papa had a tiresome dinner-party, and we were obliged to stay, you know," cried Rose, the lively sister, shaking out the pretty dress, and glancing at herself in the mirror, as she fluttered about the room like a butterfly.

"We were dying to come, and so charmed when you asked us, for we haven't seen you this age, darling," added Blanche, the pensive one, smoothing her blonde curls after a fresh embrace.

"I'm sorry the Ulsters couldn't come to keep Christmas with us, for we have no gentlemen but Jasper, Frank Annon and the major. Sad, isn't it?" said Octavia, with a look of despair, which caused a fresh peal of laughter.

"One apiece, my dear, it might be worse;" and Rose privately decided to appropriate Sir Jasper.

"Where is your cousin?" asked Blanche, with a sigh of sentimental interest.

"He is here, of course. I forget him, but he is not on the flirting list, you know. We must amuse him, and not expect him to amuse us, though really, all the capital suggestions and plans for merry-making always come from him."

"He is better, I hope?" asked both sisters, with real sympathy, making their young faces womanly and sweet.

"Yes, and has hopes of entire recovery. At least, they tell him so, though Doctor Ashley said there was no chance of it."

"Dear, dear, how sad! Shall we see him, Tavia?"

"Certainly; he is able to be with us now in the evening, and enjoys society as much as ever. But please take no notice of his infirmity, and make no inquiries beyond the usual 'How do you do.' He is sensitive, and hates to be considered an invalid more than ever."

"How charming it must be to take care of him, he is so accomplished and delightful. I quite envy you," said Blanche, pensively.

"Sir Jasper told us that the General and Mrs. Snowdon were coming. I hope they will, for I've a most intense curiosity to see her—" began Rose.

"Hush, she is here with mamma! Why curious? What is the mystery? for you look as if there was one," questioned Octavia, under her breath.

The three charming heads bent toward one another, as Rose replied, in a whisper:

"If I knew, I shouldn't be inquisitive. There was a rumor that she married the old general in a fit of pique, and now repents. I asked mamma once, but she said such matters were not for young girls to hear, and not a word more would she say. N'importe, I have wits of my own, and I can satisfy myself. The gentlemen are coming! Am I all right, dear?" And the three glanced at one another with a swift scrutiny that nothing could escape, then grouped them-selves prettily, and waited, with a little flutter of expectation in each young heart.

In came the gentlemen, and instantly a new atmosphere seemed to pervade the drawing-room, for with the first words uttered, several romances began. Sir Jasper was taken possession of by Rose, Blanche intended to devote herself to Maurice Treherne, but Annon intercepted her, and Octavia was spared any effort at politeness by this unexpected move on the part of her lover.

"He is angry, and wishes to pique me by devoting himself to Blanche. I wish he would, with all my heart, and leave me in peace. Poor Maurice, he expects me, and I long to go to him, but must obey mamma." And Octavia went to join the group formed by my lady, Mrs. Snowdon, the general and the major.

The two young couples flirted in different parts of the room, and Treherne sat alone, watching them all with eyes that pierced below the surface, reading the hidden wishes, hopes and fears that ruled them. A singular expression sat on his face, as he turned from Octavia's clear counte-nance to Mrs. Snowdon's gloomy one. He leaned his head upon his hand, and fell into deep thought, for he was passing through one of those fateful moments which come to us all, and which may make or mar a life. Such moments come when least looked for; an unexpected meeting, a peculiar mood, some trivial circumstance or careless word produces it, and often it is gone before we realize its presence, leaving after-effects to show us what we have gained or lost. Treherne was conscious that the present hour, and the acts that filled it, possessed unusual interest, and would exert an unusual influence on his life. Before him was the good and evil genius of his nature in the guise of those two women. Edith Snowdon had already tried her power, and accident only had saved him. Octavia, all unconscious as she was, never failed to rouse and stimulate the noblest attributes of mind and heart. A year spent in her society had done much for him, and he loved her with a strange mingling of passion, reverence and gratitude. He knew why Edith Snowdon came, he felt that the old fascination had not lost its charm, and though fear was unknown to him, he was ill pleased at the sight of the beautiful, danger-ous woman. On the other hand, he saw that Lady Treherne desired her daughter to shun him and smile on Annon; he acknowledged that he had no right to win the young creature, crippled and poor as he was, and a pang of jealous pain wrung his heart as he watched her.

Then a sense of power came to him, for helpless, poor, and seemingly an object of pity, he yet felt that he held the honor, peace and happiness of nearly every person present in his hands. It was a strong temptation to this man, so full of repressed passion and power, so set apart and shut out from the more stirring duties and pleasures of life. A few words from his lips, and the pity all felt for him would be turned to fear, respect and admiration. Why not utter them, and enjoy all that was possible? He owed the Trehernes nothing; why suffer injustice, dependence, and the compassion that wounds a proud man deepest? Wealth, love, pleasure might be his with a breath, why not secure them now?

His pale face flushed, his eye kindled, and his thin hand lay clenched like a vice, as these thoughts passed rapidly through his mind. A look, a word at that moment would sway him; he felt it, and leaned forward, waiting in secret suspense for the glance, the speech which should decide him for good or ill. Who shall say what subtle instinct caused Octavia to turn and smile at him with a wistful, friendly look that warmed his heart? He met it with an answering glance, which thrilled her strangely, for love, gratitude, and some mysterious intelligence met and mingled in the brilliant yet soft expression which swiftly shone and faded in her face. What it was she could not tell, she only felt that it filled her with an indescribable emotion never experienced before. In an instant it all passed, Lady Treherne spoke to her, and Blanche Talbot addressed Maurice, wondering, as she did so, if the enchanting smile he wore was meant for her.

"Mr. Annon having mercifully set me free, I came to try to cheer your solitude; but you look as if solitude made you happier than society does the rest of us," she said, without her usual affectation, for his manner impressed her.

"You are very kind and very welcome. I do find pleasures to beguile my loneliness, which gayer people would not enjoy, and it is well that I can, else I should turn morose and tyrannical, and doom some unfortunate to entertain me all day long," he answered with a gentle curtsey which was his chief attraction to womankind.

"Pray tell me some of your devices. I'm often alone in spirit, if not so in the flesh, for Rose, though a dear girl, is not congenial, and I find no kindred soul."

A humorous glimmer came to Treherne's eyes, as the sentimental damsel beamed a soft sigh, and drooped her long lashes effectively. Ignoring the topic of "kindred souls," he answered, coldly:

"My favorite amusement is studying the people around me. It may be rude, but tied to my corner, I cannot help watching the figures around me, and discovering their little plots and plans. I'm getting very expert, and really surprise myself sometimes by the depth of my researches."

"I can believe it; your eyes look as if they possessed that gift. Pray don't study *me*." And the girl shrunk away with an air of genuine alarm.

Treherne smiled involuntarily, for he had read the secret of that shallow heart long ago, and was too generous to use the knowledge, however flattering it might be to him. In a reassuring tone, he said, turning away the keen eyes she feared:

"I give you my word I never will, charming as it might be to study the white pages of a maidenly heart. I find plenty of others to read, so rest tranquil, Miss Blanche."

"Who interests you most just now?" asked the girl, coloring with pleasure at his words. "Mrs. Snowdon looks like one who has a romance to be read, if you have the skill."

"I have read it. My lady is my study just now. I thought I knew her well, but of late she puzzles me. Human minds are more full of mysteries than any written book and more changeable than the cloud-shapes in the air."

"A fine old lady, but I fear her so intensely I should never dare to try to read her, as you say." Blanche looked towards the object of discussion, as she spoke, and added, "Poor Tavia, how forlorn she seems. Let me ask her to join us, may I?"

"With all my heart," was the quick reply.

Blanche glided away, but did not return, for my lady kept her as well as her daughter.

"That test satisfies me; well, I submit for a time, but I think I can conquer my aunt yet." And with a patient sigh, Treherne turned to observe Mrs. Snowdon.

She now stood by the fire, talking with Sir Jasper, a handsome, reckless, generous-hearted young gentleman, who very plainly showed his great admiration for the lady. When he came, she suddenly woke up from her listless mood, and became as brilliantly gay as she had been unmistakably melancholy before. As she chatted, she absently pushed to and fro a small antique urn of bronze on the chimney-piece, and in doing so, she more than once gave Treherne a quick, significant glance, which he answered at last by a somewhat haughty nod. Then, as if satisfied, she ceased toying with the ornament, and became absorbed in Sir Jasper's gallant badinage.

The instant her son approached Mrs. Snowdon, Madame Mère grew anxious, and leaving Octavia to her friends and lover, she watched Jasper. But her surveillance availed little, for she could neither see nor hear anything amiss, yet could not rid herself of the feeling that some mutual understanding existed between them. When the party broke up for the night, she lingered till all were gone but her son and nephew.

"Well, madame-ma-mère, what troubles you?" asked Sir Jasper, as she looked anxiously into his face before bestowing her good-night kiss.

"I cannot tell; yet I feel ill at ease. Remember, my son, that you are the pride of my heart, and any sin or shame of yours would kill me. Good-night, Maurice." And with a stately bow she swept away.

Lounging with both elbows on the low chimney-piece, Sir Jasper smiled at his mother's fears, and said to his cousin, the instant they were alone:

"She is worried about E. S. Odd, isn't it, what instinctive antipathies women take to one another?"

"Why did you ask E. S. here?" demanded Treherne.

"My dear fellow, how could I help it? My mother wanted the general, my father's friend, and of course his wife must be asked also. I couldn't tell my mother that the lady had been a most arrant coquette, to put it mildly, and had married the old man in a pet, because my cousin and I declined to be ruined by her."

"You *could* have told her what mischief she makes wherever she goes, and for Octavia's sake, have deferred the general's visit for a time. I warn you, Jasper, harm will come of it."

"To whom, you or me?"

"To both, perhaps, certainly to you. She was disappointed once when she lost us both by wavering between your title and my supposed fortune. She is miserable with the old man, and her only hope is in his death, for he is very feeble. You are free, and doubly attractive now, so beware, or she will entangle you before you know it."

"Thanks, Mentor, I've no fear, and shall merely amuse myself for a week—they stay no longer." And with a careless laugh, Sir Jasper strolled away.

"Much mischief may be done in a week, and this is the beginning of it," muttered Treherne, as he raised himself to look under the bronze vase for the note. It was gone!

Chapter III

Who Was It?

Who had taken it? This question tormented Treherne all that sleepless night. He suspected three persons, for only these had approached the fire after the note was hidden. He had kept his eye on it, he thought, till the stir of breaking up. In that moment it must have been removed by the major, Frank Annon, or my lady; Sir Jasper was out of the question, for he never touched an ornament in the drawing-room since he had awkwardly demolished a whole *étagère* of costly trifles, to his mother's and sister's great grief. The major evidently suspected something, Annon was jealous, and my lady would be glad of a pretext to remove her daughter from his reach. Trusting to his skill in reading faces, he waited impatiently for morning, resolving to say nothing to any one but Mrs. Snowdon, and from her merely to inquire what the note contained.

Treherne usually was invisible till lunch, often till dinner, therefore, fearing to excite suspicion by unwonted activity, he did not appear till noon. The mail-bag had just been opened, and every one was busy over their letters, but all looked up to exchange a word with the new comer, and Octavia impulsively turned to meet him, then checked herself and hid her suddenly-crimsoned face behind a newspaper. Treherne's eye took in everything, and saw at once in the unusually late arrival of the mail, a pretext for discovering the pilferer of the note.

"All have letters but me, yet, I expected one last night. Major, have you got it among yours?" and, as he spoke, Treherne fixed his penetrating eyes full on the person he addressed.

With no sign of consciousness, no trace of confusion, the major carefully turned over his pile, and replied in the most natural manner:

"Not a trace of it; I wish there was, for nothing annoys me more, than any delay or mistake about my letters."

"He knows nothing of it," thought Treherne, and turned to Annon, who was deep in a long epistle from some intimate friend, with a talent for imparting news, to judge from the reader's interest.

"Annon, I appeal to you, for I *must* discover who has robbed me of my letter."

"I have but one, read it, if you will, and satisfy yourself," was the brief reply.

"No, thank you, I merely asked, in joke; it is, doubtless, among my lady's. Jasper's letters and mine often get mixed, and my lady takes care of his for him. I think you must have it, aunt."

Lady Treherne looked up impatiently.

"My dear Maurice, what a coil about a letter! We none of us have it, so do not punish us for the sins of your correspondent or the carelessness of the post."

"She was not the thief, for she is always intensely polite when she intends to thwart me," thought Treherne, and apologizing for his rudeness in disturbing them, he rolled himself to his nook in a sunny window, and became apparently absorbed in a new magazine.

Mrs. Snowdon was opening the general's letters for him, and, having finished her little task, she roamed away into the library, as if in search of a book. Presently returning with one, she approached Treherne, and putting it into his hand, said, in her musically distinct voice:

"Be so kind as to find for me the passage you spoke of last night. I am curious to see it."

Instantly comprehending her stratagem he opened it with apparent carelessness, secured the tiny note laid among the leaves, and, selecting a passage at hazard returned her book and resumed his own. Behind the cover of it he unfolded and read these words:

"I understand, but do not be anxious; the line I left was merely this—'I must see you alone, tell me when and where.' No one can make much of it, and I will discover the thief before dinner. Do nothing, but watch to whom I speak first on entering, when we meet in the evening, and beware of that person."

Quietly transferring the note to the fire, with the wrapper of the magazine, he dismissed the matter from his mind, and left Mrs. Snowdon to play detective as she pleased, while he busied himself about his own affairs.

It was a clear, bright, December day, and when the young people separated to prepare for a ride, while the general and the major sunned themselves on the terrace, Lady Treherne said to her nephew:

"I am going for an airing in the pony carriage; will you be my escort, Maurice?"

"With pleasure," replied the young man, well knowing what was in store for him.

My lady was unusually taciturn and grave, yet seemed anxious to say something which she found difficult to utter. Treherne saw this, and ended an awkward pause by dashing boldly into the subject which occupied both.

"I think you want to say something to me about Tavie, aunt; am I right?"

"Yes."

"Then let me spare you the pain of beginning, and prove my sincerity by openly stating the truth, as far as I am concerned. I love her very dearly, but I am not mad enough to dream of telling her so. I know that it is impossible, and I relinquish my hopes. Trust me, I will keep silent and see her marry Annon without a word of complaint, if you will it. I see by her altered manner, that you have spoken to her, and that my little friend and nurse is to be mine no longer. Perhaps you are wise, but, if you do this on my account, it is in vain—the mischief is done, and while I live I shall love my cousin. If you do it to spare her, I am dumb, and will go away rather than cause her a care or pain."

"Do you really mean this, Maurice?" And Lady Treherne looked at him with a changed and softened face.

Turning upon her, Treherne showed her a countenance full of suffering and sincerity, of resignation and resolve, as he said, earnestly:

"I do mean it; prove me in any way you please. I am not a bad fellow, aunt, and I desire to be better. Since my misfortune I've had time to test many things, myself among others, and in spite of many faults, I do cherish the wish to keep my soul honest and true, even though my body be a wreck. It is easy to say these things, but in spite of temptation, I think I can stand firm, if you trust me."

"My dear boy, I do trust you, and thank you gratefully for this frankness. I never forget that I owe Jasper's life to you, and never expect to repay that debt. Remember this when I seem cold or unkind, and remember, also, that I say now, had you been spared this affliction, I would gladly have given you my girl. But—"

"But, aunt, hear one thing," broke in Treherne; "they tell me that any sudden and violent shock of surprise, joy or sorrow may do for me what they hope time will achieve. I said nothing of this, for it is but a chance; yet, while there is any hope, need I utterly renounce Octavia?"

"It is hard to refuse, and, yet, I cannot think it wise to build upon a chance so slight. Once let her have you, and both are made unhappy, if the hope fail. No, Maurice, it is better to be generous, and leave her free to make her own happiness elsewhere. Annon loves her, she is heart-whole, and will soon learn to love him, if you are silent. My poor boy, it seems cruel, but I must say it."

"Shall I go away, aunt?" was all his answer, very firmly uttered, though his lips were white.

"Not yet, only leave them to themselves, and hide your trouble if you can. Yet, if you prefer, you shall go to town, and Benson shall see that you are comfortable. Your health will be a reason, and I will come, or write often, if you are homesick. It shall depend on you, for I want to be just and kind in this hard case. You shall decide."

"Then I will stay. I can hide my love; and to see them together will soon cease to wound me, if Octavia is happy."

"So let it rest then, for a time. You shall miss your companion as little as possible, for I will try to fill her place. Forgive me, Maurice, and pity a mother's solicitude, for these two are the last of many children, and I am a widow now."

Lady Treherne's voice faltered, and, if any selfish hope or plan lingered in her nephew's mind, that appeal banished it and touched his better nature. Pressing her hand he said gently:

"Dear aunt, do not lament over me, I am one set apart for afflictions, yet I will not be conquered by them. Let us forget my youth and be friendly counsellors together for the good of the two whom we both love. I must say a word about Jasper, and you will not press me to explain more than I can without breaking my promise."

"Thank you, thank you! It is regarding that woman, I know. Tell me all you can; I will not be importunate, but I disliked her the instant I saw her, beautiful and charming as she seems."

"When my cousin and I were in Paris, just before my illness, we met her. She was with her father then, a gay old man, who led a life of pleasure, and was no fit guardian for a lovely daughter. She knew our story, and, having fascinated both, paused to decide which she would accept; Jasper, for his title, or me, for my fortune. This was before my uncle changed his will, and I believed myself his heir; but, before she made her choice, something (don't ask me what, if you please,) occurred to send us from Paris. On our return voyage we were wrecked, and then came my illness, disinheritance and helplessness. Edith Dubarry heard the story, but rumor reported it falsely, and she believed both of us had lost the fortune. Her father died penniless, and in a moment of despair she married the general, whose wealth surrounds her with the luxury she loves, and whose failing health will soon restore her liberty—"

"And then, Maurice?" interrupted my lady.

"She hopes to win Jasper, I think."

"Never! we must prevent that at all costs. I had rather see him dead before me, than the husband of such a woman. Why is she permitted to visit homes like mine? I should have been told this sooner," exclaimed my lady, angrily.

"I should have told you had I known it, and I reproved Jasper for his neglect. Do not be needlessly troubled, aunt, there is no blemish on Mrs. Snowdon's name, and, as the wife of a brave and honorable man, she is received without question; for beauty, grace or tact like hers can make their way anywhere. She stays but a week, and I will devote myself to her; this will save Jasper, and, if necessary, convince Tavie of my indifference"—then he paused to stifle a sigh.

"But yourself, have you no fears for your own peace, Maurice? You must not sacrifice happiness or honor, for me or mine."

"I am safe; I love my cousin, and that is my shield. Whatever happens remember that I tried to serve you, and sincerely endeavored to forget myself."

"God bless you, my son! let me call you so, and feel that, though I deny you my daughter, I give you heartily a mother's care and affection."

Lady Treherne was as generous as she was proud, and her nephew had conquered her by confidence and submission. He acted no part, yet, even in relinquishing all, he cherished a hope that he might yet win the heart he coveted. Silently they parted, but from that hour a new and closer bond existed between the two, and exerted an unsuspected influence over the whole household.

Maurice waited with some impatience for Mrs. Snowdon's entrance, not only because of his curiosity to see if she had discovered the thief, but because of the part he had taken upon himself to play. He was equal to it, and felt a certain pleasure in it, for a three-fold reason. It would serve his aunt and cousin, would divert his mind from its own cares, and, perhaps, by making Octavia jealous, waken love; for, though he had chosen the right, he was but a man, and, moreover, a lover.

Mrs. Snowdon was late, she always was, for her toilet was elaborate, and she liked to enjoy its effects upon others. The moment she entered, Treherne's eye was on her, and to his intense surprise and annoyance she addressed Octavia, saying blandly:

"My dear Miss Treherne, I've been admiring your peacocks. Pray let me see you feed them to-morrow. Miss Talbot says it is a charming sight."

"If you are on the terrace just after lunch, you will find them there, and may feed them yourself, if you like," was the cool, civil reply.

"She looks like a peacock herself, in that splendid green and gold dress, doesn't she?" whispered Rose to Sir Jasper, with a wicked laugh.

"Faith, so she does. I wish Tavie's birds had voices like Mrs. Snowdon's; their squalling annoys me, intensely."

"I rather like it, for it is honest, and no malice or mischief is hidden behind it. I always distrust those smooth, sweet voices; they are insincere. I like a full, clear tone; sharp, if you please, but decided and true."

"Well said, Octavia, I agree with you, and your own is a perfect sample of the kind you describe." And Treherne smiled as he rolled by to join Mrs. Snowdon who evidently waited for him, while Octavia turned to her brother to defend her pets.

"Are you sure? How did you discover?" said Maurice, affecting to admire the lady's bouquet, as he paused beside her.

"I suspected it the moment I saw her this morning. She is no actress; and dislike, distrust and contempt were visible in her face when we met. Till you so cleverly told me my note was lost, I fancied she was disturbed about her brother or—you."

A sudden pause and a keen glance followed the last softly-uttered word, but Treherne met it with an inscrutable smile and a quiet:

"Well, what next?"

"The moment I learned that you did not get the note I was sure she had it, and knowing that she must have seen me put it there, in spite of her apparent innocence, I quietly asked her for it. This surprised her, this robbed the affair of any mystery, and I finished her perplexity by sending it to the major the moment she returned it to me, as if it had been intended for him. She begged pardon, said her brother was thoughtless, and she watched over him lest he should get into mischief; professed to think I meant the line for him, and behaved like a charming simpleton, as she is."

"Quite a tumult about nothing. Poor little Tavie! you doubtlessly frightened her so that we may safely correspond hereafter."

"You may give me an answer now, and here."

"Very well, meet me on the terrace to-morrow morning; the peacocks will make the meeting natural enough. I usually loiter away an hour or two there, in the sunny part of the day."

"But the girl?"

"I'll send her away."

"You speak as if it would be an easy thing to do."

"It will, both easy and pleasant."

"Now you are mysterious or uncomplimentary. You either care nothing for a *tête-à-tête* with her, or you will gladly send her out of my way. Which is it?"

"You shall decide. Can I have this?"

She looked at him, as he touched a rose with a warning glance, for the flower was both an emblem of love and of silence. Did he mean to hint that he recalled the past, or to warn her that some one was near? She leaned from the shadow of the curtain where she sat, and caught a glimpse of a shadow gliding away.

"Who was it?" she asked, below her breath.

"A Rose," he answered, laughing; then, as if the danger was over, he said, "How will you account to the major for the message you sent him?"

"Easily by fabricating some interesting perplexity in which I want sage counsel. He will be flattered, and by seeming to take him into my confidence, I can hoodwink the excellent man to my heart's content, for he annoys me by his odd way of mounting guard over me at all times. Now take me in to dinner, and be your former delightful self."

"That is impossible," he said, yet proved that it was not.

Chapter IV

Feeding the Peacocks

It was indeed a charming sight, the twelve stately birds perched on the broad stone balustrade, or prancing slowly along the terrace, with the sun gleaming on their green and golden necks and the glories of their gorgeous plumes, wide-spread, or sweeping like rich trains behind them. In pretty contrast to the splendid creatures, was their young mistress, in her simple morning dress, and fur-trimmed hood and mantle, as she stood feeding the tame pets from her hand, calling their fanciful names, laughing at their pranks, and heartily enjoying the winter sunshine, the fresh wind, and the girlish pastime. As Treherne slowly approached, he watched her with lover's eyes, and found her very sweet and blithe, and dearer in his sight than ever. She had shunned him carefully all the day before, had parted at night with a hasty hand-shake, and had not come as usual to bid him good-morning in the library. He had taken no notice of the change as yet, but now, remembering his promise to his aunt, he resolved to let the girl know that he fully understood the relation which henceforth was to exist between them.

"Good-morning, cousin; shall I drive you away, if I take a turn or two here?" he said, in a cheerful tone, but with a half-reproachful glance.

She looked at him an instant, then went to him with extended hand, and cheeks rosier than before, while her frank eyes filled, and her voice had a traitorous tremor in it, as she said, impetuously:

"I *will* be myself for a moment, in spite of everything. Maurice, don't think me unkind, don't reproach me, nor ask my leave to come where I am. There is a reason for the change you see in me; it's not caprice, it is obedience."

"My dear girl, I know it; I meant to speak of it, and show you that I understand. Annon is a good fellow, as worthy of you as any man can be, and I wish you all the happiness you deserve."

"Do you?" and her eyes searched his face keenly.

"Yes; do you doubt it?" and so well did he conceal his love, that neither face, voice nor manner betrayed a hint of it.

Her eyes fell, a cloud passed over her clear countenance, and she withdrew her hand, as if to caress the hungry bird that gently pecked at the basket she held. As if to change the conversation, she said, playfully:

"Poor Argus, you have lost your fine feathers, and so all desert you, except kind little Juno, who never forgets her friends. There, take it all, and share between you."

Treherne smiled, and said, quickly:

"I am a human Argus, and you have been a kind little Juno to me since I lost my plumes. Continue to be so, and you will find me a very faithful friend."

"I will." And, as she answered, her old smile came back, and her eyes met his again.

"Thanks! Now we shall get on happily. I don't ask nor expect the old life—that is impossible. I knew that when lovers came, the friend would fall into the background; and I am content to be second, where I have so long been first. Do not think you neglect me; be happy with your lover, dear, and when you have no pleasanter amusement, come and see old Maurice."

She turned her head away, that he might not see the angry color in her cheeks, the trouble in her eyes, and when she spoke, it was to say, petulantly:

"I wish Jasper and mamma would leave me in peace. I hate lovers, and want none. If Frank teases, I'll go into a convent, and so be rid of him."

Maurice laughed, and turned her face towards himself, saying, in his persuasive voice:

"Give him a trial first, to please your mother. It can do no harm, and may amuse you. Frank is already lost, and, as you are heart-whole, why not see what you can do for him? I shall have a new study, then, and not miss you so much."

"You are very kind; I'll do my best. I wish Mrs. Snowdon would come, if she is coming; I've an engagement at two, and Frank will look tragical, if I'm not ready. He is teaching me billiards, and I really like the game, though I never thought I should."

"That looks well. I hope you'll learn a double lesson, and Annon find a docile pupil in both."

"You are very pale this morning; are you in pain, Maurice?" suddenly asked Octavia, dropping the tone of assumed ease and gayety under which she had tried to hide her trouble.

"Yes; but it will soon pass. Mrs. Snowdon is coming; I saw her at the hall-door a moment ago. I will show her the peacocks, if you want to go. She wont mind the change, I dare say, as you don't like her, and I do."

"No, I am sure of that. It was an arrangement, perhaps? I understand. I will not play Mademoiselle De Trop."

Sudden fire shone in the girl's eyes, sudden contempt curled her lip, and a glance full of meaning went from her cousin to the door, where Mrs. Snowdon appeared, waiting for her maid to bring her some additional wrappings.

"You allude to the note you stole. How came you to play that prank, Tavie?" asked Treherne, tranquilly.

"I saw her put it under the urn. I thought it was for Jasper, and I took it," she said, boldly.

"Why for Jasper?"

"I remembered his speaking of meeting her long ago, and describing her beauty enthusiastically—and so did you."

"You have a good memory."

"I have for everything concerning those I love. I observed her manner of meeting my brother, his devotion to her, and, when they stood laughing together before the fire, I felt sure that she wished to charm him again."

"Again? Then she did charm him once?" asked Treherne, anxious to know how much Jasper had told his sister.

"He always denied it, and declared that you were the favorite."

"Then why not think the note for me?" he asked.

"I do now," was the sharp answer.

"But she told you it was for the major, and sent it."

"She deceived me; I am not surprised. I am glad Jasper is safe, and I wish you a pleasant *tête-à-tête.*"

Bowing with unwonted dignity, Octavia sat down her basket, and walked away in one direction, as Mrs. Snowdon approached in another.

"I have done it now," sighed Treherne, turning from the girlish figure, to watch the stately creature who came sweeping towards him with noiseless grace.

Brilliancy and splendor became Mrs. Snowdon; she enjoyed luxury, and her beauty made many things becoming, which, in a plainer woman, would have been out of taste, and absurd. She had wrapped herself in a genuine Eastern burnouse of scarlet, blue and gold; the hood drawn over her head framed her fine face in rich hues, and the great gilt tassels shone against her rippling black hair. She wore it with grace, and the barbaric splendor of the garment became her well. The fresh air touched her cheeks with a delicate color; her usually gloomy eyes were brilliant now, and the smile that patted her lips was full of happiness.

"Welcome, Cleopatra!" cried Treherne, with difficulty repressing a laugh, as the peacocks screamed and fled before the rustling amplitude of her drapery.

"I might reply by calling you Thaddeus of Warsaw, for you look very romantic and Polish with your pale, pensive face, and your splendid furs," she answered, as she paused beside him, with admiration very visibly expressed in her eyes.

Treherne disliked the look, and rather abruptly said, as he offered her the basket of bread:

"I have disposed of my cousin, and offered to do the honors of the peacocks. Here they are—will you feed them?"

"No, thank you—I care nothing for the fowls, as you know; I came to speak to you," she said, impatiently.

"I am at your service."

"I wish to ask you a question or two—is it permitted?"

"What man ever refused Mrs. Snowdon a request?"

"Nay, no compliments; from you they are only satirical evasions. I was deceived when abroad, and rashly married that old man; tell me truly how things stand?"

"Jasper has all, I have nothing."

"I am glad of it."

"Many thanks for the hearty speech. You at least speak sincerely," he said, bitterly.

"I do, Maurice—I do; let me prove it."

Treherne's chair was close beside the balustrade. Mrs. Snowdon leaned on the carved railing, with her back to the house, and her face screened by a tall urn. Looking steadily at him, she said, rapidly and low:

"You thought I wavered between you and Jasper, when we parted two years ago. I did; but it was not between title and fortune that I hesitated. It was between duty and love. My father, a fond, foolish old man, had set his heart on seeing me a lady. I was his all; my beauty was his delight, and no untitled man was deemed worthy of me. I loved him tenderly. You may doubt this, knowing how selfish, reckless and vain I am, but I have a heart, and, with better training, had been a better woman. No matter, it is too late now. Next my father, I loved you. Nay, hear me—I *will* clear myself in your eyes. I mean no wrong to the general. He is kind, indulgent, generous; I respect him—I am grateful, and while he lives, I shall be true to him."

"Then be silent now. Do not recall the past, Edith; let it sleep, for both our sakes," began Treherne; but she checked him imperiously.

"It shall, when I am done. I loved you, Maurice; for, of all the gay, idle, pleasure-seeking men I saw about me, you were the only one who seemed to have a thought beyond the folly of the hour. Under the seeming frivolity of your life, lay something noble, heroic and true. I felt that you had a purpose, that your present mood was but transitory—a young man's holiday, before the real work of his life began. This attracted, this won me; for even in the brief regard you then gave me, there was an earnestness no other man had shown. I wanted your respect; I longed to earn your love, to share your life, and prove that even in my neglected nature slept the power of cancelling a frivolous past by a noble future. O Maurice, had you lingered one week more, I never should have been the miserable thing I am!"

There her voice faltered and failed, for all the bitterness of lost love, peace and happiness sounded in the pathetic passion of that exclamation. She did not weep; for tears seldom dimmed those tragical eyes of hers; but she wrung her hands in mute despair, and looked down into the frost-blighted gardens below, as if she saw there a true symbol of her own ruined life. Treherne uttered not a word, but set his teeth with an almost fierce glance towards the distant figure of Sir Jasper, who was riding gayly away, like one unburdened by a memory or a care. Hurriedly Mrs. Snowdon went on:

"My father begged and commanded me to choose your cousin; I could not break his heart, and asked for time, hoping to soften him. While I waited, that mysterious affair hurried you from Paris, and then came the wreck, the illness, and the rumor that old Sir Jasper had disinherited both nephews. They told me you were dying, and I became a passive instrument in my father's hands. I promised to recall and accept your cousin; but the old man died before it was done, and then I cared not what became of me. General Snowdon was my father's friend; he pitied me; he saw my desolate, destitute state, my despair and helplessness. He comforted, sustained and saved me. I was grateful; and when he offered me his heart and home, I accepted them. He knew I had no love to give; but as a friend, a daughter, I would gladly serve him, and make his declining years as happy as I could. It was all over, when I heard that you were alive, afflicted and poor. I longed to come and live for you. My new bonds became heavy fetters then, my wealth oppressed me, and I was doubly wretched—for I dared not tell my trouble, and it nearly drove me mad. I have seen you now; I know that you are happy; I read your cousin's love, and see a peaceful life in store for you. This must content me, and I must learn to bear it as I can."

She paused, breathless and pale, and walked rapidly along the terrace, as if to hide or control the agitation that possessed her. Treherne still sat silent, but his heart leaped within him, as he thought:

"She sees that Octavia loves me! A woman's eye is quick to detect love in another, and she asserts what I begin to hope. My cousin's manner just now, her dislike of Annon, her new shyness with me; it may be true, and if it is— Heaven help me—what am I saying! I must not hope, nor wish, nor dream; I must renounce and forget."

He leaned his head upon his hand, and sat so till Mrs. Snowdon rejoined him, pale, but calm and self-possessed. As she drew near, she marked his attitude, the bitter sadness of his face, and hope sprang up within her. Perhaps she was mistaken; perhaps he did not love his cousin; perhaps he still remembered the past, and still regretted the loss of the heart she had just laid bare before him. Her husband was failing, and might die any day, and then, free, rich, beautiful and young, what might she not become to Treherne, helpless, poor and ambitious. With all her faults, she was generous, and this picture charmed her fancy, warmed her heart, and comforted her pain.

"Maurice," she said, softly, pausing again beside him, "if I mistake you and your hopes, it is because I dare ask nothing for myself; but if ever a time shall come when I have liberty to give or help, ask of me *anything*, and it is gladly yours."

He understood her, pitied her, and, seeing that she found consolation in a distant hope, he let her enjoy it while she might. Gravely, yet gratefully, he spoke, and pressed the hand extended to him with an impulsive gesture.

"Generous as ever, Edith, and impetuously frank. Thank you for your sincerity, your kindness, and the affection you once gave me. I say 'once,' for now duty, truth and honor bar us from each other. My life must be solitary, yet I shall find work to do, and learn to be content. You owe all devotion to the good old man who loves you, and will not fail him, I am sure. Leave the future and the past, but let us make the present what it may be—a time to forgive and forget, to take heart and begin anew. Christmas is a fitting time for such resolves, and the birth of friendship such as ours may be."

Something in his tone and manner struck her, and, eyeing him with soft wonder, she exclaimed:

"How changed you are!"

"Need you tell me that?" And he glanced at his helpless limbs with a bitter yet pathetic look of patience.

"No, no—not so! I mean in mind, not body. Once you were gay and careless, eager and fiery, like Jasper; now you are grave and quiet, or cheerful, and so very kind. Yet, in spite of illness and loss, you seem twice the man you were, and something wins respect, as well as admiration and—love."

Her dark eyes filled, as the last word left her lips, and the beauty of a touched heart shone in her face. Maurice looked up quickly, asking, with sudden earnestness:

"Do you see it? Then it is true. Yes, I *am* changed, thank God! and she has done it."

"Who?" demanded his companion, jealously.

"Octavia. Unconsciously, yet surely, she has done much for me, and this year of seeming loss and misery has been the happiest, most profitable of my life. I have often heard that afflictions were the best teachers, and I believe it now."

Mrs. Snowdon shook her head sadly.

"Not always; they are tormentors to some. But don't preach, Maurice; I am still a sinner, though you incline to sainthood, and I have one question more to ask. What was it that took you and Jasper so suddenly away from Paris?"

"That I can never tell you."

"I shall discover it for myself, then."

"It is impossible."

"Nothing is impossible to a determined woman."

"You can neither wring, surprise nor bribe this secret from the two persons who hold it. I beg of you to let it rest," said Treherne, earnestly.

"I have a clew, and I shall follow it; for I am convinced that something is wrong, and you are—"

"Dear Mrs. Snowdon, are you so charmed with the birds, that you forget your fellow-beings, or so charmed with one fellow-being that you forget the birds?"

As the sudden question startled both, Rose Talbot came along the terrace, with hands full of holly, and a face full of merry mischief, adding, as she vanished:

"I shall tell Tavie that feeding the peacocks is such congenial amusement for lovers, she and Mr. Annon had better try it."

"Saucy gipsey!" muttered Treherne.

But Mrs. Snowdon said, with a smile of double meaning:

"Many a true word is spoken in jest."

Chapter V

Under the Mistletoe

Unusually gay and charming the three young friends looked dressed alike in fleecy white, with holly wreaths in their hair, as they slowly descended the wide oaken stairway arm in arm. A footman was lighting the hall lamps, for the winter dusk gathered early, and the girls were merrily chatting about the evening's festivity, when suddenly a loud, long shriek echoed through the hall. A heavy glass shade fell from the man's hand with a crash, and the young ladies clung to one another aghast, for mortal terror was in the cry, and a dead silence followed it.

"What was it, John?" demanded Octavia, very pale, but steady in a moment.

"I'll go and see, miss." And the man hurried away.

"Where did the dreadful scream come from?" asked Rose, collecting her wits as rapidly as possible.

"Above us somewhere. O, let us go down among people; I am frightened to death," whispered Blanche, trembling and faint.

Hurrying into the parlor, they found only Annon and the major, both looking startled, and both staring out of the windows.

"Did you hear it? What could it be? Don't go and leave us!" cried the girls in a breath, as they rushed in.

The gentlemen had heard, couldn't explain the cry, and were quite ready to protect the pretty creatures who clustered about them like frightened fawns. John speedily appeared, looking rather wild, and as eager to tell his tale as they to listen.

"It's Patty, one of the maids, miss, in a fit. She went up to the north gallery to see that the fires was right, for it takes a power of wood to warm the gallery even enough for dancing, as you know, miss. Well, it was dark, for the fires was low and her candle went out as she whisked open the door, being flurried, as the maids always is when they go in there. Half way down the gallery she says she heard a rustling, and stopped. She's the pluckiest of 'em all, and she called out, 'I see you!' thinking it was some of us trying to fright her. Nothing answered, and she went on a bit, when suddenly the fire flared up one flash, and there right before her was the ghost."

"Don't be foolish, John. Tell us what it was," said Octavia, sharply, though her face whitened and her heart sunk as the last word passed the man's lips.

"It was a tall, black figger, miss, with a dead-white face and a black hood. She see it plain, and turned to go away, but she hadn't gone a dozen steps when there it was again before her, the same tall, dark thing with the dead-white face looking out from the black hood. It lifted its arm as if to hold her, but she gave a spring and dreadful screech, and ran to Mrs. Benson's room, where she dropped in a fit."

"How absurd to be frightened by the shadows of the figures in armor that stand along the gallery," said Rose, boldly enough, though she would have declined entering the gallery without a light.

"Nay, I don't wonder, it's a ghostly place at night. How is the poor thing?" asked Blanche, still hanging on the major's arm in her best attitude.

"If mamma knows nothing of it, tell Mrs. Benson to keep it from her, please. She is not well, and such things annoy her very much," said Octavia, adding, as the man turned away, "Did any one look in the gallery after Patty told her tale?"

"No, miss, I'll go and do it myself; I'm not afraid of man, ghost or devil, saving your presence, ladies," replied John.

"Where is Sir Jasper?" suddenly asked the major.

"Here I am. What a deuce of a noise some one has been making. It disturbed a capital dream. Why, Tavie, what is it?" And Sir Jasper came out of the library with a sleepy face and tumbled hair.

They told him the story, whereat he laughed heartily, and said the maids were a foolish set to be scared by a shadow. While he still laughed and joked, Mrs. Snowdon entered, looking alarmed, and anxious to know the cause of the confusion.

"How interesting! I never knew you kept a ghost. Tell me all about it, Sir Jasper, and soothe our nerves by satisfying our curiosity," she said, in her half-persuasive, half-commanding way, as she seated herself on Lady Treherne's sacred sofa.

"There's not much to tell, except that this place used to be an abbey, in fact as well as in name. An ancestor founded it, and for years the monks led a jolly life here, as one may see, for the cellar is twice as large as the chapel, and much better preserved. But another ancestor, a gay and gallant baron, took a fancy to the site for his castle, and, in spite of prayers, anathemas, and excommunication, he turned the poor fellows out, pulled down the abbey and built this fine old place. Abbot Boniface, as he left his abbey, uttered a heavy curse on all who should live here, and vowed to haunt us till the last Treherne vanished from the face of the earth. With this amiable threat the old party left Baron Roland to his doom, and died as soon as he could in order to begin his cheerful mission."

"Did he haunt the place?" asked Blanche, eagerly.

"Yes, most faithfully from that time to this. Some say many of the monks still glide about the older parts of the abbey, for Roland spared the chapel and the north gallery which joined it to the modern building. Poor fellows, they are welcome and once a year they shall have a chance to warm their ghostly selves by the great fires always kindled at Christmas in the gallery."

"Mrs. Benson once told me that when the ghost walked, it was a sure sign of a coming death in the family. Is that true?" asked Rose, whose curiosity was excited by the expression of Octavia's face, and a certain uneasiness in Sir Jasper's manner in spite of his merry mood.

"There is a stupid superstition of that sort in the family, but no one except the servants believes it, of course. In times of illness some silly maid or croaking old woman can easily fancy they see a phantom, and, if death comes, they are sure of the ghostly warning. Benson saw it before my father died, and old Roger, the night my uncle was seized with apoplexy. Patty will never be made to believe that this warning does not forebode the death of Maurice or myself, for the gallant spirit leaves the ladies of our house to depart in peace. How does it strike you, cousin?"

Turning, as he spoke, Sir Jasper glanced at Treherne who had entered while he spoke.

"I am quite skeptical and indifferent to the whole affair, but I agree with Octavia, that it is best to say nothing to my aunt, if she is ignorant of the matter. Her rooms are a long way off, and, perhaps, she did not hear the confusion."

"You seem to hear everything; you were not with us when I said that." And Octavia looked up with an air of surprise.

Smiling significantly, Treherne answered:

"I hear, see and understand many things that escape others. Jasper, allow me to advise you to smooth the hair which your sleep has disarranged. Mrs. Snowdon, permit me, this rich velvet catches the least speck." And with his handkerchief he delicately brushed away several streaks of white dust which clung to the lady's skirt.

Sir Jasper turned hastily on his heel and went to remake his toilet; Mrs. Snowdon bit her lip, but thanked Treherne sweetly and begged him to fasten her glove. As he did so, he said softly:

"Be more careful next time; Octavia has keen eyes, and the major may prove inconvenient."

"I have no fear that *you* will," she whispered back, with a malicious glance.

Here the entrance of my lady put an end to the ghostly episode, for it was evident that she knew nothing of it. Octavia slipped away to question John, and learn that no sign of a phantom was to be seen. Treherne devoted himself to Mrs. Snowdon, and the major entertained my lady, while Sir Jasper and the girls chatted apart.

It was Christmas-eve, and a dance in the great gallery was the yearly festival at the abbey. All had been eager for it, but the maid's story seemed to have lessened their enthusiasm, though no one would own it. This annoyed Sir Jasper, and he exerted himself to clear the atmosphere by affecting gayety he did not feel. The moment the gentlemen came in after dinner he whispered to his mother, who rose, asked the general for his arm, and led the way to the north gallery whence the sound of music now proceeded. The rest followed in a merry procession, even Treherne, for two footmen carried him up the great stairway, chair and all.

Nothing could look less ghostly now than the haunted gallery. Fires roared up a wide chimney at either end, long rows of figures clad in armor stood on each side, one mailed hand grasping a lance, the other bearing a lighted candle, a device of Sir Jasper's. Narrow windows pierced in the thick walls let in gleams of wintry moonlight; ivy, holly and evergreen glistened in the ruddy glow of mingled firelight and candle-shine. From the arched stone roof hung tattered banners and in the midst depended a great bunch of mistletoe. Red-cushioned seats stood in recessed window nooks, and from behind a high-covered screen of oak sounded the blithe air of Sir Roger de Coverly.

With the utmost gravity and stateliness my lady and the general led off the dance, for, according to the good old fashion, the men and maids in their best array joined the gentlefolk and danced with their betters in a high state of pride and bashfulness. Sir Jasper twirled the old housekeeper till her head spun round and round, and her decorous skirts rustled stormily; Mrs. Snowdon captivated the gray-haired butler by her condescension, and John was made a proud man by the hand of his young mistress. The major came out strong among the pretty maids, and Rose danced the footmen out of breath long before the music paused.

The merriment increased from that moment, and when the general surprised my lady by gallantly saluting her as she unconsciously stood under the mistletoe, the applause was immense. Every one followed the old gentleman's example, as fast as opportunities occurred, and the young ladies soon had as fine a color as the house-maids. More dancing, games, songs and all manner of festival devices filled the evening, yet, under cover of the gayety more than one little scene was enacted that night, and in an hour of seeming frivolity the current of several lives was changed.

By a skillful manœuvre Annon led Octavia to an isolated recess, as if to rest after a brisk game, and, taking advantage of the auspicious hour, pleaded his suit. She heard him patiently, and when he paused, said slowly, yet decidedly, and with no sign of maiden hesitation:

"Thanks for the honor you do me, but I cannot accept it, for I do not love you. I think I never can."

"Have you tried?" he asked, eagerly.

"Yes, indeed I have. I like you as a friend, but no more. I know mamma desires it, that Jasper hopes for it, and I try to please them, but love will not be forced, so what can I do?" And she smiled in spite of herself at her own blunt simplicity.

"No, but it can be cherished, strengthened, and in time won, with patience and devotion. Let me try, Octavia; it is but fair, unless you have already learned from another the lesson I hope to teach. Is it so?"

"No, I think not, I do not understand myself as yet, I am so young, and this so sudden; give me time, Frank."

She blushed and fluttered now, looked half angry, half beseeching, and altogether lovely.

"How much time shall I give? It cannot take long to read a heart like yours, dear." And fancying her emotion a propitious omen he assumed the lover in good earnest.

"Give me time till the New Year. I will answer then, and, meantime, leave me free to study both myself and you. We have known each other long, I own, but, still, this changes everything, and makes you seem another person. Be patient, Frank, and I will try to make my duty a pleasure."

"I will, God bless you for the kind hope, Octavia; it has been mine for years, and if I lose it, it will go hardly with me."

Later in the evening General Snowdon stood examining the antique screen. In many places the carved oak was pierced quite through, so that voices were audible from behind it. The musicians had gone down to supper, the young folk were quietly busy at the other end of the ball, and as the old gentleman admired the quaint carving, the sound of his own name caught his ear. The housekeeper and butler still remained, though the other servants had gone, and sitting cosily behind the screen chatted in low tones believing themselves secure.

"It *was* Mrs. Snowdon, Adam, as I'm a living woman, though I wouldn't say it to any one but you. She and Sir Jasper were here wrapped in cloaks, and up to mischief I'll be bound. She is a beauty, but I don't envy her, and there'll be trouble in the house if she stays long."

"But how do you know, Mrs. Benson, she was here? Where's your proof, mum?" asked the pompous butler.

"Look at this, and then look at the outlandish trimming of the lady's dress. You men are so dull about such matters you'd never observe these little points. Well, I was here first after Patty, and my light shone on this jet ornament lying near where she saw the spirit. No one has any such tasty trifles but Mrs. Snowdon, and these are all over her gown. If that aint proof, what is?"

"Well, admitting it, I then say what on earth should she and master be up here for, at such a time?" asked the slow-witted butler.

"Adam, we are old servants of the family, and to you I'll say what tortures shouldn't draw from one to another. Master has been wild, as you know, and it's my belief that he loved this lady abroad. There was a talk of some mystery, or misdeed, or misfortune, more than a year ago, and she was in it. I'm loth to say it, but I think master loves her still, and she him. The general is an old man, she is but young, and so spirited and winsome she can't in reason care for him as for a fine, gallant gentleman like Sir Jasper. There's trouble brewing, Adam, mark my words, there's trouble brewing for the Trehernes."

So low had the voices fallen that the listener could not have caught the words had not his ear been strained to the utmost. He did hear all, and his wasted face flashed with the wrath of a young man, then grew pale and stern as he turned to watch his wife. She stood apart from the others talking to Sir Jasper, who looked unusually handsome and debonair, as he fanned her with a devoted air.

"Perhaps it is true," thought the old man, bitterly. "They are well matched, were lovers once, no doubt, and long to be so again. Poor Edith, I was very blind." And with his gray head bowed upon his breast, the general stole away, carrying an arrow in his brave old heart.

"Blanche, come here and rest, you will be ill to-morrow; and I promised mamma to take care of you." With which elder-sisterly command Rose led the girl to an immense old chair, which held them both. "Now listen to me, and follow my advice, for I am wise in my generation, though not yet gray. They are all busy, so leave them alone, and let me show you what is to be done."

Rose spoke softly, but with great resolution, and nodded her pretty head so energetically, that the holly-berries came rolling over her white shoulders.

"We are not as rich as we might be, and must establish ourselves as soon and as well as possible. I intend to be Lady Treherne, you can be the Honorable Mrs. Annon, if you give your mind to it."

"My dear child, are you mad?" whispered Blanche.

"Far from it, but you will be, if you waste your time on Maurice. He is poor, and a cripple, though very charming, I admit. He loves Tavie, and she will marry him, I am sure. She can't endure Frank, but tries to because my lady commands it. Nothing will come of it, so try your fascinations and comfort the poor man; sympathy now will foster love hereafter."

"Don't talk so here, Rose, some one will hear us," began her sister, but the other broke in briskly:

"No fear, a crowd is the best place for secrets. Now remember what I say, and make your game while the ball is rolling. Other people are careful not to put their plans into words, but I'm no hypocrite, and say plainly what I mean. Bear my sage counsel in mind, and act wisely. Now come and begin."

Treherne was sitting alone by one of the great fires, regarding the gay scene with serious air. For him there was neither dancing nor games; he could only roam about catching glimpses of forbidden pleasures, impossible delights, and youthful hopes forever lost to him. Sad but not morose was his face, and to Octavia it was a mute reproach which she could not long resist. Coming up, as if to warm herself, she spoke to him in her usually frank and friendly way, and felt her heart beat fast when she saw how swift a change her cordial manner wrought in him.

"How pretty your holly is; do you remember how we used to go and gather it for festivals like this when we were happy children?" he asked, looking up at her with eyes full of tender admiration.

"Yes, I remember. Every one wears it to-night as a badge, but you have none. Let me get you a bit, I like to have you one of us in all things."

She leaned forward to break a green sprig from the branch over the chimney-piece; the strong draught drew in her fleecy skirt, and in an instant she was enveloped in flames.

"Maurice, save me, help me!" cried a voice of fear and agony, and before any one could reach her, before he himself knew how the deed was done, Treherne had thrown himself from his chair, wrapt the tiger skin tightly about her, and knelt there clasping her in his arms heedless of fire, pain or the incoherent expressions of love that broke from his lips.

Chapter VI

~

Miracles

G reat was the confusion and alarm which reigned for many minutes, but
when the panic subsided two miracles appeared. Octavia was entirely
uninjured, and Treherne was standing on his feet; a thing which for months
he had not done without crutches. In the excitement of the moment, no one
observed the wonder; all were crowding about the girl, who, pale and breathless but now self-possessed, was the first to exclaim, pointing to her cousin,
who had drawn himself up, with the help of his chair, and leaned there
smiling, with a face full of intense delight.

"Look at Maurice!—O Jasper, help him or he'll fall!"

Sir Jasper sprung to his side and put a strong arm about him, while a
chorus of wonder, sympathy and congratulation rose about them.

"Why, lad, what does it mean? Have you been deceiving us all this time?"
cried Jasper, as Treherne leaned on him, looking exhausted but truly happy.

"It means that I am not to be a cripple all my life; that they did not
deceive me when they said a sudden shock might electrify me with a more
potent magnetism than any they could apply. It *has*, and if I am cured I owe it
all to you, Octavia."

He stretched his hands to her with a gesture of such passionate gratitude
that the girl covered her face to hide its traitorous tenderness, and my lady
went to him, saying, brokenly, as she embraced him with maternal warmth:

"God bless you for this act, Maurice, and reward you with a perfect cure.
To you I owe the lives of both my children; how can I thank you as I ought?"

"I dare not tell you yet," he whispered, eagerly, then added, "I am growing
faint, aunt, get me away before I make a scene."

This hint recalled my lady to her usual state of dignified self-possession.
Bidding Jasper and the major help Treherne to his room without delay, she
begged Rose to comfort her sister, who was sobbing hysterically, and as they
all obeyed her, she led her daughter away to her own apartment; for the
festivities of the evening were at an end. At the same time Mrs. Snowdon and
Annon bade my lady good-night, as if they also were about to retire, but as
they reached the door of the gallery Mrs. Snowdon paused and beckoned
Annon back. They were alone now, and standing before the fire which had so
nearly made that Christmas-eve a tragical one, she turned to him with a face

full of interest and sympathy as she said, nodding towards the blackened shreds of Octavia's dress, and the scorched tiger skin which still lay at their feet:

"That was both a fortunate and an unfortunate little affair, but I fear Maurice's gain will be your loss. Pardon my frankness for Octavia's sake; she is a fine creature, and I long to see her given to one worthy of her. I am a woman to read faces quickly; I know that your suit does not prosper as you would have it, and I desire to help you—may I?"

"Indeed you may, and command any service of me in return. But to what do I owe this unexpected friendliness?" cried Annon, both grateful and surprised.

"To my regard for the young lady, my wish to save her from an unworthy man."

"Do you mean Treherne?" asked Annon, more and more amazed.

"I do. Octavia must not marry a gambler!"

"My dear lady, you labor under some mistake; Treherne is by no means a gambler. I owe him no good-will, but I cannot hear him slandered."

"You are generous, but I am not mistaken. Can you, on your honor, assure me that Maurice never played?"

Mrs. Snowdon's keen eyes were on him, and he looked embarrassed for a moment, but answered, with some hesitation:

"Why, no, I cannot say that, but I can assure you that he is not an habitual gambler. All young men of his rank play more or less, especially abroad. It is merely an amusement with most, and among men is not considered dishonorable or dangerous. Ladies think differently, I believe, at least in England."

At the word "abroad," Mrs. Snowdon's face brightened, and she suddenly dropped her eyes, as if afraid of betraying some secret purpose.

"Indeed we do, and well we may, many of us having suffered from this pernicious habit. I have had especial cause to dread and condemn it, and the fear that Octavia should in time suffer what I have suffered as a girl, urges me to interfere where otherwise I should be dumb. Mr. Annon, there was a rumor that Maurice was forced to quit Paris, owing to some dishonorable practices at the gaming-table. Is this true?"

"Nay, don't ask me; upon my soul I cannot tell you. I only know that something was amiss, but what I never learned. Various tales were whispered at the clubs, and Sir Jasper indignantly denied them all. The bravery with which Maurice saved his cousin, and the sad affliction which fell upon him, silenced the gossip, and it was soon forgotten."

Mrs. Snowdon remained silent for a moment, with brows knit in deep thought, while Annon uneasily watched her. Suddenly she glanced over her shoulder, drew nearer, and whispered, cautiously:

"Did the rumors of which you speak charge him with"—and the last word was breathed into Annon's ear almost inaudibly. He started, as if some new light broke on him, and stared at the speaker with a troubled face for an instant, saying, hastily:

"No, but now you remind me that when an affair of that sort was discussed the other day Treherne looked very odd, and rolled himself away, as if it didn't interest him. I can't believe it, and yet it may be something of the kind. That would account for old Sir Jasper's whim, and Treherne's steady denial of any knowledge of the cause. How in Heaven's name did you learn this?"

"My woman's wit suggested it, and my woman's will shall confirm or destroy the suspicion. My lady and Octavia evidently know nothing, but they shall if there is any danger of the girl's being won by him."

"You would not tell her!" exclaimed Annon.

"I will, unless you do it," was the firm answer.

"Never! To betray a friend, even to gain the woman I love, is a thing I cannot do; my honor forbids it."

Mrs. Snowdon smiled scornfully.

"Men's code of honor is a strong one, and we poor women suffer from it. Leave this to me; do your best, and if all other means fail, you may be glad to try my device to prevent Maurice from marrying his cousin. Gratitude and pity are strong allies, and if he recovers, his strong will will move heaven and earth to gain her. Good-night." And leaving her last words to rankle in Annon's mind, Mrs. Snowdon departed to endure sleepless hours full of tormenting memories, new-born hopes, and alternations of determination and despair.

Treherne's prospect of recovery filled the whole house with delight, for his patient courage and unfailing cheerfulness had endeared him to all. It was no transient amendment, for day by day he steadily gained strength and power, passing rapidly from chair to crutches, from crutches to a cane and a friend's arm, which was always ready for him. Pain returned with returning vitality, but he bore it with a fortitude that touched all who witnessed it. At times motion was torture, yet motion was necessary lest the torpidity should return, and Treherne took his daily exercise with unfailing perseverance, saying, with a smile, though great drops stood upon his forehead:

"I have something dearer even than health to win. Hold me up, Jasper, and let me stagger on, in spite of everything, till my twelve turns are made."

He remembered Lady Treherne's words, "If you were well, I'd gladly give my girl to you." This inspired him with strength, endurance, and a happiness which could not be concealed. It overflowed in looks, words and acts; it infected every one, and made these holidays the blithest the old abbey had seen for many a day.

Annon devoted himself to Octavia, and in spite of her command to be left in peace till the New Year, she was very kind—so kind that hope flamed up in his heart, though he saw that something like compassion often shone on him from her frank eyes, and her compliance had no touch of the tender docility which lovers long to see. She still avoided Treherne, but so skillfully that few observed the change but Annon and himself. In public Sir Jasper appeared to worship at the sprightly Rose's shrine, and she fancied her game was prospering well. But had any one peeped behind the scenes it would have been discovered that during the half hour before dinner, when every one was in their dressing-rooms and the general taking his nap, a pair of ghostly, black figures flitted about the haunted gallery, where no servant ventured without orders. The major fancied himself the only one who had made this discovery, for Mrs. Snowdon affected Treherne's society in public, and was assiduous in serving and amusing the "dear convalescent," as she called him. But the general did not sleep; he too watched and waited, longing yet dreading to speak, and hoping that this was but a harmless freak of Edith's, for her caprices were many, and till now he had indulged them freely. This hesitation disgusted the major, who, being a bachelor, knew little of women's ways, and less of their powers of persuasion. The day before New Year he took a sudden resolution, and demanded a private interview with the general.

"I have come on an unpleasant errand, sir," he abruptly began, as the old man received him with an expression which rather daunted the major. "My friendship for Lady Treherne, and my guardianship of her children, makes me jealous of the honor of the family. I fear it is in danger, sir; pardon me for saying it, but your wife is the cause."

"May I trouble you to explain, Major Royston," was all the general's reply, as his old face grew stern and haughty.

"I will, sir, briefly. I happen to know from Jasper that there were love passages between Miss Dubarry and himself a year or more ago in Paris. A whim parted them, and she married. So far no reproach rests upon either, but since she came here it has been evident to others as well as myself that Jasper's affection has revived, and that Mrs. Snowdon does not reject and reprove it as she should. They often meet, and from Jasper's manner I am convinced that mischief is afloat. He is ardent, headstrong and utterly regardless of the world's opinion in some cases. I have watched them, and what I tell you is true."

"Prove it!"

"I will. They meet in the north gallery, wrapt in dark cloaks, and play ghost if any one comes. I concealed myself behind the screen last evening at dusk, and satisfied myself that my suspicions were correct. I heard little of their conversation, but that little was enough."

"Repeat it, if you please."

"Sir Jasper seemed pleading for some promise which she reluctantly gave, saying, 'While you live I will be true to my word with every one but him. He will suspect, and it will be useless to keep it from him.' 'He will shoot me for this if he knows I am the traitor,' expostulated Jasper. 'He shall not know that; I can hoodwink him easily, and serve my purpose also.' 'You are mysterious, but I leave all to you and wait for my reward; when shall I have it, Edith?' She laughed, and answered so low I could not hear, for they left the gallery as they spoke. Forgive me, general, for the pain I inflict. You are the only person to whom I have spoken, and you are the only person who can properly and promptly prevent this affair from bringing open shame and scandal on an honorable house. To you I leave it, and will do my part with this infatuated young man if you will withdraw the temptation which will ruin him."

"I will, thank you, major; trust to me, and by to-morrow I will prove that I can act as becomes me."

The grief and misery in the general's face touched the major; he silently wrung his hand and went away, thanking Heaven more fervently than ever that no cursed coquette of a woman had it in her power to break his heart.

While this scene was going on above, another was taking place in the library. Treherne sat there alone, thinking happy thoughts evidently, for his eyes shone and his lips smiled as he mused, while watching the splendors of a winter sunset. A soft rustle and the faint scent of violets warned him of Mrs. Snowdon's approach, and a sudden foreboding told him that danger was near. The instant he saw her face his fear was confirmed, for exultation, resolve and love met and mingled in the expression it wore. Leaning in the window recess, where the red light shone full on her lovely face and queenly figure, she said, softly yet with a ruthless accent below the softness:

"Dreaming dreams, Maurice, which will never come to pass, unless I will it. I know your secret, and I shall use it to prevent the fulfilment of the foolish hope you cherish."

"Who told you?" he demanded, with an almost fierce flash of the eye and an angry flush.

"I discovered it, as I warned you I should. My memory is good, I recall the gossip of long ago, I observe the faces, words and acts of those whom I suspect, and unconscious hints from them give me the truth."

"I doubt it;" and Treherne smiled securely.

She stooped and whispered one short sentence into his ear. Whatever it was it caused him to start up with a pale, panic-stricken face, and eye her as if she had pronounced his doom.

"Do you doubt it now?" she asked, coldly.

"He told you! Even your skill and craft could not discover it alone," he muttered.

"Nay, I told you nothing was impossible to a determined woman; I needed no help, for I knew more than you think."

He sank down again in a despairing attitude and hid his face, saying, mournfully:

"I might have known you would hunt me down and dash my hopes when they were surest. How will you use this unhappy secret?"

"I will tell Octavia, and make her duty less hard. It will be kind to both of you, for even with her this memory would mar your happiness; and it saves her from the shame and grief of discovering, when too late, that she has given herself to a—"

"Stop!" he cried, in a tone that made her start and pale, as he rose out of his chair white with a stern indignation which awed her for a moment. "You shall not utter that word—you know but half the truth, and if you wrong me or trouble the girl I will turn traitor also, and tell the general the game you are playing with my cousin. You feign to love me as you feigned before, but his title is the bait now as then, and you fancy that by threatening to mar my hopes you will secure my silence, and gain your end."

"Wrong, quite wrong. Jasper is nothing to me: I use *him* as a tool, not you. If I threaten, it is to keep you from Octavia, who cannot forgive the past and love you for yourself, as I have done all these miserable months. You say I know but half the truth, tell me the whole and I will spare you."

If ever a man was tempted to betray a trust it was Treherne then. A word, and Octavia might be his; silence, and she might be lost; for this woman was in earnest, and possessed the power to ruin his good name forever. The truth leaped to his lips and would have passed them, had not his eye fallen on the portrait of Jasper's father. This man had loved and sheltered the orphan all his life, had made of him a son, and, dying, urged him to guard and serve and save the rebellious youth he left, when most needing a father's care.

"I promised, and I will keep my promise at all costs," sighed Treherne, and with a gesture full of pathetic patience he waved the fair tempter from him, saying, steadily, "I will never tell you, though you rob me of that which is dearer than my life. Go and work your will, but remember that when you might have won the deepest gratitude of the man you profess to love, you chose instead to earn his hatred and contempt."

Waiting for no word of hers, he took refuge in his room, and Edith Snowdon sank down upon the couch, struggling with contending emotions of love and jealousy, remorse and despair. How long she sat there she could not tell; an approaching step recalled her to herself, and looking up she saw Octavia. As the girl approached down the long vista of the drawing-rooms, her youth and beauty, innocence and candor, touched that fairer and more gifted woman with an envy she had never known before. Something in the girl's face struck her instantly; a look of peace and purity, a sweet serenity more winning than loveliness, more impressive than dignity or grace. With a smile on her lips, yet a half-sad, half-tender light in her eyes, and a cluster of pale winter roses in her hand, she came on till she stood before her rival, and offering the flowers, said, in words as simple as sincere:

"Dear Mrs. Snowdon, I cannot let the last sun of the old year set on any misdeeds of mine for which I may atone. I have disliked, distrusted, and misjudged you, and now I come to you in all humility to say forgive me."

With the girlish abandon of her impulsive nature Octavia knelt down before the woman who was plotting to destroy her happiness, laid the roses like a little peace-offering on her lap, and with eloquently pleading eyes waited for pardon. For a moment Mrs. Snowdon watched her, fancying it a well-acted ruse to disarm a dangerous rival; but in that sweet face there was no art: one glance showed her that. The words smote her to the heart and won her in spite of pride or passion, as she suddenly took the girl into her arms, weeping repentant tears. Neither spoke, but in the silence each felt the barrier which had stood between them vanishing, and each learned to know the other better in that moment than in a year of common life. Octavia rejoiced that the instinct which had prompted her to make this appeal had not misled her, but assured her that behind the veil of coldness, pride and levity which this woman wore, there was a heart aching for sympathy and help and love. Mrs. Snowdon felt her worser self slip from her, leaving all that was true and noble to make her worthy of the test applied. Art she could meet with equal art, but nature conquered her, for spite of her misspent life and faulty character, the germ of virtue, which lives in the worst, was there, only waiting for the fostering sun and dew of love to strengthen it, even though the harvest be a late one.

"Forgive you!" she cried, brokenly. "It is I who should ask forgiveness of you—I who should atone, confess and repent. Pardon *me*, pity me, love me, for I am more wretched than you know."

"Dear, I do with heart and soul. Believe it, and let me be your friend," was the soft answer.

"God knows I need one!" sighed the poor woman, still holding fast the only creature who had wholly won her. "Child, I am not good, but not so bad that I dare not look in your innocent face and call you friend. I never had one of my own sex, I never knew my mother; and no one ever saw in me the possibility of goodness, truth and justice but you. Trust and love and help me, Octavia, and I will reward you with a better life, if I can do no more."

"I will, and the new year shall be happier than the old."

"God bless you for that prophecy; may I be worthy of it."

Then as a bell warned them away, the rivals kissed each other tenderly, and parted friends. As Mrs. Snowdon entered her room, she saw her husband sitting with his gray head in his hands, and heard him murmur despairingly to himself:

"My life makes her miserable; but for the sin of it I'd die to free her."

"No, live for me, and teach me to be happy in your love."

The clear voice startled him, but not so much as the beautiful changed face of the wife who laid the gray head on her bosom, saying, tenderly:

"My kind and patient husband, you have been deceived. From me you shall know all the truth, and when you have forgiven my faulty past, you shall see how happy I will try to make your future."

Chapter VII

A Ghostly Revel

B less me, how dull we all are to-night," exclaimed Rose, as the younger portion of the party wandered listlessly about the drawing-rooms that evening, while my lady and the major played an absorbing game of piquet, and the general dozed peacefully at last.

"It is because Maurice is not here; he always keeps us going, for he is a fellow of infinite resources," replied Sir Jasper, suppressing a yawn.

"Have him out then," said Annon.

"He wont come; the poor lad is blue to-night, in spite of his improvement. Something is amiss, and there is no getting a word from him."

"Sad memories afflict him, perhaps," sighed Blanche.

"Don't be absurd, dear, sad memories are all nonsense; melancholy is always indigestion, and nothing is so sure a cure as fun," said Rose, briskly. "I'm going to send in a polite invitation begging him to come and amuse us. He'll accept, I haven't a doubt."

The message was sent, but to Rose's chagrin a polite refusal was returned.

"He *shall* come. Sir Jasper, do you and Mr. Annon go as a deputation from us, and return without him at your peril," was her command.

They went, and while waiting their re-appearance the sisters spoke of what all had observed.

"How lovely Mrs. Snowdon looks to-night. I always thought she owed half her charms to her skill in dress, but she never looked so beautiful as in that plain black silk, with those roses in her hair," said Rose.

"What has she done to herself?" replied Blanche. "I see a change, but can't account for it. She and Tavie have made some beautifying discovery, for both look altogether uplifted and angelic all of a sudden."

"Here come the gentlemen, and, as I'm a Talbot, they haven't got him!" cried Rose, as the deputation appeared, looking very crestfallen. "Don't come near me," she added, irefully, "you are disloyal cowards, and I doom you to exile till I want you. *I* am infinite in resources as well as this recreant man, and come he shall. Mrs. Snowdon, would you mind asking Mr. Treherne to suggest something to wile away the rest of this evening? we are in despair, and can think of nothing, and you are all-powerful with him."

"I must decline, since he refuses you," was the decided answer, as Mrs. Snowdon moved away.

"Tavie, dear, do go; we *must* have him; he always obeys you, and you would be such a public benefactor, you know."

Without a word Octavia wrote a line and sent it by a servant. Several minutes passed, and the gentlemen began to lay wagers on the success of her trial. "He will not come for me, you may be sure," said Octavia. As the words passed her lips he appeared.

A general laugh greeted him, but taking no notice of the jests at his expense, he turned to Octavia, saying, quietly, "What can I do for you, cousin?"

His colorless face and weary eyes reproached her for disturbing him, but it was too late for regret, and she answered, hastily:

"We are in want of some new and amusing occupation to wile away the evening. Can you suggest something appropriate?"

"Why not sit round the hall fire and tell stories, while we wait to see the old year out, as we used to do long ago?" he asked, after a moment's thought.

"I told you so! there it is, just what we want." And Sir Jasper looked triumphant.

"It's capital—let us begin at once. It is after ten now, so we shall not have long to wait," cried Rose, and taking Sir Jasper's arm, she led the way to the hall.

A great fire always burned there, and in winter time thick carpets and curtains covered the stone floor and draped the tall windows. Plants blossomed in the warm atmosphere, and chairs and lounges stood about invitingly. The party was soon seated, and Treherne was desired to begin.

"We must have ghost-stories, and in order to be properly thrilling and effective, the lights must be put out," said Rose, who sat next him, and spoke first, as usual.

This was soon done, and only a ruddy circle of fire-light was left to oppose the rapt gloom that filled the hall, where shadows now seemed to lurk in every corner.

"Don't be very dreadful, or I shall faint away," pleaded Blanche, drawing nearer to Annon, for she had taken her sister's advice, and laid close siege to that gentleman's heart.

"I think your nerves will bear my little tale," replied Treherne. "When I was in India, four years ago, I had a very dear friend in my regiment—a Scotchman; I'm half Scotch myself, you know, and clannish, of course.

Gordon was sent up the country on a scouting expedition, and never returned. His men reported that he left them one evening to take a survey, and his horse came home bloody and riderless. We searched, but could not find a trace of him, and I was desperate to discover and avenge his murder. About a month after his disappearance, as I sat in my tent one fearfully hot day, suddenly the canvas door-flap was raised and there stood Gordon. I saw him as plainly as I see you, Jasper, and should have sprung to meet him, but something held me back. He was deathly pale, dripping with water, and in his bonny blue eyes was a wild, woful look that made my blood run cold. I stared dumbly, for it was awful to see my friend so changed and so unearthly. Stretching his arm to me he took my hand, saying, solemnly, 'Come!' The touch was like ice; an ominous thrill ran through me; I started up to obey, and he was gone."

"A horrid dream, of course. Is that all?" asked Rose.

With his eyes on the fire, and his left hand half extended, Treherne went on, as if he had not heard her:

"I thought it was a fancy, and soon recovered myself, for no one had seen or heard anything of Gordon, and my native servant lay just outside my tent. A strange sensation remained in the hand the phantom touched. It was cold, damp and white. I found it vain to try to forget this apparition; it took strong hold of me; I told Yermid, my man, and he bid me consider it a sign that I was to seek my friend. That night I dreamed I was riding up the country in hot haste; what led me I know not, but I pressed on and on, longing to reach the end. A half-dried river crossed my path, and riding down the steep bank to ford it, I saw Gordon's body lying in the shallow water looking exactly as the vision looked. I woke in a strange mood, told the story to my commanding officer, and, as nothing was doing just then, easily got leave of absence for a week. Taking Yermid, I set out on my sad quest. I thought it folly, but I could not resist the impulse that drew me on. For seven days I searched, and the strangest part of the story is that all that time I went on exactly as in the dream, seeing what I saw then, and led by the touch of a cold hand on mine. On the seventh day I reached the river, and found my friend's body."

"How horrible!—is it really true?" cried Mrs. Snowdon.

"As true as I am a living man; nor is that all; this left hand of mine never has been warm since that time. See and feel for yourselves."

He opened both hands, and all satisfied themselves that the left was smaller, paler and colder than the right.

"Pray some one tell another story to put this out of my mind; it makes me nervous," said Blanche.

"I'll tell one, and you may laugh to quiet your nerves. I want to have mine done with, so that I can enjoy the rest with a free mind." With these words Rose began her tale in the good old fashion.

"Once upon a time, when we were paying a visit to my blessed grandmamma, I saw a ghost in this wise: The dear old lady was ill with a cold and kept her room, leaving us to mope, for it was very dull in the great lonely house. Blanche and I were both homesick, but didn't like to leave till she was better, so we ransacked the library and solaced ourselves with all manner of queer books. One day I found grandmamma very low and nervous, and evidently with something on her mind. She would say nothing, but the next day was worse, and I insisted on knowing the cause, for the trouble was evidently mental. Charging me to keep it from Blanche, who was, and is, a sad coward, she told me that a spirit had appeared to her two successive nights. 'If it comes a third time, I shall prepare to die,' said the foolish old lady. 'No you wont, for I'll come and stay with you and lay your ghost,' I said. With some difficulty I made her yield, and after Blanche was asleep I slipped away to grandmamma, with a book and candle for a long watch, as the spirit didn't appear till after midnight. She usually slept with her door unlocked, in case of fire or fright, and her maid was close by. That night I locked the door, telling her that spirits could come through the oak if they chose, and I preferred to have a fair trial. Well, I read and chatted and dozed till dawn and nothing appeared, so I laughed at the whole affair, and the old lady pretended to be convinced that it was all a fancy. Next night I slept in my own room, and in the morning was told that not only grandmamma but Janet had seen the spirit. All in white, with streaming hair, a pale face and a red streak at the throat. It came and parted the bed curtains, looking in a moment, and then vanished. Janet had slept with grandmamma, and kept a lamp burning on the chimney, so both saw it. I was puzzled, but not frightened; I never am, and I insisted on trying again. The door was left unlocked, as on the previous night, and I lay with grandmamma, a light burning as before. About two she clutched me as I was dropping off. I looked, and there, peeping in between the dark curtains, was a pale face with long hair all about it, and a red streak at the throat. It was very dim, the light being low, but I saw it, and after one breathless minute sprang up, caught my foot, fell down with a crash, and by the time I was round the bed, not a vestige of the thing appeared. I was angry, and vowed I'd succeed at all

hazards, though I'll confess I was just a bit daunted. Next time Janet and I sat
up in easy chairs, with bright lights burning, and both wide awake with the
strongest coffee we could make. As the hour drew near we got nervous, and
when the white shape came gliding in Janet hid her face. I didn't, and after
one look was on the point of laughing, for the spirit was Blanche walking in
her sleep. She wore a coral necklace in those days, and never took it off, and
her long hair half hid her face, which had the unnatural, uncanny look
somnambulists always wear. I had the sense to keep still and tell Janet what to
do, so the poor child went back unwaked, and grandmamma's spirit never
walked again for I took care of that."

"Why did you haunt the old lady?" asked Annon, as the laughter ceased.

"I don't know, unless it was that I wanted to ask leave to go home, and
was afraid to do it awake, so tried when asleep. I shall not tell any story, as I
was the heroine of this, but will give my turn to you, Mr. Annon," said
Blanche, with a soft glance, which was quite thrown away, for the gentleman's
eyes were fixed on Octavia, who sat on a low ottoman at Mrs. Snowdon's
feet, in the full glow of the fire-light.

"I've had very small experience in ghosts, and can only recall a little fright
I once had when a boy at college. I'd been out to a party, got home tired,
couldn't find my matches, and retired in the dark. Towards morning I woke,
and glancing up to see if the dim light was dawn or moonshine I was
horrified to see a coffin standing at the bed's foot. I rubbed my eyes to be
sure I was awake, and looked with all my might. There it was, a long black
coffin, and I saw the white plate in the dusk, for the moon was setting and
my curtain was not drawn. 'It's some trick of the fellows,' I thought; 'I'll not
betray myself, but keep cool.' Easy to say but hard to do, for it suddenly
flashed into my mind that I might be in the wrong room. I glanced about,
but there were the familiar objects as usual, as far as the indistinct light
allowed me to see, and I made sure by feeling on the wall at the bed's head
for my watch-case. It was there, and mine beyond a doubt, being peculiar in
shape and fabric. Had I been to a college wine-party I could have accounted
for the vision, but a quiet evening in a grave professor's well-conducted
family could produce no ill effects. 'It's an optical illusion, or a prank of my
mates; I'll sleep and forget it,' I said, and for a time endeavored to do so, but
curiosity overcame my resolve, and soon I peeped again. Judge of my horror
when I saw the sharp white outline of a dead face, which seemed to be
peeping up from the coffin. It gave me a terrible shock, for I was but a lad
and had been ill. I hid my face, and quaked like a nervous girl, still thinking it

some joke, and too proud to betray fear lest I should be laughed at. How long I lay there I don't know, but when I looked again the face was farther out and the whole figure seemed rising slowly. The moon was nearly down, I had no lamp, and to be left in the dark with that awesome thing was more than I could bear. Joke or earnest, I must end the panic, and bolting out of my room I roused my neighbor. He told me I was mad or drunk, but lit a lamp and returned with me, to find my horror only a heap of clothes thrown on the table in such a way that, as the moon's pale light shot in, it struck upon my black student's gown, with a white card lying on it, and produced the effect of a coffin and plate. The face was a crumpled handkerchief, and what seemed hair a brown muffler. As the moon sunk, these outlines changed, and, incredible as it may seem, grew like a face. My friend not having had the fright enjoyed the joke, and 'coffins' was my sobriquet for a long while."

"You get worse and worse. Sir Jasper, do vary the horrors by a touch of fun, or I shall run away," said Blanche, glancing over her shoulder nervously.

"I'll do my best, and tell a story my uncle used to relate of his young days. I forget the name of the place, but it was some little country town famous among anglers. My uncle often went to fish, and always regretted that a deserted house near the trout stream was not occupied, for the inn was inconveniently distant. Speaking of this one evening, as he lounged in the landlady's parlor, he asked why no one took it and let the rooms to strangers in the fishing season. 'For fear of the ghostissess, your honor,' replied the woman, and proceeded to tell him that three distinct spirits haunted the house. In the garret was heard the hum of a wheel and the tap of high-heeled shoes, as the ghostly spinner went to and fro. In a chamber sounded the sharpening of a knife, followed by groans and the drip of blood. The cellar was made awful by a skeleton sitting on a half-buried box and chuckling fiendishly. It seems a miser lived there once, and was believed to have starved his daughter in the garret, keeping her at work till she died. The second spirit was that of the girl's rejected lover, who cut his throat in the chamber, and the third of the miser who was found dead on the money-chest he was too feeble to conceal. My uncle laughed at all this, and offered to lay the ghosts if any one would take the house.

"This offer got abroad, and a crusty old fellow accepted it, hoping to turn a penny. He had a pretty girl, whose love had been thwarted by the old man, and whose lover was going to sea in despair. My uncle knew this and pitied the young people. He had made acquaintance with a wandering artist, and

the two agreed to conquer the prejudices against the house by taking rooms
there. They did so, and after satisfying themselves regarding the noises,
consulted a wise old woman as to the best means of laying the ghosts. She
told them if any young girl would pass a night in each haunted room, praying
piously the while, that all would be well. Peggy was asked if she would do it,
and being a stout-hearted lass she consented, for a round sum, to try it. The
first night was in the garret, and Peggy, in spite of the prophecies of the
village gossips, came out alive, though listeners at the door heard the weird
humming and tapping all night long. The next night all went well, and from
that time no more sharpening, groaning or dripping was heard. The third
time she bade her friends good-by, and wrapped in her red cloak, with a
lamp and prayer-book, went down into the cellar. Alas for pretty Peggy!
when day came she was gone, and with her the miser's empty box, though his
bones remained to prove how well she had done her work.

"The town was in an uproar, and the old man furious. Some said the devil
had flown away with her, others that the bones were hers, and all agreed that
henceforth another ghost would haunt the house. My uncle and the artist did
their best to comfort the father, who sorely reproached himself for thwarting
the girl's love, and declared that if Jack would find her he should have her.
But Jack had sailed, and the old man 'was left lamenting.' The house was
freed from its unearthly visitors, however, for no ghost appeared, and when
my uncle left, old Martin found money and letter informing him that Peggy
had spent her first two nights preparing for flight, and on the third had gone
away to marry and sail with Jack. The noises had been produced by the
artist, who was a ventriloquist, the skeleton had been smuggled from the
surgeons, and the whole thing was a conspiracy to help Peggy and accommodate the fishermen."

"It is evident that roguery is hereditary," laughed Rose, as the narrator
paused.

"I strongly suspect that Sir Jasper the second was the true hero of that
story," added Mrs. Snowdon.

"Think what you like, I've done my part, and leave the stage for you,
madame."

"I will come last. It is your turn, dear."

As Mrs. Snowdon softly uttered the last word, and Octavia leaned upon
her knee with an affectionate glance, Treherne leaned forward to catch a
glimpse of the two changed faces, and looked as if bewildered when both
smiled at him, as they sat hand in hand while the girl told her story.

"Long ago a famous actress suddenly dropped dead at the close of a splendidly-played tragedy. She was carried home, and preparations were made to bury her. The play had been gotten up with great care and expense, and a fine actor was the hero. The public demanded a repetition, and an inferior person was engaged to take the dead lady's part. A day's delay had been necessary, but when the night came the house was crowded. They waited both before and behind the curtain for the debut of the new actress, with much curiosity. She stood waiting for her cue, but as it was given, to the amazement of all, the great tragedienne glided upon the stage. Pale as marble, and with a strange fire in her eyes, strange pathos in her voice, strange power in her acting, she went through her part, and at the close vanished as mysteriously as she came. Great was the excitement that night, and intense the astonishment and horror next day when it was whispered abroad that the dead woman never had revived, but had laid in her coffin before the eyes of watchers all the evening, when hundreds fancied they were applauding her at the theatre. The mystery never was cleared up, and Paris was divided by two opinions; one that some person marvellously like Madame Z. had personated her for the sake of a sensation; the other that the ghost of the dead actress, unable to free itself from the old duties so full of fascination to an ambitious and successful woman, had played for the last time the part which had made her famous."

"Where did you find that, Tavie? It's very French, and not bad if you invented it," said Sir Jasper.

"I read it in an old book, where it was much better told. Now, Edith, there is just time for your tale."

As the word "Edith" passed her lips, again Treherne started and eyed them both, and again they smiled, as Mrs. Snowdon caressed the smooth cheek leaning on her knee, and looking full at him began the last recital.

"You have been recounting the pranks of imaginary ghosts; let me show you the workings of some real spirits, evil and good, that haunt every heart and home, making its misery or joy. At Christmas time, in a country house, a party of friends met to keep the holidays, and very happily they might have done so had not one person marred the peace of several. Love, jealousy, deceit and nobleness were the spirits that played their freaks with these people. The person of whom I speak was more haunted than the rest, and much tormented, being willful, proud and jealous. Heaven help her, she had had no one to exorcise these ghosts for her, and they goaded her to do much harm. Among these friends there were more than one pair of lovers, and much tangling of plots and plans, for hearts are wayward and mysterious things, and cannot love as duty bids or prudence counsels. This woman held the key to all the secrets of the house, and having a purpose to gain, she used her power selfishly, for a time. To satisfy a doubt, she feigned a fancy for a gentleman who once did her the honor of admiring her, and, to the great scandal of certain sage persons, permitted him to show his regard for her, knowing that it was but a transient amusement on his part as well as upon hers. In the hands of this woman lay a secret which could make or mar the happiness of the best and dearest of the party. The evil spirits which haunted her urged her to mar their peace and gratify a sinful hope. On the other side, honor, justice and generosity prompted her to make them happy, and while she wavered there came to her a sweet enchantress who, with a word, banished the tormenting ghosts forever, and gave the haunted woman a talisman to keep her free henceforth."

There the earnest voice faltered, and with a sudden impulse Mrs. Snowdon bent her head and kissed the fair forehead which had bent lower and lower as she went on. Each listener understood the truth, lightly veiled in that hasty fable, and each found in it a different meaning. Sir Jasper frowned and bit his lips, Annon glanced anxiously from face to face, Octavia hid hers, and Treherne's flashed with sudden intelligence, while Rose laughed low to herself, enjoying the scene. Blanche, who was getting sleepy, said, with a stifled gape:

"That is a very nice, moral little story, but I wish there had been some real ghosts in it."

"There was, will you come and see them?"

As she put the question, Mrs. Snowdon rose abruptly, wishing to end the *séance*, and beckoning them to follow glided up the great stairway. All obeyed, wondering what whim possessed her, and quite ready for any jest in store for them.

Chapter VIII

~

Jasper

She led them to the north gallery, and pausing at the door, said, merrily: "The ghost, or ghosts rather, for there were two, which frightened Patty were Sir Jasper and myself, meeting to discuss certain important matters which concerned Mr. Treherne. If you want to see spirits we will play phantom for you, and convince you of our power."

"Good, let us go and have a ghostly dance, as a proper finale of our revel," answered Rose, as they flocked into the long hall.

At that moment the great clock struck twelve, and all paused to bid the old year adieu. Sir Jasper was the first to speak, for, angry with Mrs. Snowdon, yet thankful to her for making a jest to others of what had been earnest to him, he desired to hide his chagrin under a gay manner, and taking Rose round the waist was about to waltz away, as she proposed, saying, cheerily:

"Come one and all, and dance the new year in,"

when a cry from Octavia arrested him, and turning he saw her stand, pale and trembling, pointing to the far end of the hall.

Eight narrow gothic windows pierced either wall of the north gallery. A full moon sent her silvery light strongly in upon the eastern side, making broad bars of brightness across the floor. No fires burned there now, and wherever the moonlight did not fall deep shadows lay. As Octavia cried out, all looked, and all distinctly saw a tall, dark figure moving noiselessly across the second bar of light far down the hall.

"Is it some jest of yours?" asked Sir Jasper of Mrs. Snowdon, as the form vanished in the shadow.

"No, upon my honor, I know nothing of it! I only meant to relieve Octavia's superstitious fears by showing her our pranks," was the whispered reply, as Mrs. Snowdon's cheek paled, and she drew nearer to Jasper.

"Who is there?" called Treherne, in a commanding tone.

No answer, but a faint, cold breath of air seemed to sigh along the arched roof and die away as the dark figure crossed the third streak of moonlight. A strange awe fell upon them all, and no one spoke, but stood watching for the appearance of the shape. Nearer and nearer it came, with soundless steps, and as it reached the sixth window its outlines were distinctly visible. A tall, wasted figure, all in black, with a rosary hanging from the girdle, and a dark beard half concealing the face.

"The Abbot's ghost, and very well got up," said Annon, trying to laugh but failing decidedly, for again the cold breath swept over them, causing a general shudder.

"Hush!" whispered Treherne, drawing Octavia to his side with a protecting gesture.

Once more the phantom appeared and disappeared, and as they waited for it to cross the last bar of light that lay between it and them, Mrs. Snowdon stepped forward to the edge of the shadow in which they stood, as if to confront the apparition alone. Out of the darkness it came, and in the full radiance of the light it paused. Mrs. Snowdon, being nearest, saw the face first, and uttering a faint cry dropped down upon the stone floor, covering up her eyes. Nothing human ever wore a look like that of the ghastly, hollow-eyed, pale-lipped countenance below the hood. All saw it and held their breath as it slowly raised a shadowy arm and pointed a shrivelled finger at Sir Jasper.

"Speak, whatever you are, or I'll quickly prove whether you are man or spirit!" cried Jasper fiercely, stepping forward as if to grasp the extended arm, that seemed to menace him alone.

An icy gust swept through the hall, and the phantom slowly receded into the shadow. Jasper sprung after it, but nothing crossed the second stream of light, and nothing remained in the shade. Like one possessed by a sudden fancy he rushed down the gallery to find all fast and empty, and to return looking very strangely. Blanche had fainted away and Annon was bearing her out of the hall. Rose was clinging to Mrs. Snowdon, and Octavia leaned against her cousin, saying, in a fervent whisper:

"Thank God it did not point at you!"

"Am I then dearer than your brother?" he whispered back.

There was no audible reply, but one little hand involuntarily pressed his, though the other was outstretched toward Jasper, who came up white and startled but firm and quiet. Affecting to make light of it, he said, forcing a smile, as he raised Mrs. Snowdon:

"It is some stupid joke of the servants, let us think no more of it. Come, Edith, this is not like your usual self."

"It was nothing human, Jasper; you know it as well as I. O, why did I bring you here to meet the warning phantom that haunts your house!"

"Nay, if my time is near the spirit would have found me out wherever I might be. I have no faith in that absurd superstition—I laugh at and defy it. Come down and drink my health in wine from the Abbot's own cellar."

But no one had heart for further gayety, and finding Lady Treherne already alarmed by Annon, they were forced to tell her all, and find their own bewilderment deepened by her unalterable belief in the evil omen.

At her command the house was searched, the servants cross-questioned, and every effort made to discover the identity of the apparition. All in vain; the house was as usual, and not a man or maid but turned pale at the idea of entering the gallery at midnight. At my lady's request, all promised to say no more upon the mystery, and separated at last to such sleep as they could enjoy.

Very grave were the faces gathered about the breakfast table next morning, and very anxious the glances cast on Sir Jasper as he came in, late as usual, looking uncommonly blithe and well. Nothing serious ever made a deep impression on his mercurial nature. Treherne had more the air of a doomed man, being very pale and worn, in spite of an occasional gleam of happiness as he looked at Octavia. He haunted Jasper like a shadow all the morning, much to that young gentleman's annoyance, for both his mother and sister hung about him with faces of ill-dissembled anxiety. By afternoon his patience gave out, and he openly rebelled against the tender guard kept over him. Ringing for his horse he said, decidedly:

"I'm bored to death with the solemnity which pervades the house to-day, so I'm off for a brisk gallop, before I lose my temper and spirits altogether."

"Come with me in the pony carriage, Jasper. I've not had a drive with you for a long while, and should enjoy it so much," said my lady, detaining him.

"Mrs. Snowdon looks as if she needed air to revive her roses, and the pony carriage is just the thing for her, so I will cheerfully resign my seat to her," he answered, laughing, as he forced himself from his mother's hand.

"Take the girls in the clarence, we all want a breath of air, and you are the best whip we know. Be gallant, and say yes, dear."

"No, thank you, Tavie, that wont do. Rose and Blanche are both asleep, and you are dying to go and do likewise, after your vigils last night. As a man and a brother I beg you'll do so, and let me ride as I like."

"Suppose you ask Annon to join you—" began Treherne, with well-assumed indifference; but Sir Jasper frowned and turned sharply on him, saying, half-petulantly, half-jocosely:

"Upon my life I should think I was a boy or a baby, by the manner in which you mount guard over me to-day. If you think I'm going to live in daily fear of some mishap, you are all much mistaken. Ghost or no ghost, I shall make merry while I can; a short life and a jolly one has always been my motto, you know, so fare you well till dinner time."

They watched him gallop down the avenue, and then went their different ways, still burdened with a nameless foreboding. Octavia strolled into the conservatory, thinking to refresh herself with the balmy silence which pervaded the place, but Annon soon joined her, full of a lover's hopes and fears.

"Miss Treherne, I have ventured to come for my answer. Is my New Year to be a blissful or a sad one?" he asked, eagerly.

"Forgive me if I give you an unwelcome reply, but I must be true, and so regretfully refuse the honor you do me," she said, sorrowfully.

"May I ask why?"

"Because I do not love you."

"And you do love your cousin," he cried, angrily, pausing to watch her half-averted face.

She turned it fully towards him, and answered, with her native sincerity:

"Yes, I do, with all my heart, and now my mother will not thwart me, for Maurice has saved my life, and I am free to devote it all to him."

"Happy man, I wish I had been a cripple!" sighed Annon, then with a manful effort to be just and generous, he added, heartily, "Say no more, he deserves you; I want no sacrifice to duty; I yield, and go away, praying Heaven to bless you now and always."

He kissed her hand and left her to seek my lady and make his adieux, for no persuasion could keep him. Leaving a note for Sir Jasper, he hurried away, to the great relief of Treherne, and the deep regret of Blanche, who, however, lived in hopes of another trial later in the season.

"Here comes Jasper, mamma, safe and well," cried Octavia, an hour or two later, as she joined her mother on the terrace, where my lady had been pacing restlessly to and fro nearly ever since her son rode away.

With a smile of intense relief she waved her handkerchief, as he came clattering up the drive, and seeing her, he answered with hat and hand. He usually dismounted at the great-hall door, but a sudden whim made him ride along the wall that lay below the terrace, for he was a fine horseman, and Mrs. Snowdon was looking from her window. As he approached, the peacocks fled screaming, and one flew up just before the horse's eyes as his master was in the act of dismounting. The spirited creature was startled, sprang part way up the low, broad steps of the terrace, and being sharply checked, slipped, fell, and man and horse rolled down together.

Never did those who heard it forget the cry that left Lady Treherne's lips as she saw the fall. It brought out both guests and servants, to find Octavia recklessly struggling with the frightened horse, and my lady down upon the stones with her son's bleeding head in her arms.

They bore in the senseless, shattered body, and for hours tried everything that skill and science could devise to save the young man's life. But every effort was in vain, and as the sun set Sir Jasper lay dying. Conscious at last, and able to speak, he looked about him with a troubled glance, and seemed struggling with some desire that overmastered pain and held death at bay.

"I want Maurice," he feebly said, at length.

"Dear lad, I'm here," answered his cousin's voice, from a seat in the shadow of the half-drawn curtains.

"Always near when I need you. Many a scrape have you helped me out of, but this is beyond your power," and a faint smile passed over Jasper's lips as the past flitted before his mind. But the smile died, and a groan of pain escaped him as he cried, suddenly, "Quick! let me tell it before it is too late! Maurice never will, but bear the shame all his life that my dead name may be untarnished. Bring Edith; she must hear the truth."

She was soon there, and lying in his mother's arms, one hand in his cousin's, and one on his sister's bent head, Jasper rapidly told the secret which had burdened him for a year.

"I did it; I forged my uncle's name when I had lost so heavily at play that I dared not tell my mother, or squander more of my own fortune. I deceived Maurice, and let him think the cheque a genuine one; I made him present it and get the money, and when all went well I fancied I was safe. But my uncle discovered it secretly, said nothing, and believing Maurice the forger, disinherited him. I never knew this till the old man died, and then it was too late. I confessed to Maurice, and he forgave me; he said, 'I am helpless now, shut out from the world, with nothing to lose or gain, and soon to be forgotten by those who once knew me, so let the suspicion of shame, if any such there be, still cling to me, and do you go your way, rich, happy, honorable and untouched by any shadow on your fame.' Mother, I let him do it, unconscious as he was that many knew the secret sin, and fancied him the doer of it."

"Hush, Jasper, let it pass; I can bear it; I promised your dear father to be your stanch friend through life, and I have only kept my word."

"God knows you have, but now my life ends, and I cannot die till you are cleared. Edith, I told you half the truth, and you would have used it against him had not some angel sent this girl to touch your heart. You have done your part to atone for the past, now let me do mine. Mother, Tavie loves him, he has risked life and honor for me, repay him generously and give him this."

With feeble touch Sir Jasper tried to lay his sister's hand in Treherne's, as he spoke; Mrs. Snowdon helped him, and as my lady bowed her head in silent acquiescence, a joyful smile shone on the dying man's face.

"One more confession, and then I am ready," he said, looking up into the face of the woman whom he had loved with all the power of a shallow nature. "It was a jest to you, Edith, but it was bitter earnest to me, for I loved you, sinful as it was. Ask your husband to forgive me, and tell him it was better I should die than live to mar a good man's peace. Kiss me once, and make him happy for my sake."

She touched his cold lips with remorseful tenderness, and in the same breath registered a vow to obey that dying prayer.

"Tavie dear, Maurice, my brother, God bless you both. Good-by, mother, he will be a better son than I have been to you." Then, the reckless spirit of the man surviving to the last, Sir Jasper laughed faintly, as he seemed to beckon some invisible shape, and died saying, gayly, "Now, Father Abbot, lead on, I'll follow you."

A year later three weddings were celebrated on the same day and in the same church. Maurice Treherne, a well man, led up his cousin. Frank Annon rewarded Blanche's patient siege by an unconditioned surrender, and, to the infinite amusement of Mrs. Grundy, Major Royston publicly confessed himself out-generaled by merry Rose. The triple wedding feast was celebrated at Treherne Abbey, and no uncanny visitor marred its festivities, for never again was the north gallery haunted by the ghostly Abbot.

Perilous Play

Editor's Note: Even a writer as skilled as Alcott must have found it difficult to rework the gothic formula imaginatively in thriller after thriller. "Perilous Play" represents one of her most startling variations on gothic themes. In lieu of the usual menacing villain, it depicts an otherwise decent man whose affections run to lust under the influence of drugs. Although surprisingly modern by today's standards, Alcott's portrayal of cultured men and women dipping into hashish like so many after-dinner mints must have seemed scandalous when it was published in 1869.

If some one does not propose a new and interesting amusement, I shall die of ennui!" said pretty Belle Daventry, in a tone of despair. "I have read all my books, used up all my Berlin wools, and it's too warm to go to town for more. No one can go sailing yet, as the tide is out; we are all nearly tired to death of cards, croquet, and gossip, so what shall we do to while away this endless afternoon? Doctor Meredith, I command you to invent and propose a new game in five minutes."

"To hear is to obey," replied the young man, who lay in the grass at her feet, as he submissively slapped his forehead, and fell a-thinking with all his might.

Holding up her finger to preserve silence, Belle pulled out her watch, and waited with an expectant smile. The rest of the young party, who were indolently scattered about under the elms, drew nearer, and brightened visibly, for Doctor Meredith's inventive powers were well known, and something refreshingly novel might be expected from him. One gentleman did not stir, but, then, he lay within ear-shot, and merely turned his fine eyes from the sea to the group before him. His glance rested a moment on Belle's piquant figure, for she looked very pretty with her bright hair blowing in the wind, one plump white arm extended to keep order, and one little foot, in a distracting slipper, just visible below the voluminous folds of her dress. Then the glance passed to another figure, sitting somewhat apart in a cloud of white muslin, for an airy burnoose floated from head and shoulders, showing only a singularly charming face. Pale, and yet brilliant, for the Southern eyes were magnificent, the clear olive cheeks contrasted well with darkest hair; lips like a pomegranate flower, and delicate, straight brows, as mobile as the lips. A cluster of crimson flowers, half falling from the loose black braids, and a golden bracelet of Arabian coins on the slender wrist, were the only ornaments she wore, and became her better than the fashionable frippery of her companions. A book lay on her lap, but her eyes, full of a passionate melancholy, were fixed on the sea, which glittered round an island green and flowery as a summer paradise. Rose St. Just was as beautiful as her Spanish mother, but had inherited the pride and reserve of her English father; and this pride was the thorn which repelled lovers from the human flower. Mark Done sighed as he looked, and, as if the sigh, low as it was, roused her from her reverie, Rose flashed a quick glance at him, took up her book, and went on reading the legend of "The Lotus Eaters."

"Time is up now, doctor," cried Belle, pocketing her watch with a flourish.

"Ready to report," answered Meredith, sitting up, and producing a little box of tortoise-shell and gold.

"How mysterious! What is it? Let me see, first!" And Belle removed the cover, looking like an inquisitive child. "Only bonbons; how stupid! That won't do, sir. We don't want to be fed with sugar-plums. We demand to be amused."

"Eat six of these despised bonbons, and you *will* be amused in a new, delicious and wonderful manner," said the young doctor, laying half a dozen on a green leaf, and offering them to her.

"Why, what are they?" she asked, looking at them askance.

"Hasheesh; did you never hear of it?"

"Oh, yes; it's that Indian stuff which brings one fantastic visions, isn't it?

I've always wanted to see and taste it, and now I will," cried Belle, nibbling at one of the bean-shaped comfits with its green heart.

"I advise you not to try it. People do all sorts of queer things when they take it. I wouldn't for the world," said a prudent young lady, warningly, as all examined the box and its contents.

"Six can do no harm, I give you my word. I take twenty before I can enjoy myself, and some people even more. I've tried many experiments, both on the sick and the well, and nothing ever happened amiss, though the demonstrations were immensely interesting," said Meredith, eating his sugar-plums with a tranquil air, which was very convincing to others.

"How shall I feel?" asked Belle, beginning on her second comfit.

"A heavenly dreaminess comes over one, in which they move as if on air. Everything is calm and lovely to them: no pain, no care, no fear of anything, and while it lasts one feels like an angel half-asleep."

"But if one takes too much, how then?" said a deep voice, behind the doctor.

"Hum! Well, that's not so pleasant, unless one likes phantoms, frenzies, and a touch of nightmare, which seems to last a thousand years. Ever try it, Done?" replied Meredith, turning toward the speaker, who was now leaning on his arm, and looking interested.

"Never. I'm not a good subject for experiments. Too nervous a temperament to play pranks with."

"I should say ten would be about your number. Less than that seldom affects men. Ladies go off sooner, and don't need so many. Miss St. Just, may I offer you a taste of Elysium? I owe my success to you," said the doctor, approaching her deferentially.

"To me! And how?" she asked, lifting her large eyes with a slight smile.

"I was in the depths of despair when my eye caught the title of your book, and I was saved. For I remembered that I had hasheesh in my pocket."

"Are you a lotus-eater?" she said, permitting him to lay the six charmed bonbons on the page.

"My faith, no! I use it for my patients. It is very efficacious in nervous disorders, and is getting to be quite a pet remedy with us."

"I do not want to forget the past, but to read the future. Will hasheesh help me to do that?" asked Rose, with an eager look, which made the young man flush, wondering if he bore any part in her hopes of that veiled future.

"Alas, no. I wish it could, for I, too, long to know my fate," he answered, very low, as he looked into the lovely face before him.

The soft glance changed to one of cool indifference, and Rose gently brushed the hasheesh off her book, saying, with a little gesture of dismissal:

"Then I have no desire to taste Elysium."

The white morsels dropped into the grass at her feet; but Doctor Meredith let them lie, and turning sharply, went back to sun himself in Belle's smiles.

"I've eaten all mine, and so has Evelyn. Mr. Norton will see goblins, I know, for he has taken quantities. I'm glad of it, for he don't believe in it, and I want to have him convinced by making a spectacle of himself for our amusement," said Belle, in great spirits at the new plan.

"When does the trance come on?" asked Evelyn, a shy girl, already rather alarmed at what she had done.

"About three hours after you take your dose, though the time varies with different people. Your pulse will rise, heart beat quickly, eyes darken and dilate, and an uplifted sensation will pervade you generally. Then these symptoms change, and the bliss begins. I've seen people sit or lie in one position for hours, rapt in a delicious dream, and wake from it as tranquil as if they had not a nerve in their bodies."

"How charming! I'll take some every time I'm worried. Let me see. It's now four, so our trances will come about seven, and we will devote the evening to manifestations," said Belle.

"Come, Done, try it. We are all going in for the fun. Here's your dose," and Meredith tossed him a dozen bonbons, twisted up in a bit of paper.

"No, thank you; I know myself too well to risk it. If you are all going to turn hasheesh-eaters, you'll need some one to take care of you, so I'll keep sober," tossing the little parcel back.

It fell short, and the doctor, too lazy to pick it up, let it lie, merely saying, with a laugh:

"Well, I advise any bashful man to take hasheesh when he wants to offer his heart to any fair lady, for it will give him the courage of a hero, the eloquence of a poet, and the ardor of an Italian. Remember that, gentlemen, and come to me when the crisis approaches."

"Does it conquer the pride, rouse the pity, and soften the hard hearts of the fair sex?" asked Done.

"I dare say now is your time to settle the fact, for here are two ladies who have imbibed, and in three hours will be in such a seraphic state of mind that 'No' will be an impossibility to them."

"Oh, mercy on us; what *have* we done? If that's the case, I shall shut myself up till my foolish fit is over. Rose, you haven't taken any; I beg you to mount guard over me, and see that I don't disgrace myself by any nonsense. Promise me you will," cried Belle, in half real, half feigned alarm at the consequences of her prank.

"I promise," said Rose, and floated down the green path as noiselessly as a white cloud, with a curious smile on her lips.

"Don't tell any of the rest what we have done, but after tea let us go into the grove and compare notes," said Norton, as Done strolled away to the beach, and the voices of approaching friends broke the summer quiet.

At tea, the initiated glanced covertly at one another, and saw, or fancied they saw, the effects of the hasheesh, in a certain suppressed excitement of manner, and unusually brilliant eyes. Belle laughed often, a silvery ringing laugh, pleasant to hear; but when complimented on her good spirits, she looked distressed, and said she could not help her merriment; Meredith was quite calm, but rather dreamy; Evelyn was pale, and her next neighbor heard her heart beat; Norton talked incessantly, but as he talked uncommonly well, no one suspected anything. Done and Miss St. Just watched the others with interest, and were very quiet, especially Rose, who scarcely spoke, but smiled her sweetest, and looked very lovely.

The moon rose early, and the experimenters slipped away to the grove, leaving the outsiders on the lawn as usual. Some bold spirit asked Rose to sing, and she at once complied, pouring out Spanish airs in a voice that melted the hearts of her audience, so full of fiery sweetness or tragic pathos was it. Done seemed quite carried away, and lay with his face in the grass, to hide the tears that would come; till, afraid of openly disgracing himself, he started up and hurried down to the little wharf, where he sat alone, listening to the music with a countenance which plainly revealed to the stars the passion which possessed him. The sound of loud laughter from the grove, followed by entire silence, caused him to wonder what demonstrations were taking place, and half resolved to go and see. But that enchanting voice held him captive, even when a boat put off mysteriously from a point near by, and sailed away like a phantom through the twilight.

Half an hour afterward, a white figure came down the path, and Rose's voice broke in on his midsummer night's dream. The moon shone clearly now, and showed him the anxiety in her face as she said hurriedly:

"Where is Belle?"

"Gone sailing, I believe."

"How could you let her go? She was not fit to take care of herself."

"I forgot that."

"So did I; but I promised to watch over her, and I must. Which way did they go?" demanded Rose, wrapping the white mantle about her, and running her eye over the little boats moored below.

"You will follow her?"

"Yes."

"I'll be your guide, then. They went toward the lighthouse; it is too far to row; I am at your service. Oh, say yes," cried Done, leaping into his own skiff, and offering his hand persuasively.

She hesitated an instant and looked at him. He was always pale, and the moonlight seemed to increase this pallor, but his hat-brim hid his eyes, and his voice was very quiet. A loud peal of laughter floated over the water, and, as if the sound decided her, she gave him her hand and entered the boat. Done smiled triumphantly as he shook out the sail, which caught the freshening wind, and sent the boat dancing along a path of light.

How lovely it was! All the indescribable allurements of a perfect summer night surrounded them; balmy airs, enchanting moonlight, distant music, and, close at hand, the delicious atmosphere of love, which made itself felt in the eloquent silences that fell between them. Rose seemed to yield to the subtle charm, and leaned back on the cushioned seat, with her beautiful head uncovered, her face full of dreamy softness, and her hands lying loosely clasped before her. She seldom spoke, showed no further anxiety for Belle, and soon seemed to forget the object of her search, so absorbed was she in some delicious thought which wrapped her in its peace.

Done sat opposite, flushed now, restless, and excited, for his eyes glittered; the hand on the rudder shook, and his voice sounded intense and passionate, even in the utterance of the simplest words. He talked continually and with unusual brilliancy, for, though a man of many accomplishments, he was too indolent or too fastidious to exert himself, except among his peers. Rose seemed to look without seeing, to listen without hearing, and, though she smiled blissfully, the smiles were evidently not for him.

On they sailed, scarcely heeding the bank of black cloud piled up in the horizon, the rising wind, or the silence which proved their solitude. Rose moved once or twice, and lifted her hand as if to speak, but sank back mutely, and the hand fell again, as if it had not energy enough to enforce her wish. A cloud sweeping over the moon, a distant growl of thunder, and the slight gust that struck the sail, seemed to rouse her. Done was singing now like one inspired, his hat at his feet, hair in disorder, and a strangely rapturous expression in his eyes, which were fixed on her. She started, shivered, and seemed to recover herself with an effort.

"Where are they?" she asked, looking vainly for the island heights and the other boat.

"They have gone to the beach, I fancy, but we will follow." As Done leaned forward to speak, she saw his face, and shrank back with a sudden flush, for in it she read clearly what she had felt, yet doubted until now. He saw the tell-tale blush and gesture, and said impetuously: "You know it now; you cannot deceive me longer, nor daunt me with your pride! Rose, I love you, and dare tell you so to-night!"

"Not now—not here—I will not listen. Turn back, and be silent, I entreat you, Mr. Done," she said, hurriedly.

He laughed a defiant laugh, and took her hand in his, which was burning and throbbing with the rapid heat of his pulse.

"No, I *will* have my answer here, and now, and never turn back till you give it; you have been a thorny Rose, and given me many wounds. I'll be paid for my heartache with sweet words, tender looks, and frank confessions of love, for, proud as you are, you do love me, and dare not deny it."

Something in his tone terrified her; she snatched her hand away, and drew beyond his reach, trying to speak calmly, and to meet coldly the ardent glances of the eyes which were strangely darkened and dilated with uncontrollable emotion.

"You forget yourself. I shall give no answer to an avowal made in such terms. Take me home instantly," she said, in a tone of command.

"Confess you love me, Rose."

"Never!"

"Ah! I'll have a kinder answer, or——" Done half rose and put out his hand to grasp and draw her to him, but the cry she uttered seemed to arrest him with a sort of shock. He dropped into his seat, passed his hand over his eyes, and shivered nervously, as he muttered in an altered tone: "I meant nothing; it's the moonlight; sit down, I'll control myself—upon my soul I will!"

"If you do not, I shall go overboard. Are you mad, sir?" cried Rose, trembling with indignation.

"Then, I shall follow you, for I *am* mad, Rose, with love—hasheesh!"

His voice sank to a whisper, but the last word thrilled along her nerves, as no sound of fear had ever done before. An instant she regarded him with a look which took in every sign of unnatural excitement, then she clasped her hands with an imploring gesture, saying, in a tone of despair:

"Why did I come! How will it end? Oh, Mark, take me home before it is too late!"

"Hush! Be calm; don't thwart me, or I may get wild again. My thoughts are not clear, but I understand you. There, take my knife, and if I forget myself, kill me. Don't go overboard; you are too beautiful to die, my Rose!"

He threw her the slender hunting-knife he wore, looked at her a moment with a far-off look, and trimmed the sail like one moving in a dream. Rose took the weapon, wrapped her cloak closely about her, and, crouching as far away as possible, kept her eye on him, with a face in which watchful terror contended with some secret trouble and bewilderment more powerful than her fear.

The boat moved round, and began to beat up against wind and tide; spray flew from her bow, the sail bent and strained in the gusts that struck it with perilous fitfulness. The moon was nearly hidden by scudding clouds, and one-half the sky was black with the gathering storm. Rose looked from threatening heavens to treacherous sea, and tried to be ready for any danger, but her calm had been sadly broken, and she could not recover it. Done sat motionless, uttering no word of encouragement, though the frequent flaws almost tore the rope from his hand, and the water often dashed over him.

"Are we in any danger?" asked Rose at last, unable to bear the silence, for he looked like a ghostly helmsman, seen by the fitful light, pale now, wild-eyed, and speechless.

"Yes, great danger."

"I thought you were a skillful boatman."

"I am when I am myself; now I am rapidly losing the control of my will, and the strange quiet is coming over me. If I had been alone I should have given up sooner, but for your sake I've kept on."

"Can't you work the boat?" asked Rose, terror-struck by the changed tone of his voice, the slow, uncertain movements of his hands.

"No. I see everything through a thick cloud; your voice sounds far away, and my one desire is to lay my head down and sleep."

"Let me steer—I can, I must!" she cried, springing toward him, and laying her hand on the rudder.

He smiled and kissed the little hand, saying, dreamily, "You could not hold it a minute; sit by me, love; let us turn the boat again, and drift away together—anywhere, anywhere out of the world."

"Oh, Heaven, what will become of us!" and Rose wrung her hands in real despair. "Mr. Done—Mark—dear Mark, rouse yourself and listen to me. Turn, as you say, for it is certain death to go on so. Turn, and let us drift down to the lighthouse; they will hear and help us. Quick, take down the sail, get out the oars, and let us try to reach there before the storm breaks."

As Rose spoke, he obeyed her like a dumb animal; love for her was stronger even than the instinct of self-preservation, and for her sake he fought against the treacherous lethargy which was swiftly overpowering him. The sail was lowered, the boat brought round, and with little help from the ill-pulled oars, it drifted rapidly out to sea with the ebbing tide.

As she caught her breath after this dangerous manœuvre was accomplished, Rose asked, in a quiet tone, she vainly tried to render natural:

"How much hasheesh did you take?"

"All that Meredith threw me. Too much; but I was possessed to do it, so I hid the roll and tried it," he answered, peering at her with a weird laugh.

"Let us talk; our safety lies in keeping awake, and I dare not let you sleep," continued Rose, dashing water on her own hot forehead with a sort of desperation.

"Say you love me; that would wake me from my lost sleep, I think. I have hoped and feared, waited and suffered so long. Be pitiful, and answer, Rose."

"I do; but I should not own it now."

So low was the soft reply, he scarcely heard it, but he felt it, and made a strong effort to break from the hateful spell that bound him. Leaning forward, he tried to read her face in a ray of moonlight breaking through the clouds: he saw a new and tender warmth in it, for all the pride was gone, and no fear marred the eloquence of those soft, Southern eyes.

"Kiss me, Rose, then I shall believe it. I feel lost in a dream, and you, so changed, so kind, may be only a fair phantom. Kiss me, love, and make it real."

As if swayed by a power more potent than her will, Rose bent to meet his lips. But the ardent pressure seemed to startle her from a momentary oblivion of everything but love. She covered up her face, and sank down, as if overwhelmed with shame, sobbing through passionate tears:

"Oh, what am I doing? I am mad, for I, too, have taken hasheesh."

What he answered she never heard, for a rattling peal of thunder drowned his voice, and then the storm broke loose. Rain fell in torrents, the wind blew fiercely, sky and sea were black as ink, and the boat tossed from wave to wave almost at their mercy. Giving herself up for lost, Rose crept to her lover's side and clung there, conscious only that they would bide together through the perils their own folly brought them. Done's excitement was quite gone now; he sat like a statue, shielding the frail creature whom he loved, with a smile on his face, which looked awfully emotionless when the lightning gave her glimpses of its white immobility. Drenched, exhausted, and half senseless with danger, fear and exposure, Rose saw at last a welcome glimmer through the gloom, and roused herself to cry for help.

"Mark, wake and help me! Shout, for God's sake—shout and call them, for we are lost if we drift by!" she cried, lifting his head from his breast, and forcing him to see the brilliant beacons streaming far across the troubled water.

He understood her, and springing up, uttered shout after shout, like one demented. Fortunately, the storm had lulled a little; the lighthouse-keeper heard and answered. Rose seized the helm, Done the oars, and with one frantic effort, guided the boat into quieter waters, where it was met by the keeper, who towed it to the rocky nook which served as harbor.

The moment a strong, steady face met her eyes, and a gruff, cheery voice hailed her, Rose gave way, and was carried up to the house, looking more like a beautiful drowned Ophelia than a living woman.

"Here, Sally, see to the poor thing; she's had a rough time on't. I'll take care of her sweetheart—and a nice job I'll have, I reckon, for if he ain't mad or drunk, he's had a stroke of lightenin, and looks as if he wouldn't get his hearin' in a hurry," said the old man, as he housed his unexpected guests, and stood staring at Done, who looked about him like one dazed. "You jest turn in yonder and sleep it off, mate. We'll see to the lady, and right up your boat in the morning," the old man added.

"Be kind to Rose. I frightened her. I'll not forget you. Yes, let me sleep and get over this cursed folly as soon as possible," muttered this strange visitor.

Done threw himself down on the rough couch and tried to sleep, but every nerve was overstrained, every pulse beating like a trip-hammer, and everything about him was intensified and exaggerated with awful power. The thunder-shower seemed a wild hurricane, the quaint room a wilderness peopled with tormenting phantoms, and all the events of his life passed before him in an endless procession, which nearly maddened him. The old man looked weird and gigantic, his own voice sounded shrill and discordant, and the ceaseless murmur of Rose's incoherent wanderings haunted him like parts of a grotesque but dreadful dream.

All night he lay motionless, with staring eyes, feverish lips, and a mind on the rack, for the delicate machinery which had been tampered with, revenged the wrong by torturing the foolish experimenter. All night Rose wept and sung, talked and cried for help in a piteous state of nervous excitement, for with her the trance came first, and the after-agitation was increased by the events of the evening. She slept at last, lulled by the old woman's motherly care, and Done was spared one tormenting fear, for he dreaded the consequences of this folly on her, more than upon himself.

As day dawned he rose, haggard and faint, and staggered out. At the door he met the keeper, who stopped him to report that the boat was in order, and a fair day coming. Seeing doubt and perplexity in the old man's eye, Done told him the truth, and added that he was going to the beach for a plunge, hoping by that simple tonic to restore his unstrung nerves.

He came back feeling like himself again, except a dull headache, and a heavy sense of remorse weighing on his spirits, for he distinctly recollected all the events of the night. The old woman made him eat and drink, and in an hour he felt ready for the homeward trip.

Rose slept late, and when she woke, soon recovered herself, for her dose had been a small one. When she had breakfasted and made a hasty toilet, she professed herself anxious to return at once. She dreaded, yet longed to see Done, and when the time came, armed herself with pride, feeling all a woman's shame at what had passed, and resolving to feign forgetfulness of the incidents of the previous night. Pale and cold as a statue she met him, but the moment he began to say, humbly, "Forgive me, Rose," she silenced him with an imperious gesture and the command:

"Don't speak of it; I only remember that it was very horrible, and wish to forget it all as soon as possible."

"All, Rose?" he asked, significantly.

"Yes, *all*. No one would care to recall the follies of a hasheesh dream," she answered, turning hastily to hide the scarlet flush that would rise, and the eyes that would fall before his own.

"*I* never can forget, but I will be silent if you bid me."

"I do. Let us go. What will they think at the island? Mr. Done, give me your promise to tell no one, now or ever, that I tried that dangerous experiment. I will guard your secret also." She spoke eagerly, and looked up imploringly.

"I promise," and he gave her his hand, holding her own with a wistful glance, till she drew it away, and begged him to take her home.

Leaving hearty thanks and a generous token of their gratitude, they sailed away with a fair wind, finding in the freshness of the morning a speedy cure for tired bodies and excited minds. They said little, but it was impossible for Rose to preserve her coldness. The memory of the past night broke down her pride, and Done's tender glances touched her heart. She half hid her face behind her hand, and tried to compose herself for the scene to come, for, as she approached the island, she saw Belle and her party waiting for them on the shore.

"Oh, Mr. Done, screen me from their eyes and questions as much as you can! I'm so worn out and nervous, I shall betray myself. You will help me?" and she turned to him with a confiding look, strangely at variance with her usual calm self-possession.

"I'll shield you with my life, if you will tell me why you took the hasheesh," he said, bent on knowing his fate.

"I hoped it would make me soft and lovable, like other women. I'm tired of being a lonely statue," she faltered, as if the truth was wrung from her by a power stronger than her will.

"And I took it to gain courage to tell my love. Rose, we have been near death together; let us share life together, and neither of us be any more lonely or afraid."

He stretched his hand to her with his heart in his face, and she gave him hers with a look of tender submission, as he said, ardently:

"Heaven bless hasheesh, if its dreams end like this!"

Love and Self-Love

Editor's Note: Alcott wrote her thrillers from many different perspectives, including those of the betrayed lover, the menaced heroine, and even the beguiled hero.
"Love and Self-Love," which appeared in the *Atlantic Monthly* in 1860, is one of the
earliest stories in which she attempts to relate female experience from a male per-
spective. It begins on a note that is unusual with Alcott: The male and female
characters are already redeemed through the power of love. In her later gothic
narratives, male-viewpoint characters usually discover the incompatibility of male
and female interests.

riendless, when you are gone? But, Jean, you surely do not mean that
Effie has no claim on any human creature, beyond the universal one of
common charity?" I said, as she ceased, and lay panting on her pillows,
with her sunken eyes fixed eagerly upon my own.

"Ay, Sir, I do; for her grandfather has never by word or deed acknowledged her, or paid the least heed to the letter her poor mother sent him from
her dying bed seven years ago. He is a lone old man, and this child is the last
of his name; yet he will not see her, and cares little whether she be dead or
living. It's a bitter shame, Sir, and the memory of it will rise up before him
when he comes to lie where I am lying now."

"And you have kept the girl safe in the shelter of your honest home all these years? Heaven will remember that, and in the great record of good deeds will set the name of Adam Lyndsay far below that of poor Jean Burns," I said, pressing the thin hand that had succored the orphan in her need.

But Jean took no honor to herself for that charity, and answered simply to my words of commendation.

"Sir, her mother was my foster-child; and when she left that stern old man for love of Walter Home, I went, too, for love of her. Ah, dear heart! she had sore need of me in the weary wanderings which ended only when she lay down by her dead husband's side and left her bairn to me. Then I came here to cherish her among kind souls where I was born; and here she has grown up, an innocent young thing, safe from the wicked world, the comfort of my life, and the one thing I grieve at leaving when the time that is drawing very near shall come."

"Would not an appeal to Mr. Lyndsay reach him now, think you? Might not Effie go to him herself? Surely, the sight of such a winsome creature would touch his heart, however hard."

But Jean rose up in her bed, crying, almost fiercely—

"No, Sir! no! My child shall never go to beg a shelter in that hard man's house. I know too well the cold looks, the cruel words, that would sting her high spirit and try her heart, as they did her mother's. No, Sir—rather than that, she shall go with Lady Gower."

"Lady Gower? What has she to do with Effie, Jean?" I asked, with increasing interest.

"She will take Effie as her maid, Sir. A hard life for my child! but what can I do?" And Jean's keen glance seemed trying to read mine.

"A waiting-maid? Heaven forbid!" I ejaculated, as a vision of that haughty lady and her three wild sons swept through my mind.

I rose, paced the room in silence for a little time, then took a sudden resolution, and, turning to the bed, exclaimed—

"Jean, I will adopt Effie. I am old enough to be her father; and she shall never feel the want of one, if you will give her to my care."

To my surprise, Jean's eager face wore a look of disappointment as she listened, and with a sigh replied—

"That's a kind thought, Sir, and a generous one; but it cannot be as you wish. You may be twice her age, but still too young for that. How could Effie look into that face of yours, so bonnie, Sir, for all it is so grave, and, seeing never a wrinkle on the forehead, nor a white hair among the black, how could she call you father? No, it will not do, though so kindly meant. Your friends would laugh at you, Sir, and idle tongues might speak ill of my bairn."

"Then what can I do, Jean?" I asked, regretfully.

"Make her your wife, Sir."

I turned sharply and stared at the woman, as her abrupt reply reached my ear. Though trembling for the consequences of her boldly spoken wish, Jean did not shrink from my astonished gaze; and when I saw the wistfulness of that wan face, the smile died on my lips, checked by the tender courage which had prompted the utterance of her dying hope.

"My good Jean, you forget that Effie is a child, and I a moody, solitary man, with no gifts to win a wife or make home happy."

"Effie is sixteen, Sir—a fair, good lassie for her years; and you—ah, Sir, *you* may call yourself unfit for wife and home, but the poorest, saddest creature in this place knows that the man whose hand is always open, whose heart is always pitiful, is not the one to live alone, but to win and to deserve a happy home and a true wife. Oh, Sir, forgive me, if I have been too bold; but my time is short, and I love my child so well, I cannot leave the desire of my heart unspoken, for it is my last."

As the words fell brokenly from her lips, and tears streamed down her pallid cheek, a great pity took possession of me, the old longing to find some solace for my solitary life returned again, and peace seemed to smile on me from little Effie's eyes.

"Jean," I said, "give me till to-morrow to consider this new thought. I fear it cannot be; but I have learned to love the child too well to see her thrust out from the shelter of your home to walk through this evil world alone. I will consider your proposal, and endeavor to devise some future for the child which shall set your heart at rest. But before you urge this further, let me tell you that I am not what you think me. I am a cold, selfish man, often gloomy, often stern—a most unfit guardian for a tender creature like this little girl. The deeds of mine which you call kind are not true charities; it frets me to see pain, and I desire my ease above all earthly things. You are grateful for the little I have done for you, and deceive yourself regarding my true worth; but of one thing you may rest assured—I am an honest man, who holds his name too high to stain it with a false word or a dishonorable deed."

"I do believe you, Sir," Jean answered, eagerly. "And if I left the child to you, I could die this night in peace. Indeed, Sir, I never should have dared to speak of this, but for the belief that you loved the girl. What else could I think, when you came so often and were so kind to us?"

"I cannot blame you, Jean; it was my usual forgetfulness of others which so misled you. I was tired of the world, and came hither to find peace in solitude. Effie cheered me with her winsome ways, and I learned to look on her as the blithe spirit whose artless wiles won me to forget a bitter past and a regretful present." I paused; and then added, with a smile, "But, in our wise schemes, we have overlooked one point: Effie does not love me, and may decline the future you desire me to offer her."

A vivid hope lit those dim eyes, as Jean met my smile with one far brighter, and joyfully replied—

"She *does* love you, Sir; for you have given her the greatest happiness she has ever known. Last night she sat looking silently into the fire there with a strange gloom on her bonnie face, and, when I asked what she was dreaming of, she turned to me with a look of pain and fear, as if dismayed at some great loss, but she only said, "He is going, Jean! What shall I do?"

"Poor child! she will miss her friend and teacher, when I'm gone; and I shall miss the only human creature that has seemed to care for me for years," I sighed—adding, as I paused upon the threshold of the door, "Say nothing of this to Effie till I come to-morrow, Jean."

I went away, and far out on the lonely moor sat down to think. Like a weird magician, Memory led me back into the past, calling up the hopes and passions buried there. My childhood—fatherless and motherless, but not unhappy; for no wish was ungratified, no idle whim denied. My boyhood— with no shadows over it but those my own wayward will called up. My manhood—when the great joy of my life arose, my love for Agnes, a mid-summer dream of bloom and bliss, so short-lived and so sweet! I felt again the pang that wrung my heart when she coldly gave me back the pledge I thought so sacred and so sure, and the music of her marriage-bells tolled the knell of my lost love. I seemed to hear them still wafted across the purple moor through the silence of those fifteen years.

My life looked gray and joyless as the wide waste lying hushed around me, unblessed with the verdure of a single hope, a single love; and as I looked down the coming years, my way seemed very solitary, very dark.

Suddenly a lark soared upward from the heath, cleaving the silence with its jubilant song. The sleeping echoes woke, the dun moor seemed to smile, and the blithe music fell like dew upon my gloomy spirit, wakening a new desire.

"What this bird is to the moor might little Effie be to me," I thought within myself, longing to possess the cheerful spirit which had power to gladden me.

"Yes," I mused, "the old home will seem more solitary now than ever; and if I cannot win the lark's song without a golden fetter, I will give it one, and while it sings for love of me it shall not know a want or fear."

Heaven help me! I forgot the poor return I made my lark for the sweet liberty it lost.

All that night I pondered the altered future Jean had laid before me, and the longer I looked the fairer it seemed to grow. Wealth I cared nothing for; the world's opinion I defied; ambition had departed, and passion I believed lay dead—then why should I deny myself the consolation which seemed offered to me? I would accept it; and as I resolved, the dawn looked in at me, fresh and fair as little Effie's face.

I met Jean with a smile, and, as she read its significance aright, there shone a sudden peace upon her countenance, more touching than her grateful words.

Effie came singing from the burn-side, as unconscious of the change which awaited her as the flowers gathered in her plaid and crowning her bright hair.

I drew her to my side, and in the simplest words asked her if she would go with me when Jean's long guardianship was ended. Joy, sorrow, and surprise stirred the sweet composure of her face, and quickened the tranquil beating of her heart. But as I ceased, joy conquered grief and wonder; for she clapped her hands like a glad child, exclaiming—

"Go with you, Sir? Oh, if you knew how I long to see the home you have so often pictured to me, you would never doubt my willingness to go."

"But, Effie, you do not understand. Are you willing to go with me as my wife?" I said—with a secret sense of something like remorse, as I uttered that word, which once meant so much to me, and now seemed such an empty title to bestow on her.

The flowers dropped from the loosened plaid, as Effie looked with a startled glance into my face; the color left her cheeks, and the smile died on her lips, but a timid joy lit her eye, as she softly echoed my last words—

"Your wife? It sounds very solemn, though so sweet. Ah, Sir, I am not wise or good enough for that!"

A child's humility breathed in her speech, but something of a woman's fervor shone in her uplifted countenance, and sounded in the sudden tremor of her voice.

"Effie, I want you as you are," I said—"no wiser, dear—no better. I want your innocent affection to appease the hunger of an empty heart, your blithe companionship to cheer my solitary home. Be still a child to me, and let me give you the protection of my name."

Effie turned to her old friend, and, laying her young face on the pillow close beside the worn one grown so dear to her, asked, in a tone half pleading, half regretful—

"Dear Jean, shall I go so far away from you and the home you gave me when I had no other?"

"My bairn, I shall not be here, and it will never seem like home with old Jean gone. It is the last wish I shall ever know, to see you safe with this good gentleman who loves my child. Go, dear heart, and be happy; and Heaven bless and keep you both!"

Jean held her fast a moment, and then, with a whispered prayer, put her gently away. Effie came to me, saying, with a look more eloquent than her meek words—

"Sir, I will be your wife, and love you very truly all my life."

I drew the little creature to my breast, and felt a tender pride in knowing she was mine. Something in the shy caress those soft arms gave touched my cold nature with a generous warmth, and the innocence of that confiding heart was an appeal to all that made my manhood worth possessing.

Swiftly those few weeks passed, and when old Jean was laid to her last sleep, little Effie wept her grief away upon her husband's bosom, and soon learned to smile in her new English home. Its gloom departed when she came, and for a while it was a very happy place. My bitter moods seemed banished by the magic of the gentle presence that made sunshine there, and I was conscious of a fresh grace added to the life so wearisome before.

I should have been a father to the child, watchful, wise, and tender; but old Jean was right—I was too young to feel a father's calm affection or to know a father's patient care. I should have been her teacher, striving to cultivate the nature given to my care, and fit it for the trials Heaven sends to all. I should have been a friend, if nothing more, and given her those innocent delights that make youth beautiful and its memory sweet.

I was a master, content to give little, while receiving all she could bestow.

Forgetting her loneliness, I fell back into my old way of life. I shunned the world, because its gayeties had lost their zest. I did not care to travel, for home now possessed a charm it never had before. I knew there was an eager face that always brightened when I came, light feet that flew to welcome me, and hands that loved to minister to every want of mine. Even when I sat engrossed among my books, there was a pleasant consciousness that I was the possessor of a household sprite whom a look could summon and a gesture banish. I loved her as I loved a picture or a flower—a little better than my horse and hound—but far less than I loved my most unworthy self.

And she—always so blithe when I was by, so diligent in studying my desires, so full of simple arts to win my love and prove her gratitude—she never asked for any boon, and seemed content to live alone with me in that still place, so utterly unlike the home she had left. I had not learned to read that true heart then. I saw those happy eyes grow wistful when I went, leaving her alone; I missed the roses from her cheek, faded for want of gentler care; and when the buoyant spirit which had been her chiefest charm departed, I fancied, in my blindness, that she pined for the free air of the Highlands, and tried to win it back by transient tenderness and costly gifts. But I had robbed my lark of heaven's sunshine, and it could not sing.

I met Agnes again. She was a widow, and to my eye seemed fairer than when I saw her last, and far more kind. Some soft regret seemed shining on me from those lustrous eyes, as if she hoped to win my pardon for that early wrong. I never could forget the deed that darkened my best years, but the old charm stole over me at times, and, turning from the meek child at my feet, I owned the power of the stately woman whose smile seemed a command.

I meant no wrong to Effie, but, looking on her as a child, I forgot the higher claim I had given her as a wife, and, walking blindly on my selfish way, I crushed the little flower I should have cherished in my breast.

"Effie, my old friend Agnes Vaughan is coming here to-day; so make yourself fair, that you may do honor to my choice; for she desires to see you, and I wish my Scotch harebell to look lovely to this English rose," I said, half playfully, half earnestly, as we stood together looking out across the flowery lawn, one summer day.

"Do you like me to be pretty, Sir?" she answered, with a flush of pleasure on her upturned face. "I will try to make myself fair with the gifts you are always heaping on me; but even then I fear I shall not do you honor, nor please your friend, I am so small and young."

A careless reply was on my lips, but, seeing what a long way down the little figure was, I drew it nearer, saying, with a smile, which I knew would make an answering one—

"Dear, there must be the bud before the flower; so never grieve, for your youth keeps my spirit young. To me you may be a child forever; but you must learn to be a stately little Madam Ventnor to my friends."

She laughed a gayer laugh than I had heard for many a day, and soon departed, intent on keeping well the promise she had given. An hour later, as I sat busied among my books, a little figure glided in, and stood before me with its jewelled arms demurely folded on its breast. It was Effie, as I had never seen her before. Some new freak possessed her, for with her girlish dress she seemed to have laid her girlhood by. The brown locks were gathered up, wreathing the small head like a coronet; aërial lace and silken vesture shimmered in the light, and became her well. She looked and moved a fairy queen, stately and small.

I watched her in a silent maze, for the face with its shy blushes and downcast eyes did not seem the childish one turned frankly to my own an hour ago. With a sigh I looked up at Agnes's picture, the sole ornament of that room, and when I withdrew my gaze the blooming vision had departed. I should have followed it to make my peace, but I fell into a fit of bitter musing, and forgot it till Agnes's voice sounded at my door.

She came with a brother, and seemed eager to see my young wife; but Effie did not appear, and I excused her absence as a girlish freak, smiling at it with them, while I chafed inwardly at her neglect, forgetting that I might have been the cause.

Pacing down the garden paths with Agnes at my side, our steps were arrested by a sudden sight of Effie fast asleep among the flowers. She looked a flower herself, lying with her flushed cheek pillowed on her arm, sunshine glittering on the ripples of her hair, and the changeful lustre of her dainty dress. Tears moistened her long lashes, but her lips smiled, as if in the blissful land of dreams she had found some solace for her grief.

"A 'Sleeping Beauty' worthy the awakening of any prince!" whispered Alfred Vaughan, pausing with admiring eyes.

A slight frown swept over Agnes's face, but vanished as she said, with that low-toned laugh that never seemed unmusical before—

"We must pardon Mrs. Ventnor's seeming rudeness, if she welcomes us with graceful scenes like this. A child-wife's whims are often prettier than the world's formal ways; so do not chide her, Basil, when she wakes."

I was a proud man then, touched easily by trivial things. Agnes's pitying manner stung me, and the tone in which I wakened Effie was far harsher than it should have been. She sprang up; and with a gentle dignity most new to me received her guests, and played the part of hostess with a grace that well atoned for her offence.

Agnes watched her silently as she went before us with young Vaughan, and even I, ruffled as my temper was, felt a certain pride in the loving creature who for my sake conquered her timidity and strove to do me honor. But neither by look nor word did I show my satisfaction, for Agnes demanded the constant service of lips and eyes, and I was only too ready to devote them to the woman who still felt her power and dared to show it.

All that day I was beside her, forgetful in many ways of the gentle courtesies I owed the child whom I had made my wife. I did not see the wrong then, but others did, and the deference I failed to show she could ask of them.

In the evening, as I stood near Agnes while she sang the songs we both remembered well, my eye fell on a mirror that confronted me, and in it I saw Effie bending forward with a look that startled me. Some strong emotion controlled her, for with lips apart and eager eyes she gazed keenly at the countenances she believed unconscious of her scrutiny.

Agnes caught the vision that had arrested the half-uttered compliment upon my lips, and, turning, looked at Effie with a smile just touched with scorn.

The color rose vividly to Effie's cheek, but her eyes did not fall—they sought my face, and rested there. A half-smile crossed my lips; with a sudden impulse I beckoned, and she came with such an altered countenance I fancied that I had not seen aright.

At my desire she sang the ballads she so loved, and in her girlish voice there was an undertone of deeper melody than when I heard them first among her native hills; for the child's heart was ripening fast into the woman's.

Agnes went, at length, and I heard Effie's sigh of relief when we were left alone, but only bid her "go and rest," while I paced to and fro, still murmuring the refrain of Agnes's song.

The Vaughans came often, and we went often to them in the summer-home they had chosen near us on the river-bank. I followed my own wayward will, and Effie's wistful eyes grew sadder as the weeks went by.

One sultry evening, as we strolled together on the balcony, I was seized with a sudden longing to hear Agnes sing, and bid Effie come with me for a moonlight voyage down the river.

She had been very silent all the evening, with a pensive shadow on her face and rare smiles on her lips. But as I spoke, she paused abruptly, and, clenching her small hands, turned upon me with defiant eyes—crying, almost fiercely—

"No, I will not go to listen to that woman's songs. I hate her! yes, more than I can tell! for, till she came, I thought you loved me; but now you think of her alone, and chide me when I look unhappy. You treat me like a child; but I am not one. Oh, Sir, be more kind, for I have only you to love!"—and as her voice died in that sad appeal, she clasped her hands before her face with such a burst of tears that I had no words to answer her.

Disturbed by the sudden passion of the hitherto meek girl, I sat down on the wide steps of the balcony and essayed to draw her to my knee, hoping she would weep this grief away as she had often done a lesser sorrow. But she resisted my caress, and, standing erect before me, checked her tears, saying, in a voice still trembling with resentment and reproach—

"You promised Jean to be kind to me, and you are cruel; for when I ask for love, you give me jewels, books, or flowers, as you would give a pettish child a toy, and go away as if you were weary of me. Oh, it is not right, Sir! and I cannot, no, I will not bear it!"

If she had spared reproaches, deserved though they were, and humbly pleaded to be loved, I should have been more just and gentle; but her indignant words, the sharper for their truth, roused the despotic spirit of the man, and made me sternest when I should have been most kind.

"Effie," I said, looking coldly up into her troubled face, "I have given you the right to be thus frank with me; but before you exercise that right, let me tell you what may silence your reproaches and teach you to know me better. I desired to adopt you as my child; Jean would not consent to that, but bid me marry you, and so give you a home, and win for myself a companion who should make that home less solitary. I could protect you in no other way, and I married you. I meant it kindly, Effie; for I pitied you—ay, and loved you, too, as I hoped I had fully proved."

"You have, Sir—oh, you have! But I hoped I might in time be more to you than a dear child," sighed Effie, while softer tears flowed as she spoke.

"Effie, I told Jean I was a hard, cold man"—and I was one as those words passed my lips. "I told her I was unfitted to make a wife happy. But she said you would be content with what I could offer; and so I gave you all I had to bestow. It was not enough; yet I cannot make it more. Forgive me, child, and try to bear your disappointments as I have learned to bear mine."

Effie bent suddenly, saying, with a look of anguish, "Do you regret that I am your wife, Sir?"

"Heaven knows I do, for I cannot make you happy," I answered, mournfully.

"Let me go away where I can never grieve or trouble you again! I will—

indeed, I will—for anything is easier to bear than this. Oh, Jean, why did you leave me when you went?"—and with that despairing cry Effie stretched her arms into the empty air, as if seeking that lost friend.

My anger melted, and I tried to soothe her, saying gently, as I laid her tear-wet cheek to mine—

"My child, death alone must part us two. We will be patient with each other, and so may learn to be happy yet."

A long silence fell upon us both. My thoughts were busy with the thought of what a different home mine might have been, if Agnes had been true; and Effie—God only knows how sharp a conflict passed in that young heart! I could not guess it till the bitter sequel of that hour came.

A timid hand upon my own aroused me, and, looking down, I met such an altered face, it touched me like a mute reproach. All the passion had died out, and a great patience seemed to have arisen there. It looked so meek and wan, I bent and kissed it; but no smile answered me as Effie humbly said—

"Forgive me, Sir, and tell me how I can make you happier. For I am truly grateful for all you have done for me, and will try to be a docile child to you."

"Be happy yourself, Effie, and I shall be content. I am too grave and old to be a fit companion for you, dear. You shall have gay faces and young friends to make this quiet place more cheerful. I should have thought of that before. Dance, sing, be merry, Effie, and never let your life be darkened by Basil Ventnor's changeful moods."

"And you?" she whispered, looking up.

"I will sit among my books, or seek alone the few friends I care to see, and never mar your gayety with my gloomy presence, dear. We must begin at once to go our separate ways; for, with so many years between us, we can never find the same paths pleasant very long. Let me be a father to you, and a friend—I cannot be a lover, child."

Effie rose and went silently away; but soon came again, wrapped in her mantle, saying, as she looked down at me, with something of her former cheerfulness—

"I am good now. Come and row me down the river. It is too beautiful a night to be spent in tears and naughtiness."

"No, Effie, you shall never go to Mrs. Vaughan's again, if you dislike her so. No friendship of mine need be shared by you, if it gives you pain."

"Nothing shall pain me any more," she answered, with a patient sigh. "I will be your merry girl again, and try to love Agnes for your sake. Ah! do come, *father*, or I shall not feel forgiven."

Smiling at her April moods, I obeyed the small hands clasped about my own, and through the fragrant linden walk went musing to the river-side.

Silently we floated down, and at the lower landing-place found Alfred Vaughan just mooring his own boat. By him I sent a message to his sister, while we waited for her at the shore.

Effie stood above me on the sloping bank, and as Agnes entered the green vista of the flowery path, she turned and clung to me with sudden fervor, kissed me passionately, and then stole silently into the boat.

The moonlight turned the waves to silver, and in its magic rays the face of my first love grew young again. She sat before me with water-lilies in her shining hair, singing as she sang of old, while the dash of falling oars kept time to her low song. As we neared the ruined bridge, whose single arch still cast its heavy shadow far across the stream, Agnes bent toward me, softly saying—

"Basil, you remember this?"

How could I forget that happy night, long years ago, when she and I went floating down the same bright stream, two happy lovers just betrothed? As she spoke, it all came back more beautiful than ever, and I forgot the silent figure sitting there behind me. I hope Agnes had forgotten, too; for, cruel as she was to me, I never wished to think her hard enough to hate that gentle child.

"I remember, Agnes," I said, with a regretful sigh. "My voyage has been a lonely one since then."

"Are you not happy, Basil?" she asked, with a tender pity thrilling her low voice.

"Happy?" I echoed, bitterly—"how can I be happy, remembering what might have been?"

Agnes bowed her head upon her hands, and silently the boat shot into the black shadow of the arch. A sudden eddy seemed to sway us slightly from our course, and the waves dashed sullenly against the gloomy walls; a moment more and we glided into calmer waters and unbroken light. I looked up from my task to speak, but the words were frozen on my lips by a cry from Agnes, who, wild-eyed and pale, seemed pointing to some phantom which I could not see. I turned—the phantom was Effie's empty seat. The shining stream grew dark before me, and a great pang of remorse wrung my heart as that sight met my eyes.

"Effie!" I cried, with a cry that rent the stillness of the night, and sent the name ringing down the river. But nothing answered me, and the waves rippled softly as they hurried by. Far over the wide stream went my despairing glance, and saw nothing but the lilies swaying as they slept, and the black arch where my child went down.

Agnes lay trembling at my feet, but I never heeded her—for Jean's dead voice sounded in my ear, demanding the life confided to my care. I listened, benumbed with guilty fear, and, as if summoned by that weird cry, there came a white flash through the waves, and Effie's face rose up before me.

Pallid and wild with the agony of that swift plunge, it confronted me. No cry for help parted the pale lips, but those wide eyes were luminous with a love whose fire that deathful river could not quench.

Like one in an awful dream, I gazed till the ripples closed above it. One instant the terror held me—the next I was far down in those waves, so silver fair above, so black and terrible below. A brief, blind struggle passed before I grasped a tress of that long hair, then an arm, and then the white shape, with a clutch like death. As the dividing waters gave us to the light again, Agnes flung herself far over the boat-side and drew my lifeless burden in; I followed, and we laid it down, a piteous sight for human eyes to look upon. Of that swift voyage home I can remember nothing but the still face on Agnes's breast, the sight of which nerved my dizzy brain and made my muscles iron.

For many weeks there was a darkened chamber in my house, and anxious figures gliding to and fro, wan with long vigils and the fear of death. I often crept in to look upon the little figure lying there, to watch the feverish roses blooming on the wasted cheek, the fitful fire burning in the unconscious eyes, to hear the broken words so full of pathos to my ear, and then to steal away and struggle to forget.

My bird fluttered on the threshold of its cage, but Love lured it back, for its gentle mission was not yet fulfilled.

The *child* Effie lay dead beneath the ripples of the river, but the *woman* rose up from that bed of suffering like one consecrated to life's high duties by the bitter baptism of that dark hour.

Slender and pale, with serious eyes and quiet steps, she moved through the home which once echoed to the glad voice and dancing feet of that vanished shape. A sweet sobriety shaded her young face, and a meek smile sat upon her lips, but the old blithesomeness was gone.

She never claimed her childish place upon my knee, never tried the winsome wiles that used to chase away my gloom, never came to pour her innocent delights and griefs into my ear, or bless me with the frank affection which grew very precious when I found it lost.

Docile as ever, and eager to gratify my lightest wish, she left no wifely duty unfulfilled. Always near me, if I breathed her name, but vanishing when I grew silent, as if her task were done. Always smiling a cheerful farewell when I went, a quiet welcome when I came. I missed the April face that once watched me go, the warm embrace that greeted me again, and at my heart the sense of loss grew daily deeper as I felt the growing change.

Effie remembered the words I had spoken on that mournful night; remembered that our paths must lie apart—that her husband was a friend, and nothing more. She treasured every careless hint I had given, and followed it most faithfully. She gathered gay, young friends about her, went out into the brilliant world, and I believed she was content.

If I had ever felt she was a burden to the selfish freedom I desired, I was punished now, for I had lost a blessing which no common pleasure could replace. I sat alone, and no blithe voice made music in the silence of my room, no bright locks swept my shoulder, and no soft caress assured me that I was beloved.

I looked for my household sprite in girlish garb, with its free hair and sunny eyes, but found only a fair woman, graceful in rich attire, crowned with my gifts, and standing afar off among her blooming peers. I could not guess the solitude of that true heart, nor see the captive spirit gazing at me from those steadfast eyes.

No word of the cause of that despairing deed passed Effie's lips, and I had no need to ask it. Agnes was silent, and soon left us, but her brother was a frequent guest. Effie liked his gay companionship, and I denied her nothing—nothing but the one desire of her life.

So that first year passed; and though the ease and liberty I coveted were undisturbed, I was not satisfied. Solitude grew irksome, and study ceased to charm. I tried old pleasures, but they had lost their zest—renewed old friendships, but they wearied me. I forgot Agnes, and ceased to think her fair. I looked at Effie, and sighed for my lost youth.

My little wife grew very beautiful to me, for she was blooming fast into a gracious womanhood. I felt a secret pride in knowing she was mine, and watched her as I fancied a fond brother might, glad that she was so good, so fair, so much beloved. I ceased to mourn the plaything I had lost, and something akin to reverence mingled with the deepening admiration of the man.

Gay guests had filled the house with festal light and sound one winter's night, and when the last bright figure had vanished from the threshold of the door, I still stood there, looking over the snow-shrouded lawn, hoping to cool the fever of my blood, and ease the restless pain that haunted me.

I shut out the keen air and wintry sky, at length, and silently ascended to the deserted rooms above. But in the soft gloom of a vestibule my steps were stayed. Two figures, in a flowery alcove, fixed my eye. The light streamed full upon them, and the fragrant stillness of the air was hardly stirred by their low tones.

Effie was there, sunk on a low couch, her face bowed upon her hands; and at her side, speaking with impassioned voice and ardent eyes, leaned Alfred Vaughan.

The sight struck me like a blow, and the sharp anguish of that moment proved how deeply I had learned to love.

"Effie, it is a sinful tie that binds you to that man; he does not love you, and it should be broken—for this slavery will wear away the life now grown so dear to me."

The words, hot with indignant passion, smote me like a wintry blast, but not so coldly as the broken voice that answered them—

"He said death alone must part us two, and, remembering that, I cannot listen to another love."

Like a guilty ghost I stole away, and in the darkness of my solitary room struggled with my bitter grief, my new-born love. I never blamed my wife—that wife who had heard the tender name so seldom, she could scarce feel it hers. I had fettered her free heart, forgetting it would one day cease to be a child's. I bade her look upon me as a father; she had learned the lesson well; and now what right had I to reproach her for listening to a lover's voice, when her husband's was so cold? What mattered it that slowly, almost unconsciously, I had learned to love her with the passion of a youth, the power of a man? I had alienated that fond nature from my own, and now it was too late.

Heaven only knows the bitterness of that hour—I cannot tell it. But through the darkness of my anguish and remorse that newly kindled love burned like a blessed fire, and, while it tortured, purified. By its light I saw the error of my life: self-love was written on the actions of the past, and I knew that my punishment was very just. With a child's repentant tears, I confessed it to my Father, and He solaced me, showed me the path to tread, and made me nobler for the blessedness and pain of that still hour.

Dawn found me an altered man; for in natures like mine the rain of a great sorrow melts the ice of years, and their hidden strength blooms in a late harvest of patience, self-denial, and humility. I resolved to break the tie which bound poor Effie to a joyless fate; and gratitude for a selfish deed, which wore the guise of charity, should no longer mar her peace. I would atone for the wrong I had done her, the suffering she had endured; and she should never know that I had guessed her tender secret, nor learn the love which made my sacrifice so bitter, yet so just.

Alfred came no more; and as I watched the growing pallor of her cheek, her patient efforts to be cheerful and serene, I honored that meek creature for her constancy to what she deemed the duty of her life.

I did not tell her my resolve at once, for I could not give her up so soon. It was a weak delay, but I had not learned the beauty of a perfect self-forgetfulness; and though I clung to my purpose steadfastly, my heart still cherished a desperate hope that I might be spared this loss.

In the midst of this secret conflict, there came a letter from old Adam Lyndsay, asking to see his daughter's child; for life was waning slowly, and he desired to forgive, as he hoped to be forgiven when the last hour came. The letter was to me, and, as I read it, I saw a way whereby I might be spared the hard task of telling Effie she was to be free. I feared my new-found strength would desert me, and my courage fail, when, looking on the woman who was dearer to me than my life, I tried to give her back the liberty whose worth she had learned to know.

Effie should go, and I would write the words I dared not speak. She would be in her mother's home, free to show her joy at her release, and smile upon the lover she had banished.

I went to tell her; for it was I who sought her now, who watched for her coming and sighed at her departing steps—I who waited for her smile and followed her with wistful eyes. The child's slighted affection was atoned for now by my unseen devotion to the woman.

I gave the letter, and she read it silently.

"Will you go, love?" I asked, as she folded it.

"Yes—the old man has no one to care for him but me, and it is so beautiful to be loved."

A sudden smile touched her lips, and a soft dew shone in the shadowy eyes, which seemed looking into other and tenderer ones than mine. She could not know how sadly I echoed those words, nor how I longed to tell her of another man who sighed to be forgiven.

"You must gather roses for these pale cheeks among the breezy moorlands, dear. They are not so blooming as they were a year ago. Jean would reproach me for my want of care," I said, trying to speak cheerfully, though each word seemed a farewell.

"Poor Jean! how long it seems since she kissed them last!" sighed Effie, musing sadly, as she turned her wedding-ring.

My heart ached to see how thin the hand had grown, and how easily that little fetter would fall off when I set my captive lark at liberty.

I looked till I dared look no longer, and then rose, saying—

"You will write often, Effie, for I shall miss you very much."

She cast a quick look into my face, asking, hurriedly—

"Am I to go alone?"

"Dear, I have much to do and cannot go; but you need fear nothing; I shall send Ralph and Mrs. Prior with you, and the journey is soon over. When will you go?"

It was the first time she had left me since I took her from Jean's arms, and I longed to keep her always near me; but, remembering the task I had to do, I felt that I must seem cold till she knew all.

"Soon—very soon—to-morrow—let me go to-morrow, Sir. I long to be away!" she cried, some swift emotion banishing the calmness of her usual manner, as she rose, with eager eyes and a gesture full of longing.

"You shall go, Effie," was all I could say; and with no word of thanks, she hastened away, leaving me so calm without, so desolate within.

The same eagerness possessed her all that day; and the next she went away, clinging to me at the last as she had clung that night upon the river-bank, as if her grateful heart reproached her for the joy she felt at leaving my unhappy home.

A few days passed, bringing me the comfort of a few sweet lines from Effie, signed "Your child." That sight reminded me, that, if I would do an honest deed, it should be generously done. I read again the little missive she had sent, and then I wrote the letter which might be my last—with no hint of my love, beyond the expression of sincerest regard and never-ceasing interest in her happiness; no hint of Alfred Vaughan; for I would not wound her pride, nor let her dream that any eye had seen the passion she so silently surrendered, with no reproach to me and no shadow on the name I had given into her keeping. Heaven knows what it cost me, and Heaven, through the suffering of that hour, granted me an humbler spirit and a better life.

It went, and I waited for my fate as one might wait for pardon or for doom. It came at length—a short, sad letter, full of meek obedience to my will, of penitence for faults I never knew, and grateful prayers for my peace.

My last hope died then, and for many days I dwelt alone, living over all that happy year with painful vividness. I dreamed again of those fair days, and woke to curse the selfish blindness which had hidden my best blessing from me till it was forever lost.

How long I should have mourned thus unavailingly I cannot tell. A more sudden, but far less grievous loss befell me. My fortune was nearly swept away in the general ruin of a most disastrous year.

This event roused me from my despair and made me strong again—for I must hoard what could be saved, for Effie's sake. She had known a cruel want with me, and she must never know another while she bore my name. I looked my misfortune in the face and ceased to feel it one; for the diminished fortune was still ample for my darling's dower, and now what need had I of any but the simplest home?

Before another month was gone, I was in the quiet place henceforth to be mine alone, and nothing now remained for me to do but to dissolve the bond that made my Effie mine. Sitting over the dim embers of my solitary hearth, I thought of this, and, looking round the silent room, whose only ornaments were the things made sacred by her use, the utter desolation struck so heavily upon my heart, that I bowed my head upon my folded arms, and yielded to the tender longing that could not be repressed.

The bitter paroxysm passed, and, raising my eyes, the clearer for that stormy rain, I beheld Effie standing like an answer to my spirit's cry.

With a great start, I regarded her, saying, at length, in a voice that sounded cold, for my heart leaped up to meet her, and yet must not speak—

"Effie, why are you here?"

Wraith-like and pale, she stood before me, with no sign of emotion but the slight tremor of her frame, and answered my greeting with a sad humility—

"I came because I promised to cleave to you through health and sickness, poverty and wealth, and I must keep that vow till you absolve me from it. Forgive me, but I knew misfortune had befallen you, and, remembering all you had done for me, came, hoping I might comfort when other friends deserted you."

"Grateful to the last!" I sighed, low to myself, and, though deeply touched, replied with the hard-won calmness that made my speech so brief—

"You owe me nothing, Effie, and I most earnestly desired to spare you this."

Some sudden hope seemed born of my regretful words, for, with an eager glance, she cried—

"Was it that desire which prompted you to part from me? Did you think I should shrink from sharing poverty with you who gave me all I own?"

"No, dear—ah, no!" I said, "I knew your grateful spirit far too well for that. It was because I could not make your happiness, and yet had robbed you of the right to seek it with some younger and some better man."

"Basil, what man? Tell me; for no doubt shall stand between us now!"

She grasped my arm, and her rapid words were a command.

I only answered, "Alfred Vaughan."

Effie covered up her face, crying, as she sank down at my feet—

"Oh, my fear! my fear! Why was I blind so long?"

I felt her grief to my heart's core; for my own anguish made me pitiful, and my love made me strong. I lifted up that drooping head and laid it down where it might never rest again, saying, gently, cheerily, and with a most sincere forgetfulness of self—

"My wife, I never cherished a harsh thought of you, never uttered a reproach when your affections turned from a cold, neglectful guardian, to find a tenderer resting-place. I saw your struggles, dear, your patient grief, your silent sacrifice, and honored you more truly than I can tell. Effie, I robbed you of your liberty, but I will restore it, making such poor reparation as I can for this long year of pain; and when I see you blest in a happier home, my keen remorse will be appeased."

As I ceased, Effie rose erect and stood before me, transformed from a timid girl into an earnest woman. Some dormant power and passion woke; she turned on me a countenance aglow with feeling, soul in the eye, heart on the lips, and in her voice an energy that held me mute.

"I feared to speak before," she said, "but now I dare anything, for I have heard you call me 'wife,' and seen that in your face which gives me hope. Basil, the grief you saw was not for the loss of any love but yours; the conflict you beheld was the daily struggle to subdue my longing spirit to your will; and the sacrifice you honor but the renunciation of all hope. I stood between you and the woman whom you loved, and asked of death to free me from that cruel lot. You gave me back my life, but you withheld the gift that made it worth possessing. You desired to be freed from the affection which only wearied you, and I tried to conquer it; but it would not die. Let me speak now, and then I will be still forever! Must our ways lie apart? Can I never be more to you than now? Oh, Basil! oh, my husband! I have loved you very truly from the first! Shall I never know the blessedness of a return?"

Words could not answer that appeal. I gathered my life's happiness close to my breast, and in the silence of a full heart felt that God was very good to me.

Soon all my pain and passion were confessed. Fast and fervently the tale was told; and as the truth dawned on that patient wife, a tender peace transfigured her uplifted countenance, until to me it seemed an angel's face.

"I am a poor man now," I said, still holding that frail creature fast, fearing to see her vanish, as her semblance had so often done in the long vigils I had kept—"a poor man, Effie, and yet very rich, for I have my treasure back again. But I am wiser than when we parted; for I have learned that love is better than a world of wealth, and victory over self a nobler conquest than a continent. Dear, I have no home but this. Can you be happy here, with no fortune but the little store set apart for you, and the knowledge that no want shall touch you while I live?"

And as I spoke, I sighed, remembering all I might have done, and dreading poverty for her alone.

But with a gesture, soft, yet solemn, Effie laid her hands upon my head, as if endowing me with blessing and with gift, and answered, with her steadfast eyes on mine—

"You gave me your home when I was homeless; let me give it back, and with it a proud wife. I, too, am rich; for that old man is gone and left me all. Take it, Basil, and give me a little love."

I gave not little, but a long life of devotion for the good gift God had bestowed on me—finding in it a household spirit the daily benediction of whose presence banished sorrow, selfishness, and gloom, and, through the influence of happy human love, led me to a truer faith in the Divine.

Ariel

A Legend of the Lighthouse

Editor's Note: Most of Alcott's heroines have hearts of gold, but few shine as
bright as Ariel March's in "Ariel: A Legend of the Lighthouse." Raised to adulthood
on an island off the New England coast, she is obviously a fusion of the characters
Ariel and Miranda from Shakespeare's *The Tempest*, and intended to represent innocence untouched by the world at large. Alcott was fond of showing in her thrillers
how true virtue was not only incorruptible, but even infectious: Ariel's purity draws
her true love to her, transforms her self-serving competitor into a friend, and makes
her nemesis into a character deserving of pity.

I

Good morning, Mr. Southesk. Aren't you for the sea, to-day?"

"Good morning, Miss Lawrence. I am only waiting for my boat
to be off."

As he answered her blithe greeting, the young man looked up from the
rock where he was lounging, and a most charming object rewarded him for
the exertion of lifting his dreamy eyes. Some women have the skill to make
even a bathing costume graceful and picturesque; and Miss Lawrence knew
that she looked well in her blue suit, with loosened hair blowing about her

handsome face, glimpses of white ankles through the net-work of her bath-
ing-sandals, and a general breeziness of aspect that became her better than
the most elaborate toilet she could make. A shade of disappointment was
visible on receiving the answer to her question, and her voice was slightly
imperious, for all its sweetness, as she said, pausing beside the indolent figure
that lay basking in the sunshine.

"I meant bathing, not boating, when I spoke of the sea. Will you not
join our party and give us another exhibition of your skill in aquatic gymnas-
tics?"

"No, thank you; the beach is too tame for me; I prefer deep water, heavy
surf and a spice of danger, to give zest to my pastime."

The languid voice was curiously at variance with the words; and Miss
Lawrence almost involuntarily exclaimed—

"You are the strangest mixture of indolence and energy I ever knew! To see
you now, one would find it difficult to believe the stories told of your feats
by land and sea; yet I know that you deserve your soubriquet of 'Bayard,' as
well as the other they give you of *'Dolce far niente.'* You are as changeable as the
ocean which you love so well; but we never see the moon that rules your ebb
and flow."

Ignoring the first part of her speech, Southesk replied to the last sentence
with sudden animation.

"I am fond of the sea, and well I may be, for I was born on it, both my
parents lie buried in it, and out of it my fate is yet to come."

"Your fate?" echoed Miss Lawrence, full of the keenest interest, for he
seldom spoke of himself, and seemed anxious to forget the past in the
successful present, and the promising future. Some passing mood made him
unusually frank, for he answered, as his fine eyes roved far across the glittering
expanse before them—

"Yes, I once had my fortune told by a famous wizard, and it has haunted
me ever since. I am not superstitious, but I cannot help attaching some
importance to her prediction:

> 'Watch by the sea-shore early and late,
> For out of its depths will rise your fate,
> Both love and life will be darkly crossed,
> And a single hour see all won or lost.'

"That was the prophecy; and though I have little faith in it, yet I am
irresistibly drawn toward the sea, and continually find myself watching and
waiting for the fate it is to bring me."

"May it be a happy one."

All the imperiousness was gone from the woman's voice, and her eyes turned as wistfully as her companion's, to the mysterious ocean which had already brought *her* fate. Neither spoke for a moment. Southesk, busied with some fancy of his own, continued to scan the blue waves that rolled to meet the horizon, and Helen scanned his face with an expression which many men would have given much to have awakened, for the world said that Miss Lawrence was as proud and cold as she was beautiful. Love and longing met and mingled in the glance she fixed on that unconscious countenance; and once, with an involuntary impulse, her small hand was raised to smooth away the wind-tossed hair that streaked his forehead, as he sat with uncovered head, smiling to himself—forgetful of her presence. She caught back her hand in time and turned away to hide the sudden color that dyed her cheeks at the momentary impulse which would have betrayed her to a less absorbed companion. Before she could break the silence, there came a call from a group gathered on the smoother beach beyond, and, glad of another chance to gain her wish, she said, in a tone that would have won compliance from any man except Southesk,

"They are waiting for us; can I not tempt you to join the mermaids yonder, and let the boat wait till it's cooler?"

But he shook his head with a wilful little gesture, and looked about him for his hat, as if eager to escape, yet answered smiling—

"I've a prior engagement with the mermaid of the island, and, as a gallant man, must keep it, or expect shipwreck on my next voyage. Are you ready, Jack?" he added, as Miss Lawrence moved away, and he strolled toward an old boatman, busy with his wherry.

"In a jiffy, sir. So you've seen her, have you?" said the man, pausing in his work.

"Seen whom?"

"The marmaid at the island."

"No; I only fabricated that excuse to rid myself of the amiable young ladies who bore me to death. You look as if you had a yarn to spin; so spin away while you work, for I want to be off."

"Well, sir, I jest thought you'd like to know that there *is* a marmaid down there, as you're fond of odd and pretty things. No one has seen her but me, or I should a heard of it, and I've told no one but my wife, being afraid of Rough Ralph, as we call the lighthouse-keeper. He don't like folks comin' round his place; and if I said a word about the marmaid, every one would go swarmin' to the island to hunt up the pretty creeter, and drive Ralph into a rage."

"Never mind Ralph; tell me how and where you saw the mermaid; asleep in your boat, I fancy."

"No, sir; wide awake and sober. I had a notion one day to row round the island, and take a look at the chasm, as they call a great split in the rock that stands up most as high as the lighthouse. It goes from top to bottom of the Gull's Perch, and the sea flows through it, foamin' and ragin' like mad, when the tide rises. The waves have worn holes in the rocks on both sides of the chasm, and in one of these basins I see the marmaid, as plain as I see you."

"What was she doing, Jack?"

"Singin' and combin' her hair; so I knew she was gennywine."

"Her hair was green or blue, of course," said Southesk, with such visible incredulity that old Jack was nettled and answered gruffly,

"It was darker and curlier than the lady's that's jest gone; so was her face handsomer, her voice sweeter, and her arms whiter; believe it or not as you please."

"How about the fins and scales, Jack?"

"Not a sign of 'em, sir. She was half in the water, and had on some sort of a white gown, so I couldn't see whether there were feet or a tail. But I'll swear I saw her; and I've got her comb to prove it."

"Her comb! let me see it, and I shall find it easier to believe the story," said the young man, with a lazy sort of curiosity.

Old Jack produced a dainty little comb, apparently made of a pearly shell, cut and carved with much skill, and bearing two letters on its back.

"Faith! it *is* a pretty thing, and none but a mermaid could have owned it. How did you get it?" asked Southesk, carefully examining the delicate lines and letters, and wishing that the tale could be true, for the vision of the fair-faced mermaiden pleased his romantic fancy.

"It was this way, sir," replied Jack. "I was so took aback that I sung out before I'd had a good look at her. She see me, give a little screech, and dived out of sight. I waited to see her come up, but she didn't; so I rowed as nigh as I dared, and got the comb she'd dropped; then I went home and told my wife. She advised me to hold my tongue and not go agin, as I wanted to; so I give it up; but I'm dreadful eager to have another look at the little thing, and I guess you'd find it worth while to try for a sight of her."

"I can see women bathing without that long row, and don't believe Ralph's daughter would care to be disturbed again."

"He aint got any, sir—neither wife nor child; and no one on the island but him and his mate—a gruff chap that never comes ashore, and don't care for nothin' but keepin' the lantern tidy."

Southesk stood a moment measuring the distance between the mainland and the island, with his eye, for Jack's last speech gave an air of mystery to what before had seemed a very simple matter.

"You say Ralph is not fond of having visitors, and rarely leaves the lighthouse; what else do you know about him?" he asked.

"Nothing, sir, only he's a sober, brave, faithful man that does his duty well, and seems to like that bleak, lonesome lighthouse more than most folks would. He's seen better days, I guess, for there's something of the gentleman about him in spite of his rough ways. Now she's ready, sir, and you're just in time to find the little marmaid doin' up her hair."

"I want to visit the lighthouse, and am fond of adventures, so I think I'll follow your advice. What will you take for this comb, Jack?" asked Southesk, as the old man left his work, and the wherry danced invitingly upon the water.

"Nothing from you, sir; you're welcome to it, for my wife's fretted ever since I had it, and I'm glad to be rid of it. It aint every one I give it to, or tell about what I saw; but you've done me more'n one good turn, and I'm eager to give you a bit of pleasure to pay for 'em. On the further side of the island you'll find the chasm. It's a dangerous place, but you're a reg'lar fish; so I'll risk you. Good luck, and let me know how you get on."

"What do you suppose the letters stand for?" asked Southesk, as he put the comb in his pocket, and trimmed his boat.

"Why, 'A. M.' stands for a Mermaid; don't it?" answered Jack, soberly.

"I'll find another meaning for them before I come back. Keep your secret, and I'll do the same, for I want the mermaid all to myself."

With a laugh the young man skimmed away, deaf to the voices of the fashionable syrens, who vainly endeavored to detain him, and blind to the wistful glances following the energetic figure that bent to the oars with a strength and skill which soon left the beach and its gay groups far behind.

The lighthouse was built on the tallest cliff of the island, and the only safe landing-place appeared to be at the foot of the rock, whence a precipitous path and an iron ladder led to the main entrance of the tower. Barren and forbidding it looked, even in the glow of the summer sun, and remembering Ralph's dislike of visitors, Southesk resolved to explore the chasm alone, and ask leave of no one. Rowing along the craggy shore he came to the enormous rift that cleft the rocks from top to bottom. Bold and skillful as he was he dared not venture very near, for the tide was coming in, and each advancing billow threatened to sweep the boat into the chasm, where angry waves chafed and foamed, filling the dark hollow with a cloud of spray and reverberating echoes that made a mellow din.

Intent on watching the splendid spectacle he forgot to look for the mermaid, till something white flashed by, and turning with a start he saw a human face rise from the sea, followed by a pair of white arms, that beckoned as the lips smiled and the bright eyes watched him while he sat motionless, till, with a sound of musical laughter, the phantom vanished.

Uttering an exclamation, he was about to follow, when a violent shock made him reel in his seat, and a glance showed him the peril he was in, for the boat had drifted between two rocks; the next wave would shatter it.

The instinct of self-preservation being stronger than curiosity, he pulled for his life and escaped just in time.

Steering into calmer water he took an observation, and decided to land if possible, and search the chasm where the water-sprite or bathing-girl had seemed to take refuge. It was some time, however, before he found any safe harbor, and with much difficulty he at last gained the shore, breathless, wet and weary.

Guided by the noise of the waves he came at length to the brink of the precipice and looked down. There were ledges and crannies enough to afford foothold for a fearless climber, and full of the pleasurable excitement of danger and adventures, Southesk swung himself down with a steady head, strong hand and agile foot. Not many steps were taken when he paused suddenly, for the sound of a voice arrested him. Fitfully it rose and fell through the dash of advancing and retreating billows, but he heard it distinctly, and with redoubled eagerness looked and listened.

Half-way down the chasm lay a mass of rock, firmly wedged between the two sides by some convulsion of nature which had hurled it there. Years had evidently passed since it fell, for a tree had taken root and shot up, fed by a little patch of earth, and sheltered from wind and storm in that secluded spot. Wild vines, led by their instinct for the light, climbed along either wall and draped the cliff with green. Some careful hand had been at work, however, for a few hardy plants blossomed in the almost sunless nook; every niche held a delicate fern, every tiny basin was full of some rare old weed, and here and there a suspended shell contained a tuft of greenish moss, or a bird's eggs, or some curious treasure gathered from the deep. The sombre verdure of the little pine concealed a part of this airy nest, but from the hidden nook the sweet voice rose singing a song well suited to the scene—

"Oh, come unto the yellow sands."

Feeling as if he had stepped into a fairy tale, the young man paused with suspended breath till the last soft note and its softer echo had died away, then he noiselessly crept on. Soon his quick eye discovered a rope ladder, half hidden by the vines and evidently used as a path to the marine bower below. Availing himself of it he descended a few steps, but not far, for a strong gust blew up the rift, and swaying aside the leafy screen disclosed the object of his search. No mermaid but a young girl, sitting and singing like a bird in her green nest.

As the pine waved to and fro, Southesk saw that the unknown sat in a thoughtful attitude, looking out through the wide rift into the sunny blue beyond. He saw, too, that a pair of small, bare feet shone white against the dark bottom of a rocky basin, full of newly fallen rain; that a plain grey gown defined the lithe outlines of a girlish figure, and that the damp dark rings of hair were fastened back with a pretty band of shells.

So intent on looking was he that he leaned nearer and nearer, till a sudden gesture caused the comb to slip from his pocket and fall into the basin with a splash that roused the girl from her reverie. She started, seized it eagerly, and looking upward exclaimed with a joyful accent,

"Why, Stern, where did you find my comb?"

There was no answer to her question, and the smile died on her lips, for instead of Stern's rough, brown countenance she saw, framed in green leaves, a young and comely face.

Blonde and blue-eyed, flushed and eager, the pleasant apparition smiled down upon her with an aspect which brought no fear, but woke wonder and won confidence by the magic of a look. Only a moment did she see it; then the pine boughs came between them. The girl sprang up, and Southesk, forgetting safety in curiosity, leaped down.

He had not measured the distance; his foot slipped and he fell, striking his head with a force that stunned him for a moment. The cool drip of water on his forehead roused him, and he soon collected himself, although somewhat shaken by his fall. Half-opening his eyes he looked into a dark yet brilliant face, of such peculiar beauty that it struck and charmed him at a single glance. Pity, anxiety and alarm were visible in it, and glad of a pretext for prolonging the episode, he resolved to feign the suffering he did not feel.

With a sigh he closed his eyes again, and for a moment lay enjoying the soft touch of hands about his head, the sound of a quickly-beating heart near him, and the pleasant consciousness that he was an object of interest to this sweet-voiced unknown. Too generous to keep her long in suspense, he soon raised his head and looked about him, asking faintly,

"Where am I?"

"In the chasm, but quite safe with me," replied a fresh young voice.

"Who is this gentle 'me' whom I mistook for a mermaid, and whose pardon I ask for this rude intrusion?"

"I'm Ariel, and I forgive you willingly."

"Pretty name—is it really yours?" asked Southesk, feeling that his simplest manner was the surest to win her confidence, for the girl spoke with the innocent freedom of a child.

"I have no other, except March, and that is not pretty."

"Then, 'A. M.' on the comb does not mean 'A mermaid,' as old Jack thought when he gave it to me?"

A silvery laugh followed his involuntary smile, as, still kneeling by him, Ariel regarded him with much interest, and a very frank expression of admiration in her beautiful eyes.

"Did you come to bring it back to me?" she asked, turning the recovered treasure in her hand.

"Yes; Jack told me about the pretty water-sprite he saw, so I came to find her, and am not yet sure that you're not a Lurelei, for you nearly wrecked me, and vanished in a most unearthly manner."

"Ah!" she said, with the blithe laugh again, "I lead the life of a mermaid though I'm not one, and when I'm disturbed I play pranks, for I know every cranny of the rocks, and learned swimming and diving from the gulls."

"Flying also, I should think, by the speed with which you reached this nook, for I made all haste, and nearly killed myself, as you see."

As he spoke, Southesk tried to rise, but a sharp tingle in his arm made him pause, with an exclamation of pain.

"Are you much hurt? Can I do anything more for you?" and the voice was womanly pitiful, as the girl watched him.

"I've cut my arm, I think, and lamed my foot; but a little rest will set them right. May I wait here a few minutes, and enjoy your lovely rest; though it's no place for a clumsy mortal like me?"

"Oh, yes; stay as long as you please, and let me bind up your wound. See how it bleeds."

"You are not afraid of me then?"

"No; why should I be?" and the dark eyes looked fearlessly into his as Ariel bent to examine the cut. It was a deep one, and he fancied she would cry out or turn pale; but she did neither, and having skilfully bound a wet handkerchief about it, she glanced from the strong arm and shapely hand to their owner's face, and said, naively,

"What a pity there will be a scar."

Southesk laughed outright, in spite of the smart, and, leaning on the uninjured arm, prepared to enjoy himself, for the lame foot was a fiction.

"Never mind the scar. Men consider them no blemish, and I shall be prouder of this than half a dozen others I have, because by means of it I get a glimpse into fairy land. Do you live here on foam and sunshine, Ariel?"

"No; the lighthouse is my home now."

There was evident reluctance in her manner. She seemed to weigh her words, yet longed to speak out, and it was plain to see that the new-comer was very welcome to her solitude. With all his boldness, Southesk unconsciously tempered his manner with respect, and neither by look nor tone caused any touch of fear to disturb the innocent creature whose retreat he had discovered.

"Then you are Ralph's daughter, as I fancied?" he went on, putting his questions with an engaging air that was hard to resist.

"Yes."

Again she hesitated, and again seemed eager to confide even in a stranger, but controlled the impulse, and gave brief replies to all home questions.

"No one knows you are here, and you seem to lead a hidden life like some enchanted princess. It only needs a Miranda to make a modern version of the Tempest." He spoke half aloud, as if to himself, but the girl answered readily—

"Perhaps I am to lead you to her as the real Ariel led Ferdinand to his Miranda, if you've not already found her."

"Why, what do you know of Shakespeare? and how came you by your pretty name?" asked Southesk, wondering at the look and tone which suddenly gave the girl's face an expression of elfish intelligence.

"I know and love Shakespeare better than any of my other books, and can sing every song he wrote. How beautiful they are! See, I have worn out my dear book with much reading."

As she spoke, from a dry nook in the rock she drew a dilapidated volume, and turned its pages with a loving hand, while all the innocent sweetness returned to her young face, lending it new beauty.

"What a charming little sprite it is," thought Southesk, adding aloud, with an irresistible curiosity that banished politeness,

"And the name, how came that?"

"Father gave it to me." There she paused, adding hastily, "He loves Shakespeare as well as I do, and taught me to understand him."

"Here's a romantic pair, and a mystery of some sort, which I'll amuse myself by unravelling, if possible," he thought, and put another question— "Have you been here long?"

"No; I only spend the hot hours here."

"Another evasion. I shall certainly be driven into asking her, point blank, who and what she is," said Southesk to himself, and, to avoid temptation, returned to the comb which Ariel still held.

"Who carved that so daintily? I should like to bespeak one for myself it is so pretty."

"I carved it, and was very happy at my work. It's hard to find amusement on this barren island, so I invent all sorts of things to wile away the time."

"Did you invent this hanging garden and make this wilderness blossom?" asked Southesk, trying the while to understand the lights and shadows that made her face as changeful as an April sky.

"Yes, I did it, and spend half my time here, for here I escape seeing people on the beach, and so forget them."

A little sigh followed, and her eyes turned wistfully to the dark rift, that gave her but a glimpse of the outer world.

"You can scarcely see the beach, much less the people on it, I should think," said Southesk, wondering what she meant.

"I can see well with the telescope from the tower, and often watch the people on the shore—they look so gay and pretty."

"Then, why wish to forget them?"

"Because since they came it is more lonely than before."

"Do you never visit the mainland? Have you no friends or companions to enliven your solitude?"

"No."

Something in the tone in which the monosyllable was uttered checked further inquiries, and prompted him to say smilingly:

"Now it is your turn; ask what you will."

But Ariel drew back, answering with an air of demure propriety that surprised him more than her self-possession or her rebuke.

"No, thank you, it is ill-bred to question strangers."

Southesk colored at the satirical glance she gave him, and rising, he made his most courtly bow, saying, with a pleasant mixture of candor and contrition:

"Again I beg pardon for my rudeness. Coming so suddenly upon a spirit singing to itself between sea and sky, I forgot myself, and fancied the world's ways out of place. Now I see my mistake, and though it spoils the romance, I will call you Miss March, and respectfully take my leave."

The silvery laugh broke in on the last sentence, and in her simplest manner Ariel replied:

"No, don't call me that nor go away, unless you are quite out of pain. I like your rudeness better than your politeness, for it made you seem like a pleasant boy, and now you are nothing but a fine gentleman."

Both amused and relieved by her reply, he answered, half in jest, half in earnest,

"Then, I'll be a boy again, and tell you who I am, as you are too well-bred to ask, and it is but proper to introduce myself. Philip Southesk by name, gentleman by birth, poet by profession; but I don't deserve the title, though certain friendly persons do me the honor to praise a few verses I once wrote. Stay, I forgot two things that ladies usually take an interest in. Fortune ample—age four-and-twenty."

"You did not ask me either of these two questions," said Ariel, with a flicker of merriment in her eyes, as she glanced up rather shyly at the would-be boy, who now stood straight and tall before her.

"No; even in the midst of my delusion I remembered that one never ventures to put the last of those questions to a woman—the first I cared nothing about."

"I like that," said the girl in her quick way, adding frankly, "I am poor, and seventeen."

She half rose as she spoke, but hastily sat down again, recollecting her bare feet. The change of color, and an anxious look toward a pair of little shoes that lay near by, suggested to Southesk a speedy withdrawal, and, turning toward the half-hidden ladder, he said, lingering in the act of going:

"Good-by; may I come again, if I come properly, and do not stay too long? Poets are privileged persons, you know, and this is a poet's paradise."

She looked pleased, yet troubled, and answered reluctantly:

"You are very kind to say so, but I cannot ask you to come again, for father would be displeased, and it is best for me to go on as before."

"But why hide yourself here? Why not enjoy the pleasures fitting for your age, instead of watching them afar off, and vainly longing for them?" exclaimed Southesk impetuously, for the eloquent eyes betrayed what the tongue would not confess.

"I cannot tell you."

As she spoke her head was bowed upon her hands, her abundant hair veiled her face, and as it fell the little chaplet of shells dropped at Southesk's feet.

"Forgive me; I have no right to question you, and will not disturb your solitude again, unless your father is willing. But give me some token to prove that I have really visited an enchanted island, and heard Ariel sing. I returned the comb, may I have this in exchange?"

He spoke playfully, hoping to win a smile of pardon for his last trespass. She looked up quite calm again, and freely gave him the chain of shells for which he asked. Then he sprang up the precipitous path, and went his way, but his parting glance showed him the fair face still wistfully watching him from the green gloom of Ariel's nest.

II

In the lower room of the lighthouse sat three persons, each apparently busy with his own thoughts, yet each covertly watching the others. Ralph March, a stern, dark-browed, melancholy-looking man, leaned back in his chair, with one hand above his eyes, which were fixed on Ariel, who sat near the narrow window cut in the thick wall, often gazing out upon the sea, glowing with the gold and purple of a sunset sky, but oftener stealing a glance toward her father, as if she longed to speak yet dared not. The third occupant of the room was a rough, sturdy-looking man, whose age it was hard to discover, for an unsightly hump disfigured his broad shoulders, and a massive head was set upon a stunted body. Shaggy-haired, tawny-bearded and bronzed by wind and weather he was a striking, not a pitiful figure, for his herculean strength was visible at a glance, and a somewhat defiant expression seemed to repel compassion and command respect. Sitting in the doorway, he appeared to be intent on mending a torn net, but his keen eye went stealthily from father to daughter, as if trying to read their faces. The long silence that had filled the room was broken by March's deep voice, saying suddenly, as he dropped his hand and turned to Ariel:

"Are you sick or sad, child, that you sigh so heavily?"

"I'm lonely, father."

Something in the plaintive tone and drooping figure touched March's heart, and, drawing the girl to his knee, he looked into her face with a tender anxiety that softened and beautified his own.

"What can I do for you, dear? Where shall I take you to make you forget your loneliness?—or whom shall I bring here to enliven you?"

Her eyes woke and her lips parted eagerly, as if a wish was ready, but some fear restrained its utterance, and, half averting her face, she answered meekly:

"I ought to be contented with you, and I try to be, but sometimes I long to do as others do, and enjoy my youth while it lasts. If you liked to mingle with people I should love to try it; as you do not, I'll endeavor to be happy where I am."

"Poor child, it is but natural, and I am selfish to make a recluse of you, because I hate the world. Shall we leave the island and begin our wandering life again?"

"Oh, no; I like the island now, and could be quite contented if I had a young companion. I never have had, and did not know how pleasant it was until two days ago."

Her eyes turned toward the open door, through which the Gull's Perch was visible, with the chasm yawning near it, and again she sighed. March saw where she looked; a frown began to gather, but some gentler emotion checked his anger, and with a sudden smile he said, stroking her smooth cheek:

"Now I know the wish you would not tell, the cause of your daily watch from the tower, and the secret of these frequent sighs. Silly child, you want young Southesk to return, yet dare not ask me to permit it."

Ariel turned her face freely to his, and leaning confidingly upon his shoulder, answered with the frankness he had taught her,

"I do wish he'd come again, and I think I deserve some reward for telling you all that happened, for bidding him go away, and for being so careful what I said."

"Hard tasks, I know, especially the last, for such an open creature as my girl. Well, you shall be rewarded, and if he come again you may see him, and so will I."

"Oh, thank you, father, that is so kind. But you look as if you thought he would not come."

"I am afraid he has already forgotten all about the lonely island and the little barefooted maiden he saw on it. Young men's memories are treacherous things, and curiosity once gratified, soon dies."

But Ariel shook her head, as if refusing to accept the ungracious thought, and surprised her father by the knowledge of human nature which she seemed to have learned by instinct, for she answered gravely, yet hopefully:

"I think he *will* come, simply because I forbade it. He is a poet, and cares for things that have no charm for other men. He liked my nest, he liked to hear me sing, and his curiosity was not gratified, because I only told enough to make him eager for more. I have a feeling that he will come again, to find that the island is not always lonely, nor the girl always barefooted."

Her old blithe laugh broke out again as she glanced from the little mirror that reflected the glossy waves of her hair, bound with a band of rosy coral, to the well-shod feet that peeped from below the white hem of her gown. Her father watched her fondly, as she swept him a stately curtsey, looking so gay and lovely that he could not but smile and hope her wish might be granted.

"Little vanity," he said, "who taught you to make yourself so bonny, and where did you learn these airs and graces? Not from Stern or me, I fancy."

"Ah, I have not looked through the telescope and watched the fine ladies in vain, it seems, since you observe the change. I study fashion and manners at a disadvantage, but I am an apt scholar, I find. Now I'm going up to watch and wait for my reward."

As she ran up the winding-stairs that led to the great lantern, and the circular balcony that hung outside, Stern said, with the freedom of one privileged to speak his mind:

"The girl is right; the boy will come again, and mischief will grow out of it."

"What mischief?" demanded March.

"Do you suppose he can see her often and not love her?" returned Stern, almost angrily.

"Let him love her."

"Do you mean it? After hiding her so carefully, will you let her be won by this romantic boy, if his fancy last? You are making a false step, and you'll repent of it."

"I have already made a false step, and I do repent of it; but it's not this one. I have tried to keep Ariel a child, and she was happy until she became a woman. Now the old simple life is not enough for her, and her heart craves its right. I live only for her, and if her happiness demands the sacrifice of the seclusion I love, I shall make it—shall welcome anyone who can give her pleasure, and promote any scheme that spares her from the melancholy that curses me."

"Then you are resolved to let this young man come if he choose, and allow her to love him, as she most assuredly will?"

"Yes, chance brought him here at first, and if inclination brings him again let it be so. I have made inquiries concerning him, and am satisfied. He is Ariel's equal in birth, is fitted to make her happy, and has already wakened an unusual interest in her mind. Sooner or later I must leave her; she is alone in the world, and to whom can I confide her so safely as to a husband."

A dark flush had passed over Stern's face as he listened, and more than once impetuous words seemed to have risen to his lips, to be restrained by set teeth and an emotion of despair.

March saw this, and it seemed to confirm his purpose, though he made no comment on it, and abruptly closed the conversation; for, as Stern began—

"I warn you, sir————" he interrupted him, saying with decision:

"No more of this; I have had other warnings than yours, and must listen to them, for the time is not far distant when I must leave the child alone, unless I give her a guardian soon. Wild as my plan may seem, it is far safer than to take her into the world, for here I can observe this young man, and shape her future as I will. You mean kindly, Stern, but you cannot judge for me nor understand my girl as I do. Now, leave me, I must go and rest."

Stern's black eyes glowed with an ireful spark, and he clenched his strong hands as if to force himself to silence, as he went away without a word, while March passed into an inner room, with the melancholy expression deeper than ever on his face.

For a few moments the deserted room was silent and solitary, but presently a long shadow fell athwart the sunny floor, and Southesk stood in the open doorway, with a portfolio and a carefully folded parcel underneath his arm. Pausing to look about him for some one to address, the sound of Ariel's voice reached his ear, and, as if no other welcome were needed, he followed it as eagerly as before. Stealing up the steep stairs, he came into the many-windowed tower, and on the balcony saw Ariel straining her eyes through a telescope, which was pointed toward the beach he had left an hour ago. As he lingered, uncertain how to accost her, she dropped the glass, exclaiming with a sigh of weariness and disappointment,

"No, he is not there!" In the act she turned, saw him, and uttered a little cry of delight, while her face brightened beautifully as she sprang forward, offering her hand with a gesture as graceful as impulsive, saying joyfully—

"I knew you would come again!"

Well pleased at such a cordial welcome, he took the hand, and still holding it, asked in that persuasive voice of his—

"For whom were you looking, Ariel?"

She colored, and turned her traitorous eyes away, yet answered with an expression of merry mischief that was very charming—

"I looked for Ferdinand!"

"And here he is," replied Southesk, laughing at her girlish evasion. "Though you forbade my return, I was obliged to break my promise, because I unconsciously incurred a debt which I wish to discharge. When I asked you for those pretty shells I did not observe that they were strung on a little gold chain, and afterward it troubled me to think I had taken a gift of value. Much as I want to keep it, I shall not like to do so unless you will let me make some return for that, and for the hospitality you showed me. May I offer you this, with many thanks?"

While speaking rapidly, he had undone the parcel, and put into her hands a beautiful volume of Shakespeare, daintily bound, richly illustrated, and bearing on the fly-leaf a graceful little poem to herself. So touched and delighted was she that she stood silent, reading the musical lines, glancing at the pictured pages, and trying to summon words expressive enough to convey her thanks. None came that suited her, but her eyes filled, and she exclaimed with a grateful warmth that well repaid the giver.

"It is too beautiful for me, and you are too kind! How did you know I wanted a new book, and would have chosen one like this?"

"I am glad I guessed so well, and now consider the mermaid's rosary my own. But tell me, did you ask if I might come again, or did you leave it to me?"

"I tell my father everything, and when I spoke of you again to-day, much to my surprise, he said you might come if you chose. But he added that you'd probably forgotten all about the island by this time."

"And you knew I had not—thank you for that. No; so far from forgetting, I've dreamed about it ever since, and should have returned before had not my arm been too lame for rowing, and I would not bring any intruder but myself. I want to sketch your nest, for some day it will get into verse, and I wish to keep it fresh before me. May I?"

"I shall be very proud to see it drawn, and to read the poem if it is as sweet as this. I think I like your songs better than Shakespeare's."

"What a compliment! It is I who am proud now. How beautiful it is up here; one feels like a bird on this airy perch. Tell me what those places are that look so like celestial cities in this magical light?"

Willingly she obeyed, and standing at her side he listened, feeling the old enchantment creep over him as he watched the girl, who seemed to glow and brighten like a flower at the coming of the sun. Nor did the charm lie in her beauty alone; language, mien, and manner betrayed the native refinement which comes from birth and breeding, and, despite her simple dress, her frank ways, and the mystery that surrounded her, Southesk felt that this lighthouse-keeper's daughter was a gentlewoman, and every moment grew more interested in her.

Presently he professed a desire to sketch a picturesque promontory not far distant; and, seated on the step of the narrow door, he drew industriously, glancing up now and then at Ariel, who leaned on the balustrade turning the pages of her book with her loveliest expression, as she read a line here and there, sung snatches of the airs she loved so well, or paused to talk, for her companion wasted little time in silence. Place, hour, and society suited him to a charm, and he luxuriated in the romance and the freedom, both being much enhanced by the strong contrast between this hour and those he had been spending among the frivolous crowds at the great hotel. He took no thought for the future but heartily enjoyed the present, and was in his gayest, most engaging mood as he feasted his eyes on the beauty all about him while endeavoring to copy the graceful figure and spirited face before him.

Quite unconscious of his purpose she pored over the book, and presently exclaimed, as she opened on a fine illustration of the Tempest—

"Here we all are! Prospero is not unlike my father, but Ferdinand is much plainer than you. Here's Ariel swinging in a vine, as I've often done, and Caliban watching her as Stern watches me. He is horrible here, however, and my Caliban has a fine face, if one can get a sight of it when he is in good humor."

"You mean the deformed man who glowered at me as I landed? I want much to know who he is, but I dare not ask, lest I get another lesson in good manners," said Southesk, with an air of timidity belied by his bold, bright eyes.

"I'll tell you without asking. He is the lighthouse-keeper, for my father only helps him a little, because he likes the wild life. People call him the master, as he goes to the mainland for all we need instead of Stern, who hates to be seen, poor soul."

"Thank you," returned Southesk, longing to ask more questions, and on the alert for any hint that might enlighten him regarding this peculiar pair.

Ariel went back to her book, smiling to herself, as she said, after a long look at one figure in the pictured group—

"This Miranda is very charming, but not so queenly as yours."

"Mine!" ejaculated Southesk, with as much amusement as surprise. "How do you know I have one?"

"She came here to look for you," stealing a glance at him from under her long lashes.

"The deuce, she did! When—how? Tell me about it, for, upon my honor, I don't know who you mean," and Southesk put down his pencil to listen.

"Yesterday a boatman rowed a lady down here, and though the steep path and the ladder rather daunted her at first, she climbed up, and asked to see the lighthouse. Stern showed it, but she was not soon satisfied, and peered about as if bent on searching every corner. She asked many questions, and examined the book for visitors' names, which hangs below. Yours was not there, but she seemed to suspect that you had been here, and Stern told her that it was so. It was not like him, but he was unusually gracious, though he said nothing about father and myself, and when she had roamed up and down for a long time, the lady went away."

"Was she tall and dark, with fine eyes and proud air?" asked Southesk, with a frown.

"Yes; but I thought she could be very sweet and gentle when she chose, she changed so as she spoke of you."

"Did she see you, Ariel?"

"No; I ran away and hid, as I always do when strangers come; but I saw her, and longed to know her name, for she would not give it, so I called her your Miranda."

"Not she! Her name is Helen Lawrence, and I wish she was——" He checked himself, looking much annoyed, yet ashamed of his petulant tone, and added, with a somewhat disdainful smile—"less inquisitive. She must have come while I was in the city searching for your book, but she never breathed a word of it to me. I shall feel like a fly in a cobweb if she keeps such close watch over me."

"Why did she think you had been here? Did you tell her?" asked Ariel, looking as if she quite understood Miss Lawrence's motive in coming, and rather enjoyed her disappointment.

"That puppy, Dr. Haye, who dressed my arm, and found your handkerchief on it, made a story out of nothing, and set the gossips chattering. The women over yonder have nothing else to do, so a fine romance was built up, founded on the wounded arm, the little handkerchief, and the pretty chain, of which Haye caught a glimpse. Miss Lawrence must have bribed old Jack to tell her where I'd been, for I told no one, and stole off to-day so carefully that I defy them to track me here."

"Thank you for remembering that we did not wish to be disturbed; but I am sorry that you have been annoyed, and hope this handsome Helen will not come again. You think her handsome, don't you?" asked the girl, in the demure tone that she sometimes used with much effect.

"Yes; but she is not to my taste. I like spirit, character, and variety of expression in a face more than mere beauty of coloring or outline. One doesn't see faces like hers in one's dreams, or imagine it at one's fireside; it is a fine picture—not the image of the woman one would live and die for."

A soft color had risen to Ariel's cheek as she listened, wondering why those few words sounded so sweet to her. Southesk caught the fleeting emotion, and made the likeness perfect with a happy stroke or two. Pausing to survey his work with pleasure, he said low to himself—

"What more does it need?"

"Nothing—it is excellent."

The paper fluttered from his hand as a man's voice answered, and turning quickly, he saw March standing behind him. He knew who it was at once, for several times he had passed on the beach this roughly-dressed, stern-faced man, who came and went as if blind to the gaiety all about him. Now, the change in him would have greatly surprised his guest had not his interviews with Ariel prepared him for any discovery, and when March greeted him with the air and manner of a gentleman, he betrayed no astonishment, but, giving his name, repeated his desire to sketch the beauties of the island, and asked permission to do so. A satirical smile passed over March's grave face, as he glanced from the paper he had picked up to the bare cliffs below, but his tone was very courteous as he replied—

"I have no right to forbid any one to visit the island, though its solitude was the attraction that brought me here. But poets and painters are privileged; so come freely, and if your pen and pencil make it too famous for us we can emigrate to a more secluded spot, for we are only birds of passage."

"There shall be no need of that, I assure you, sir. Its solitude is as attractive to me as to yourself, and no word or act of mine shall destroy the charm," Southesk spoke eagerly, adding, with a longing glance at the paper which March still held: "I ventured to begin with the island's mistress, and, with your permission, I will finish it as you pronounce it good."

"It is excellent, and I shall be glad to bespeak a copy, for I've often tried to sketch my will-o'-the-wisp, but never succeeded. What magic did you use to keep her still so long?"

"This, father," and Ariel showed her gift, as she came to look over his shoulder, and smile and blush to see herself so carefully portrayed.

Southesk explained, and the conversation turning upon poetry, glided smoothly on till the deepening twilight warned the guest to go, and more than ever charmed and interested, he floated homeward to find Miss Lawrence waiting for him on the beach, and to pass her with his coolest salutation.

From that day he led a double life—one gay and frivolous for all the world to see, the other sweet and secret as a lover's first romance. Hiring a room at a fisherman's cottage that stood in a lonely nook, and giving out that he was seized with a fit of inspiration, he secluded himself whenever he chose, without exciting comment or curiosity. Having purchased the old couple's silence regarding his movements, he came and went with perfect freedom, and passers-by surveyed with respectful interest the drawn curtains behind which the young poet was believed to be intent on songs and sonnets, while, in reality, he was living a sweeter poem than any he could write far away on the lighthouse tower, or hidden in the shadowy depths of Ariel's nest. Even Helen was deceived, for, knowing that hers were the keenest eyes upon him, he effectually blinded them for the time by slowly changing his former indifference to the gallant devotion which may mean much or little, yet which is always flattering to a woman, and doubly so to one who loves and waits for a return. Her society was more agreeable to him than that of the giddy girls and *blasé* men about him, and believing that the belle of several seasons could easily guard the heart that many had besieged, he freely enjoyed the intercourse which their summer sojourn facilitated, all unconscious of the hopes and fears that made those days the most eventful of her life.

Stern was right; the young man could not see Ariel without loving her. For years, he had roamed about the world, heart-free; but his time came at last, and he surrendered without a struggle. For a few weeks he lived in an enchanted world, too happy to weigh consequences or dread disappointment. There was no cause for doubt or fear—no need to plead for love—because the artless girl gave him her heart as freely as a little child, and reading the language of his eyes, answered eloquently with her own. It was a poet's wooing; summer, romance, beauty, innocence and youth—all lent their charms, and nothing marred its delight. March watched and waited hopefully, well pleased at the success of his desire; and seeing in the young man the future guardian of his child, soon learned to love him for his own sake as well as hers. Stern was the only cloud in all this sunshine; he preserved a grim silence, and seemed to take no heed of what went on about him; but, could the cliffs have spoken, they might have told pathetic secrets of the lonely man who haunted them by night, like a despairing ghost; and the sea might have betrayed how many tears, bitter as its own billows, had been wrung from a strong heart that loved, yet knew that the passion never could be returned.

The mystery that seemed at first to surround them no longer troubled him, for a few words from March satisfied him that sorrow and misfortune made them seek solitude, and shun the scenes where they had suffered most. A prudent man would have asked more, but Southesk cared nothing for wealth or rank, and with the delicacy of a generous nature, feared to wound by questioning too closely. Ariel loved him; he had enough for all, and the present was too blissful to permit any doubts of the past—any fears for the future.

So the summer days rolled on, sunny and serene, as if tempests were unknown, and brought, at last, the hour when Southesk longed to claim Ariel for his own, and show the world the treasure he had found.

Full of this purpose, he went to his tryst one golden August afternoon, intent on seeing March first, that he might go to Ariel armed with her father's consent. But March was out upon the sea, where he often floated aimlessly for hours, and Southesk found no one but Stern, busily burnishing the great reflectors until they shone again.

"Where is Ariel?" was the young man's second question, though usually it was the first.

"Why ask me, when you know better than I where to find her," Stern answered harshly, as he frowned over the bright mirror that reflected both his own and the happy lover's face; and too light-hearted to resent a rude speech, Southesk went smiling away to find the girl, waiting for him in the chasm.

"What pretty piece of work is in hand, to-day, busy creature?" he said, as he threw himself down beside her with an air of supreme content.

"I'm stringing these for you, because you carry the others so constantly they will soon be worn out," she answered, busying herself with a redoubled assiduity, for something in his manner made her heart beat fast and her color vary. He saw it, and fearing to agitate her by abruptly uttering the ardent words that trembled on his lips, he said nothing for a moment, but leaning on his arm, looked at her with lover's eyes, till Ariel, finding silence more dangerous than speech, said hastily, as she glanced at a ring on the hand that was idly playing with the many-colored shells that strewed her lap,

"That is a curious old jewel; are those your initials on it?"

"No, my father's;" and he held it up for her to see.

"R. M., where is the S. for Southesk?" she asked, examining it with girlish curiosity.

"I shall have to tell you a little story all about myself in order to explain that. Do you care to hear it?"

"Yes, your stories are always pleasant; tell it, please."

"Then, you must know that I was born on the long voyage to India, and nearly died immediately after. The ship was wrecked, and my father and mother were lost; but, by some miracle, my faithful nurse and I were saved. Having no near relatives in the world, an old friend of my father's adopted me, reared me tenderly, and dying, left me his name and fortune."

"Philip Southesk is not your true name, then?"

"No; I took it at my good old friend's desire. But you shall choose which name you will bear, when you let me put a more precious ring than this on the dear little hand I came to ask you for. Will you marry Philip Southesk or Richard Marston, my Ariel?"

If she had leaped down into the chasm the act would not have amazed him more than the demonstration which followed these playful, yet tender words. A stifled exclamation broke from her, all the color died out of her face, in her eyes grief deepened to despair, and when he approached her she shrunk from him with a gesture of repulsion that cut him to the heart.

"What is it? Are you ill? How have I offended you? Tell me, my darling, and let me make my peace at any cost," he cried, bewildered by the sudden and entire change that had passed over her.

"No, no; it is impossible. You must not call me that. I must not listen to you. Go—go at once, and never come again. Oh, why did I not know this sooner?" and, covering up her face, she burst into a passion of tears.

"How could you help knowing that I loved you when I showed it so plainly—it seemed hardly necessary to put it into words. Why do you shrink from me with such abhorrence? Explain this strange change, Ariel. I have a right to ask it," he demanded distressfully.

"I can explain nothing till I have seen my father. Forgive me. This is harder for me to hear than it ever can be for you," she answered through her grief, and in her voice there was the tenderest regret, as well as the firmest resolution.

"You do not need your father to help you. Answer whether you love me, and that is all I ask. Speak, I conjure you." He took her hands and made her look at him. There was no room for doubt; one look assured him, for her heart spoke in her eyes before she answered, fervently as a woman, simply as a child:

"I love you more than I can ever tell."

"Then, why this grief and terror? What have I said to trouble you? Tell me that, also, and I am content."

He had drawn her toward him as the sweet confession left her lips, and was already smiling with the happiness it gave him; but Ariel banished both smile and joy by breaking from his hold, pale and steady as if tears had calmed and strengthened her, saying, in a tone that made his heart sink with an ominous foreboding of some unknown ill:

"I must not answer you without my father's permission. I have made a bitter mistake in loving you, and I must amend it if I can. Go now, and come again to-morrow; then I can speak and make all clear to you. No, do not tempt me with caresses; do not break my heart with reproaches, but obey me, and whatever comes between us, oh, remember that I shall love you while I live."

Vain were all his prayers and pleadings, questions and commands: some power more potent than love kept her firm through the suffering and sorrow of that hour. At last he yielded to her demand, and winning from her a promise to set his heart at rest early on the morrow, he tore himself away, distracted by a thousand vague doubts and dreads.

III

~

Asleepless night, an hour or two of restless pacing to and fro upon the beach, then the impatient lover was away upon his fateful errand, careless of observation now, and rowing as he had never rowed before. The rosy flush of early day shone over the island, making the grim rocks beautiful, and Southesk saw in it a propitious omen; but when he reached the lighthouse a sudden fear dashed his sanguine hopes, for it was empty. The door stood open—no fire burned upon the hearth, no step sounded on the stairs, no voice answered when he called, and the dead silence daunted him.

Rapidly searching every chamber, shouting each name, and imploring a reply, he hurried up and down like one distraught, till but a single hope remained to comfort him. Ariel might be waiting at the chasm, though she had bid him see her father first. Bounding over the cliffs, he reached the dearest spot the earth held for him, and looking down saw only desolation. The ladder was gone, the vines torn from the walls, the little tree lay prostrate; every green and lovely thing was crushed under the enormous stones that some ruthless hand had hurled upon them, and all the beauty of the rock was utterly destroyed as if a hurricane had swept over it.

"Great heavens! who has done this?"

"I did."

Stern spoke, and standing on the opposite side of the chasm, regarded Southesk with an expression of mingled exultation, hatred and defiance, as if the emotions which had been so long restrained had found a vent at last.

"But why destroy what Ariel loved?" demanded the young man, involuntarily retreating a step from the fierce figure that confronted him.

"Because she has done with it, and no other shall enjoy what she has lost."

"Done with it," echoed Southesk, forgetting everything but the fear that oppressed him. "What do you mean? Where is she? For God's sake end this horrible suspense."

"She is gone, never to return," and as he answered, Stern smiled a smile of bitter satisfaction in the blow he was dealing the man he hated.

"Where is March?"

"Gone with her."

"Where are they gone?"

"I will never tell you."

"When did they go, and why? Oh! answer me!"

"At dawn, and to shun you."

"But why let me come for weeks and then fly me as if I brought a curse with me?"

"Because you are what you are."

Questions and answers had been too rapidly exchanged to leave time for anything but intense amazement and anxiety. Stern's last words arrested Southesk's impetuous inquiries and he stood a moment trying to comprehend that enigmatical reply. Suddenly he found a clue, for in recalling his last interview with Ariel, he remembered that for the first time he had told her his father's name. The mystery was there—that intelligence, and not the avowal of his love, was the cause of her strange agitation, and some unknown act of the father's was now darkening the son's life. These thoughts flashed through his mind in the drawing of a breath, and with them came the recollection of Ariel's promise to answer him.

Lifting the head that had sunk upon his breast, as if this stroke fell heavily, he stretched his hands imploringly to Stern, exclaiming:

"Did she leave no explanation for me, no word of comfort, no farewell? Oh! be generous, and pity me; give me her message and I will go away, never to disturb you any more."

"She bade me tell you that she obeyed her father, but her heart was yours forever, and she left you this."

With a strong effort at self-control, Stern gave the message, and slowly drew from his breast a little parcel, which he flung across the chasm. It fell at Southesk's feet, and tearing it open a long, dark lock of hair coiled about his fingers with a soft caressing touch, reminding him so tenderly of his lost love, that for a moment he forgot his manhood, and covering up his face, cried in a broken voice:

"Oh! Ariel, come back to me—come back to me!"

"She never will come back to you; so cast yourself down among the ruins yonder, and lament the ending of your love dream, like a romantic boy, as you are."

The taunting speech, and the scornful laugh that followed it calmed Southesk better than the gentlest pity. Dashing away the drops he turned on Stern with a look that showed it was fortunate the chasm parted the two men, and answered in a tone of indomitable resolve:

"No, I shall not lament, but find and claim her as my own, even if I search the world till I am grey, and a thousand obstacles be between us. I leave the ruins and the tears to you, for I am rich in hope and Ariel's love."

Then they parted, Southesk full of the energy of youth, and a lover's faith in friendly fortune, sprang down the cliffs, and shot away across the glittering bay on his long search, but Stern, with despair for his sole companion, flung himself on the hard bosom of the rocks, struggling to accept the double desolation which came upon his life.

"An early row and an early ride without a moment's rest between. Why, Mr. Southesk, we shall not dare to call you *dolce far niente* any more," began Miss Lawrence, as she came rustling out upon the wide piazza, fresh from her morning toilette, to find Southesk preparing to mount his fleetest horse; but as he turned to bow silently the smile vanished from her lips, and a keen anxiety banished the gracious sweetness from her face.

"Good heavens, what has happened?" she cried, forgetting her self-betrayal in alarm at the haggard countenance she saw.

"I have lost a very precious treasure, and I am going to find it. Adieu;" and he was gone without another word.

Miss Lawrence was alone, for the gong had emptied halls and promenades of all but herself, and she had lingered to caress the handsome horse until its master came. Her eye followed the reckless rider until he vanished, and as it came back to the spot where she had caught that one glimpse of his altered face, it fell upon a little case of curiously-carved and scented Indian wood. She took it up, wondering that she had not seen it fall from his pocket as he mounted, for she knew it to be his, and opening it, found the key to his variable moods and frequent absences of late. The string of shells appeared first, and examining it with a woman's scrutiny, she found letters carved on the inside of each. Ten rosy shells—ten delicate letters, making the name Ariel March. A folded paper came next, evidently a design for a miniature to form a locket for the pretty chain, for in the small oval, drawn with all a lover's skill, was a young girl's face, and underneath, in Southesk's hand, as if written for his eye alone, the words, "My Ariel." A long, dark lock of hair and a little knot of dead flowers were all the case held beside.

"This is the mermaid old Jack told me of, this is the muse Southesk has been wooing, and this is the lost treasure he has gone to find."

As she spoke low to herself, Helen made a passionate gesture as if she would tear and trample on the relics of this secret love, but some hope or purpose checked her, and concealing the case, she turned to hide her trouble in solitude, thinking as she went:

"He will return for this; till then I must wait."

But Southesk did not return, for the lesser loss was forgotten in the greater, and he was wandering over land and sea, intent upon a fruitless quest. Summer passed, and Helen returned to town still hoping and waiting with a woman's patience for some tidings of the absentee.

Rumor gossiped much about the young poet—the eccentricities of genius—and prophesied an immortal work as the fruit of such varied and incessant travel.

But Helen knew the secret of his restlessness, and while she pitied his perpetual disappointment she rejoiced over it, sustaining herself with the belief that a time would come when he would weary of this vain search, and let her comfort him. It did come; for, late in the season, when winter gaieties were nearly over, Southesk returned to his old haunts, so changed that curiosity went hand in hand with sympathy.

He gave no reason for it but past illness; yet it was plain to see the malady of his mind. Listless, taciturn, and cold, with no trace of his former energy except a curiously vigilant expression of the eye and a stern folding of the lips, as if he was perpetually looking for something and perpetually meeting with disappointment. This was the change which had befallen the once gay and *debonair* Philip Southesk.

Helen Lawrence was among the first to hear of his return, and to welcome him, for, much to her surprise, he came to see her on the second day, drawn by the tender recollections of a past with which she was associated.

Full of the deepest joy at beholding him again, and the gentlest pity for his dejection, Helen had never been more charming than during that interview.

Eager to assure herself of the failure which his face betrayed, she soon inquired, with an air and accent of the friendliest interest:

"Was your search successful, Mr. Southesk? You left so suddenly, and have been so long away I hoped the treasure had been found, and that you had been busy putting that happy summer into song for us."

The color rose to Southesk's forehead, and fading left him paler than before, as he answered with a vain attempt at calmness:

"I shall never find the thing I lost, and never put that summer into song, for it was the saddest of my life;" then, as if anxious to change the direction of her thoughts, he said abruptly, "I am on another quest now, looking for a little case which I think I dropped the day I left you, but whether at the hotel or on the road I cannot tell. Did you hear anything of such a trifle being found?"

"No. Was it of much value to you?"

"Of infinite value now, for it contains the relics of a dear friend lately lost."

Helen had meant to keep what she had found, but his last words changed her purpose, for a thrill of hope shot through her heart, and, turning to a cabinet behind her, she put the case into his hand, saying in her softest tone:

"I heard nothing of it because I found it, believed it to be yours, and kept it sacred until you came to claim it, for I did not know where to find you."

Then, with a woman's tact, she left him to examine his recovered treasure, and, gliding to an inner room, she busied herself among her flowers till he rejoined her.

Sooner than she had dared to hope he came, with signs of past emotion on his face, but much of his old impetuosity of manner, as he pressed her hand, saying warmly:

"How can I thank you for this? Let me atone for my past insincerity by confessing the cause of it; you have found a part of my secret, let me add the rest. I need a confidant, will you be mine?"

"Gladly, if it will help or comfort you."

So, sitting side by side under the passion flowers, he told his story, and she listened with an interest that insensibly drew him on to fuller confidences than he had intended.

When he had described the parting, briefly yet very eloquently, for voice, eye, and gesture lent their magic, he added, in an altered tone, and with an expression of pathetic patience:

"There is no need to tell you how I searched for them, how often I thought myself upon their track, how often they eluded me, and how each disappointment strengthened my purpose to look till I succeeded, though I gave years to the task. A month ago I received this, and knew that my long search was ended."

He put a worn letter into her hand, and with a beating heart Helen read:

Ariel is dead. Let her rest in peace, and do not pursue me any longer, unless you would drive me into my grave as you have driven her.

RALPH MARCH.

A little paper, more worn and stained than the other, dropped from the letter as Helen unfolded it, and seeing a woman's writing, she asked no permission, but read it eagerly, while Southesk sat with hidden face, unaware that he had given her that sacred farewell.

"Good-by, good-by," it said, in hastily-written letters, blurred by tears that had fallen long ago. "I have obeyed my father to the last, but my heart is yours for ever. Believe this, and pray, as I do, that you may meet again your Ariel."

A long silence followed, for the simple little note had touched Helen deeply, and while she could not but rejoice in the hope which this discovery gave her, she was too womanly a woman not to pity the poor child who had loved and lost the heart she coveted. As she gently laid the letter back in Southesk's hand, she asked, turning her full eyes on his:

"Are you sure that this is true?"

"I cannot doubt it, for I recognise the writing of both, and I know that neither would lend themselves to a fraud like this. No; I must accept the hard truth, and bear it as I can. My own heart confirms it, for every hope dies when I try to revive it, and the sad belief remains unshaken" was the spiritless reply.

Helen turned her face away, to hide the passionate joy that glowed in it; then, veiling her emotion with the tenderest sympathy, she gave herself up to the sweet task of comforting the bereaved lover. So well did she perform her part, so soothing did he find her friendly society, that he came often and lingered long, for with her, and her alone, he could talk of Ariel. She never checked him, but listened to the distasteful theme with unwearied patience, till, by insensible degrees and unperceived allurements, she weaned him from these mournful reminiscences, and woke a healthier interest in the present. With feminine skill she concealed her steadily-increasing love under an affectionate friendliness, which seemed a mute assurance that she cherished no hopes for herself, but knew that his heart was still Ariel's. This gave him confidence in her, while the new and gentle womanliness which now replaced her former pride, made her more attractive and more dangerous. Of course, the gossips gave them to one another, and Southesk felt aggrieved, fearing that he must relinquish the chief comfort of his solitary life. But Helen showed such supreme indifference to the clack of idle tongues, and met him with such unchanged composure, that he was reassured, and by remaining lost another point in this game of hearts.

With the summer came an unconquerable longing to revisit the island. Helen detected this wish before he uttered it, and, feeling that it would be vain to oppose it, quietly made her preparations for the sea-side, though otherwise she would have shunned it, fearing the old charm would revive and undo her work. Such visible satisfaction appeared in Southesk's face when she bade him good-by for a time, that she departed, sure that he would follow her to that summer haunt as to no other. He did follow, and resolving to have the trial over at once, during their first stroll upon the beach Helen said, in the tone of tranquil regard which she always used with him:

"I know you are longing to see your enchanted island again, yet, perhaps, dread to go alone. If it is so, let me go with you, for, much as I desire to see it, I shall never dare to trespass a second time."

Her voice trembled a little as she spoke—the first sign of emotion she had betrayed for a long time. Remembering that he had deceived her once, and recalling all he owed her since, Southesk felt that she had been very generous, very kind, and gratitude warmed his manner as he answered, turning toward the boats, which he had been eyeing wistfully:

"How well you understand me, Helen. Thank you for giving me courage to revisit the ruins of my little paradise. Come with me, for you are the only one who knows how much I have loved and lost. Shall we go now?"

"Blind and selfish, like a true man," thought Helen, with a pang, as she saw his eye kindle and the old elasticity return to his step as he went on before her. But she smiled and followed, as if glad to serve him, and a keen observer might have added, "patient and passionate, like a true woman."

Little was said between them as they made the breezy voyage. Once Southesk woke out of a long reverie, to say, pausing on his oars:

"A year to-day since I first saw Ariel."

"A year to-day since you told me that your fate was to come to you out of the sea," and Helen sighed involuntarily as she contrasted the man before her with the happy dreamer who smiled up at her that day.

"Yes, and it has come even to the hour when all was to be won or lost," he answered, little dreaming that the next hour was to verify the prophecy more perfectly than any in the past.

As they landed, he said, beseechingly:

"Wait for me at the lighthouse; I must visit the chasm alone, and I have no desire to encounter Stern, if I can help it."

"Why not?" asked Helen, wondering at his tone.

"Because he loved her, and could not forgive me that I was more beloved than he."

"I can pity him," she said, below her breath, adding, with unusual tenderness of manner—

"Go, Philip; I know how to wait."

"And I to thank you for it."

The look he gave her made her heart leap, for he had never bent such a one on her before, yet she feared that the memory of his lost love stirred and warmed him, not a dawning passion for herself, and would have wrung her hands in despair could she have known how utterly she was forgotten, as Southesk strode across the cliffs, almost as eagerly as if he knew that Ariel waited for him in her nest. It was empty; but something of its former beauty had been restored to it, for the stones were gone, green things were struggling up again, and the ladder was replaced.

"Poor Stern, he has repented of his frantic act, and tried to make the nest beautiful again as a memorial of her," thought Southesk; and descending, he threw himself down upon the newly-piled moss to dream his happy dream again, and fancy Ariel was there.

Well for him that he did not see the wrathful face that presently peered over the chasm's edge, as Stern watched him with the air of a man driven to desperation. The old hatred seemed to possess him with redoubled violence, and some new cause for detestation appeared to goad him with a hidden fear. More than once he sprang up and glanced anxiously behind him, as if he was not alone; more than once he laid his sinewy hands on a ponderous stone near by, as if tempted to hurl it down the chasm; and more than once he ground his teeth, like some savage creature who sees a stronger enemy approaching to deprive him of his prey.

The tide was coming in, the sky was over-cast, and a gale was rising; but though Southesk saw, heard and heeded nothing about him, Stern found hope in the gathering storm; for some evil spirit seemed to have been born of the tempest that raged within him, and to teach him how to make the elements his friends.

"Mr. Southesk."

Philip leaped to his feet as if a pistol had been fired at his ear, and saw Stern standing beside him with an air of sad humility, that surprised him more than the sight of his grey hair and haggard face. Pity banished resentment, and offering his hand, he said, with a generous oblivion of their parting words—

"Thank you for the change you have wrought here, and forgive me that I come back to see it once before I go away for ever. We both loved her; let us comfort one another."

A sudden color passed over Stern's swarthy face, he drew a long breath as he listened, and clenched one hand behind him as he put the other into Southesk's, answering in the same suppressed tone and with averted eyes—

"You know it, then, and try to submit as I do?"

Philip's lips were parted to reply, but no words followed, for a faint, far-off sound was heard, a woman's voice singing—

"Oh, come unto the yellow sands!"

Southesk turned pale, believing for an instant that Ariel's spirit came to welcome him; but the change in Stern's face, and the look of baffled rage and despair that played up in his eyes, betrayed him. Clutching his arm, the young man cried out, trembling with a sudden conviction—

"You have lied to me; she is not dead!"

What passed in Stern's heart during the second in which the two stood face to face, it would be impossible to tell, but with an effort that shook his strong body, he wrenched himself away and controlled his desperate desire to send his rival down the gulf. Some thought seemed to flash across him, calming the turbulence of his nature like a spell; and assuming the air of one defeated, he said slowly—

"I have lost, and I confess, I did lie to you, for March never sent the letter. I forged it, knowing that you would believe it if I added the note Ariel left for you a year ago. I could not give it to you then, but kept it with half the lock of hair. You followed them, but I followed you, and more than once thwarted you when you had nearly found them. As time passed, your persistence and her suffering began to soften March; I saw this, and tried to check you by the story of her death."

"Thank God I came, else I should never have recovered her. Give her up, Stern; she is mine, and I claim her."

Southesk turned to spring up the ladder, with no thought now but to reach Ariel; Stern arrested him, by saying with grim reluctance—

"You'll not find her, for she will not come here any more, but sit below by the basin where you saw her first. You can reach her by climbing down the steps I have made. Nay, if you doubt me, listen."

He did listen, and as the wind swept over the chasm, clearer and sweeter came the sound of that beloved voice. Southesk hesitated no longer, but swung himself recklessly downward, followed by Stern, whose black eyes glittered with a baleful light as they watched the agile figure going on before him. When they reached the basin, full to overflowing with the rising tide, they found the book her lover gave her and the little comb he knew so well, but no Ariel.

"She has gone into the cave for the weeds and shells you used to like. I'll wait for you; there is no need of me now."

Again Southesk listened; again he heard the voice, and followed it without a thought of fear; while Stern, seating himself on one of the fragments of rock cleared from the rest, leaned his head despondently upon his hand, as if his work was done.

The cave, worn by the ceaseless action of the waves at high tide, wound tortuously through the cliff to a lesser opening on the other side. Glancing rapidly into the damp nooks on either hand, Southesk hurried through this winding passage, which grew lower, narrower and darker toward the end, yet Ariel did not appear, and, standing still, he called her. Echo after echo caught up the word, and sent it whispering to and fro, but no human voice replied, though still the song came fitfully on the wind that blew coldly through the cave.

"She has ventured on to watch the waves boil in the Kelpie's Cauldron. Imprudent child, I'll punish her with a kiss," thought Southesk, smiling to himself, as he bent his tall head and groped his way toward the opening. He reached it, and looked down upon a mass of jagged rocks, over and among which the great billows dashed turbulent and dark with the approaching storm. Still no Ariel; and as he stood, more clearly than ever sounded her voice, above him now.

"She has not been here, but has climbed the Gull's Perch to watch the sky as we used to do. I have wasted all this time. Curse Stern's stupidity!"

In a fever of impatience he retraced his steps, stopping suddenly as his feet encountered a pool which had not been there when he came.

"Ah! the tide is nearer in than I thought. Thank heaven, my darling is not here!" he said, and hurried round a sharp corner, expecting to see the entrance before him. It was not there! A ponderous stone had been rolled against it, effectually closing it, and permitting only a faint ray of light to penetrate this living tomb. At first he stood panic-stricken at the horrible death that confronted him; then he thought of Stern, and in a paroxysm of wrath dashed himself against the rock, hoping to force it outward. But Stern's immense strength had served him well; and while his victim struggled vainly, wave after wave broke against the stone, wedging it more firmly still, yet leaving crevices enough for the bitter waters to flow in, bringing sure death to the doomed man, unless help came speedily from without. Not till the rapidly advancing tide drove him back did Southesk desist; then drenched, breathless and bruised he retreated to the lesser opening, with a faint hope of escape that way. Leaning over the Cauldron, he saw that the cliff sunk sheer down, and well he knew that a leap there would be fatal. As far up as he could see, the face of the cliff offered foothold for nothing but a bird. He shouted till the cave rang, but no answer came, though Ariel's song began again, for the same wind that brought her voice to him bore his away from her. There was no hope unless Stern relented, and being human, he might have, had he seen the dumb despair that seized his rival as he lay waiting for death, while far above him the woman whom he loved unconsciously chanted a song he taught her, little dreaming it would be his dirge.

Left alone, Helen entered the lighthouse, and looked about her with renewed interest. The room was empty, but through a half-open door she saw a man sitting at a table covered with papers. He seemed to have been writing, but the pen had dropped from his hand, and leaning back in his deep chair he appeared to be asleep. His face was turned from her; yet when she advanced, he did not hear her, and when she spoke, he neither stirred nor answered. Something in the attitude and silence of the unknown man alarmed her; involuntarily she stepped forward and laid her hand on his. It was icy cold, and the face she saw had no life in it. Tranquil and reposeful, as if death had brought neither pain nor fear, he lay there with his dead hand on the paper, which some irresistible impulse had prompted him to write. Helen's eye fell on it, and despite the shock of this discovery, a single name made her seize the letter and devour its contents, though she trembled at the act and the solemn witness of it.

"To Philip Southesk:

"Feeling that my end is very near, and haunted by a presentiment that it will be sudden—perhaps solitary—I am prompted to write what I hope to say to you if time is given me to reach you. Thirty years ago your father was my dearest friend, but we loved the same beautiful woman and he won her, unfairly I believed and in the passionate disappointment of the moment I swore undying hatred to him and his. We parted and never met again, for the next tidings I received were of his death. I left the country and was an alien for years; thus I heard no rumor of your birth and never dreamed that you were Richard Marston's son till I learned it through Ariel. Her mother, like yours, died at her birth. I reared her with jealous care, for she was my all, and I loved her with the intensity of a lonely heart, you came; I found that you could make her happy. I knew that my life was drawing to a close; I trusted you and I gave her up. Then I learned your name, and at the cost of breaking my child's heart I kept my sinful oath. For a year you have followed me with unwearied patience; for a year Ariel's fading youth has pleaded silently, and for a year I have been struggling to harden myself against both. But love has conquered hate, and standing in the shadow of death I see the sin and folly of the past. I repent and retract my oath, I absolve Ariel from the promise I exacted, I freely give her to the man she loves, and may God deal with him as he deals with her.   RALPH MARCH, June————"

There the pen had fallen, blotting the date; but Helen saw only the last two lines and her hand closed tighter on the paper as if she felt that it would be impossible to give it up. Forgetting everything but that she held her rival's fate in her grasp, she yielded to the terrible temptation, and thrusting the paper into her bosom glided away like a guilty creature to find Southesk and prevent him from discovering that the girl lived, if it was not too late. He was nowhere to be seen, and crossing the rude bridge that spanned the chasm she ventured to call him as she passed round the base of the tall rock named the Gull's Perch. A soft voice answered her, and turning a sharp angle she came upon a woman who sat alone looking down into the Kelpie's Cauldron that foamed far below. She had half risen with a startled look at the sound of a familiar name, and as Helen paused to recover herself, Ariel asked half imploringly, half imperiously—

"Why do you call Philip? Tell me, is he here?"

But for the paper in her breast Helen would have answered no, and trusted all to chance; now, feeling sure that the girl would keep her promise more faithfully than her father had kept his oath, unless he absolved her from it, she answered:

"Yes, but I implore you to shun him. He thinks you dead; he has learned to love me, and is happy. Do not destroy my hope, and rob me of my hard-won prize, for you cannot reward him unless you break the solemn promise you have given."

Ariel covered up her face, as if confessing the hard truth, but love clamored to be heard, and, stretching her hands to Helen, she cried:

"I will not come between you; I will keep my word; but let me see him once, and I will ask no more. Where is he? I can steal a look at him unseen; then you may take him away for ever, if it must be so."

Trying to silence the upbraidings of her conscience, and thinking only of her purpose, Helen could not refuse this passionate prayer, and, pointing toward the chasm, she said anxiously:

"He went to the place you made so dear to him, but I do not see him now, nor does he answer when I call. Can he have fallen down that precipice?"

Ariel did not answer, for she was at the chasm's brink, looking into its gloom with eyes that no darkness could deceive. No one was there, and no sound answered the soft call that broke from her lips, but the dash of water far below. Glancing toward the basin, with a sudden recollection of the precious book left there, she saw, with wonder, that the stone where she had sat was gone, and that the cavern's mouth was closed. Stern's hat lay near her, and as her eye fell on it, a sudden horror shook her, for he had left her, meaning to return, yet had not come, and was nowhere to be seen.

"Have you seen Stern?" she asked, grasping Helen's arm, with a face of pale dismay.

"I saw him climbing the ladder, as if he was going to bind up his hands, which were bleeding. He looked wet and wild, and, as he did not see me, I did not speak. Why do you ask?"

"Because I fear he has shut Philip in the cave, where the rising tide will drown him. It is too horrible to believe; I must be sure."

Back she flew to the seat she had left, and flinging herself down on the edge of the sloping cliff, she called his name till she was hoarse and trembling with the effort. Once a faint noise seemed to answer, but the wind swept the sound away, and Helen vainly strained her ear to catch some syllable of the reply. Suddenly Ariel sprung up, with a cry:

"He is there! I see the flutter of his handkerchief! Help me, and we will save him."

She was gone as she spoke, and before Helen could divine her purpose or steady her own nerves, Ariel was back again, dragging the rope ladder, which she threw down, and began to tear up the plaid on which she had been sitting.

"It is too short, and even these strips will not make it long enough. What can I give to help?" cried Helen, glancing at the frail silks and muslins which composed her dress.

"You can give nothing, and there is not time to go for help. I shall lengthen it in this way."

Tying back the hair that blew about her face, and gathering the rope on her arm, Ariel slid over the edge of the cliff, and unstartled by Helen's cry of alarm, climbed with wary feet along a perilous path, where one mis-step would be her last. Half-way down a ledge appeared where a tree had once grown; the pine was blasted and shattered now, but the roots held fast, and to these Ariel hung the ladder, with a stone fastened to the lower end to keep the wind from blowing it beyond the opening. Straight as a plummet it fell, and for a moment neither woman breathed; then a cry broke from both, for the ropes tightened, as if a hand tried the strength of that frail road. Another pause of terrible suspense, and out from the dark cave below came a man, who climbed swiftly upward, regardless of the gale that nearly tore the ladder from his hold, the hungry sea that wet him with its spray, the yielding roots that hardly bore his weight, or the wounded hands that marked his way with blood, for his eyes were fixed on Ariel, and on his face, white with the approach of a cruel death, shone an expression brighter than a smile, as he neared the brave girl who lent all her strength to save him, with one arm about the tree, the other clutching the ladder as if she defied all danger to herself.

Kneeling on the cliff above, Helen saw all this, and when Southesk stood upon the ledge, with Ariel gathered to the shelter of his arms, her heart turned traitor to her will, remorse made justice possible, love longed to ennoble itself by sacrifice, and all that was true and tender in her nature pleaded for the rival who had earned happiness at such a cost. One sharp pang, one moment of utter despair, followed by utter self-forgetfulness, and Helen's temptation became a triumph that atoned for an hour's suffering and sin.

What went on below her she never knew, but when the lovers came to her, spent yet smiling, she gave the paper to Southesk, and laid her hand on Ariel's head with a gesture soft and solemn, as she said, wearing an expression that made her fine face strangely beautiful:

"You have won him and you deserve him; for you are nobler than I. Forgive me, Philip; and when you are happiest, remember that, though sorely tempted, I resisted, hoping to grow worthier to become your friend."

Even while she spoke he had caught the meaning of the paper, and Ariel guessed it from his face before she, too, read the words that set her free. But her tears of joy changed to tears of grief when Helen gently broke to her the sad fact of her father's death, trying to comfort her so tenderly that, by the blessed magic of sympathy, all bitterness was banished from her own sore heart. As they turned to leave that faithful cliff, Stern confronted them with an aspect that daunted even Southesk's courage. Calm with the desperate calmness of one who had staked his last throw and lost it, he eyed them steadily a moment; then with a gesture too sudden to be restrained, he snatched Ariel to him—kissed her passionately, put her from him, and springing to the edge of the cliff, turned on Southesk, saying in an accent of the intensest scorn, as he pointed downward to the whirlpool below—

"Coward! you dared not end your life when all seemed lost, but waited for a woman to save you. I will show you how a brave man dies." And as the last words left his lips he was gone.

Years have passed since then; Ariel has long been a happy wife; Philip's name has become a household word on many lips, and Helen's life has grown serenely cheerful, though still solitary. But so the legend runs: Stern yet haunts the island; for the lighthouse-keepers tell of a wild and woeful phantom that wanders day and night among the cliffs and caverns by the sea. Sometimes they see it, in the strong glare of the lantern, leaning on the balcony, and looking out into the night, as if it watched and waited to see some ship come sailing by. Often those who visit the Kelpie's Cauldron are startled by glimpses of a dark, desperate face that seems to rise and mock them with weird scorn. But oftenest a shadowy shape is seen to flit into the chasm, wearing a look of human love and longing, as it vanishes in the soft gloom of Ariel's nest.

A Whisper
in the Dark

Editor's Note: Although only her third published thriller, "A Whisper in the Dark" is Alcott's gothic masterpiece: a tale of innocence imperiled that incorporates disinheritance, murder, madness, skeletons in the family closet, and other sensational elements into a fast-paced narrative. Almost a quarter century after it appeared in 1863, Alcott described it to publisher Thomas Niles as "rather a lurid tale," and suggested that she preface its reprint with the explanation that it was a sample of the "necessity stories" Jo March contributed to the tabloids in *Little Women*. The tale is one of the few anonymously published thrillers that Alcott publicly admitted to writing.

As we rolled along, I scanned my companion covertly, and saw much to interest a girl of seventeen. My uncle was a handsome man, with all the polish of foreign life fresh upon him; yet it was neither comeliness nor graceful ease which most attracted me; for even my inexperienced eye caught glimpses of something stern and sombre below these external charms, and my long scrutiny showed me the keenest eye, the hardest mouth, the subtlest smile I ever saw—a face which in repose wore the look which comes to those who have led lives of pleasure and learned their emptiness. He seemed intent on some thought that absorbed him, and for a time rendered him forgetful of my presence, as he sat with folded arms, fixed eyes, and restless lips. While I looked, my own mind was full of deeper thought than it had ever been before; for I was recalling, word for word, a paragraph in that half-read letter—

"At eighteen Sybil is to marry her cousin, the compact having been made between my brother and myself in their childhood. My son is with me now, and I wish them to be together during the next few months, therefore my niece must leave you sooner than I at first intended. Oblige me by preparing her for an immediate and final separation, but leave all disclosures to me, as I prefer the girl to remain ignorant of the matter for the present."

That displeased me. Why was I to remain ignorant of so important an affair? Then I smiled to myself, remembering that I did know, thanks to the wilful curiosity that prompted me to steal a peep into the letter that Madame Bernard had pored over with such an anxious face. I saw only a single paragraph, for my own name arrested my eye; and, though wild to read all, I had scarcely time to whisk the paper back into the reticule the forgetful old soul had left hanging on the arm of her chair. It was enough, however, to set my girlish brain in a ferment, and keep me gazing wistfully at my uncle, conscious that my future now lay in his hands; for I was an orphan and he my guardian, though I had seen him but seldom since I was confided to madame a six years' child. Presently my uncle became cognizant of my steady stare, and returned it with one as steady for a moment, then said, in a low, smooth tone, that ill accorded with the satirical smile that touched his lips—

"I am a dull companion for my little niece. How shall I provide her with pleasanter amusement than counting my wrinkles or guessing my thoughts?"

I was a frank, fearless creature, quick to feel, speak, and act, so I answered readily—

"Tell me about my cousin Guy. Is he as handsome, brave, and clever as madame says his father was when a boy?"

My uncle laughed a short laugh, touched with scorn, whether for madame, himself, or me I could not tell, for his countenance was hard to read.

"A girl's question and artfully put; nevertheless I shall not answer it, but let you judge for yourself."

"But, sir, it will amuse me and beguile the way. I feel a little strange and forlorn at leaving madame, and talking of my new home and friends will help me to know and love them sooner. Please tell me, for I've had my own way all my life, and can't bear to be crossed."

My petulance seemed to amuse him, and I became aware that he was observing me with a scrutiny as keen as my own had been; but I smilingly sustained it, for my vanity was pleased by the approbation his eye betrayed. The evident interest he now took in all I said and did was sufficient flattery for a young thing, who felt her charms and longed to try their power.

"I, too, have had my own way all my life; and as the life is double the length, the will is double the strength of yours, and again I say no. What next, mademoiselle?"

He was blander than ever as he spoke, but I was piqued, and resolved to try coaxing, eager to gain my point, lest a too early submission now should mar my freedom in the future.

"But that is ungallant, uncle, and I still have hopes of a kinder answer, both because you are too generous to refuse so small a favor to your 'little niece,' and because she can be charmingly wheedlesome when she likes. Won't you say yes now, uncle?" and, pleased with the daring of the thing, I put my arm about his neck, kissed him daintily, and perched myself upon his knee with most audacious ease.

He regarded me mutely for an instant, then holding me fast deliberately returned my salute on lips, cheeks, and forehead, with such warmth that I turned scarlet and struggled to free myself, while he laughed that mirthless laugh of his till my shame turned to anger, and I imperiously commanded him to let me go.

"Not yet, young lady. You came here for your own pleasure, but shall stay for mine, till I tame you as I see you must be tamed. It is a short process with me, and I possess experience in the work; for Guy, though by nature as wild as a hawk, has learned to come at my call as meekly as a dove. Chut! what a little fury it is!"

I was just then; for exasperated at his coolness, and quite beside myself, I had suddenly stooped and bitten the shapely white hand that held both my own. I had better have submitted; for slight as the foolish action was, it had an influence on my after-life as many another such has had. My uncle stopped laughing, his hand tightened its grasp, for a moment his cold eye glittered and a grim look settled round the mouth, giving to his whole face a ruthless expression that entirely altered it. I felt perfectly powerless. All my little arts had failed, and for the first time I was mastered. Yet only physically;

my spirit was rebellious still. He saw it in the glance that met his own, as I sat erect and pale, with something more than childish anger. I think it pleased him, for swiftly as it had come the dark look passed, and quietly, as if we were the best of friends, he began to relate certain exciting adventures he had known abroad, lending to the picturesque narration the charm of that peculiarly melodious voice, which soothed and won me in spite of myself, holding me intent till I forgot the past; and when he paused I found that I was leaning confidentially on his shoulder, asking for more, yet conscious of an instinctive distrust of this man whom I had so soon learned to fear yet fancy.

As I was recalled to myself, I endeavored to leave him; but he still detained me, and, with a curious expression, produced a case so quaintly fashioned that I cried out in admiration, while he selected two cigarettes, mildly aromatic with the herbs they were composed of, lit them, offered me one, dropped the window, and leaning back surveyed me with an air of extreme enjoyment, as I sat meekly puffing and wondering what prank I should play a part in next. Slowly the narcotic influence of the herbs diffused itself like a pleasant haze over all my senses; sleep, the most grateful, fell upon my eyelids, and the last thing I remember was my uncle's face dreamily regarding me through a cloud of fragrant smoke. Twilight wrapped us in its shadows when I woke, with the night wind blowing on my forehead, the muffled roll of wheels sounding in my ear, and my cheek pillowed upon my uncle's arm. He was humming a French *chanson* about "Love and Wine, and the Seine to-morrow!" I listened till I caught the air, and presently joined him, mingling my girlish treble with his flute-like tenor. He stopped at once, and, in the coolly courteous tone I had always heard in our few interviews, asked if I was ready for lights and home.

"Are we there?" I cried; and looking out saw that we were ascending an avenue which swept up to a pile of buildings that rose tall and dark against the sky, with here and there a gleam along its gray front.

"Home at last, thank Heaven!" And springing out with the agility of a young man, my uncle led me over a terrace into a long hall, light and warm, and odorous with the breath of flowers blossoming here and there in graceful groups. A civil, middle-aged maid received and took me to my room, a bijou of a place, which increased my wonder when told that my uncle had chosen all its decorations and superintended their arrangement. "He understands women," I thought, handling the toilet ornaments, trying luxurious chair and lounge, and ending by slipping my feet into the scarlet and white Turkish slippers, coquettishly turning up their toes before the fire. A few moments I

gave to examination, and, having expressed my satisfaction, was asked by my
maid if I would be pleased to dress, as "the master" never allowed dinner to
wait for any one. This recalled to me the fact that I was doubtless to meet my
future husband at that meal, and in a moment every faculty was intent upon
achieving a grand toilette for this first interview. The maid possessed skill
and taste, and I a wardrobe lately embellished with Parisian gifts from my
uncle which I was eager to display in his honor.

When ready, I surveyed myself in the long mirror as I had never done
before, and saw there a little figure, slender, yet stately, in a dress of foreign
fashion, ornamented with lace and carnation ribbons which enhanced the
fairness of neck and arms, while blonde hair, wavy and golden, was gathered
into an antique knot of curls behind, with a carnation fillet, and below a
blooming dark-eyed face, just then radiant with girlish vanity and eagerness
and hope.

"I'm glad I'm pretty!"

"So am I, Sybil."

I had unconsciously spoken aloud, and the echo came from the doorway
where stood my uncle, carefully dressed, looking comelier and cooler than
ever. The disagreeable smile flitted over his lips as he spoke, and I started,
then stood abashed, till beckoning, he added in his most courtly manner—

"You were so absorbed in the contemplation of your charming self, that
Janet answered my tap and took herself away unheard. You are mistress of my
table now: it waits; will you come down?"

With a last touch to that unruly hair of mine, a last, comprehensive glance
and shake, I took the offered arm and rustled down the wide staircase, feeling
that the romance of my life was about to begin. Three covers were laid, three
chairs set, but only two were occupied, for no Guy appeared. I asked no
questions, showed no surprise, but tried to devour my chagrin with my
dinner, and exerted myself to charm my uncle into the belief that I had
forgotten my cousin. It was a failure, however, for that empty seat had an
irresistible fascination for me, and more than once, as my eye returned from
its furtive scrutiny of napkin, plate, and trio of colored glasses, it met my
uncle's and fell before his penetrative glance. When I gladly rose to leave him
to his wine—for he did not ask me to remain—he also rose, and, as he held
the door for me, he said—

"You asked me to describe your cousin: you have seen one trait of his
character to-night; does it please you?"

I knew he was as much vexed as I at Guy's absence, so quoting his own words I answered saucily—

"Yes; for I'd rather see the hawk free than coming tamely at your call, uncle."

He frowned slightly, as if unused to such liberty of speech, yet bowed when I swept him a stately little curtsey and sailed away to the drawing-room, wondering if my uncle was as angry with me as I was with my cousin. In solitary grandeur I amused myself by strolling through the suite of handsome rooms henceforth to be my realm, looked at myself in the long mirrors, as every woman is apt to do when alone and in costume, danced over the mossy carpets, touched the grand piano, smelt the flowers, fingered the ornaments on *étagère* and table, and was just giving my handkerchief a second drench of some refreshing perfume from a filigree flask that had captivated me, when the hall door was flung wide, a quick step went running up-stairs, boots tramped overhead, drawers seemed hastily opened and shut, and a bold, blithe voice broke out into a hunting song in a tone so like my uncle's that I involuntarily flew to the door, crying—

"Guy is come!"

Fortunately for my dignity, no one heard me, and hurrying back I stood ready to skim into a chair and assume propriety at a minute's notice, conscious, meanwhile, of the new influence which seemed suddenly to gift the silent house with vitality, and add the one charm it needed—that of cheerful companionship. "How will he meet me? and how shall I meet him?" I thought, looking up at the bright-faced boy, whose portrait looked back at me with a mirthful light in the painted eyes and a trace of his father's disdainful smile in the curves of the firm-set lips. Presently the quick steps came flying down again, past the door, straight to the dining-room opposite, and, as I stood listening with a strange flutter at my heart, I heard an imperious young voice say rapidly—

"Beg pardon, sir, unavoidably detained. Has she come? Is she bearable?"

"I find her so. Dinner is over, and I can offer you nothing but a glass of wine."

My uncle's voice was frostily polite, making a curious contrast to the other, so impetuous and frank, as if used to command or win all but one.

"Never mind the dinner! I'm glad to be rid of it; so I'll drink your health, father, and then inspect our new ornament."

"Impertinent boy!" I muttered, yet at the same moment resolved to deserve his appellation, and immediately grouped myself as effectively as possible, laughing at my folly as I did so. I possessed a pretty foot, therefore one little slipper appeared quite naturally below the last flounce of my dress; a bracelet glittered on my arm as it emerged from among the lace and carnation knots; that arm supported my head. My profile was well cut, my eyelashes long, therefore I read with face half averted from the door. The light showered down, turning my hair to gold; so I smoothed my curls, retied my snood, and, after a satisfied survey, composed myself with an absorbed aspect and a quickened pulse to await the arrival of the gentlemen.

Soon they came. I knew they paused on the threshold, but never stirred till an irrepressible, "You are right, sir!" escaped the younger. Then I rose prepared to give him the coldest greeting, yet I did not. I had almost expected to meet the boyish face and figure of the picture; I saw, instead, a man comely and tall. A dark moustache half hid the proud mouth; the vivacious eyes were far kinder, though quite as keen as his father's, and the freshness of unspoiled youth lent a charm which the older man had lost for ever. Guy's glance of pleased surprise was flatteringly frank, his smile so cordial, his "Welcome, cousin!" such a hearty sound, that my coldness melted in a breath, my dignity was all forgotten, and before I could restrain myself I had offered both hands with the impulsive exclamation—

"Cousin Guy, I know I shall be very happy here! Are you glad I have come?"

"Glad as I am to see the sun after a November fog."

And, bending his tall head, he kissed my hand in the graceful foreign fashion he had learned abroad. It pleased me mightily, for it was both affectionate and respectful. Involuntarily I contrasted it with my uncle's manner, and flashed a significant glance at him as I did so. He understood it, but only nodded with the satirical look I hated, shook out his paper and began to read. I sat down again, careless of myself now; and Guy stood on the rug, surveying me with an expression of surprise that rather nettled my pride.

"He is only a boy, after all; so I need not be daunted by his inches or his airs. I wonder if he knows I am to be his wife, and likes it."

The thought sent the color to my forehead, my eyes fell, and despite my valiant resolution, I sat like any bashful child before my handsome cousin. Guy laughed a boyish laugh as he sat down on his father's footstool, saying, while he warmed his slender brown hands—

"I beg your pardon, Sybil. (We won't be formal, will we?) But I haven't seen a lady for a month, so I stare like a boor at sight of a silk gown and high-bred face. Are those people coming, sir?"

"If Sybil likes, ask her."

"Shall we have a flock of people here to make it gay for you, cousin, or do you prefer our quiet style better; just riding, driving, lounging, and enjoying life, each in his own way? Henceforth it is to be as you command in such matters."

"Let things go on as they have done, then. I don't care for society, and strangers wouldn't make it gay to me, for I like freedom; so do you, I think."

"Ah, don't I!"

A cloud flitted over his smiling face, and he punched the fire, as if some vent were necessary for the sudden gust of petulance that knit his black brows into a frown, and caused his father to tap him on the shoulder with the bland request, as he rose to leave the room—

"Bring the portfolios and entertain your cousin; I have letters to write, and Sybil is too tired to care for music to-night."

Guy obeyed with a shrug of the shoulder his father touched, but lingered in the recess till my uncle, having made his apologies to me, had left the room; then my cousin rejoined me, wearing the same cordial aspect I first beheld. Some restraint was evidently removed, and his natural self appeared. A very winsome self it was, courteous, gay, and frank, with an undertone of deeper feeling than I thought to find. I watched him covertly, and soon owned to myself that he was all I most admired in the ideal hero every girl creates in her romantic fancy; for I no longer looked upon this young man as my cousin, but my lover, and through all our future intercourse this thought was always uppermost, full of a charm that never lost its power.

Before the evening ended Guy was kneeling on the rug beside me, our two heads close together, while he turned the contents of the great portfolio spread before us, looking each other freely in the face, as I listened and he described, both breaking into frequent peals of laughter at some odd adventure or comical mishap in his own travels, suggested by the pictured scenes before us. Guy was very charming, I my blithest, sweetest self, and when we parted late, my cousin watched me up the stairs with still another, "Good-night, Sybil," as if both sight and sound were pleasant to him.

"Is that your horse Sultan?" I called from my window next morning, as I looked down upon my cousin, who was coming up the drive from an early gallop on the moors.

"Yes, bonny Sybil; come and admire him," he called back, hat in hand, and a quick smile rippling over his face.

I went, and, standing on the terrace, caressed the handsome creature, while Guy said, glancing up at his father's undrawn curtains—

"If your saddle had come, we would take a turn before 'my lord' is ready for breakfast. This autumn air is the wine you women need."

I yearned to go, and when I willed the way soon appeared; so careless of bonnetless head and cambric gown, I stretched my hands to him, saying boldly—

"Play young Lochinvar, Guy; I am little and light; take me up before you and show me the sea."

He liked the daring feat, held out his hand, I stepped on his boot toe, sprang up, and away we went over the wide moor, where the sun shone in a cloudless heaven, the lark soared singing from the green grass at our feet, and the September wind blew freshly from the sea. As we paused on the upland slope, that gave us a free view of the country for miles, Guy dismounted, and, standing with his arm about the saddle to steady me in my precarious seat, began to talk.

"Do you like your new home, cousin?"

"More than I can tell you!"

"And my father, Sybil?"

"Both yes and no to that question, Guy; I hardly know him yet."

"True, but you must not expect to find him as indulgent and fond as many guardians would be to such as you. It's not his nature. Yet you can win his heart by obedience, and soon grow quite at ease with him."

"Bless you! I'm that already, for I fear no one. Why, I sat on his knee yesterday and smoked a cigarette of his own offering, though madame would have fainted if she had seen me; then I slept on his arm an hour, and he was fatherly kind, though I teased him like a gnat."

"The deuce he was!" with which energetic expression Guy frowned at the landscape and harshly checked Sultan's attempt to browse, while I wondered what was amiss between father and son, and resolved to discover; but, finding the conversation at an end, started it afresh, by asking—

"Is any of my property in this part of the country, Guy? Do you know I am as ignorant as a baby about my own affairs; for, as long as every whim was gratified and my purse full, I left the rest to madame and uncle, though the first hadn't a bit of judgment, and the last I scarcely knew. I never cared to ask questions before, but now I am intensely curious to know how matters stand."

"All you see is yours, Sybil," was the brief answer.

"What, that great house, the lovely gardens, these moors, and the forest stretching to the sea? I'm glad! I'm glad! But where, then, is your home, Guy?"

"Nowhere."

At this I looked so amazed, that his gloom vanished in a laugh, as he explained, but briefly, as if this subject were no pleasanter than the first—

"By your father's will you were desired to take possession of the old place at eighteen. You will be that soon; therefore, as your guardian, my father has prepared things for you, and is to share your home until you marry."

"When will that be, I wonder?" and I stole a glance from under my lashes, wild to discover if Guy knew of the compact and was a willing party to it. His face was half averted, but over his dark cheek I saw a deep flush rise, as he answered, stooping to pull a bit of heather—

"Soon, I hope, or the gentleman sleeping there below will be tempted to remain a fixture with you on his knee as 'madame my wife.' He is not your own uncle, you know."

I smiled at the idea, but Guy did not see it; and seized with a whim to try my skill with the hawk that seemed inclined to peck at its master, I said demurely—

"Well, why not? I might be very happy if I learned to love him, as I should, if he were always in that kindest mood of his. Would you like me for a little mamma, Guy?"

"No!" short and sharp as a pistol shot.

"Then you must marry and have a home of your own, my son."

"Don't, Sybil! I'd rather you didn't see me in a rage, for I'm not a pleasant sight, I assure you; and I'm afraid I shall be in one if you go on. I early lost my mother, but I love her tenderly, because my father is not much to me, and I know if she had lived I should not be what I am."

Bitter was his voice, moody his mien, and all the sunshine gone at once. I looked down and touched his black hair with a shy caress, feeling both penitent and pitiful.

"Dear Guy, forgive me if I pained you. I'm a thoughtless creature, but I'm not malicious, and a word will restrain me if kindly spoken. My home is always yours, and when my fortune is mine you shall never want, if you are not too proud to accept help from your own kin. You are a little proud, aren't you?"

"As Lucifer, to most people. I think I should not be to you, for you understand me, Sybil, and with you I hope to grow a better man."

He turned then, and through the lineaments his father had bequeathed him I saw a look that must have been his mother's, for it was womanly, sweet, and soft, and lent new beauty to the dark eyes, always kind, and just then very tender. He had checked his words suddenly, like one who has gone too far, and with that hasty look into my face had bent his own upon the ground, as if to hide the unwonted feeling that had mastered him. It lasted but a moment, then his old manner returned, as he said gayly—

"There drops your slipper. I've been wondering what kept it on. Pretty thing! They say it is a foot like this that oftenest tramples on men's hearts. Are you cruel to your lovers, Sybil?"

"I never had one, for madame guarded me like a dragon, and I led the life of a nun; but when I do find one I shall try his mettle well before I give up my liberty."

"Poets say it is sweet to give up liberty for love, and they ought to know," answered Guy, with a sidelong glance.

I liked that little speech, and recollecting the wistful look he had given me, the significant words that had escaped him, and the variations of tone and manner constantly succeeding one another, I felt assured that my cousin was cognizant of the family league, and accepted it, yet, with the shyness of a young lover, knew not how to woo. This pleased me, and, quite satisfied with my morning's work, I mentally resolved to charm my cousin slowly, and enjoy the romance of a genuine wooing, without which no woman's life seems complete—in her own eyes, at least. He had gathered me a knot of purple heather, and as he gave it I smiled my sweetest on him, saying—

"I commission you to supply me with nosegays, for you have taste, and I love wild-flowers. I shall wear this at dinner in honor of its giver. Now take me home; for my moors, though beautiful, are chilly, and I have no wrapper but this microscopic handkerchief."

Off went his riding-jacket, and I was half smothered in it. The hat followed next, and as he sprung up behind I took the reins, and felt a thrill of delight in sweeping down the slope with that mettlesome creature tugging at the bit, that strong arm round me, and the happy hope that the heart I leaned on might yet learn to love me.

The day so began passed pleasantly, spent in roving over house and grounds with my cousin, setting my possessions in order, and writing to dear old madame. Twilight found me in my bravest attire, with Guy's heather in my hair, listening for his step, and longing to run and meet him when he came. Punctual to the instant he appeared, and this dinner was a far different one from that of yesterday, for both father and son seemed in their gayest and most gallant mood, and I enjoyed the hour heartily. The world seemed all in tune now, and when I went to the drawing-room I was moved to play my most stirring marches, sing my blithest songs, hoping to bring one at least of the gentlemen to join me. It brought both, and my first glance showed me a curious change in each. My uncle looked harassed and yet amused, Guy looked sullen and eyed his father with covert glances.

The morning's chat flashed into my mind, and I asked myself, "Is Guy jealous so soon?" It looked a little like it, for he threw himself upon a couch and lay there silent and morose; while my uncle paced to and fro, thinking deeply, while apparently listening to the song he bade me finish. I did so, then followed the whim that now possessed me, for I wanted to try my power over them both, to see if I could restore that gentler mood of my uncle's, and assure myself that Guy cared whether I was friendliest with him or not.

"Uncle, come and sing with me; I like that voice of yours."

"Tut, I am too old for that; take this indolent lad instead, his voice is fresh and young, and will chord well with yours."

"Do you know that pretty *chanson* about 'Love and Wine, and the Seine to-morrow,' cousin Guy?" I asked, stealing a sly glance at my uncle.

"Who taught you that?" and Guy eyed me over the top of the couch with an astonished expression which greatly amused me.

"No one; uncle sang a bit of it in the carriage yesterday. I like the air, so come and teach me the rest."

"It is no song for you, Sybil. You choose strange entertainment for a lady, sir."

A look of unmistakable contempt was in the son's eye, of momentary annoyance in the father's, yet his voice betrayed none as he answered, still pacing placidly along the room—

"I thought she was asleep, and unconsciously began it to beguile a silent drive. Sing on, Sybil; that Bacchanalian snatch will do you no harm."

But I was tired of music now they had come, so I went to him, and, passing my arm through his, walked beside him, saying with my most persuasive aspect—

"Tell me about Paris, uncle; I intend to go there as soon as I'm of age, if you will let me. Does your guardianship extend beyond that time?"

"Only till you marry."

"I shall be in no haste, then, for I begin to feel quite homelike and happy here with you, and shall be content without other society; only you'll soon tire of me, and leave me to some dismal governess, while you and Guy go pleasuring."

"No fear of that, Sybil; I shall hold you fast till some younger guardian comes to rob me of my merry ward."

As he spoke, he took the hand that lay upon his arm into a grasp so firm, and turned on me a look so keen, that I involuntarily dropped my eyes lest he should read my secret there. Eager to turn the conversation, I asked, pointing to a little miniature hanging underneath the portrait of his son, before which he had paused—

"Was that Guy's mother, sir?"

"No, your own."

I looked again, and saw a face delicate yet spirited, with dark eyes, a passionate mouth, and a head crowned with hair as plenteous and golden as my own; but the whole seemed dimmed by age, the ivory was stained, the glass cracked, and a faded ribbon fastened it. My eyes filled as I looked, and a strong desire seized me to know what had defaced this little picture of the mother whom I never knew.

"Tell me about her, uncle; I know so little, and often long for her so much. Am I like her, sir?"

Why did my uncle avert his eyes as he answered—

"You are a youthful image of her, Sybil."

"Go on please, tell me more; tell me why this is so stained and worn; you know all, and surely I am old enough now to hear any history of pain and loss."

Something caused my uncle to knit his brows, but his bland voice never varied a tone as he placed the picture in my hand and gave me this brief explanation—

"Just before your birth your father was obliged to cross the Channel, to receive the last wishes of a dying friend; there was an accident; the vessel foundered, and many lives were lost. He escaped, but by some mistake his name appeared in the list of missing passengers; your mother saw it, the shock destroyed her, and when your father returned he found only a mother-less little daughter to welcome him. This miniature, which he always carried with him, was saved with his papers at the last moment; but though the sea-water ruined it he would never have it copied or retouched, and gave it to me when he died in memory of the woman I had loved for his sake. It is yours now, my child; keep it, and never feel that you are fatherless or motherless while I remain."

Kind as was both act and speech, neither touched me, for something seemed wanting. I felt, yet could not define it, for then I believed in the sincerity of all I met.

"Where was she buried, uncle? It may be foolish, but I should like to see my mother's grave."

"You shall some day, Sybil," and a curious change came over my uncle's face as he averted it.

"I have made him melancholy, talking of Guy's mother and my own; now I'll make him gay again if possible, and pique that negligent boy," I thought, and drew my uncle to a lounging-chair, established myself on the arm thereof, and kept him laughing with my merriest gossip, both of us apparently unconscious of the long dark figure stretched just opposite, feigning sleep, but watching us through half-closed lids, and never stirring except to bow silently to my careless "Good-night."

As I reached the stairhead, I remembered that my letter to madame, full of the frankest criticisms upon people and things, was lying unsealed on the table in the little room my uncle had set apart for my boudoir; fearing servants' eyes and tongues, I slipped down again to get it. The room adjoined the parlors, and just then was lit only by a ray from the hall lamp. I had secured the letter, and was turning to retreat, when I heard Guy say petulantly, as if thwarted yet submissive—

"I *am* civil when you leave me alone; I *do* agree to marry her, but I won't be hurried or go a-wooing except in my own way. You know I never liked the bargain, for it's nothing else; yet I can reconcile myself to being sold, if it relieves you and gives us both a home. But, father, mind this, if you tie me to that girl's sash too tightly I shall break away entirely, and then where are we?"

"I should be in prison and you a houseless vagabond. Trust me, my boy, and take the good fortune which I secured for you in your cradle. Look in pretty Sybil's face, and resignation will grow easy; but remember time presses, that this is our forlorn hope, and for God's sake be cautious, for she is a headstrong creature, and may refuse to fulfil her part if she learns that the contract is not binding against her will."

"I think she'll not refuse, sir; she likes me already. I see it in her eyes; she has never had a lover, she says, and according to your account a girl's first sweetheart is apt to fare the best. Besides, she likes the place, for I told her it was hers, as you bade me, and she said she could be very happy here, if my father was always kind."

"She said that, did she? little hypocrite! For your father, read yourself, and tell me what else she babbled about in that early *tête-à-tête* of yours."

"You are as curious as a woman, sir, and always make me tell you all I do and say, yet never tell me any thing in return, except this business, which I hate, because my liberty is the price, and my poor little cousin is kept in the dark. I'll tell her all, before I marry her, father."

"As you please, hot-head. I am waiting for an account of the first love passage, so leave blushing to Sybil and begin."

I knew what was coming and stayed no longer, but caught one glimpse of the pair, Guy in his favorite place, erect upon the rug, half-laughing, half-frowning as he delayed to speak, my uncle serenely smoking on the couch; then I sped away to my own room, thinking, as I sat down in a towering passion—

"So he does know of the baby betrothal and hates it, yet submits to please his father, who covets my fortune—mercenary creatures! I can annul the contract, can I? I'm glad to know that, for it makes me mistress of them both. I like you already, do I? and you see it in my eyes. Coxcomb! I'll be the thornier for that. Yet I do like him; I do wish he cared for me, I'm so lonely in the world, and he can be so kind."

So I cried a little, brushed my hair a good deal, and went to bed, resolving to learn all I could when, where, and how I pleased, to render myself as charming and valuable as possible, to make Guy love me in spite of himself, and then say yes or no, as my heart prompted me.

That day was a sample of those that followed, for my cousin was by turns attracted or repelled by the capricious moods that ruled me. Though conscious of a secret distrust of my uncle, I could not resist the fascination of his manner when he chose to exert its influence over me; this made my little plot easier of execution, for jealousy seemed the most effectual means to bring my wayward cousin to subjection. Full of this fancy, I seemed to tire of his society, grew thorny as a briar-rose to him, affectionate as a daughter to my uncle, who surveyed us both with that inscrutable glance of his, and slowly yielded to my dominion as if he had divined my purpose and desired to aid it. Guy turned cold and gloomy, yet still lingered near me as if ready for a relenting look or word. I liked that, and took a wanton pleasure in prolonging the humiliation of the warm heart I had learned to love, yet not to value as I ought, until it was too late.

One dull November evening as I went wandering up and down the hall, pretending to enjoy the flowers, yet in reality waiting for Guy, who had left me alone all day, my uncle came from his room, where he had sat for many hours with the harassed and anxious look he always wore when certain foreign letters came.

"Sybil, I have something to show and tell you," he said, as I garnished his button-hole with a spray of heliotrope, meant for the laggard, who would understand its significance, I hoped. Leading me to the drawing-room, my uncle put a paper into my hands, with the request—

"This is a copy of your father's will; oblige me by reading it."

He stood watching my face as I read, no doubt wondering at my composure while I waded through the dry details of the will, curbing my impatience to reach the one important passage. There it was, but no word concerning my power to dissolve the engagement if I pleased; and, as I realized the fact, a sudden bewilderment and sense of helplessness came over me, for the strange law terms seemed to make inexorable the paternal decree which I had not seen before. I forgot my studied calmness, and asked several questions eagerly.

"Uncle, did my father really command that I should marry Guy, whether we loved each other or not?"

"You see what he there set down as his desire; and I have taken measures that you *should* love one another, knowing that few cousins, young, comely, and congenial, could live three months together without finding themselves ready to mate for their own sakes, if not for the sake of the dead and living fathers to whom they owe obedience."

"You said I need not, if I didn't choose; why is it not here?"

"I said that? Never, Sybil!" and I met a look of such entire surprise and incredulity it staggered my belief in my own senses, yet also roused my spirit, and, careless of consequences, I spoke out at once—

"I heard you say it myself the night after I came, when you told Guy to be cautious, because I could refuse to fulfil the engagement, if I knew that it was not binding against my will."

This discovery evidently destroyed some plan, and for a moment threw him off his guard; for, crumpling the paper in his hand, he sternly demanded—

"You turned eavesdropper early; how often since?"

"Never, uncle; I did not mean it then, but, going for a letter in the dark, I heard your voices, and listened for an instant. It was dishonorable, but irresistible; and, if you force Guy's confidence, why should not I steal yours? All is fair in war, sir, and I forgive as I hope to be forgiven."

"You have a quick wit and a reticence I did not expect to find under that frank manner. So you have known your future destiny all these months, then, and have a purpose in your treatment of your cousin and myself?"

"Yes, uncle."

"May I ask what?"

I was ashamed to tell; and, in the little pause before my answer came, my pique at Guy's desertion was augmented by anger at my uncle's denial of his own words the ungenerous hopes he cherished, and a strong desire to perplex and thwart him took possession of me, for I saw his anxiety concerning the success of this interview, though he endeavored to repress and conceal it. Assuming my coldest mien, I said—

"No, sir, I think not; only I can assure you that my little plot has succeeded better than your own."

"But you intend to obey your father's wish, I hope, and fulfil your part of the compact, Sybil?"

"Why should I? It is not binding, you know, and I'm too young to lose my liberty just yet; besides, such compacts are unjust, unwise. What right had my father to mate me in my cradle? how did he know what I should become, or Guy? how could he tell that I should not love some one else better? No! I'll not be bargained away like a piece of merchandise, but love and marry when I please!"

At this declaration of independence my uncle's face darkened ominously, some new suspicion lurked in his eye, some new anxiety beset him; but his manner was calm, his voice blander than ever as he asked—

"Is there then, some one whom you love? Confide in me, my girl."

"And if there were, what then?"

"All would be changed at once, Sybil. But who is it? Some young lover left behind at madame's?"

"No, sir."

"Who, then? You have led a recluse life here. Guy has no friends who visit him, and mine are all old, yet you say you love."

"With all my heart, uncle."

"Is this affection returned, Sybil?"

"I think so."

"And it is not Guy?"

I was wicked enough to enjoy the bitter disappointment he could not conceal at my decided words, for I thought he deserved that momentary pang; but I could not as decidedly answer that last question, for I would not lie, neither would I confess just yet; so, with a little gesture of impatience, I silently turned away, lest he should see the tell-tale color in my cheeks. My uncle stood an instant in deep thought, a slow smile crept to his lips, content returned to his mien, and something like a flash of triumph glittered for a moment in his eye, then vanished, leaving his countenance earnestly expec- tant. Much as this change surprised me, his words did more, for, taking both my hands in his, he gravely said—

"Do you know that I am your uncle by adoption and not blood, Sybil?"

"Yes, sir; I heard so, but forgot about it," and I looked up at him, my anger quite lost in astonishment.

"Let me tell you, then. Your grandfather was childless for many years, my mother was an early friend, and when her death left me an orphan, he took me for his son and heir. But two years from that time, your father was born. I was too young to realize the entire change this might make in my life. The old man was too just and generous to let me feel it, and the two lads grew up together like brothers. Both married young, and when you were born a few years later than my son, your father said to me, 'Your boy shall have my girl, and the fortune I have innocently robbed you of shall make us happy in our children.' Then the family league was made, renewed at his death, and now destroyed by his daughter, unless—Sybil, I am forty-five, you not eighteen, yet you once said you could be very happy with me, if I were always kind to you. I can promise that I will be, for I love you. My darling, you reject the son, will you accept the father?"

If he had struck me, it would scarcely have dismayed me more. I started up, and snatching away my hands hid my face in them, for after the first tingle of surprise an almost irresistible desire to laugh came over me, but I dared not, and gravely, gently he went on—

"I am a bold man to say this, yet I mean it most sincerely. I never meant to betray the affection I believed you never could return, and would only laugh at as a weakness; but your past acts, your present words, give me courage to confess that I desire to keep my ward mine for ever. Shall it be so?"

He evidently mistook my surprise for maidenly emotion, and the sudden- ness of this unforeseen catastrophe seemed to deprive me of words. All thought of merriment or ridicule was forgotten in a sense of guilt, for if he feigned the love he offered it was well done, and I believed it then. I saw at once the natural impression conveyed by my conduct; my half confession and the folly of it all oppressed me with a regret and shame I could not master. My mind was in dire confusion, yet a decided "No" was rapidly emerging from the chaos, but was not uttered; for just at this crisis, as I stood with my uncle's arm about me, my hand again in his, and his head bent down to catch my answer, Guy swung himself gayly into the room. A glance seemed to explain all, and in an instant his face assumed that expression of pale wrath so much more terrible to witness than the fiercest outbreak; his eye grew fiery, his voice bitterly sarcastic, as he said—

"Ah, I see; the play goes on, but the actors change parts. I congratulate you, sir, on your success, and Sybil on her choice. Henceforth I am *de trop*, but before I go allow me to offer my wedding gift. You have taken the bride, let me supply the ring."

He threw a jewel-box upon the table, adding, in that unnaturally calm tone that made my heart stand still:

"A little candor would have spared me much pain, Sybil; yet I hope you will enjoy your bonds as heartily as I shall my escape from them. A little confidence would have made me your ally, not your rival, father. I have not your address; therefore I lose, you win. Let it be so. I had rather be the vagabond this makes me than sell myself, that you may gamble away that girl's fortune as you have your own and mine. You need not ask me to the wedding, I will not come. Oh, Sybil, I so loved, so trusted you!"

And with that broken exclamation he was gone.

The stormy scene had passed so rapidly, been so strange and sudden, Guy's anger so scornful and abrupt, I could not understand it, and felt like a puppet in the grasp of some power I could not resist; but as my lover left the room I broke out of the bewilderment that held me, imploring him to stay and hear me.

It was too late, he was gone, and Sultan's tramp was already tearing down the avenue. I listened till the sound died, then my hot temper rose past control, and woman-like asserted itself in vehement and voluble speech: I was angry with my uncle, my cousin, and myself, and for several minutes poured forth a torrent of explanations, reproaches, and regrets, such as only a passionate girl could utter.

My uncle stood where I had left him when I flew to the door with my vain cry; he now looked baffled, yet sternly resolved, and as I paused for breath his only answer was—

"Sybil, you ask me to bring back that headstrong boy; I cannot; he will never come. This marriage was distasteful to him, yet he submitted for my sake, because I have been unfortunate, and we are poor. Let him go, forget the past, and be to me what I desire, for I loved your father and will be a faithful guardian to his daughter all my life. Child, it must be—come, I implore, I command you."

He beckoned imperiously as if to awe me, and held up the glittering betrothal ring as if to tempt me. The tone, the act, the look put me quite beside myself. I did go to him, did take the ring, but said as resolutely as himself—

"Guy rejects me, and I have done with love. Uncle, you would have deceived me, used me as a means to your own selfish ends. I will accept neither yourself nor your gifts, for now I despise both you and your commands;" and, as the most energetic emphasis I could give to my defiance, I flung the ring, case and all, across the room; it struck the great mirror, shivered it just in the middle, and sent several loosened fragments crashing to the floor.

"Great heavens! is the young lady mad?" exclaimed a voice behind us. Both turned and saw Dr. Karnac, a stealthy, sallow-faced Spaniard, for whom I had an invincible aversion. He was my uncle's physician, had been visiting a sick servant in the upper regions, and my adverse fate sent him to the door just at that moment with that unfortunate exclamation on his lips.

"What do you say?"

My uncle wheeled about and eyed the new-comer intently as he repeated his words. I have no doubt I looked like one demented, for I was desperately angry, pale and trembling with excitement, and as they fronted me with a curious expression of alarm on their faces, a sudden sense of the absurdity of the spectacle came over me; I laughed hysterically a moment, then broke into a passion of regretful tears, remembering that Guy was gone. As I sobbed behind my hands, I knew the gentlemen were whispering together and of me, but I never heeded them, for as I wept myself calmer a comforting thought occurred to me; Guy could not have gone far, for Sultan had been out all day, and though reckless of himself he was not of his horse, which he loved like a human being; therefore he was doubtless at the house of an humble friend near by. If I could slip away unseen, I might undo my miserable work, or at least see him again before he went away into the world, perhaps never to return. This hope gave me courage for any thing, and dashing away my tears I took a covert survey. Dr. Karnac and my uncle still stood before the fire, deep in their low-toned conversation; their backs were toward me, and, hushing the rustle of my dress, I stole away with noiseless steps into the hall, seized Guy's plaid, and, opening the great door unseen, darted down the avenue.

Not far, however; the wind buffeted me to and fro, the rain blinded me, the mud clogged my feet and soon robbed me of a slipper; groping for it in despair, I saw a light flash into the outer darkness; heard voices calling, and soon the swift tramp of steps behind me. Feeling like a hunted doe, I ran on, but before I had gained a dozen yards my shoeless foot struck a sharp stone, and I fell half-stunned upon the wet grass of the wayside bank. Dr. Karnac reached me first, took me up as if I were a naughty child, and carried me back through a group of staring servants to the drawing-room, my uncle following with breathless entreaties that I would be calm, and a most uncharacteristic display of bustle.

I was horribly ashamed; my head ached with the shock of the fall, my foot bled, my heart fluttered, and when the doctor put me down the crisis came, for as my uncle bent over me with the strange question, "My poor girl, do you know me?" an irresistible impulse impelled me to push him from me, crying passionately—

"Yes, I know and hate you; let me go! let me go, or it will be too late!" then, quite spent with the varying emotions of the last hour, for the first time in my life I swooned away.

Coming to myself, I found I was in my own room, with my uncle, the doctor, Janet, and Mrs. Best, the housekeeper, gathered about me, the latter saying, as she bathed my temples—

"She's a sad sight, poor thing, so young, so bonny, and so unfortunate. Did you ever see her so before, Janet?"

"Bless you, no, ma'am; there was no signs of such a tantrum when I dressed her for dinner."

"What do they mean? did they never see any one angry before?" I dimly wondered, and presently, through the fast disappearing stupor that had held me, Dr. Karnac's deep voice came distinctly, saying—

"If it continues, you are perfectly justified in doing so."

"Doing what?" I demanded sharply, for the sound both roused and irritated me, I disliked the man so intensely.

"Nothing, my dear, nothing," purred Mrs. Best, supporting me as I sat up, feeling weak and dazed, yet resolved to know what was going on. I was "a sad sight" indeed; my drenched hair hung about my shoulders, my dress was streaked with mud, one shoeless foot was red with blood, the other splashed and stained, and a white, wild-eyed face completed the ruinous image the opposite mirror showed me. Every thing looked blurred and strange, and a feverish unrest possessed me, for I was not one to subside easily after such a mental storm. Leaning on my arm, I scanned the room and its occupants with all the composure I could collect. The two women eyed me curiously yet pitifully; Dr. Karnac stood glancing at me furtively as he listened to my uncle, who spoke rapidly in Spanish as he showed the little scar upon his hand. That sight did more to restore me than the cordial just administered, and I rose erect, saying abruptly—

"Please, everybody, go away; my head aches, and I want to be alone."

"Let Janet stay and help you, dear; you are not fit," began Mrs. Best; but I peremptorily stopped her.

"No, go yourself, and take her with you; I'm tired of so much stir about such foolish things as a broken glass and a girl in a pet."

"You will be good enough to take this quieting draught before I go, Miss Sybil."

"I shall do nothing of the sort, for I need only solitude and sleep to be perfectly well," and I emptied the glass the doctor offered into the fire. He shrugged his shoulders with a disagreeable smile, and quietly began to prepare another draught, saying—

"You are mistaken, my dear young lady; you need much care, and should obey, that your uncle may be spared further apprehension and anxiety."

My patience gave out at this assumption of authority; and I determined to carry matters with a high hand, for they all stood watching me in a way which seemed the height of impertinent curiosity.

"He is not my uncle! never has been, and deserves neither respect nor obedience from me! I am the best judge of my own health, and you are not bettering it by contradiction and unnecessary fuss. This is my house, and you will oblige me by leaving it, Dr. Karnac; this is my room, and I insist on being left in peace immediately."

I pointed to the door as I spoke; the women hurried out with scared faces; the doctor bowed and followed, but paused on the threshold, while my uncle approached me, asking in a tone inaudible to those still hovering round the door—

"Do you still persist in your refusal, Sybil?"

"How dare you ask me that again? I tell you I had rather die than marry you!"

"The Lord be merciful to us! just hear how she's going on now about marrying master. Ain't it awful, Jane?" ejaculated Mrs. Best, bobbing her head in for a last look.

"Hold your tongue, you impertinent creature!" I called out; and the fat old soul bundled away in such comical haste I laughed, in spite of languor and vexation.

My uncle left me, and I heard him say as he passed the doctor—

"You see how it is."

"Nothing uncommon; but that virulence is a bad symptom," answered the Spaniard, and closing the door locked it, having dexterously removed the key from within.

I had never been subjected to restraint of any kind; it made me reckless at once, for this last indignity was not to be endured.

"Open this instantly!" I commanded, shaking the door. No one answered, and after a few ineffectual attempts to break the lock I left it, threw up the window and looked out; the ground was too far off for a leap, but the trellis where summer-vines had clung was strong and high, a step would place me on it, a moment's agility bring me to the terrace below. I was now in just the state to attempt any rash exploit, for the cordial had both strengthened and excited me; my foot was bandaged, my clothes still wet; I could suffer no new damage, and have my own way at small cost. Out I crept, climbed safely down, and made my way to the lodge as I had at first intended. But Guy was not there; and, returning, I boldly went in at the great door, straight to the room where my uncle and the doctor were still talking.

"I wish the key of my room," was my brief command. Both started as if I had been a ghost, and my uncle exclaimed—

"You here! how in Heaven's name came you out?"

"By the window. I am no child to be confined for a fit of anger. I will not submit to it; to-morrow I shall go to madame; till then I will be mistress in my own house. Give me the key, sir."

"Shall I?" asked the doctor of my uncle, who nodded with a whispered—

"Yes, yes; don't excite her again."

It was restored, and without another word I went loftily up to my room, locked myself in, and spent a restless, miserable night. When morning came, I breakfasted above stairs, and then busied myself packing trunks, burning papers, and collecting every trifle Guy had ever given me. No one annoyed me, and I saw only Janet, who had evidently received some order that kept her silent and respectful, though her face still betrayed the same curiosity and pitiful interest as the night before. Lunch was brought up, but I could not eat, and began to feel that the exposure, the fall, and excitement of the evening had left me weak and nervous, so I gave up the idea of going to madame till the morrow; and, as the afternoon waned, tried to sleep, yet could not, for I had sent a note to several of Guy's haunts, imploring him to see me; but my messenger brought word that he was not to be found, and my heart was too heavy to rest.

When summoned to dinner, I still refused to go down; for I heard Dr. Karnac's voice, and would not meet him, so I sent word that I wished the carriage early the following morning, and to be left alone till then. In a few minutes, back came Janet, with a glass of wine set forth on a silver salver, and a card with these words—

"Forgive, forget, for your father's sake, and drink with me, 'Oblivion to the past.' "

It touched and softened me. I knew my uncle's pride, and saw in this an entire relinquishment of the hopes I had so thoughtlessly fostered in his mind. I was passionate, but not vindictive. He had been kind, I very wilful. His mistake was natural, my resentment ungenerous. Though my resolution to go remained unchanged, I was sorry for my part in the affair; and remembering that through me his son was lost to him, I accepted his apology, drank his toast, and sent him back a dutiful "Good-night."

I was unused to wine. The draught I had taken was powerful with age, and, though warm and racy to the palate, proved too potent for me. Still sitting before my fire, I slowly fell into a restless drowse, haunted by a dim dream that I was seeking Guy in a ship, whose motion gradually lulled me into perfect unconsciousness.

Waking at length, I was surprised to find myself in bed, with the shimmer of daylight peeping through the curtains. Recollecting that I was to leave early, I sprang up, took one step and remained transfixed with dismay, for the room was not my own! Utterly unfamiliar was every object on which my eyes fell. The place was small, plainly furnished, and close, as if long unused. My trunks stood against the wall, my clothes lay on a chair, and on the bed I had left trailed a fur-lined cloak I had often seen on my uncle's shoulders. A moment I stared about me bewildered, then hurried to the window—it was grated!

A lawn, sere and sodden, lay without, and a line of sombre firs hid the landscape beyond the high wall which encompassed the dreary plot. More and more alarmed, I flew to the door and found it locked. No bell was visible, no sound audible, no human presence near me, and an ominous foreboding thrilled cold through nerves and blood, as, for the first time, I felt the paralyzing touch of fear. Not long, however. My native courage soon returned, indignation took the place of terror, and excitement gave me strength. My temples throbbed with a dull pain, my eyes were heavy, my limbs weighed down by an unwonted lassitude, and my memory seemed strangely confused; but one thing was clear to me, I must see somebody, ask questions, demand explanations, and get away to madame without delay.

With trembling hands I dressed, stopping suddenly, with a cry; for, lifting my hands to my head, I discovered that my hair, my beautiful, abundant hair, was gone! There was no mirror in the room, but I could feel that it had been shorn away close about face and neck. This outrage was more than I could bear, and the first tears I shed fell for my lost charm. It was weak, perhaps, but I felt better for it, clearer in mind and readier to confront whatever lay before me. I knocked and called. Then, losing patience, shook and screamed; but no one came or answered me, and, wearied out at last, I sat down and cried again in impotent despair.

An hour passed, then a step approached, the key turned, and a hard-faced woman entered with a tray in her hand. I had resolved to be patient, if possible, and controlled myself to ask quietly, though my eyes kindled, and my voice trembled with resentment—

"Where am I, and why am I here against my will?"

"This is your breakfast, miss; you must be sadly hungry," was the only reply I got.

"I will never eat till you tell me what I ask."

"Will you be quiet, and mind me if I do, miss?"

"You have no right to exact obedience from me, but I'll try."

"That's right. Now all I know is that you are twenty miles from the Moors, and came because you are ill. Do you like sugar in your coffee?"

"When did I come? I don't remember it."

"Early this morning; you don't remember because you were put to sleep before being fetched, to save trouble."

"Ah, that wine! Who brought me here?"

"Dr. Karnac, miss."

"Alone?"

"Yes, miss; you were easier to manage asleep than awake, he said."

I shook with anger, yet still restrained myself, hoping to fathom the mystery of this nocturnal journey.

"What is your name, please?" I meekly asked.

"You can call me Hannah."

"Well, Hannah, there is a strange mistake somewhere. I am not ill—you see I am not—and I wish to go away at once to the friend I was to meet to-day. Get me a carriage and have my baggage taken out."

"It can't be done, miss. We are a mile from town, and have no carriages here; besides, you couldn't go if I had a dozen. I have my orders, and shall obey 'em."

"But Dr. Karnac has no right to bring or keep me here."

"Your uncle sent you. The doctor has the care of you, and that is all I know about it. Now I have kept my promise, do you keep yours, miss, and eat your breakfast, else I can't trust you again."

"But what is the matter with me? How can I be ill and not know or feel it?" I demanded, more and more bewildered.

"You look it, and that's enough for them as is wise in such matters. You'd have had a fever, if it hadn't been seen to in time."

"Who cut my hair off?"

"I did; the doctor ordered it."

"How dared he? I hate that man, and never will obey him."

"Hush, miss, don't clench your hands and look in that way, for I shall have to report every thing you say and do to him, and it won't be pleasant to tell that sort of thing."

The woman was civil, but grim and cool. Her eye was unsympathetic, her manner business-like, her tone such as one uses to a refractory child, half-soothing, half-commanding. I conceived a dislike to her at once, and resolved to escape at all hazards, for my uncle's inexplicable movements filled me with alarm. Hannah had left my door open, a quick glance showed me another door also ajar at the end of a wide hall, a glimpse of green, and a gate. My plan was desperately simple, and I executed it without delay. Affecting to eat, I presently asked the woman for my handkerchief from the bed. She crossed the room to get it. I darted out, down the passage, along the walk, and tugged vigorously at the great bolt of the gate, but it was also locked. In despair I flew into the garden, but a high wall enclosed it on every side; and as I ran round and round, vainly looking for some outlet, I saw Hannah, accompanied by a man as gray and grim as herself, coming leisurely toward me, with no appearance of excitement or displeasure. Back I would not go; and, inspired with a sudden hope, swung myself into one of the firs that grew close against the wall. The branches snapped under me, the slender tree swayed perilously, but up I struggled, till the wide coping of the wall was gained. There I paused and looked back. The woman was hurrying through the gate to intercept my descent on the other side, and close behind me the man, sternly calling me to stop. I looked down; a stony ditch was below, but I would rather risk my life than tamely lose my liberty, and with a flying leap tried to reach the bank; failed, fell heavily among the stones, felt an awful crash, and then came an utter blank.

For many weeks I lay burning in a fever, fitfully conscious of Dr. Karnac and the woman's presence; once I fancied I saw my uncle, but was never sure, and rose at last a shadow of my former self, feeling pitifully broken, both mentally and physically. I was in a better room now, wintry winds howled without, but a generous fire glowed behind the high closed fender, and books lay on my table.

I saw no one but Hannah, yet could wring no intelligence from her beyond what she had already told, and no sign of interest reached me from the outer world. I seemed utterly deserted and forlorn, my spirit was crushed, my strength gone, my freedom lost, and for a time I succumbed to despair, letting one day follow another without energy or hope. It is hard to live with no object to give zest to life, especially for those still blest with youth, and even in my prison-house I soon found one quite in keeping with the mystery that surrounded me.

As I sat reading by day or lay awake at night, I became aware that the room above my own was occupied by some inmate whom I never saw. A peculiar person it seemed to be; for I heard steps going to and fro, hour after hour, in a tireless march, that wore upon my nerves, as many a harsher sound would not have done. I could neither tease nor surprise Hannah into any explanation of the thing, and day after day I listened to it, till I longed to cover up my ears and implore the unknown walker to stop, for Heaven's sake. Other sounds I heard and fretted over: a low monotonous murmur, as of some one singing a lullaby; a fitful tapping, like a cradle rocked on a carpetless floor; and at rare intervals cries of suffering, sharp but brief, as if forcibly suppressed. These sounds, combined with the solitude, the confinement, and the books I read, a collection of ghostly tales and weird fancies, soon wrought my nerves to a state of terrible irritability, and wore upon my health so visibly that I was allowed at last to leave my room.

The house was so well guarded that I soon relinquished all hope of escape, and listlessly amused myself by roaming through the unfurnished rooms and echoing halls, seldom venturing into Hannah's domain; for there her husband sat, surrounded by chemical apparatus, poring over crucibles and retorts. He never spoke to me, and I dreaded the glance of his cold eye, for it looked unsoftened by a ray of pity at the little figure that sometimes paused a moment on his threshold, wan and wasted as the ghost of departed hope.

The chief interest of these dreary walks centred in the door of the room above my own, for a great hound lay before it, eying me savagely as he rejected all advances, and uttering his deep bay if I approached too near. To me this room possessed an irresistible fascination. I could not keep away from it by day, I dreamed of it by night, it haunted me continually, and soon became a sort of monomania, which I condemned, yet could not control, till at length I found myself pacing to and fro as those invisible feet paced overhead. Hannah came and stopped me, and a few hours later Dr. Karnac appeared. I was so changed that I feared him with a deadly fear. He seemed to enjoy it; for in the pride of youth and beauty I had shown him contempt and defiance at my uncle's, and he took an ungenerous satisfaction in annoying me by a display of power. He never answered my questions or entreaties, regarded me as being without sense or will, insisted on my trying various mixtures and experiments in diet, gave me strange books to read, and weekly received Hannah's report of all that passed. That day he came, looked at me, said, "Let her walk," and went away, smiling that hateful smile of his.

Soon after this I took to walking in my sleep, and more than once woke to find myself roving lampless through that haunted house in the dead of night. I concealed these unconscious wanderings for a time, but an ominous event broke them up at last, and betrayed them to Hannah.

I had followed the steps one day for several hours, walking below as they walked above; had peopled that mysterious room with every mournful shape my disordered fancy could conjure up; had woven tragical romances about it, and brooded over the one subject of interest my unnatural life possessed with the intensity of a mind upon which its uncanny influence was telling with perilous rapidity. At midnight I woke to find myself standing in a streak of moonlight, opposite the door whose threshold I had never crossed. The April night was warm, a single pane of glass high up in that closed door was drawn aside, as if for air; and, as I stood dreamily collecting my sleep-drunken senses, I saw a ghostly hand emerge and beckon, as if to me. It startled me broad awake, with a faint exclamation and a shudder from head to foot. A cloud swept over the moon, and when it passed the hand was gone, but shrill through the keyhole came a whisper that chilled me to the marrow of my bones, so terribly distinct and imploring was it.

"Find it! for God's sake find it before it is too late!"

The hound sprang up with an angry growl; I heard Hannah leave her bed near by, and, with an inspiration strange as the moment, I paced slowly on with open eyes and lips apart, as I had seen "Amina" in the happy days when kind old madame took me to the theatre, whose mimic horrors I had never thought to equal with such veritable ones. Hannah appeared at her door with a light, but on I went in a trance of fear; for I was only kept from dropping in a swoon by the blind longing to fly from that spectral voice and hand. Past Hannah I went, she following; and, as I slowly laid myself in bed, I heard her say to her husband, who just then came up—

"Sleep-walking, John; it's getting worse and worse, as the doctor foretold; she'll settle down like the other presently, but she must be locked up at night, else the dog will do her a mischief."

The man yawned and grumbled; then they went, leaving me to spend hours of unspeakable suffering, which aged me more than years. What was I to find? where was I to look? and when would it be too late? These questions tormented me; for I could find no answers to them, divine no meaning, see no course to pursue. Why was I here? what motive induced my uncle to commit such an act? and when should I be liberated? were equally unanswerable, equally tormenting, and they haunted me like ghosts. I had no power to exorcise or forget. After that I walked no more, because I slept no more; sleep seemed scared away, and waking dreams harassed me with their terrors. Night after night I paced my room in utter darkness—for I was allowed no lamp—night after night I wept bitter tears wrung from me by anguish, for which I had no name; and night after night the steps kept time to mine, and the faint lullaby came down to me as if to soothe and comfort my distress. I felt that my health was going, my mind growing confused and weak, my thoughts wandered vaguely, memory began to fail, and idiocy or madness seemed my inevitable fate; but through it all my heart clung to Guy, yearning for him with a hunger that would not be appeased.

At rare intervals I was allowed to walk in the neglected garden, where no flowers bloomed, no birds sang, no companion came to me but surly John, who followed with his book or pipe, stopping when I stopped, walking when I walked, keeping a vigilant eye upon me, yet seldom speaking except to decline answering my questions. These walks did me no good, for the air was damp and heavy with vapors from the marsh; for the house stood near a half-dried lake, and hills shut it in on every side. No fresh winds from upland moor or distant ocean ever blew across the narrow valley; no human creature visited the place, and nothing but a vague hope that my birthday might bring some change, some help, sustained me. It did bring help, but of such an unexpected sort that its effects remained through all my after-life. My birth-day came, and with it my uncle. I was in my room, walking restlessly—for the habit was a confirmed one now—when the door opened, and Hannah, Dr. Karnac, my uncle, and a gentleman whom I knew to be his lawyer, entered, and surveyed me as if I were a spectacle. I saw my uncle start and turn pale; I had never seen myself since I came, but, if I had not suspected that I was a melancholy wreck of my former self, I should have known it then, such sudden pain and pity softened his ruthless countenance for a single instant. Dr. Karnac's eye had a magnetic power over me; I had always felt it, but in my present feeble state I dreaded, yet submitted to it with a helpless fear that should have touched his heart—it was on me then, I could not resist it, and paused fixed and fascinated by that repellent yet potent glance. Hannah pointed to the carpet worn to shreds by my weary march, to the walls which I had covered with weird, grotesque, or tragic figures to while away the heavy hours, lastly to myself, mute, motionless, and scared, saying, as if in confirmation of some previous assertion—

"You see, gentlemen, she is, as I said, quiet, but quite hopeless."

I thought she was interceding for me; and, breaking from the bewilder-ment and fear that held me, I stretched my hands to them, crying with an imploring cry—

"Yes, I *am* quiet! I *am* hopeless! Oh, have pity on me before this dreadful life kills me or drives me mad!"

Dr. Karnac came to me at once with a black frown, which I alone could see; I evaded him, and clung to Hannah, still crying frantically—for this seemed my last hope—

"Uncle, let me go! I will give you all I have, will never ask for Guy, will be obedient and meek if I may only go to madame and never hear the feet again, or see the sights that terrify me in this dreadful room. Take me out! for God's sake take me out!"

My uncle did not answer me, but covered up his face with a despairing gesture, and hurried from the room; the lawyer followed, muttering pitifully, "Poor thing! poor thing!" and Dr. Karnac laughed the first laugh I had ever heard him utter as he wrenched Hannah from my grasp and locked me in alone. My one hope died then, and I resolved to kill myself rather than endure this life another month; for now it grew clear to me that they believed me mad, and death of the body was far more preferable than that of the mind. I think I *was* a little mad just then, but remember well the sense of peace that came to me as I tore strips from my clothing, braided them into a cord, hid it beneath my mattress, and serenely waited for the night. Sitting in the last twilight I thought to see in this unhappy world, I recollected that I had not heard the feet all day, and fell to pondering over the unusual omission. But, if the steps had been silent in that room, voices had not, for I heard a continuous murmur at one time: the tones of one voice were abrupt and broken, the other low, yet resonant, and that, I felt assured, belonged to my uncle. Who was he speaking to? what were they saying? should I ever know? and even then, with death before me, the intense desire to possess the secret filled me with its old unrest.

Night came at last; I heard the clock strike one, and, listening to discover if John still lingered up, I heard through the deep hush a soft grating in the room above, a stealthy sound that would have escaped ears less preternaturally alert than mine. Like a flash came the thought, "Some one is filing bars or picking locks: will the unknown remember me and let me share her flight?" The fatal noose hung ready, but I no longer cared to use it, for hope had come to nerve me with the strength and courage I had lost. Breathlessly I listened; the sound went on, stopped, a dead silence reigned; then something brushed against my door, and, with a suddenness that made me tingle from head to foot like an electric shock, through the keyhole came again that whisper, urgent, imploring, and mysterious—

"Find it! for God's sake find it before it is too late!" then fainter, as if breath failed, came the broken words, "The dog—a lock of hair—there is yet time."

Eagerness rendered me forgetful of the secrecy I should preserve, and I cried aloud, "What shall I find? where shall I look?" My voice, sharpened by fear, rang shrilly through the house, Hannah's quick tread rushed down the hall, something fell, then loud and long rose a cry that made my heart stand still, so helpless, so hopeless was its wild lament. I had betrayed and I could not save or comfort the kind soul who had lost liberty through me. I was frantic to get out, and beat upon my door in a paroxysm of impatience, but no one came; and all night long those awful cries went on above, cries of mortal anguish, as if soul and body were being torn asunder. Till dawn I listened, pent in that room which now possessed an added terror; till dawn I called, wept, and prayed, with mingled pity, fear, and penitence, and till dawn the agony of that unknown sufferer continued unabated. I heard John hurry to and fro, heard Hannah issue orders with an accent of human sympathy in her hard voice; heard Dr. Karnac pass and repass my door, and all the sounds of confusion and alarm in that once quiet house. With daylight all was still, a stillness more terrible than the stir; for it fell so suddenly, remained so utterly unbroken, that there seemed no explanation of it but the dread word "death."

At noon Hannah, a shade paler, but grim as ever, brought me some food, saying she forgot my breakfast, and when I refused to eat, yet asked no questions, she bade me go into the garden and not fret myself over last night's flurry. I went, and, passing down the corridor, glanced furtively at the door I never saw without a thrill; but I experienced a new sensation then, for the hound was gone, the door was open, and, with an impulse past control, I crept in and looked about me. It was a room like mine, the carpet worn like mine, the windows barred like mine; there the resemblance ended, for an empty cradle stood beside the bed, and on that bed, below a sweeping cover, stark and still a lifeless body lay. I was inured to fear now, and an unwholesome craving for new terrors seemed to have grown by what it fed on: an irresistible desire led me close, nerved me to lift the cover and look below—a single glance—then, with a cry as panic-stricken as that which rent the silence of the night, I fled away, for the face I saw was a pale image of my own. Sharpened by suffering, pallid with death, the features were familiar as those I used to see; the hair, beautiful and blonde as mine had been, streamed long over the pulseless breast, and on the hand, still clenched in that last struggle, shone the likeness of a ring I wore, a ring bequeathed me by my father. An awesome fancy that it was myself assailed me; I had plotted death, and, with the waywardness of a shattered mind, I recalled legends of spirits returning to behold the bodies they had left.

Glad now to seek the garden, I hurried down, but on the threshold of the great-hall door was arrested by the sharp crack of a pistol; and, as a little cloud of smoke dispersed, I saw John drop the weapon and approach the hound, who lay writhing on the bloody grass. Moved by compassion for the faithful brute whose long vigilance was so cruelly repaid, I went to him, and, kneeling there, caressed the great head that never yielded to my touch before. John assumed his watch at once, and leaning against a tree cleaned the pistol, content that I should amuse myself with the dying creature, who looked into my face with eyes of almost human pathos and reproach. The brass collar seemed to choke him as he gasped for breath, and, leaning nearer to undo it, I saw, half hidden in his own black hair, a golden lock wound tightly round the collar, and so near its color as to be unobservable, except upon a close inspection. No accident could have placed it there; no head but mine in that house wore hair of that sunny hue—yes, one other, and my heart gave a sudden leap as I remembered the shining locks just seen on that still bosom.

"Find it—the dog—the lock of hair," rung in my ears, and swift as light came the conviction that the unknown help was found at last. The little band was woven close, I had no knife, delay was fatal, I bent my head as if lamenting over the poor beast and bit the knot apart, drew out a folded paper, hid it in my hand, and rising strolled leisurely back to my own room, saying I did not care to walk till it was warmer. With eager eyes I examined my strange treasure-trove; it consisted of two strips of thinnest paper, without address or signature, one almost illegible, worn at the edges and stained with the green rust of the collar; the other fresher, yet more feebly written, both abrupt and disjointed, but terribly significant to me. This was the first—

"I have never seen you, never heard your name, yet I know that you are young, that you are suffering, and I try to help you in my poor way. I think you are not crazed yet, as I often am; for your voice is sane, your plaintive singing not like mine, your walking only caught from me, I hope. I sing to lull the baby whom I never saw; I walk to lessen the long journey that will bring me to the husband I have lost—stop! I must not think of those things or I shall forget. If you are not already mad, you will be; I suspect you were sent here to be made so; for the air is poison, the solitude is fatal, and Karnac remorseless in his mania for prying into the mysteries of human minds. What devil sent you I may never know, but I long to warn you. I can devise no way but this; the dog comes into my room sometimes, you sometimes pause at my door and talk to him; you may find the paper I shall hide about his collar. Read, destroy, but obey it. I implore you to leave this house before it is too late."

The other paper was as follows—

"I have watched you, tried to tell you where to look, for you have not found my warning yet, though I often tie it there and hope. You fear the dog, perhaps, and my plot fails; yet I know by your altered step and voice that you are fast reaching my unhappy state; for I am fitfully mad, and shall be till I die. To-day I have seen a familiar face; it seems to have calmed and strengthened me, and, though he would not help you, I shall make one desperate attempt. I may not find you, so leave my warning to the hound, yet hope to breathe a word into your sleepless ear that shall send you back into the world the happy thing you should be. Child! woman! whatever you are, leave this accursed house while you have power to do it."

That was all; I did not destroy the papers, but I obeyed them, and for a week watched and waited till the propitious instant came. I saw my uncle, the doctor, and two others, follow the poor body to its grave beside the lake, saw all depart but Dr. Karnac, and felt redoubled hatred and contempt for the men who could repay my girlish slights with such a horrible revenge. On the seventh day, as I went down for my daily walk, I saw John and Dr. Karnac so deep in some uncanny experiment that I passed out unguarded. Hoping to profit by this unexpected chance, I sprang down the steps, but the next moment dropped half-stunned upon the grass; for behind me rose a crash, a shriek, a sudden blaze that flashed up and spread, sending a noisome vapor rolling out with clouds of smoke and flame. Aghast, I was just gathering myself up, when Hannah fled out of the house, dragging her husband sense-less and bleeding, while her own face was ashy with affright. She dropped her burden beside me, saying, with white lips and a vain look for help where help was not—

"Something they were at has burst, killed the doctor, and fired the house! Watch John till I get help, and leave him at your peril!" then flinging open the gate she sped away.

"Now is my time," I thought, and only waiting till she vanished, I boldly followed her example, running rapidly along the road in an opposite direc-tion, careless of bonnetless head and trembling limbs, intent only upon leaving that prison-house far behind me. For several hours I hurried along that solitary road; the spring sun shone, birds sang in the blooming hedges, green nooks invited me to pause and rest, but I heeded none of them, steadily continuing my flight, till spent and footsore I was forced to stop a moment by a wayside spring. As I stooped to drink, I saw my face for the first time in many months, and started to see how like that dead one it had grown, in all but the eternal peace which made that beautiful in spite of suffering and age. Standing thus and wondering if Guy would know me, should we ever meet, the sound of wheels disturbed me. Believing them to be coming from the place I had left, I ran desperately down the hill, turned a sharp corner, and before I could check myself passed a carriage slowly ascending. A face sprang to the window, a voice cried "Stop!" but on I flew, hoping the traveller would let me go unpursued. Not so, however; soon I heard fleet steps following, gaining rapidly, then a hand seized me, a voice rang in my ears, and with a vain struggle I lay panting in my captor's hold, fearing to look up and meet a brutal glance. But the hand that had seized me tenderly drew me close, the voice that had alarmed cried joyfully—

"Sybil, it is Guy! lie still, poor child, you are safe at last."

Then I knew that my surest refuge was gained, and, too weak for words, clung to him in an agony of happiness, which brought to his kind eyes the tears I could not shed.

The carriage returned; Guy took me in, and for a time cared only to soothe and sustain my worn soul and body with the cordial of his presence, as we rolled homeward through a blooming world, whose beauty I had never truly felt before. When the first tumult of emotion had subsided, I told the story of my captivity and my escape, ending with a passionate entreaty not to be returned to my uncle's keeping, for henceforth there could be neither affection nor respect between us.

"Fear nothing, Sybil; madame is waiting for you at the Moors, and my father's unfaithful guardianship has ended with his life."

Then with averted face and broken voice Guy went on to tell his father's purposes, and what had caused this unexpected meeting. The facts were briefly these: The knowledge that my father had come between him and a princely fortune had always rankled in my uncle's heart, chilling the ambitious hopes he cherished even in his boyhood, and making life an eager search for pleasure in which to drown his vain regrets. This secret was suspected by my father, and the household league was formed as some atonement for the innocent offence. It seemed to soothe my uncle's resentful nature, and as years went on he lived freely, assured that ample means would be his through his son. Luxurious, self-indulgent, fond of all excitements, and reckless in their pursuit, he took no thought for the morrow till a few months before his return. A gay winter in Paris reduced him to those straits of which women know so little; creditors were oppressive, summer friends failed him, gambling debts harassed him, his son reproached him, and but one resource remained, Guy's speedy marriage with the half-forgotten heiress. The boy had been educated to regard this fate as a fixed fact, and submitted, believing the time to be far distant; but the sudden summons came, and he rebelled against it, preferring liberty to love. My uncle pacified the claimants by promises to be fulfilled at my expense, and hurried home to press on the marriage, which now seemed imperative. I was taken to my future home, approved by my uncle, beloved by my cousin, and, but for my own folly, might have been a happy wife on that May morning when I listened to this unveiling of the past. My mother had been melancholy mad since that unhappy rumor of my father's death; this affliction had been well concealed from me, lest the knowledge should prey upon my excitable nature and perhaps induce a like misfortune. I believed her dead, yet I had seen her, knew where her solitary grave was made, and still carried in my bosom the warning she had sent me, prompted by the unerring instinct of a mother's heart. In my father's will a clause was added just below the one confirming my betrothal, a clause decreeing that, if it should appear that I inherited my mother's malady, the fortune should revert to my cousin, with myself a mournful legacy, to be cherished by him whether his wife or not. This passage, and that relating to my freedom of choice, had been omitted in the copy shown me on the night when my seeming refusal of Guy had induced his father to believe that I loved him, to make a last attempt to keep the prize by offering himself, and, when that failed, to harbor a design that changed my little comedy into the tragical experience I have told.

Dr. Karnac's exclamation had caused the recollection of that clause respecting my insanity to flash into my uncle's mind—a mind as quick to conceive as fearless to execute. I unconsciously abetted the stratagem, and Dr. Karnac was an unscrupulous ally, for love of gain was as strong as love of science; both were amply gratified, and I, poor victim, was given up to be experimented upon, till by subtle means I was driven to the insanity which would give my uncle full control of my fortune and my fate. How the black plot prospered has been told; but retribution speedily overtook them both, for Dr. Karnac paid his penalty by the sudden death that left his ashes among the blackened ruins of that house of horrors, and my uncle had preceded him. For before the change of heirs could be effected my mother died, and the hours spent in that unhealthful spot insinuated the subtle poison of the marsh into his blood; years of pleasure left little vigor to withstand the fever, and a week of suffering ended a life of generous impulses perverted, fine endowments wasted, and opportunities for ever lost. When death drew near, he sent for Guy (who, through the hard discipline of poverty and honest labor, was becoming a manlier man), confessed all, and implored him to save me before it was too late. He did, and when all was told, when each saw the other by the light of this strange and sad experience—Guy poor again, I free, the old bond still existing, the barrier of misunderstanding gone—it was easy to see our way, easy to submit, to forgive, forget, and begin anew the life these clouds had darkened for a time.

Home received me, kind madame welcomed me, Guy married me, and I was happy; but over all these years, serenely prosperous, still hangs for me the shadow of the past, still rises that dead image of my mother, still echoes that spectral whisper in the dark.

V. V.;

or, Plots and Counterplots

Editor's Note: "My sinners always have a good spot somewhere," Alcott once wrote of her fictional characters—but that was three years before she created scheming *femme fatale* Virginie Varens in her self-described "blood & thunder story" "V. V.; or, Plots and Counterplots." Virginie is the most devious of all heroines to appear in Alcott's thrillers, and the tale is a *tour de force* of misdirected passion and jealousy. Alcott wrote the story in 1865 as a diversion from her frustrating inability to sell her literary novel *Moods,* and one almost senses that she poured into Virginie's character some of her own passion to be taken seriously as a writer.

Chapter I

Won and Lost

I n the green room of a Parisian theatre a young man was pacing to and fro, evidently waiting with impatience for some expected arrival. The room was empty, for the last performance of a Grande Spectacle was going on, and the entire strength of the company in demand. Frequent bursts of barbaric music had filled the air; but now a brief lull had fallen, broken only by the soft melody of flutes and horns. Standing motionless, the young man listened with a sudden smile, an involuntary motion of the head, as if in fancy he saw and followed some object of delight. A storm of applause broke in on the last notes of the air. Again and again was it repeated, and when at length it died away, trumpet, clarion and drum resumed their martial din, and the enchanting episode seemed over.

Suddenly, framed in the dark doorway, upon which the young man's eyes were fixed, appeared an apparition well worth waiting for. A sylph she seemed, costumed in fleecy white and gold; the star that glittered on her forehead was less brilliant than her eyes; the flowers that filled her graceful arms were out-rivalled by the blooming face that smiled above them; the ornaments she wore were forgotten in admiration of the long blonde tresses that crowned her spirited little head, and when the young man welcomed her she crossed the room as if borne by the shining wings upon her shoulders.

"My Virginie, how long they kept you," began the lover, as this beautiful girl leaned against him, flushed and panting, but radiant with the triumphs of the hour.

"Yes, for they recalled me many times; and see—not one bouquet without a *billet doux* or gift attached!"

"I have much to say, Virginie, and you give me no time but this. Where is Victor?"

"Safe for many minutes; he is in the Pas de Enfer, and then we are together in the Pas des Deesses. Behold! another offer from the viscount. Shall I accept?"

While speaking she had been rifling the flowers of their attractive burdens, and now held up a delicately scented note with an air half serious, half gay. Her lover crushed the paper in his hand, and answered, hotly:

"You will refuse, or I shall make the viscount a different sort of offer. His devotion is an insult, for you are mine!"

"Not yet, monsieur. Victor has the first claim. And see; he has set his mark upon me."

Pushing up a bracelet, she showed two dark letters stamped or tattooed on the white flesh.

"And you permitted him to disfigure you? When, Virginie, and why?"

"Ah, that was years ago when I cared nothing for beauty, and clung to Victor as my only friend, letting him do what he would, quite content to please him, for he was very kind, and I, poor child, was nothing but a burden. A year ago we were betrothed, and next year he hopes to marry—for we do well now, and I shall then be eighteen."

"You will not marry him, then why deceive him, Virginie?"

"Yes, but I may if no one else will offer me a name as he does. I do not love him, but he is useful; he guards me like a dragon, works for me, cherishes me, and keeps me right when from mere youth and gaiety of heart I might go astray. What then? I care nothing for lovers; they are false and vain, they annoy me, waste my time, keep Victor savage, and but for the *éclat* it gives one, I would banish all but—" She finished the sentence with a caress more eloquent than any words, and before he could speak, added, half tenderly, half reproachfully, while the flowers strayed down upon the ground—"Not one of all these came from you. I thought you would remember me on this last night."

Passionately kissing the red lips so near his own, the lover answered:

"I did remember you, but kept my gift to offer when we were alone."

"That is so like you! A thousand thanks. Now give it to me."

With a pretty gesture of entreaty, she held out her little hand, and the young man put his own into it, saying, earnestly:

"I offer this in all sincerity, and ask you to be my wife."

A brilliant smile flashed over her face, and something like triumph shone in her eyes as she clasped the hand in both her own, exclaiming with mingled delight and incredulity:

"You ask that of *me*, the *danseuse*, friendless, poor and humble? Do you *mean* it, Allan? Shall I go with you to Scotland, and be 'my lady' by-and-by? *Ciel!* it is incredible."

"Yes, I mean it. Passion has conquered pride, and for love's sake I can forgive, forget anything but degradation. That you shall never know; and I thank Victor that his jealous vigilance has kept you innocent through all the temptation of a life like yours. The viscount offers you an establishment and infamy; I offer you an honorable name and a home with my whole heart. Which shall it be, Virginie?"

She looked at him keenly—saw a young and comely face, now flushed and kindled with the ardor of a first love. She had seen many such waiting for her smile; but beyond this she saw truth in the honest eyes, read a pride on the forehead that no dishonor could stain, and knew that she might trust one whose promises were never broken. With a little cry of joy and gratitude she laid her face down on the generous hand that gave so much, and thanked Heaven that the desire of her life was won. Gathering her close, Allan whispered, with a soft cheek against his own:

"My darling, we must be married at once, or Victor will discover and betray us. All is arranged, and this very night we may quit Paris for a happy honeymoon in Italy. Say yes, and leave the rest to me."

"It is impossible! I cannot leave my possessions behind me; I must prepare a little. Wait till to-morrow, and give me time to think."

She spoke resolutely; the young man saw that his project would fail unless he yielded the point, and controlling his impatience, he modified his plan and won her by the ease of that concession.

"I will not hurry you, but, Virginie, we must be married to-night, because all is prepared, and delay may ruin us. Once mine, Victor has no control over you, and my friends will have no power to part us. Grant me this boon, and you shall leave Paris when you will."

She smiled, and agreed to it, but did not confess that the chief reason of her reluctance to depart so suddenly was a desire to secure the salary which on the morrow would be paid her for a most successful but laborious season. Mercenary, vain and hollow-hearted as she was, there was something so genuine in the perfect confidence, the ardent affection of her lover, that it won her respect and seemed to gift the rank which she aspired to attain with a redoubled charm.

"Now tell me your plan, and tell me rapidly, lest Victor should divine that we are plotting and disturb us," she said, with the look of exultation still gleaming in her eyes.

"It is this. Your engagement ends to-night, and you have made no new one. You have spoken of going into the country to rest, and when you vanish people will believe that you have gone suddenly to rusticate. Victor is too proud to complain, and we will leave a penitent confession behind us to appease him."

"He will be terrible, Allan."

"You have a right to choose, I to protect you. Have no fear; we shall be far beyond his reach when he discovers his mistake. I asked you of him honorably once, and he refused with anger."

"He never told me that. We are requited, so let him rave. What next?"

"When your last dance is over, change your dress quickly, and instead of waiting here for your cousin, as usual, slip out by the private door. I shall be there with a carriage, and while Victor is detained searching for you, we will be married, and I shall take you home to gather up these precious possessions of yours. You will do this, Virginie?"

"Yes."

"Your courage will not fail when I am gone, and some fear of Victor keep you?"

"Bah! I fear nothing now."

"Then I am sure of you, and I swear you never shall regret your confidence; for as soon as my place is made at home, you shall be received there as my honored wife."

"Are you very sure that you *will* be forgiven?" she asked, anxiously, as if weighing possibilities even then.

"I *am* sure of pardon after the first anger is over, for they love me too much to disinherit or banish me, and they need only see you to be won at once."

"This marriage, Allan—it will be a true one? You will not deceive me; for if I leave Victor I shall have no friend in the wide world but you."

The most disloyal lover could not have withstood the pleading look, the gesture of appeal which accompanied her words, and this one, who harbored no treachery, assured her with solemn protestations and the most binding vows.

A few moments were spent in maturing their plan, and Virginie was just leaving him with the words "To-morrow" on her lips, when an animated flame of fire seemed to dart into the room. It was a youth whose scarlet and silver costume glowed and glittered in the light, as with one marvellous bound he crossed the room and stood before them. Supple, sinewy and slight was the threatening figure which they saw; dark and defiant the face, with fierce, black eyes, frowning brows, and the gleam of set teeth between lips parted by a muttered malediction. Lovely as the other apparition had been, this was far more striking, for it seemed full of the strong grace and beauty of the fallen angel whom it represented. The *pose* was magnificent; a flaming crown shone in the dark hair, and filmy pinions of scarlet flecked with silver drooped from shoulder to heel. So fiery and fierce he looked, it was little wonder that one lover drew back and the other uttered an exclamation of surprise. Instantly recovering herself, however, Virginie broke into a blithe laugh and airily twirled away beyond the reach of Victor's outstretched hand.

"It is late; you are not dressed—you will be disgraced by a failure. Go!" he said, with an air of command.

"Au revoir, monsieur; I leave Paris with you." And as she uttered the words with a glance that pointed their double meaning, Virginie vanished.

Turning to the long mirror behind him, the young gentleman replaced his hat, resettled in his button-hole the flower just given him, tranquilly drew on his gloves, saying as he strolled toward the door:

"I shall return to my box to witness this famous Pas des Deesses. Virginie, Lucille and Clotilde, upon my word, Paris, you will find it difficult to decide upon which of the three goddesses to bestow the golden apple."

Not a word spoke Victor, till the sound of steps died away. Then he departed to his dressing-room, moodily muttering as he went:

"To-morrow, she said. They intend to meet somewhere. Good! I will prevent *that*. There has been enough of this—it must end, and Virginie shall keep her promise. I will stand guard to-night and watch them well to-morrow."

Three hours later, breathless and pale with fatigue and rage, Victor sprung up the stairs leading to his cousin's chamber in the old house by the Seine. A lamp burned in a niche beside her door, a glass of wine and a plate of fruit stood there, also, waiting, as usual, for him. As his eye fell upon these objects a long sigh of relief escaped him.

"Thank Heaven, she has come home, then. Yet hold! It may be but a ruse to prevent my discovering her absence. Virginie! cousin! are you there?"

He struck upon the door lightly at first, then vehemently, and to his great joy a soft, sleepy voice replied:

"Who calls?"

"It is Victor. I missed you, searched for you, and grew anxious when I found you gone. Why did you not wait, as usual?"

"Mademoiselle Clotilde offered me a seat in her carriage, and I gladly accepted it. She was set down first, and it is a long distance there and back, you know. Now let me rest; I am very tired."

"Good-night, my heart," answered Victor, adding, in a tone of pain and tenderness, as he turned away, "Mon Dieu! how I love that girl, and how she tortures me! Rest well, my cousin; I shall guard your sleep."

Hour after hour passed, and still a solitary figure paced to and fro with noiseless feet along the narrow terrace that lay between the ancient house and the neglected garden sloping to the river. Dawn was slowly breaking in the east when the window of Virginie's chamber opened cautiously, and her charming head appeared. The light was very dim, and shadows still lay dark upon the house; but Victor, coming from the water gate whither he had been drawn by the sound of a passing boat, heard the soft movement, glided behind a group of shrubs and eyed the window keenly, remembering that now it was "to-morrow." For a moment the lovely face leaned out, looking anxiously across terrace, street and garden. The morning air seemed to strike cold on her uncovered shoulders, and with a shiver she was drawing back, when a man's hand laid a light cloak about her, and a man's head appeared beside her own.

"Imprudent! Go quickly, or Victor will be stirring. At noon I shall be ready," she said, half aloud, and as she withdrew the curtain fell.

With the bound of a wounded tiger, Victor reached the terrace, and reckless of life or limb, took the short road to his revenge. The barred shutters of a lower window, the carved ornaments upon the wall, and the balcony that hung above, all offered foot- and hand-hold for an agile climber like himself, as, creeping upward like a stealthy shadow, he peered in with a face that would have appalled the lovers had they seen it. They did not, for standing near the half-opened door, they were parting as Romeo and Juliet parted, heart to heart, cheek to cheek, and neither saw nor heard the impending doom until the swift stroke fell. So sure, so sudden was it, that Virginie knew nothing, till, with a stifled cry, her lover started, swayed backward from her arms, and dyeing her garments with his blood, fell at her feet, stabbed through the heart.

An awful silence followed, for Virginie uttered no cry of alarm, made no gesture of flight, showed no sign of guilt; but stood white and motionless as if turned to stone. Soon Victor grasped her arm and hissed into her ear:

"Traitoress! I could find it in my heart to lay you there beside him. But no; you shall live to atone for your falsehood to me and mourn your lover."

Something in the words or tone seemed to recall her scattered senses and rouse her to a passionate abhorrence of him and of his deed. She wrenched herself from his hold, saying vehemently, though instinctively below her breath:

"No; it is you who shall atone! He was my husband, not my lover. Look if I lie!"

He did look as a trembling hand was stretched toward him over that dead form. On it he saw a wedding-ring, and in it the record of the marriage which in a single night had made her wife and widow. With an ejaculation of despair he snatched the paper as if to tear and scatter it; but some sudden thought flashed into his mind, and putting the record in his bosom, he turned to Virginie with an expression that chilled her by its ominous resolve.

"Listen," he said, "and save yourself while you may; for I swear that if you raise your voice, lift your hand against me, or refuse to obey me now, that I will denounce you as the murderer of that man. You were last seen with him, were missed by others beside me last night. There lies his purse; here is the only proof of your accursed marriage, and if I call in witnesses, which of us looks most like an assassin, you or I?"

She listened with a terror-stricken face, glanced at her bloody garments, knew that she was in the power of a relentless man, and clasped her hands with a gesture of mute supplication and submission.

"You are wise," he said. "Apart we are both in danger; together we may be strong and safe. I have a plan—hear it and help me to execute it, for time is life now. You have spoken to many of going into the country; it shall be so, but we will give our departure the appearance of a sudden thought, a lover's flight. Leave everything behind you but money and jewels. That purse will more than pay the sum you cannot claim. While I go to fling this body into the river to tell no tales till we are safe, do you destroy all traces of the deed, prepare yourself for travelling, and guard the room in silence until I come. Remember! One sign of treachery, one cry for help, and I denounce you where my word will have much weight and yours none."

She gave him her hand upon the dark bargain, and covering up her face to hide the tragic spectacle, she heard Victor leave the room with his awful burden.

When he returned, she was nearly ready, for though moving like one in a ghastly dream, bewildered by the sudden loss of the long coveted, just won prize, and daunted by the crime whose retribution a word might bring upon herself, she still clung to life and its delights with the tenacity of a selfish nature, a shallow heart. While she finished her hasty preparations, Victor set the room in order, saw that the red witnesses of the crime were burnt, and dashed off a gay note to a friend, enclosing money for all obligations, explaining their sudden flight as an innocent ruse to escape congratulations on their hasty marriage, and promising to send soon for such possessions as were left behind them. Then, leaving the quiet room to be forever haunted by the memory of a night of love, and sin, and death, like two pale ghosts they vanished in the dimness of the dawn.

Chapter II

Earl's Mystery

Four ladies sat in the luxurious privacy of Lady Lennox's boudoir, wiling away the listless hour before dinner with social chat. Dusk was deepening, but firelight filled the room with its warm glow, flickering on mirrors, marbles, rich hues and graceful forms, and bathing the four faces with unwonted bloom.

Stately Diana Stuart leaned on the high back of the chair in which sat her aunt and chaperone, the Honorable Mrs. Berkeley. On the opposite side of the wide hearth a slender figure lounged in the deep corner of a couch, with a graceful abandon which no Englishwoman could hope to imitate. The face was hidden by a hand screen, but a pair of ravishing feet were visible, and a shower of golden hair shone against the velvet pillow. Directly before the fire sat Lady Lennox, a comely, hospitable matron, who was never so content as when she could gather her female guests about her and refresh herself with a little good-natured gossip. She had evidently been discussing some subject which interested her hearers, for all were intently listening, and all looked eager for more, when she said, with a significant nod:

"Yes, I assure you there *is* a mystery in that family. Lady Carrick has known them all her life, and from what she has dropped from time to time, I quite agree with her in believing that something has gone wrong."

"Dear Lady Lennox, pray go on! There is nothing so charming as a family mystery when the narrator can give a clue to her audience as I am sure you can," exclaimed the lady on the couch in a persuasive voice which had a curious ring to it despite its melody.

"That is just what I cannot do, Mrs. Vane. However, I will gladly tell you all I know. This is in strict confidence, you understand."

"Certainly!" "Upon my honor!" "Not a word shall pass my lips!" murmured the three listeners, drawing nearer, as Lady Lennox fixed her eyes upon the fire and lowered her voice.

"It is the custom in ancient Scottish families for the piper of the house, when dying, to put the pipes into the hand of the heir to name or title. Well, when old Dougal lay on his deathbed, he called for Earl, the fourth son—"

"What a peculiar name!" interrupted Mrs. Berkeley.

"It was not his proper name, but they called him so because of his strong resemblance to the pictures of the great earl, Black Douglas. They continue to call him so to this day, and I really don't know whether his name is Allan, Archie or Alex, for they are all family names, and one cannot remember which belongs to whom. Now the eldest son was Robert, and Dougal should have called for him, because the title and the fortune always go to the eldest son of the eldest son. But no, Earl must come; and into his hands the pipes were put, with a strange prophecy that no heir would enjoy the title but a year until it came to him."

"Was the prediction fulfilled?" asked Diana.

"To the letter. This was five or six years ago, and not one year has passed without a death, till now a single feeble life is all that stands between Earl and the title. Nor was this all. When his father died, though he had laid insensible for days, he rose up in his bed at the last and put upon Earl's hand the iron ring which is their most precious heirloom, because it belonged to the ancient earl. This, too, should have gone to Robert; but the same gift of second sight seemed given to the father as to the servant, and these strange things made a deep impression upon the family, as you may suppose."

"That is the mystery, then?" said Mrs. Vane, with an accent of disappointment in her voice.

"Only a part of it. I am not superstitious, so the prediction and all the rest of it don't trouble me much, but what occurred afterward does. When Earl was one-and-twenty he went abroad, was gone a year, and came home so utterly and strangely changed that every one was amazed at the alteration. The death of a cousin just then drew people's attention from him, and when that stir was over the family seemed to be reconciled to the sad change in him. Nothing was said, nothing ever transpired to clear up the matter; and to this day he has remained a cold, grave, peculiar man, instead of the frank, gay fellow he once was."

"He met with some loss in an affair of the heart, doubtless. Such little tragedies often mar a young man's peace for years—perhaps for life."

As Mrs. Vane spoke she lowered her screen, showing a pair of wonderfully keen and brilliant eyes fixed full upon Diana. The young lady was unconscious of this searching glance as she intently regarded Lady Lennox, who said:

"That is my opinion, though Lady Carrick never would confirm it, being hampered by some promise to the family, I suspect, for they are almost as high and haughty now as in the olden time. There was a vague rumor of some serious entanglement at Paris, but it was hushed up at once, and few gave it credence. Still, as year after year passed, and Earl remains unmarried, I really begin to fear there was some truth in what I fancied an idle report."

Something in this speech seemed to ruffle Mrs. Berkeley; a look of intelligence passed between her and her niece as she drew herself up, and before Diana could speak, the elder lady exclaimed, with an air of mystery:

"Your ladyship does Mr. Douglas great injustice, and a few months, weeks, perhaps, will quite change your opinion. We saw a good deal of him last season before my poor brother's death took us from town, and I assure you that he is free to address any lady in England. More I am not at liberty to say at present."

Lady Lennox looked politely incredulous, but Diana's eyes fell and a sudden color bathed her face in a still deeper bloom than that which the firelight shed over it. A slight frown contracted Mrs. Vane's beautiful brows as she watched the proud girl's effort to conceal the secret of her heart. But the frown faded to a smile of intelligent compassion as she said, with a significant glance that stung Diana like an insult:

"Dear Miss Stuart, pray take my screen. This glowing fire is ruining your complexion."

"Thank you. I need no screens of any sort."

There was a slight emphasis upon the "I," and a smile of equal significance curled her lips. If any taunt was intended it missed its mark, for Mrs. Vane only assumed a more graceful *pose*, saying with a provoking little air of superior wisdom:

"There you are wrong, for our faces are such traitors, that unless we have learned the art of self-control, it is not best for us to scorn such harmless aids as fans, screens and veils. Emotions are not wellbred, and their demonstrations are often as embarrassing to others as to ourselves."

"That, doubtless, is the reason why you half conceal your face behind a cloud of curls. It certainly is a most effectual mask at times," replied Diana, pushing back her own smooth bands of hair.

"Thanks for the suggestion. I wonder it never occurred to me before," sweetly answered Mrs. Vane, adding, as she gathered up the dishevelled locks, "My poor hair is called a great ornament, but indeed it is a great trial both to Gabrielle and to myself."

Lady Lennox touched a long tress that rolled down the pillow, saying, with motherly admiration:

"My dear, I promised Mrs. Berkeley she should see this wonderful hair of yours, for she could not believe my account of it. The dressing-bell will ring directly, so you may gratify us without making more work for Gabrielle."

"Willingly, dear Lady Lennox; anything for you!"

As she spoke with affectionate good will, Mrs. Vane rose, drew out a comb or two, and a stream of golden hair rippled far below her knee. Mrs. Berkeley exclaimed, and Diana praised, while watching with a very natural touch of envy the charming picture the firelight showed her. In its full glow stood Mrs. Vane; against the deep purple of her dress glittered the golden mass, and a pair of lovely hands parted the shining veil from a face whose beauty was as peculiar and alluring as the mingled spirit and sweetness of her smile.

"A thousand pardons! I thought your ladyship was alone."

A deep voice broke the momentary silence, and a tall figure paused upon the threshold of the softly opened door. All started, and with a little cry of pleasure and surprise, Lady Lennox hurried forward to greet her guest.

"My dear Earl, this is a most inhospitable welcome. George should have apprised me of your arrival."

"He is a lazy fellow, as he bade me find you here. I tapped, but receiving no reply, fancied the room empty and peeped to make sure. Pray accept my apologies; and put me out if I intrude."

The voice of Mr. Douglas was remarkably calm, his manner stately yet cordial, and his dark eyes went rapidly from face to face with a glance that seemed to comprehend the scene at once.

"Not in the least," said Lady Lennox, heartily. "Let me present you to Mrs. Berkeley, Miss Stuart, and—why, where is she? The poor little woman has run away in confusion, and must receive your apologies by-and-by."

"We must run away, also, for it is quite time to dress." And with a most gracious smile Mrs. Berkeley led her niece away before the gentleman should have time to note her flushed face and telltale eyes.

"You did not mention the presence of those ladies in your ladyship's letter," began Douglas, as his hostess sat down and motioned him to do likewise.

"They came unexpectedly, and you have met before, it seems. You never mentioned that fact, Earl," said Lady Lennox, with a sharp glance.

"Why should I? We only met a few times last winter, and I quite forgot that you knew them. But pray tell me who was the fair one with golden locks, whom I frightened away?"

"The widow of Colonel Vane."

"My dear lady, do you mean to tell me that child is a widow?"

"Yes; and a very lovely one, I assure you. I invited you here expressly to fall in love with her, for George and Harry are too young."

"Thank you. Now be so kind as to tell me all about her, for I knew Vane before he went to India."

"I can only tell you that he married this lady when she was very young, took her to India, and in a year she returned a widow."

"I remember hearing something of an engagement, but fancied it was broken off. Who was the wife?"

"A Montmorenci; noble but poor, you know. The family lost everything in the revolution, and never regained their former grandeur. But one can see at a glance that she is of high birth—high enough to suit even a Douglas."

"Ah, you know our weakness, and I must acknowledge that the best blood in France is not to be despised by the best blood in Scotland. How long have you known her?"

"Only a few months; that charming Countess Camareena brought her from Paris, and left her when she returned. Mrs. Vane seemed lonely for so young a thing; her family are all gone, and she made herself so agreeable, seemed so grateful for any friendship, that I asked her here. She went into very little society in London, and was really suffering for change and care."

"Poor young lady! I will do my best to aid your friendly purpose—for Vane's sake, if not for her own," said Douglas, evidently continuing the subject, lest her ladyship should revert to the former one.

"That reminds me to give you one warning: Never speak to her or before her of the colonel. He died three or four years ago; but when I mentioned him, she implored me to spare her all allusion to that unhappy past, and I have done so. It is my belief that he was not all she believed him to be, and she may have suffered what she is too generous to complain of or confess."

"I doubt that; for when I knew him, though weak on some points, Vane was an excellent fellow. She wears no weeds, I observe."

"You have a quick eye, to discover that in such an instant," replied Lady Lennox, smiling.

"I could scarcely help looking longest at the most striking figure of the group."

"I forgive you for it. She left off her weeds by my advice, for the sombre colors seemed to oppress and sadden her. Three or four years is long enough to mourn one whom she did not wholly love, and she is too young to shroud herself in sables for a lifetime."

"Has she fortune?"

"The colonel left her something handsome, I suspect, for she keeps both man and maid, and lives as becomes her rank. I ask no questions, but I feel deeply for the poor child, and do my best for her. Now tell me about home, and your dear mother."

Earl obeyed, and entertained his hostess till the dressing-bell rang.

Chapter III

The Iron Ring

When Douglas entered the drawing-rooms, he was instantly seized upon by Major Mansfield, and while he stood listening with apparent interest to that gentleman's communications, he took a survey of the party before him. The elder ladies were not yet down; Harry Lennox was worshipping Diana with all the frank admiration of a lad of eighteen, and Mrs. Vane was pacing up and down the rooms on the arm of George Lennox, the young master of the house. Few little women would have appeared to advantage beside the tall guardsman: but Mrs. Vane moved with a dignity that seemed to add many inches to her almost fairy-like stature, and make her a fit companion for her martial escort. Everything about her was peculiar and piquant. Her dress was of that vivid, silvery green, which is so ruinous to any but the purest complexion, so ravishing when worn by one whose fresh bloom defies all hues. The skirt swept long behind her, and the Pompadour waist, with its flowing sleeves, displayed a neck and arms of dazzling fairness, half concealed by a film of costly lace. No jewels but an antique opal ring, attached by a slender chain to a singular bracelet, or wide band of enchased gold. A single deep-hued flower glowed on her bosom, and in that wonderful hair of hers, a chaplet of delicate ferns seemed to gather back the cloud of curls, and encircle coil upon coil of glossy hair, that looked as if it burdened her small head.

The young man watched her so intently that the major soon observed his pre-occupation, and paused in the middle of his account of a review, to ask, good-naturedly:

"Well, what do you think of the bewitching widow?"

"She reminds me of a little green viper," replied Douglas, coolly.

"The deuce she does! What put such an odd fancy into your head?" asked the major.

"The color of her gown, her gliding gait, her brilliant eyes, and poor George's evident fascination."

"Faith! I see the resemblance, and you've expressed my feeling exactly. Do you know I've tried to fall in love with that woman, and, upon my soul, I can't do it!"

"She does not care to fascinate you, perhaps."

"Neither does she care to charm George, as I happen to know; yet you see what a deuce of a state he's getting into."

"His youth prevents his seeing the danger before it is too late; and there you have the advantage, major."

"We shall see how you will prosper, Douglas; for you are neither a lad of twenty, like George, nor an old fellow of forty, like me, and, if rumor does not lie, you have had 'experiences,' and understand womankind."

Though he spoke in a tone of raillery, the major fixed a curious eye upon his companion's countenance. But the dark, handsome face remained inscrutably calm, and the only answer he received was a low—

"Hush! they are coming. Present me, and I'll see what I can make of her."

Now Douglas was undoubtedly the best *parti* of the season, and he knew it. He was not a vain man, but an intensely proud one—proud of his ancient name, his honorable race, his ancestral home, his princely fortune; and he received the homage of both men and women as his due. Great, therefore, was his surprise at the little scene which presently occurred, and very visible was his haughty displeasure.

Lennox and his fair companion approached, the one bending his tall head to listen ardently, the other looking up with a most tempting face, as she talked rapidly, after softening a hard English phrase by an entrancing accent. The major presented his friend with much *empressement*, and Douglas was prepared to receive the gracious greeting which women seldom failed to give him. But scarcely pausing in her progress, Mrs. Vane merely glanced at him, as his name was mentioned, returned his bow with a slight inclination, and rustled on as if quite oblivious that a direct descendant of the great Scotch earl had been presented to her.

The major stifled an irrepressible laugh at this unexpected rebuff, and took a malicious pleasure in watching his friend's eye kindle, his attitude become more stately as he talked on, and deigned to take no notice of an act which evidently much annoyed and amazed him. Just then Lady Lennox entered, and dinner was announced. George beckoned, and Douglas reluctantly joined him.

"As host, I am obliged to take Mrs. Berkeley down; Harry has monopolized Miss Stuart, and the major belongs to my mother—so I must reluctantly relinquish Mrs. Vane to you."

Being a wellbred man, Douglas could only bow, and offer his arm. Mrs. Vane made George happy by a smile, as he left her, then turned to Douglas with a "May I trouble you?" as she gave him her fan and handkerchief to hold, while she gathered up her train and took his arm, as unconcernedly as if he had been a footman. Though rather piqued by her nonchalance, Douglas found something half amusing, half captivating in her demeanor; for, much as he had been courted and admired, few women were ever quite at ease with the highborn gentleman, whose manners were so coldly charming, whose heart seemed so invulnerable. It was a new sensation to be treated like other men, and set to serve an imperious lady, who leaned upon his arm as if she needed its support, and tranquilly exacted the small courtesies which hitherto had been left to his own good will and pleasure to offer.

Whatever the secret of his past might be, and however well he might conceal his real self behind a grave demeanor, Douglas had not yet lost his passion for beautiful women, and though no word was spoken during the short transit from drawing-room to dinner-table, the power of loveliness and womanhood made itself felt beyond a doubt. The touch of a fair hand on his arm, the dazzle of white shoulders at his side, the soft scent of violets shaken from the folds of lace and cambric which he held, the glimpse of a dainty foot, and the glance of a vivacious eye, all made the little journey memorable. When they took their places, the hauteur had melted from his manner, the coldness from his face, and, with his courtliest air, he began a conversation which soon became absorbing—for Mrs. Vane talked with the grace of a Frenchwoman, and the intelligence of an Englishwoman.

When the gentlemen rejoined the ladies, they were found examining some antique jewels, which Lady Lennox had been prevailed upon to show.

"How well those diamonds look in Diana's dark hair. Ah, my dear, a coronet becomes you vastly. Does it not?" said Mrs. Berkeley, appealing to Douglas, who was approaching.

"So well, that I hope you will soon see one rightfully there, madam," he answered, with a glance that made Diana's eyes fall, and Mrs. Berkeley look radiant.

Mrs. Vane saw the look, divined its meaning, and smiled a strange smile, as she looked down upon the jewels that strewed her lap. Mrs. Berkeley mistook her attitude for one of admiration and envy, and said:

"You wear no ornaments but flowers, I observe; from choice, doubtless, for, as you are the last of your race, you must possess many of the family relics."

Mrs. Vane looked up, and answered with an indescribable mixture of simplicity and dignity:

"I wear flowers, because I have no other ornaments. My family paid the price of loyalty with both life and fortune; but I possess one jewel which I value above all these—a noble name."

A banished princess might have so looked, so spoken, as, gathering up the glittering mass in her white hands, she let it fall again, with an air of gentle pride. Douglas gave her a glance of genuine admiration, and Diana took the diamonds from her hair, as if they burdened her. Mrs. Berkeley saw that her shot had failed, but tried again, only to be more decidedly defeated.

"Very prettily done, my dear; but I really thought you were going to say that your most valuable jewel was the peculiar bracelet you wear. Is there any charming legend or mystery concerning it? I fancied so, because you never take it off, however out of taste it may be; and otherwise, your dress is always perfect."

"I wear it in fulfilment of a vow, and the beauty of the ring atones for the ugliness of the bracelet. Does it not?"

As she spoke, Mrs. Vane extended an exquisitely moulded arm and hand to Douglas, who answered with most unusual gallantry:

"The beauty of the arm would render any fetter an ornament."

He bent to examine the jewel, as he spoke, and Mrs. Vane whispered, below her breath:

"You have offended Diana; pray make your peace. I should be desolated to think my poor arm had estranged you, even for an hour."

So entirely was he thrown off his guard by this abrupt address, that he whispered, eagerly:

"Do my actions interest her? Have I any cause for hope? Does she—"

There he paused, recovered his self-possession, but not his countenance—for an angry flush stained his dark cheek, and he fixed a look upon Mrs. Vane that would have daunted any other woman. She did not seem to see it, for her head drooped till her face was hidden, and she sat absently playing with the little chain that shone against her hand. George Lennox looked

fiercely jealous; Diana turned pale; Mrs. Berkeley frowned, and good, unconscious Lady Lennox said, blandly:

"Apropos to heirlooms and relics, I was telling these ladies about your
famous iron ring, Earl. I wish you had it here to show them."

"I am happy to be able to gratify your ladyship's wish. I never leave home
without it, for I use it as my seal. I will ring for it."

Mrs. Vane lifted her head, with an air of interest, as Douglas gave an
order, and his servant presently put a small, steel-bound case into his hand.
Opening this with a key that hung upon his watch-guard, he displayed the
famous relic. Antique, rusty and massive it was, and on its shield the boar's
head, and the motto of the house.

"You say you use this as a signet ring; why do you not have your arms cut
on some jewel, and set in a more graceful setting? This device is almost
effaced, and the great ring anything but ornamental to one's hand or chate-
laine," said Mrs. Vane, curiously examining the ring, as it was passed to her.

"Because I am superstitious, and believe that an especial virtue lies in this
ancient bit of iron. The legend goes that no harm can befall its possessor,
and as I have gone scathless so far, I hold fast to the old faith."

As Douglas turned to hear and answer Mrs. Vane's question, Harry
Lennox, with the freedom of a boy, had thrown back the lid of the case,
which had been opened with peculiar care, and, lifting several worn papers,
disclosed two objects that drew exclamations of surprise from several of the
party. A satin slipper, of fairy-like proportions, with a dull, red stain upon its
sole, and what looked like a ring of massive gold, till the lad lifted it, when
coil after coil unwound, till a long curl of human hair touched the ground.

"My faith! that is the souvenir of the beautiful *danseuse*, Virginie Varens,
about whom you bored me with questions, when you showed me that several
years ago," said the major, staring with all his eyes.

Mrs. Vane had exclaimed with the rest, but her color faded perceptibly,
her eye grew troubled, and when Harry leaned toward her to compare the
long tress with her own, she shrunk back with a shudder. Diana caught a
muttered ejaculation from Douglas, saw Mrs. Vane's discomposure, and fixed
a scrutinizing gaze upon her. But in a moment those obedient features
resumed their former calm, and, with a little gesture of contrition, Mrs. Vane
laid the long curl beside one of her own, saying, tranquilly:

"Pardon, that I betrayed an instinctive shrinking from anything plebeian.
The hair of the dancer is lighter than mine, you see; for this is pure gold, and

mine is fast deepening to brown. Let me atone for my rudeness thus; and believe me, I can sympathize, for I, too, have loved and lost."

While speaking, she had refolded the lock, and, tying it together with a little knot of ribbon from her dress, she laid it back into its owner's hand, with a soft glance and a delicate dropping of the voice at the last words. If it was a bit of acting, it was marvellously well done, and all believed it to be a genuine touch of nature. Diana looked consumed with curiosity, and Douglas answered, hastily:

"Thanks for the pity, but I need none. I never saw this girl, and as for love—"

He paused there, as if words unfit for time and place were about to pass his lips. His eye grew fierce, and his black brows lowered heavily, leaving no doubt on the mind of any observer that hate, not love, was the sentiment with which he now regarded the mysterious *danseuse*. An uncomfortable pause followed, as Douglas relocked the case, and put it in his pocket, forgetting, in his haste, the ring he had slipped upon his finger.

Feeling that some unpleasant theme had been touched upon, Lady Lennox asked for music. Diana coldly declined, but Mrs. Vane readily turned to the piano. The two elder ladies and the major went to chat by the fire; Lennox took his brother aside to administer a reproof, and Douglas, after a moment of moody thoughtfulness, placed himself beside Diana on the couch which stood just behind Mrs. Vane. She had begun with a brilliant overture, but suddenly passed to a softer movement, and filled the room with the whispering melody of a Venetian barcarole. This seeming caprice was caused by an intense desire to overhear the words of the pair behind her. But though she strained her keen ear to the utmost, she caught only broken fragments of their low-toned conversation, and these fragments filled her with disquiet.

"Why so cold, Miss Stuart? One would think you had forgotten me."

"I fancied the forgetfulness was yours."

"I never shall forget the happiest hours of my life. May I hope that you recall those days with pleasure?"

There was no answer, and a backward glance showed Mrs. Vane Diana's head bent low, and Douglas watching the deepening color on her half-averted cheek, with an eager, ardent glance. More softly murmured the boat song, and scarcely audible was the whispered entreaty:

"I have much to say; you will hear me to-morrow, early, in the park?"

A mute assent was given, and, with the air of a happy lover, Douglas left her, as if fearing to say more, lest their faces should betray them. Then the barcarole ended as suddenly as it begun, and Mrs. Vane resumed the stormy overture, playing as if inspired by a musical frenzy. So pale was she when she left the instrument, that no one doubted the fact of her needing rest, as, pleading weariness, she sank into a deep chair, and, leaning her head upon her hand, sat silent for an hour.

As they separated for the night, and Douglas stood listening to his young host's arrangements for the morrow, a singular-looking man appeared at the door of an ante-room, and, seeing them, paused where he stood, as if waiting for them to precede him.

"Who is that, George? What does he want?" said Douglas, drawing his friend's attention to the dark figure, whose gleaming eyes belied his almost servile posture of humility and respect.

"O, that is Mrs. Vane's man, Jitomar. He was one of the colonel's Indian servants, I believe. Deaf and dumb, but harmless, devoted and invaluable—*she* says. A treacherous-looking devil, to my mind," replied Lennox.

"He looks more like an Italian than an Indian, in spite of his Eastern costume and long hair. What is he after now?" asked Earl.

"Going to receive the orders of his mistress. I would gladly change places with him, heathen as he is, for the privilege of serving her. Good-night."

As George spoke, they parted, and while the dark servant watched Douglas going up the wide oaken stairs, he shook his clenched hand after the retreating figure, and his lips moved as if he muttered something low between his teeth.

A few moments afterward, as Earl sat musing over his fire, there came a tap at his door. Having vainly bidden the knocker to enter, he answered the summons, and saw Jitomar obsequiously offering a handkerchief. Douglas examined it, found the major's name, and, pointing out that gentleman's room, further down the corridor, he returned the lost article with a nod of thanks and dismissal. While he had been turning the square of cambric in his hands, the man's keen eyes had explored every corner of the room. Nothing seemed to escape them, from the ashes on the hearth, to a flower which Diana had worn, now carefully preserved in water; and once a gleam of satisfaction glittered in them, as if some desired object had met their gaze. Making a low obeisance, he retired, and Douglas went to bed, to dream waking dreams till far into the night.

The great-hall clock had just struck one, and sleep was beginning to conquer love, when something startled him wide awake. What it was he could not tell, but every sense warned him of some impending danger. Sitting up in his bed, he pushed back the curtains, and looked out. The night-lamp burned low, the fire had faded, and the room was full of dusky shadows. There were three doors; one led to the dressing-room, one to the corridor, and the third was locked on the outside. He knew that it opened upon a flight of narrow stairs, that communicated with the library, having been built for the convenience of a studious Lennox, long ago.

As he gazed about him, to his great amazement this door was seen to move. Slowly, noiselessly, it opened, with no click of lock, no creak of hinge. Almost sure of seeing some ghostly visitant enter, he waited, mute and motionless. A muffled hand and arm appeared, and, stretching to their utmost, seemed to take something from the writing-table that stood near this door. It was a human hand, and, with a single leap, Douglas was half way across the room. But the door closed rapidly, and as he laid his hand upon it, the key turned in the lock. He demanded who was there, but not a sound replied; he shook the door, but the lock held fast; he examined the table, but nothing seemed gone, till, with an ominous thrill, he missed the iron ring. On reaching his chamber, he had taken it off, meaning to restore it to its place; had laid it down, to put Diana's rose in water; had forgotten it, and now it was gone!

Flinging on dressing-gown and slippers, and taking a pistol from his travelling-case, he left his room. The house was quiet as a tomb, the library empty, and no sign of intruders visible, till, coming to the door itself, he found that the rusty lock had been newly oiled, for the rusty key turned noiselessly, and the hinges worked smoothly, though the dust that lay thickly everywhere, showed that this passage was still unused. Stepping into his room, Douglas gave a searching glance about him, and in an instant an expression of utter bewilderment fell upon his face, for there, on the exact spot which had been empty five minutes ago, there lay the iron ring!

Chapter IV

A Shred of Lace

Long before any of the other guests were down, Diana stole into the garden on her way to the park. Hope shone in her eyes, smiles sat on her lips, and her heart sang for joy. She had long loved in secret; had believed and despaired alternately, and now her desire was about to be fulfilled, her happiness assured by a lover's voice. Hurrying through the wilderness of autumn flowers, she reached the shrubbery that divided park and garden. Pausing an instant, to see if any one awaited her beyond, she gave a great start, and looked as if she had encountered a ghost.

It was only Mrs. Vane; she often took early strolls in the park, followed by her man; Diana knew this, but had forgotten it in her new bliss. She was alone now, and as she seemed unconscious of her presence, Diana would have noiselessly withdrawn, had not a glimpse of Mrs. Vane's face arrested and detained her. As if she had thrown herself down in a paroxysm of distress, sat Mrs. Vane, with both hands tightly clasped; her white lips were compressed, and in her eyes was a look of mingled pain, grief and despair. The most careless observer would have detected the presence of some great anxiety or sorrow, and Diana, made generous by the assurance of her own happiness, for the first time felt a touch of pity for the woman of whom she had been both envious and jealous. Forgetting herself, she hastened forward, saying, kindly:

"Are you suffering, Mrs. Vane? What can I do for you?"

Mrs. Vane started as if she had been shot, sprung to her feet, and, putting out her hands as if to keep the other off, cried, almost incoherently:

"Go back! go back, and save yourself! For me you can do nothing—it is too late!"

"Indeed, I hope not. Tell me your trouble, and let me help you if I can," urged Diana, shocked yet not alarmed by the wildness of Mrs. Vane's look and manner.

But she only clasped her hands before her face, saying, despairingly:

"You could help both of us—but at what a price!"

"No price will be too costly, if I can honorably pay it. I have been unjust, unkind; forgive it, and confide in me; for, indeed, I pity you."

"Ah, if I dared!" sighed Mrs. Vane. "It seems impossible, and yet I ought—for you, not I, will suffer most from my enforced silence."

She paused an instant, seemed to calm herself by strong effort, and, fixing her mournful eyes upon Diana, she said, in a strangely solemn and impressive manner:

"Miss Stuart, if ever a woman needed help and pity, it is I. You have misjudged, distrusted and disliked me; I freely forgive this, and long to save you, as I alone can do. But a sacred promise fetters me—I dare not break it; yet if you will pledge your word to keep this interview secret, I will venture to give you one hint, one warning, which may save you from destroying your peace forever. Will you give me this assurance?"

Diana shrunk back, disturbed and dismayed by the appeal and the requirement. Mrs. Vane saw her hesitation, and wrung her hands together in an agony of impotent regret:

"I knew it—I feared it! you will not trust me—you will not let me ease my conscience by trying to save another woman from the fate that darkens all my life. Go your way, then, and when the bitter hour comes, remember that I tried to save you from it, and you would not hear me."

"Stay, Mrs. Vane! I do trust you—I will listen; and I give you my word that I will conceal this interview. Speak quickly—I must go," cried Diana, won to compliance even against her wishes.

"Stoop to me—not even the air must hear what I breathe. Ask Allan Douglas the mystery of his life, before you marry him, else you will rue the hour that you became his wife."

"Allan Douglas! You know his name? You know the secret of his past?" exclaimed Diana, lost in wonder.

"My husband knew him, and I—Hush! some one is coming. Quick! escape into the park, or your face will betray you. I can command myself; I will meet and accost whoever comes."

Before the rapid whisper ended, Diana was gone, and when Douglas came hastening to his tryst, he, too, found Mrs. Vane alone—and he, too, paused a moment, surprised to see her there. But the picture he saw was a very different one from that which arrested Diana. Great indeed must have been Mrs. Vane's command of countenance, for no trace of agitation was visible, and never had she looked more lovely than now, as she stood with a handful of flowers in the white skirt of her dress, her bright hair blowing in the wind, her soft eyes fixed on vacancy, while a tranquil smile proved that her thoughts were happy ones. So young, so innocent, so blithe she looked, that Douglas involuntarily thought, with a touch of self-reproach:

"Pretty creature! what injustice my ungallant simile did her last night! I ask her pardon." Then aloud, as he approached, "Good-morning, Mrs. Vane. I am off for an early stroll."

With the shy grace, the artless glance of a child, she looked up at him, offering a flower, and saying, as she smilingly moved on:

"May it be a pleasant one."

It was not a pleasant one, however; and perhaps Mrs. Vane's wish had been sweetly ironical. Diana greeted her lover coldly, listened to his avowal with an air of proud reserve, that contrasted strangely with the involuntary betrayals of love and joy that escaped her. Entirely laying aside the chilly gravity, the lofty manner, which was habitual to him, Douglas proved that he could woo ardently, and forget the pride of the man in the passion of the lover. But when he sued for a verbal answer to his prayer, although he thought he read assent in the crimson cheek half turned away, the downcast eyes that would not meet his own, and the quick flutter of the heart that beat under his hand, he was thunderstruck at the change which passed over Diana. She suddenly grew colorless and calm as any statue, and, freeing herself from his hold, fixed a searching look upon him, while she said, slowly and distinctly:

"When you have told me the mystery of your life, I will give my answer to your love—not before."

"The mystery of my life!" he echoed, falling back a step or two, with such evident discomposure in face and manner, that Diana's heart sank within her, though she answered, steadily:

"Yes; I must know it, before I link my fate with yours."

"Who told you that I had one?" he demanded.

"Lady Lennox. I had heard the rumor before, but never gave it thought till she confirmed it. Now I wait for your explanation."

"It is impossible to give it; but I swear to you, Diana, that I am innocent of any act that could dishonor my name, or mar your peace, if it were known. The secret is not mine to tell; I have promised to keep it, and I cannot forfeit my word, even for your sake. Be generous; do not let mere curiosity or pique destroy my hopes, and make you cruel when you should be kind."

So earnestly he spoke, so tenderly he pleaded, that Diana's purpose wavered, and would have failed her, had not the memory of Mrs. Vane's strange warning returned to her, bringing with it other memories of other mysterious looks, hints and acts which had transpired since Douglas came. These recollections hardened her heart, confirmed her resolution, and gave her power to appear inexorable to the last.

"You mistake my motive, sir. Neither curiosity nor pique influenced me, but a just and natural desire to assure myself that in trusting my happiness to your keeping, I am not entailing regret upon myself, remorse upon you. I must know all your past, before I endanger my future; clear yourself from the suspicions that have long clung to you, and I am yours; remain silent, and we are nothing to each other from this day forth."

Her coldness chilled his passion, her distrust irritated his pride; all the old hauteur returned fourfold, his eye grew hard, his voice bitter, and his whole manner showed that his will was as inflexible as hers.

"Are you resolved on making this unjust, ungenerous test of my affection, Miss Stuart?"

"I am."

"You have no faith in my honor, then?—no consideration for the hard strait in which my promise places me?—no compassion for the loss I must sustain in losing the love, respect and confidence of the woman dearest to me?"

"Assure me that you are worthy of love, respect, confidence, and I gladly accord them to you."

"I cannot, in the way you demand. Will nothing else satisfy you?"

"Nothing!"

"Then, in your own words, we are nothing to one another from this day forth. Farewell, Diana!"

With an involuntary impulse, she put out her hand to detain him as he turned away. He took it, and, bending, kissed it, with a lingering fondness that nearly conquered her. The act, the look that accompanied it, the tremor of the lips that performed it, touched the poor girl's heart, and words of free acceptance were rising to her lips, when, as he bent, a miniature, suspended by a chain of mingled hair and gold, swung forward from its hiding-place in his breast, and though she saw no face, the haste with which he replaced it roused all her suspicions again, and redoubled all her doubts. Scorning herself for her momentary weakness, the gesture of recall was changed to one of dismissal, as she withdrew her hand, and turned from him, with a quiet—

"Farewell, then, forever!"

"One moment," he pleaded; "do not let us destroy the peace of both our lives by an unhappy secret which in no way but this can do us harm. Bear with me for a few days, Diana; think over this interview, remember my great love for you, let your own generous nature appeal to your pride, and perhaps time may show you that it is possible to love, trust and pardon me."

Glad of any delay which should spare her the pain of an immediate separation, she hesitated a moment, and then, with feigned reluctance, answered:

"My visit was to have ended with the coming week; I will not shorten it, but give you till then to reconsider your decision, and by a full confession secure your happiness and my own."

Then they parted—not with the lingering adieux of happy lovers, but coldly, silently, like estranged friends—and each took a different way back, instead of walking blissfully together, as they had thought to do.

"Why so *triste*, Diana? One would think you had seen a ghost in the night, you look so pale and solemn. And, upon my word, Mr. Douglas looks as if he had seen one also," said Mrs. Berkeley, as they all gathered about the breakfast-table, two hours later.

"I did see one," answered Douglas, generously distracting general attention from Diana, who could ill sustain it.

"Last night?" exclaimed Mrs. Berkeley, full of interest at once.

"Yes, madam—at one o'clock last night."

"How charming! Tell us all about it; I dote upon ghosts, yet never saw one," said Mrs. Vane.

Douglas narrated his adventure. The elder ladies looked disturbed, Diana incredulous; and Mrs. Vane filled the room with her silvery laughter, as Harry protested that no ghost belonged to the house, and George explained the mystery as being the nightmare.

"I never have it; neither do I walk in my sleep, and seldom dream," replied Douglas. "I perfectly remember rising, partially dressing, and going down to the library, up the private stairs, and examining the door. This may be proved by the key, now changed to my side of the lock, and the train of wax which dropped from my candle as I hurried along."

"What woke you?" asked Mrs. Vane.

"I cannot tell; some slight sound, probably, although I do not remember hearing any, and fancy it was an instinctive sense of danger."

"That door could not have been opened without much noise, for the key was rusted in the lock. We tried to turn it the other day, and could not, so were forced to go round by the great gallery to reach that room."

Diana spoke, and for the first time since they parted in the park, Douglas looked at and addressed her.

"You have explored the private passage, then, and tried the door? May I ask when?"

"Harry was showing us the house; anything mysterious pleased us, so we went up, tried the rusty key, and, finding it immovable, we came down again."

"Of whom was the party composed?"

"My aunt, Mrs. Vane, and myself, accompanied by Harry."

"Then I must accuse Harry of the prank, for both key and lock have been newly oiled, and the door opens easily and noiselessly, as you may prove, if you like. He must have had an accomplice among the house-maids, for it was a woman's hand that took the ring. She doubtless passed it to him, and while I was preparing to sally forth, both ran away—one to hide, the other to wait till I left my room, when he slipped in and restored the ring. Was that it, Hal?"

As Douglas spoke, all looked at Harry; but the boy shook his head, and triumphantly appealed to his brother.

"George will tell you that your accusation is entirely unjust; and as he sat up till dawn, writing poetry, I could not have left him without his knowledge."

"True, Hal—you had nothing to do with it, I know. Did you distinctly see the hand that purloined your ring, Earl?" asked Lennox, anxious to divert attention from the revelation of his poetical amusements.

"No; the room was dusky, and the hand muffled in something dark. But it was no ghostly hand, for as it was hastily withdrawn when I sprang up, the wrapper slipped aside, and I saw white human flesh, and the outlines of a woman's arm."

"Was it a beautiful arm?" asked Lennox, with his eyes upon Mrs. Vane's, which lay like a piece of sculptured marble against the red velvet cushion of her chair.

"Very beautiful, I should say; for in that hasty glimpse it looked too fair to belong to any servant, and when I found this hanging to the lock, I felt assured that my spirit was a lady, for house-maids do not wear anything like this, I fancy;" and Douglas produced a shred of black lace, evidently torn from some costly flounce or scarf.

The ladies put their heads together over the scrap, and all pronounced it quite impossible for any dressing-maid to have come honestly by such expensive trimming as this must have been.

"It looks as if it had belonged to a deeply scalloped flounce," said Mrs. Vane. "Who of us wears such? Miss Stuart, you are in black; have I not seen you with a trimming like this?"

"You forget—I wear no trimming but crape. This never was part of a flounce, it is the corner of a shawl. You see how unequally rounded the two sides are; and no flounce was ever scalloped so deeply as this," returned Diana.

"How acute you are, Di! It is, so I really believe. See how exactly this bit compares with the corner of my Shetland breakfast-shawl, made to imitate lace. Who wears a black lace shawl? Neither Di nor myself," said Mrs. Berkeley.

"Mrs. Vane often wears one."

Diana uttered the name with significance, and Douglas stirred a little, as if she had put into words some vague idea of his own. Mrs. Vane shrugged her shoulders, sipped her coffee, and answered, tranquilly:

"So does Lady Lennox; but I will bear all the suspicions of phantom folly, and when I dress for dinner will put on every rag of lace I possess, so that you may compare this bit, and prove me guilty if it gives you pleasure. Though what object I could have in running about in the dark, oiling door-locks, stealing rings and frightening gentlemen, is not as clear to me as it appears to be to you—probably because I am not as much interested in the sufferer."

Diana looked embarrassed, Lady Lennox grave, and, as if weary of the subject, Douglas thrust the shred of lace into his waistcoat pocket, and proposed a riding-party. Miss Stuart preferred driving her aunt in the pony-carriage, but Mrs. Vane accepted the invitation, and made George Lennox wretched by accepting the loan of one of Earl's horses in preference to his own, which she had ridden the day before. When she appeared, ready for the expedition, glances of admiration shone in the eyes of all the gentlemen, even the gloomy Douglas, as he watched her, wondering if the piquant figure before him could be the same that he had seen in the garden, looking like a lovely, dreaming child. Her black habit, with its velvet facings, set off her lithe figure to a charm; her hair shone like imprisoned sunshine through the scarlet net that held it, and her face looked bewilderingly brilliant and arch in the shadow of a cavalier hat, with its graceful plume.

As Douglas bent to offer his hand in mounting her, she uttered an exclamation of pain, and caught at his arm to keep herself from falling. Involuntarily he sustained her, and for an instant she leaned upon him, with her face hidden in his breast, as if to conceal some convulsion of suffering.

"My dear Mrs. Vane, what is it? Let me take you in—shall I call for help?" began Douglas, much alarmed. But she interrupted him, and, looking up with a faint smile, answered quietly, as she attempted to stand alone:

"It is nothing but a cramp in my foot. It will be over in a moment; Gabrielle fastened my boot too tightly—let me sit down, and I will loosen it."

"Allow me; lean upon my shoulder; it will take but a moment."

Down knelt Douglas, and, with one hand lightly touching his shoulder to steady herself, the other still closely folded, as if not yet out of pain, Mrs. Vane stood glancing from under her long lashes at Diana, who was waiting in the hall for her aunt, and observing the scene in the avenue with ill-concealed anxiety. The string was in a knot, and Douglas set about his little service very leisurely, for the foot and ankle before him were the most perfect he had ever seen. While so employed, Jitomar, Mrs. Vane's man, appeared, and, tossing him the gloves she had taken off, she signed to him to bid her maid bring her another pair, as some slight blemish in these had offended her fastidious taste. He comprehended with difficulty, it seemed, for words were useless to a deaf mute, and the motions of his mistress's hands appeared at first without meaning to him. The idea came with a flash, and, bowing, he bounded into the house, with his white robes streaming, and his scarlet slippers taking him along as if enchanted, while the grooms stared and wondered, and Mrs. Vane laughed.

Jitomar hurried to his lady's room, delivered his message, and while Gabrielle went down with a fresh pair of gloves, he enacted a curious little scene in the deserted chamber. Carefully unfolding the discarded gloves, he took from the inside of one of them the shred of lace that Douglas had put into his waistcoat pocket at the breakfast-table. He examined it with a peculiar smile; then, going to a tiger-skin rug that lay beside the bed, he lifted it, and produced a black lace shawl, which seemed to have been hastily hidden there. One corner was gone; but laying the torn bit in its place, it fitted exactly, and, as if satisfied, Jitomar refolded both, put them in his pocket, glided to his own room, prepared himself for going out, and, unob- served by any one, took the next train to London. Mrs. Vane meanwhile had effaced the memory of her first failure, by mounting her horse alone, with an elasticity and grace that filled her escort with astonishment and admiration. Laughing her enchanting laugh, she settled herself in the saddle, touched her hat to Lady Lennox, and cantered away with Douglas, while Harry followed far behind, for George had suddenly remembered that an engagement would prevent his joining them, having no mind to see Mrs. Vane absorbed by another.

As they climbed a long hill, Mrs. Vane suddenly paused in her witty badinage, and after a thoughtful moment, and a backward glance at Harry, who followed apparently out of earshot, she said, earnestly yet timidly:

"Mr. Douglas, I desire to ask a favor of you—not for myself, but for the sake of one who is dear to both of us."

"Mrs. Vane can ask no favor that I shall not be both proud and happy to grant for her own sake," returned Earl, eyeing her with much surprise.

"Well, then, I shall be most grateful if you will shun me for a few days; ignore my presence as far as possible, and so heal the breach which I fear I may unconsciously have caused between Miss Stuart and yourself."

"I assure you that you are mistaken regarding the cause of the slight coolness between us, and it is impossible to ignore the existence of Mrs. Vane, having once had the happiness of seeing her."

"Ah, you take refuge in evasion and compliment, as I feared you would; but it is my nature to be frank, and I shall compass my end by leaving you no subterfuge and no power to deny me. I met you both this morning, and read a happy secret in your faces; I hoped when next I saw you, to find your mutual happiness secured. But, no—I found you grave and cold; saw trouble in your eyes, jealousy and pain in Diana's. I have seen the latter sentiment in her eyes before, and could not but think that I was the unhappy cause of this estrangement. She is peculiar; she does not like me, will not let me love her, and wounds me in many ways. I easily forgive her, for she is not happy, and I long to help her, even against her will—therefore I speak to you."

"Again I assure you that you are wrong. Diana is jealous, but not of you alone, and she has placed me in a cruel strait. I, too, will be frank, and confess that she will not listen to me, unless I betray a secret that is not my own."

"You will not do this, having sworn to keep it?"

"Never! A Douglas cannot break his word."

"I comprehend now," said Mrs. Vane. "Diana wishes to test her power, and you rebel. It is but natural in both; yet I beseech you not to try her too much, because at a certain point she will become unmanageable. She comes of an unhappy race, and desperate things have been done in her family. Guard your secret, for honor demands it, but take my warning and shun me, that you may add nothing to the trouble she has brought upon herself."

"I have no wish to do so; but she also must beware of testing her power too severely, for I am neither a patient nor an humble man, and my will is inflexible when once I am resolved. She should see this, should trust me, and let us both be happy."

"Ah, if she truly loved, she would; for then one believes blindly, can think no ill, fear no wrong, desire no confidence that is not freely given. She does not know the bliss of loving with one's whole heart and soul, and asking no

happier fate than to live for the man whose affection makes a heaven anywhere."

They had paused on the brow of the hill to wait for Harry, and as she
spoke, Mrs. Vane's face kindled with a glow that made it doubly beautiful;
for voice, eyes, lips and gesture all betrayed how well *she* could love. Douglas
regarded her with a curious consciousness of attraction and repulsion, feeling
that had he met her before he saw and loved Diana, he never should have
given his peace into the keeping of that exacting girl. An involuntary sigh
escaped him; Mrs. Vane brightened instantly, saying:

"Nay, do not fall back into your gloomy mood again, or I shall think that
I have increased, not lessened, your anxiety. I came to cheer you if I could, for
though I have done with love myself, it gives me the sincerest satisfaction to
serve those who are just beginning to know its pleasant pain."

She was smiling as she spoke, but the lovely eyes lifted to her companion's
face were full of tears. Remembering her loneliness, her loss, and with a
grateful sense of all she desired to do for him, Douglas ungloved and offered
her his hand, with an impulsive gesture, saying, warmly:

"You are very kind; I thank you, and feel already comforted by the
thought that though I may have lost a lover, I have gained a friend."

Here Harry came up brimful of curiosity, for he had seen and heard more
than they knew. After this they all rode on together, and when Douglas
dismounted Mrs. Vane, she whispered:

"Remember, you are to shun me, no matter how pointedly. I shall forgive
you, and she will be the happier for our little ruse."

This speech, as well as the first uttered by Mrs. Vane when their serious
conversation began, was overheard by Harry, and when Diana carelessly asked
him if he had enjoyed his ride, he repeated the two remarks, hoping to gain
some explanation of them before he told his brother, whose cause he heartily
espoused. He knew nothing of Miss Stuart's love, and made her his confidant without a suspicion of the pang he was inflicting. She bade him forget
what he had heard, but could not do so herself, and all that day those two
sentences rang through her mind, unceasingly.

Pausing that evening, in the hall, to examine one of the ancient portraits
hanging there, Douglas heard a soft rustle, and turning, saw Mrs. Vane
entering, as if from a moonlight stroll on the balcony. The night was cool,
and over her head was drawn a corner of the black lace shawl that drooped
from her shoulders. Her dress of violet silk was trimmed with a profusion of

black lace, and wonderfully becoming to white skin and golden hair, was the delicate tint and its rich decoration. Douglas went to meet her, saying, as he offered his arm:

"You see how well I keep my word; now let me reward myself by taking you in. But, first, pray tell me if this is a picture of Sir Lionel?"

He led her to the portrait that had excited his curiosity, and while she told him some little legend of it, he still lingered, held as much by the charm of the living voice as by the exploits of the dead knight. Standing thus, arm-in-arm, alone, and engrossed in one another, neither, apparently, saw Diana pausing on the threshold of the library with an expression of deep displeasure in her face. Douglas did not see her; Mrs. Vane did, though not a sign betrayed it, except that in an instant her whole expression changed. As Douglas looked up at the picture, she looked up at him with love, grief, pain and pity visibly contending in her beautiful face; then suddenly withdrawing her arm, she said:

"I forgot, we are strangers now. Let me enter alone." And gliding from him with bent head, she passed into the drawing-room.

Much amazed at her abrupt flight, Earl looked after her, saw Diana watching him, and inexpressibly annoyed by the *contretemps*, he started, colored, bowed coldly, and followed Mrs. Vane without a word. For a moment, Diana lingered with her head in her hands, thinking disconsolately:

"What secret lies between them? She leaned and looked as if she had a right there. He is already more at ease with her than me, although they met but yesterday. Have they not met before? She asked some favor 'for the sake of one dear to both.' Who is it? He must shun her that some one may be happy, though deceived. Is that I? She knows his mystery, has a part in it, and I am to be kept blind. Wait a little! I too, can plot, and watch, and wait. I can read faces, fathom actions, and play a part, though my heart breaks in doing it."

All that evening she watched them; saw that Douglas did shun Mrs. Vane; also that he feigned unconsciousness of her own keen scrutiny, and seemed endeavoring to chase from her mind the memory of the morning's interview, or the evening's discovery. She saw Mrs. Vane act surprise, pique and displeasure at his seeming desertion, and console herself by making her peace with Lennox. To others, Diana appeared unusually animated and care-free, but never had an evening seemed so interminable, and never had she so gladly hailed the hour of separation.

She was standing by Lady Lennox, when Mrs. Vane came up to say good-night. Her ladyship did not like Diana, and did both love and pity the lonely little widow, who had endeared herself in so many ways. As she swept a curtsey with the old-fashioned reverence that her hostess liked, Lady Lennox drew her nearer, and kissed her with motherly affection, saying playfully, as she did so:

"No pranks to-night among the spirits, my dear, else these friends will think you and I are witches in good earnest."

"That reminds me, I have kept my promise, and Mr. Douglas can compare his telltale bit with my mother's, and, as you see, very precious in every respect."

Gravely exploring one pocket after another, Earl presently announced, with some chagrin, that the bit was lost, blown away while riding, probably. So nothing could be done, and Mrs. Vane was acquitted of lending her laces to the household ghost. Diana looked disappointed, and taking up a corner of the shawl, said, as she examined it narrowly:

"As I remember the shred, it matched this pattern exactly. It is a peculiar one, and I observed it well. I wish the bit were not lost, for if people play such games with your clothes they may take equal liberties with mine."

Seeing suspicion in her eyes, Mrs. Vane gathered the four corners of the shawl together, and with great care, spread each over her violet skirt before Diana. Not a fracture appeared, and when she had done the same with every atom of trimming on her dress, she drew her slender figure up with an air of proud dignity, asking, almost sternly:

"Am I acquitted of this absurd charge, Miss Stuart?"

Entirely disconcerted by the quickness with which her distrust had been seen and exposed, Diana could only look guilty, apologize, and find herself convicted of an unjust suspicion. Mrs. Vane received her atonement graciously, and wrapping her shawl about her, went away to bed, with a mischievous smile shining in her eyes, as she bowed to Douglas, whose glance followed her till the last glimpse of the violet dress disappeared.

Chapter V

~

Treason

The week passed gaily enough, externally, but to several of the party, it was a very dreary and very memorable week. George Lennox basked in the light of Mrs. Vane's smiles, and his mother began to hope that Douglas would not take her at her word, but leave her son to woo and win the bonny widow, if he could. Earl watched and waited for Diana to relent, pleading with his eyes, though never a word of submission or appeal passed his lips. And poor Diana, hoping to conquer him, silenced the promptings of her reason, and stood firm, when a yielding look, a tender word, would have overcome his pride, and healed the breach. She suffered much, but told no one her pain till the last day came. Then, driven by the thought that a few hours would seal her fate, she resolved to appeal to Mrs. Vane. She knew the mystery; she professed to pity her. She was a woman, and to her this humiliation would not be so hard, this confession so impossible.

Diana haunted the hall and drawing-rooms all that morning, hoping to find Mrs. Vane alone. At last, just before lunch, she caught her playing with Earl's spaniel, while she waited for Lennox to bring her hat from the garden seat where she had left it.

"Be so kind as to take a turn with me on the balcony, Mrs. Vane. I wish much to say a few words to you," began Diana, with varying color and anxious eyes, as she met her at the great-hall door.

"With pleasure. Give me your arm, and let us have our little chat quite comfortably together. Can I do anything for you, my dear Miss Stuart? Pray speak freely, and, believe me, I desire to be your friend."

So kind, so cordial was the tone, the look, that poor Diana felt comforted at once; and bending her stately head to the bright one at her side, she said, with a sad humility, which proved how entirely her love had subdued her pride:

"I hope so, Mrs. Vane, for I need a friend. You, and you alone, can help me. I humble myself to you; I forget my own misgivings. I endeavor to see in you only a woman younger, yet wiser than myself, who, knowing my sore necessity, will help me by confessing the share she bears in the secret that is destroying my peace."

"I wish I could! I wish I dared! I have thought of it often; have longed to do it at all costs; and then remembering my vow, I have held my peace!"

"Assure me of one thing and I will submit. I will ask Allan to forgive me, and I will be happy in my ignorance, if I can. He told me that this mystery would not stain his honor, nor mar my peace if it were known. Mrs. Vane, is this true?" asked Diana, solemnly.

"No; a man's honor is not tarnished in his eyes by treachery to a woman, and he believes that a woman's peace will not be marred by the knowledge that in God's sight she is not his wife, although she may be in the eyes of the world."

"Mrs. Vane, I conjure you to tell me what you mean! I have a right to know; it is your duty to save me from sin and sorrow if you can, and I will make any promise you exact to keep eternally secret whatever you may tell me. If you fear Douglas, he shall never know that you have broken your vow, whether I marry or discard him. Have pity upon me, I implore you, for this day must make or mar my life!"

Few women could have withstood the desperate urgency of Diana's prayer; Mrs. Vane did not. A moment she stood, growing paler as some purpose took shape in her mind, then drew her companion onward, saying, hurriedly, as George Lennox appeared in the avenue:

"Invite me to drive out alone with you after lunch, and then you shall know all. But O, Miss Stuart, remember that you bring the sorrow upon yourself if you urge this disclosure. I cannot think it right to see you give yourself to this man without a protest; but you may curse me for destroying your faith in him, while powerless to kill your love. Go now, and if you retract your wish, be silent; I shall understand."

They parted, and when Lennox came up, the balcony was deserted.

"My love, you get so pale and spiritless that I am quite reconciled to our departure; for the air here does not suit you, and we must try the sea-shore," said Mrs. Berkeley, as they rose from the table after lunch.

"I shall be myself again soon, aunt. I need more exercise, and if Mrs. Vane will allow me, I should enjoy a long drive with her this afternoon," returned Diana, growing still paler as she spoke.

Mrs. Vane bowed her acceptance, and as she left the room, a curious shiver seemed to shake her from head to foot as she pressed her hands together, and hurried to her chamber.

The two ladies drove in silence, till Diana said, abruptly:

"I am ready, Mrs. Vane; tell me all, and spare nothing."

"Your solemn oath first, that living or dying, you will never reveal to any human soul what I shall tell you." And as she spoke, Mrs. Vane extended her hand.

Diana gave her own, and took the oath which the other well knew she would keep inviolate.

"I shall not torture you by suspense," Mrs. Vane began, "but show you at once why I would save you from a greater suffering than the loss of love. Miss Stuart, read that, and learn the mystery of your lover's life."

With a sudden gesture, she took from her bosom a worn paper, and unfolding it, held before the other's eyes the marriage record of Allan Douglas and Virginie Varens. Not a word passed Diana's lips, but with the moan of a broken heart, she covered up her face, and slowly, tremulously, the voice at her side went on:

"You see here the date of that mysterious journey to Paris, from which he returned an altered man. There, too, is his private seal. That long lock of hair, that stained slipper, belonged to Virginie; and though he said he had never seen her, the lie cost him an effort, and well it might, for I sat there before him, and I am Virginie."

Diana's hands dropped from her pallid face, as she shrunk away from her companion, yet gazed at her like one fascinated by an awful spell.

"Hear my story, and then judge between us," the voice continued, so melancholy, yet so sweet that tears came to the listener's eyes, as the sad story was unfolded. "I am of a noble family, but was left so poor, so friendless, that but for a generous boy, I should have perished in the streets of Paris. He was a dancer, his poor earnings could not support us both. I discovered this, and in my innocence, thought no labor degrading that lessened my great debt to him. I, too, had become a dancer. I had youth, beauty, health and a grateful heart to help me on. I made money. I had many lovers, but Victor kept me safe, for he, too, loved, but in secret, till he was sure I could give him love, not gratitude. Then Allan came, and I forgot the world about me; for I loved, as only a girl of seventeen can love the first man who had touched her heart. He offered me his hand and honorable name, for I was as well born as himself, and even in my seeming degradation, he respected me. We were married, and for a year, I was as happy as an angel. Then my boy was born, and for a time I lost my beauty. That cooled Allan's waning passion. Some fear of consequences, some late regret for his rash act, came over him, and made him very bitter to me when I most needed tenderness. He told me that our marriage had been without witnesses, that our faith was different, and that vows pronounced before a Catholic priest alone were not binding upon him. That he was weary of me, and having been recalled to Scotland, he desired to return as free as he went. If I would promise solemnly to conceal the truth, he would support the boy and me abroad, until I chose to marry; that I must destroy the record of the deed, and never claim him, or he would denounce me as an impostor, and take away the boy. Miss Stuart, I was very ignorant and young; my heart was broken, and I believed myself dying. For the child's sake, I promised all things, and he left me; but remorse haunted him, and his peace was poisoned from that hour."

"And you? You married Colonel Vane?" whispered Diana, holding her breath to listen.

"No, I have never married, for in my eyes, that ceremony made me Allan's wife, and I shall be so till I die. When most forlorn, Colonel Vane found me. He was Allan's friend; he had seen me with him, and when we met again, he pitied me; and finding that I longed to hide myself from the world, he took me to India under an assumed name, as the widow of a friend. My boy went with me, and for a time, I was as happy as a desolate creature could be. Colonel Vane desired to marry me; for, though I kept my promise, he suspected that I had been deceived, and cruelly deserted, and longed to atone for his friend's perfidy by his own devotion. I would not marry him; but when he was dying, he begged me to take his name as a shield against a curious world, to take his fortune, and give my son the memory of a father when his own had cast him off. I did so; and no one knew me there except under my false name. It was believed that I had married him too soon after my first husband's death, to care to own it at once, and when I came to England, no one denied me the place I chose to fill."

"O, why did you come?" cried Diana, with a tearless sob.

"I came because I longed to know if Allan had forgotten me, if he had married, and left his poor boy fatherless. I saw him last winter, saw that you loved him, feared that he would love you, and when I learned that both were coming here, I resolved to follow. It was evident that Allan had not forgotten me, that he had suffered as well as I; and perhaps if he could bring himself to brave the pity, curiosity and criticism of the world, he might yet atone for his deceit, and make me happy. We had met in London; he had told me to remember my vow; had confessed that he still loved me, but dared not displease his haughty family by owning me; had seen his boy, and reiterated his promise to provide for us as long as we were silent. I saw him no more till we met here, and this explains all that has seemed so strange to you. It was I who entered his room, but not to juggle with the ring. He invented that tale to account for the oiled lock, and whatever stir might have been overheard. I went to implore him to pause before he pledged himself to you. He would not yield, having gone too far to retract with honor, he said. Then I was in despair; for well I knew that if ever the knowledge of this passage in his life should come to you, that you would feel as I feel, and regard that first marriage as sacred in God's eye, whatever the world might say. I gave him one more opportunity to spare you by the warning I whispered in the park. That has delayed the wrong, but you would have yielded had not other things roused suspicion of me. I had decided to say no more, but let you two tangle your fates as you would. Your appeal this morning conquered me, and I have broken every vow, dared every danger, to serve and save you. Have I done all this in vain?"

"No; let me think, let me understand—then I will act."

For many minutes they rolled on silently, two pale, stern-faced women, sitting side by side looking out before them, with fixed eyes that saw nothing but a hard task performed, a still harder one yet to be done. Diana spoke first, asking, sharply:

"Do you intend to proclaim your wrong, and force your husband to do you justice?"

"No, I shall not ask that of him again, but I shall do my best to prevent any other woman from blindly sacrificing her happiness by marrying him, unconscious of my claim. For the boy's sake I have a right to do this."

"You have. I thank you for sparing me the affliction of discovering that man's perfidy too late. Where is your boy, Mrs. Douglas?"

Steadily she spoke; and when her lips pronounced the name she had hoped to make her own, a stern smile passed across her white face, and left a darker shadow behind. Mrs. Vane touched her lips with a warning gesture, saying pitifully, yet commandingly:

"Never call me that until he gives me the right to bear it openly. You ask for my boy; will you come and see him? He is close by; I cannot be parted from him long, yet must conceal him, for the likeness to his father would betray me at once, if we were seen together."

Turning down a grassy lane, Mrs. Vane drove on till the way became too narrow for the carriage. Here they alighted, and climbing a wooded path, came to a lonely cottage in a dell.

"My faithful Jitomar found this safe nook for me, and brings me tidings of my darling every day," whispered Mrs. Vane, as she stole along the path that wound round the house.

Turning a sharp corner, a green, lawn-like bit of ground appeared. On a vine-covered seat sat an old French *bonne*, knitting as she nodded in the sun. But Diana saw nothing but a little figure tossing butter-cups into the air, and catching them as they fell, with peals of childish laughter. A three-year-old boy it was, with black curls blowing round a bold, bright face, where a healthful color glowed through the dark skin, and brilliant eyes sparkled under a brow so like that other, that she could not doubt that this was Allan's son. Just then the boy spied his mother, and with a cry of joy ran to her, to be gathered close, and covered with the tenderest caresses.

There was no acting here, for genuine mother love transformed Mrs. Vane from her usual inexplicable self into a simple woman, whose heart was bound up in the little creature whom she loved with the passionate fondness of an otherwise cold and superficial nature.

Waving off the old *bonne* when she would have approached, Mrs. Vane turned to Diana, asking:

"Are you satisfied?"

"Heaven help me, yes!"

"Is he not like his father? See, the very shape of his small hands, the same curve to his baby-mouth. Stay, you shall hear him speak. Darling, who am I?"

"Mama, my dear mama," replied the little voice.

"And who is this?" asked Mrs. Vane, showing a miniature of Douglas.

"O, papa! when will he come again?"

"God only knows, my poor baby. Now kiss mama, and then go and make a pretty daisy chain against I come next time. See, love, here are bonbons and new toys, show them to Babette. Quick, let us slip away, Miss Stuart."

As the boy ran to his nurse, the ladies vanished, and in silence regained the carriage. Only one question and answer passed between them, as they drove rapidly homeward.

"Diana, what will you do?"

"Go to-morrow, and in silence. It is all over between us, forever. Mrs. Vane, I envy you, I thank you, and I could almost *hate* you for the kind yet cruel deed you have done this day."

A gloomy darkness settled down on her altered face; despair sat in her eyes, and death itself could not have stricken hope, energy and vitality out of it more utterly than the bitter truth which she had wrung from her companion.

George Lennox and Douglas were waiting at the door, and both ran down to help them alight. Diana dragged her veil over her face, while Mrs. Vane assumed an anxious, troubled air as the carriage stopped, and both gentlemen offered a hand to Miss Stuart. Putting Earl's aside with what seemed almost rude repugnance, she took George's arm, hurried up the steps, and as her foot touched the threshold of the door, she fell heavily forward in a swoon. Douglas was springing toward her, when a strong grasp detained him, and Mrs. Vane whispered, as she clung to his arm tremblingly and pale:

"Do not touch her; she must not see you; it will kill her."

"Good heavens! what is the cause of this?" he asked, as Lennox carried Diana in, and help came flocking at his call.

"O, Mr. Douglas, I have had an awful drive! She terrified me so by her wild conversation, her fierce threats of taking her own life, that I drove home in an agony. You saw how she repulsed you, and rushed away to drop exhausted in the hall; imagine what it all means, and spare me the pain of telling you."

She spoke breathlessly, and glanced nervously about her, as if still in fear. Earl listened, half bewilderingly at first, then, as her meaning broke upon him, his dark cheek whitened, and he looked aghast.

"You do not mean that she is mad?" he whispered, recalling her fierce gesture, and the moody silence she had preserved for many days.

"No, O no, I dare not say that *yet*; but I fear that her mind is unsettled by long brooding over one unhappy thought, and that the hereditary taint may be upon the point of showing itself. Poor girl!"

"Am I the cause of this outbreak? Is our disagreement the unhappy thought that has warped her reason? What shall I, what ought I to do?" Earl asked, in great distress, as Diana's senseless body was carried up the stairs, and her aunt stood wringing her hands, while Lady Lennox despatched a servant for medical help.

"Do nothing but avoid her, for she says your presence tortures her. She will go to-morrow. Let her leave quietly, and when absence has restored her, take any steps toward a reconciliation that you think best. Now I must go to her, do not repeat what I have said. It escaped me in my agitation, and may do her harm if she learns that her strange behaviour is known."

Pressing his hand with a sympathizing glance, Mrs. Vane hurried in, and for an hour busied herself about Diana so skilfully, that the physician sent all the rest away, and gave his directions to her alone. When recovered from her faint, Diana lay like one dead, refusing to speak or move, yet taking obediently whatever Mrs. Vane offered her, as if a mutual sorrow linked them together with a secret bond. At dusk she seemed to fall asleep, and leaving Gabrielle to watch beside her, Mrs. Vane went down to join the others at a very quiet meal.

Chapter VI

A Dark Death

The party separated early. Diana was still sleeping, and leaving her own maid to watch in the dressing-room between their chambers, Mrs. Berkeley went to bed. As he passed down the gallery to his apartment, Earl heard Mrs. Vane say to the maid, "If anything happens in the night, call me." The words made him anxious, and instead of going to bed, he sat up writing letters till very late. It was past midnight, when the sound of a closing door broke the long silence that had filled the house. Stepping into the gallery, he listened. All was still, and nothing stirred but the heavy curtain before the long window at the end of the upper hall; this swayed to and fro in the strong current of air that swept in. Fearing that the draught might slam other doors and disturb Diana, he went to close it.

Pausing a moment to view the gloomy scene without, Douglas was startled by an arm flung violently about his neck, lips pressed passionately to his own, and a momentary glimpse of a woman's figure dimly defined on the dark curtain that floated backward from his hand. Silently and suddenly as it came, the phantom went, leaving Douglas so amazed, that for an instant he could only stare dumbly before him, half breathless, and wholly bewildered by the ardor of that mysterious embrace. Then he sprang forward to discover who the woman was and whither she had gone. But, as if blown outward by some counter-draught, the heavy curtain wrapped him in its fold, and when he had freed himself, neither ghost nor woman was visible.

Earl was superstitious, and for a moment he fancied the spirit of Diana had appeared to him, foretelling her death. But a second thought assured him that it was a human creature, and no wraith, for the soft arms had no deathly chill in them, the lips were warm, living breath had passed across his face, and on his cheek he felt a tear that must have fallen from human eyes. The light had been too dim to reveal the partially shrouded countenance, or more than a tall and shadowy outline, but with a thrill of fear he thought, "It was Diana, and she is mad!"

Taking his candle, he hurried to the door of the dressing-room, tapped softly, and when the sleepy maid appeared, inquired if Miss Stuart still slept.

"Yes, sir, like a child; it does one's heart good to see her."

"You are quite sure she is asleep?"

"Bless me, yes, sir; I've just looked at her, and she hasn't stirred since I looked an hour ago."

"Does she ever walk in her sleep, Mrs. Mason?"

"Dear, no, sir."

"I thought I saw her just now in the upper gallery. I went to shut the great window, lest the wind should disturb her, and some one very like her certainly stood for a moment at my side."

"Lord, sir! you make my blood run cold. It couldn't have been her, for she never left her bed, much less her room."

"Perhaps so; never mind; just look again, and tell me if you see her, then I shall be at ease."

Mrs. Mason knew that her young lady loved the gentleman before her, and never doubted that he loved her, and so considering his anxiety quite natural and proper, she nodded, crept away, and soon returned, saying, with an air of satisfaction:

"She's all right, sir, sleeping beautifully. I didn't speak, for once when I looked at her she said, quite fierce: 'Go away, and let me be until I call you.' So I've only peeped through the curtain since. I see her lying with her face to the wall, and the coverlet drawn comfortably round her."

"Thank God! she is safe. Excuse my disturbing you, Mrs. Mason, but I was very anxious. Be patient and faithful in your care of her; I shall remember it. Good-night."

"Handsome creeter! how fond he is of her, and well he may be, for she dotes on him, and they'll make a splendid couple. Now I'll finish my nap, and then I'll have a cup of tea."

With a knowing look and a chilly shiver, Mrs. Mason re-settled herself in a luxurious chair and was soon dozing tranquilly.

Douglas meanwhile returned to his room, after a survey of the house, and went to bed thinking with a smile and a frown, that if all spirits came in such an amicable fashion, the fate of a ghost-seer was not a hard one.

In the dark hour just before the dawn, a long, shrill cry rent the silence, and brought every sleeper under that roof out of his bed, trembling and with fright. The cry came from Diana's room, and in a moment the gallery, dressing-room and chamber were filled with pale faces and half-dressed figures, as ladies and gentlemen, men and maids, came flocking in, all asking, breathlessly:

"What is it? O, what is it?"

Mrs. Berkeley lay on the floor in strong hysterics, and Mrs. Mason, instead of attending to her, was beating her hands distractedly together, and running wildly about the room, as if searching for something she had lost. Diana's bed was empty, with the clothes flung one way and the pillows another, and every sign of strange disorder, but its occupant was nowhere to be seen.

"Where is she?" "What has happened?" "Why don't you speak?" cried the terrified beholders.

A sudden lull fell upon the excited group, as Mrs. Vane, white, resolute and calm, made her way through the crowd, and laying her hand on Mrs. Mason's shoulder, commanded her to stand still and explain the mystery. The poor soul endeavored to obey, but burst into tears, and dropping on her knees, poured out her story in a passion of penitent despair.

"You left her sleeping, ma'am, and I sat as my lady bid me, going now and then to look at miss. The last time I drew the curtains, she looked up and said, sharp and short, 'Let me be in peace, and don't disturb me till I call you.' After that, I just peeped through the crack, and she seemed quiet. You know I told you so, sir, when you came to ask, and O, my goodness me, it wasn't her at all, sir, and she's gone! she's gone!"

"Hush! stop sobbing, and tell me how you missed her. Gabrielle and Justine, attend to Mrs. Berkeley; Harry, go at once and search the house. Now, Mrs. Mason."

Mrs. Vane's clear, calm voice seemed to act like a spell on the agitation of all about her, and the maids obeyed, Harry, with the men-servants hurried away, and Mrs. Mason more coherently, went on:

"Well, ma'am, when Mr. Douglas came to the door asking if miss was here, thinking he saw her in the hall, I looked again, and thought she lay as I'd left her an hour before. But O ma'am, it wasn't her, it was the piller that she'd fixed like herself, with the coverlet pulled round it, like she'd pulled it round her own head and shoulders when she spoke last. It looked all right, the night-lamp being low, and me so sleepy, and I went back to my place, after setting Mr. Douglas's mind at rest. I fell asleep, and when I woke, I ran in here to make sure she was safe, for I'd had a horrid dream about seeing her laid out, dead and dripping, with weeds in her hair, and her poor feet all covered with red clay, as if she'd fallen into one of them pits over yonder. I ran in here, pulled up the curtain, and was just going to say, 'Thank the Lord,' when, as I stooped down to listen if she slept easy, I saw she wasn't there. The start took my wits away, and I don't know what I did, till my lady came running in, as I was tossing the pillows here and there to find her, and when I told what had happened, my lady gave one dreadful scream, and went off in a fit."

There was a dead silence for a moment, as Mrs. Mason relapsed into convulsive sobbing, and every one looked into each other's frightened faces. Douglas leaned on Lennox, as if all the strength had gone out of him, and George stood aghast. Mrs. Vane alone seemed self-possessed, though an awful anxiety blanched her face, and looked out at her haggard eyes.

"What did you see in the hall?" she asked of Douglas. Briefly he told the incident, and Lady Lennox clasped her hands in despair, exclaiming:

"She has destroyed herself, and that was her farewell."

"Your ladyship is mistaken, I hope, for among the wild things she said this afternoon, was a longing to go home at once, as every hour here was torture to her. She may have attempted this in her delirium. Look in her wardrobe, Mrs. Mason, and see what clothes are gone. That will help us in our search. Be calm, I beg of you, my lady; I am sure we shall find the poor girl soon."

"It's no use looking, ma'am; she's gone in the clothes she had on, for she wouldn't let me take 'em off her. It was a black silk with crape trimmings, and her black mantle's gone, and the close crape bonnet. Here's her gloves just where they dropped when we laid her down in her faint."

"Is her purse gone?" asked Mrs. Vane.

"It's always in her pocket, ma'am, when she drives out, she likes to toss a bit of money to the little lads that open gates, or hold the ponies while she gets flowers, and such like. She was so generous, so kind, poor dear!"

Here Harry came in, saying that no trace of the lost girl was visible in the house. But as he spoke, Jitomar's dark face and glittering eyes looked over his shoulder with an intelligent motion, which his mistress understood, and put into words.

"He says that one of the long windows in the little breakfast-room is unfastened and ajar. Go, gentlemen, at once, and take him with you, he is as keen as a hound, and will do good service. It is just possible that she may have remembered the one o'clock mail train, and taken it. Inquire, and if you find any trace of her, let us know without delay."

In an instant they were gone, and the anxious watchers left behind, traced their progress by the glimmer of the lantern, which Jitomar carried low, that he might follow the print her flying feet had left here and there in the damp earth.

A long hour passed, then Harry and the Indian returned, bringing the good news that a tall lady in black had been seen at the station alone, had not been recognized, being veiled, and had taken the mail train to London. Douglas and Lennox had at once ordered horses, and gone with all speed to catch an early train that left a neighboring town in an hour or two. They would trace and discover the lost girl, if she was in London.

"There can be no doubt that it was she, no lady would be travelling alone at such an hour, and the station people say that she seemed in great haste. Now let us compose ourselves, hope for the best, and comfort her poor aunt."

As Mrs. Vane spoke, Harry frankly looked his admiration of the cheerful, courageous little woman, and his mother took her arm, saying, affectionately:

"My dear, what should we do without you, for you have the nerves of a man, the quick wit of a woman, and presence of mind enough for us all."

The dreary day dawned, and slowly wore away. A dull rain fell, and a melancholy wind sighed among the yellowing leaves. All occupations flagged, all failed, except the one absorbing hope. The servants loitered, unreproved, and gossiped freely among themselves about the sad event. The ladies sat in Mrs. Berkeley's room, consoling her distress, while Harry haunted the station, waiting for an arrival or a telegram. At noon, the latter came.

"The lady in black not Diana. On another scent now. If that fails, home at night."

No one knew how much they leaned upon this hope, until it failed and all was uncertainty again. Harry searched house, garden, park and river-side, but found no trace of the lost girl beyond the point where her footsteps ended on the hard gravel of the road. So the long afternoon wore on, and at dusk the gentlemen returned, haggard, wet and weary, bringing no tidings of good cheer. The lady in black proved to be a handsome young governess, called suddenly to town by her father's dangerous illness. The second search was equally fruitless, and nowhere had Diana been seen.

Their despondent story was scarcely ended, when the bell rang. Every servant in the house sprang to answer it, and every occupant of the drawing-room listened breathlessly. A short parley followed the ring; then an aston-ished footman showed in a little farmer lad, with a bundle under his arm.

"He wants to see my lady, and would come in," said the man, lingering, as all eyes were fixed on the new-comer.

The boy looked important, excited and frightened, but when Lady Lennox bade him to do his errand without fear, he spoke up briskly, though his voice shook a little, and he now and then gave a nervous clutch at the bundle under his arm.

"Please, my lady, mother told me to come up as soon as ever I got home, so I ran off right away, knowing you'd be glad to hear something, even if it warn't good."

"Something about Miss Stuart, you mean?"

"Yes, my lady, I know where she is."

"Where? speak quickly, you shall be well paid for your tidings."

"In the pit, my lady," and the boy began to cry.

"No!"

Douglas spoke, and turned on the lad a face that stopped his crying, and sent the words to his lips faster than he could utter them, so full of mute entreaty was its glance of anguish.

"You see, sir, I was here this noon, and heard about it. Mrs. Mason's dream scared me, 'cause my brother was drowned in the pit. I couldn't help thinking of it all the afternoon, and when work was down, I went home that way. The first thing I saw was tracks in the red clay, coming from the lodge way. The pit has overflowed, and made a big pool, but just where it's deepest, the tracks stopped, and there I found these."

With a sudden gesture of the arm, he shook out the bundle; a torn mantle, heavily trimmed, and a crushed crape bonnet dropped upon the floor. Lady Lennox sank back in her chair, and George covered up his face with a groan; but Earl stood motionless, and Mrs. Vane looked as if the sight of these relics had confirmed some wordless fear.

"Perhaps she is not there, however," she said, below her breath. "She may have wandered on, and lost herself. O, let us look!"

"She *is* there, ma'am, I see her sperrit," and the boy's eyes dilated as they glanced fearfully about him while he spoke. "I was awful scared when I see them things, but she was good to me, and I loved her, so I took 'em up, and went on round the pool, meaning to strike off by the great ditch. Just as I got to the bit of brush that grows down by the old clay pits, something flew right up before me, something like a woman, all black but a white face and arms. It gave a strange screech, and seemed to go out of sight all in a minute, like as if it vanished in the pits. I know it warn't a real woman, it flew so, and looked so awful when it wailed, as granny says the sperrits do."

The boy paused, till Douglas beckoned solemnly, and left the room, with the one word, "Come!"

The brothers went, the lad followed, Mrs. Vane hid her face in Lady Lennox's lap, and neither stirred nor spoke for one long, dreadful hour.

"They are coming," whispered Mrs. Vane, when at length her quick ear caught the sound of many approaching feet. Slowly, steadily they came on, across the lawn, up the steps, through the hall; then there was a pause.

"Go and see if she is found, I cannot," implored Lady Lennox, spent and trembling, with the long suspense.

There was no need to go, for as she spoke, the wail of women's voices filled the air, and Lennox stood in the doorway with a face that made all questions needless.

He beckoned, and Mrs. Vane went to him as if her feet could hardly bear her, while her face might have been that of a dead woman, so white and stony had it grown. Drawing her outside, he said:

"My mother must not see her yet. Mrs. Mason can do all that is necessary, if you will give her orders, and spare my mother the first sad duties. Douglas bade me come for you, for you are always ready."

"I will come; where is she?"

"In the library. Send the servants away, in pity to poor Earl. Harry cannot bear it, and it kills me to see her looking so."

"You found her there?"

"Yes, quite underneath the deepest water of the pool. That dream was surely sent by Heaven. Are you faint? Can you bear it?"

"I can bear anything. Go on."

Poor Diana! there she lay, a piteous sight, with stained and dripping garments, slimy weeds entangled in her long hair, a look of mortal woe stamped on her dead face, for the blue lips were parted, as if by the passage of the last painful breath, and the glassy eyes seemed fixed imploringly upon some stern spectre, darker and more dreadful even than the desperate death she had sought and found.

A group of awe-stricken men and sobbing women stood about her. Harry leaned upon the high arm of the couch where they had laid her, with his head down upon his arm, struggling to control himself, for he had loved her with a boy's first love, and the horror of her end unmanned him. Douglas sat at the head of the couch, holding the dead hand, and looking at her with a white, tearless anguish, which made his face old and haggard, as with the passage of long and heavy years.

With an air of quiet command, and eyes that never once fell on the dead girl, Mrs. Vane gave a few necessary orders, which cleared the room of all but the gentlemen and herself. Laying her hand softly on Earl's shoulder, she said, in a tone of tenderest compassion:

"Come with me, and let me try to comfort you, while George and Harry take the poor girl to her room, that these sad tokens of her end may be removed, and she made beautiful for the eyes of those who love her."

He heard, but did not answer in words, for waving off the brothers, Earl took his dead love in his arms, and carrying her to her own room, laid her down tenderly, kissed her pale forehead with one lingering kiss, and then without a word shut himself into his own apartment.

Mrs. Vane watched him go with a dark glance, followed him up-stairs, and when his door closed, muttered low to herself:

"He loved her better than I knew, but she has made my task easier than I dared to hope it would be, and now I can soon teach him to forget."

A strange smile passed across her face as she spoke, and still, without a glance at the dead face, left the chamber for her own, whither Jitomar was soon summoned, and where he long remained.

Chapter VII

The Footprint by the Pool

Three sad and solemn days had passed, and now the house was still again. Mr. Berkeley had removed his wife, and the remains of his niece, and Lennox had gone with him. Mrs. Vane devoted herself to her hostess, who had been much affected by the shock, and to Harry, who was almost ill with the excitement and the sorrow. Douglas had hardly been seen, except by his own servant, who reported that he was very quiet, but in a stern and bitter mood, which made solitude his best comforter. Only twice had he emerged during those troubled days. Once, when Mrs. Vane's sweet voice came up from below singing a sacred melody in the twilight, he came out and paced to and fro in the long gallery, with a softer expression than his face had worn

since the night of Diana's passionate farewell. The second time was in answer
to a tap at his door, on opening which he saw Jitomar, who with the graceful
reverence of his race, bent on one knee, as with dark eyes full of sympathy, he
delivered a lovely bouquet of the flowers Diana most loved, and oftenest
wore. The first tears that had been seen there softened Earl's melancholy eyes,
as he took the odorous gift, and with a grateful impulse stretched his hand to
the giver. But Jitomar drew back with a gesture which signified that his
mistress sent the offering, and glided away. Douglas went straight to the
drawing-room, found Mrs. Vane alone, and inexpressibly touched by her
tender thought of him, he thanked her warmly, let her detain him for an hour
with her soothing conversation, and left her, feeling that comfort was possible when such an angel administered it.

On the third day, impelled by an unconquerable wish to re-visit the lonely
spot hereafter and forever to be haunted by the memory of that tragic death,
he stole out, unperceived, and took his way to the pool. It lay there, dark and
still under a gloomy sky; its banks trampled by many hasty feet, and in one
spot the red clay still bore the impress of the pale shape drawn from the
water on that memorable night. As he stood there, he remembered the lad's
story of the spirit which he believed he had seen. With a dreary smile at the
superstition of the boy, he followed his tracks along the bank as they
branched off toward the old pits, now half filled with water by recent rains.
Pausing where the boy had paused when the woman's figure sprang up before
him with its eldritch cry, Douglas looked keenly all about, wondering if it
were possible for any human being to vanish as the lad related. Several yards
from the clump of bushes and coarse grass at his feet, lay the wide pit;
between it and the spot where he stood, stretched a smooth bed of clay,
unmarked by the impress of any step, as he at first thought. A second and
more scrutinizing glance showed him the print of a human foot on the very
edge of the pit. Stepping lightly forward, he examined it. Not the boy's track,
for he had not passed the bushes, but turned and fled in terror, when the
phantom seemed to vanish. It was a child's footprint, apparently, or that of a
very small woman; probably the latter, for it was a slender, shapely print, cut
deep into the yielding clay, as if by the impetus of a desperate spring. But
whither had she sprung? Not across the pit, for that was impossible to any
but a very active man, or a professional gymnast of either sex. Douglas took
the leap, and barely reached the other side, though a tall, agile man. Nor did
he find any trace of the other leaper, though the grass that grew to the very
edge on that side, might have concealed a lighter, surer tread than his own.

With a thrill of suspicion and dread, he looked down into the turbid water of the pit, asking himself if it were possible that two women had found their death so near together on that night? The footprint was not Diana's; hers was larger, and utterly unlike; whose was it, then? With a sudden impulse, he cut a long, forked pole, and searched the depths of the pit. Nothing was found; again and again he plunged in the pole and drew it carefully up, after sweeping the bottom in all directions. A dead branch, a fallen rod, a heavy stone were all he found.

As he stood pondering over the mysterious mark, having re-crossed the pit, some slight peculiarity in it suddenly seemed to give it a familiar aspect. Kneeling down, he examined it minutely, and as he looked, an expression of perplexity came into his face, while he groped for some recollection in the dimness of the past, the gloom of the present.

"Where have I seen a foot like this, so dainty, so slender, yet so strong, for the tread was firm here, the muscles wonderfully elastic to carry this unknown woman over that wide gap? Stay! it was not a foot, but a shoe that makes this mark so familiar. Who wears a shoe with a coquettish heel like this stamped here in the clay? A narrow sole, a fairy-like shape, a slight pressure downward at the toe, as if the wearer walked well and lightly, yet danced better than she walked? Good heavens? can it be? That word 'danced' makes it clear to me—but it is impossible—unless—can she have discovered me, followed me, wrought me fresh harm, and again escaped me? I will be satisfied at all hazards, and if I find her, Virginie shall meet a double vengeance for a double wrong."

Up he sprang, as these thoughts swept through his mind, and like some one bent on some all-absorbing purpose, he dashed homeward through bush and brake, park and garden, till, coming to the lawn, he restrained his impetuosity, but held on his way, turning neither to the right nor the left till he stood in his own room. Without pausing for breath, he snatched the satin slipper from the case, put it in his breast, and hurried back to the pool. Making sure that no one followed him, he cautiously advanced, and bending, laid the slipper in the mould of that mysterious foot. It fitted exactly! Outline, length, width, even the downward pressure at the toe corresponded, and the sole difference was in the depth of heel, as if the walking boot or shoe had been thicker than the slipper.

Bent on assuring himself, Douglas pressed the slipper carefully into the smooth clay beside that other print, and every slight peculiarity was repeated with wonderful accuracy.

"I am satisfied," he muttered, adding, as he carefully effaced both the little tracks, "no one must follow this out but myself. I have sworn to find her and her accomplice, and henceforth, it shall be the business of my life to keep my vow."

A few moments he stood, buried in dark thoughts and memories, then putting up the slipper, he bent his steps toward the home of little Wat, the farmer's lad. He was watering horses at the spring, his mother said, and Douglas strolled that way, saying he desired to give the boy something for the intelligence he brought three days before. Wat lounged against the wall, while the tired horses slowly drank their fill, but when he saw the gentleman approaching, he looked troubled, for his young brain had been sadly perplexed by the late events.

"I want to ask you a few questions, Wat; answer me truly, and I will thank you in a way you will like better than words," began Douglas, as the boy pulled off his hat, and stood staring.

"I'm ready; what will I say, sir?" he asked.

"Tell me just what sort of a thing or person the spirit looked like when you saw it by the pit?"

"A woman, sir, all black but her face and arms."

"Did she resemble the person we were searching for?"

"No, sir; leastways, I never saw miss looking so; in course she wouldn't when she was alive you know."

"Did the spirit look like the lady afterwards? when we found her, I mean?"

The boy pondered a minute, seemed perplexed, but answered slowly, as he grew a little pale:

"No, sir, then she looked awful, but the spirit seemed scared-like, and screamed as any woman would if frightened."

"And she vanished in the pit, you say?"

"She couldn't go nowhere else, sir, 'cause she didn't turn."

"Did you see her go down into the water, Wat?"

"No, sir, I only see her fly up out of the bushes, looking at me over her shoulder, and giving a great leap, as light and easy as if she hadn't no body. But it startled me, so that I fell over backwards, and when I got up, she was gone."

"I thought so. Now tell me, was the spirit large or small?"

"I didn't mind, but I guess it wasn't very big, or them few bushes wouldn't have hid it from me."

"Was its hair black or light?"

"Don't know, sir, a hood was all over its head, and I only see the face."

"Did you mind the eyes?"

"They looked big and dark, and scared me horridly."

"You said the face was handsome but white, I think?"

"I didn't say anything about handsome, sir, it was too dark to make out much, but it was white, and when she threw up her arms, they looked like snow. I never see any live lady with such white ones."

"You did not go down to the edge of the pit to leap after her, did you?"

"Lord, no, sir. I just scud the other way, and never looked back till I see the lodge."

"Is there any strange lady down at the inn, or staying anywhere in the village?"

"Not as I know, sir. I'm down there every day, and guess I'd hear of it if there was. Do you want to find any one, sir?"

"No, I thought your spirit might have been some live woman, whom you frightened as much as she did you. Are you quite sure it was not?"

"I shouldn't be sure, if she hadn't flown away so strange, for no woman could go over the pit, and if she'd fell in, I'd have heard the splash."

"So you would. Well, let the spirit go, and keep away from the pit and the pool, lest you see it again. Here is a golden 'thank you,' my boy, so good-by."

"O, sir, that's a deal too much! I'm heartily obliged. Be you going to leave these parts, please, sir?"

"Not yet; I've much to do before I go."

Satisfied with his inquiries, Douglas went on, and Wat, pulling on his torn hat, as the gentleman disappeared, fell to examining the bit of gold that had been dropped into his brown palm.

"Do you want another, my lad?" said a soft voice behind him, and, turning quickly, he saw a man leaning over the wall, just below the place where he had lounged a moment before.

The man was evidently a gipsey; long black hair hung about a brown face with black eyes, a crafty mouth and glittering teeth. His costume was picturesquely ragged and neglected, and in his hand he held a stout staff. Bending further over, he eyed the boy with a nod, repeating his words in a smooth, low tone, as he held up a second half sovereign between his thumb and finger.

"Yes, I do," answered Wat, sturdily, as he sent his horses trotting homeward with a chirrup and a cut of his long whip.

"Tell me what the gentleman said, and you shall have it," whispered the gipsey.

"You might have heard for yourself, if you'd been where you are a little sooner," returned Wat, edging toward the road—for there was something about the swarthy-faced fellow that he did not like, in spite of his golden offer.

"I was there," said the man, with a laugh; "but you spoke so low I couldn't catch it all."

"What do you want to know for?" demanded Wat.

"Why, perhaps I know something about that spirit woman he seemed to be asking about, and if I do, he'd be glad to hear it, wouldn't he? Now I don't want to go and tell him myself, for fear of getting into trouble, but I might tell you, and you could do it. Only I must know what he said, first, because perhaps he has found out for himself what I could tell him."

"What are you going to give me that for, then?" asked Wat, much reassured.

"Because you are a clever little chap, and were good to some of my people here once upon a time. I'm rich, though I don't look it, and I'd like to pay for the news you give me. Out with it, and then here's another yellow boy for you."

Wat was entirely conquered by the grateful allusion to a friendly little act of his own on the previous day, and willingly related his conversation with Douglas, explaining as he went on. The gipsey questioned and cross-questioned, and finished the interview by saying, with a warning glance:

"He's right; you'd better not tell any one you saw the spirit—it's a bad sign, and if it's known, you'll find it hard to get on in the world. Now here's your money; catch it, and then I'll tell you my story."

The coin came singing through the air, and fell into the road not far from Wat's feet. He ran to pick it up, and when he turned to thank the man, he was gone as silently and suddenly as he had come. The lad stared in a maze, listened, searched, but no gipsey was heard or seen, and poor bewildered Wat scampered home as fast as his legs could carry him, believing that he was bewitched.

That afternoon Douglas wrote a long letter, directed it to "Monsieur Antoine Dupres, Rue Saint Honoré, Paris," and was about to seal it, when a servant came to tell him that Mrs. Vane desired her adieux, as she was leaving for town by the next train. Anxious to atone for his seeming negligence, not having seen her that day, and therefore being in ignorance of her intended departure, he hastily dropped a splash of wax on his important letter, and leaving it upon his table, hurried down to see her off. She was already in the hall, having bidden Lady Lennox farewell in her boudoir—for her ladyship was too poorly to come down. Harry was giving directions about the baggage, and Gabrielle chattering her adieux in the housekeeper's room.

"My dear Mrs. Vane, forgive my selfish sorrow, when you are settled in town, let me come to thank you for the great kindness you have shown me through these dark days."

Douglas spoke warmly; he pressed the hand she gave him in both his own, and gratitude flushed his pale face with a glow that restored all its lost comeliness. Mrs. Vane dropped her beautiful eyes, and answered, with a slight quiver of the lips that tried to smile:

"I have suffered for you, if not with you, and I need no thanks for the sympathy that was involuntary. Here is my address; come to me when you will, and be assured that you will always find a welcome."

He led her to the carriage, assiduously arranging all things for her comfort, and when she waved a last adieu, he seized the little hand, regardless of Harry, who accompanied her, and kissed it warmly, as he said:

"I shall not forget, and shall see you soon."

The carriage rolled away, and Douglas watched it, saying to the groom, who was just turning stableward:

"Does not Jitomar go with his mistress?"

"No, sir; he's to take some plants my lady gave Mrs. Vane, so he's to go in a later train—and good riddance to the sly devil, I say," added the man, under his breath, as he walked off.

Had he turned his head a moment afterward, he would have been amazed at the strange behaviour of the gentleman he had left behind him. Happening to glance downward, Douglas gave a start, stooped suddenly, examined something on the ground, and as he rose, struck his hands together like one in great perplexity or exultation, while his face assumed a singular expression of mingled wonder, pain and triumph. Well it might, for there, clearly defined in the moist earth, was an exact counterpart of the footprint by the pool.

Chapter VIII

〜

On the Trail

The packet from Havre was just in. It had been a stormy trip, and all the passengers hurried ashore, as if glad to touch English soil. Two gentlemen lingered a moment, before they separated to different quarters of the city. One was a stout, gray-haired Frenchman, perfectly dressed, blandly courteous and vivaciously grateful, as he held the other's hand, and poured out a stream of compliments, invitations and thanks. The younger man was evidently a Spaniard, slight, dark and dignified, with melancholy eyes, a bronzed, bearded face, and a mien as cool and composed as if he had just emerged from some elegant retreat, instead of the cabin of an over-crowded packet, whence he had been tossing about all day.

"It is a thousand pities that we do not go on together; but remember I am under many obligations to Signor Arguelles, and I implore that I may be allowed to return them during my stay. I believe you have my card; now au revoir, and my respectful compliments to madame your friend."

"Adieu, Monsieur Dupont—we shall meet again."

The Frenchman waved his hand, the Spaniard raised his hat, and they separated.

Antoine Dupres, for it was he, drove at once to a certain hotel, asked for M. Douglas, sent up his name, and was at once heartily welcomed by his friend, with whom he sat in deep consultation till very late.

Arguelles was set down at the door of a lodging-house, in a quiet street, and, admitting himself by means of a latch-key, he went noiselessly up-stairs, and looked about him. The scene was certainly a charming one, though somewhat peculiar. A bright fire filled the room with its ruddy light; several lamps added their milder shine, and the chamber was a flush of color, for carpet, chairs and tables were strewn with brilliant costumes. Wreaths of artificial flowers strewed the floor; mock jewels glittered here and there; a lyre, a silver bow and arrow, a slender wand of many colors, a pair of ebony castanets; a gaily decorated tambourine lay on the couch; little hats, caps, bodices, jackets, skirts, boots, slippers, and clouds of rosy, blue, white and green tulle were heaped, hung and scattered everywhere. In the midst of this gay confusion, stood a figure in perfect keeping with it. A slight, blooming girl of eighteen, she looked, evidently an actress—for though busily sorting the contents of two chests that stood before her, she was *en costume,* as if she had been reviewing her wardrobe, and had forgotten to take off the various parts of different suits which she had tried on. A jaunty hat of black velvet, turned up with a white plume, was stuck askew on her blonde head; scarlet boots, with brass heels, adorned her feet; a short white satin skirt was oddly contrasted with a blue and silver Hussar jacket, and a flame-colored silk domino completed her piquant array.

A smile of tenderest joy and admiration lighted up the man's dark features, as he leaned in, watching the pretty creature purse up her lips and bend her brows, in deep consideration, over a faded pink and black Spanish dress, just unfolded.

"Madame, it is I."

He closed the door behind him, as he spoke, and advanced with open arms. The girl dropped the garment she held, turned sharply, and surveyed the new-comer with little surprise, but much amusement, for suddenly clapping her hands, she broke into a peal of laughter, exclaiming, as she examined him:

"My faith! you are superb. I admire you thus; the melancholy is becoming, the beard ravishing, and the *tout ensemble* beyond my hopes. I salute you, Signor Juan Arguelles."

"Come, then, and embrace me. So long away, and no tenderer welcome than this, my heart?"

She shrugged her white shoulders, and submitted to be drawn close, kissed and caressed with ardor, by her husband or lover, asking a multitude of questions the while, and smoothing the petals of a crumpled camellia, quite unmoved by the tender names showered upon her, the almost fierce affection that glowed in her companion's face, and lavished itself in demonstrations of delight at regaining her.

"But tell me, darling, why do I find you at such work? Is it wise or needful?"

"It is pleasant, and I please myself now. I have almost lived here since you have been gone. At my aunt's in the country, they say, at the other place. The rooms there were dull; no one came, and at last I ran away. Once here, the old mania returned; I was mad for the gay life I love, and while I waited, I played at carnival."

"Were you anxious for my return? Did you miss me, *cariña?*"

"That I did, for I needed you, my Juan," she answered, with a laugh. "Do you know we must have money? I am deciding which of my properties I will sell, though it breaks my heart to part with them. Mother Ursule will dispose of them, and as I shall never want them again, they must go."

"Why will you never need them again? There may be no course but that in the end."

"My husband will never let me dance, except for my own pleasure," she answered, dropping a half humble, half mocking courtesy, and glancing at him with a searching look.

Juan eyed her gloomily, as she waltzed away, clinking her brass heels together, and humming a gay measure in time to her graceful steps. He shook his head, threw himself wearily into a chair, and leaned his forehead upon his hand. The girl watched him over her shoulder, paused, shook off the jaunty hat, dropped the red domino, and, stealing toward him, perched herself upon his knee, peering under his hand with a captivating air of penitence, as she laid her arm about his neck, and whispered in his ear:

"I meant you, *mon ami*, and I will keep my promise, by-and-by, when all is as we would have it. Believe me, and be gay again, because I do not love you when you are grim and grave, like an Englishman."

"Do you ever love me, my—"

She stopped his mouth with a kiss, and answered, as she smoothed the crisp black curls off his forehead:

"You shall see how well I love you, by-and-by."

"Ah, it is always 'by-and-by,' never now. I have a feeling that I never shall possess you, even if my long service ends this year. You are so cold, so treacherous, I have no faith in you, though I adore you, and shall until I die."

"Have I ever broken the promise made so long ago?"

"You dare not, for you know that the penalty of treason is death."

"Death for you, not for me. I am wiser now; I do not fear you, but I need you, and at last I think—I love you."

As she added the last words, the black frown that had darkened the man's face lifted suddenly, and the expression of intense devotion returned to make it beautiful. He turned that other face upward, scanned it with those magnificent eyes of his, now soft and tender, and answered, with a sigh that ended in a smile:

"It would be death for me to find that, after all I have suffered, done and desired for you, there was no reward but falsehood and base ingratitude. It must not be so; and in that thought I will find patience to work on for one whom I try to love for your sake."

A momentary expression of infinite love and longing touched the girl's face, and filled her eyes with tenderness. But it passed, and settling herself more comfortably, she asked:

"How have you prospered since you wrote? Well, I know, else I should have read it at the first glance."

"Beyond my hopes. We crossed together; we are friends already, and shall meet as such. It was an inspiration of yours, and has worked like a charm. Monsieur from the country has not yet appeared, has he?"

"He called when I was out. I did not regret it, for I feel safer when you are by, and it is as well to whet his appetite by absence."

"How is this to end? As we last planned?"

"Yes; but not yet. We must be sure, and that we can only be through himself. Leave it to me. I know him well, and he is willing to be led, I fancy. Now I shall feed you, for it occurs to me that you are fasting. See, I am ready for you."

She left him, and ran to and fro, preparing a dainty little supper, but on her lips still lay a smile of conscious power, and in the eyes that followed her, still lurked a glance of disquiet and distrust.

Mrs. Vane was driving in the park—not in her own carriage, for she kept none—but having won the hearts of several amiable dowagers, their equipages were always at her command. In one of the most elegant of these she was reclining, apparently unconscious of the many glances of curiosity and admiration fixed upon the lovely face, enshrined in the little black tulle bonnet, with its fall of transparent lace to heighten her blonde beauty.

Two gentlemen were entering the great gate, as she passed by for another turn; one of them pronounced her name, and sprang forward. She recognized the voice, ordered the carriage to stop, and when Douglas came up, held out her hand to him, with a smile of welcome. He touched it, expressed his pleasure at meeting her, and added, seeing her glance at his companion:

"Permit me to present my friend, Monsieur Dupont, just from Paris, and happy in so soon meeting a fair countrywoman."

Dupres executed a superb bow, and made his compliments in his mother tongue. Mrs. Vane listened with an air of pretty perplexity, and answered, in English, while she gave him her most beaming look:

"Monsieur must pardon me that I have forgotten my native language so sadly that I dare not venture to use it in his presence. My youth was spent in

Spain, and since then England or India has been my home; but to this dear country I most cordially welcome any friend of M. Douglas."

As she turned to Earl, and listened to his tidings of Lady Lennox, Dupres fixed a searching glance upon her. His keen eye ran over her from head to foot, and nothing seemed to escape his scrutiny. Her figure was concealed by a great mantle of black velvet; her hair waved plainly away under her bonnet; the heavy folds of her dress flowed over her feet, and her delicately gloved hands lay half buried in the deep lace of her handkerchief. She was very pale, her eyes were languid, her lips sad even in smiling, and her voice had lost its lightsome ring. She looked older, graver, more pensive and dignified than when Douglas last saw her.

"You have been ill, I fear?" he said, regarding her with visible solicitude, while his friend looked down, yet marked every word she uttered.

"Yes, quite ill; I have been through so much in the last month, that I can hardly help betraying it in my countenance. A heavy cold, with fever, has kept me a prisoner till these few days past, when I have driven out, being still too feeble to walk."

Earl was about to express his sorrow, when Dupres exclaimed:

"Behold! it is he—the friend who so assuaged the tortures of that tempestuous passage. Let me reward him by a word from M. Douglas, and a smile from madame. Is it permitted?"

Scarcely waiting for an assent, the vivacious gentleman darted forward, and arrested the progress of a gentleman who was bending at the moment to adjust his stirrup. A few hasty words and emphatic gestures prepared the stranger for the interview, and with the courtesy of a Spaniard, he dismounted, and advanced bare-headed, to be presented to madame. It was Arguelles; and even Douglas was struck with his peculiar beauty, and the native pride that was but half veiled by the southern softness of his manners. He spoke English well, but when Mrs. Vane addressed him in Spanish, he answered with a flash of pleasure that proved how grateful to him was the sound of his own melodious tongue.

Too wellbred to continue the conversation in a language which excluded the others, Mrs. Vane soon broke up the party by inviting Douglas and his friend to call upon her that evening, adding, with a glance toward the Spaniard:

"It will gratify me to extend the hospitalities of an English home to Señor Arguelles, if he is a stranger here, and to enjoy again the familiar sound of the language which is dearer to me than my own."

Three hats were lifted, and three grateful gentlemen expressed their thanks with smiles of satisfaction; then the carriage rolled on, the señor galloped off, looking very like some knightly figure from a romance, and Douglas turned to his companion with an eager, "Tell me, is it she?"

"No; Virginie would be but one-and-twenty, and this woman must be thirty if she is a day, ungallant that I am to say so of the charming creature."

"You have not seen her to advantage, Antoine. Wait till you meet her again to-night in full toilet, and then pronounce. She has been ill; even I perceive the great change this short time has wrought, for we parted only ten days ago," said Douglas, disappointed, yet not convinced.

"It is well; we will go; I will study her, and if it be that lovely devil, we will cast her out, and so avenge the past. But you see, this Spaniard is to be there; he may serve us, for he will be enslaved at once, if she uses those fine eyes of hers as she did just now; and while she captivates Arguelles, Dupres will captivate her in a less charming manner. I own that those eyes of hers *are* like Virginie's in shape and color, but not in expression, for they are pensive and soft; the girl's were brilliant as stars, and as cold," replied Dupres.

"You are sure you would remember her again?"

"I have little doubt of it; for though I never spoke with her, I have heard her speak often, have watched her, night after night, and from my boy, who adored her, have learned many a small trait of character, which will serve me now. I am so changed, I fancy she would not recall me, even if I gave my own name, but it is better to conceal myself behind that altered syllable for a time."

"I wish it had been possible to bring Gustave."

"Unwise, unsafe; the boy is better out of the affair; for though he might be quicker to discover, he would be less secure in the keeping of the secret. Such is her power over men, that a glance, a touch, a tone, would win him back to her side, and we should be wounded with our own weapon. Let him rest tranquil with his little wife, and forget the *grande passion* of his school-days," replied the Frenchman, as they strolled on.

At nine o'clock, a cab left Douglas at the door of a handsome house in a West End square. A servant in livery admitted him, and, passing up one flight of stairs, richly carpeted, softly lighted, and decorated with flowers, he entered a wide doorway, hung with curtains of blue damask, and found himself in a charming room. Directly opposite, hung a portrait of Colonel Vane, a handsome, soldierly man, with such a cordial smile upon the painted lips, that his friend involuntarily smiled in answer, and advanced, as if to greet his host.

"Would that he were here to welcome you."

The voice was at his side, and there stood Mrs. Vane. But not the woman whom he met in Lady Lennox's drawing-room; that was a young and bloom-ing creature, festally arrayed—this a pale, sad-eyed widow, in her weeds. Never, surely, had weeds been more becoming, for the black dress, in spite of its nun-like simplicity, had an air of elegance that many a ball-dress lacks, and the widow's cap was a mere froth of tulle, encircling the fair face, and concealing all the hair but two plain bands upon the forehead. Not an ornament was visible but a tiny pearl brooch which Douglas himself had given his friend long ago, and a wedding-ring upon the hand that once had worn the opal also. She, too, was looking upward toward the picture, and for an instant a curious pause fell between them.

The apartment was an entire contrast to the gay and brilliant drawing-rooms he had been accustomed to see. Softly lighted by the pale flame of antique lamps, the eye was relieved from the glare of gas, while the graceful blending of blue and silver, in furniture, hangings and decorations, pleased one as a change from the more garish colors so much in vogue. A few rare pictures leaned from the walls; several statues stood cool and still in remote recesses; from the curtained entrance of another door was blown the odorous breath of flowers, and the rustle of leaves, the drip of falling water, betrayed the existence of a conservatory close at hand.

"No wonder you were glad to leave the country, for a home like this," said Douglas, as she paused.

"Yes, it is pleasant to be here; but I should tell you that it is not my own. My kind friend, Lady Leigh, is in Rome for the winter, and knowing that I was a homeless little creature, she begged me to stay here, and keep both servants and house in order till she came again. I was very grateful, for I dread the loneliness of lodgings, and having arranged matters to suit my taste, I shall nestle here till spring tempts me to the hills again."

She spoke quite simply, and seemed as thankful for kindness as a solitary child. Despite his suspicions, and all the causes for distrust—nay, even hatred, if his belief was true—Douglas could not resist the wish that she might be proved innocent, and somewhere find the safe home her youth and beauty needed. So potent was the fascination of her presence, that when with her his doubts seemed unfounded, and so great was the confusion into which his mind was thrown by these conflicting impressions, that his native composure quite deserted him at times. It did so then, for, leaning nearer, as they sat together on a couch, he asked, almost abruptly:

"Why do I find you so changed, in all respects, that I scarcely recognize my friend just now?"

"You mean this?" and she touched her dress. "As you have honored me with the name of friend, I will speak frankly, and explain my seeming caprice. At the desire of Lady Lennox, I laid aside my weeds, and found that I could be a gay, young girl again, but with that discovery came another, which made me regret the change, and resolve to return to my sad garb."

"You mean that you found the change made you too beautiful for George's peace? Poor lad—I knew his secret, and now I understand your sacrifice," Earl said, as she paused, too delicate to betray her young lover, who had asked and been denied.

She colored beautifully, and sat silent; but Douglas was possessed by an irresistible desire to probe her heart as deeply as he dared, and quite unconscious that interest lent his voice and manner an unusual warmth, he asked, thinking only of poor George:

"Was it not possible to spare both yourself and him? You see I use a friend's privilege to the utmost."

She still looked down, and the color deepened visibly in her smooth cheek, as she replied:

"It was not possible, nor will it ever be, for him."

"You have not vowed yourself to an eternal widowhood, I trust?"

She looked up suddenly, as if to rebuke the persistent questioner, but something in his eager face changed her own expression of displeasure into one of half-concealed confusion.

"No; it is so sweet to be beloved, that I have not the courage to relinquish the hope of retasting the happiness so quickly snatched from me before."

Douglas rose suddenly, and paced down the room, as if attracted by a balmy gust that just then came floating in. But in truth, he fled from the syren by his side, for, despite the bitter past, the late loss, the present distrust, something softer than pity, warmer than regard, seemed creeping into his heart, and the sight of the beautiful, blushing face made his own cheek burn with a glow such as his love for Diana had never kindled. Indignant at his own weakness, he paused half way down the long room, wheeled about, and came back, saying, with his accustomed tone of command disguised by a touch of pity:

"Come and do the honors of your little paradise. I am restless to-night, and the splash of that fountain has a soothing sound that tempts me to draw nearer."

She went with him, and, standing by the fountain's brim, talked tranquilly of many things, till the sound of voices caused them to look toward the drawing-room. Two gentlemen were evidently coming to join them, and Earl said, with a smile:

"You have not asked why I came alone; yet your invitation included Arguelles and Dupont."

Again the blush rose to her cheek, and she answered, hastily, as she advanced to meet her guests:

"I forgot them; now I must atone for my rudeness."

Down the green vista came the gentlemen—the stout Frenchman tripping on before, the dark Spaniard walking behind, with a dignity of bearing that made his companion's gait more ludicrous by comparison. Compliments were exchanged, and then, as the guests expressed a desire to linger in the charming spot, Mrs. Vane led them on, doing the honors with her accustomed grace. Busied in translating the names of remarkable plants into Spanish for Arguelles, they were somewhat in advance of the other pair, and after a sharp glance or two at Douglas, Dupres paused behind a young orange-tree, saying, in a low whisper:

"You are going fast, Earl. Finish this business soon, or it will be too late for anything but flight."

"No fear; but what can *I* do? I protest I never was so bewildered in my life. Help me, for Heaven's sake, and do it at once!" replied Douglas, with a troubled and excited air.

"Chut! you English have no idea of *finesse;* you bungle sadly. See, now, how smoothly I will discover all I wish to know." Then aloud, as he moved on, "I assure you, *mon ami,* it is an orange, not a lemon-tree. Madame shall decide the point, and award me yonder fine flower, if I am right."

"Monsieur is correct, and here is the prize."

As she spoke, Mrs. Vane lifted her hand to break the flower which grew just above her. As she stretched her arm upward, her sleeve slipped back, and on her white wrist shone the wide bracelet once attached to the opal ring. As if annoyed by its exposure, she shook down her sleeve with a quick gesture, and before either gentleman could assist her, she stepped on a low seat, gathered the azalea, and turned to descend. Her motion was sudden, the seat frail; it broke as she turned, and she would have fallen, had not Arguelles sprung forward and caught her hands. She recovered herself instantly, and apologizing for her awkwardness, presented the flower with a playful speech. To Earl's great surprise, Dupres received it without his usual flow of compliments, and bowing, silently settled it in his button-hole, with such a curious expression that his friend fancied he had made some unexpected discovery. He had—but not what Douglas imagined, as he lifted his brows inquiringly when Mrs. Vane and her escort walked on.

"Hush!" breathed Dupres in answer; "ask her where Jitomar is, in some careless way."

"Why?" asked Earl, recollecting the man for the first time.

But his question received no reply, and the entrance of a servant with refreshments offered the desired pretext for the inquiry.

"Where is your handsome Jitomar? His oriental face and costume would give the finishing touch to this Eastern garden of palms and lotus-flowers," said Douglas, as he offered his hostess a glass of wine, when they paused at a rustic table by the fountain.

"Poor Jitomar—I have lost him!" she replied.

"Dead?" exclaimed Earl.

"O, no; and I should have said, Happy Jitomar, for he is on his way home to his own palms and lotus-flowers. He dreaded another winter here so much, that when a good opportunity offered for his return, I let him go, and have missed him sadly ever since—for he was a faithful servant to me."

"Let us drink the health of this good and faithful servant, and wish him a prosperous voyage to the torrid land where he belongs," cried Dupres, as he touched his glass to that of Arguelles, who looked somewhat bewildered, both by the odd name and the new ceremony.

By some mishap, as Dupres turned to replace his glass upon the table, it slipped from his hand, and fell into the fountain, with a splash that caused a little wave to break over the basin's edge, and wet Mrs. Vane's foot with an unexpected bath.

"Great heavens—what carelessness! A thousand pardons! Madame, permit me to repair the damage, although it is too great an honor for me, *maladroit* that I am," exclaimed the Frenchman, with a gesture of despair.

Mrs. Vane shook her dress, and assured him that no harm was done; but nothing could prevent the distressed gentleman from going down upon his knees, and with his perfumed handkerchief removing several drops of water from the foot of his hostess—during which process he discovered that, being still an invalid, she wore quilted black silk boots, with down about the tops;

also that though her foot was a very pretty one, it was by no means as small as that of Virginie Varens.

When this small stir was over, Mrs. Vane led the way back to the saloon, and here Douglas was more than ever mystified by Dupres's behaviour. Entirely ignoring madame's presence; he devoted himself to Arguelles, besetting him with questions regarding Spain, his own family, pursuits and tastes; on all of which points the Spaniard satisfied him, and accepted his various invitations for the coming days, looking much at their fair hostess the while, who was much engrossed with Douglas, and seemed quite content.

Arguelles was the first to leave, and his departure broke up the party. As Earl and Dupres drove off together, the former exclaimed, in a fever of curiosity:

"Are you satisfied?"

"Entirely."

"She is not Virginie, then?"

"On the contrary, she *is* Virginie, I suspect."

"You suspect? I thought you were entirely satisfied."

"On another point, I am. She baffles me somewhat, I confess, with her woman's art in dress. But I shall discover her yet, if you let me conduct the affair in my own way. I adore mystery; to fathom a secret, trace a lie, discover a disguise, is my delight. I should make a superb detective. Apropos to that, promise me that you will not call in the help of your blundering constabulary, police, or whatever you name them, until I give the word. They will destroy the *éclat* of the *dénouement*, and annoy me by their stupidity."

"I leave all to you, and regret that the absence of this Jitomar should complicate the affair. What deviltry is he engaged in now, do you think? Not travelling to India, of course, though she told it very charmingly."

His companion whispered three words in his ear. Earl fell back, and stared at him, exclaiming, presently:

"It is impossible!"

"Nothing is impossible to me," returned the other, with an air of conviction. "That point is clear to my mind; one other remains, and being more difficult, I must consider it. But have no fear; this brain of mine is fertile in inventions, and by morning will have been inspired with a design which will enchant you by its daring, its acuteness, its romance."

Chapter IX

Midnight

For a week the three gentlemen haunted the house of the widow, and were much together elsewhere. Dupres was still enthusiastic in praise of his new-made friend, but Douglas was far less cordial, and merely courteous when they met. To outside observers, this seemed but natural, for the world knew nothing of his relations to Diana, nor the sad secret that existed between himself and Mrs. Vane. And when it was apparent that the Spaniard was desperately in love with that lady, Douglas could not but look coldly upon him as a rival, for, according to rumor, the latter gentleman was also paying court to the bewitching widow. It was soon evident which was the favored lover, for despite the dark glances and jealous surveillance of Arguelles, Mrs. Vane betrayed, by unmistakable signs, that Douglas possessed a power over her which no other man had ever attained. It was impossible to conceal it, for when the great passion for the first time possessed her heart, all her art was powerless against this touch of nature, and no timid girl could have been more harassed by the alternations of hope and fear, and the effort to hide her passion.

Going to their usual rendezvous somewhat earlier than usual one evening, Dupres stopped a moment in an ante-room to exchange a word with Gabrielle, the coquettish maid, who was apt to be in the way when the Frenchman appeared. Douglas went on to the drawing-room, expecting to find Mrs. Vane alone. The apartment was empty, but the murmur of voices was audible in the conservatory, and going to the curtained arch, he was about to lift the drapery that had fallen from its fastening, when through a little crevice in the middle, he saw two figures that arrested him, and, in spite of certain honorable scruples, held him motionless where he stood.

Mrs. Vane and the Spaniard were beside the fountain; both looked excited. Arguelles talked vehemently; she listened with a hard, scornful expression, and made brief answers that seemed to chafe and goad him bitterly. Both spoke Spanish, and even if they had not, so low and rapid were their tones, that nothing was audible but the varied murmur rising or falling as the voices alternated. From his gestures, the gentleman seemed by turns to reproach, entreat, command; the lady to recriminate, refuse and defy. Once she evidently announced some determination that filled her companion with de-

spair; then she laughed, and in a paroxysm of speechless wrath he broke from
her, hurrying to the farthest limits of the room, as if unconscious whither he
went, and marking with scattered leaves and flowers the passage of his reckless steps.

As he turned from her, Mrs. Vane dipped her hands in the basin and laid
them on her forehead, as if to cool some fever of the brain, while such a
weight of utter weariness came over her, that in an instant ten years seemed to
be added to her age. Her eyes roved restlessly to and fro, as if longing to
discover some method of escape from the danger or the doubt that oppressed
her.

A book from which Douglas had read to her, lay on the rustic table at her
side, and as her eye fell on it, all her face changed beautifully; hope, bloom
and youth returned, as she touched the volume with a lingering touch, and
smiled a smile in which love and exultation blended. A rapid-step announced
the Spaniard's return; she caught her hand away, mused a moment, and when
he came back to her, she spoke in a softer tone, while her eyes betrayed that
now she pleaded for some boon, and did not plead in vain. Seizing both her
hands in a grasp more firm than tender, Arguelles seemed to extort some
promise from her with sternest aspect. She gave it reluctantly; he looked but
half satisfied, even though she drew his tall head down and sealed her
promise with a kiss; and when she bade him go, he left her with a gloomy air,
and some dark purpose stamped upon his face.

So rapidly had this scene passed, so suddenly was it ended, that Douglas
had barely time to draw a few paces back, before the curtain was pushed
aside, and Arguelles stood in the arch. Unused to the dishonorable practices
to which he had lent himself for the completion of a just work, Earl's face
betrayed him. The Spaniard saw that the late interview had not been without
a witness, and forgetting that they had spoken in an unknown tongue, for a
moment he looked perfectly livid with fear and fury. Some recollection
suddenly seemed to reassure him, but the covert purpose just formed appeared to culminate in action, for, with ungovernable hatred flaming up in his
eyes, he said, in a suppressed voice that scarcely parted his white lips:

"Eavesdropper and spy! I spit upon you!" And advancing one step struck
Douglas full in the face.

It had nearly been his last act, for burning with scorn and detestation, Earl
took him by the throat, and was about to execute swift retribution for both
the old wrong and the new, when Dupres came between them, whispering, as
he wrenched Earl's arm away:

"Hold! remember where you are. Come away, señor, I am your friend in this affair. It shall be arranged. Douglas, remain here, I entreat you."

As he spoke, Dupres gave Earl a warning glance, and drew Arguelles swiftly from the house. Controlling a desperate desire to follow, Douglas remembered his promise to let his friend conduct the affair in his own way, and by a strong effort composed himself, though his cheek still tingled with the blow, and his blood burned within him. The whole encounter had passed noiselessly, and when, after a brief pause, Douglas entered the conservatory, Mrs. Vane still lingered by the fountain, unconscious of the scene which had just transpired. She turned to greet the new-comer with extended hand, and it was with difficulty that he restrained the rash impulse to strike it from him. The very effort to control this desire made the pressure of his own hand almost painful, as he took that other, and the strong grasp sent a thrill of joy to Mrs. Vane's heart, as she smiled and glowed under his glance like a flower at the coming of the sun. The inward excitement, which it was impossible to wholly subdue, manifested itself in Earl's countenance and manner more plainly than he knew, and would have excited some of ill in his companion's mind, had not love blinded her, and left room for none but prophecies of good. A little tremble of delight agitated her, and the eyes that once were so coldly bright and penetrating, now were seldom lifted to the face that she had studied so carefully, not long ago. After the first greetings, she waited for him to speak, for words would not come at her will when with him; but he stood thoughtfully, dipping his hand into the fountain as she had done, and laying the wet palm against his cheek, lest its indignant color should betray the insult he had just received.

"Did you meet Señor Arguelles as you came in?" she asked presently, as the pause was unbroken.

"He passed me, and went out."

"You do not fancy him, I suspect."

"I confess it, Mrs. Vane."

"And why?"

"Need I tell *you?*"

The words escaped him involuntarily, and had she seen his face just then, her own would have blanched with fear. But she was looking down, and as he spoke the traitorous color rose to her forehead, though she ignored the betrayal by saying, with an accent of indifference:

"He will not annoy you long. To-morrow he fulfils some engagement with a friend in the country, and in the evening will take leave of me."

"He is about to return to Spain, then?"

"I believe so, I did not question him."

"You will not bid him adieu without regret?"

"With the greatest satisfaction, I assure you, for underneath that Spanish dignity of manner lurks fire, and I have no desire to be consumed." And the sigh of relief that accompanied her words was the most sincere expression of feeling that had escaped her for weeks.

Anxious to test his power to the utmost, Douglas pursued the subject, though it was evidently distasteful to her. Assuming an air of lover-like anxiety, he half timidly, half eagerly inquired:

"Then when he comes again to say farewell, you will not consent to go with him to occupy the 'castle in Spain' which he has built up for himself during this short week?"

He thought to see some demonstration of pleasure at the jealous fear his words implied, but her color faded suddenly, and she shivered as if a chilly gust had blown over her, while she answered briefly, with a little gesture of the hand as she set the topic decidedly aside:

"No, he will go alone."

There was a momentary pause, and in it something like pity knocked at the door of Earl's heart, for with all his faults he was a generous man, and as he saw this woman sitting there, so unconscious of impending danger, so changed and beautiful by one true sentiment, his purpose wavered, a warning word rose to his lips, and with an impetuous gesture he took her hand, and turned away with an abrupt:

"Pardon me—it is too soon—I will explain hereafter."

The entrance of a servant with coffee seemed to rouse him into sudden spirits and activity, for begging Mrs. Vane to sit and rest, he served her with assiduous care.

"Here is your own cup of violet and gold; you see I know your fancy even in trifles. Is it right? I took such pains to have it as you like it," he said, as he presented the cup with an air of tender solicitude.

"It does not matter, but one thing you have forgotten, I take no sugar," she answered, smiling as she tasted.

"I knew it, yet the line 'Sweets to the sweet' was running in my head, and so I unconsciously spoiled your draught. Let me retrieve the error?"

"By no means. I drink to you," and lifting the tiny cup to her lips, she emptied it with a look which proved that his words had already retrieved the error.

He received the cup with a peculiar smile, looked at his watch, and exclaimed, regretfully:

"It is late, and I should go, yet—"

"No, not yet; stay and finish the lines you began yesterday. I find less beauty in them when I read them to myself," she answered, detaining him.

Glad of an excuse to prolong his stay, Earl brought the book, and sitting near her, lent to the poem the sonorous music of his voice.

The last words came all too soon, and when Douglas rose, Mrs. Vane bade him good-night with a dreamy softness in her eyes which caused a gleam of satisfaction to kindle in his own. As he passed through the ante-room, Gabrielle met him with a look of anxious though mute inquiry in her face. He answered it with a significant nod, a warning gesture, and she let him out, wearing an aspect of the deepest mystery.

Douglas hurried to his rooms, and there found Dupres with Major Mansfield, who had been put in possession of the secret, and the part he was expected to play in its unravelling.

"What in heaven's name did you mean by taking the wrong side of the quarrel, and forcing me to submit quietly to such an indignity?" demanded Earl, giving vent to the impatience which had only been curbed till now, that he might perform the portion of the plot allotted to him.

"Tell me first have you succeeded?" said Dupres.

"I have."

"You are sure?"

"Beyond a doubt."

"It is well, I applaud your dexterity. Behold the major, he knows all, he is perfect in his role, now hear yours. You will immediately write a challenge."

"It is impossible! Antoine, you are daft to ask me to meet that man."

"Bah! I ask you to meet, but not to honor him by blowing his brains out. He is a dead shot, and thirsts for your blood, but look you, he will be disappointed. We might arrest him this instant, but he will confess nothing, and that clever creature will escape us. No, my little arrangement suits me better."

"Time flies, Dupres, and so perhaps may this crafty hind that you are about to snare," said the major, whose slow, British wits were somewhat confused by the Frenchman's *finesse.*

"It is true; see then, my Earl. In order that our other little affair may come smoothly off without interference from our friend, I propose to return to the señor, whom I have lately left writing letters, and amuse myself by keeping him at home to receive your challenge, which the major will bring about twelve. Then we shall arrange the affair to take place at sunrise, in some secluded spot out of town. You will be back here by that time, you will agree to our plans, and present yourself at the appointed time, when the *grand dénouement* will take place with much *éclat*."

"Am I not to know more?" asked Douglas.

"It would be well to leave all to me, for you will act your part better if you do not know the exact programme, because you do not perform so well with monsieur as with madame. But if you must know, the major will tell you, while you wait for Hyde and the hour. I have seen him, he has no scruples; I have insured his safety, and he will not fail us. Now the charming billet to the señor, and I go to my post."

Douglas wrote the challenge; Dupres departed in buoyant spirits, and while Earl waited for the stranger Hyde, the major enlightened him upon the grand finale.

The city clocks were striking twelve, as two men masked and cloaked, passed up the steps of Mrs. Vane's house, and entered noiselessly. No light beamed in the hall, but scarcely had they closed the door behind them, when a glimmer shone from above, and at the stair-head appeared a woman beckoning. Up they stole, as if shod with velvet, and the woman flitted like a shadow before them, till they reached a door in the second story. Opening this, she motioned them to enter, and as they passed in, she glided up another flight, as if to stand guard over her sleeping fellow-servants.

One of the men was tall and evidently young, the other, a bent and withered little man, whose hands trembled slightly as he adjusted his mask, and peered about him. A large, still room, lighted by a night-lamp burning behind its shade, richly furnished, and decorated with warm hues, that produced the effect of mingled snow and fire. A luxurious nest it seemed, and a fit inmate of it looked the beautiful woman asleep in the shadow of the crimson-curtained bed. One white arm pillowed her head; from the little cap that should have confined it, flowed a mass of golden hair over neck and shoulders; the long lashes lay dark against her cheek; the breath slept upon her lips, and perfect unconsciousness lent its reposeful charm to both face and figure.

Noiselessly advancing, the taller man looked and listened, for a moment, as if to assure himself that this deep slumber was not feigned; then he beckoned the other to bring the lamp. It flickered as the old man took it up, but he trimmed the wick, removed the shade, and a clear light shone across the room. Joining his companion, he too looked at the sleeping beauty, shook his gray head, and seemed to deplore some fact that marred the pretty picture in his sight.

"Is there no danger of her waking, sir?" he whispered, as the light fell on her face.

"It is impossible for an hour yet. The bracelet is on that wrist; we must move her, or you cannot reach it," returned the other, and with a gentle touch drew the left arm from underneath her head.

She sighed in her sleep, knit her brows, as if a dream disturbed her, and turning on her pillow, all the bright hair fell about her face, but could not hide the glitter of the chain about her neck. Drawing it forth, the taller man started, uttered an exclamation, dragged from his own bosom a duplicate of the miniature hanging from that chain, and compared the two with trembling intentness. Very like they were, those two young faces, handsome, frank, and full of boyish health, courage and blithesomeness. One might have been taken a year after the other, for the brow was bolder, the mouth graver, the eye more steadfast, but the same charm of expression appeared in both, making the ivory oval more attractive even to a stranger's eye than the costly setting, or the initial letters "A. D." done in pearls upon the back. A small silver key hung on the chain the woman wore, and as if glad to tear his thoughts from some bitter reminiscence, the man detached this key, and glanced about the room, as if to discover what lock it would fit.

His action seemed to remind the other of his own task, for setting down the lamp on the little table where lay a prayer-book, a bell and a rosary, he produced a case of delicate instruments and bunch of tiny keys, and bending over the bracelet, examined the golden padlock that fastened it. While he carefully tried key after key upon that miniature lock, the chief of this mysterious inspection went to and fro with the silver key, attempting larger locks. Nowhere did it fit, till in passing the toilet table, his foot brushed its draperies aside, disclosing a quaint, foreign-looking casket of ebony and silver. Quick as thought it was drawn out and opened, for here the key did its work. In the upper tray lay the opal ring in its curiously thick setting, beside it a seal, rudely made from an impression in wax of his own iron ring, and a paper bearing its stamp. The marriage record was in his hand, and he longed to keep or destroy it, but restrained the impulse; and lifting the tray, found below two or three relics of his friend Vane, and some childish toys, soiled and broken, but precious still.

"A child! Good God! what have I done!" he said to himself, as the lid fell from his hand.

"Hush, come and look, it is off," whispered the old man and hastily restoring all things to their former order, the other relocked and replaced the casket, and obeyed the call.

For a moment a mysterious and striking picture might have been seen in that quiet room. Under the crimson canopy lay the fair figure of the sleeping woman, her face half hidden by the golden shadow of her hair, her white arm laid out on the warm-hued coverlet, and bending over it, the two masked men, one holding the lamp nearer, the other pointing to something just above the delicate wrist, now freed from the bracelet which lay open beside it. Two distinctly traced letters were seen, "V. V.," and underneath a tiny true-lover's knot, in the same dark lines. The man who held the lamp examined the brand with minutest care, then making a gesture of satisfaction, he said:

"It is enough, I am sure now. Put on the bracelet, and come away, there is nothing more to be done to-night."

The old man skilfully replaced the hand, while the other put back locket and key, placed the lamp where they found it, and with a last look at the sleeper, whose unconscious helplessness appealed to them for mercy, both stole away as noiselessly as they had come. The woman reappeared the instant they left the room, lighted them to the hall door, received some reward that glittered, as it passed from hand to hand, and made all fast behind them, pausing a moment in a listening attitude, till the distant roll of a carriage assured her that the maskers were safely gone.

Chapter X

In the Snare

The first rays of the sun fell on a group of five men, standing together on a waste bit of ground in the environs of London. Major Mansfield and Dupres were busily loading pistols, marking off the distance, and conferring together with a great display of interest. Douglas conversed tranquilly with the surgeon in attendance, a quiet, unassuming man, who stood with his hand in his pocket, as if ready to produce his case of instruments at a moment's notice. The Spaniard was alone, and a curious change seemed to have passed over him. The stately calmness of his demeanor was gone, and he paced to and fro with restless steps, like a panther in his cage. A look of almost savage hatred lowered on his swarthy face; desperation and despair alternately glowed and gloomed in his fierce eyes, and the whole man wore a look of one who after long restraint yields himself utterly to the dominion of some passion, dauntless and indomitable as death. Once he paused, drew from his pocket an ill-spelt, rudely-written letter, which had been put into his hand by a countryman, as he left his hotel, re-read the few lines it contained, and thrust it back into his bosom, muttering:

"All things favor me; this was the last tie that bound her, now we must stand or fall together."

"Señor, we are prepared," called Dupres, advancing, pistol in hand, to place his principal, adding, as Arguelles dropped hat and cloak, "our custom may be different from yours, but give heed, and at the word 'three,' fire."

"I comprehend, monsieur," and a dark smile passed across the Spaniard's face as he took his place, and stretched his hand to receive the weapon.

But Dupres drew back a step—and with a sharp, metallic click, around that extended wrist snapped a handcuff. A glance showed Arguelles that he was lost, for on his right stood the counterfeit surgeon, with the well-known badge now visible on his blue coat, behind him Major Mansfield, armed, before him Douglas, guarding the nearest outlet of escape, and on his left Dupres, radiant with satisfaction, exclaiming, as he bowed with grace:

"A thousand pardons, M. Victor Varens, but this little ruse was inevitable."

Quick as a flash, that freed left hand snatched the pistol from Dupres, aimed it at Douglas, and it would have accomplished its work, had not the Frenchman struck up the weapon. But the ball was sped, and as the pistol turned in his hand, the bullet lodged in Victor's breast, sparing him the fate he dreaded more than death. In an instant, all trace of passion vanished, and with a melancholy dignity that nothing could destroy, he offered his hand to receive the fetter, saying calmly, while his lips whitened, and a red stain dyed the linen on his breast:

"I am tired of my life; take it."

They laid him down, for, as he spoke, consciousness ebbed away. A glance assured the major that the wound was mortal, and carefully conveying the senseless body to the nearest house, Douglas and the detective remained to tend and guard the prisoner, while the other gentlemen posted to town to bring a genuine surgeon and necessary help, hoping to keep life in the man till his confession had been made.

At nightfall, Mrs. Vane, or Virginie, as we may now call her, grew anxious for the return of Victor, who was to bring her tidings of the child, because she dared not visit him just now herself. Not only anxious was she, but inwardly intensely excited, for she, too, had taken a desperate resolution to break the tie that bound her to her cousin. She had promised him the heart he had waited for so long, but that promise never would be kept, for when he came to claim its fulfilment, she had determined to reward his constancy with the swift and painless death, which she would offer him in the draught he drank to the success of their last venture. Victor gone, the secret of her life was hers alone, she thought, and this hard-won liberty would leave her free to accept the name she coveted; for once his wife, Douglas would never dare proclaim the past, when she should be made known to him as her real self. She had pondered over the design, the hope, until the one had grown too familiar to daunt her, the other, too precious to relinquish; and now she waited with feverish impatience to do and dare anything for the accomplishment of her desire.

When dressed for the evening, she dismissed Gabrielle, opened the antique casket, and put on the opal ring, carefully attaching the little chain that fastened it securely to her bracelet, for the ring was too large for the delicate hand that wore it. For a moment, she remained kneeling before this repository of her secrets and her sins, with a troubled look, that deepened as she touched one object after another, seeming to recall the various parts they had played.

With a heavy sigh she laid her head down on her knee, and if tears fell, none saw them, if she prayed, none heard the prayer, and if the spirit of good that lingers in the most unrepentant beckoned her on to penitence, there was no sign of submission, for when she rose, her face was cold and quiet, and with steady feet she went down to the drawing-room to meet her lover and her victim.

But there, as elsewhere, some reproachful memory seemed to start up and haunt the present with a vision of the past. She passed her hand across her eyes, as if she saw again the little room, where in the gray dawn she had left her husband lying dead, and she sank into a seat, groaning half aloud:

"O, if I could forget!"

A bell rang from below, but she did not hear it; steps came through the drawing-room, yet she did not heed them; and Douglas stood before her, but she did not see him till he spoke. So great was her surprise, that with all her power of dissimulation she would have found difficulty in concealing it, had not the pale gravity of the new-comer's face afforded a pretext for alarm.

"You startled me at first, and now you look as if you brought ill news," she said, with a vain effort to assume her usual gaiety.

"I do," was the brief reply.

"The señor? Is he with you? I am waiting for him."

"Wait no longer, he will never come."

"Where is he?"

"Quiet in his shroud."

He thought to see her shrink and pale before the blow, but she did neither; she grasped his arm, searched his face, and whispered, with a look of relief, not terror, in her own:

"You have killed him?"

"No, his blood is not upon my head; he killed himself."

She covered up her face, and from behind her hands he heard her murmur:

"Thank God, he did not come! I am spared that."

While he pondered over the words, vainly trying to comprehend them, she recovered herself, and turning to him, said quite steadily, though very pale:

"This is awfully sudden; tell me how it came to pass. I am not afraid to hear."

"I will tell you, for you have a right to know. Sit, Mrs. Vane; it is a long tale, and one that will try your courage to the utmost."

She shot a quick glance at him, saw that his face was grave and stern, yet his voice was calm, his eye pitiful, and with the thought, "He would not look so if he knew all. I am safe," she sat down, leaning her elbow on the table, with one hand arched above her eyes, as if to shield them from the light. Douglas placed himself opposite, folded his arms before him, and bending toward her, fixed and held her wavering glance with his own steadfast gaze. She could not escape nor conquer it, and before a word left his lips an instinctive foreboding warned her that in the next hour all would be lost or won.

"Six years ago I went abroad to meet my cousin Allan," Douglas began, speaking slowly, almost sternly. "He was my senior by a year, but we so closely resembled each other that we were often taken for twin brothers. Alike in person, character, temper and tastes, we were never so happy as when together, and we loved one another as tenderly as women love. For nearly a year, we roamed east and west, then our holiday was over, for we had promised to return. One month more remained; I desired to revisit Switzerland, Allan to remain in Paris, so we parted for a time, each to our own pleasures, appointing to meet on a certain day at a certain place. I never saw him again, for when I reached the spot where he should have met me, I found only a letter, saying that he had been called from Paris suddenly, but that I should receive further intelligence before many days. I waited, but not long. Visiting the Morgue that very week, I found my poor Allan waiting for me there. His body had been taken from the river, and the deep wound in his breast showed that foul play was at the bottom of the mystery. Night and day I labored to clear up the mystery, but labored secretly, lest publicity should warn the culprits, or bring dishonor upon our name, for I soon found that Allan had led a wild life in my absence, and I feared to make some worse discovery than a young man's follies. I did so; for it appeared that he had been captivated by a singularly beautiful girl, a *danseuse,* had privately married her, and both had disappeared with a young cousin of her own. Her apartments were searched, but all her possessions had been removed, and nothing remained but a plausible letter, which would have turned suspicion from the girl to the cousin, had not the marriage been discovered, and in her room two witnesses against them. The handle of a stiletto, half consumed in the ashes, which fitted the broken blade entangled in the dead man's clothes, and, hidden by the hangings of the bed, a woman's slipper, with a blood stain on the sole. Ah, you may well shudder, Mrs. Vane; it is an awful tale."

"Horrible! Why tell it?" she asked, pressing her hand upon her eyes, as if to shut out some image too terrible to look upon.

"Because it concerns our friend Arguelles, and explains his death," replied Earl, in the same slow, stern voice. She did not look up, but he saw that she listened breathlessly, and grew paler still behind her hand.

"Nothing more was discovered then. My cousin's body was sent home, and none but our two families ever knew the truth. It was believed by the world that he died suddenly of an affection of the heart—poor lad! it was the bitter truth—and whatever rumors were afloat regarding his death, and the change it wrought in me, were speedily silenced at the time, and have since died away. Over the dead body of my dearest friend, I vowed a solemn vow to find his murderer and avenge his death. I have done both."

"Where? How?"

Her hand dropped, and she looked at him with a face that was positively awful in its unnatural calmness.

"Arguelles was Victor Varens. I suspected, watched, ensnared him, and would have let the law avenge Allan's death, but the murderer escaped by his own hand."

"Well for him that it was so. May his sins be forgiven. Now let us go elsewhere, and forget this dark story and its darker end."

She rose as she spoke, and a load seemed lifted off her heart; but it fell again, as Douglas stretched his hand to detain her, saying:

"Stay, the end is not yet told. You forget the girl."

"She was innocent—why should she suffer?" returned the other, still standing as if defying both fear and fate.

"She was *not* innocent—for she lured that generous boy to marry her, because she coveted his rank and fortune, not his heart, and when he lay dead, left him to the mercies of wind and wave, while she fled away to save herself. But that cruel cowardice availed her nothing, for though I have watched and waited long, at length I have found her, and at this moment her life lies in my hand—for you and Virginie are one!"

As he spoke, his outstretched hand closed with an ominously significant gesture. But like a hunted creature driven to bay, she turned on him with an air of desperate audacity, saying, haughtily:

"Prove it!"

"I will."

For a moment they looked at one another. In his face she saw pitiless resolve; in hers he read passionate defiance.

"Sit down, Virginie, and hear the story through. Escape is impossible—the house is guarded, Dupres waits in yonder room, and Victor can no longer help you with quick wit or daring hand. Submit quietly, and do not force me to forget that you are my cousin's—wife."

She obeyed him, and as the last words fell from his lips, a new hope sprang up within her, the danger seemed less imminent, and she took heart again, remembering the child, who might yet plead for her, if her own eloquence should fail.

"You ask me to prove that fact, and evidently doubt my power to do it; but well as you have laid your plots, carefully as you have erased all traces of your former self, and skilfully as you have played your new part, the truth has come to light, and through many winding ways I have followed you, till my labor ends here. Let me show you where you have failed, and how your own arts have helped to snare you and your accomplice. When you fled from

Paris, Victor, whose mother was a Spaniard, took you to Spain, and there, among his kindred, your boy was born."

"Do you know that, too?" she cried, lost in wonder at the quiet statement of what she believed to be known only to herself, her dead cousin, and those far-distant kindred who had succored her in her need.

"I know everything," Earl answered, with an expression that made her quail; then a daring spirit rose up in her, as she remembered more than one secret, which she now felt to be hers alone.

"Not everything, my cousin; you are keen and subtle, but I excel you, though you win this victory, it seems."

So cool, so calm she seemed, so beautifully audacious she looked, that Earl could only resent the bold speech with a glance, and proceed to prove the truth of his second assertion with the first.

"You suffered the sharpest poverty, but Victor respected your helplessness, forgave your treachery, supplied your wants as far as possible, and when all other means failed, left you there, while he went to earn bread for you and your boy. Virginie, I never can forgive him my cousin's death, but for his faithful, long-suffering devotion to you, I honor him, sinner though he was."

She shrugged her shoulders, with an air of indifference or displeasure, took off the widow's cap, no longer needed for a disguise, and letting loose the cloud of curls that seemed to love to cluster round her charming face, she lay back in her chair with all her former graceful ease, saying, as she fixed her lustrous eyes upon the man she meant to conquer yet:

"I let him love me, and he was content. What more could I do, for I never loved *him?*"

"Better for him that you did not, and better for poor Allan that he never lived to know that it was impossible for you to love."

Earl spoke bitterly, but Virginie bent her head till her face was hidden, as she murmured:

"Ah, if it were impossible, this hour would be less terrible, the future far less dark."

He heard the soft lament, divined its meaning, but abruptly continued his story, as if he ignored the sorrowful fact which made her punishment heavier from his hand than from any other.

"While Victor was away, you wearied of waiting, you longed for the old life of gaiety and excitement, and, hoping to free yourself from him, you stole away, and for a year were lost to him. Your plan was to reach France, and, under another name, dance yourself into some honest man's heart and home, making him your shield against all danger. You did reach France, but weary, ill, poor, and burdened with the child, you failed to find friends or help, till some evil fortune threw Vane in your way. You had heard of him from Allan, knew his chivalrous nature, his passion for relieving pain or sorrow, at any cost to himself, and you appealed to him for charity. A piteous story of a cruel husband, desertion, suffering and destitution you told him; he believed it, and being on the point of sailing for India, offered you the place of companion to a lady sailing with him. Your tale was plausible, your youth made it pathetic, your beauty lent it power, and the skill with which you played the part of a sad gentlewoman won all hearts, and served your end successfully. Vane loved you, wished to marry you, and would have done so had not death prevented. He died suddenly; you were with him, and though his last act was to make generous provision for you and the boy, some devil prompted you to proclaim yourself his wife, as soon as he was past denying it. He was a solitary man, with few friends and no relatives; therefore no one dared demand proofs from you, had they suspected you. None did; Vane's peculiar character explained any seeming mystery in the affair; his love for you was well known among those with whom you lived, and your statement was believed."

He paused a moment to watch her, for she was evidently racking her brain to discover how he had gained such accurate information of her past. Victor had sworn never to betray her, living or dying; hitherto he had kept his word with strictest fidelity, and she could not believe that he had turned traitor at last.

"You are a magician," she said, suddenly. "I have thought so before; now I am sure of it, for you must have transported yourself to India, to make these discoveries."

"No—India came to me in the person of a Hindoo, and from him I learned these facts," replied Douglas, slow to tell her of Victor's perfidy, lest he should put her on her guard, and perhaps lose some revelation, which, in her ignorance, she might make. Fresh bewilderment seemed to fall upon her, and with intensest interest she listened, as that ruthless voice went on.

"Your plan was this: From Vane you had learned much of Allan's family, and the old desire to be 'my lady,' returned more strongly than before. Your brain was fertile in expedients, you acquired the polish of good society with ease, your eventful life gave you the advantages of courage, craft, and great skill in reading characters, and moulding your own to suit your purposes. Once in England, you hoped to make your way as Colonel Vane's widow, and if no safe, sure opportunity appeared of claiming your boy's right, you resolved to gain your end by wooing and winning another Douglas. You were on the point of starting, with poor Vane's fortune in your power (for he left no will, and you were prepared to produce forged papers, if your possession was questioned in England), when Victor found you. He had traced you with the instinct of a faithful dog, though his heart was nearly broken by your cruel desertion. You saw that he could serve you; you appeased his anger and silenced his reproaches by renewed promises to be his when the boy was acknowledged, if he would aid you in that project. At the risk of his life, this devoted slave consented, and, disguised as an Indian servant, came with you to England. On the way, you met and won the good graces of the Countess Camareena; she introduced you to the London world, and you began your career as a lady under the best auspices. Money, beauty, art, served you well, and as an unfortunate descendant of the noble house of Montmorenci, you were received by those who would have shrunk from you as you once did from the lock of hair of the plebeian French *danseuse*, found in Allan's dead bosom."

A scornful smile touched Earl's lips as he uttered the last words with a look that hurt her like a blow, and forced from her a truthful bit of history that otherwise would never have escaped her.

"I *am* noble," she cried, with an air that proved it; "for though my mother was a peasant, my father was a prince, and better blood than that of the Montmorencis flows in my veins. It ill becomes you to taunt me with low birth, for there is a blot on your own escutcheon, and the proud Lady of Lochleven was a king's mistress."

He could not deny it, and her woman's tongue avenged her wounded pride, as the hot blushes on Earl's cheek betrayed. But he only answered with a slight bow, which might be intended as a mocking obeisance in honor of her questionable nobility, or a grave dismissal of the topic.

"From this point the tale is unavoidably egotistical," he said; "for through Lady Lennox you heard of me, learned that I was the next heir to the title, and began at once to weave the web in which I was to be caught. You easily understood what was the mystery of my life, as it was called among the gossips, and that knowledge was a weapon in your hands, which you did not fail to use. You saw that Diana loved me, soon learned my passion for her, and set yourself to separate us, without one thought of the anguish it would bring us, one fear of the consequences of such wrong to yourself. You bade her ask of me a confession that I could not make, having given my word to Allan's mother that her son's memory should not be tarnished by the betrayal of the rash act that cost his life. That parted us; then you told her a tale of skilfully mingled truth and falsehood, showed her the marriage record on which a name and date appeared to convict me, took her to see the boy whose likeness to his father, and therefore to myself, completed the cruel deception, and drove that high-hearted girl to madness and to death."

"I did not kill her! On my soul, I never meant it! I was terror-stricken when we missed her, and knew no peace nor rest till she was found. Of this deed I am innocent—I swear it to you on my knees."

The haunting horror of that night seemed again to overwhelm her; all her courage and composure to desert her, and she fell down upon her knees before him, enforcing her denial with clasped hands, imploring eyes and trembling voice. But Douglas drew back with a gesture of repugnance that wounded her more deeply than his sharpest word, and from that moment all traces of compassion vanished from his countenance, which wore the relentless aspect of a judge who resolves within himself no longer to temper justice with mercy.

"Stand up," he said; "I will listen to no appeal, believe no oath, let no touch of pity soften my heart for your treachery, your craft, your sin, deserve nothing but the heavy retribution you have brought upon yourself. Diana's death lies at your door, as much as if you had stabbed her with the same dagger that took Allan's life. It may yet be proved that you beguiled her to that fatal pool, for you were seen there, going to remove all trace of her, perhaps. But in your hasty flight you left traces of yourself behind you, as you sprang away with an agility that first suggested to me the suspicion of Virginie's presence. I tried your slipper in the footprint, and it fitted too exactly to leave me in much doubt of the truth of my wild conjecture. I had never seen you. Antoine Dupres knew both Victor and yourself. I sent for him, but before the letter went, Jitomar, your spy, read the address, feared that some peril menaced you both, and took counsel with you how to delude the new-comer, if any secret purpose lurked behind our seeming friendliness. You devised a scheme that would have baffled us, had not accident betrayed Victor. In the guise of Arguelles he met Dupres in Paris, returned with him, and played his part so well that the Frenchman was entirely deceived, never dreaming of being sought by the very man who would most desire to shun him. You, too, disguised yourself, with an art that staggered my own senses, and perplexed Dupres, for our masculine eyes could not fathom the artifices of costume, cosmetics, and consummate acting. We feared to alarm you by any open step, and resolved to oppose craft to craft, treachery to treachery. Dupres revels in such intricate affairs, and I yielded, against my will, till the charm of success drew me on with increasing eagerness and spirit. The day we first met here, in gathering a flower you would have fallen, had not the Spaniard sprung forward to save you; that involuntary act betrayed him, for the momentary attitude he assumed recalled to Dupres the memory of a certain pose which the dancer Victor often assumed. It was too peculiar to be accidental, too striking to be easily forgotten, and the entire unconsciousness of its actor was a proof that it was so familiar as to be quite natural. From that instant Dupres devoted himself to the Spaniard; this first genuine delusion put Victor off his guard with Antoine, and Antoine's feigned friendship was so adroitly assumed that no suspicion woke in Victor's mind till the moment when, instead of offering him a weapon with which to take my life, he took him prisoner."

"He is not dead, then? You lie to me; you drive me wild with your horrible recitals of the past, and force me to confess against my will. Who told you these things? The dead alone could tell you what passed between Diana and myself."

Still on the ground, as if forgetful of everything but the bewilderment of seeing plot after plot unfolded before her, she had looked up and listened with dilated eyes, lips apart, and both hands holding back the locks that could no longer hide her from his piercing glance. As she spoke, she paled and trembled with a sudden fear that clutched her heart, that Diana was not dead, for even now she clung to her love with a desperate hope that it might save her. Calm and cold as a man of marble, Douglas looked down upon her, so beautiful in all her abasement, and answered, steadily:

"You forget Victor. To him all your acts, words, and many of your secret thoughts were told. Did you think his love would endure forever, his patience never tire, his outraged heart never rebel, his wild spirit never turn and rend you? All day I have sat beside him, listening to his painful confessions, painfully but truthfully made, and with his last breath he cursed you as the cause of a wasted life, an ignominious death. Virginie, this night your long punishment begins, and that curse is a part of it."

"O, no, no! You will have mercy, remembering how young, how friendless

I am? For Allan's sake you will pity me; for his boy's sake you will save me; for your own sake you will hide me from the world's contempt?"

"What mercy did you show poor Diana?—what love for Allan?—what penitence for your child's sake?—what pity for my grief? I tell you, if a word would save you, my lips should not utter it!"

He spoke passionately now, and passionately she replied, clinging to him, though he strove to tear his hands away.

"You have heard Victor's confession, now hear mine. I *have* longed to repent; I did hope to make my life better, for my baby's sake, and O, I did pity you, till my cold heart softened and grew warm. I should have given up my purpose, repaid Victor's fidelity, and gone away to grow an honest, happy, humble woman, if I had not loved *you*. That made me blind, when I should have been more keen-sighted than ever; that kept me here to be deceived, betrayed, and that should save me now."

"It will not; and the knowledge that I detest and despise you, is to add bitterness to your threefold punishment; the memory of Allan, Victor and Diana is another part of it, and here is the heaviest blow which Heaven inflicts as a retribution that will come home to you."

As he spoke, Douglas held to her a crumpled paper, stained with a red stain, and torn with the passage of a bullet that ended Victor's life. She knew the writing, sprung up to seize it, read the few lines, and when the paper fluttered to the ground, the white anguish of her face betrayed that the last blow *had* crushed her as no other could have done. She dropped into a seat, with the wail of tearless woe that breaks from a bereaved mother's heart as she looks on the dead face of the child who has been her idol, and finds no loving answer there.

"My baby gone—and I not there to say good-by! O, my darling, I could have borne anything but this!"

So utterly broken did she seem, so wild and woful did she look, that Douglas had not the heart to add another pang to her sharp grief by any word of explanation or compassion. Silently he poured out a glass of wine and placed it nearer, then resumed his seat, and waited till she spoke. Soon she lifted up her head, and showed him the swift and subtle blight that an hour had brought upon her. Life, light and beauty seemed to have passed away, and a pale shadow of her former self alone remained. Some hope or some resolve had brought her an unnatural calmness, for her eyes were tearless, her face expressionless, her voice tranquil, as if she had done with life, and neither pain nor passion could afflict her now.

"What next?" she said, and laid her hand upon the glass, but did not lift it to her lips, as if the former were too tremulous, or the latter incapable of receiving the draught.

"Only this," he answered, with a touch of pity in his voice. "I will not have my name handed from mouth to mouth, in connection with an infamous history like this. For Allan's sake, and for Diana's, I shall keep it secret, and take your punishment into my hands. Victor I leave to a wiser Judge than any human one; the innocent child is safe from shame and sorrow, but you must atone for the past with the loss of liberty and your whole future. It is a more merciful penalty than the law would exact, were the truth known, for you are spared public contempt, allowed time for repentance, and deprived of nothing but the liberty which you have so cruelly abused."

"I thank you. Where is my prison to be?"

She took the glass into her hand, yet still held it suspended, as she waited for his answer, with an aspect of stony immobility that troubled him.

"Far away in Scotland I own a gray old tower, all that now remains of an ancient stronghold. It is built on the barren rock, where it stands like a solitary eagle's eyrie, with no life near it but the sound of the wind, the scream of the gulls, the roll of the sea that foams about it. There, with my faithful old servants you shall live, cut off from all the world, but not from God, and when death comes to you, may it find you ready and glad to go, an humble penitent, more fit to meet your little child than now."

A long, slow tremor shook her from head to foot, as word by word her merciful yet miserable doom was pronounced, leaving no hope, no help but the submission and repentance which it was not in her nature to give. For a moment she bowed her head, while her pale lips moved, and her hands, folded above the glass, were seen to tremble as if some fear mingled even in her prayers. Then she sat erect, and fixing on him a glance in which love, despair and defiance mingled, she said, with all her former pride and spirit, as she slowly drank the wine:

"Death cannot come too soon; I go to meet it."

Her look, her tone, awed Douglas, and for a moment he regarded her in silence, as she sat there, leaning her bright head against the dark velvet of the cushioned chair. Her eyes were on him, still brilliant and brave, in spite of all that had just past; a disdainful smile curved her lips, and one fair arm lay half extended on the table, as it fell when she put the glass away. On this arm the bracelet shone; he pointed to it, saying, with a meaning glance:

"I know that secret, as I know all the rest."

"Not all; there is one more that you have not discovered—yet."

She spoke very slowly, and her lips seemed to move reluctantly, while a strange pallor fell upon her face, and the fire began to die out of her eyes, leaving them dim, but beautifully tender.

"You mean the mystery of the iron ring; but I learned that last night, when, with an expert companion, I entered your room, where you lay buried in the deep sleep produced by the drugged coffee which I gave you. I saw my portrait on your neck, as I wear Allan's, ever since we gave them to each other, long ago, and beside the miniature, the silver key that opened your quaint treasure-casket. I found the wax impression of my signet, taken, doubtless, on the night when, as a ghost, you haunted my room; I found the marriage record, stamped with that counterfeit seal, to impose upon Diana; I found relics of Vane, and of your child, and when Hyde called me, I saw and examined the two letters on your arm, which he had uncovered by removing the bracelet from it."

He paused there, expecting some demonstration. None appeared; she leaned and listened, with the same utter stillness of face and figure, the same fixed look and deathly pallor. He thought her faint and spent with the excitement of the hour, and hastened to close the interview, which had been so full of contending emotions to them both.

"Go now, and rest," he said. "I shall make all necessary arrangements here, all proper explanations to Lady Leigh. Gabrielle will prepare for your departure in the morning; but let me warn you not to attempt to bribe her, or to deceive me by any new ruse, for now escape is impossible."

"I have escaped!"

The words were scarcely audible, but a glance of exultation flashed from her eyes, then faded, and the white lids fell, as if sleep weighed them down. A slight motion of the nerveless hand that lay upon the table drew Earl's attention, and with a single look those last words were explained. The opal ring was turned inward on her finger, and some unsuspected spring had been touched, when she laid her hands together; for now in the deep setting appeared a tiny cavity, which had evidently contained some deadly poison. The quick and painless death that was to have been Victor's had fallen to herself, and, unable to endure the fate prepared for her, she had escaped, when the net seemed most securely drawn about her. Horror-stricken, Douglas called for help; but all human aid was useless, and nothing of the fair, false Virginie remained, but a beautiful, pale image of repose.

Enigmas

Editor's Note: False and concealed identities abound in Alcott's thrillers, and in the short mystery "Enigmas" they achieve a level of complexity unique in all her writing. The story features not only a deceitful, voyeuristic narrator with whom the reader is meant to identify, but also a character of ambiguous sexuality whose appeal causes others to doubt the propriety of their own emotions. Alcott pulls off the tale's multiple charades through a carefully misdirected narrative.

I bought my roll that day off the quiet woman who kept the bakeshop near my poor lodging. I liked her ways; she always folded my purchase in a tidy paper, received my three cents with a little bow and a softly spoken "Thank you," which dignified the paltry transaction and cost my pride no pang. At the corner I paused to decide where I should dine. A simple process, one would fancy, for the bread composed my meal. But, not being a Franklin, I objected to consuming the roll in public, and had two free dining-rooms to choose from—the Park in fine weather, a certain reading-room in stormy. A drop of rain decided me, and I strolled leisurely away to the latter refuge, for hunger had not yet reached its unendurable stage.

The room was deserted by all occupants but the librarian and one old gentleman, consulting a file of foreign newspapers. I slipped into an alcove, devoured my dinner behind a book, and then fell to brooding moodily over the desperate state of my finances and prospects, the first consisting of a single dollar, the last of slow starvation or manual labor, if I could bring myself to it. An abrupt exclamation from the old gentleman roused me, for it had a hopeful sound.

"Page, who copied this? I'd like to secure such a penman."

"Don't know, I'm sure, sir," responded Page. "Among so many clerks it's impossible to tell. I'll inquire if you like."

"No; I couldn't have him, if you did. But if you happen to hear of any good copyist who, for a moderate sum, would do a job for me, let me know, Page."

"I will, sir."

The old gentleman put down the list of newly arrived books which he had been examining, and drew on his gloves. As he approached my alcove a sudden impulse prompted me to step out and address him.

"Pardon me, sir, but necessarily overhearing your request, I venture to offer myself for trial."

"Have you any references or recommendations to offer, eh?" asked the old gentleman, pausing.

I had an excellent one which I had vainly offered to many persons for the last month. He read the very flattering letter from a well-known scholar whom I had served as secretary for a year, and seemed inclined to try me.

"Hum—quite correct—very satisfactory. Give me a sample of your writing; here's pen and paper."

I obeyed, and laying a sheet of paper upon the open book I had been reading, dashed off my signature in several different styles.

"Very good; the plainest suits me best. What's this? So you understand Italian, do you?"

"Yes, sir; perfectly, I believe."

The old gentleman meditated, and while doing so scanned my face with a pair of keen eyes, in which I could discover nothing but curiosity. I gratified it by saying, briefly:

"Mine is the old story, sir. I am a gentleman's son, poor, proud and friendless now, in want of employment, and ready to do anything for my daily bread."

"Anything, young man?" asked the old gentleman, almost startling me with the energy of his emphasis on that first word.

"Anything but crime, sir. I am in a strait where one does not hesitate long between almost any humiliation and absolute want."

I spoke as forcibly as he had done; it seemed to please him, for the stony immobility of his face relaxed, and a curious expression of satisfaction crept over it.

"Come to me to-morrow at ten. There is my address."

And, thrusting a card into my hand, the old gentleman walked away.

Precisely at ten o'clock on the morrow I presented myself at Mr. North's door, and was speedily set at work in his very comfortable office. The whole affair was rather peculiar, but I liked it the better for that, and the more eccentric the old lawyer appeared the more I desired to remain with him, though copying deeds was not exciting. He seemed to take a fancy to me, engaged me for a week, kept me busy till Saturday evening, and then astonished me by informing me for what secret service I was next intended.

As the clock struck five Mr. North wiped his pen, wheeled about in his chair, and sat waiting till I finished my last page.

"Mr. Clyde, I have a proposition to make," he began, as I looked up. "It will surprise you, but I have no explanation to give, and you can easily refuse. I have not intended keeping you from the first, but desired to test your capabilities before offering you a better situation. A certain person wishes an amanuensis; I think you eminently fitted for the post. You wish independence, agreeable duties and the surroundings of a gentleman. This place will give you all of these, for the salary is liberal, the labor light, the society excellent. One condition, however, is annexed to your acceptance. If you will pledge me your word to keep that condition a secret, whether you accept it or not, I will mention it."

"I do, sir."

"For reasons, the justice and importance of which you would acknowledge if I were at liberty to divulge them, I desire a reliable report of what passes in this person's house. I think you are fitted for that post also. A week ago you told me you were ready to do anything for your bread which was not a crime; this is none. Do you accept the place and the condition?"

"I am to play the spy, am I, sir?"

"Exactly, to any extent that your interest, ingenuity and courage prompt you. It is necessary that I should have a daily witness of the events that occur in that family for the next month at least, perhaps longer. I know the task I offer you is both a mysterious and somewhat difficult one, but if you will rely upon the word of an old man who has little more to expect of life, I assure you that no wrong is meditated, and that you will never have cause to regret your compliance. Let me add that at the end of your service, be it short or long, you will receive five hundred dollars, and be subjected to no questions, no detention, no danger or suspicion of any kind."

"But, sir, am I to work utterly in the dark?"

"Utterly."

"Am I never to know what mysterious purpose I am forwarding?"

"Never."

"Can I, ought I to pledge myself to such blind obedience?"

"I believe you can and ought; it is for you to decide whether you will."

Not a feature of the old man's face had varied from its usual colorless immobility; his keen eye searched me while he spoke, and when he paused he sat motionless, with no sign of impatience, as I rapidly considered the strange compact offered me. I rebelled a little at the dishonorable part of it, yet I was conscious of a secret interest and delight in the mysterious mission. The place seemed a tempting one, the bribe a fortune, the security reliable, for Mr. North was as much in my power as I in his. As if cognizant of the doubt and desire between which I was wavering, he said, abruptly:

"You are well-born, well-bred, comely, discreet and acute. Too proud to bear poverty, too poor to be overnice. A man exactly fitted to the place, though others may be found as competent, less scrupulous and more eager for both the enterprise and the reward."

"Hardly, sir. I accept."

The only sign of satisfaction which he gave was a closer pressure of the long thin hands loosely folded on his knee.

"Good! now listen, and bear these instructions carefully in mind. This place is ten miles out of the city; here is the address. On Monday evening go there, ask for Mr. Bernard Noel, and present your letter of recommendation. On no account mention my name or ever betray that you have any knowledge of me. Another thing remember, use your Italian as far as the comprehending of it when spoken by others, but deny that you possess that accomplishment if asked."

"Am I sure of being accepted, sir?"

"Yes, I think so. You have only to say that you saw and have answered an advertisement in last week's *Times.* Such a one appeared—stay, put it in your letter. Now look at this and give me your attention."

He turned to his table, produced a small locked portfolio and explained its purpose as I stood beside him. Several quires of peculiarly thin smooth paper lay within a package of envelopes directed in a strange hand to A. Z. Clyde, a seal with a skull for its device, and a stick of iron-gray sealing-wax completed the contents of the portfolio.

"You will record upon this paper the principal events, impressions or discoveries of each day, beginning with your first interview on Monday. Every Saturday you will send me your weekly report in one of the envelopes directed to an imaginary relative of your own. Secure each carefully with this wax and seal, and post them as privately as possible, without attracting attention by too much precaution."

"I shall remember, sir."

"You are to ask no questions, show no especial interest in what passes about you, and on no account betray that you keep this private record. You have wit, courage, great command of countenance, and will soon discover how to use these helps. Let nothing surprise, alarm or baffle you, and keep faith with me unless you desire ruin instead of reward. Now go, and let me hear from you on Saturday."

He rose, offered me a check, the portfolio and his hand. I accepted all three, and with our usual brief but courteous adieux we parted, the old man to brood doubtless over his strange secret, the young one to hope that in the unknown family he should find some solution of this first enigma.

JUNE 1ST.—Having received no directions as to the form into which I am to put my record, I choose the simple one of the diary as the easiest to myself, perhaps the most interesting to the eyes for which these pages are written.

According to agreement I came hither to-night at nine o'clock, being belated by an accident on the way. A grave, soldierly servant ushered me into a charming room, airy, softly lighted and exquisitely furnished, yet somewhat foreign in its elegant simplicity. It was empty, and wandering about it while waiting, I discovered a lady in an adjoining room. As she seemed unconscious of my presence, I began my surveillance by taking a careful survey. Leaning in a deep chair, I only caught the outline of her figure; for over her silvery gray dress she wore a large white cashmere, as if an invalid, and forced to guard herself even from the mild night air. Gray hair waved away on either side her pale cheeks, under a delicate lace cap, which fell in a point upon her fore-head. A deep green shade concealed her eyes, leaving visible only the contour of a rounded chin and feminine mouth. She was knitting, and I observed that her little hands were covered nearly to the finger-tips with quaint black silk mits, such as ancient ladies wore. There was something melancholy yet attractive about this figure, so delicate, so womanly, so sadly afflicted, for I felt that she was blind.

Absorbed in watching her, I was rather startled by a rustling among the shrubs that grew about the open French window behind me, and turned to see a young man entering from the garden. Somewhat embarrassed at being discovered peeping, I hastily inferred that the new-comer was a son of Mr. Bernard Noel, and introduced myself rather awkwardly.

"I came in answer to an advertisement in the *Times*, sir. I sent my name to Mr. Noel; but it is late; your father, perhaps, is not disengaged?"

What a singular look flashed upon me out of the dark eyes that were scrutinising my face, and what a singular smile accompanied the words:

"I am Bernard Noel."

I murmured an apology, presented my letter, and while he read it sat examining my future patron, wondering the while that such a lad should need an amanuensis. I say lad, for at the first glance he looked eighteen; a second caused me to suspect that he was some years older. Every inch a gentleman, for high-breeding makes itself manifest at a glance. Of middle height, slender and boyish in figure, yet with no boyish awkwardness to mar the easy grace of his address or attitude. The light shone full upon his face, and in that momentary pause I studied it. Dark curling hair framed a broad, harmoniously rounded forehead; black brows lay straight above those Southern eyes of his, now veiled by sweeping lashes; the nose was spirited and haughty; the mouth grave and strong, perhaps rendered more so by a slight moustache that shaded it. Even his dress interested me, as if I were a woman, though nothing could have been simpler or more becoming. A black velvet *paletot*, dark trousers, collar turned over a ribbon; an aristocratically small foot, perfectly shod, and a single ring on a handsome hand that held the letter. An almost instantaneous impression took possession of me that this youth was both older than he looked and wiser than his years. Whether some deep experience had matured him, or the presence of genius thus manifested itself, I could not so soon decide, but felt instinctively attracted and interested in the unconscious person whom I had been set to watch.

Presently he looked up, saying in a peculiarly clear and penetrating voice:

"This is entirely satisfactory, Mr. Clyde; let me hope that the situation may prove so to yourself for Mr. Lord has conferred honor in allowing me to secure the services of a 'a fine scholar and an accomplished gentleman.'"

He bowed with a glance that turned the quotation to a compliment, then continued with a gracious gravity that was very charming, from the contrast of youth with the native dignity which sat so gracefully upon this boyish master of a household:

"It is too late for the return train; you will remain to-night, and perhaps send for your luggage to-morrow. I am impatient to see my work begun, for time presses."

"I am entirely at your service, Mr. Noel."

"Thanks. You will find us a quiet family; we see no society just now, for my cousin is an invalid, and my present pursuits require solitude. I hoped to have finished my task myself, but my health will not permit of such close confinement; therefore I shall leave the pen to you, and take a holiday."

Anxious to discover what my duties were to be, I put the question in the form of a surmise.

"I shall be doubly glad to take it up if, as I infer, it is to be used for the transcribing of some maiden work, perhaps."

A slight flush rose to the young man's cheek, colorless before; his eyes fell like a shy girl's, and his lips broke into a sudden smile, seemingly against his will, for he checked it with a frown, and answered, with a curious blending of pleasure, pride and reserve:

"Yes, it is my maiden work, but as we shall both be heartily tired of the thing before we are done with it, let us drop that subject for the present, if you please."

"Sensitive and shy, like most young authors," thought I, apologising, with an air of contrition. Setting the topic aside with a little wave of the hand, Mr. Noel said, more cordially:

"Your rooms are in the east wing, and I hope will be agreeable to you. Madame Estavan's health and my own wayward habits prevent much regularity in our daily life, but this need not disturb you. We breakfast in our own rooms, lunch when we please, and dine at five. You will oblige me by ordering the two first meals at whatever hours best suit your appetite and convenience, and by joining us at dinner; for in so small a family ceremony is unnecessary, and social intercourse better for us all."

"What hours do you prefer to have devoted to my duties, sir?" I asked, finding no difficulty in uttering the respectful monosyllable, for my six and twenty years seemed to give me no superiority over this stripling not yet out of his teens, perhaps.

"I am in my study early these summer mornings, finding an hour or two then more profitable than later in the day. Let us say from eight to four, or half after, with a recess at noon for rest and refreshment. The garden and west wing are sacred to madame, but the rest of the house and grounds are open to you, and the evenings at your disposal, unless you prefer to write. When not otherwise engaged, we are usually in the drawing-room after dinner, if you care to join us."

Another singular expression passed over his face just then; reluctance and regret, audacity and pain, all seemed to meet and mingle in it, but it was gone before I could define the predominant emotion, and his countenance was like a cold, pale mask again.

I expressed my satisfaction at these arrangements, and while I spoke he watched me intently, so intently that I felt my color rising, a most unwonted manifestation, and doubly annoying just then; for, conscious of my secret mission, a sense of guilt haunted me which was anything but tranquillizing, with those searching eyes full upon me. I think the blush did me good service, however, for as if some doubt had disturbed his mind, my apparent bashfulness seemed to reassure him. He said nothing, but a slight fold in his forehead smoothed itself away, and an aspect of relief overspread his features so visibly that I made a mental note of the fact, and resolved to support the character of a simple-minded, diffident scholar, rather than a man of the world, as by so doing I should doubtless secure many opportunities which might otherwise be denied me.

Here madame called "Bernard!" and he went in to her. Without leaving my seat I saw him bend over her more like a son than a cousin, heard her ask several questions in a lowered voice, the answers to which she received with a silvery little laugh as blithe as any girl's. Then she rose, saying aloud in a slow, mild voice, with a pleasant accent in it:

"Take me in, *chéri*, and present monsieur, then ring for Pierre, that we have coffee."

Drawing his arm through hers, Mr. Noel led her to the larger room, established her in an armchair, and presented me, with the anxious look again apparent. Madame was very French, pensively courteous, and so gracefully helpless that I soon found myself waiting upon her almost as zealously as her cousin, who watched my compassionate attentions with that inscrutable smile of his. The soldierly servant handed coffee, and the slight constraint which unavoidably exists at the beginning of an acquaintance was fast wearing off when an incident occurred which effectually broke up our interview.

I was approaching madame with her ball, which had rolled from her lap, when Mr. Noel, who stood beside her, suddenly bent forward, as if attracted by something that alarmed him; for, dropping his cup, he whispered a single word and threw her shawl across her face. It sounded like "paint" or "faint," was probably the latter, for with a slight cry, more expressive of alarm than pain, madame fell into his arms, and without a word he carried her away, leaving me transfixed with astonishment.

He was back again directly, looking quite composed, and with the brief explanation that madame was accustomed to such turns, he presently asked if I would like to write the order for my luggage, that it might be dispatched early in the morning. Accepting the hint, I bade him good-night, and was soon installed by the old servant in two charming rooms on the ground floor of the west wing, where I now sit, concluding first report.

JUNE 2D.—Breakfasted in my room, and punctually at eight o'clock tapped at the door which Pierre had pointed out the night before as belonging to "master's study." Mr. Noel bade me enter, and obeying, I found him busied in a deep recess, divided from the room by damask curtains. These being partially undrawn, discovered a wide window, looking on the garden, a writing-chair and table, a tall cabinet and couch, and a literary strew of books, MSS., ponderous dictionaries and portfolios. The room itself was plainly furnished, quiet, cool and shady, while the same atmosphere of refinement and repose pervaded it that had impressed me elsewhere, and which seemed rather some peculiar charm of its possessor than the result of taste or time. Mr. Noel bade me good-morning with a chilly courtesy, which would have instantly recalled the relations between us had I been inclined to forget them. Pointing to a second writing-table, whereon all necessary appliances were laid ready, he handed me a pile of MS., saying, as he half reluctantly loosed his hold upon it:

"Many freaks and whims are permitted to young authors, you know, Mr. Clyde. One of mine is to leave my book unchristened till it is ready to be dressed in type. I will not impose the first chapters upon you, but you may begin where my patience gave out. Copy a few pages as a sample, I will come and look at them presently."

He returned to his nook, and employed himself so noiselessly that I soon forgot his presence. The instant his back was turned my eye ran down the page before me, and what I read confirmed my fancy that Mr. Noel was a genius. That one sheet amazed me, for it gave evidence of a power, insight and culture hardly credible in one so young. The book was no romance, poem, satire or essay, but a most remarkable work upon Italian history and politics. A strange subject for a boy to choose, and still more marvellous was his treatment of it. I was fairly staggered as I read on at the learning, research and eloquence each fine paragraph displayed. No wonder his cheeks are colorless, his eyes full of fire, his air both lofty and languid, when that young brain of his has wrought such sentences. No wonder he is proud, knowing himself endowed with such a gift and the power to use it. This explains the fascination of his presence, the charm of his manner, the indefinable some-thing which attracts one's eye, arrests one's interest, yet restrains one's curios-ity by an involuntary respect for that attribute which is "divine when young."

I should have gone on reading in a maze of admiration and incredulity, had not the recollection of his request set me writing with my utmost celerity and elegance. Soon I became absorbed and forgot everything but the smoothly flowing words, that seemed to glide from my pen as if to music, for the theme was liberty, and the writer was a poet as well as patriot and philosopher. Pausing to take a long breath, I became aware that Mr. Noel was at my side. He saw my excited face, my evident desire to break into a rapture. It seemed to touch and please him, for he came nearer, asking, wistfully yet shily:

"Do you like it?"

"I have no words to express how much. It is well that you laid an embargo on my tongue, for otherwise I should never be done praising."

His face glowed, his eye shone, and he offered me his hand with that enchanting smile of his.

"I thank you, I shall remember this." Then, as if to check me and himself he examined my copy of his own hastily written MS.

"This is beautifully done. I hardly know my pages when freed from the blots and blemishes grown so familiar to me. Do you find it very tiresome?"

"On the contrary, most delightful yet most tantalising, for I long to read when I should be writing. Mr. Noel, I am utterly amazed that such a book should be produced by so young a man."

"I might say I did not write it, for my father bequeathed me his spirit; and if these pages possess truth, eloquence or beauty, the praise belongs to him— not me."

Softly, almost solemnly he spoke, without confusion or conceit; pride unmarred by any tinge of vanity he probably showed, but seemed as if he had entirely forgotten himself in his work, and would accept no commendation but through that. He appeared to fall into a little reverie, and I sat silent, my eyes fixed on the shapely hand resting against the table as he stood. I was not thinking of it, but it annoyed him; for, with an almost petulant gesture, he flung down the pages he had held, thrust both hands deep into the pockets of his *paletot*, turned sharply on his heel and went into his alcove. I heard him stirring there for several minutes, as if putting his papers under lock and key, then reappearing, he said gravely:

"You will find lunch in the dining-room whenever you like it. I must take madame for her drive now; we shall meet at dinner."

He went, and soon after I saw a pony carriage roll down the avenue. I wrote till noon, when feeling hungry I set off on an exploring expedition, as Mr. Noel had forgotten to mention where the dining-room was, and I did not care to ring up a servant. A wide hall ran the whole length of the house, opening upon the garden in the rear. Four doors appeared; the two opposite were open and belonged to the drawing-rooms; I was standing on the thresh-old of the third, and the fourth evidently led to the dining-room. I chose to ignore that fact and satisfy my curiosity by prowling elsewhere. I might never have so good an opportunity again; the master and mistress were away, no one would suspect a stranger, and if I met the servants ignorance would be a fair excuse. Having assumed the part of spy, I wished to play it well, and being forbidden to question persons, must gain information from inanimate things, if possible. Two cross passages led from the main hall, one to my rooms, the other to the west wing. This, of course, I took, softly opening the first door that appeared; madame's apartment, for the gray silk dress and white shawl lay across a chair. A rapid survey satisfied me, and I passed to the next; Mr. Noel's, though I should scarcely have guessed it but for the hat upon the lounge, the pistols beside the bed, and the gentleman's dressing-case on the toilette. The windows were heavily curtained, the furniture luxurious, and an air of almost feminine elegance pervaded it. Two things struck me; the first was a dainty work-basket in a lounging-chair, so near me that I could see the exquisitely fine stitching on the wristband that lay in it. Madame was blind, no other woman appeared—who did it? The second discovery was more important. Opposite the door where I stood appeared another half open, showing a flight of thickly carpeted stairs winding upward. A blaze of June sunshine streamed down them, the odor of flowers came to me with a balmy gust, and in the act of stealing forward to see what was above, I was arrested by a soft voice exclaiming in Italian:

"Ah, I am so tired of this; devise some new amusement, or I shall die of weariness."

"My darling, so am I," replied a deeper voice; "but remembering our reward, I can have patience. Come to me and let us talk of our next letter, it is due to-day."

"No; it makes me sad to think of that unless I must, and Heaven knows I need all the cheerfulness and courage I possess."

"Poor little heart, you do. Sing to me while I work, and so forget imprisonment and trouble."

"That is my only pleasure now. But I am thirsty, I want a draught of wine, and Pierre has forgotten me," murmured the female voice.

"No, love, he never will do that. I was obliged to send him to the St. Michaels, that they might be told of this man's arrival and conduct matters with double discretion," answered the man.

"Poor Pierre! he has to serve us now as butler, gardener, errand-boy and sentinel. His life must be almost as wearisome as mine," sighed the other.

"Now you are growing sorrowful again. Kiss me, Clarice, and let me find a happier face when I return; I am going for the wine."

There was a rustle, a murmur and a pause, but I heard no more; for gliding like a shadow down the hall, I bolted into the dining-room and began to devour the first viand that came to hand. Here was a discovery! the deeper voice I heard was Mr. Noel's, and the softer one not madame's. Hers was sweet and slow, his youthful and vivacious, plaintive and petulant by turns. Noel's was unmistakable, though now it varied from passionate melancholy to an infinite tenderness, a caressing tone that would have soothed and won any woman by its magic. I had barely time to compose myself before he entered, started at seeing me, then laughed and explained.

"Pardon! I have lived so much alone that I had forgotten the addition to my household for the moment. Let me fill your glass."

I had opened my lips to reply when a strain of music floated past the window, and involuntarily I paused to listen.

"Ah! 'Casta Diva,' and exquisitely given."

As I spoke I saw Mr. Noel's hand tighten round the decanter he held, and again that peculiar glance flashed upon me as he said:

"You understand Italian, then?"

"Yes," was on my lips, but the recollection of my promise checked it, and I answered with an accent of regret, "I wish I did."

Mr. Noel raised his glass to his lips, as if to conceal the smile that parted them, a smile which doubtless signified, "So do not I," but he said aloud:

"You recognised the air rather than the words, I fancy."

"Yes, madame possesses a wonderful voice."

"Madame is an accomplished woman."

With which unsatisfactory reply he strolled to the window, plate in hand, and stood there listening. I ate in silence, but watched him covertly, recalling what I had lately heard, and finding in his appearance further confirmation of the suspicion which had come to me. His eyes had met mine but once; on his cheek burned a color not born of the summer heat; his grave mouth was soft and smiling, as if the kiss he asked for still remained upon his lips, and the music of that sweeter language seemed to linger in his voice. He looked a lover, and I felt that he was one, for genius rapidly matures both head and heart, unhampered by restraints of custom, age or race. How else explain the presence of the unknown singer, upon whom I had heard him lavish such tender names with more than brotherly affection? I confess the fancy charms me, for my own loveless life has been so bare of romance I am ready to find interest and pleasure in another man's experience, while the mystery which surrounds this strange youth and my relations with him make it doubly alluring.

As I rose to return to my work the act seemed to rouse him; approaching the table he carefully selected a cake and fruit, filled a glass with iced claret, and arranging them on a silver salver, added a handful of flowers from a vase near by, and carried it away, saying with a half-sad, half-mirthful look:

"Madame likes me to wait on her, and is as fond of delicate attentions as a girl."

Till nearly five I wrote, then dressed for dinner, and when summoned found my host and hostess waiting for me. A well-appointed table, a well-served meal and one occurrence at its close are all that is necessary to record of this episode. Noel sat beside his cousin, waiting on her with a quiet devotion beautiful to see. Pierre hovered about both with a respectfully protective air, which became the venerable servant who seemed to eye me rather jealously, as if he feared a rival in his young master's confidence. It was a silent meal, for Noel was not loquacious, and madame seemed sad. I did my best, but the rôle I had taken was not one to allow of much conversation, and long pauses followed short dialogues.

We were just rising when Pierre entered bringing a basket of hot-house flowers, which he delivered to his master, with the message:

"For madame, with Mrs. St. Michael's compliments."

Madame uttered no thanks, made no gesture of pleasure, but every particle of color faded from her face as she seemed to listen for Noel's answer. He too was paler, and the hand extended for the basket trembled visibly, yet he answered with unwonted animation:

"She is very kind; cousin, I will take them to your room for you. Mr. Clyde, I have an engagement for this evening; but drawing-room, library and lawn are at your service."

"The last shall be first, thank you, and I will enjoy the sunset out of doors."

With that I took myself away; Pierre closed the door behind me, and as I turned into the passage to my rooms I fancied I heard the click of a key turning in the lock. I got my hat, passed out at one of the long windows of my little parlor, and strolled towards the lawn along the terrace which lay close before the house. My steps were noiseless on the turf, and as I passed the windows of the dining-room I snatched a hasty look, which showed me the basket overturned upon the floor, madame with her shade at her feet and her face hidden in her hands, Mr. Noel reading a letter aloud, and Pierre listening intently, with a napkin still over his arm.

They did not see me, all being absorbed, and with my curiosity still further piqued, I wearied myself with conjectures as I surveyed the exterior of the house, the occupants of which already inspired me with such interest.

A rambling English cottage in a nest of verdure. A lawn slopes to the road in front, a garden lies behind, a lane runs parallel with the garden-wall on the right, and a grove of pines rises soberly against the sky upon the left. Curious to locate the room of the unknown, I struck into the lane, scrutinising the left wing as I walked. To my surprise, no upper windows appeared. An ancient grape-vine covered the western wall, trained away from the lower casements, but completely masking the space above and wandering over half the roof. Looking closer, I soon discovered a large aperture in the roof, half hidden by the leaves; the sash evidently lowered from within, and this explains the flood of sunshine and the odorous gust that floated down the stairway which I now long to mount. Having looked till my eyes ached, I roamed away into the fields which lie between the solitary cottage and the town.

As I came up the avenue on my return Mr. Noel passed me, driving rapidly; he did not see me, for his hat was pulled down low upon his forehead, but his mouth looked grim, his whole figure erect and resolute. I watched him out of sight, went in and read for an hour, then to my room and secret diary. It is past midnight now, but Mr. Noel has not yet returned.

JUNE 3D.—Found the young gentleman in his alcove and my work laid ready when I went to the study this morning. He looked up and answered my salutation as I entered, then seated himself behind his curtain, and I saw no more of him for an hour. At the end of that time the perfect silence that reigned in the recess arrested my attention, and caused me to suspect that he had slipped away through the window. I was just meditating a peep when accident supplied me with a genuine excuse. A little gust of air blew in from the garden, rustling the papers on his table; one was wafted beyond the curtain, and almost to my feet. I waited a moment for him to reclaim it, but nothing stirred, and quite sure that he was gone, I examined it. A closely covered sheet written in Italian it proved to be, and a moment's inspection showed me that it was a part of the work I was copying, though in a different and bolder hand. Stepping to the recess to restore it, I was startled by discovering Mr. Noel asleep in his chair. Very worn and tired he looked, though younger than ever in his sleep, and on the page upon his desk lay drops that looked like tears. Seeing that his slumber was deep, I ventured to look well about me. The half-written sheet on which his pen still lay, as it dropped from his drowsy hand, was a translation of the very page I held. Others lay on the table, and in the cabinet which now stood open I spied three piles of MS. A hasty glance showed me the missing chapters copied in his graceful hand, a heap of blurred and hasty translation, and a worn, stained MS. in the same bold writing, the same language as the truant leaf. Farther I dared not look, but crept back to my seat, and fell to wondering why the boy wrote in Italian, and suffered no one to translate it but himself. Were he other than he is I should suspect him of a literary theft or some double-dealing with another's work. But Bernard Noel seems incapable of deceit, and his look, his manner when speaking of it assure me that it is rightfully his own, whatever his reasons may be for so laborious a process. My reflections were suddenly interrupted by hearing him rouse, and seeing him pull aside the curtain to ascertain if I was there. He looked half bewildered by sleep, but began to collect the papers, carefully arranged them in the cabinet, locked it, and stepped out into the garden, where I saw him pacing thoughtfully to and fro for half an hour. That was the last of him for to-day, for he and madame dined at the St. Michaels, as Pierre informed me when five o'clock found me the sole partaker of an excellent dinner. They returned at nine, and the invisible musician has been singing for an hour.

JUNE 6TH.—For four days nothing has occurred worth recording, as I have been almost entirely alone. Mr. Noel hands me a chapter or two each morning, receives my copy at night, and only the necessary directions are asked and given. Madame has not been visible, ill I am told, yet her cousin looks tranquil, and no nurse or physician has been summoned to my knowledge. Very brief and silent are our interviews at dinner, and not once have I found the drawing-room occupied of an evening. No one calls, but Mr. Noel drives out often and returns late. My days have been spent at the writing-table, my evenings in my own room or solitary walks about the country. Returning from one of these, I saw the window under the vines brilliantly lighted, and resolved to satisfy my curiosity the first moonless night. This ends my first week's record; I trust it is satisfactory, and that out of my own darkness I have given light.

JUNE 7TH.—To-day, being Sunday, I asked Mr. Noel, when I met him at lunch, in which of the three churches, over the hill, I should find his pew.

"In none; I go nowhere just now. My cousin cannot, and I join her in a little service here at home," he said slowly; adding instantly, as if afraid I should expect to be included in that domestic service: "My friend, Mrs. St. Michael, will be happy to do the honors of her husband's chapel. I have spoken to her, and she expects you."

I thanked him, went to church, found the pastor a dull preacher, though apparently an excellent and pious gentleman; his wife a grave, motherly lady who received me with courtesy, examined me with interest, and, as we came out together, asked me how I liked her neighbors.

"Mr. Noel seems an eccentric but most charming young man and madame a wonderfully cheerful sufferer," I replied.

"Genius has many privileges, and eccentricity is one, you know," replied the lady, adding, rather guardedly: "Madame Estavan is younger than she seems, and manifold afflictions cannot wholly darken her bright spirit. May I trouble you to give my regards to her, and tell Mr. Noel I will see him to-morrow?"

At dinner I delivered the messages; Mr. Noel turned graver than before on receiving his, and madame turned gay. I was glad to see her so, and did my best to interest her, observing that her cousin often took the word from her lips, and that Pierre's usually expressionless face wore an aspect of uneasiness. In drawing out her handkerchief madame dropped an ebony rosary. No one heard it fall for it slipped noiselessly through the folds of her dress, and no one saw it but myself. Pierre was busy at the sideboard, and, stooping, I lifted and returned it to her. She received it with the exclamation:

"*Ciel!* How careless I am grown! I thought I put it by after mass."

"Madame is a Catholic, one sees."

The words slipped from me involuntarily, her answer seemed to do the same.

"Oh, yes; in truth I am, and so is————"

A heavy silver fork clanged down into Mr. Noel's plate, and madame started at the clatter, leaving her sentence unfinished.

"Pardon, cousin; if you are forgetful, I am awkward. You were about to say, 'and so is Pierre.'"

Noel spoke quite naturally, but I suspect madame caught some warning from his tone, for the color mounted to her forehead as she eagerly assented.

"Surely, yes. Whom else could I mean? Not you, my too Protestant and English Bernard."

Poor lady, she overdid the matter sadly, and that anxious emphasis upon the words "Protestant" and "English" convinced me that Noel was neither, though but for this I never should have suspected it. As if anxious to banish it from my mind, he led the way to the drawing-room, and, as all madame's spirits had departed, exerted himself to entertain us both. In conversation I found him witty, earnest and frank, but in the midst of an animated description of foreign life he checked himself, and going to the grand piano gave us fragments from the sacred music of the great masters, with an ease and brilliancy that captivated me. I was heartily enjoying this treat when, as if doomed to make scenes, madame suddenly gave a loud cry and darted out upon the lawn, exclaiming:

"He has come! *Mon père! Mon père!*"

For an instant Noel stared aghast, then sprung after her, looking as wild as she. I followed to the terrace, and, standing there, heard, through the stillness of the twilight, madame sobbing and her cousin chiding. He spoke Italian, but low and rapid as were his words, I caught them brokenly.

"I cannot trust you—you have no control of face, voice, mind or manner. You knew it was impossible—he cannot come for weeks yet—I will have no more of this."

"Forgive me. It is this life which destroys my nerves; it is unnatural. I cannot bear it. Let it end for me," sobbed madame.

"It shall," almost sternly answered he. "Rest content, I will ask no more of you; it is selfish, unwise. I can bear and do alone; you have suffered enough."

"It is not that; it is the suspense, the deceit, the danger that dismays me. I can act no part. Send me away for a little; you will be freer, happier, safer, without me, as you know."

"I shall, and so will you. To-morrow St. Michael will receive you, and a few weeks will end all. Now compose yourself, go to your room, and leave me to explain your flight to Clyde."

I slipped round to the hall door and met him there with, I flatter myself, well-acted concern. Madame passed me with a murmured:

"Monsieur, I have known loss, it haunts me; forgive the malady of a broken heart."

Noel gave her into the charge of a grave, elderly woman, whom I now saw for the first time, and who came hurrying up with Pierre. As she departed the old servant hastily explained that it was he who had peeped and startled madame.

"Then madame is not wholly blind?" I asked, quickly, for there he paused and looked confused. Noel answered, tranquilly:

"It is only a partial loss. You may go, Pierre; you are forgiven. But let us have no more of this, for madame's sake."

The old man gladly withdrew and his master added, as I bade him good-night:

"My cousin needs change. I shall take her to town to-morrow. We have friends there, and her state demands better care than I can give her. We shall leave early, but I will prepare matters for you, as I shall not return till late."

A long sigh of relief broke from him as he turned away, and on my soul I pitied him; for it is my belief that madame is not only a little mad, but some refugee whom he is befriending, and who, in spite of gratitude, finds it hard to lead a life of concealment under the same roof with some fair, frail lover of this fascinating boy.

JUNE 8TH.—Found the house silent as a tomb, and fancy the sound of carriage wheels which half woke me at dawn was the only farewell I shall receive from poor madame. A long, quiet day. Noel returned at dusk, and went straight to his room. I seized my hat, concealed myself in the lane and watched the leafy window. Presently it blazed with light, and but for the appearance of Pierre in the garden I should have been tempted to execute my resolve at once. Hearing the rattle of the chain that holds the gate, I sprang into the footpath which turns into the lane from the fields. Pierre showed small surprise at meeting me, as these meadows are my favorite walk, and my assumption of simplicity has quite blindfolded this old watchdog. Anxious to see how he would explain it, I asked, as if just discovering the window:

"What is that light among the leaves, does the roof burn?"

"Oh, no, monsieur, it is my master's studio. He paints as he does everything else—divinely. For that room he took the cottage; an artist built it, and though he does little now, he often lounges there at night."

The answer came so readily, and seemed so natural an explanation I could not but believe it, and saying I should go in and read, I left him. From my window I watched him far along the avenue, he and the maids chatting in the grove, knew that madame's nurse had gone with her from a word Pierre dropped at dinner, and felt that my time had come. It was a moonless evening, fast deepening into night; a light wind was blowing that filled the air with rustling sounds, and the house was quite deserted for the time. I had no fear—excitement is my element, daring my delight, and I desired to earn my liberal reward for this dishonorable but alluring service.

Leaving my hat behind me, I crept to the western wing, with every sense alert. Not by the vines did I ascend, but by a slender Norway pine, whose stem, being branchless for many feet above the ground, seemed to forbid approach by that means. Practice made me agile, and I was soon upon the first bough which touched the roof. With catlike steps I picked my way, crouching low and making no sound louder than the whispers of the wind. The window was closed, and all I heard was a murmur of voices, but parting the leaves at one shaded corner I lay flat and looked down.

A long, lofty room was below, full of light, soft colors, lovely shapes, but how furnished I cannot tell, for its occupants absorbed me instantly. Stretched his full length on a couch lay Noel, looking like a luxuriously indolent young sultan, in crimson dressing-gown and Turkish slippers. He was laughing, and till then I had never seen the real beauty of his face; some cloud of reserve, distrust or melancholy had veiled it from me, but at last I saw the boy's true self, and felt that nothing was impossible to such as he. His white throat was bare, his black curls tumbled, his hands clasped above his head, and as he laughed he hummed a sprightly air, in which a softer voice joined fitfully.

At first he alone was visible, but soon down the long room came a woman dancing like an elf. Great heavens! how beautiful she was! She wore some foreign dress, brilliant and piquant, a lovely neck and arms shone white against the gold and scarlet of her bodice, and bare rosy feet scarcely seemed to touch the carpet. Dark eyes glittered through a stream of rippling gold hair, a sweet, red mouth was smiling, and as she danced the bloom no art can give deepened beautifully on her cheek.

With a deep obeisance and a ringing laugh she ended her pretty part of

Bayadere, and dropping on a cushion beside the couch, talked vivaciously while gathering up her hair. Noel caressed the bright head which presently leaned against his pillow, sobering slowly as the thoughtful look stole back into his face. Clarice—for this was doubtless she—seemed to chide him, to try and win the gay mood back again, but vainly; for rising on his elbow he began to speak earnestly, so earnestly that his companion soon grew as intent as he. I would have given worlds to have caught a word, but not one reached me, and but for the emphatic gestures of the pair should have gathered nothing of their meaning. He evidently urged something from which she shrank, yet in the end acceded to with tears and eloquently sorrowful eyes. Noel seemed satisfied, and with the fondest gestures dried the tears, consoled the grief, and endeavored to make light of it. A deep lounging-chair stood before an easel, on which shone the image of this sweet-voiced girl. A dainty little supper was spread beside the chair, and drawing his model—for such I now suspect Clarice to be—into the velvet nest beside him, Noel made merry over it like one content, and yet not heartily at ease.

It was a prettier picture than any he will ever paint; both so young, so blithe and beautiful, so loving and beloved, so free and rich in all that makes life pleasant. I felt like one shut out from some sweet Paradise as I lay looking from the dimness of the night upon this happy pair, while they nestled there together, drinking from the same glass, eating from the same plate, serving one another with such charming zeal, and forgetting all things but themselves.

Utterly oblivious of the outer world, Pierre's voice nearly caused me to betray myself, so suddenly did it break the hush.

"Catherine, has Monsieur Clyde come in?"

"Yes, long ago; his light is out."

The speakers were in the garden, and waiting till the door closed upon them I crept to the pine, half slid, half fell in my haste, and safely regained my room.

JUNE 9TH.—Mrs. St. Michael came, had a brief interview with Mr. Noel on the lawn, which was prudent but unsatisfactory to me, for I learned nothing from it. Saw no more of him till dinner, when he told me he should pass the evening out. At eight he drove away, and curious to know when he returned, I amused myself with a book till nearly midnight, then wearying of it, put out my light and sat musing in the dark. The night was cloudy, close and warm, and finding all still I presently went out into the lane, wondering if Clarice, too, watched and waited for his return. The window was dark, but just as I turned from it I was alarmed by the sound of wheels close by. I recognised the light roll of the pony carriage, though it was deadened by the turf, for to my dismay it was evidently coming not up the avenue but along the lane. Fearing to be seen if I attempted to get in, I sprang behind the hedge, and holding my breath, saw the carriage pause before the door in the garden-wall. A man leaped out, seemed to listen, then admitted himself both to the garden and the house, as the sound of a cautiously lifted window suggested. Quite breathless with interest I waited, and sooner than I expected the man reappeared, not alone now, for a slender female figure clung to him. I could just see the outline of their figures, the white gleam of their faces, but I knew them at once by the few words rapidly exchanged in Italian.

"How still it is; have you no fear?"

"I have done with fear, Clarice."

"And I with captivity, thank God!"

"I shall miss you sadly, dear."

"Not for long, your wife will comfort you."

A little laugh accompanied the words, and like spectres of the shadowy hour, house, carriage, man and woman vanished in the gloom.

Here is a clue at last; Noel will marry, and for this purpose clears his house of all encumbrances; poor madame and the lovely model must give place to some woman whom he unwillingly marries—if his face and manner are to be relied on. Why he does so is a mystery like himself, but I will yet fathom both.

June 10th.—It is well that I was prepared beforehand, else the announcement made to me this evening would have filled me with uncontrollable surprise. Mr. Noel wrote steadily all day, was unusually taciturn at dinner, and amused himself at the piano till twilight fell. I had been pacing up and down the hall enjoying his music, when it ceased abruptly, and coming out he joined me in my promenade. The hall was not lighted, except by the softened gleam of shaded lamps in the drawing-room. I instantly observed the anxious look I have learned to know, and by the slight embarrassment of his usually easy manner I inferred that he both wished and feared to speak. Presently fixing his eyes full upon me, he said slowly, as if weighing every word, and marking its effect:

"Mr. Clyde, as an inmate of my house, I feel that it is but right for me to tell you of an approaching event, which, however, will not materially change my mode of life nor your own—I am about to marry."

He so evidently expected me to be surprised that I instantly feigned what I should yesterday have really felt. Stopping in my walk, I exclaimed:

"Married! you are very young for that experience;" there I checked myself and began the proper congratulations. He cut them short by asking:

"How old do you believe me to be?"

"You look eighteen, your book says forty," I answered, laughing.

"I am of age, however, and though young to marry, have neither parents nor guardians to forbid it if they would."

"It will be soon I infer, as you do me the honor of announcing it to me?"

"On Saturday."

"You mentioned that this event would make no change in my present mode of life—I am then to continue my copying as usual during your absence?"

"I shall be absent but a day. It will be a very private affair, and my—Mrs. Noel will return with me at once."

A little pause fell between us. I was contrasting his cool, quiet manner now with the loverlike expression he had worn when with Clarice, and felt more than ever convinced that for some weighty reason he was doing violence to his own heart. He seemed conscious that, having said so much, he should say more, and presently added, still in the same measured tone:

"Madame's departure leaves me lonely. My attachment is no sudden one, for I have loved Hortense from her babyhood. She, too, is an orphan, and both being solitary, we see no wisdom in delaying to secure our happiness. Mrs. St. Michael is a mutual friend, and at her house we shall be married in the quietest manner, for the few relatives we possess are far distant, and Hortense dreads strangers."

Here Pierre came in, bringing a dainty little note, which he delivered with a smile. Noel took it eagerly, wished me good-night, and hurried away to the west wing. I wish that I, too, were a lover!

June 12th.—Since our conversation in the hall I have scarcely seen Mr. Noel, and therefore have little to record. For an hour or two he has sat in his alcove, then dressed and driven away to the St. Michaels, where I suspect the bride-elect has already arrived. To-day was the wedding-day, and I waited with intense impatience for the coming of the young pair. Not that I expected to be invited to join them so soon, if ever, but because I was burning with curiosity to see the woman for whom he had discarded poor Clarice, and had no scruples about gratifying myself in any way that offered.

At five I went to my dinner, found Pierre polishing the plate, but no appearance of food.

"Master will dine at seven to-day, and hopes monsieur will not be incommoded by the change," he said.

"Am I to join them as usual, then?" I asked, surprised.

"Oh, yes; the arrival of young madame will alter nothing but Monsieur Noel's spirits, I believe."

At half-past six o'clock a carriage rolled up the avenue, and from behind a group of larches on the lawn I watched the arrival. Pierre came smiling to the door as Noel led a lady up the steps. A slender, dainty little lady she seemed, but her face was hidden by the white veil which covered her blonde bonnet, and all I could discover of her figure, under a flowing white burnouse, was that it was slight and graceful. She was evidently very young; for as she entered the house she clapped her hands and danced down the long hall, as if overjoyed to be at home. Noel stood an instant talking with his old servant, and I caught a glimpse of his face, and very little like the countenance of a bridegroom did it look.

As both went in I returned to my room, and half an hour afterwards was summoned to dinner.

Twilight had come on and lamps were lit. The table shone with damask, glass and silver, flowers glowed everywhere, and the lustres filled the room with a festal breadth of light. But none of these things caught my eye on entering, for standing in the deep window were Noel and his bride. His arm was about her, and leaning there as if content, he looked down at her as she held out an almost childishly lovely hand, and seemed laughing blithely at the wedding-ring upon it. Both turned as I came in, and, with the color mounting to his very forehead, Noel said:

"Mr. Clyde, allow me to present you to—my wife."

Well for me that a bow was all sufficient, and that my command of countenance was great, or I should have betrayed myself beyond repair, for Mrs. Noel was Clarice! There could be no doubt of it. The face was peculiar even in its beauty, and not easily forgotten. There was the rippling, golden hair, dark eyes, sweet red mouth and blooming cheek—even the smile was the same, brilliant and brief, the voice unchanged, vivacious, yet musically soft. The dress was simple white, yet above the flowers in the bosom shone the fair shoulders I had seen, and the round arm that lay on Noel's wore the very bracelet that had flashed upon Clarice's but a little while ago. Noel eyed me narrowly, but I believe my face was impenetrable, as I uttered my congratulations after the surprise of that first glimpse had passed.

Half shily, half daringly, Mrs. Noel glanced at me, and as I paused she drew her husband towards the table like an impatient child.

"Come, Bernard, Pierre is waiting, and I am so hungry. That is a sadly unromantic admission for a bride to make, but it is true. Besides, I want to play mistress, and begin to realise that I am free from all restraints but yours, *mon ami*."

We sat down, and a most charming mistress did she prove herself. So gay, so graceful, so frankly fond of her husband, so courteous to me, and now and then, as if the novelty of her position overcame her, so sweetly shy and blushing, that before the meal was over I found myself forgetting all the past and full of admiration for this most captivating little creature. Noel seemed to own the charm as well. The cloud lifted, and again I saw the beautiful blithe nature which he seems to hide and hold in check. He laughed as gaily as his young wife, drank her health more than once, and was more cordial to me than I believed it possible for him to be. Both seemed to forget who and what I was, to make me one of them, and freely to shed the light of their new happiness upon the lonely stranger.

My heart reproached me for my treachery, yet I did not repent, nor shall I till my mission ends. Strange as all has been here, I am fast learning to respect and love this gifted boy, to look leniently upon his peculiarities, and even commend this last act, whatever its causes and consequences may be. It is evident that he loves his wife passionately, and she loves him with a confiding tenderness which will not be concealed: I felt like one in fairyland, and when they went into the drawing-room longed to follow, yet dared not, till Mrs. Noel, looking backward, beckoned me with an imperious little gesture that was irresistible.

"There is no need of your deserting your old haunts because I have come, Mr. Clyde," she said, looking up at me with eyes that seemed to read the desire I felt. "Bernard and I have known each other for so many years, have been together so much, and loved each other from our childhood, that the putting on of this ring seems to make no change in us. We care nothing for the world's ways, and rule this little kingdom as we will. You are a gentleman, you like my————" she paused, laughed delightsomely, and added, "my husband's book, and help him as he would be helped; therefore you are our friend, as such you must live with us, and let two children profit by your age and wisdom."

This friendly speech, so warmly, gracefully delivered, quite touched and won my heart, and I at once accepted both the offer and the hand outstretched to me. Hardly waiting till my thanks were spoken, little madame danced away to the piano and broke into a song. If anything were needed to convince me of her identity with Clarice this would have done it, for the marvellous voice could not be feigned. With a malicious fancy to see how Noel would bear an allusion to the falsehood he once told me, I said, carelessly:

"Although I heard but indistinctly at the time, Mrs. Noel's voice reminds me strongly of Madame Estavan's when she sang 'Casta Diva.' "

Smiling the smile that makes his face so young, he answered, with a mirthful look at the golden-haired, white-robed figure at the instrument:

"Well it may, for madame is a near relation of my little wife's, whose voice was trained by her. Hortense, come out upon the lawn, I want to show you your nest by moonlight."

She came to him with the airy motion which seems habitual to her, and, hanging on his arm, went out, along the terrace, looking a fit inmate of this enchanting and enchanted place.

JUNE 14TH.—I take the liberty of noting only such events as seem important or mysterious, and therefore when my days are solitary leave them blank. Yesterday the young couple fully proved themselves "a pair of children," for they danced and sang all through the house, haunted garden, grove and lawn, drove, walked and rested, always together and always happy. Mrs. Noel seemed like a bird let loose, her husband enjoyed her joy and gave himself a holiday, for mind as well as heart; for he never came into the study, but leaned in at the window, giving his directions while his wife stuck roses in his buttonhole. Perhaps my eyes looked wistful; I suspect they did, for suddenly she stepped in and came to me, saying, as she put a flower on my desk and then tripped away again:

"You, too, shall have one, because you are the wise and busy man. See, I give you this fully opened rose; it suits you best. Bernard must have the little white ones, because they are like me."

As I waited their coming in the dining-room, a few hours later, from the window I saw Mrs. St. Michael's servant come up the avenue and hand a packet to Noel, who was loitering there while madame dressed. The man went back. Noel read a brief note, hastily unfolded the newspaper which composed the packet, and seemed to dart at once upon some particular passage. I saw him stand motionless and intent a moment, then drop the paper, turn as if to enter, and fall, face downwards, on the grass.

Darting out, I raised his head to my knee, loosened his collar, and while wondering at the smile still lingering on his pale lips, I snatched a glance at the note, for the paper was still crushed in his hand. Only three lines:

"I go at once to London. Be prepared at all times. Another week and your long task is over, my brave child."

It was Mrs. St. Michael's hand. I had seen it on sundry notes of invitation, but whatever clue I might have found by searching the paper was lost, for Noel opened his eyes the instant I touched his clenched hand. To my utter amazement his face grew almost fierce as he staggered to his feet and thrust me off.

"Have you read it? What have I done? How came you here?"

He spoke as if hardly conscious of what he said; yet, through all the agitation of his manner and the incoherency of his speech, some strange happiness was plainly visible.

"My dear sir, I have read nothing. See, the note lies under your feet and the paper is in your hand. I saw you fall and ran to help you. Should I have left you here to startle Mrs. Noel?"

The composure of my manner reassured him, but, as if wonders would never cease, he clasped his hands before his face, and great tears fell between his slender fingers as he wept like a woman for a moment. I involuntarily put my arm about him, for he trembled, and, as if the act were comforting, he leaned against me till the paroxysm passed. Presently he was himself again, and looked up half grateful, half ashamed. His eyes fell before mine; he saw the note at his feet, and, as if self were forgotten in some returning thought, he caught it up, saying, slowly, and with still downcast eyes:

"Forgive my folly and my harshness; I am not strong, and sudden tidings overcome me. Let me explain, for I hate mystery."

So, eager to learn, I did not refuse, and he added, after reading the note aloud, much to my surprise:

"This is from my kind neighbor; she goes to London about my book. I am to be prepared to deliver it at any moment, and that is the long task that will be ended in another week."

Nothing could be simpler, and yet I did not believe the explanation. Why? Because I have learned to know this young man's face so well that its expressions are familiar now, and not once did his eyes meet mine while speaking, nor did he once allude to the paper still crumpled in the hand behind him. I could not but accept it, however, and as Mrs. Noel was seen coming out to us, her husband started, thrust both note and newspaper into his pocket, hastily smoothed his disordered locks upon his forehead, and said, fixing on me a look that was almost stern:

"Oblige me by saying nothing of this to my wife at present. I will tell her later. Give me your arm, please, and be so kind as to attract her attention from me for a little."

I obeyed in all things, but Mrs. Noel was not deceived; her first glance at her husband caused her to turn as pale as he, but some look or gesture unperceived by me restrained her, and she endeavored to appear unconscious of anything amiss. Pierre also looked expectant, was unusually awkward in his duties, and evidently eager to get me away. The instant dinner was over all three vanished, yet not together, and with every appearance of anxiety to be unobserved.

JUNE 17TH.—But one thing has absorbed the household for the last three days, and that has been the book. Such genuine interest and haste cannot be feigned, and I must believe that Noel spoke the truth. The study is no longer deserted, for not only has he written steadily himself, but merry little madame labors also, staining her pretty fingers with ink, flushing her sweet face with energetic struggles to keep up with our swifter pens, and making the once quiet room a bright and busy place.

"It must be done before the week is out, if we give our nights as well as our days to it. Help me through this task, Clyde, and ask any recompense when it is done."

Never had Noel spoken to me with such energy, such familiarity; his eagerness seemed to put new strength into my hands, his confidence to warm my heart with an almost brotherly affection for him. We did work, silently for the most part, but how rapidly you may understand when I say that to-night the book is done. I have just left the study very weary, yet heartily sorry that my share of the work is over, for Mr. Noel tells me he may not need me but a little longer. This unexpected note of Mrs. St. Michael's seems to have precipitated matters, and my task ends before the month is out.

JUNE 18TH.—The clue is found, and the mystery solved. Last night, being weary, I slept unusually sound, but woke suddenly, sure that some one called me. The moon had set, a light shower pattered on the leaves, and a fresh wind blew in. While drowsily thinking that I must rise and close my window, there came a light tap on the glass of the one nearest me, which was already shut. I sat up and listened; cautious footsteps brushed across the turf, and as if my movements had assured some one of my presence, a voice breathed softly:

"Pierre! Clarice! Bernard!"

"Who's there?" I cried, but nothing answered, and again the stealthy footsteps caught my ear. I sprang to the window, strained eye and ear, waited and wondered for nearly an hour, but no sound reached me, and I reluctantly compelled myself to think it all a delusion, for these names had been sounding through my dreams.

This morning I stepped out upon the terrace early, as I often do, but took only a single step, for there in the black mould under my closed windows were footprints not my own. Peculiar footprints were they; one large, but shapely, the other smaller, and evidently made by a foot deformed in some way. Long I looked at them, but could find no solution of the matter, so strolled on looking for more. None appeared, and I was just turning back to ring for breakfast, when Mrs. Noel came flying down the hall, her hair loose upon her shoulders, her muslin wrapper half on, and terror in her face. Seeing me, she cried:

"Where is he? Bernard? Have you seen him? He is gone!"

"Gone! How? When? What has happened, Mrs. Noel?"

"I want Pierre," she cried, beating her hands distractedly together. "He too is gone, the maids tell me. What shall I do? Help me, Mr. Clyde! Look for them; oh, look for them!"

"Where shall I look? Tell me more; I cannot help you till I understand."

"It was so warm last night that I left Bernard and went to madame's room. I heard nothing, knew nothing till I awoke and found him gone. I looked and called, I sent for Pierre, but he too had deserted me, and now I have no hope but in you."

Her white face dropped upon my arm as the last words left her lips, and she clung to me, sobbing like a frightened child.

"Let us go to his room, he may have left some paper, some trace that will serve us. Be of good heart, dear Mrs. Noel; I will help you with all my wit, strength and soul."

"You are so kind! Come, then—stay, I must go first—the room is in sad disorder."

Hurrying before me, she ran into the west wing; I followed when she called me, and looked vainly for some trace to explain Noel's absence.

"He never walks so early, never till now has gone even to the grove without telling me. Why did I leave him? Oh, my darling, what has happened to take you from—"

There she paused abruptly, for I beckoned. The long window was open, and glancing out, I had seen upon the newly gravelled walk footprints like those I had seen before. Others were beside them now, slender and small. Mrs. Noel looked, rushed out regardless of her disarray, dropped on her knees and scrutinised the prints, then rose, and carefully compared the smaller one with her own pretty foot thrust stockingless into an embroidered slipper. It seemed to satisfy her; a long sigh of relief followed, yet she began to tremble as her eye wandered far beyond the garden-walls. I said nothing of my nocturnal visitor, and waited for her to speak. In a moment she recovered her self-possession, brushed away the larger footprints with a rapid gesture, and gathering her wrapper closer about her, she turned to me with a gentle dignity I had never seen in her till now.

"I have no longer any fear for him," she said. "These tracks show that Pierre is with him. They plan some surprise for me. Thank you, Mr. Clyde, and let me apologise for my foolish fright."

More mystified than ever, I was turning away, when Noel sprang in at the window, rosy, radiant and wonderfully altered. Wherein the change lay I could not tell, but I felt it so strongly that I stood staring dumbly, while his wife explained my somewhat embarrassing situation, and chid him for his flight.

"My dearest, I only went to the St. Michaels. The good gentleman had one of his sudden attacks near morning, and sent for me; Pierre would not let me go alone; I feared to distress you, so we slipped away, hoping to be back before you awoke."

This statement, like several others, sounded probable, yet I doubted it, and observed that while he spoke he looked steadily at his wife, who looked as steadily at him. Of course I retired after that, and nothing more was said, even when we met as usual.

All day I wrote, copying several fine poems, which I suspect have been lately written, as they are of love. Mr. Noel has seemed more unlike his former self even than he did at dawn, and his wife has been in a state of joyful restlessness which infected us all. Something wonderfully exciting had evidently happened, and something ardently desired was evidently to take place at night; for as I left the drawing-room this evening I heard Noel whisper, as if to check some impatient glance or gesture of his wife's:

"Wait a few hours more, darling. It will not be safe for him to come till twelve."

That was enough for me; out went my light, and having carefully tumbled my bed that it might appear to have been occupied, I sat down by my window, waiting till the house was quiet. At half-past eleven I crept out, and looked to see what windows were still lighted. None but the studio showed a ray. There, then, this joyful meeting was probably to take place. Up I crept, but before I could set foot upon the roof the wind brought me the sound of steps coming to the gate. Motionless I sat, hidden in the sombre verdure of the pine, as two tall figures entered, crept to the window of Noel's room, and disappeared. One was Pierre I knew, by a suppressed hem; the other was almost gigantic, seen through the pale mist that rolled up from the river. An unequal motion in the gait suggested a limp, and as they vanished I caught the faint echo of a voice very like Noel's, but far deeper and manlier than his.

Fearing that Pierre might stand guard, I remained where I was for some time, then crept to my former loophole, and looked down.

A magnificent old man was sitting in the easy-chair with Clarice upon his knee, both her arms were about his neck, and tears of joy were streaming, for she smiled as they fell, and seemed to have no words to express her happiness.

Another woman knelt beside the chair, her face uplifted, tearless, but how nobly beautiful! As I looked my heart stood still, then leaped with an excitement almost uncontrollable, for with a shock of recognition I knew that this was Noel, and that Noel was a woman. The black locks were parted on the forehead now, the dark moustache was gone, the loose *paletot* was replaced by some flowing dress, from whose deep purple sleeves came arms whose white grace would have convinced me had the face been hidden.

Dizzy with bewilderment and a strange satisfaction which I could not analyse, I stared down upon the three, seeing, hearing, yet scarcely comprehending for a time. This stately man was their father; it needed no words to tell me that, for Clarice's eyes were dark and lustrous as his; Noel's—I can call her by no other name—Noel's grave, sweet mouth was a perfect miniature of his, and the features of both have a strong though softened resemblance to those finer ones whose reposeful strength was beautifully touched by tenderness. An Italian evidently, for though his figure far exceeded the lithe slenderness which usually characterises this race, there was the olive hue, the Southern eye, the fire, the grace which colder climates seldom produce. Gray-haired, worn and old he looked; yet suffering, thought and care seemed to have aged him more than years, for his voice had a youthful ring, his gestures the vigor of a man still in his prime. The right foot was smaller than the left, and slightly deformed, as if by some accident, and one of the daughters had laid a cushion for this weak and weary foot, the sight of which confirmed my suspicion that I saw the midnight visitor whose tracks I had found beneath my window.

The first words that reached me after a pause were Noel's, and I held my breath to hear, for the flutelike tenor I had learned to love was softened with a womanly tone, and now I knew why the seeming boy had been so silent when I was by. As if continuing some subject dropped for a momentary overflow of emotion:

"*Padre mìo*, I will tell you how it has fared with us since they drove us from your prison doors. Good old Annunciata took us home, but remembering my promise to you to fly at once to your old comrade Pierre in Paris, we went. He was all you believed he would be, father, friend, counsellor and guard. He feared to keep us there, begged us to come to England, and in some safe disguise wait here till you could join us, if your captivity did not end in death.

"As we planned what would be the easiest, safest disguise for each to assume, I bethought me that if we were searched, for when it was discovered that the proscribed book had disappeared with us we should be described as two Italian girls; if we separated each might be found, and apart, our apprehensions for each other would be unbearable. Now, if we could lose our identity altogether, and appear in a new land exactly opposite to what we had been in the old, we should be doubly safe, and could help you without fear. I recalled our wandering life before you knew Clarice's mother, when you and I roamed over Italy and France as a peasant and his little son. I made so excellent a boy, and liked the part so well, you know, I cried when forced to give it up; but in my strait I remembered it, and resolved to be, not a little lad, but a half-grown youth, and train myself to dare all things for your sake. Clarice could not if she would, having neither courage, stature, nor voice, poor, timid darling as she is! therefore she should personate aunt Clotilde, whom she used to mock, and her French accent would serve her well. Show papa how perfectly you looked it, naughty girl."

Up sprang Clarice, ran below, and in a moment Madame Estavan appeared. Great heavens, how blind I have been! No matter, that is over now, and a light I never dreamed of has dawned for me. Let me finish speedily. The three happy souls within laughed gaily as the mock invalid repeated her graceful helplessness, and deplored her sufferings with the pensive airs with which madame had won my sympathy. Soon Noel, or Monica as I should now call her—ah, the sweet Italian name!—continued her narration, leaning on the high back of her father's chair, caressing his gray head with a fond reverence that was beautiful to see.

"Pierre was unknown, circumspect, and the dear soul insisted upon coming with us. He knew the St. Michaels, and had done them a service when they were in Paris years ago; he wrote to them, for they were true as gold; they prepared all things for us, and in this quiet nook we have lived through these weary months."

"But this young man, to whom I nearly betrayed myself last night, what of him? how came he here? You would only hear my story then, now finish yours, my man-hearted girl."

How her face glowed at that, half with pride at the praise, half with shame at the part she had played so well; as if with her woman's garb she had assumed her woman's nature.

"Papa, see what we have done while waiting for you. Here, translated, fairly copied and ready for your last touches, is the dear book, written with such enthusiasm, lived for, suffered for, and now to be enjoyed in this free land when all danger has gone by, and honor, fame and love are to be reaped at last."

What passed below for a few minutes I shall never know, for my own eyes grew too dim for seeing, as the daughter who had dared and done so much laid her gift in her father's hands, and her head upon her father's knee. When next I looked the precious gift was at his feet, the beloved giver in his arms, and with the two fair faces looking up into his own, the happy man was listening to that chapter of the romance in which I played a part. Clarice spoke now.

"This dear Monica nearly killed herself with working at it all last winter, and when the spring arrived Mrs. St. Michael and myself began to pray and urge and work upon her to consent that we should either put the copying out or have some person here. At length we prevailed; she would not part with her charge even then for a time, but having grown bold through many successful trials, she consented to have a clerk at home. We were dying for society; we dared not go out much, because I could not play my part well, and made sad blunders by forgetting that I was blind and ill. She might have gone anywhere in this dull place, for none would guess her, but she would not do that for fear of mishaps. Both longed for some change, and when we advertised were wild to see who would come. This Clyde appeared; Monica liked him; he seemed well-bred, simple, unsuspecting and sincere. In time we found him accomplished, assiduous and a most agreeable inmate. Was it not so, *cara sposa?*"

Infinitely mischievous and merry looked Mrs. Noel, as she glanced up at her blushing sister, who half averted her face, and answered with a traitorous softness in her tone:

"Yes, too agreeable for our peace of mind, perhaps. Now let me finish, for I have ill things to tell of you and of myself. Papa, Clarice forgot her part continually; she never would be careful, and kept me in a fever of fear. The first night he came a lock of her bright hair nearly betrayed her, another time she dropped her rosary, and calmly owned that we were Catholics. I took refuge behind her, for in a Frenchwoman it was nothing strange, but in me who desired to pass for an English youth it was not to be allowed. Mrs. St. Michael often tried us by her overanxiety, and sent your letters in all manner of strange ways, till I bid her do it simply, for Clarice was always in a tremor when anything arrived from them, lest a letter should appear when least expected. I too was more than once on the point of telling all, for Clyde was very faithful, very kind, and oh! papa, I longed so for a wiser, stronger friend than either my good Pierre or the St. Michaels. When the paper came which announced the release of those who suffered for Italy, and your name was among them, I could not bear it. Clyde helped me, and was so patient, so unsuspicious and so tender that it broke my heart to tell another of those falsehoods. But till I knew how free, how safe you were I would not breathe a whisper of the truth."

"Poveretta! it was too hard a task, too heavy a burden for your loving heart. You shall be rewarded, my daughter, in this world if your old father can do it, and in the next where your mother waits to receive you into Paradise." A little pause, then the proud father asked with a smile so like his daughter's I seemed to see an elder Noel, "Tell me why this mock marriage was performed?"

"It never would have been had we known how soon you would arrive. But Clarice endangered all things; I could not send Clyde away when that part of my venture failed, for the book was not done; she would not leave me, yet pined here in confinement after madame's shadow departed. Nor could she appear as my sister, for I had said to various persons when I came that I had no family. Neither could she stay openly with me as a friend, because I would not have a breath of scandal or the faintest blemish on her maiden fame. We were in despair, when it occurred to me, that, as I assumed the rôle of a wayward genius—that I was forced to do, owing to the book and the secluded life I led—I might marry and play a little game of love and matrimony. It was foolish, perhaps hazardous, but I won them all to it, and brought my wife home, as happy as a bird when the cage is open and the sky cloudless."

"Lean nearer, my daughter, and answer truly. Did this shadow of love arise from any longing in your own heart for the substance? Have not these quiet summer days, passed in the society of this young man, been hazardous to something more valuable than my safety? Will you not find the same longing to lean upon, to confide in the new friend lingering under the woman's robe as warmly, as strongly, as when this gentle bosom hid itself behind a man's vest? Tell me, Monica, do you love this Clyde?"

There was no answer, but her face was hidden, and before the mute confession could be accepted she sprang up, as if pride struggled with maiden love and shame, and came towards me. Then I saw her face, and knew that the strange sentiment of affection, reverence and admiration I had felt for her when I believed her to be a singularly gifted and noble boy was unsuspected love; that the blushes, the reserve, the anxiety which I fancied arose from other causes, in truth proceeded from a like suddenly up-springing, swiftly growing passion, whose chief charm lay in its blindness. These thoughts whirled through my brain as I listened, and when I saw that familiar yet sweetly altered countenance unconsciously betraying to me what it struggled to conceal from those nearer yet not dearer I could scarcely contain myself, and some half audible exclamation broke from me. She caught it, looked up, seemed to see my face as it vanished. No sound betrayed that she had recognised me, and so brief was the glimpse that I flattered myself she could scarcely think she saw a human visage through the thickest growing leaves. Like a guilty yet most happy ghost, I swiftly, silently regained my room, and dashed into bed. Not a moment too soon, for barely had I got my breath when a light step drew near and paused at the door. My heart beat as if it would betray me, when the door opened, and the invisible being evidently paused upon the threshold listening. I bore the suspense till I could bear it no longer, and stirred noisily in my bed. Then quietly as it had opened the door closed, and the steps withdrew.

Mr. North, I am your spy no longer, and the record which I now dispatch is the last you will ever receive from me, for I break the compact and relinquish the reward you offer.

* * *

Those last words were written in the hush of dawn on that morning after the discovery, for I was eager to be done with my now insupportable task, and as Monica had said that her father was past all danger, I feared no harm would follow the delivery of that final record. I had waited impatiently for the first ray of light that I might make it, and when it was written paused for the page to dry. That pause was fatal, for worn out with a sleepless night and the excitement of the preceding hours, my eyes closed, my head fell on my arms, and lost I all consciousness in a deep slumber, which must have lasted for an hour, as when I awoke the sun shone in upon me. Intent on posting my letter unobserved as usual, I looked for it, and seeing it wished that I had never wakened.

There it lay with its infamous purpose clearly confessed in its closing lines, and on it a bank-note, a slip of paper, all three stabbed through by the tiny dagger that pinned them to their place. I knew the dagger, had seen it on Monica's study-table, and admired its dainty workmanship; I knew the sharp Italian writing on the paper, for I had seen it day after day; I knew whose eyes had read my words, whose hand had stabbed the treacherous sheet, whose contempt had spared me for a remorse sharper than any pang of death. The slip held these words:

"We are gone for ever, leaving despair for the lover, wages for the tool, a friend for the traitor."

How long I sat there I cannot tell. The sun came up, the world woke, and life went on about me, but mine seemed to have ended.

A dull hope woke at last within me, and I went wandering through the house, looking for that which I shall never find. Every room was deserted, but that of the grim maid, Catherine; and from her I got no help, but a curt request to breakfast and go, as she had orders to close the house, and return to her former mistress, Mrs. St. Michael. "Were they there?" I asked. No, they were miles away now, and she would have no questions put to her. My one refuge was Mr. North, and to him I hurried. His office was closed. I knew his house, and ran to it. Crape shrouded the knocker, and when I was admitted it was to find him dead. The day before a strange gentleman had called, had a long interview, and when he went Mr. North was found speechless in his chair. He never had revived, and died at dawn. His secret had died with him, and through all these weary years I have never gleaned a hint of it; never seen Monica; never regained my peace of mind, nor found rest from pondering miserably over these unsolved Enigmas.

A Laugh and a Look

Editor's Note: By the time Alcott began writing her thrillers, it was de rigueur that even the most convoluted mystery prove to have a simple solution by the story's end. "A Laugh and a Look," first published in 1868, appears to fit this pattern: It presents the reader with a series of clues that seem to point to a sinister murder conspiracy, then offers an explanation that ties all of the story's events into a neat, innocuous bundle. Or does it? Readers must judge for themselves whether this richly enigmatic tale is a simple case of misinterpreted motives or Alcott's deliberate toying with reader expectations for a happy ending.

I

There was music in the Park that night, and I ventured out, for my room was solitary, and my still delicate health made parties distasteful to me. The May night was lovely, with its balmy air, young moon, and the vernal freshness which wakes vague longings even in the least romantic hearts. Leaning against a tree, I listened to the music, watched the wandering groups about me, and dreamed the dreams that young men love. A sudden laugh disturbed my reverie; it was a peculiar laugh, and I involuntarily turned my head to see whose lips uttered it. Just the other side of the tree stood a tall young man, with a slender little woman leaning on his arm. They were talking earnestly, he bending down, she looking up; but I could see neither face distinctly, for the light was dim, his hat-brim hid his features, and hers were concealed by a dark vail. They stood somewhat apart from the crowd, yet evidently fancied they were enjoying the freedom from observation which such a time and place permitted.

"If my husband knew of this, he would be wild," the lady said, in a tone that contrasted strangely with her burst of merriment.

"But, my angel, he must *not* know. So far, you have played your part divinely, but you must guard your voice and eyes, else you'll betray the truth, fine actress as you are. You look at me too much, speak to me with too soft an accent, and your manner at times would inevitably proclaim our secret to the old man if he were not so unsuspicious and obtuse."

"I do my best, but when with you, I forget myself. You must remind me by a look, and show me how to deceive with an innocent face. Ah, me, what madness it all is!"

She drooped her head, and her voice became inaudible as a burst of drums and trumpets broke in on the softer melody of flutes and horns.

"You will surely meet me there in August, Mab?" were the next words that reached my eager ear.

"I will, without fail; you know my poor old dear denies me nothing, and is too busy then to leave town, so we may lay our plans in peace. No one we know will be there, and we can both enjoy our freedom and make it profitable."

"We will, and defy the world. My love, you'll not repent?" asked the man, tenderly.

"Never! with me, as with you, it is 'all for love, or the world well lost.' "

"The steamer sails in September, we must make the most of our time, for I shall be in despair to go without you," said the young man, in an entirely altered tone, when I could hear again.

"Poor Vaughn, he little dreams what's in store for him," and the musical laugh made me shudder, so full of heartless mirth did it sound.

"Privy conspiracy and rebellion suits you, Mab. You've a talent for *finesse*, that quite appalls me sometimes, sinner as I am. Don't you feel remorse when you sit on your husband's knee, and remember that we are about to destroy his peace?"

"A little, Val; but he needs change and excitement; this will give it to him, and he'll soon forget the rest. He'd forgive me the unpardonable sin if I played penitence, for in his eyes the queen can do no wrong. He loves me too much; he never should have married me; I am too young to make him really happy," and a sigh shook the gossamer vail.

"I always thought and said so, you remember, for I meant to have you myself. And so I will, in spite of heaven and earth, an old man's mortgage and a woman's fears."

The fervor of the last sentence sent an odd thrill through me, as I saw the speaker seize the little hand that lay on his arm.

"Don't be absurd, Val; remember where you are. This is no place for that sort of thing," said the lady, glancing hastily about her.

"There's a good deal of it, nevertheless; this is a capital stage for lovers to rehearse on," returned the man, nodding toward several pairs of humble sweethearts near them.

"I'm tired; take me home. It's getting late, and Vaughn will wonder where we are."

"Come and get an ice first. I want something cool, and a sight of your face to set me up for my night's work."

"I hate to think of you in that dreadful place, night after night. When will you give it up, dear Valentine?"

"In another month or two I shall be free; then hey for Paris and Queen Mab!"

The music ceased as they moved on, and in a moment the crowd broke up, streaming away in four directions toward the four great gates.

I meant to follow to see the faces of this pair, for I was in a fever of excitement, and I rushed after them, regardless of the jostlings I both received and gave.

For a time the tall figure of the man served to guide me, but in the crush at the southern gate I lost him, and after chasing several stalwart gentlemen, I hurried to the most fashionable saloon. Here I waited an hour, prowling about or lounging over a cup of coffee, and watching all new-comers, till it occurred to me that this mysterious Val and Mab would not desire to be seen together, and had doubtless gone to some less frequented cafe.

Provoked at my own stupidity, I turned toward home, but feeling that I should not sleep, I stepped into the theatre, hoping to quiet myself by a wholesome laugh with the great comedian playing there.

It was a benefit night, and getting interested, I remained till the long performance was over. It was past midnight as I went toward the river, near which my lodgings were just then, and as I turned a corner, I saw something that made me pause suddenly.

A tall man, wrapped in a curious dark cloak, stood under a lamp, apparently examining some object in his hand. It looked like a pistol, and the air and the dress of the man were suspicious. The place was solitary, for the streets were new, and many of the houses unoccupied. I was still weak and very nervous, and following an involuntary impulse, I stepped into a dark doorway, hoping he would pass me unobservantly.

As I stood there, a carriage turned the other corner, and as if he was as anxious to escape observation as myself, the man threw off his cloak and sprang up the steps of the door where I was standing.

The suddenness of the meeting startled both. I uttered an exclamation; he sprang back, and would have fallen, had I not caught his hand. In the drawing of a breath, he was on his feet, and wrenching himself from my hold, darted away.

I stood a moment to recover myself, and was about to hurry off in an opposite direction, when a little bright object attracted my attention. I picked it up, and stopping under the light, found it to be a tiny silver imp, curiously wrought and attached to a broken silver chain, an inch or two long.

I was just going to pocket it, when I was horror-struck to perceive on my hand the stain of blood. It came from no wound of my own, but evidently from the man whose hand I had grasped. I stared at it an instant, then dashed home and into bed, feeling as if I had committed a murder, and the police were on my track.

The imprudence and excitement of that night caused a relapse, and I was a prisoner for several weeks. When able to care and ask for news, I learned that the latest sensation had been the assault and robbery of a Mr. Vaughn, one of the richest and most respected merchants in the city. He had been detained at his counting-room late one night, and returning with a large sum of money about him, had been stabbed, robbed, and left for dead by some unseen person.

The offender had been discovered, after much difficulty, and was awaiting his trial, stoutly denying the act, and refusing to give up the money.

On reading the account in an old paper, the date of the outrage struck me, May 14th. That was the date of my last walk, and my encounter with the bloody-handed man.

It interested me intensely, but finding that Mr. Vaughn was recovering, and the offender was taken, I resolved to save myself any further excitement or fatigue, and as my testimony was now valueless, I held my tongue. I had some curiosity to see the culprit, for the impression I received from him in the instant we stood face to face, was of a young and handsome man; blackbearded, pale, and remarkably tall. On inquiring about the prisoner, however, I learned that he was a short, stout, fair man, quite the reverse of my mysterious party. After that I let the matter drop, but often thought of it, and often wondered if the young couple in the Park were in any way connected with the injured Vaughn, for the two affairs were curiously connected in my mind from that time forth.

II

Early in August I went to the seashore to recruit, choosing a quiet place, once fashionable, but now deserted by all but a few faithful *habitués* who came for health, not gayety. I had lounged through one week, and was beginning to long for some object of interest, when my wish was suddenly granted.

Coming up from the beach one evening, I approached the house from the rear, thinking to shorten the way, and as I passed a room in the wing, I was arrested by the sound of a laugh. I remembered it at once, for it was too peculiar to be forgotten, and I paused with a half-uttered exclamation on my lips. The French windows were open, and a soft gust of wind swayed the muslin drapery far enough aside to show me a lovely young woman, leaning on the shoulder of a man, into whose averted face she was looking with an expression of mingled joy and anxiety. I saw no more, for the curtain fell, and I stole away, longing to hear what that fresh voice was saying.

"What new arrivals are there?" I asked of Mrs. Wayne, a motherly matron, who had expressed an interest in me, because I resembled a son of hers.

"No one but little Mrs. Vaughn and her cousin, Valentine Devon," answered Mrs. Wayne.

"Is she related to the old gentleman who was robbed and wounded last May?"

"Slightly; she is his wife."

"That young creature! why, he is old enough to be her father."

"You know them, then?"

"Not at all; I never saw Mr. Vaughn, and merely caught a glimpse of her just now. She doesn't look as if she came for her health. By Jove, it's August, and the time they planned to meet!"

My incoherent exclamation was caused by a sudden recollection of the words spoken in the Park by the unknown pair; and in a moment I was as excited as before, and actually grateful that fate had thrown them in my way again. So absorbed was I in my discovery, that I stood before Mrs. Wayne, deaf to her surprised inquiry of what I meant by that odd speech. Her curiosity was increased a moment afterward, for, as we still stood in the hall, a voice said, courteously, behind me:

"Will you allow me to pass?"

And, turning abruptly at the sound, I found myself face to face with the tall, darkly-bearded man whose bloody hand had grasped my own. I must have looked even more startled than I felt, for Mrs. Wayne exclaimed:

"Bless me, what is it?"

And the stranger half-paused in passing, as if arrested by my strange expression.

"I beg pardon; it is nothing; a momentary dizziness," I muttered, turning away, quite upset by this sudden rencontre.

There was no doubt of it, for, brief as that glimpse had been, the face I saw that night was clearly impressed upon my memory. The figure, carriage, and expression were the same; the look of wild surprise just seen was a shadow of the startled glance he gave me as he started back when I seized him.

At dinner my eye glanced down the long table and saw the pair at the end, entirely absorbed in each other.

Mrs. Vaughn was younger and lovelier even than I thought, and Devon a fine-looking fellow. No one but Mrs. Wayne knew them, and they seemed to care very little what any one thought, evidently bent on enjoying their freedom.

As we strolled about on the long piazzas, after dinner, Mrs. Wayne kept her promise and introduced me to Devon. While the two ladies chatted, we smoked and discussed meerschaums, as young men have a weakness for doing. I admired his, which was of a peculiar and foreign style, richly carved and ornamented with silver. A tiny Cupid sat on the cover to the bowl, and as I examined it, he said, carelessly:

"That is not in keeping with the rest of the ornaments, which are gro-tesque rather than pretty, you see. Originally there was an imp there—a capital little fellow, but I lost him, and filled his place with that fat cherub."

"Something in this style, perhaps," I said, showing the silver imp that hung from my watchguard, fixing my eyes on his face as I spoke.

"By Jove! that's the image of my Puck! Where did that come from, if I may ask?" he exclaimed, with unfeigned surprise.

"I found it in the street. I dare say it is yours, and I'll return it in a week or two if you care for it," I said, coolly, dropping my guard again.

"Thank you. I do care for it, as my pet pipe is imperfect without it. But I am to sail in ten days for Europe, so if you can spare it I'll gladly replace it with any trinket you fancy," he answered, smiling, yet looking at me with an odd expression.

"You shall have it in time, I assure you," and with a glance still more peculiar than his own, I turned to talk with Mrs. Vaughn. "If this weather holds, you will have a charming voyage," I said, as Mrs. Wayne addressed herself to Devon.

"Voyage! I'm not going abroad," she answered, with well-acted surprise.

"I beg pardon. I fancied it was a party, from something I heard. Your cousin goes alone, then?"

"Alone—unless my husband is persuaded to join him. But that is not probable," and an irrepressible sigh escaped her.

"I hope he is quite recovered from the wounds he received last winter."

As I spoke I fixed my eye on Devon; he did not turn, but I saw his hand close on the meerschaum with such a sudden pressure that the amber mouthpiece snapped.

"Oh, yes; he is entirely himself again, and as devoted to business as ever," answered Mrs. Vaughn, looking from me to her cousin with evident uneasiness.

Mrs. Wayne, with a woman's quick instinct, perceived that something was amiss between us and adroitly changed the conversation. Nothing more was said, but I was satisfied that my suspicions were correct, and not wishing to rouse theirs, I never alluded to the subject, but watched them closely all that week.

They drove, walked, and were much together, and more than once I caught a look, a word, that confirmed my belief in their treachery to the good old man who trusted them.

One evening as I came up the unfrequented path from the beach, I heard Devon passionately declaring that he could not leave her, and Mabel tearfully beseeching him to remember the duty she owed her husband.

"By Jove, it's too bad!" I muttered, much excited. "She wants to do right in spite of her love for this man, and he tempts her. She needs a friend to help her, even against her will, and the struggle that is wearing upon her. Mrs. Wayne is a gossip, so it won't do to ask her advice, for the story would be all over town in a day. No; I'll write to the old man, and let him manage the affair as he likes. It's none of my business, of course, and I shall get into trouble, I dare say; but as fate has mixed me up in the matter, I'll do a man's duty to the injured old party. She don't know that Devon is the ruffian who robbed her husband, but I believe he was, for his looks, his occupation, his bloody hands, and the coincidence of time and place are all against him. I'll inform Mr. Vaughn that I have a clue to the real offender; I'll get him down here privately, and tell him all."

In a fever of virtuous indignation I hurried to my room, and feeling that no time was to be lost, wrote an urgent letter to Mr. Vaughn, begging him to come down by the late train the next night and I would meet him to impart some most important information concerning the robbery and other matters of vital interest.

After the letter was gone and my ardor had somewhat subsided, I began to doubt the wisdom of my act, and to wish it were not past recall. However, I comforted myself by thinking of the wrong and suffering I hoped to spare the old man by what might seem my officious meddling, and soon worked myself into a state of stern complacency at the important part I was playing in this little drama.

My manner must have been peculiar that evening and the next day, for even Mrs. Vaughn observed it, and usually she took no more notice of me than if I had been a child.

Devon looked worried, and both were evidently preparing to leave, though neither spoke of it.

When evening came I stole away to the station, and was rather alarmed to see Mr. Vaughn alight, followed by a person whom I knew to be a policeman without his badge.

The old gentleman seemed rather excited, and my courage began to fail as the affair approached a climax. Telling him I wished to speak to him in private, the officer was left below, and we went quietly to my room.

There I told him all, and was much amazed at the utter incredulity of the old man. He wouldn't believe a word of it, though I repeated the scene in the Park, the midnight meeting, and showed the little ornament which Devon owned and which proved that he had been abroad that night in a strange dress and with bloody hands.

As I repeated, explained, and expostulated, Mr. Vaughn's faith began to waver. His own memory evidently brought up certain inexplicable and unusual events, words, or acts of the young pair and as he recalled them, his face darkened, his manner changed, and doubt slowly began to creep into his unsuspicious mind.

"Will you come with me and repeat this story before them? You accuse them of heinous offenses; they should have the privilege of clearing themselves. This you owe us all, for, having stirred in the affair, you must help to clear it up."

He said this after a long pause, during which he sat with his hands over his pale face, evidently suffering much in even admitting for an hour any doubt of his young wife.

His unbelief rather nettled me, and feeling sure of my facts, I consented, having a private pique against both Devon and Mrs. Vaughn for the supreme indifference with which they treated me, evidently regarding me as a boy.

I led the way to Mabel's apartments, and, finding my tap unanswered, was about to knock louder, when Mr. Vaughn abruptly opened the door and entered.

A feeling of triumph possessed me, for the scene before us confirmed a part of my charge most conclusively.

Mrs. Vaughn sat on the little balcony in the moonlight, and leaning toward her, with both her hands in his, was Devon, saying, in a low, passionate tone:

"My darling, why pause? The old man's claim can easily be set aside, nay, ought to be, for you love me, and I—"

There he stopped short, sprang to his feet, and stood looking at us in blank surprise.

Mabel hesitated an instant, as if something in our faces daunted her; then came forward with a smile, exclaiming, frankly:

"Why, Vaughn, dear, what a surprise you give me!"

"So I see, and I have still other equally unpleasant surprises for you, madame," he answered, coldly, putting out his hand as if to keep her off, as he eyed her with anger, grief and distrust in his sincere old face.

"I don't understand," she faltered, shrinking back with a bewildered air.

"I do, and fancy we have that young gentleman to thank for this unexpected visit," cried Devon, glancing at me with a significant expression.

"You are right. Speak, if you please, sir," and Mr. Vaughn drew me forward with a decided gesture.

It was a hard task, but there was no help for me, and I blundered through it as briefly as possible.

Judge of my chagrin, amazement, and wrath, when, as my tale ended, the young couple broke into a laugh, and seemed overwhelmed with amusement instead of shame.

Peal after peal rang through the room, while we stood blankly looking from each other to the merry pair, who vainly tried to speak.

As Mabel dropped exhausted into a seat, Devon wiped the tears from his eyes, and with frequent interruptions of mirth, explained the mystery, at least his part of it.

"My dear sir," he cried, ignoring me, "the night you were attacked I was at the Medical College till late, busy in the dissecting-room. You see, we are forbidden to stay after a certain hour, but sometimes, when the students have an interesting subject, they bribe the janitor not to turn off the gas at the usual time, and then stay and work as long as they like. I did it for the first time that night, and being new to the thing, was a trifle nervous when I found myself alone in the great room at midnight, with six or eight dead bodies laid out around me. I worked away till a groan startled me, and, to my horror, one of the bodies began to move under the sheet. In my alarm I cut my hand, dropped my instruments, and made for the door as a ghastly face looked at me from a distant table.

"At that moment the gas went out, and I bolted down-stairs into the street, forgetting my black linen dissecting-gown, my red hands, and the janitor, who, I afterward discovered, was in the joke, got up by some of my mates. I was half way home before I thought of my suspicious appearance; I stopped a minute in a quiet street, meaning to light my pipe and roll up my gown. Hearing some one approach, I stepped into a doorway to escape observation, and there I met that—person, whom I fancied a policeman."

With a scornful glance at me, he turned his back, and Mabel took up the tale.

"Let me explain the part of the silly mystery which most affects me. Vaughn, dear, we were getting up a little play for your birthday, and farewell party for Val—a French play, in which a young wife is tempted to leave her old husband; but she learns his worth, she truly loves him, and she cannot go. I've fancied now and then that you were a little jealous of Val, dear; that you forgot we were brought up like brother and sister and freely show our affection, never dreaming of harm. The conversation this gentleman over-heard was half earnest and half quotations from the play. The scenes he has taken the trouble to watch were rehearsals which we came here to have quietly, out of your way. Oh, my dear, kind husband, don't doubt me, don't believe any slander, foolish officious boys may invent. Forgive my little secret, and take me to your heart again!"

It was impossible to doubt that truthful, earnest, loving face, and Mabel was gathered close in her husband's arms.

Devon turned and looked at me. My pitiable mortification and distress touched his heart. He came to me, and frankly offering his hand, said with a hearty laugh:

"My good fellow, I don't bear malice, though, upon my life, you'd got up a nice little tragedy for my benefit. Let me recommend you to curb your romantic tendencies, and busy yourself about something safer and more useful than your neighbors' affairs."

"Well said, Val. It's all right, young man; we'll say no more; and on the whole, I'm not sure I don't thank you for your meddling, since the half hour's heartache you've given me has cured my jealousy forever," said Mr. Vaughn, kindly, as he kissed his young wife.

"You've spoilt my little surprise, but I forgive you, and as your punishment, ask you to come and see the play, in the rehearsals of which you've taken such deep interest," added Mabel, with a half compassionate, half mirthful glance in her beautiful eyes.

I could only stammer my thanks, regrets, and apologies, and retire as speedily as possible.

"You may dismiss the officer who is waiting to take Val in charge," said Mr. Vaughn, as I bowed myself out, and with the sound of a general burst of merriment ringing in my ears, I rushed away, vowing I'd see my fellowmen to the deuce before I'd meddle in their affairs again.

About the Author

Louisa May Alcott was born in 1832 to a Concord, Massachusetts, family who numbered Ralph Waldo Emerson and Henry David Thoreau among their closest friends. The second oldest of the four Alcott daughters, she developed early on a passion for reading and writing, and published her first book, *Flower Fables*, in 1855. She held a variety of occupations in her lifetime: servant, hospital nurse, and editor of a children's magazine. Her experiences at these different positions became subject matter for essays and stories that she published in leading magazines and newspapers of the day. Between 1858 and 1877, she wrote over thirty thrillers for popular periodicals, which were mostly published anonymously. In this same period, she published her serious literary novels *Moods* and *Success*. Her novel *Little Women*, published in 1868, was an instant best-seller and led to a number of sequels, including *Little Men* in 1871. She never married, and died in 1888.

Stefan Dziemianowicz has helped compile over thirty story collections and anthologies, including the *100 Little* series published by Barnes & Noble Books. He is also the editor of *Necrofile: The Review of Horror Fiction.*

Susie Mee has edited an anthology of southern women writers called *Downhome* and published a novel, *The Girl Who Loved Elvis,* as well as a collection of poetry, *The Undertaker's Daughter.* Born in Georgia, she currently lives in New York City.